The Old Man and the Boy

The Old Man's Boy Grows Older

The Old Man
and the Boy

ROBERT RUARK

illustrated with line drawings

BY WALTER DOWER

Stackpole Books

The Classics of American Sport Series

Printed in the United States of America

10 9 8 7 6 5 4 3 2 1

This edition is reprinted by arrangement with Henry Holt and Company, Inc.

Cover design by Tracy Patterson
Cover illustration by Deborah Bond

Library of Congress Cataloging-in-Publication Data

Ruark, Robert Chester, 1915–1965.
     The old man and the boy; The old man's boy grows older.

     (The Classics of American sport series)
     I. Ruark, Robert Chester, 1915–1965. Old man's
boy grows older. 1989.   II. Title.   III. Title: Old
man's boy grows older.   IV. Series.
PS3535.U150428   1989   813'.54   88-28503
ISBN 0-8117-2297-X

This book is for the memory of

my grandfathers, Captain Edward Hall Adkins and Hanson

Kelly Ruark; for my father, Robert Chester Ruark, Sr.;

and for all the honorary uncles, black and white,

who took me to raise

AUTHOR'S NOTE

Anybody who reads this book is bound to realize that I had a real fine time as a kid.

R.R.

Contents

Introduction

In these cloudy days of a world composed in equal parts of hydrocarbons, hyperbole, and hypocrisy, there are still a few hideouts where any professional small boy can lose himself in a double-dram dose of the good old days. One of the best ways to do this, by my reckoning, is to settle down in front of a fatwood fire with a wet dog, pour a little of the Old Man's nerve tonic, and get stuck into Robert Ruark's two great classics, *The Old Man and the Boy* and *The Old Man's Boy Grows Older.* If you're fresh out of wet dogs and fatwood, you can substitute a palm tree or a tree house, either of which will do in an emergency.

Although I have read and reread this priceless pair until my old copies look as if they have spent a week in a box full of bird dog pups, I have never really been able to decide what they were: pure philosophy or just plain nostalgia in a Tiffany setting with baguettes of humor and adventure, the realities of the joys of living and the dignity of dying. After all this pawing over the pair, or at least *The Old Man and the Boy*, since 1957, when it first appeared, I have decided that Ruark wrote them both more or less for the sheer hell of it. Of course, the money they made didn't hurt too much, but if you read him closely, he will tell you how easy these masterpieces were to write as the memories came flooding back to him like high tide during one of the October northers that brought the big fish into the cuts off the roiled beaches of his beloved North Carolina.

Robert Ruark was a hopeless, incurable romantic. A man could suffer worse afflictions. Still, as the twig is bent, so grows the tree, and the Old Man must have been a mighty fine twig bender. Certainly nobody had a greater influence on the Boy's short life than did his grandfather, Captain Edward "Ned" Hall Adkins, a registered ship's master, hunter, fisherman, and full-time gentleman. In his own seventy-odd years of wanderings through the odd corners of the earth and the pages of great books, he gained knowledge and a sense of honor that came to rest in a grandson who could coax a dream from a jack-hammered Underwood like Rubenstein tickled a Steinway.

To reiterate here the things he taught the Boy would be to plunk my thumb into the icing of a beautiful chocolate cake. It might taste as good later, but it wouldn't come to the table as prettily. I'll leave it to you to cut the slice.

The Old Man's and the Boy's adventuring is one thing, but how about the Boy himself? As the Old Man might have put it, his grandson indeed spent a life hearing the owl and seeing the elephant. Robert Chester Ruark, Ned would have told you, got hisself whelped in Wilmington, North Carolina, a passel of years ago, back in 1915, persactly. Probably to keep the young Visigoth out of their hair, his parents took to sending the Boy on vacations and weekends to the parole of his maternal grand-father in a small coastal town where the Old Man and Miss Lottie, the Boy's grandmother, lived. These were the years that produced most of the material for both these books, although much of *The Old Man's Boy Grows Older* is as charming a squirrel-head stew of memories relative to the Old Man's teachings as is the first book.

If I'm not getting icing on my moustache here, I would venture that the two most important lessons the Cap'm imbued in the only semi-tame Boy were probably those of seeing instead of looking and the power of reading. That the influence was pretty effective might be deduced by the fact that Ruark entered the University of North Carolina at the age of fifteen. Turned loose on the world in 1935 as a journalism major, he already had a job through school on a newspaper where, despite living in one suit and two pairs of shoes for four years, he worked as reporter, editor, subscription salesman, and ad manager for the Depression days' duke's ransom of ten dollars a week.

Times were plenty tough before the war, but over the five years since school the Boy kicked, bit, cussed, and scratched his way through several Washington D.C. newspapers, rising from copyboy to sportswriter with a stipend of twenty-five dollars a week. During World War II, Ruark was a gunnery officer on munitions ships, and also tried his hand at some magazine pieces. His experiences at sea show up in most of the thirteen books that bear his name.

It was a star-sequined night aboard a floating bomb in the Pacific, probably off Guam. Ruark was smoking quietly in one of the safe areas—the navy being dry and no compass alcohol available—when the great strategem for his postwar career hit him in the skull like an eight-inch shell. What, he considered, was the largest group of people he could either entrance or enrage into buying his work? What was the weak point of this group? He decided women and their vanity were the answers. It was a doozie of an idea. And it worked.

In 1945, out of the navy, Ruark talked Scripps-Howard into giving him a shot at reporting. It was mostly sport at first but he soon got his own column and started his war with American womanhood. It was a proper blitzkrieg and, depending upon which source you want to believe, he received 2,500 or 22,000 letters the first week from outraged females and go-gettem-boy males, largely servicemen outraged at what had happened to the fashions and attitudes of their gals while they were off throttling Huns or doing rude things to the Japanese.

Robert Chester Ruark, never, ever looked back.

Now a proper society columnist with white-lightning venom, he traveled all over the world gathering material for the column, which became syndicated, beating the tar off ten dollars a week and one suit. In about 1952, Ruark, probably because of the influence of his late grandfather and their wayward adventures and the fact that he had now turned relative Old Man himself, began his love affair with that most possessive of steamy mistresses: Africa. She never let him go. It was the beginning of a Ruark very much different from the clever, glib columnist writing about fingernail polish and the goings-on at the 21 Club or Toots Shore's. Along with these two books, it was the side of Ruark I liked best.

His first African work was *Horn of the Hunter*, the grand tale of several months playing Allan Quatermain with the then-unknown professional hunter, Harry Selby. It was probably the most significant work since Hemingway's "Green Hills" or "The Short Happy Life of Francis Macomber." Despite the kick he got out of hunting the "Big Five" dangerous African animals, he discovered that there was, indeed, a sixth: the Mau Mau. And this led to his first smash novel, *Something of Value*.

Incidentally, nobody has ever seemed to notice that although the great artist Walter Dower illustrated *The Old Man and The Boy* and *The Old Man's Boy Grows Older*, Ruark was hardly second class with ink in any medium. The vignette line drawings in *Horn of the Hunter* were his own work. I doubt the National Academy would have tapped him but I think they're fine representative Africana.

Ruark wrote from the hip and he used a very large caliber. His many safaris over months in east Africa, particularly in Kenya and what was then Tanganyika (now Tanzania), led to another literary whopper, *Uhuru*.

The winds of change, however, had howled themselves from a gentle Indian Ocean zephyr into a saber-toothed typhoon that came very close indeed to blowing off Robert Ruark's head. Over the years, he had written some rather uncomplimentary prose about folks who became Presidents for Life and former Mau Mau terrorists now legitimate generals with main streets in Nairobi named after them. Bwana Ruark left East Africa — I am told by mutual friends of ours — quietly, late at night, and with very little luggage. But, like most things in Africa, it's business as usual; the only place I have ever seen a complete set of Ruark books for sale was at Nairobi Airport.

The Portuguese Overseas Province of Mozambique became Ruark's new haven, where he undertook half a dozen long safaris with my dear old pal, Wally Johnson. Hunting in Mozambique on a commercial scale for safaris was just opening in the early sixties, and the place was a hunter's paradise. But, as Wally tells me, Ruark had had enough of lions and elephants: he shot warthogs and birds almost exclusively and used the camp named after him as a writing base.

There have been odd similarities in Ruark's life and mine. I once met him at a cocktail party in New York when I was in my tender twenties, some years before I decided to inflict my own pen upon the unsuspecting public. I doubt that the Great Man would have remembered the encounter, as he was successfully courting his fifth dry martini and had become slightly overserved. Of course, my brush with literary grandeur was brief, as everybody there wanted to meet Robert Ruark. I did notice, however, that his moustache was a whisker scraggly, that he was starting to bald, and that he had wonderfully red eyes. I immediately went home, grew a scruffy lip piece, let a lot of my hair fall out, and discovered how much fun it is to maintain rosy eyes. A couple of years later, wouldn't you know it, I was a writer! It wasn't hard at all once I knew how to go about it.

Yet, it is odd. Ruark made Harry Selby famous as a professional hunter. I worked for Harry as a professional hunter some years later in Botswana. The godson Ruark speaks of is Harry's son, Mark, who used to spend a lot of time with me in the old days in the Okavango Swamps. He, too, is a professional hunter now. Mark still has a genuine no-kidding Rigby 7 x 57mm rifle given to him by Ruark, that particular iron having been one of "Karamojo" Bell's.

He doesn't appear in a Ruark book, but Wally Johnson is the subject of my own latest effort, *The Last Ivory Hunter*. Wally told me more of Ruark than any encyclopedia could have.

The biggest problem I had when I began writing was that I had read too *much* Ruark. Imitation may be the most sincere flattery in most things, but not in writing. Trouble was, I was very careful *not* to imitate him because we tended to write a great deal on the same subjects, especially Africana. Every time I wanted to describe something, I usually found that old Bwana Bob had done it neater, tighter, and better.

I have, I flatter myself, a special understanding for *The Old Man and the Boy* and *The Old Man's Boy Grows Older*. Both my grandfathers had died years before I was born, but I had a mighty fine pair in my father and my brother, Tom, who had nine years on me. When you're ten that qualifies him as an ancient. My woodcock and grouse were the Boy's quail and doves, but we shared the French ducks in Baldwin's Marsh, the icy cider sold on the roadside, and the training of pussyfooted English setters. His puppy drum and weakfish were my brook, brown, and rainbow trout in the Rockaway River, the Glen, and the Salmonid Club. Tom and I may have had to drive eighty miles downstate to the Jersey Shore for the bluefish, but ours were bigger and I swear they tasted better. Sheepshead and croakers? Hell, those Carolina boys were amateurs. Few were the June evenings Tom and I didn't release eighty to one hundred sag-bellied largemouths and a couple of amateur barracuda pickerel on Lake Valhalla in northern New Jersey. Old Wally Johnson even remarked once that we look and talk alike. But I would say the similarity ends with the prose. I haven't quite got to the Spanish castle stage yet.

Oops. I can hear the Old Man now, spitting a long amber

squirt into the flames of Hades, muttering, "Come on, now, you Willie-off-the-pickle-boat. This is supposed to be about the Boy 'n me. Hie on with what you're supposed to be doin'. Please."

As I mentioned, there are thirteen Ruark books, starting with *Grenadine Etching* in 1947 and ending with *The Honey Badger*, which was published shortly after he got a good look at the Eternity he spent most of his youth pondering. Two other collections of his work were published posthumously: *Use Enough Gun*, dealing with his African and Asian adventures, and another book, appropriately named *Women*.

Ruark whacked up his life between Africa in general and London, New York, a couple of dozen unpronounceable places and, mainly, Spain. He invited Wally Johnson and Wally's son, Walter, Jr. there for at least one long stay in Spain and I am assured that the Bwana's home in the snoozy little pueblo of Palámos could be called nothing *but* a castle. It was decorated with the things Ruark always wrote about: fine weapons, ashtrays the size of ashcans, comfortable man-furniture, fireplaces you could burn witches in, a kitchen that would not have embarrassed his beloved 21 Club and, everywhere, the trophies of a short lifetime of the chase.

Ruark dominated the area as the resident mogul for fifteen years, until 1965. That summer, at age forty-nine, he "became ill," was flown to London, and, on July first, rejoined company with the Old Man and a passel of half-Injun moonshiners, poachers, surf casters, and quail shooters. Whether he headed off north or south is not known. I suspect the latter: he would have wanted to be with his friends.

I don't know, beyond speculation, what Robert Ruark died of, but I have always suspected it might have had something to do with the fate of his last hero, Alec Barr, of *The Honey Badger*. After all, he did finish the book quite shortly before his death. He sure knew a lot about cancer, but then, he always was a fine researcher. Seems to me that if he didn't want us told, then it's none of our business. At least, I think that's the way the Old Man would have put it.

Ruark's remains were returned to Palámos, where they were interred. It may well be that no man ever so deserved the eternal farewell penned by Robert Louis Stevenson, in "Requiem":

Here he lies where he longed to be;
Home is the sailor, home from the sea,
And the hunter home from the hill.

PETER HATHAWAY CAPSTICK

THE OLD MAN AND THE BOY

1

It Takes a Gentleman to Approach Another Gentleman

The Old Man knows pretty near close to everything. And mostly he ain't painful with it. What I mean is that he went to Africa once when he was a kid, and he shot a tiger or two out in India, or so he says, and he was in a whole mess of wars here and yonder. But he can still tell you why the quail sleep at night in a tight circle or why the turkeys always fly uphill.

The Old Man ain't much to look at on the hoof. He's got big ears that flap out and a scrubby mustache with light yellow tobacco stains on it. He smokes a crook-stem pipe and he shoots an old pump gun that looks about as battered as he does. His pants wrinkle and he spits pretty straight in the way people used to spit when most grown men chewed Apple tobacco.

The thing I like best about the Old Man is that he's willing to talk about what he knows, and he never talks down to a kid, which is me, who wants to know things. When you are as old as the Old Man, you know a lot of things that you forgot you ever knew, because they've been a part of you so long. You forget that a young'un hasn't had as hard a start on the world as you did, and you don't bother to spread the information around. You forget that other people might be curious about what you already knew and forgot.

Like the other day when we called the dogs and the Old Man and I went out into the woods to see if there were any quail around. Turned out there were some quail around. Pete, who is the pointer, whirled around like he was crazy, and then he stuck his tail straight up in the air and settled down in a corner of the peafield as if he planned to spend the winter.

"I ain't shooting much these days," the Old Man said. "You'd better do it for me. Take my gun, and walk in past Pete now. Walk gentle, kick up the birds without making the dog nervous, and let's us see can you get one bird. Don't worry about the second bird. Just concentrate on the first one. You got to kill the first one before you can shoot the second one. It's what we call a rule of thumb. Suppose you try it to see if it works."

I walked in past Pete, and the birds came up like rockets on the Fourth, and I did what most people do at first. I shot at all of them, all at the same time. I fired both barrels and nothing dropped. At all.

I looked at the Old Man, and he looked back at me, kind of sorrowful. He shook his head, reached for his pipe, and made a great to-do about tamping down the tobacco and lighting it with a kitchen match.

"Son," he said, "I missed a lot of birds in my time, and I will miss some more if I shoot at enough of them. But there is one thing I know that you might as well learn now. Nobody can kill the whole covey—not even if they shoot the birds on the ground running down a row in a cornfield. You got to shoot them one at a time."

The Old Man said we ought to give the dogs a little more

time, because the birds wouldn't be moving as singles the very moment they hit and they left most of their body scent up in the air, anyhow; so why didn't we sit while he smoked his pipe and then we would go put up the singles. The Old Man said he didn't know what I would be when I grew up, and didn't care a lot, but he said I might as well learn to respect quail, if only for practice in the respect of people.

This little bobwhite, the Old Man told me, was a gentleman, and you had to approach him as gentleman to gentleman. You had to cherish him and look after him and make him very important in his own right, because there weren't many of him around and he was worthy of respectful shooting. The way you handled quail sort of kicked back on you.

Figure it this way, the Old Man said. A covey of quail is a member of your family. You treat it right, and it stays there with you for all the years you live. It works in and around your garden, and it eats the bugs and it whistles every evening and cheers you up. It keeps your dogs happy, because they've got something to play with; and when you shoot it you shoot it just so many, and then you don't shoot it any more that year, because you got to leave some seed birds to breed you a new covey for next year. There ain't nothing as nice as taking the gun down off the hook and calling up the dogs and going out to look for a covey of quail you got a real good chance to find, the Old Man said. The little fellow doesn't weigh but about five ounces, but every ounce of him is pure class. He's smart as a whip, and every time you go up against him you're proving something about yourself.

I never knew a man that hunted quail that didn't come out of it a little politer by comparison, the Old Man said. Associating with gentlemen can't hurt you. If you intend to hunt quail, you have to keep remembering things—like, well, like you can't shoot rabbits in front of the dog, or you'll take his mind off the quail.

And then you have to worry about the dogs some, too. A dog that won't backstand a point—"honor it" is the word—a dog that won't concede to another dog is a useless dog, and you might as well shoot him. One of the troubles with the world is that everybody is crowding and pushing and shoving, and if your dog hasn't got any manners he hasn't got any real right to be a dog.

The same way with a dog that chases rabbits. If he's a hound, let him go chase rabbits. But a setter dog or a pointer dog hasn't got any right to indulge himself in chasing rabbits. It is what the people in Washington call a nonessential luxury. A dog or a man has got to do what he has got to do to earn his keep, and he has got to do it right.

The Old Man smiled and sucked at his pipe. "I mind well a little setter bitch named Lou," he said. "Belonged to an old friend of mine named Joe Hesketh. She was about as dumb a bitch as ever I saw in the field. But she was loyal. She was real loyal. She was a backstanding kind of bitch.

"Joe's real bird-finding dog was a big old Gordon setter who was as black as your hat. He was named Jet. He looked like a charred stump when he pointed a bird. He was as stanch as a stump and as black as a stump. So Lou spent her whole life pointing stumps. You would walk through the broom grass in the savannas, and there was poor old Lou, froze solid on a burnt stump. There wasn't much Lou could do except backstand, but that was the backstandingest bitch I ever saw. She made a career out of it and never got to hate it. Her eyes failed her finally, and she got killed. She backstood a fireplug in the middle of a busy street, and she wouldn't break her point for an automobile that was coming along in a hurry."

The Old Man smiled some more, in the gentle, evil way he had, and made a new essay for himself.

"Fellow can learn a lot about living from watching dogs," he said. "Like about snakes and terrapins. The best bird dog in the world will point a terrapin, and he will point a snake. But he won't back off from a terrapin. He will point a snake and walk backward away from it. This is what the dog would call a public service. But when a good bird dog points a rabbit, he cocks his ears peculiar and looks over his shoulder at you with a real guilty look, like he was stealing an apple from the fruit-stand, and you know he expects a licking. He knows. He knows it just as he knows it when he gets himself all roused up and runs through a covey of birds. Or when he hard-mouths a dead bird when he knows it's wrong. Never underestimate a dog. If he's got sense enough to be bred from a family with a nose and a sense of decency, any mistake you let him make is *your* fault."

The Old Man said that he had kind of gotten off the subject of quail, which is a way he has of explaining that even an old man can get wrought up, and then he came back to the original subject. He said that any man with brains would never change a covey of quail from the original acre that they loved to live in.

The quail is a member of the family, the Old Man said again. He expects to get fed, like any other member of the family. So you plant him some field peas or some ground peas or some lespedeza or something, and you leave it there for him to eat. You plant it close to a place he can fly to hide in. A bobwhite is pretty well set in his habits. He will walk off from where he roosted, but he likes to fly home. It is a damned shame, the Old Man said, that the human race wouldn't take a tip from this.

But there is a stupid thing about quail like there is about people, the Old Man said. He won't let well enough alone. He starts a war and puts himself out of business just like we do, which is why we have wars and famines and even game laws, which I am basically in favor of, because they keep people and birds careful. If you don't lay the law of sound economics on a quail bird, he will start fights in the family and inbreed himself, and eventually he will kill himself off. The cock birds fight and the hen birds cannibalize the eggs, and all of a sudden where you had birds there ain't any.

This is no good for anybody, including the birds, the bugs, and you. Not to mention the dogs. So you shoot 'em down to a reasonable minimum each year. Let's say there is a covey of twenty. You shoot 'em down to half. The foxes will get some and wild tame-cats will get some more, and of the two clutches they try to hatch that year the weather will get one. But if you cherish 'em enough and don't get greedy, you can keep them in the back yard forever.

Just before I met your grandmother, the Old Man said, I dug into a place down South and I was interested in dogs. I lived there thirty years, and I trained all the dogs that I owned on the same covey of birds in the same back yard. While I trained the dogs I trained some young'uns, too.

This used to be called *laissez faire* by the French. I trained the birds to stay close to the house. I trained the dogs to be polite to the birds in the nesting season. I trained the children to be polite to the dogs while the dogs were being polite to the birds. I never shot over these birds more than three times a year, and I never shot more than three out of the covey at once. And I never shot the covey down to less than 50 per cent. And I planted the food for them all the time, the Old Man said. They were guests in the house, so to speak.

There's a lot I could tell you about birds, the Old Man said, but I find I'm talking too much lately. If you can remember to take your time and never shoot at the whole covey, if you can remember to keep them fed right, and if you can remember to make your dogs respect the birds—well, hell, the Old Man said, what I just delivered was a sermon about respect. I might say that it will cover most situations, whether it's bobwhite, dogs, or people.

"This ain't a very expensive gun," the Old Man said. "It's not a handmade gun, and it hasn't got any fancy engraving on it. But it'll shoot where you hold her, and if you hold her true she'll kill what you're aiming at. Some day when you go to work and get rich, you can take a trip to England and buy yourself a set of matched doubles, or you can get a special job built in this country with a lot of gold birds dogs on it. But for you to learn to shoot with, this is all the gun you need right now."

It was maybe the most beautiful gun a boy ever had, especially if he was only eight years old at the time and the Old Man had decided he could be trusted with a dangerous firearm. A little 20-gauge, it was only a twenty-dollar gun, but twenty dollars was a lot of money in those days and you could buy an awful lot with it.

The Old Man stuffed his pipe and stuck it under his mustache, and sort of cocked his big stick-out ears at me, like a setter dog looking at a rabbit he ain't supposed to recognize socially.

"In a minute," he said, "I aim to whistle up the dogs and let you use this thing the best way you can. But before we go out to the woods I want to tell you one thing: you have got my reputation in your hands right now. Your mother thinks I'm a damned old idiot to give a shirt-tail boy a gun that is just about as tall as the boy is. I told her I'd be personally responsible for you and the gun and the way you use it. I told her that any time a boy is ready to learn about guns is the time he's ready, no matter how young he is, and you can't start too young to learn how to be careful. What you got in your hands is a dangerous weapon. It can kill you, or kill me, or kill a dog. You always got to remember that when the gun is loaded it makes a potential killer out of the man that's handling it. Don't you ever forget it."

I said I wouldn't forget it. I never did forget it.

The Old Man put on his hat and whistled for Frank and Sandy. We walked out back of the house where the tame covey was. It was a nice November day, with the sun warm and the breeze not too stiff, and still some gold and red left in the leaves. We came to a fence, a low barbed-wire fence, and I climbed it, holding the gun high up with one hand and gripping the fence post with the other. I was halfway over when the barbed wire sort of caught in the crotch of my pants and the Old Man hollered.

"Whoa!" the Old Man said. "Now, ain't you a silly sight, stuck on a bob-wire fence with a gun waving around in the breeze and one foot in the air and the other foot on a piece of limber wire?"

"I guess I am, at that," I said.

"I'm going to be pretty naggy at you for a while," the Old Man said. "When you do it wrong, I'm going to call you. I know you haven't loaded the gun yet, and that no matter what happens nobody is going to get shot because you decide to climb a fence with a gun in your hand. But if you make a habit out of it, some day you'll climb one with the loads in the gun and your foot'll slip and the trigger'll catch in the bob-wire and the gun'll go off and shoot you or me or somebody else, and then it'll be too late to be sorry.

"There's a lot of fences around woods and fields," he said. "You'll be crossing fences for the rest of your life. You might as well start now to do it right. When you climb a fence, you lay the gun on the ground, under the fence, with the safety on, ten foot away from where you intend to cross the fence. You got the muzzle sticking in the opposite direction from where you're going. After you've crossed the fence you go back and pick up the gun, and look at it to see if the safety is still on. You make a habit of this, too. It don't cost nothing to look once in a while and see if the safety's on."

We walked on for a spell until we hit the corner of the cornfield. Old Sandy, the lemon-and-white setter, was sailing around with his nose in the air, taking the outside edge, and Frank, who was pretty old and slow, was making some serious game with his nose on the ground. In a minute Sandy got a message and went off at a dead gallop. He pulled up in full stride and froze by a clump of gallberry bushes. Frank picked up a little speed on the trail and headed up to Sandy. He raised his head once and saw Sandy on the point and stood him stiff and pretty. Maybe you've seen prettier pictures. I haven't.

"Can I really shoot it now?" I said.

"Load her up," the Old Man said. "Then walk in, and when the birds get up pick out one and shoot him."

I loaded and walked up to the dogs and slipped off the safety catch. It made a little click that you could hardly hear. But the Old Man heard it.

"Whoa," he said. "Give me the gun."

I was mystified and my feelings were hurt, because it was *my* gun. The Old Man had given it to me, and now he was taking it away from me. He switched his pipe to the outboard corner of his mustache and walked in behind the dogs. He wasn't looking at the ground where the birds were. He was looking straight ahead of him, with the gun held across his body at a 45-degree angle. The birds got up, and the Old Man jumped the gun up. As it came up his thumb flicked the safety off and the gun came smooth up under his chin and he seemed to fire the second it got there. About twenty-five yards out a bird dropped in a shower of feathers.

"Fetch," the Old Man said, unloading the other shell.

"Why'd you take the gun away from me?" I yelled. I was mad as a wet hen. "Dammit, it's my gun. It ain't your gun."

"You ain't old enough to cuss yet," the Old Man said. "Cussing is a prerogative for adults. You got to earn the right to cuss, like you got to earn the right to do most things. Cussing is for emphasis. When every other word is a swear word it just gets to be dull and don't mean anything any more. I'll tell you why I took the gun away from you. You'll never forget it, will you?"

"You bet I won't forget it," I said, still mad and about to cry.

"I told you I was going to nag you some, if only to satisfy your mother. This is part of the course. You'll never walk into a covey of birds or anything else any more without remembering the day I took your new gun away from you."

"I don't even know why you took it," I said. "What'd I do wrong then?"

"Safety catch," he said. "No reason in the world for a man to go blundering around with the catch off his gun. You don't know the birds are going to get up where the dog says they are. Maybe they're running on you. So the dog breaks point and you stumble along behind him and fall in a hole or trip over a rock and the gun goes off—blooey."

"You got to take it off some time if you're planning to shoot something," I said.

"Habit is a wonderful thing," the Old Man said. "It's just as easy to form good ones as it is to make bad ones. Once they're made, they stick. There's no earthly use of slipping the safety off a gun until you're figuring to shoot it. There's plenty of time to slip it off while she's coming to your shoulder after the birds are up. Shooting a shotgun is all reflexes, anyhow.

"The way you shoot it is simply this: You carry her across your body, pointing away from the man you're shooting with. You look straight ahead. When the birds get up, you look at a bird. Then your reflexes work. The gun comes up under your eye, and while it's coming up your thumb slips the safety and your finger goes to the trigger, and when your eye's on the bird and your finger's on the trigger the gun just goes off and the bird drops. It is every bit as simple as that if you start at it right. Try it a few times and snap her dry at a pine cone or something."

I threw the gun up and snapped. The gun went off with a horrid roar and scared me so bad I dropped it on the ground.

"Uh huh," the Old Man said sarcastically. "I thought you might have enough savvy to check the breech and see if she was loaded before you dry-fired her. If you had, you'd have seen that I slipped that shell back when you weren't looking. You mighta shot me or one of the dogs, just taking things for granted."

That ended the first lesson. I'm a lot older now, of course, but I never forgot the Old Man taking the gun away and then palming that shell and slipping it back in the gun to teach me caution. All the words in the world wouldn't have equaled the object lesson he taught me just by those two or three things. And he said another thing as we went back to the house: "The older you get, the carefuller you'll be. When you're as old as I am, you'll be so scared of a firearm that every young man you know will call you a damned old maid. But damned old maids don't shoot the heads off their friends in duck blinds or fire blind into a bush where a deer walked in and then go pick up their best buddy with a hole in his chest."

We went back to the house and up to the Old Man's room. He stirred up the fire and reached into a closet and brought out a bottle of old corn liquor. He poured himself half a glassful and sipped at it. He smacked his lips.

"Long as we're on the subject," he said, "when you get bigger, I suppose you'll start to smoke and drink this stuff. Most people do. You might remember that nobody ever got hurt with a gun if he saved his drinking for the fireside after the day's hunt was over, with the guns cleaned and in a rack or in a case. I notice you ain't broken your gun yet, let alone clean it, and it's standing in a corner for a child to get ahold of or a dog to knock over. I suggest you clean her now. That way you know there aren't any shells left in her. That way she don't rust. And since you have to break her to clean her, you might as well put her in her case."

Maybe you think the Old Man was cranky, because I did then, but I don't any more. I've seen just about everything happen with a gun. One fellow I know used to stand like Dan'l Boone with his hands crossed on the muzzle of his shotgun, and one day something mysterious happened and the gun went off and now he hasn't got any hands any more, which makes it inconvenient for him.

I've seen drunks messing with "unloaded" guns and the guns go off in the house, sobering everybody up. An automatic went crazy on me in a duck blind one day and fired every shot in its magazine. Habit had the gun pointed away from the other fellow, or I'd of shot his head off with a gun that was leaping like a crazy fire hose. I saw a man shoot his foot nearly off with a rifle he thought he'd ejected all the cartridges out of. I saw another man on a deer hunt fire into a bush a buck went into and make a widow out of his best friend's wife.

The Old Man nagged at me and hacked at me for about three years. One time I forgot and climbed a fence with a loaded gun, and he took a stick to me.

"You ain't too big to be beat," he said, "if you ain't adult enough to remember what I told you about guns and fences. This'll hurt your feelings, even if it don't hurt your hide."

When I was eleven, the Old Man stole my little 20-gauge from me. He grinned sort of evilly and announced that he was an Indian giver in the best and strongest sense. I was puzzled, but not very, because the Old Man was a curious cuss and a kind of devious mover. I went back to my bedroom later, and on the bed was a 16-gauge double with a leather case that had my name on it. There were engravings of quail and dogs in silver on the sides and my name on the silver butt plate.

The Old Man was taking a drink for his nervous stomach when I busted into his room with the new gun clutched in my hands. He grinned over the glass.

"That there's your graduation present," he said. "It's been three years since we started this business, and you ain't shot me, you, or the dogs. I figure it's safe to turn you loose now. But I'll take that one away from you if you get too big for your britches and start waving it around careless."

I'm big enough to cuss now, and I've seen a lot of silly damned fools misusing guns and scaring the daylights out of careful people. But they never had the Old Man for a tutor. Some people ain't as lucky as other people.

2

A Walk in the Woods

It was the kind of day when a walk seems necessary, and the Old Man and I just sort of fell into step and started out for the woods without much plan or purpose. It's nice to just walk if you aren't going any place in particular or in a hurry, and we weren't particular or in a hurry. We weren't looking for anything special, either.

"It's a real funny thing," the Old Man said as we traced the river around to where you either have to swim or cut across high in the sandy hills. "A man can spend his life with his eyes open and never see a dingdong thing. Most people just stumble through this foolish business called life, bright-eyed and bushy-tailed, but when the old boy upstairs whacks you with the scythe you ain't seen anything much. I thought we'd spend some part of this summer getting you accustomed to seeing things instead of just registering them and forgetting them, like a damn camera."

We heard some chittering high in a tree and stepped quietly around it on the pine needles. Two squirrels were chasing each other happily back and forth on the branches, disregarding the strangers at the foot of the tree.

"Whoa," the Old Man said. "Let me read you a little lecture on love and its evil effects on things in general. That's a girl squirrel and a boy squirrel up there. They are squirrels in love, for this is the time of year for it. Look at 'em cavort. In the fall when the leaves come off, one would be flattened on the opposite side of the tree and t'other would already have departed for other countries.

"But not now. Love has come to the squirrel kingdom, and they don't care anything about anything but whatever a squirrel thinks about when he's in love. I'm not going to shoot 'em, but you could bag the pair with a slingshot and they wouldn't know what hit 'em. This is known as losing your head over a lady, which is fatal whether you're a squirrel or a boy."

"Yessir," I said.

When the Old Man has an attack of philosophy coming on, all you can do is hold still and listen. This was one of the philosophical days. We sat down quietly and observed the squirrels at play.

The Old Man fired up his pipe and ran his fingers over his tobacco-stained mustache. Squirrels, he said, were always a puzzle to him. Some were red and some were gray, and some were cat squirrels and the big black-and-gray ones were fox squirrels, as big as a tabby cat and with teeth like a beaver.

"I try to figure out what God had in mind," he said, "when He made all the different kind of things, and I can't for the life of me decide why He made so many different kinds of squirrels. It seems to me that if you were just going to make squirrels you'd cut 'em all to the same mold and forget the whole business. But He made a lot of little people and big people and people of all sorts of colors and languages; so I guess He just had to balance off with squirrels. With everything you see it's the same. All kinds of sharks. All kinds of deer and quail and rabbits and people. Puzzles me some. Look there!"

He jerked his gnarled thumb up to where the squirrels were playing and a new boy came on the scene. He was a dirty off-white cat squirrel, an albino. He leaped down on the limb, his bushy tail waving, and almost immediately the fun stopped. Three squirrels—the male and female and another male—took out after the white squirrel. They snarled in a squirrelly fashion, and the big male bit him. He let out a loud *chirr* and took off through the tree tops, all three of the other squirrels chasing him and sort of growling.

"Never saw that before," the Old Man remarked casually. "Seen a lot of strange color variations in a lot of animals, but never saw an albino squirrel before. But did you notice how all three of the other ones lit out after him? You know why?"

"No, sir," I said.

"It was because he was different," the Old Man answered. "The Lord played a trick on him and made him white, when all the other squirrels you know are red, gray, or black. He's a curiosity in the squirrel world. All the other squirrels look at him and say to each other, 'What's this, a white squirrel? Must be a foreigner.' And then they light out after him. Must be tough, being a white squirrel. Every squirrel's hand against him. I suppose after he's run away enough, if somebody don't kill him, he'll wish he was born an alligator or a turtle or something, instead of a squirrel with bad luck enough to be born a strange color."

I was beginning to get tired of squirrels. I wanted a little more action and a little less philosophy.

"Let's go get the car," I said, "and go on over to Caswell and spend the night in the shack. The moon's about right for the turtles to be laying, isn't it?"

"I surmise so," the Old Man said. "I think that's a very good idea. Sea turtles can be very interesting, especially when the moon is nigh full and the old girl comes up to bury her eggs in the sand. You never saw that, did you?"

"No, sir," I said. "You always said you were going to take me on a turtle hunt, but you never did. Can we go now?"

"Sure," the Old Man said. "Let's go crank up the Liz."

We had a little shack over on Caswell, which is a big island. Not much of a shack. Just a one-roomer made out of rough boards and tar paper, but it had a sloppy kind of makeshift kitchen built off the big room and enough space above the big room to sleep a whole squad of people if they didn't mind roughing it under the eaves. It was right on the beach, and the waves lapped up to the front door. I loved going over there, whether it was fishing or poaching the squirrels that lived on the Government part or just hearing the ocean. Lots of times I'd seen the big herringbone tracks the turtles made when they came up to lay, but I never was lucky enough to see one of the turtles laying.

Lots of people don't like turtle eggs, because there's no way you can cook them long enough to get the whites to solidify and they wind up kind of gooey. But I like 'em. The way you eat 'em is to boil them about five minutes until the yolk gets hard, and then you pinch off the top of the leathery skin, shove a little butter and pepper and salt on top, and then squeeze the bottom. That's where the dimple is, the dimple you can't ever iron out of the egg. It tastes remarkable fine that way if you don't think too hard about the white.

Once in a while the Old Man had fetched home a mess from somebody who had caught a turtle in the process of laying them, and he educated me into not being afraid to eat things that ain't quite as pretty as steak or cake. He said he didn't have any patience whatsoever with people who wouldn't eat oysters or snails or suchlike truck just because they were a little off the beaten track.

We drove over slow to Caswell and stirred up a pretty simple dinner, and while the Old Man was messing around with the kerosene stove I peeled off my pants and took a swim. The Old

Man had the finishing touches on the food when I came out of the ocean, and was muttering to himself. He was muttering about how men were always better cooks than women, because they didn't fuss about it and were content to cook a couple of things and not go around fretting about six or seven courses. As usual, it was ham and eggs. The Old Man says that when God made hens and pigs He could have quit right there, because ham, eggs, and hominy are all a man needs to sustain life.

We ate and went out in front of the little shack to watch the moon rise, and pretty soon up she came out of the ocean. The Old Man said he reckoned that it wasn't Venus who came out of the ocean at all, for the Greeks to look at, but it was probably one drunk Greek watching the moon rise and he got it all mixed up with women.

"And I might as well educate you right now," the Old Man remarked. "Don't ever let me hear you calling her the Venus de Milo. Her name was Aphrodite, and she came from the Greek island of Melos. Venus is Roman and Milo is in Italy, and the word *de* is French. It's remarkable how much inaccuracy can come down through the ages."

The moon was tilting a little higher before the Old Man finished with a lecture on the Greeks and the Romans and historians in general, and was starting on the Egyptians and the pyramids when we decided to go look for a turtle. I was barefoot, walking in the firm, grainy, cold, wet sand down close to where the waves were lapping, and the night was so bright that you could have read a book. I didn't mention this to the Old Man, because he would probably have sent me off to find a book, just to see if I was exaggerating.

There's something pretty wonderful about a beach in the nighttime, with nobody around to make a lot of noises, and the gulls crying quiet, and the waves lapping soft and contented on the shore. I walked along looking for turtle tracks, and I got to thinking sort of like the Old Man. When God made water and mountains, I thought, He sure knew what He was doing.

We only walked about a mile when we came on some fresh turtle tracks. The flipper marks were still crumbly on the sand, and there were no other marks leading back down to the ocean. We followed the tracks—as easy as following a tractor—and came to where the dunes started, where the sea oats quit growing, and there she was. She was durn near as big as the dining room table.

She had dug a deep hole and had let down a sort of tube for the eggs to fall out of. The hole was dug big at the bottom and little at the top. She had it about half-filled with the eggs, which were dropping out of her at a rate of about six a minute. She had a big curved nose that made her look like an old parrot, and her half-filmed-over eyes were full of tears. I don't know why a turtle weeps when she lays her eggs, unless it's because it hurts. But she cries like a wife who's mad at her husband and wants to make a point of it.

Turtles are real peculiar critters. The male, they say, is a lot smaller than the female, and he never, ever comes out of the ocean. He lives there and they breed there, and when the mama's ready to lay her eggs she comes out of the sea, crawls painfully up the beach, and digs herself a hole. Then she drops those eggs out of a tube, and when she's through she covers up the hole and toddles off back into the sea. The sun warms the eggs and hatches them, and when the little turtles bust out of the leathery shells they head straight for the water. I'd think that even a turtle would want to hang around and see what her kids looked like, but evidently they're not curious.

While Aphrodite (I named her this, to show the Old Man I hadn't forgotten his lecture) was weeping and laying her eggs I looked her over. She was about six feet long and four feet wide in the shell, and she had busted barnacles on her as big as soup plates. And a lot of moss, like an old piling that's been in the water a long time. I asked the Old Man how old he figured she was, and he said he didn't know, but from the look of her she was older than Grandma.

She finally finished her chores and covered up the hole,

swinging her flippers like a bulldozer shoving earth, and when she had it tamped down she headed for the sea.

"Ride her," the Old Man said, "like that other mythological character that rode the bull out to sea and never come home."

I rode her. I climbed on her back and she wobbled down to the water. I stayed on her back until she started to swim and to head for deep water. Then I went back and we dug open the hole and counted the eggs. There was 137, a little bigger than big walnuts and each one with the same little dimple.

"We'll just take a couple of dozen," the Old Man said. "Leave the rest to hatch into turtles. Would be a shame to make the old girl do all that work for nothing. We'll have 'em for breakfast tomorrow, and try to come back when the little ones hatch, but cuss me if I know how long it takes for a turtle to get itself borned."

We walked home slow in the moonlight, with my cap full of new turtle eggs and nobody talking. When we went to bed, with the surf booming and the gulls screaming and the moon still high, I fell asleep thinking that I could have stayed home and gone to the movies, and I was awful glad I hadn't.

3

A Duck Looks Different to Another Duck

It was one of those November weeks when the skies were about the color of putty and the wind bored holes in you, and even down South there was a little feeling of snow in the air. The clouds were very low and the gray river was chopping straight up and down. One night after supper the Old Man checked his barometer and said it was dropping some.

"I guess you don't know much about ducks," he said. "Tomorrow looks like it's going to be real nasty. Some sleet and mebbe a little snow flurry. Stiff north wind and a choppy river. They'll be flying, and they'll be flying low. Maybe we better get up early and break you in on ducks, now you're a quail expert."

The Old Man grinned at me and I grinned back. I was a very

chesty young fellow since yesterday afternoon. It was the first time I had ever got a limit on quail. It had been one of those wet days with the birds holding good for the dogs and the singles scattering just right in the broom grass. I was shooting the new 16-gauge double the Old Man had given me and taking my time. I got two sets of doubles on the covey rises and only missed with both barrels once. When I shot the fifteenth bird, even the dogs looked pleased, but they didn't look as pleased as I did.

"Just because you know about this quail business now," the Old Man said, "don't go thinking that the same thing applies to ducks. Quail are reflexes, like I told you. There isn't time to do any figuring. But ducks are ballistics."

"What's a ballistic?" I asked him.

The Old Man had a lot of big words he liked to spring with no explanation, just waiting for me to ask him. He said curiosity was necessary to intelligence, and that curiosity never killed the cat. The cat died from stupidity, he said, or mebbe an overdose of mice.

"A ballistic," he said, "is sort of hard to explain. Let's see can I. Suppose you take the speed of a bird and the angle of flight and the speed of wind and the direction of the wind and the height of the bird and the size of the shot pattern and the speed of the shot or the strength of the powder, and then you grind them all up in one mill and the right answer comes out. Maybe that ain't the book definition, but it's my definition. I can explain it easier to you after you've missed a few ducks."

We got up the next morning away before dawn, and it was so cold your breath was standing out in front of you and your ears felt like they'd drop off if anybody touched 'em. Getting out of that warm bed and into ice-cold long drawers and into your pants and your ice-cold hip boots was torture.

When I got downstairs, the Old Man was in the kitchen. He had a fire going in the stove—one of those old, big, square wood burners that lit up rosy when she really got to jumping, and warmed up the room like a furnace. The Old Man had his pipe going, and he was busting some eggs into the skillet over pieces of bread that were already sizzling in bacon fat. He had some strips of fried bacon laid out on a tin plate, and the coffee-pot was talking on the back of the stove.

"Ain't nothing quite as cold as a cold duck hunter," he said, "unless maybe it's a cold, *hungry* duck hunter. You can build a fire in your belly with some hot vittles that'll spread all through you and keep your insides warm even if your ears and hands are cold. I allus say if a man eats a big breakfast he don't have to worry about dinner. Come and git it."

The Old Man laid out the eggs on the fried bread, with the yolks broken and soaked down into and bubbling up from the bread, which wasn't crunchy like toast but was part of the egg and the bacon grease, and he put the bacon strips across the eggs and poured the coffee. We ate about six eggs apiece, and I don't know of anything that tastes as good as eggs cooked that way when it's cold as sin outside but warm inside the room. They don't make that kind of coffee any more, either, coffee percolated in a tin percolator until it's got some body to it and you can smell it all over the house.

After we finished, the Old Man went over to the crockery cookie jar, winked at me, and stole about two dozen of Miss Lottie's yesterday's baking off the top, picked up two apples and two oranges, and made a little package of them. He took down a thermos jug and poured the rest of the coffee in it, and filled a quart milk bottle with water from the pump on the back porch. He put on his mackinaw and his old wool cap with the ear flaps and reached for his pump gun and announced that we were ready to go duckin'.

We walked down through the cold night, with the stars still bright when you could see them through the racing clouds and the little bit of moon just starting to die, down through the dead streets to the river. The roosters were just beginning to crow and the dogs beginning to stir and bark without much heart in it. It was cold down by the river, cold and black.

We went to where the Old Man kept the skiff, and he sent me

up to the bow and then untied her painter and kicked her off the bank. He said he would row her; it kept his circulation up. He said I could row her back when we came home in the sunshine, if there was any to come home in. The breeze was stiff on my back as the Old Man rowed the skiff along, her nose bouncing on the little waves and sending spray up on my neck, the spray standing like dewdrops on the stiff, hairy wool of my mackinaw. But I was warm inside me from the breakfast, just like he said I'd be.

I looked at the back of the Old Man's neck as he hunched his shoulders over the oars, and I could see his big ears standing out from the side of his head and the pipe stuck out of the corner of his mouth and the ends of his mustache blowing in the morning wind. He rowed about two miles, and then he ooched the boat around a corner of marsh grass and rested his oars. "Hand me the push pole," he said as he shipped his oars and stood up.

I reached him the push pole, which I had helped him whittle out of a piece of the toughest hickory I ever laid a barlow knife to. It was just a little limber, and you couldn't break it even if you were strong enough to bend it in a half-circle. We had sanded her down until even the bumps were smooth as glass, with not a splinter to come off in your hand.

The Old Man stood facing me in the back of the skiff, and he shoved her along until we came up into a little, shallow, sweet-water pond, with lily pads on it and all sorts of curious snaky-looking roots growing down into the black mucky bottom, where the push pole roiled up the water and made muddy puffs. The skiff sort of bubbled along on the surface. She was flat-bottomed and didn't draw much, and she just slid along. We went all the way across the pond to a little headland where the grass grew five or six foot high.

"This is as good as any," the Old Man said.

He got out, with his hip boots pulled high and hooked onto his belt with string. He braced his feet and pushed the skiff, with me in it, all the way into the grass. The grass finally jammed her bow, and he wedged her stern in with an oar, the blade sunk down deep into the ooze. "Throw me the decoys," he said.

I threw him the decoys. We didn't have more than a dozen. The Old Man had whittled them out of cork, sitting on the back steps by the fig tree and whittling very carefully. Then he had got some paints and painted them. They didn't look very much like ducks to me. I told him so. He was pretty short when he answered me.

"They look like ducks to a duck," he said. "Trouble with most people is that they always think about everything selfish. You ain't going duck hunting to shoot you. You're going to shoot ducks. From up in the sky these things will look like ducks to a duck."

The Old Man waded out, with decoys strung all over him, hanging from his hands and over his shoulders by the strings with the lead weights on the ends. He started throwing the ducks out sort of haphazard, about twenty-five yards from where I was, with one out there by itself, two or three together in one clump, a couple here and a couple there. All together they made a little half-circle around the point of grass. The wind was blowing from behind us, I noticed, and the decoys were bobbing and dancing on the water, with the wind mostly in their faces.

"Bend them reeds down over the boat so's to cover most of it from the sky," he shouted at me. "Leave us a couple of peep-holes to see through without raising up. I'll be through directly."

I cramped the reeds down so that when I was sitting down you couldn't see there was a boat or a boy in the grass, and made a couple of holes in the front and sat back. The Old Man was wading back now, and it was just coming a little light. The stars were gone, and the clouds had gathered and were very low. The wind had picked up considerable. It seemed to be getting colder.

You could hear the soft brush of the wings in the dark sky,

and occasionally a whistle as some teal passed low, chuckling. A hen mallard quarreled at a passing flock from her feeding place in a mudhole in the marsh, and the drake answered her from away high up in the sky. The rush of the wings was all around us now, and occasionally you could see a small flash of black against the lighter sky. You could hear splashes in the marsh, too, as the mallards began to sit down like motorboats in the pools where the water was shallow.

"How long before——" I started to say to the Old Man, and he cut me off.

"Might's well learn not to talk too much in a duck blind," he said. "Maybe it don't make any difference, but it takes your mind off watching. And four-fifths of shooting ducks is watching. *Shhh.* Sun's beginning to come a little now. It'll be shooting light in a minute. When you start to shoot, do it your way."

There is something about waiting just before dawn in a duck blind that makes you forget everything but the slow passage of time. Seemed to me like it never was going to get light enough to shoot. The whole sky was full of noise, and you could see the long strings of ducks, flying away high, it seemed like, but not very high because you could hear the whistle of their wings. Out on the water the decoys were bumping and rocking and making little noises in the water. One seemed to be standing on its head. Another was looking under its wing. In the half-light they looked an awful lot like ducks now. If I was a duck, I would think they were ducks too, I said to myself.

I forgot it was cold. I was looking through my peephole, trying to see ducks. The red-winged blackbirds had started to sing all over the marsh, and the bitterns began to croak and the marsh hens to rattle and the bullfrogs to growl and the ducks everywhere to quack. There was a hiss in front of us, and a swarm of teal dipped and passed low over the water, to get away, long gone. It was very light now, not even very gray any more, and a little more pink was showing on the horizon.

"You can shoot now," the Old Man said, "whenever you see anything to shoot."

I loaded up my 16-gauge with No. 6's and shoved her nose away from the Old Man, pointing the barrel over the stern. The clouds were dropping even more, and the strings of ducks had lowered in their flight until you could hear the wing beats very plainly. You could see the flicker of light on white bellies as one string wheeled over us.

"Pintails," the Old Man said. "Big ones."

In a minute he reached over and clamped my shoulder with his big, knotted hand. He nodded his head and looked straight ahead. "Mallards," he said. "Coming this way."

I looked and looked and I couldn't see anything, but in a few seconds I made out a string of dots. How he knew what they were or which way they were coming I couldn't say, but they kept getting bigger. They got closer and closer and I tensed up and half-raised my gun, but the Old Man said, "No," just as they wheeled around us and passed to the left. "They'll be back," he said, and began to gurgle and chuckle softly, like mallards do in the mud puddle in the back yard. Then he nodded to the right, and I could see the birds pass. The Old Man now began to cackle like his life depended on it. *"Gack-gack-chuckle-gurgle-gack,"* he was saying around his pipe.

The birds swung and came in to us fast. There were about twenty, with a big greenhead out in front. They set their wings, put on brakes, and, coming low over the water, dropped their feet at the outer edge of the decoys.

"Now," the Old Man said, and I lurched to my feet, bringing the gun up under my chin, with my eyes never off the big greenhead that was coming in for a landing.

As he saw me he turned and went straight up. I covered him and pulled, and he kept going. I pulled again, and he still kept going. I turned to the Old Man, shaking, pale, and sick.

"There'll always be more," the Old Man said.

I was baffled out of my mind and sick to my stomach when the big duck went off and took the other ducks with him. Those big mallards had come roaring into the decoys as though they planned to live there all their lives. The drake was as big as a goose, and so close you could make out all the gray and blue and green and yellow of him. You could see even the close-barred markings on his sides and the blue feathers on his wings, he was that close.

Once again I was wanting to cry, because I felt as if I had let the Old Man down, but then I figured I was a pretty big boy now and big boys that cry generally get their guns taken away from them; so I played it tough.

"Okay," I said. "Okay. I did it wrong again. I missed him clean and I ain't glad, but I musta done something wrong, and you might as well tell me what it was. What was it?"

The Old Man grinned, very happy. He took a lot of time lighting the big redheaded match and shielding it from the breeze as he cupped his hand around the pipe. The Old Man had times when he enjoyed cruelty.

"You did it all right," he told me. "You missed that big duck as clean as a whistle. The reason you missed him was ballistics. You remember yesterday we were talking about ballistics?"

"Yessir," I said. "But I remember that you weren't too sure about ballistics, either. Gimme some more ballistics."

All this time I was thinking: *Damn ballistics! I missed that duck, that duck as big as a turkey, as big as a house, and I don't know why. So now I get a lecture from the Old Man.*

The Old Man snickered a little more. "I think I got this ballistics drawed down to where you can understand it. I got it what they call reduced to its component parts.

"Let's say you are watering the lawn. Your Cousin Roy runs through the back yard and you got the hose in your hand and all of a sudden you would like to wet down your Cousin Roy. He could probably use a bath, but let's don't get personal.

"If the kid is running against the wind and you got a hose in your hand and you want to wet him, you got to do several different things. One, you are pointing the hose. Two, you are figuring the wind. Three, you are figuring how fast is Roy running.

"So you know that a hose will squirt only so far before it bends backward in the wind. You know that Roy can run only so fast. So if you're as smart as I think you are, you point the hose somewhere ahead of Roy, let the wind take the water stream backward, and then let Roy and the stream collide at a point you've already figured out.

"That's duck shooting. That's ballistics. Shot go from a gun like water out of a hose. The duck comes on like Roy is running. The shot goes one way, like the water goes one way. The ducks go one way, like Roy goes one way. And the wind adjusts the relationship between Roy and the water, between the shot and the ducks. Because shot always string out like water from a hose."

The Old Man settled back with that any-questions look. I had one to throw at him. "Sure, that's fine, this hose and Cousin Roy business. But the one I missed a minute ago was coming down fast and going up fast. Gimme one of them ballistics on this, that rule of thumb you're always talking about."

"It's really a shame," the Old Man said. "I hate to spoil you so early, but there was once aponst a time when I shot ducks down in Louisiana with a Cajun guide, and he told me a very wise thing. I will tell you now. When a duck is coming down, you aim at his tail. When a duck is coming up, you aim at his nose. When he is doing either one of those things but crosswise, lead him. Lead him twice as far as you think you need to lead him. That won't be far enough, but you'll probably hit him in the tail and slow him down, anyhow."

"How far is a lead, a real good lead on a duck?" I asked him. "Golly, I mean how can you make a rule out of it?"

"A lead is as far as you can swing a gun ahead of the bird," the Old Man answered. "You'll never be able to lead one far enough, because you can't pull the gun that far ahead of him in the time you've got to do it. There are all sorts of ducks that fly all sorts of speeds. Teal go off on a level line faster than most of the others. But under certain circumstances a mallard will be faster than a teal. Bluebill coming in low give you a bigger ballistic, because they look faster than they are and mostly you are shooting down at them, which means you'll shoot over 'em unless you're careful. Hell," the Old Man said, "I can't tell you how to do it. You just got to miss enough to make you automatic. And there will always be enough for you to miss. Like now. Get down, boy! We got pintails in the breeze!"

The pins came in like pins almost always come in, which is fast and undecided and not wishing to tarry unless somebody asks them. The Old Man asked them, using his pleading pintail voice this time. They swirled in a big circle and slanted low, and then they shot up in a hard, smooth skid from the water they didn't want much of anyhow. I was standing straight up in the boat when they zoomed, and when I shot I was bending backward. The pintail I was pointing at hit the water about the same time I did, because the discharge of the gun sent me tail over tip into the mucky water, mashing the reeds and back-tilting the boat. The Old Man seemed pleased at both results.

"If you can retrieve yourself," he said, "I'll go out and pick up a fine drake that you must have killed by accident. Very fine bird, the pintail. He doesn't cheat, which is more than you can say of some people. He won't eat fish on you, like a mallard will, or even like a canvasback will. And he's the best-looking duck in the business, unless you like 'em loud-colored like the French ducks, the big greenheads."

I climbed, dripping, back into the boat, scraped off some of the awful-smelling ooze, and watched the Old Man retrieve my first duck. Did you look at your first duck, or your first pheasant, real close? Ever see a bull pintail at close range?

Maybe this wasn't a very special pintail, but the gray on him was like a fine herringbone suit, and his belly was white, and the crest on his head was still ruffled. His open eye was white-rimmed, and his head was dull red-golden brown, and his tail was sharp as a dart. He was as big as a mallard and would taste just as sweet, because he was an honest duck that wouldn't cheat on you and go gormandize himself on fish.

And he was *my* pintail, my first duck, my first big duck. Sometime later I might shoot a goose or a wild turkey or almost anything, but this was my first real big duck. I hated to think that he would stiffen up and his glossy feathers would get soggy and his fine open eyes would glaze. A man's first duck is an adventure.

I still didn't know how I had shot him, except that whatever I did sent me backward, overboard. I swore I would try to do better. In the meantime I would admire my pintail. The Old Man stopped my reverie in full bloom.

"If you ain't so caught up in your own importance," he whispered, "you might be interested in the fact that there's a hull passel of mallards about to decoy in your front yard. Maybe you better figger it out for yourself."

I came out of the fog, and there among the decoys were a double dozen mallards, in the water already, two drakes out ahead, swimming into the blind, some brown-flecked hens behind, already chuckling happily and standing on their heads. Some more drakes and some more hens behind them settled down into the decoys as if they'd found friends and relatives with money. I looked at the old boy. He broke a rule and talked.

"There's three or four in line," he said. "If you were hungry, you could loose off at the lot and fill up the boat. But if you're wondering how good you can shoot, I'd recommend that you stand up and holler, 'Shoo!' and see how good you can do. It's up to you, bud."

It seemed that the Old Man was looking very intently at me, and I decided I'd better stand up and holler, "Shoo!" Which is what I did. The two drakes went out of the water in a vertical climb, and I never saw at all what the rest did. My eyes were full of mallard drakes.

I pointed the gun at the first drake's nose, as the Old Man had said. Then I pushed her ahead a couple of feet and pulled on the trigger, and the first drake came down like a sack of meal. The other one had got up high enough and had squared off and was heading for elsewhere. I led him as far as I could and pulled again, and down he came like another sack, and all of a sudden there were two big green-headed, blue-winged, yellow-billed and yellow-footed, curled-tail mallard drakes floating belly up on the pond. And they belonged to me.

"Easy, ain't it?" the Old Man said. "Once you know how, I mean."

"I think it's pretty simple," I agreed. "You make it awful easy the way you say it."

"I wouldn't get awful cocky about it, if I were you," the Old Man warned. "Not just because you got three ducks in the boat and they're all good big ducks. You'll miss a lot of ducks before you get as old as I am. You'll very likely miss some ducks today."

The Old Man was right. Some more pins came in a little later and decoyed to the Old Man's pretty-please talk as tame as bluebills. I made the same shot I had killed the mallards with, and as far as I know I never pulled a feather. Some teal came in and squished down in the decoys, and I led one a mile and he dropped like a rock. I led another the same mile, and he went on to Mexico.

There were a lot of ducks around in those days, and not much of a limit to worry about. The weather got better as the morning wore on. The clouds massed low and solid, keeping the ducks down. The open water was rough and the ducks were looking for the still-water ponds.

I burned powder until my arm was black on the muscle, but I could have shot a 10-gauge off my nose that day and never noticed the difference. The Old Man didn't coach me too much. He would just nod when I killed a hard one and shake his head when I missed an easy one. He didn't shoot anything flying. I had a lot of cripples, and he shot their heads off with his creaky old pump gun. Every time he turned a cripple over he looked sort of sad and disapproving, as if a man shouldn't go around crippling ducks because of the cost of gunpowder.

Along toward the end of the morning, when the ducks stopped about nine-thirty, as they usually do, I figured I had a pretty good grasp on the Old Man's idea of ballistics. At least I knew one thing for sure: you can't aim at it and hit it unless it's coming straight at you or going straight away, and this never really happens. A duck coming is either dipping down or slanting up, and a duck going is always heading up a little. You got to aim at where you think it'll be when the shot gets there.

It began to snow a little at ten, when the Old Man counted the ducks in the boat and said, "That's enough. We got more than we can eat at the house and give to the neighbors. Let's save some for next week, or maybe next fall."

We sat there in the marsh, with the marsh smell coming strong on the breeze and the soft flakes of snow falling, drinking what was left of the coffee and eating the apples and Miss Lottie's cookies we had stolen out of the crock. The red-winged blackbirds had shut up, and there was only an occasional string of ducks flying low under the solid clouds. It was getting colder all the time.

"We had a pretty good morning," the Old Man said. "I thought you did pretty good for an amateur. I guess you feel like celebrating some; so I suggest you row the boat home. It'll calm you down."

4

Fish Keep a Fellow
Out of Trouble

The summertime had come, as it comes swiftly in the South, with the trees heavy with summer smells and all the roses blooming in Miss Lottie's garden, and the magnolia all busted out in those great, heavy waxen blossoms that turn brown if you touch them.

The Old Man was watching us play a game of two o'cat one day, and when we wound it up he called me to one side and said he reckoned it was about time for us to go fishing. It was just a question, he said, of what kind of fishing we wanted to do.

"This is the summertime," the Old Man said. "This is not a time for heavy fishing. In the summertime you don't belong to work too hard. My idea of summertime fishing is to take a pole and a length of line and sit by a fresh-water crick and catch a black bass, or else to get in the rowboat and go find one of those big holes full of speckled trout and use a hand line on them. The whole purpose of summer fishing," the Old Man said, "is not to worry about catching fish, but to just get out of the house and set and think a little. Also, the womenfolk are very bad-tempered in the summer. The less you hang around the premises the less trouble you're apt to get in."

I said let's us row out to the channel and find us a trout hole and throw a hand line over and let the day take care of itself. The Old Man said he thought that was a fine idea, but that even summer fishing took some preparation. He dug in his pocket, and found a dime, and flipped it at me.

"You go on down to the shrimp house and buy us a dime's worth," he said, "and mind they're fresh and little. Wait for one of the boats to come in, and get them while they're still kicking. No!" he said. "On second thought, give me the dime back. We'll go catch our own. You might as well learn how to use a cast net now as any other time. It's almost as much fun as fishing, if you do it right."

I went into the kitchen to snitch the makings for some lunch and to fill the water jug, and the Old Man crawled under the house where he kept his tents and some spare boats and a side-saddle Miss Lottie used to ride, when people still rode horses sidesaddle. He came out swearing, with a crick in his back and the cast net, carefully rolled, in his hand. The Old Man had made the net himself, knotting each line in the net to form a fine, thin web, and carefully spacing each leaden sinker that hung from the hem of the net. It was a work of art. As I recall, it took him all winter, although, of course, some of the time he was working on a miniature full-rigged ship, which used up a lot more of his time when he wasn't hunting or playing the fiddle.

We walked down to the water, the Old Man carrying the net slung over his shoulder and a couple of hand lines wrapped neatly around two pieces of wood, notched at each end, with the hook bit deep into the wood and the sinker hanging free.

I had the lunch box and the water bottle and a fishing-tackle box full of extra hooks and sinkers and leaders. The Old Man was very particular about the extras. He always said that a fisherman who lost his hook might as well not be there at all unless he had another hook, and that a hunter who didn't carry some sort of spare gun was wasting his time in the woods.

The boat was hauled up high and dry on the beach with her oars under her. We flipped her over, and I walked, barefoot, of course, backward into the water, where we hauled her free and set her to bobbing in the little glittery summer wavelets. We stowed the stuff under one of the wharfs, and the Old Man took a push pole and shoved her over to the corner of the marsh, where you could smell the mud, very salty and foul, but where the little schools of mullet and shrimp were making extra wrinkles in the water. The Old Man shipped his push pole and reached for the cast net. He shook it until it hung free, like a lead-weighted skirt, and then swished it very carefully through the water to make it wet and free-running, so as not to snarl.

In case you don't know about a cast net, it's a thing like a big circular skirt, which fans out at the bottom. It has drawstrings on the bottom that come up through its narrow horn-rimmed neck. It lands flat on the water, and the lead weights carry it swiftly to the bottom. A simple twitch closes the wide bottom and makes it into a net bag, with whatever's inside trapped safe and sound. You have to use it in shallow water, of course, because it's not much good at over four or five feet deep, but throwing it is an art—I found out—and it's a deadly way of collecting your small bait with a minimum of trouble.

The Old Man stood up and flipped out his net, like a bull-fighter flipping his cape. He put one of the lead sinkers on the bottom in his mouth. Holding the drawstring in his left hand, he stretched his right hand to grab another piece of the hem, and steadied the whole three-cornered arrangement—right hand, mouth in the middle—with the left hand grabbing the outer left-hand edge of the net's hem. He carried his left hand behind him, taking that part of the net's skirt with him, crossed his right hand past his chest, and threw. The net swirled out, lovely and graceful, opening to its full diameter like a great round butterfly. It settled at full extension on the water, covering a small school of bucking shrimp. It sank, carrying the shrimp down with it, and the Old Man's left hand twitched the drawstring. Then he began to haul in the net.

The lead-weighted bottom, tucked in now from the stress of the drawstring, made a secure trap for the shrimp. As the water poured out of the net you could see the tiny little grayish-yellow shrimp fighting and kicking inside. The Old Man dumped the weighted part on the deck of the boat. He released the draw, encircled the horn ring with thumb and forefinger, and shook the net gently. Its closed bottom opened. The shrimp, a hundred or more, leaped and kicked and quivered on the deck. The Old Man scooped them up by handfuls and dropped them in a bucket of salt water.

"Now you try it," he said. " 'Tain't as easy as it looks. You got to make the net swirl out like a lady's dancing skirt when you throw her, and if you ain't careful that sinker in your mouth will pull out a couple of front teeth. Also, there's a knack to when you haul taut on the drawstring. You got to give her a chance to settle over the shrimp, but not too long, or they'll get out from under the bottom. Give her a whirl."

I spent most of the morning with that net. I hurt my teeth with the sinker. I snarled it and fouled it and twitched it too soon and didn't twitch it fast enough, or forgot to lead the swimming schools of shrimp and little mullet I was practicing on. Finally I got to where I could throw her and make her swirl, and eventually I caught a couple of pounds of shrimp and some little three-inch mullet. A lot later on I was going to have a mess of fun with that net, fishing the shallows and catching sizable fish that had come in close to feed on the bait. But this morning I just about pulled my arms out of the sockets before the Old Man said that was enough, and let's have some lunch and then go fish the ebb tide.

We rowed out a mile or so to where the water made an eddy around some rocks, and the Old Man dropped the anchor overside and let out all the slack in the line. The boat yawed around and hung in a clear place, with rapid-running water on both sides of her, and we started to unwind the fishing lines, letting them flow downstream to get the kinks dampened out. Then we hauled them back in, hand over hand, making a neat wet coil on the deck of the boat. The Old Man reached into the shrimp pot and chose a lusty kicker and threaded him on the hook, gently circling the shrimp's spine with the barb. He tossed him over the side, and I did the same with mine.

We caught fish that day. We caught big sea trout, weakfish, that had come in through the inlets, fellows going up as high as three and four pounds—big, beautiful, speckled salt-water trout with mean chins and anger at the hooks in their mouths. We caught blackfish and croakers with a grunt like an unhappy pig. We even caught some small sharks and an occasional big perch. We caught fish until our hands were chapped and cut and tired from hauling them in.

Summertime is an overrated time, I think today, full of sunburn and poison ivy and expensive vacations. But for a boy like me, at that time, summertime was a time of almost unbearable happiness. School was out, of course, and we had a song that went: "No more school, no more books, no more teachers' cross-eyed looks." Summertime was when I went to stay with the Old Man, and got loose from my ma and my pa. Summertime was June-bug time and firefly time, each tiny fly blinking his parking light on and off.

If you are a very small boy, being close to water makes the summer a marvelous thing. There is something of the kiss of the sun on dancing little waves, fresh salt breeze in your face and sun on your head, the taste of salt fresh on your lips. It was like that this day when the Old Man taught me to use the cast net and all the fish were hungry for the little gray shrimp we had caught at the edges of the steaming marshes.

The sun was low when the Old Man announced that we

had had enough and put me to the task of rowing us back to port. My face was fiery from the sun and there was salt in my pores and my hands hurt on the hard handles of the oars, but I bent my back with a right good will and listened to the Old Man, who was talking now, more or less to himself.

"The thing about fishing," the Old Man said, "is not how many fish you catch or what kind of fish. I, for one, think that making a hardheaded profession out of fishing is a waste of time, because a fish is only a fish, and when you make a lot of work out of him you lose the whole point of him.

"A fish, which you can't see, deep down in the water, is a kind of symbol of peace on earth, good will to yourself. Fishing gives a man some time to think. It gives him some time to collect his thoughts and rearrange them kind of neat, in an orderly fashion.

"Once the bait is on the hook and the boat anchored, there's nothing to interfere with thinking except an occasional bite, and even an idiot with reflexes can haul in a fish without interrupting his train of thought. This isn't true, I hasten to add, of sport fishing, game fishing, because that calls for a great deal of concentration and some skill and an awful lot of work.

"I mean that, for a rest cure for your head, you got to go fishing like we just been fishing, a holiday from yourself and all the things a man gets mixed up in. Setting out here in this boat, your ma can't get at you and your grandma can't get at you. There ain't any telephone or postal service or radio or automobiles. There ain't anything but just you and the fish, and these kind of fish are all fools. So you put a shrimp on the hook and throw it out, and if one bites you haul it in, and if one doesn't you've still had a mighty fine day in the open where it's quiet and only the sea gulls are noisy.

"Once in a while," the Old Man said, "a fellow wants to get away from everything that's complicated, and fishing is really the only way I know of to do it. Later on we'll do some serious fishing, which is work, but I don't think you ought to do it in the summertime. One of the reasons people drop dead is from doing serious things in the summertime.

"Look at us, for example," the Old Man said. "We have had us a fine day away from the women. We haven't bothered each other with a lot of problems. You learned how to throw a cast net, and this afternoon we caught a mighty pretty mess of fish. So we go home now, with all the wrinkles smoothed out of us, hungry, tired, and ready for dinner and bed. The women can't be mad at us because we weren't underfoot all day, and on top of it here are enough fish to feed the whole block. In a way we are heroes, just because we had sense enough to loaf all day without people watching us.

"One thing you will learn," the Old Man said, talking at me, "is that you must never be lazy in front of anybody. Loafing is fine, but energetic people get mad at you if you take it easy in front of them. That's one of the troubles with women. They got a dynamo in them, and they run on energy. It pure riles a woman to see a man having any fun that doesn't involve work. That's why fishing was invented, really. It takes you away from the view of industrious people. Lazy men make the best fishermen, and they usually amount to something in the end, because they have time enough to unclutter their brains and get down to the real flat basics.

"I do not admire people who are industrious all the time. They're like people who swat at gnats and miss the mosquitoes. They are always so damn busy running here and yonder on fool's errands that they never have time to settle down and cerebrate a little. Lean a little harder on them oars, boy. I'm getting powerful peckish."

We came back to the beach, and we hauled up the boat and cached the oars under her and collected the oarlocks and pulled the fish in from the string that let them swim behind us. Then we walked up the hill to the house, tired and sunburnt and rested.

When we got there, Miss Lottie was on the front porch,

agitating because we were a little late to supper, and there was some sort of telephone call from my ma that I would have had to answer if I'd been there, but now it was all settled because I wasn't there to answer it. We had some early supper —not very much, because in those days you ate heavy in the middle of the day, and supper was mostly ham and eggs and hominy and biscuits and coffee and maybe a piece of cake. I was yawning before I was through. Then the Old Man pointed to the back yard.

"Go clean those fish, son," he said. "I'm too old and tired to do it, and you might as well learn that a man who catches fish or shoots game has got to make it fit to eat before he sleeps. Otherwise it's all a waste and a sin to take it if you can't use it."

I near about went to sleep, squatting under the fig tree and cleaning those fish. I never saw so many fish. Seems to me we had caught all the fish there were. But finally they were all gutted and scaled and trimmed and washed down in salty water and stuck off in the icebox. I was sort of staggering off to bed when the Old Man hollered at me again.

"Go wash," he said. "I can smell you from here, and you smell like a consarned fish market. Miss Lottie'll raise hell if you fish up her nice clean sheets, and then we'll never be able to go fishing any more."

I went and washed and fell dead in the bed. One of the last thoughts I had was that the Old Man was right when he said that our kind of fishing wasn't work. But he meant that for *him*. He didn't mean it for me. I never worked harder in my life, but it was worth it next morning at breakfast when old Galena, the cook, brought in those trout.

5

September Song

When the autumn came to our coast, just a little ahead of the quail-shooting season, when all the summer visitors went away from Wrightsville Beach and the gray-shingled little beach houses had their windows tacked shut against the northern gales, when the skies got as gray as the shingles and a wood fire was nice at night and all the little shops closed for the long, unprofitable off season—that was when the Old Man and I got into big business with each other.

"It makes a wonderful balance of nature," the Old Man would say, eying the woodpile speculatively, which made me know all of a sudden that he was going to suggest an ax and a small boy to wield it. "When the dodlimbed tourists leave, the bluefish cannot be very far behind. There was a book along those lines, I recall, called *If Winter Comes* or some such. Except I think the writer was reading more spring than bluefish into the script."

As I remember the Old Man, he never said anything at all that you couldn't walk away from three ways and still find a fresh idea in it. I got to where I could listen to him with only one ear, separating the meat from the philosophy, and it wasn't until a lot of years later when I grew up to be a man that I found I remembered more philosophy than meat.

"It is now Labor Day," the Old Man said. "Never quite understood why they call it that, since nobody works on the week end before the Monday they named it after. But on Tuesday the boys will all be gone, and the men will be left. And the bluefish, having watched carefully from Topsail, will come in to commune with the men. Bluefish do not like summer tourists. They like people who admire nor'easters and don't mind a little rain and a squall or so.

"The first thing we will do about bluefish," the Old Man continued, "is to catch a mess of them easy, so you can learn to appreciate the other way. It's too early for them to be inshore, in the sloughs, so we will go trolling for bluefish like the rich people do, and let the boat kill them. I got a connection in the Coast Guard. We will go to Southport and leave early in the morning with Cap'n Willis."

We went on the cutter, and we went out past Caswell, out from Southport, around Frying Pan Shoals. The driver of the boat—he had to be named Midyette, because nearly all Coast Guarders come from Okracoke Island, near Hatteras, and they're all named Midyette down there—tooled the little craft so close to the edge of the shoals you could touch sand with your left hand and see ten fathom of water to your right.

The water was as clear and cool blue as in Bermuda, and the sand as white. The bell buoy was just a little bit behind you, making mournful sounds, and the lightship was over there, as lonesome as the men who lived on her. The gulls wheeled and screamed, and the gannets prowled the water looking for small bait, and off from the sand shoals you could see the big red living shoals of menhaden—pogies, we called them—that the fishing fleet preyed on to make fish-scrap fertilizer.

Here was where the mackerel (we always called them Spanish mackerel) lived, and the kingfish or horse mackerel lived. And here was where the bluefish and the sea trout came into the shallows for the small mullet and the shrimp that swarmed off the rim of the shoals.

"This is silly fishing," the Old Man said. "Don't take any sense or skill at all. All you need is a rod and some line and a hook and piece of bone to make the hook look like a minnow. Heave her over, and the bluefish fight each other for the right to take it. The speed of the boat half-kills the fish, so it is just a matter of hauling them in. Try it and see for yourself."

He handed me a light bass rod, and I flipped the bone minnow over the stern. The line hadn't paid out twenty yards when there was a strike and the rod bent double. It was pretty tough reeling, what with the boat going one way and the fish trying to go another, but I hauled him in. It was a nice bluefish, about two pounds, steely blue in the sun, with his jaw mean-looking and pugnacious and his teeth sharp. He was the first of a hundred, some smaller, which we threw back, and some bigger. One was a four-pounder.

Later on we hooked into a school of mackerel—big, streamlined, speckly fellows that have a chin like a barracuda—and it was the same story. When we finished about 10:00 A.M., we had a boat full of fish—blues, mackerel, a few bonito, and a couple of big kingfish. We had enough fish to feed the whole Coast Guard station and half of the town. Like the Old Man said, it wasn't much sport after the first dozen. But there wasn't anything wrong with them in the skillet or on the little makeshift barbecue the Old Man rigged in front of the shack.

I feel real sorry for people who never had a chance at broiled bluefish or mackerel when the fish is so fresh you have to kill him before you clean him. Some say that blues and mackerel are too fat and oily, but there are some people who don't like snails or oysters and think carrots are just dandy. The way the Old Man cooked them, they tasted better than any fish has a right to taste. He just laid them on the grill over the hot coals and left them until you could see the skin blistering and cracking and turning gold and black, with the white showing through and the grease sizzling steadily onto the coals. When he finally took them off, he had to do it with a flapjack turner; they were so tender they just fell apart. He bathed them in about half a pound of butter per fish, poured vinegar over them, and then dusted them with black pepper. I ate about four pounds of fish before I quit.

Later on in the fall, after the first steady northers had begun to cut sloughs into the beaches and it was getting chilly in the afternoons, he announced one day after lunch that it was time to *really* go fishin'.

"We'll go to Corncake," he said. "I got a hunch the puppy drum are hungry and are in those sloughs stuffin' themselves on sand fleas. This is my kind of fishin'. It ain't murder—it's *fishin'*."

He dug out two big surf rods from under the house and got a big tackle box from his bedroom. We went down to the water front and bought some salt mullet—big ones, thickly crusted with salt—and set out. We took our time. The Old Man said it was no use fishing or hunting any time except real early in the morning or late in the afternoon, because even a fish or a jack rabbit had too much sense to bustle around in the heat of the day.

It was a gray, mean day, with the spume flying and the gulls moaning low and complaining. Along about 5:00 P.M. it was chilly enough for a sweater, and the water was cold on my bare legs. The Old Man spent the first hour trying to teach me to cast, with no bait on my hook. It looked so easy, the way he did it. It looked impossible, the way I did it. He would take the rod, wade out to over his knobby old knees, bring the rod back over his shoulder, with about four feet of line running free. Then he would bring the rod up and over in one single smooth motion, with a whip on the end of the cast. The line would sing through the reel, and the heavy, pyramid-shaped sinker would go whistling out to sea for maybe forty or fifty yards and fall with a plunk right where he was aiming in the slough. Then he'd reel in, very slowly, just enough to keep his line always taut.

When I did it I either threw the sinker into the water at my feet, or jammed the reel and threw the sinker away entirely, or had a backlash right in the middle of the cast. We spent most of the early afternoon unsnarling the reel or putting iodine on the fingers I cut and knocked and line-burned. But I expect young fellows learn pretty fast to do things with their hands, and by dusk I was still clumsy but getting the line out far enough to where at least some fish were. Then the Old Man took his sawbacked ripping knife and showed me how to cut the salt mullet in strips, slicing the inch-and-a-half strips diagonally across the fish. Next he showed me how to work the hook through the strips, weaving it back and forth until the mullet was firm and only the tip of the barb showed. The reason, he said, that we used the mullet instead of fresh bait or shrimps was that the salt had toughened the skin and she'd stay on the hook in rough surf, whereas the other stuff would work off every cast.

The Old Man used a long leader made out of wire, and he hooked two leaders, two hooks, and two baits onto each line. He grinned to himself, humming quietly as he fixed the tackle. His square hands with the broken, stubby fingers and with the old man's brown liver spots on the backs looked clumsy, but they weren't. Anything he handled, from a knife to a gun to a fiddle, was handled so swift and well that it looked easy.

It was growing dark when I stepped out into the icy gray water and cast. The line went out pretty well, the baits whirling through the air, and settled into a slough with a satisfactory chunk. I began to wind her up, to get the belly out of the line, when two bolts of lightning struck. The line screamed out of the reel, and I burned some more fingers before I could get the drag on. It was like being tied fast to two horses, each with his own idea about where he was headed. It seemed that whatever was on that line was going to pull me right into the ocean. But then I began to walk slowly backward, cranking a little bit, keeping the tension on the rod by holding the tip high, the reel close to my belly, and the rod jammed under my arm.

I finally backed up to where the dunes started and the sea oats grew, and I could see the fish coming out of the water, flopping and fighting even on the silver sands. They looked big, like live logs on the beach. I started toward them now, reeling in the slack, and went down to where they lay on the sand. They were both big bluefish, three or four pounds each. I felt like I had just played four quarters of football.

I played out pretty quick, because the rod and reel were heavy and every time I cast—when I didn't backlash—two big bluefish tied into me as soon as the sinker settled. It was taking me fifteen to twenty minutes to land the ones I landed. The ones I lost didn't take so long, and I lost a good deal more than I beached.

By black dark I was cold and wet and sore all over. My hands were cut and full of burning salt, and my back ached like a dissatisfied tooth. But I had caught maybe a dozen big blues, and once a ten-pound puppy drum with the big black spot on his silver backside.

After a while I built a fire out of some driftwood, and sat down to chew on some raw mullet—which tasted delicious—and to watch the Old Man work. The moon rose, about full, and it was like something I had never seen or imagined. The Old Man would wade out and cast into the slough. He would back up, and suddenly he would strike his rod, which would bend double. He would then begin that slow and dignified backward march up the beach, fighting the fish. I was fascinated, watching what eventually emerged from the dark seas onto the moonlit sands.

He fished until midnight. Once he hooked into two drum,

and not puppies. One weighed twenty-two pounds, and the other twenty. He was nearly an hour getting them ashore, and when they finally slid up on the sand they looked as big as a couple of Coast Guard surfboats. He never took a line out of the sea without two fish on it. They were starving, I guess, because he never quit until he was exhausted, and they were still striking two at a time the second the bait hit. The Old Man has been dead a long time now, but I'll never forget the way he looked in the moonlight, horsing two channel bass onto the beach, with the birds screaming and the wind high.

"This," the Old Man said as we headed home with the car full of fish, "is what fishing can be like, where you earn your fish and don't kill him with a boat. I'd rather have two mad bluefish on the same line in a cold ocean than catch all the sailfish and marlin ever made. The only thing I know of that's better is a frisky Atlantic salmon in a cold Canadian stream, on about six ounces of fly rod. I hope you get a chance to try it some day when you're bigger."

I did get a chance when I got bigger, and it was twenty-eight pounds of salmon, and he worked me an hour and a half. But he never gave me what I got out of those first two bluefish in an angry autumn sea.

Now the summer was completely gone, and all the memories of the summer. The time of year I liked better than any other had started. You could tell in so many ways that the summer was finished—your legs didn't sweat the crease out of your Sunday pants any more, and there was just a little nip in the evening air. The dogs that had been listless and shedding hair in the sticky heat got into condition again without being dosed, and began to look hopefully at the tin Liz, like maybe a ride was indicated.

The milky smell of summer was all gone out of the air, and had been replaced by the smell of leaves burning and the tart odor of the last of the grapes. You could feel your blood sparkling inside you, no longer heavy with the summer lethargy. A hot breakfast—pancakes and sausage and eggs busted and mixed into the grits—tasted just fine. The leaves were beginning to crinkle a little on the edges, and the first norther that brought the marsh hens flapping up from flooded marshes had already come and gone. A few ducks—teal, mostly—were beginning to drop in.

I don't know if you remember clearly the unspoken promise of excitement that early autumn brings, just before frost comes to grizzle the grasses in the early morning; before the chinquapins are ripe in their burry shells, before the persimmons lose the alum taste that twists your mouth. It's sort of like the twenty-third of December—Christmas isn't quite here, but it's close enough to ruin your sleep.

This was the time when we went fishing seriously on the week ends—fishing in the cold gray sea that always carried a chop except in the long, smooth sloughs; fishing in the inlets, and fishing off a long pier that went away out into the ocean. It was called Kure's Pier, if I remember right, and it cost something, ten cents or two bits, to fish off it. I used to see a couple of hundred fishermen casting off the pier, and there was so much fishing courtesy around in those days that when a man hung into a real big channel bass all the fishermen on his side would reel in and let him work his fish to the shore.

But by and large there weren't many big ones snagged off Kure's Pier. The stuff ran little—two-pound blues and an occasional sea trout, the odd puppy drum and a whole lot of whiting, which we called Virginia mullet. The Old Man and I didn't crave company very much; we went farther down the coast from Carolina Beach past Kure's to old Fort Fisher, where the big guns used to be aimed against the Civil War blockade runners.

Down there we had the peculiar kind of solitude the Old Man loved and which I loved then, without ever knowing why we loved it. Oh, but that was a scary, desolate beach, the offset currents cutting great sloughs where the big fish lay. The silver-sandy beach came down from steep dunes as high as mountains, with just a fringe of sea oats. There weren't any houses as far as you could see. The bush was warped and gnarled by the winds that never stopped, the myrtle and the cedars and the little hunchbacked oaks twisted and tortured and ever buffeted. The thin screech of the wind was always there, and the water was cold. The rafts of sea ducks looked gloomy, and the birds always screamed louder there than on any other beach I can remember. The general air of age was heightened by the fact that you were always stumbling over an old cannon ball or a rusty saber, and the ghosts flew thick at nightfall.

We used to stop off at Kure's Pier once in a while, just to swap lies with fishing friends. We were an odd bunch, I'm forced to admit. The one I liked best was Chris—Chris Rongotis, or some such name as that—a flat-necked Greek who owned a café, naturally, in town. Chris lived to fish. The restaurant was strictly side-bar. Chris always had a joke for me, or a slab of "oppla pie" or "peenoppla pie" or "strumberry tsortcake" he'd fetched from the restaurant, and a thermos of the hottest coffee in the world. He would tell me what it was like back in Greece, and I learned three bars of the Greek national anthem. Chris just about died laughing at my Greek accent.

There were also a doctor and a dentist and a World War hero with most of himself shot loose. There were a Portygee and a Frenchman and a big blowsy old woman who wore pants and hip boots and cussed worse than anybody I ever heard when she lost a fish. I reckon it was my first real taste of the international set—except none of these internationals could have bribed their way into a parlor. The Portygee even wore big gold earrings and shaved every other Fourth of July.

If you snapped a rod or threw your last leader or ran plumb out of cut bait, somebody would come along and lend you a hand without appearing to be doing you a favor.

What I'm trying to do is tell you how nice it was in the fall, in late October and early November, when the big blues ran close ashore to feed off the minnows and the sand fleas.

Looking back, I can't think of any real big fish we caught, or any lives we saved, or anything poetic or fancy. But this I do remember—an infection I caught which, if the good Lord is willing, I never aim to get cured of. That is the feeling of wonderful contentment a man can have on a lonesome beach that is chilling itself up for winter, sort of practice-swinging to get ready for the bitter cold that's coming.

We had a little weathered gray shingle-and-clapboard cottage rented for the fall fishing. It stuck up on a high bluff just between Carolina and Kure's Beach. If you stepped too spry off the front piazza, you would tumble right down onto the brown mossed-over rocks, which weren't so much rocks as case-hardened sand. There was a rough board step—more of a ladder, actually—that you had to climb up from the beach, about fifty yards straight up.

It wasn't very grand, I must say. It had a toilet and a ramshackle stove and a bedroom and a sitting room and a fireplace. The fireplace was what made it. This fireplace drew so hard that it dang near carried the logs straight up the "chimbley." That was how I pronounced "chimney" until I was about grown, and I still think "chimbley."

This place was home, castle, sanctuary. I mind it so clear, coming in off that beach in the black night. The surf would be booming spooky and sullen, sometimes wild and angry and spume-tossing when the wind freshened. Your feet in the heavy black rubber boots sank down into the squishy sand, and you had to pull them out with a conscious effort as you walked up from the firm, moist sand at the water's edge and slogged through the deep, loose sand to the first steep rise of bluff. You would naturally be carrying a heavy surf rod and a heavy reel and a tackle box, and were generally dragging a string of fish that started out about the size of anchovies and wound up weighing more than a marlin before you got 'em home.

There would be an ache all through your shoulders from casting that heavy line with the four-ounce sinker and the big slab of cut mullet. There would be an ache in the back of your legs from wading in and then walking backward to reel in the fish. There would be cramps in your cold, salt-water-wrinkled red fingers, and your nose would be pink and running. If anybody had snapped you on the ear, the ear would have fallen off. Your feet were just plain frozen inside those clammy rubber boots, and you were salty and sandy from stem to stern.

Somehow you wrestled your gear and yourself up the steep steps in the dark, and the door would open when you moved the wooden latch. The first fellow in lit the lamps, old smoky kerosene lamps, and there wasn't any quarrel about who fixed the fire. Among the Old Man's assorted rules was one unbreakable: you never left the house unless the dishes were washed, dried, and stacked, the beds made, the floor swept and—this above all—a correct fire laid and ready for the long, yellow-shafted, red-headed kitchen match to touch it into flaring life. The Old Man said you couldn't set too much store by a fire; that a fire was all that separated man from beast, if you came right down to it. I believe him. I'd rather live in the yard than in a house that didn't have an open fireplace.

One of the chores I never minded was being the vice-president in charge of the fire detail. I loved to straggle off in the mornings, with the sun still warm and bright before the afternoon winds and clouds chilled the beach, just perusing around for firewood. We had wonderful firewood—sad and twisted old logs, dull silver-gray from salt, big scantlings and pieces of wrecked boats, and stuff like that, all bone-dry and wind-seasoned. The salt or something caused it to burn slow and steady with a blue flame like alcohol burns, and the smell was salt and sand and sea grapes and fire, together. All you needed under it was a few tight-crumpled, greasy old newspapers that the bait had been wrapped in and a lightwood knot or two, and when you nudged her with the match she went up like Chicago when the old lady's cow kicked over the lantern.

With that fire roaring you could cut out one of the lamps, because the fire made that wonderful flickering light which will ruin your eyes if you try to read by it but which, I believe, was responsible for making a President of Honest Abe. You backed up to her and warmed the seat of your pants, with your boots still on, and then turned and baked a little cold out of your chapped, wrinkled hands. Only then did you sit down and haul off the Old Man's boots, with one of his feet seized between your legs and the other in your chest, and then he helped you prize your boots off the same way.

It's funny the things you remember, isn't it? I remember a pair of ankle slippers made out of sheepskin, with the curly wool inside. I would set 'em to toast by the fire as soon as I came through the door. When I popped my bare feet into 'em, they were scorching and felt like a hot bath, a cup of coffee, and a pony for Christmas. Then some hot water on my hands, to wash off the salt and the greasy fish and the dirt. Now I started out to do the supper.

The Old Man said that in deference to his advanced years he had to take a little drink of his nerve tonic, and the least a boy could do would be to lay the table and set up the supper. I liked that, too—the Old Man sitting sprawled in a rocker in front of the fire, his feet spread whopperjawed out toward the flames, puffing on his pipe and taking a little snort and talking kind of lazy about what all had happened that day. Shucks, getting supper wasn't any trouble at all.

You just started the coffee in the tin percolator and got the butter out of the food safe and sliced off a few rounds of bread and dug up the marmalade or the jelly. We had an iron grill that we slid into the fireplace as soon as she began to coal down into nice rosy embers, and it didn't take a minute to lay the halves of yesterday's bluefish or sea trout onto the grill. About the time the fish started to crumble and fall down through the grill I'd stick a skillet full of scrambled eggs over the fire, and in about two shakes dinner was served.

Full as ticks, we'd sit and talk over the second cup of coffee, and then the Old Man would bank the fire and blow out the lamp. We'd reel off to bed, dead from fatigue and food and fire.

These trips were only on week ends, of course, because there was that business about education, which meant I was bespoken five days a week. But from Friday afternoon until Monday morning early, when the Old Man dragged me out of bed before light in order to check my fingernails and cowlick for respectability, I was a mighty happy boy.

And it's funny, as I was saying earlier, but I can't remember the fish. All I remember very clear are Chris the Greek and the cussing lady in the hip boots and the Portygee with the earrings. And how the Old Man's face looked with the fire bright against it, making it cherry red on one side and shadowed black on the other, and how the wind sounded, thrashing on the stout gray shingles that kept us safe inside from storm. I haven't lit a fire from that day to this without seeing, and even smelling a little bit, the presence of beard and bourbon and tobacco and salt air and fish and fire that went to make up the Old Man. I guess that's why some people call me a firebug.

6

Mister Howard Was a Real Gent

The week before Thanksgiving that year, one of the Old Man's best buddies came down from Maryland to spend a piece with the family, and I liked him a whole lot right from the start. Probably it was because he looked like the Old Man—ragged mustache, smoked a pipe, built sort of solid, and he treated me like I was grown up too. He was interested in 'most everything I was doing, and he admired my shotgun, and he told me a whole lot about the dogs and horses he had up on his big farm outside of Baltimore.

He and the Old Man had been friends for a whole lot of years, they had been all over the world, and they were always sitting out on the front porch, smoking and laughing quiet together over some devilment they'd been up to before I was born. I noticed they always shut up pretty quick when Miss

Lottie, who was my grandma, showed up on the scene. Sometimes, when they'd come back from walking down by the river, I could smell a little ripe aroma around them that smelled an awful lot like the stuff that the Old Man kept in his room to keep the chills off him. The Old Man's friend was named Mister Howard.

They were planning to pack up the dogs and guns and a tent and go off on a camping trip for a whole week, 'way into the woods behind Allen's Creek, about fifteen miles from town. They talked about it for days, fussing around with cooking gear, and going to the store to pick up this and that, and laying out clothes. They never said a word to me; they acted as if I wasn't there at all. I was very good all the time. I never spoke at the table unless I was spoken to, and I never asked for more than I ate, and I kept pretty clean and neat, for me. My tongue was hanging out, like a thirsty hound dog's. One day I couldn't stand it any longer.

"I want to go too," I said. "You promised last summer you'd take me camping if I behaved myself and quit stealing your cigars and didn't get drowned and——"

"What do you think, Ned?" Mister Howard asked the Old Man. "Think we could use him around the camp, to do the chores and go for water and such as that?"

"I dunno," the Old Man said. "He'd probably be an awful nuisance. Probably get lost and we'd have to go look for him, or shoot one of us thinking we were a deer, or get sick or bust a leg or something. He's always breaking something. Man can't read his paper around here for the sound of snapping bones."

"Oh, hell, Ned," Mister Howard said, "let's take him. Maybe we can teach him a couple of things. We can always get Tom or Pete to run him back in the flivver, if he don't behave."

"Well," the Old Man said, grinning, "I'd sort of planned to fetch him along all along, but I was waiting to see how long it'd take him to ask."

We crowded a lot of stuff into that old tin Liz. Mister Howard and the Old Man and me and two bird dogs and two hound dogs and a sort of fice dog who was death on squirrels and a big springer spaniel who was death on ducks. Then there were Tom and Pete, two kind of half-Indian backwoods boys who divided their year into four parts. They fished in the summer and hunted in the fall. They made corn liquor in the winter and drank it up in the spring. They were big, dark, lean men, very quiet and strong. Both of them always wore hip boots, in the town and in the woods, on the water or in their own back yards. Both of them worked for the Old Man when the fishing season was on and the pogies were running in big, red, fat-backed schools. They knew just about everything about dogs and woods and water and game that I wanted to know.

The back seat was full of dogs and people and cooking stuff and guns. There were a couple of tents strapped on top of the Liz, a big one and a small one. That old tin can sounded like a boiler factory when we ran over the bumps in the corduroy clay road. I didn't say anything as we rode along. I was much too excited; and anyhow, I figured they might decide to send me back home.

It took us a couple of hours of bumping through the long, yellow savanna-land hills before we came up to a big pond, about five hundred yards from a swamp, or branch, with a clear creek running through it. We drove the flivver up under a group of three big water oaks and parked her. The Old Man had camped there lots before, he said. There was a cleared-out space of clean ground about fifty yards square between the trees and the branch. And there was a small fireplace, or what had been a small fireplace, of big stones. They were scattered around now, all over the place. A flock of tin cans and some old bottles and such had been tossed off in the bush.

"Damned tourists," the Old Man muttered, unloading some tin pots and pans from the back of the car. "Come in here to a man's best place and leave it looking like a hogwallow. You, son, go pick up those cans and bury them some place out of my sight. Then come back here and help with the tents."

By the time I finished collecting the mess and burying it, the men had the tents laid out flat on the ground, the flaps fronting south, because there was a pretty stiff northerly wind working, and facing in the direction of the pond. Tom crawled under the canvas with one pole and a rope, and Pete lifted the front end with another pole and the other end of the rope. Mister Howard was behind with the end of Tom's rope and a peg and a maul. The Old Man was at the front with the end of Pete's rope and another stake and maul. The boys in the tent gave a heave, set the posts, and the two old men hauled taut on the ropes and took a couple of turns around the pegs.

The tent hung there like a blanket on a clothesline until Tom and Pete scuttled out and pegged her out stiff and taut from the sides. They pounded the pegs deep into the dirt, so that the lines around the notches were clean into the earth. It was a simple tent, just a canvas V with flaps fore and aft, but enough to keep the wet out. The other one went up the same way.

We didn't have any bedrolls in those days, or cots either. The Old Man gave me a hatchet and sent me off to chop the branches of the longleaf pine saplings that grew all around— big green needles a foot and a half long. While I was gone he cut eight pine stakes off an old stump, getting a two-foot stake every time he slivered off the stump, and then he cut four long oak saplings. He hammered the stakes into the ground inside the tent until he had a wide rectangle about six by eight feet. Then he split the tops of the stakes. He wedged two saplings into the stakes lengthwise, jamming them with the flat of the ax, and then he jammed two shorter saplings into the others, crosswise. He took four short lengths of heavy fishing cord and tied the saplings to the stakes, at each of the four corners, until he had a framework, six inches off the ground.

"Gimme those pine boughs," he said to me, "and go fetch more until I tell you to stop."

The Old Man took the fresh-cut pine branches, the resin

still oozing stickily off the bright yellow slashes, and started shingling them, butt to the ground. He overlapped the needles like shingles on a house, always with the leaf end up and the branch end down to the ground. It took him about fifteen minutes, but when he finished he had a six-by-eight mattress of the spicy-smelling pine boughs. Then he took a length of canvas tarpaulin and arranged it neatly over the top. There were little grommet holes in each of the four corners, and he pegged the canvas tight over the tops of the saplings that confined the pine boughs. When he was through, you could hit it with your hand and it was springy but firm.

"That's a better mattress than your grandma's got," the Old Man said, grinning over his shoulder as he hit the last lick with the ax. "All it needs is one blanket under you and one over you. You're off the ground, and dry as a bone, with pine needles to smell while you dream. It's just big enough for two men and a boy. The boy gets to sleep in the middle, and he better not thrash around and snore."

By the time he was through and I had spread the blankets, Tom and Pete had made themselves a bed in the other tent, just the same way. The whole operation didn't take half an hour from stopping the car until both tents and beds were ready.

While we were building the beds Mister Howard had strung a line between a couple of trees and had tied a loop in the long leash of each dog, running the loop around the rope between the trees and jamming it with a square knot. The dogs had plenty of room to move in, but not enough to tangle up with each other, and not enough to start to fight when they got fed. They had just room enough between each dog to be sociable and growl at each other without starting a big rumpus. Pretty soon they quit growling and lay down quietly.

We had two big canvas water bags tied to the front of the flivver, and the Old Man gestured at them. "Boys have to handle the water detail in a man's camp," he said. "Go on

down to the branch and fill 'em up at that little spillway.
Don't roil up the water. Just stretch the necks and let the
water run into the bags."

I walked down through the short yellow grass and the sparkleberry bushes to the branch, where you could hear the stream
making little chuckling noises as it burbled over the rocks in
its sandy bed. It was clear, brown water, and smelled a little
like the crushed ferns and the wet brown leaves around it and
in it. When I got back, I could hear the sound of axes off in a
scrub-oak thicket, where Tom and Pete had gone to gather
wood. Mister Howard was sorting out the guns, and the Old
Man was puttering around with the stones where the fire
marks were. He didn't look up.

"Take the hatchet and go chop me some kindling off that
lighterd-knot stump," he said. "Cut 'em small, and try not to
hit a knot and chop off a foot. Won't need much, 'bout an
armful."

When I got back with kindling, Tom and Pete were coming
out of the scrub-oak thicket with huge, heaping armfuls of old
dead branches and little logs as big as your leg. They stacked
them neatly at a respectable distance from where the Old
Man had just about finished his oven. It wasn't much of an
oven—just three sides of stones, with one end open and a few
stones at intervals in the middle. I dumped the kindling down
by him, and he scruffed up an old newspaper and rigged the
fat pine on top, in a little sharp-pointed tepee over the crumpled paper.

He put some small sticks of scrubby oak crisscross over the
fat pine, and then laid four small logs, their ends pointing in to
each other until they made a cross, over the stones and over
the little wigwam of kindling he had erected. Then he touched
a match to the paper, and it went up in a poof. The blaze licked
into the resiny lightwood, which roared and crackled into
flame, soaring in yellow spurts up to the other, stouter kindling and running eager tongues around the lips of the logs.

In five minutes it was roaring, reflecting bright red against the stones.

The Old Man got up and kicked his feet out to get the cramp out of his knees. It was just on late dusk. The sun had gone down, red over the hill, and the night chill was coming. You could see the fog rising in snaking wreaths out of the branch. The frogs were beginning to talk, and the night birds were stirring down at the edge of the swamp. A whippoorwill tuned up.

" 'Bout time we had a little snort, Howard," the Old Man said. "It's going to be chilly. Pete! Fetch the jug!"

Pete ducked into his tent and came out with a half-gallon jug of brown corn liquor. Tom produced four tin cups from the nest of cooking utensils at the foot of the tree on which they had hung the water bags, and each man poured a half-measure of the whisky into his cup. I reckoned there must have been at least half a pint in each cup. Tom got one of the water bags and tipped it into the whisky until each man said, "Whoa." They drank and sighed. The Old Man cocked an eye at me and said, "This is for when you're bigger."

They had another drink before the fire had burned down to coal, with either Tom or Pete getting up to push the burning ends of the logs closer together. When they had a solid bed of coal glowing in the center of the stones, the Old Man heaved himself up and busied himself with a frying pan and some paper packages. He stuck a coffee pot off to one side, laid out five tin plates, dribbled coffee into the pot, hollered for me to fetch some water to pour into the pot, started carving up a loaf of bread, and slapped some big thick slices of ham into the frying pan.

When the ham was done, he put the slices, one by one, into the tin plates, which had warmed through from the fire, and laid slices of bread into the bubbling ham grease. Then he broke egg after egg onto the bread, stirred the whole mess into a thick bread-egg-and-ham-grease omelet, chopped the omelet into sections, and plumped each section onto a slice of ham. He poured the steaming coffee into cups, jerked his thumb at a can of condensed milk and a paper bag of sugar, and announced that dinner was served.

He had to cook the same mess three more times and refill the coffee pot before we quit eating. It was black dark, with no moon, when we lay back in front of the fire. The owls were talking over the whippoorwills, and the frogs were making an awful fuss.

The Old Man gestured at me. "Take the dirty dishes and the pans down to the branch and wash 'em," he said. "Do it now, before the grease sets. You won't need soap. Use sand. Better take a flashlight, and look out for snakes."

I was scared to go down there by myself, through that long stretch of grass and trees leading to the swamp, but I would have died before admitting it. The trees made all sorts of funny ghostly figures, and the noises were louder. When I got back, Mister Howard was feeding the dogs and the Old Man had pushed more logs on the fire.

"You better go to bed, son," the Old Man said. "Turn in in the middle. We'll be up early in the morning, and maybe get us a turkey."

I pulled off my shoes and crawled under the blanket. I heard the owl hoot again and the low mutter from the men, giant black shapes sitting before the fire. The pine-needle mattress smelled wonderful under me, and the blankets were warm. The fire pushed its heat into the tent, and I was as full of food as a tick. Just before I died I figured that tomorrow had to be heaven.

It was awful cold when the Old Man hit me a lick in the ribs with his elbow and said, "Get up, boy, and fix that fire." The stars were still up, frosty in the sky, and a wind was whistling round the corners of the tent. You could see the fire flicker just a mite against the black background of the swamp. Mister

Howard was still snoring on his side of the pine-needle-canvas bed, and I remember that his mustache was riffling, like marsh grass in the wind. Over in Tom and Pete's tent you could hear two breeds of snores. One was squeaky, and the other sounded like a bull caught in a bob-wire fence. I crawled out from under the covers, shivering, and jumped into my hunting boots, which were stiff and very cold. Everything else I owned I'd slept in.

The fire was pretty feeble. It had simmered down into gray ash, which was swirling loosely in the morning breeze. There was just a little red eye blinking underneath the fine talcumy ashes. After kicking some of the ashes aside with my boot, I put a couple of lightwood knots on top of the little chunk of glowing coal, and then I dragged some live-oak logs over the top of the lightwood and waited for her to catch. She caught, and the tiny teeth of flame opened wide to eat the oak. In five minutes I had a blaze going, and I was practically in it. It was mean cold that morning.

When the Old Man saw the fire dancing, he woke up Mister Howard and reached for his pipe first and his boots next. Then he reached for the bottle and poured himself a dram in a tin cup. He shuddered some when the dram went down.

"I heartily disapprove of drinking in the morning," he said. "Except some mornings. It takes a man past sixty to know whether he can handle his liquor good enough to take a nip in the morning. Howard?"

"I'm past sixty too," Mister Howard said. "Pass the jug."

Tom and Pete were coming out of the other tent, digging their knuckles into sleepy eyes. Pete went down to the branch and fetched a bucket of water, and everybody washed their faces out of the bucket. Then Pete went to the fire and slapped some ham into the pan and some eggs into the skillet, set some bread to toasting, and put the coffee pot on. Breakfast didn't take long. We had things to do that day.

After the second cup of coffee—I can still taste that coffee, with the condensed milk sweet and curdled on the top and the coffee itself tasting of branch water and wood smoke—we got up and started sorting out the guns.

"This is a buckshot day," the Old Man said, squinting down the barrel of his pump gun. "I think we better get us a deer today. Need meat in the camp, and maybe we can blood the boy. Tom, Pete, you all drive the branch. Howard, we'll put the boy on a stand where a buck is apt to amble by, and then you and I will kind of drift around according to where the noise seems headed. One, t'other of us ought to get a buck. This crick is populous with deer."

The Old Man paused to light his pipe, and then he turned around and pointed the stem at me.

"You, boy," he said. "By this time you know a lot about guns, but you don't know a lot about guns and deer together. Many a man loses his wits when he sees a big ol' buck bust out of the bushes with a rockin' chair on his head. Trained hunters shoot each other. They get overexcited and just bang away into the bushes. *Mind* what I say. A deer ain't a deer unless it's got horns on its head and you can see all of it at once. We don't shoot does and we don't shoot spike bucks and we don't shoot each other. There ain't no sense to shootin' a doe or a young'un. One buck can service hundreds of does, and one doe will breed you a mess of deer. If you shoot a young'un, you haven't got much meat, and no horns at all, and you've kept him from breedin' to make more deer for you to shoot. If you shoot a man, they'll likely hang you, and if the man is me I will be awful gol-damned annoyed and come back to ha'nt you. You mind that gun, and don't pull a trigger until you can see what it is and *where* it is. *Mind*, I say."

Tom and Pete picked up their pump guns and loaded them. They pushed the load lever down so there'd be no shell in the chamber, but only in the magazine. The Old Man looked at my little gun and said, "Don't bother to load it until you get on the stand. You ain't likely to see anything to shoot for an hour or so."

Tom and Pete went over to where we had the dogs tethered

on a line strung between two trees, and he unleashed the two hounds, Bell and Blue. Bell was black-and-tan and all hound. Blue was a kind of a sort of dog. He had some plain hound, some Walker hound, and some bulldog and a little beagle and a smidgen of pointer in him. He was ticked blue and brown and black and yellow and white. He looked as if somebody spilled the eggs on the checkered tablecloth. But he was a mighty dandy deer dog, or so they said. Old Sam Watts, across the street, used to say there wasn't no use trying to tell Blue anything, because Blue had done forgot more than you knew and just got annoyed when you tried to tell him his business.

Tom snapped a short lead on Blue, and Pete snapped another one on Bell. They shouldered their guns and headed up the branch, against the wind. We let 'em walk, while the Old Man and Mister Howard puttered around, like old people and most women will. Drives a boy crazy. What I wanted to do was go and shoot myself a deer. *Now.*

After about ten minutes the Old Man picked up his gun and said, "Let's go." We walked about half a mile down the swamp's edge. The light had come now, lemon-colored, and the fox squirrels were beginning to chase each other through the gum trees. We spied one old possum in a persimmon tree, hunched into a ball and making out like nobody knew he was there. We heard a turkey gobble away over yonder somewheres, and we could hear the doves beginning to moan—*oooh—oohoo —ooooh.*

All the little birds started to squeak and chirp and twitter at each other. The dew was staunchly stiff on the grass and on the sparkleberry and gallberry bushes. It was still cold, but getting warmer, and breakfast had settled down real sturdy in my stomach. Rabbits jumped out from under our feet. We stepped smack onto a covey of quail just working its way out of the swamp, and they like to have scared me to death when they busted up under our feet. There was a lot going on in that swamp that morning.

We turned into the branch finally, and came up to a track that the Old Man said was a deer run. He looked around and spied a stump off to one side, hidden by a tangle of dead brush. From the stump you could see clear for about fifty yards in a sort of accidental arena.

"Go sit on that stump, boy," the Old Man said. "You'll hear the dogs after a while, and if a deer comes down this branch he'll probably bust out there, where that trail comes into the open, because there ain't any other way he can cross it without leaving the swamp. Don't let the dogs fool you into not paying attention. When you hear 'em a mile away, the chances are that deer will be right in your lap. Sometimes they travel as much as two miles ahead of the dogs, just slipping along, not running; just slipping and sneaking on their little old quiet toes. And stay still. A deer'll run right over you if you stay still and the smell is away from him. But if you wink an eye, he can see it two hundred yards off, and will go the other way."

I sat down on the stump. The Old Man and Mister Howard went off, and I could hear them chatting quietly as they disappeared. I looked all around me. Nothing much was going on now, except a couple of he-squirrels were having a whale of a fight over my head, racing across branches and snarling squirrel cuss words at each other. A chickadee was standing on its head in a bush and making chickadee noises. A redheaded woodpecker was trying to cut a live-oak trunk in half with his bill. A rain crow—a kind of cuckoo, it is—was making dismal noises off behind me in the swamp, and a big old yellowhammer was swooping and dipping from tree to tree.

There were some robins hopping around on a patch of burnt ground, making conversation with each other. Crows were cawing, and two doves looped in to sit in a tree and chuckle at each other. A towhee was scratching and making more noise than a herd of turkeys, and some catbirds were meowing in the low bush while a big, sassy old mocker was imitating them kind of sarcastically. Anybody who says woods are quiet is crazy. You learn how to listen. The Tower of Babel was a study period alongside of woods in the early morning.

It is wonderful to smell the morning. Anybody who's been around the woods knows that morning smells one way, high noon another, dusk still another, and night most different of all, if only because the skunks smell louder at night. Morning smells fresh and flowery and little-breezy, and dewy and spanking new. Noon smells hot and a little dusty and sort of sleepy, when the breeze has died and the heads begin to droop and anything with any sense goes off into the shade to take a nap. Dusk smells scary. It is getting colder and everybody is going home tired for the day, and you can smell the turpentine scars on the trees and the burnt-off ground and the bruised ferns and the rising wind. You can hear the folding-up, I'm-finished-for-the-day sounds all around, including the colored boys whistling to prove they ain't scared when they drive the cows home. And in the night you can smell the fire and the warm blankets and the coffee a-boil, and you can even smell the stars. I know that sounds silly, but on a cool, clear, frosty night the stars have a smell, or so it seems when you are young and acutely conscious of everything bigger than a chigger.

This was as nice a smelling morning as I can remember. It smelled like it was going to work into a real fine-smelling day. The sun was up pretty high now and was beginning to warm the world. The dew was starting to dry, because the grass wasn't clear wet any more but just had little drops on top, like a kid with a runny nose. I sat on the stump for about a half-hour, and then I heard the dogs start, a mile or more down the swamp. Bell picked up the trail first, and she sounded as if church had opened for business. Then Blue came in behind her, loud as an organ, their two voices blending—fading sometimes, getting stronger, changing direction always.

Maybe you never heard a hound in the woods on a frosty fall morning, with the breeze light, the sun heating up in the sky, and the "aweful" expectancy that something big was going to happen to you. There aren't many things like it. When the baying gets closer and closer and still closer to you, you feel as if maybe you're going to explode if something doesn't happen quick. And when the direction changes and the dogs begin to fade, you feel so sick you want to throw up.

But Bell and Blue held the scent firmly now, and the belling was clear and steady. The deer was moving steady and straight, not trying to circle and fool the dogs, but honestly running. And the noise was coming straight down the branch, with me on the other end of it.

The dogs had come so close that you could hear them panting between their bays, and once or twice one of them quit sounding and broke into a yip-yap of barks. I thought I could hear a little tippety-tappety noise ahead of them, in between the belling and the barking, like mice running through paper or a rabbit hopping through dry leaves. I kept my eyes pinned onto where the deer path opened into the clearing. The dogs were so close that I could hear them crash.

All of a sudden there was a flash of brown and two does, flop-eared, with two half-grown fawns skipped out of the brush, stopped dead in front of me, looked me smack in the face, and then gave a tremendous leap that carried them halfway across the clearing. They bounced again, white tails carried high, and disappeared into the branch behind me. As I turned to watch them go there was another crash ahead and the buck tore through the clearing like a race horse. He wasn't jumping. This boy was running like the wind, with his horns laid back against his spine and his ears pinned by the breeze he was making. The dogs were right behind him. He had held back to tease the dogs into letting his family get a start, and now that they were out of the way he was pouring on the coal and heading for home.

I had a gun with me and the gun was loaded. I suppose it would have fired if the thought had occurred to me to pull the trigger. The thought never occurred. I just watched that big buck deer run, with my mouth open and my eyes popped out of my head.

The dogs tore out of the bush behind the buck, baying out their brains and covering the ground in leaps. Old Blue looked at me as he flashed past and curled his lip. He looked as if he were saying, "This is man's work, and what is a boy doing here, spoiling my labor?" Then he dived into the bush behind the buck.

I sat there on the stump and began to shake and tremble. About five minutes later there was one shot, a quarter-mile down the swamp. I sat on the stump. In about half an hour Tom and Pete came up to my clearing.

"What happened to the buck?" Pete said. "Didn't he come past here? I thought I was going to run him right over you."

"He came past, all right," I said, feeling sick-mean, "but I never shot. I never even thought about it until he was gone. I reckon you all ain't ever going to take me along any more." My lip was shaking and now I *was* about to cry.

Tom walked over and hit me on top of the head with the flat of his hand. "Happens to everybody," he said. "Grown men and boys, both, they all get buck fever. Got to do it once before you get over it. Forget it. I seen Pete here shoot five times at a buck big as a horse last year, and missed him with all five."

There were some footsteps in the branch where the deer had disappeared, and in a minute Mister Howard and the Old Man came out, with the dogs leashed and panting.

"Missed him clean," the Old Man said cheerfully. "Had one whack at him no farther'n thirty yards and missed him slick as a whistle. That's the way it is, but there's always tomorrow. Let's us go shoot some squirrels for the pot, and we'll rest the dogs and try again this evenin'. You *see* him, boy?"

"I *saw* him," I said. "And I ain't ever going to *forget* him."

We went back to camp and tied up the hounds. We unleashed the fice dog, Jackie, the little sort of yellow fox terrier kind of nothing dog with prick ears and a sharp fox's face and a thick tail that curved up over his back. I was going with Pete to shoot some squirrels while the old gentlemen policed up the camp, rested, took a couple of drinks, and started to prepare lunch. It was pretty late in the morning for squirrel hunting, but this swamp wasn't hunted much. While I had been on the deer stand that morning the swamp was alive with them—mostly big fox squirrels, huge old fellers with a lot of black on their gray- and-white hides.

"See you don't get squirrel fever," the Old Man hollered over his shoulder as Pete and I went down to the swamp. "Else we'll all starve to death. I'm about fresh out of ham and eggs."

"Don't pay no 'tention to him, son," Pete told me. "He's a great kidder."

"Hell with him," I said. "He missed the deer, didn't he? At least *I* didn't miss him."

"That's right," Pete agreed genially. "You got to shoot at 'em to miss 'em."

I looked quick and sharp at Pete. He didn't seem to be teasing me. A cigarette was hanging off the corner of his lip, and his lean, brown, Injun-looking face was completely straight. Then we heard Jackie, yip-yapping in a querulous bark, as if somebody had just insulted him by calling him a dog.

"Jackie done treed hisself a squirrel," Pete said. "Advantage of a dog like Jackie is that when the squirrels all come down to the ground to feed, ol' Jackie rousts 'em up and makes 'em head for the trees. Then he makes so much noise he keeps the squirrel interested while we go up and wallop away at him. Takes two men to hunt squirrels this way. Jackie barks. I go around to the other side of the tree. Squirrel sees me and moves. That's when you shoot him, when he slides around on your side. Gimme your gun."

"Why?" I asked. "What'll I use to shoot the——"

"*Mine*," Pete answered. "You ain't going to stand there and tell me you're gonna use a shotgun on a squirrel? Anybody can hit a pore little squirrel with a shotgun. Besides, shotgun shells cost a nickel apiece."

I noticed Pete's gun for the first time. He had left his pump gun in camp and had a little bolt-action .22. He took my shotgun from me and handed me the .22 and a handful of cartridges.

" 'Nother thing you ought to know," Pete said as we walked up to the tree, a big blue gum under which Jackie seemed to be going mad, "is that when you're hunting for the pot you don't belong to make much more noise with guns than is necessary. You go booming off a shotgun, blim-blam, and you spook ever'-thing in the neighborhood. A .22 don't make no more noise than a stick crackin', and agin the wind you can't hear it more'n a hundred yards or thereabouts. Best meat gun in the world, a straight-shootin' .22, because it don't make no noise and don't spoil the meat. Look up yonder, on the fourth fork. There's your dinner. A big ol' fox squirrel, near-about black all over."

The squirrel was pasted to the side of the tree. Pete walked around, and the squirrel moved with him. When Pete was on the other side, making quite a lot of noise, the squirrel shifted back around to my side. He was peeping at Pete, but his shoulders and back and hind legs were on my side. I raised the little .22 and plugged him between the shoulders. He came down like a sack of rocks. Jackie made a dash for him, grabbed him by the back, shook him once and broke his spine, and sort of spit him out on the ground. The squirrel was dang near as big as Jackie.

Pete and I hunted squirrels for an hour or so, and altogether we shot ten. Pete said that was enough for five people for a couple of meals, and there wasn't no sense to shootin' if the meat had to spoil. "We'll have us some venison by tomorrow, anyways," he said. "One of us is bound to git one. You shot real nice with that little bitty gun," he said. "She'll go where you hold her, won't she?"

I felt pretty good when we went into camp and the Old Man, Mister Howard, and Tom looked up inquiringly. Pete and I started dragging fox squirrels out of our hunting coats, and the ten of them made quite a sizable pile.

"Who shot the squirrels?" the Old Man asked genially. "The dog?"

"Sure," Pete grinned. "Dog's so good we've taught him to shoot, too. We jest set down on a log, give Jackie the gun, and sent him off into the branch on his lonesome. We're planning to teach him to skin 'em and cook 'em, right after lunch. This is the best dog I ever see. Got more sense than people."

"Got more sense than *some* people," the Old Man grunted. "Come and git it, boy, and after lunch you and Jackie can skin the squirrels."

The lunch was a lunch I loved then and still love, which is why I'm never going to be called one of those epicures. This was a country hunting lunch, Carolina style. We had Vienna sausages and sardines, rat cheese, gingersnaps and dill pickles and oysterettes and canned salmon, all cold except the coffee that went with it, and that was hot enough to scald clean down to your shoes. It sounds horrible, but I don't know anything that tastes so good together as Vienna sausages and sardines and rat cheese and gingersnaps. Especially if you've been up since before dawn and walked ten miles in the fresh air.

After lunch we stretched out in the shade and took a little nap. Along about two I woke up, and so did Pete and Tom, and the three of us started to skin the squirrels. It's not much trouble, if you know how. Pete and I skinned 'em and Tom cleaned and dressed 'em. I'd pick up a squirrel by the head, and Pete would take his hind feet. We'd stretch him tight, and Pete would slit him down the stomach and along the legs as far as the feet. Then he'd shuck him like an ear of corn, pulling the hide toward the head until it hung over his head like a cape and the squirrel was naked. Then he'd just chop off the head, skin and all, and toss the carcass to Tom.

Tom made a particular point about cutting the little castor glands. Squirrel with the musk glands out is as tasty as any meat I know, but unless you take out those glands an old he-squirrel is as musky as a billy goat, and tastes like a billy goat smells. Tom cut up the carcasses and washed them clean, and I proceeded to bury the heads, hides, and guts.

The whole job didn't take forty-five minutes with the three of us working. We put the pieces of clean red meat in a covered pot, and then woke up the Old Man and Mister Howard. We were going deer hunting again.

The dogs had rested too; they had had half a can of salmon each and about three hours' snooze. It was beginning to cool off when Tom and Pete put Blue and Bell on walking leashes and we struck off for another part of the swamp, which made a Y from the main swamp and had a lot of water in it. It was a cool swamp, and Tom and Pete figured that the deer would be lying up there from the heat of the day, and about ready to start stirring out to feed a little around dusk.

I was in the process of trying to think about just how long forever was when the hounds started to holler real close. They seemed to be coming straight down the crick off to my right, and the crick's banks were very open and clear, apart from some sparkleberry and gallberry bushes. The *whoo-whooing* got louder and louder. The dogs started to growl and bark, just letting off a *woo-woo* once in a while, and I could hear a steady swishing in the bushes.

Then I could see what made the swishing. It was a buck, a big one. He was running steadily and seriously through the low bush. He had horns—my Lord, but did he have horns! It looked to me like he had a dead tree lashed to his head. I slipped off the safety catch and didn't move. The buck came straight at me, the dogs going crazy behind him.

The buck came down the water's edge, and when he got to about fifty yards I stood up and threw the gun up to my face. He kept coming and I let him come. At about twenty-five yards he suddenly saw me, snorted, and leaped to his left as if somebody had unsnapped a spring in him. I forgot he was a deer. I shot at him as you'd lead a duck or a quail on a quartering shot—plenty of lead ahead of his shoulder.

I pulled the trigger—for some odd reason shooting the choke barrel—right in the middle of a spring that had him six feet off the ground and must have been wound up to send him twenty yards, into the bush and out of my life. The gun said *boom!*

but I didn't hear it. The gun kicked but I didn't feel it. All I saw was that this monster came down out of the sky like I'd shot me an airplane. He came down flat, turning completely over and landing on his back, and he never wiggled.

The dogs came up ferociously and started to grab him, but they had sense and knew he didn't need any extra grabbing. I'd grabbed him real good, with about three ounces of No. 1 buckshot in a choke barrel. I had busted his shoulder and busted his neck and dead-centered his heart. I had let him get so close that you could practically pick the wads out of his shoulder. This was *my* buck. Nobody else had shot at him. Nobody else had seen him but me. Nobody had advised or helped. This monster was mine.

And monster was right. He was huge, they told me later, for a Carolina whitetail. He had fourteen points on his rack, and must have weighed nearly 150 pounds undressed. He was beautiful gold on his top and dazzling white on his under-neath, and his little black hoofs were clean. The circular tufts of hair on his legs, where the scent glands are, were bright russet and stiff and spiky. His horns were as clean as if they'd been scrubbed with a wire brush, gnarled and evenly forked and the color of planking on a good boat that's just been holy-stoned to where the decks sparkle.

I had him all to myself as he lay there in the aromatic, crushed ferns—all by myself, like a boy alone in a big cathedral of oaks and cypress in a vast swamp where the doves made sobbing sounds and the late birds walked and talked in the sparkleberry bush. The dogs came up and lay down. Old Blue laid his muzzle on the big buck's back. Bell came over and licked my face and wagged her tail, like she was saying, "You did real good, boy." Then she lay down and put her face right on the deer's rump.

This was our deer, and no damn bear or anything else was go-ing to take it away from us. We were a team, all right, me and Bell and Blue.

I couldn't know then that I was going to grow up and shoot

elephants and lions and rhinos and things. All I knew then was that I was the richest boy in the world as I sat there in the crushed ferns and stroked the silky hide of my first buck deer, patting his horns and smelling how sweet he smelled and admiring how pretty he looked. I cried a little bit inside about how lovely he was and how I felt about him. I guess that was just reaction, like being sick twenty-five years later when I shot my first African buffalo.

I was still patting him and patting the dogs when Tom and Pete came up one way and the Old Man and Mister Howard came up from another way. What a wonderful thing it was. when you are a kid, to have four huge, grown men—everything is bigger when you are a boy—come roaring up out of the woods to see you sitting by your first big triumph. "Smug" is a word I learned a lot later. Smug was modest for what I felt then.

"Well," the Old Man said, trying not to grin.

"Well," Mister Howard said.

"Boy done shot hisself a horse with horns," Pete said, as proud for me as if I had just learned how to make bootleg liquor.

"Shot him pretty good, too," Tom said. "Deer musta been standing still, boy musta been asleep, woke up, and shot him in self-defense."

"Was not, either," I started off to say, and then saw that all four men were laughing.

They had already checked the sharp scars where the buck had jumped, and they knew I had shot him on the fly. Then Pete turned the buck over and cut open his belly. He tore out the paunch and ripped it open. It was full of green stuff and awful smelly gunk. All four men let out a whoop and grabbed me. Pete held the paunch and the other men stuck my head right into—blood, guts, green gunk, and all. It smelled worse than anything I ever smelled. I was bloody and full of partly digested deer fodder from my head to my belt.

"That," the Old Man said as I swabbed the awful mess off me and dived away to stick my head in the crick, "makes you a grown man. You have been blooded, boy, and any time you miss a deer from now on we cut off your shirt tail. It's a very good buck, son," he said softly, "one of which you can be very, very proud."

Tom and Pete cut a long sapling, made slits in the deer's legs behind the cartilage of his knees, stuck the sapling through the slits, and slung the deer up on their backs. They were sweating him through the swamp when suddenly the Old Man turned to Mister Howard and said, "Howard, if you feel up to it, we might just as well go get *our* deer and lug him into camp. He ain't but a quarter-mile over yonder, and I don't want the wildcats working on him in that tree."

"What deer?" I demanded. "You didn't shoot this afternoon, and you missed the one you——"

The Old Man grinned and made a show of lighting his pipe. "I didn't miss him, son," he said. "I just didn't want to give you an inferiority complex on your first deer. If you hadn't of shot this one—and he's a lot better'n mine—I was just going to leave him in the tree and say nothing about him at all. Shame to waste a deer; but it's a shame to waste a boy, too."

I reckon that's when I quit being a man. I just opened my mouth and bawled. Nobody laughed at me, either.

7

Somebody Else's Turkey Tastes Better

It was pushing on for Christmas when my grandma, Miss Lottie, pursed her mouth one day after she finished pouring the coffee, and remarked that if there were any menfolk in the house worth the powder and shot to blow them to perdition they would bestir themselves and go find a couple of wild turkeys that were dumber than they were. "The price of meat," Miss Lottie said, "has gone up something terrible, and I do not propose to pay ten cents a pound for turkey. You either shoot it or you don't eat it this year."

The Old Man cut his eyes at me over the coffee cup and allowed that he would finish his coffee on the piazza, because he wanted to smoke his pipe, and Miss Lottie had some definite ideas about smoking in the house. Unless she did it herself. She had the asthma and smoked Cubeb cigarettes for her chest troubles. I broke in on Cubebs at a very early age.

"The way of a man with a woman is hard," the Old Man said when he was settled down in his rocker and had fired up the Prince Albert. "I reckon there's just nothing for us to do but leave her bed and board for a spell. It's a tough life, son, and you might as well recognize it early. Here we just got back from a hard week in the woods, up every morning before dawn, doing our own cooking, walking all day long, freezing on stumps waiting for deer to come by, and now we got to go back to the same place we left and do it all over again. My, *my*. Women are so unreasonable. If I had of suggested even mildly that maybe you and me ought to go turkey hunting, she would of found sixty different reasons to keep us home."

The Old Man knocked the dottle out of his pipe and walked laboriously upstairs. He came down five minutes later with a peculiar-looking flute thing made out of cedar and a stick of chalk in his hand. He rubbed the chalk on the cedar and moved some sliding parts, and the most lonesome piece of hen-turkey clucking I ever heard came out of it. Then he did something else to the calling apparatus, and a ferocious gobble emerged. The Old Man stuck the turkey caller in his pocket and pulled out his watch.

"I'd say four minutes, maybe five," he said softly, and when I asked him what and why, he just nodded and said to wait.

I had a dollar watch of my own, and I pulled it out to see what he was waiting for. In exactly four and one-half minutes Tom and Pete came roaring down the street, taking giant strides in their hip boots.

"Well," the Old Man said, "I was pretty near right. I estimated between four and five minutes, and you split the difference with me. I reckon you're both gettin' old. There was a time you would of been here in two minutes flat when I I sounded off on a turkey call."

Tom and Pete grinned. "We're ready to go now if you are, Ned," they said. "Lend us the boy and the flivver, and we'll be ripe to leave in an hour. Ain't nothing to do but th'ow in the tent and the guns and the food and the blankets and the shells."

"Get her ready," the Old Man said. "We can make the place by dark if we hurry, and be up in the morning. When Miss Lottie demands turkeys, I hate mightily to disappoint her."

All through this double-talky stuff I was not saying a word, because nobody had come right out to say whether I was invited or not. I was thinking of myself as a real professional about now, after having recently shot me a deer, but I knew you couldn't crowd the Old Man any and, for all I knew, he and Pete and Tom and Grandma were all in some sort of plot or other to torture me. Wouldn't be the first time it happened, either.

I helped Tom and Pete load all the duffel into the flivver, and Pete drove her up in front of the house. I just stood there and didn't say anything, looking kind of wistful like Oliver Twist asking for another helping of gruel.

"Well, boy," the Old Man said, "I see everything in this Liz but your gun. Who's going to shoot the turkeys if you don't rustle upstairs and get that 16-gauge?"

I rustled.

Tom and Pete were in the front seat and the Old Man and I were jammed into the back of the Liz. We didn't head up the main road, but went up the River Road, a back road. The Old Man addressed the back of Tom's head.

"It would seem to me," he said to nobody in particular, "that a wild thing is God's property. A turkey or a deer is born, and he ain't got any way of knowing whether he belongs to a rich man or a poor man. But a rich man will come along and buy up a great passel of land, and then go off to New York or to Paris, France, and leave the land there all by itself. Gradually the word spreads around amongst the wild critters that this here is heaven on earth, a kind of pie-in-the-sky operation for everybody. The rich man, like the feller that owns these Magnolia Acres, is off playing Willie-off-the-pickle-boat in his yacht somewhere, and what is happening? Nobody is shooting over his ground, but all the birds and animals for miles around are hived up there. The cock birds are fighting the other cock birds, and the deer are fighting the deer, and inbreeding is going on, and the first thing you know diseases will start, and then we'll have an epidemic of blacktongue or screwworm or galloping pip, and all the crittes'll die off or get inbred or something and do nobody no good in the meantime.

"Now," the Old Man said, "I'm a law-abiding man, first, last, and always. If this Willie-off-the-pickle-boat would ask me to caretake his property, I would be pleased to keep his game shot down to a reasonable balance; but as long as I ain't got a yacht and don't live in the French Riveera, there ain't much chance of him asking me. Mind, I wouldn't set foot on his property for a pretty, because it plainly says 'Posted' every whipstitch. But he don't own the other side of the road. That he don't. That's public ground. And I was just thinking that if a turkey was dumb enough to cross that road we might shoot him legal-like, since we all have hunting licenses. If this offends anybody's sense of morals, ethics, or legal tendencies, now's the time to speak up."

I could see the neckskin stretch on Tom and Pete when they grinned. The chances were pretty good that no Christmas or New Year's ever passed without a houseful of wild turkey, and I reckoned that the three had had themselves a dead-sure cinch for more years than I was born. But this was the first crack I'd had at looking at it.

We drove on for an hour or more and finally came up to the millionaire's place, which was highly fenced off on one side of the road and every tenth tree had a big "No Hunting" sign on it. We turned off a little washboarded clay road in the other direction, drove about half a mile, and came to a campsite that looked exactly like the last one I saw that the Old Man had anything to do with. He left a trade-mark on all his camps. They looked like he'd manicured them before he left. I *know; I* manicured the last one until all that was left was a neat pile of stones for the cook-fire. Everything else was either burned up or buried.

We made a swift camp, had a swift meal, built some swift beds, and went swiftly off to sleep. I hadn't even turned over good before Pete was shaking me. The moon was still high and the stars still very bright. It was four o'clock in the morning, an awful hour for anybody to get up. It was cold as Christmas in Canada. We had a cup of coffee and that was all.

"All I ask of you, young man," the Old Man said, "is to just follow me and Pete and Tom, do what we do, keep your mouth shut, try not to step on no dry sticks, sit when we sit, and when I punch you on the arm you shoot. You will know what to shoot at."

We headed off through the black woods, stepping carefully along an old deer path, Tom first, Pete second, then the Old Man, and finally me. We walked about a quarter of a mile, until we came to a little glade about a thousand yards from the main road. It had bush all around it. At the far end, away from the road, it had a suspicious-looking hump of bush that didn't look quite like the other bush. Pete and Tom and the Old Man disappeared in it. I followed. It was quite a comfortable blind, broad enough to hold four shooters, with little slits cut for the eyes to see out of and big enough to poke a gun out of. It was still dark, and my Lord, but it was cold, sitting shivering on the slick brown pine needles.

The Old Man whispered, "As soon as it comes gray light you're going to see some turkeys. They may fly in, light in trees, look around, and then come down. They don't do it so much in the morning, but I never trust a turkey. He's smarter than you are most all the time. Likely they'll walk. If it's a little flock, there'll be a gobbler and mebbe three, four, five hens. If it's a big flock, there'll be more'n one gobbler and a whole passel of hens. I want you to shoot whatever's biggest that's closest to you, when I punch you, and not before. Take a bead on his head and try to think that you're shooting a robin. No point shooting him in the white meat when his head is right there and plenty target. This one is for your grandma. Now be quiet and watch."

It came on dawn and the Old Man got out his turkey call. He fiddled with it in the gray half-light, and then he sounded off like he was the sole owner of a turkey farm. He chuckled seductively, like a hen turkey hunting a boy friend. He gobbled like a boy friend hunting a hen turkey. Then he shut himself up and never struck another note. Later he told me that the point in turkey calling was not to overdo it. If there was a turkey around that was coming to call, he'd come.

A lot of years later I sat in leopard blinds, and that was tense. But it wasn't as tense as waiting out a turkey. The turkeys never flew in. They crept in like wraiths, as fog sweeps into narrow alleys. First they weren't there, and then they were there, looking as big as cows. They came out of a little avenue in single file. The first ones were hens. Then there were some yearling gobblers. Then more hens, and finally the Chief.

They fanned out, feeding gently toward us. I suspect now that Tom and Pete had kept that clearing ankle-deep in corn against the annual T-day, but baiting was legal in those days, and anyhow they could have been eating pine mast. I didn't care, one way or the other. I was watching that gobbler, the Chief. He spread his tail like a vast fan and let out a gobble that sounded like "The Bells of St. Mary's." He gazed arrogantly around him and dared any turkey in the neighborhood to flap so much as a wattle at one of his wives and he, personally, the Chief, would tear him limb from wing. He hustled his gang along, coming straight at the blind; Pete told me later there were sixteen or seventeen turkeys in the family. I dunno. All I saw was the head man, his wattles red in the early dawn, his purplish breast as big as a feather bed, his bronze-and-black coming out in the emerging light. I never will see a moa, but this thing was bigger than any ostrich.

Finally he strutted down the center of his family, cursing quietly to himself in Turkish, and hauled up about thirty yards from the blind like a general surveying his troops. Then he let out a gobble fit to wake the millionaire in Paris, France, and stretched his neck to heaven, saying he would take on any angels that were flying around loose that morning too. That's when the Old Man punched me on the arm.

I hid his head with the front sight of the little sixteen and hauled down. When I hauled down, Tom, Pete, and the Old Man hauled down. I only hauled once. They hauled twice, but what happened in that grassy little pine glade I'm not apt to forget. My man, the Chief, was down, with his head shot off, but he was roaring around with his wings like he was a windmill gone crazy. So were exactly six other turkeys. Seven wild turkeys doing a death dance in a quiet forest glade before sunup make any pictures I ever saw of the poor souls in hell look like a quiet pastoral.

Everybody seemed to be whooping and running, including two turkeys which got up and headed for the brush, but which caught loads of No. 2 shot in their trousers and decided to stay. But for confusion I've never seen anything like it, now, then, or ever, even the one day when I was a grown man and got mixed up with nine lions. Seemed to me the whole danged countryside had turned into turkey.

What happened was that, when I assassinated the Chief, Tom and Pete and the Old Man had also picked targets and whanged off at them, killing them real dead. Then they threw the other barrel into the flock as it took off, and scored again. Like I said, only two were wounded enough to run.

I expect that set some sort of record. My victim—that turned out to be tougher than whit leather—weighed nineteen pounds, which I understand now is a lot of turkey. We had two other toms over ten pounds, and the hens were all a nice six, seven, eight pounds of plump eating.

I mean we were a sight to see when the Liz drew up in front of the house and Miss Lottie came out with that all-right-where-is-it look on her face. We slung 'em out one at a time, and even Miss Lottie couldn't keep her face straight in front of seven big new wild turkeys. We had turkey those holidays until I wished I'd never seen one. The Old Man didn't have much to say about the feat. Sometime between Christmas and New Year's he got me off to one side and muttered a parable at me.

"The trouble," he said, "with people and turkeys is not knowing which side of the road to stay on in face of temptation."

One of the great things I remember about the grown-ups who raised me was that when Christmas came around they never gave me anything I needed. By "needed" I mean to say I knew a kid next door who was always getting something worthy, like a new pair of shoes or a school suit, which may be practical and fine economy, but I never saw any romance in a roof on a house. A house belongs to have a roof, and is not supposed to get one for Christmas. When a boy gets a school suit or a new pair of shoes, they aren't a gift. They're a roof on a house.

Fair times or foul, what I got for Chistmas and birthdays was a luxury, even if it was only a pocketknife worth fifty cents. Most of the time it was considerably more, because that was before the Big Depression, and everybody had some money to spend on fun. By "everybody" I suppose I mean my own family, because the early Christmases started out with air guns and bicycles and such, and wound up with hunting boots and knives and scout axes and punching bags and shotguns. I reckon the most memorable of them all was the one when I got a blue Iver Johnson bicycle *and* a shotgun.

It was a lot of fun prowling the ten-cent stores to buy notable gifts for the grown-ups, and it was a lot of fun waiting for Santa Claus to bring you something you'd been hammering at the family about for six months, but the real fun didn't start until afterward, around the New Year's, when you were still free from school and could really concentrate on using the loot you'd found under the tree.

Christmas itself was pretty well cluttered up with grown

people—visiting aunts and cousins and stuff, largely city people come slumming to the country—and a fellow was expected to hang around with a clean face and a decent air of raising until they all cleared out and let you revert to dirty fingernails and your normal lack of hair comb. Then was when the pure fun started.

The holiday season was pretty special for me. As soon as school let out, about the twentieth, I took off for the little town where the Old Man lived, and I didn't get back to my own city until the day before school started again. For better than two weeks I lived a life like I imagine it might have been in the old English-squire days, when they hung the halls with holly and it took three men and a boy to haul in the Yule log.

I don't remember any pigs stuffed whole, with apples in their mouths, but I do know that certain expeditions had to be made by the Old Man and his willing assistant, which was your ob't sv't, and these expeditions lasted right on through the holidays.

First, there was the oyster business. Holiday time was oyster time, because there were plenty of R's in the months, and the oysters were fine and firm and fat, as big as cucumbers, with their gray-and-white shells the color of a pintail duck and the big deep-cut wrinkles running down to the scalloped edges. Maybe there isn't much romance to an oyster unless you find a pearl in one. To me oysters even without pearls are romantic.

The Old Man and I used to go out in the skiff, with the tongs, on a cold gray day when the ducks were scudding low and sitting cosy around corners of the marsh. We would take the guns, of course, because there would always be some fool duck that would wait too long to take off, and whichever one of us wasn't poling or rowing the skiff would grab a shotgun off the gunwale and haul him down. Once I saw a little animal with a head like a rat swimming, and the Old Man said, "Shoot him!" and it was a big boar mink. We skinned him out and stretched him and salted him, and the man in town gave me two dollars for his hide.

But you would go out over the wind-stirred gray waters,

with your nose and ears bitten red by the cold, and finally come to the oyster beds. You would take the tongs and grapple along until you tied into a likely clump, and up they'd come, muddy, and you would swish the full-loaded tongs back and forth in the water until most of the mud washed off, so as not to muck up the boat too much. When you had half a boatload, you poled her back, and by this time I would have had the knife out and a couple of dozen opened.

It was very simple to open those oysters. You just took the heavy back of the knife blade and crushed the thin serrated edges of the oyster, stuck the point of the knife in close to the muscle, gave your wrist a little twist, and bong, there was your oyster, lying salty and clean on the shell and still dribbling cold briny water. That water was chilly enough to numb you. While I have eaten a lot of oysters since, with a lot of contrived sauces, I don't remember any oyster tasting as good as one of those big ones that came streaming straight up out of the mud.

Getting oysters was one of the expeditions. The Christmas-tree expedition was another. They tell me people buy Christmas trees now. We scouted a cedar tree for a year in advance. It had to be just the right size and shape and hard enough to get at so that nobody else was apt to swipe it out from under your nose. Mostly, the whole family—Ma, Pa, the Old Man, the grandmas, and the dogs—all piled into the car and went to get the tree. It was a special event.

You couldn't go very early, because the tree had to endure until after New Year's. So we went about two days before Christmas; and if I had spotted the tree, I usually tried to locate it deep in a big swamp or away off in a gallberry bay so that I'd have an excuse to take a gun in case a squirrel or a deer attacked me.

The mistletoe and holly procurement was my special province. Mistletoe had to be climbed after, if it was any good, and somehow I never went after any mistletoe that wasn't hung away up in the mizzen of a cypress as big as a California redwood. You would see the little white waxy kissing berries against the dark green leaves, parasiting happily up there in the clouds, and this was fine, because it was something a boy could do that a man couldn't do. I would take a knife in my teeth—of course in my teeth, because I was Mr. Israel Hands, straight out of *Treasure Island*—and I would shoot up the rigging like a monkey and cut the mistletoe and throw it down.

The holly berries were easy to get at, since they grew on a low bush, but somehow the sight of those glowing red berries against the dark fleshy green of the sharp-bristled leaves made your heart jump high. When you finally got all the stuff home and the women went to work with it, your house smelled just like a good woods camp from the smell of the cedar, and the clean, late-afternoon swampy smell of the holly, and the smoky spice coming from a big oak or hickory log with the resin-dripping lightwood kindling crackling under it.

Women are generally a bother to a boy or a man, but around the holiday season they sure earned their keep. Miss Lottie, my grandma, was a fair hand with a stove, and between the smell of what she was cooking, the smell of the evergreens, and the smell of the strange Yule specialties that you never saw at any other time of the year, the house literally trembled with odor.

Miss Lottie would have had a couple of big fruit cakes under way since along about September—cakes as big as mill wheels, full of dark green citron and fat raisins and candied cherries and juicy currants, and soaked in enough brandy to get you giddy on a slice of it. The fruit cake lasted forever, because the Old Man would slip in and sluice her down with a fresh dollop of brandy from time to time, and if you kept her shut up in a tin box she stayed moist until June.

We had the three kinds of cake around Christmas—the black fruit cake; another kind of cake they called Sally White, which was a blond cousin to the mahogany-dark one; and then pound cake, which was made out of angel's-down and vanilla icing that broke off in wonderful slabs.

For the holidays you had oranges, which never appeared at any other time, and whose oily hides added an extra pungency to the society of odors. You had the big brown-purplish Malaga grapes and fist-sized clusters of plump wrinkled raisins, sticky and sugar-sweet, as big as taw marbles. The Old Man used to pour a little brandy over the raisins too, and then set them alight, and the great game was to see who could dart a hand in and come out, unsinged, with a decent clump.

Then all the dishes were filled with nuts—English walnuts, shelled pecans, and the special treat, the greasy, plump white Brazil nuts we called niggertoes. Flanking the nut dishes were plates full of store-bought candies: little clover-leaf-shaped mints in various bright colors and stripedy hard candies with nasty soft centers that didn't taste very good but looked real pretty.

You cannot get through a holiday menu without devoting some tender thought to the ham. This was pig that needed no apple in its maw—very special pig. My household featured three kinds of ham. One was a hard country ham, as salty as the sea and deep red and tough-tender, which had been hanging in a smokehouse since Gabriel was an apprentice trumpeter. This was what you had fried in the morning, hot and salty with the grits. Then there was a corned ham, blond in color, that was stuck full of cloves. And finally there was that light pink one, a Smithfield, but not hard, because the slices curled up at the edges and crumpled at the corners and were streaked with rivers of soft white fat.

The smells of all this stuff mixed with the wild turkeys that were cooking slowly, being basted by old Galena, the cook, and the saddles of venison that somebody was dripping wine and jelly onto, and the wild ducks taking it easy in the bake pan with carrots and onions and slices of apple—and perhaps the quail frying for the breakfast meal, to help the ham along. There was a dessert the Old Man called raisin duff, an old English seagoing dish served with a hard sauce that had enough brandy in it to arouse the adverse attention of the Anti-Saloon League.

Each day of the holiday fetched a fresh excitement: testing the new gun, breaking in the new boots—the new soft boots that

looked military but had the strap over the arch—and getting
the feel of the new mackinaw with the wetproof game pocket.
It all had a sort of electricity to it.

The men took extra time off and special hunts were arranged. If I minded my *p's* and *q's*, sometimes I would get asked
to a deer drive or a coon hunt in the cold, frosty woods, or to go
out with Tom or Pete to shoot some tame hogs run wild.
There were quail to hunt and ducks to shoot and squirrels to
tree, and every day of the holidays it was the same—wonderful.

You would come in half-dead and full-froze, and a blast of
heat and the intermingled scent of food and festivity would
smite you in the face. You went over and turned your tail to the
fire, and you heated up your hands so that the hot water
wouldn't torture them when you washed off the muck. Then
you kicked off the new boots and put your tired feet in some
sloppy slippers and crawled into a pair of softer pants and went
to the table and ate dedicatedly until you had consumed more
food than a battalion eats these days. You ate it all, and then
came back for more. The butter-soggy hot biscuits, the size of
quarters, were endless; the pickled artichokes and the watermelon preserves were only condiments. You dragged yourself
up from the table by main force, but still had the foresight to
grab a handful of raisins and a pocketful of candy in case you
got a mite peckish in the night. Why I didn't founder myself
I will never, never know.

The Old Man, as usual, tried to cram a little culture down
me on top of the turkey and the sage dressing, but I don't think
I really absorbed much. He hit me with *A Christmas Carol*,
but got nowhere, because the Messrs. Scrooge and Cratchit and
Tiny Tim were really not living in my league.

8

Old Dogs and Old Men Smell Bad

The Old Man cornered me one drizzly day after dinner—I mean the meal we ate in the middle of the day—and he said that he had an awful crick in his back and that he reckoned he was getting old and rheumaticky and that one of these days he was just going to say to hell with it and lay right down and die.

"There are two things got no place in this world," he said, "an old dog and an old man. They perform no useful function, and generally smell bad, too. It seems to me you ought to start branching out on your own hook, boy, because I have wet-nursed you long enough. My back aches and my feet hurt and I feel like a mess of quail, but I'm too feeble to go out in the wet and help you shoot 'em. It's about time you investigated the delicate art of making a dog behave himself in the woods. All you've ever done with the dogs is listen to me holler, 'Whoa!' and one of these days you will have to train dogs of your own. The best way to learn to train a dog is to let a dog that's smarter than you are train you."

It was late February, and it had been raining solidly for a week, and the rain was still coming down in spasms. A little weak sun filtered through every now and then, though; so the Old Man said he reckoned the birds were as tired of the weather as he was, and just might be out of the swamps for a breath of fresh air.

"You take Frank and Sandy," he said, "and turn 'em loose and watch 'em. The only order you got to give is to tell Sandy to hold when he tries to steal Frank's point, and he'll try to steal any covey point Frank makes. That dog is the biggest covey thief I ever knew. If he don't *whoa*, cut yourself a switch and wear him out. There are some dogs, like some people, who won't listen to reason and who respond only to a lick on the tail."

My ma took the Liz and dropped me and the animals out by a little crick named Jackie's Creek, and said she would pick us up at the bridge come sundown when she headed back from town. The dogs were raring to go. They'd been shut up for the last couple of weeks, and they craved action.

Sandy was a big lemon-and-white English setter with one red eye, and old Frank was a blue-ticked Llewellyn. They both had quality folks. As I remember, Frank had old Sir Sidney Mohawk for a grandpa. He wasn't flashy like Sandy, who thought anything under a mile was close hunting and who never had his nose on the ground in his life. He could stick that nose up in the air and wind a bird from here to Canada, if the wind was right and there was a bird in Canada.

Frank was a close hunter, and he believed that the ground was for smelling. On singles he was sure and sudden death, and if you gave him a little time no coveys were apt to escape him forever. When he froze, there were birds there. They were not over yonder; they were there, right under Frank's nose. If they ran, he ran with them, and they were still there, right under Frank's nose. He didn't point snakes and he didn't point terrapins and he didn't point rabbits. He pointed quail.

The dogs paid their respects, as dogs will, to all the trees, bushes, stumps, rocks, and footpaths that they encountered. As dogs will, they ran down the road as if they had lost a watch in it last week. Then they came back to the whistle and informed me that it was time to go to work. I waved the hand like I'd seen the Old Man do and swept it at a sad-looking cornfield. Frank looked at Sandy and Sandy looked at Frank and then they both looked at me rather wistfully. "No," they said. "This is ridiculous."

"Hie on," I ordered. "Dammit." I could cuss pretty good now when the Old Man wasn't around.

The dogs shrugged. Sandy took off and made a rectangular speed run around the edges of the field. Frank worked it diagonally one way, and then intersected himself and worked it diagonally the other way. Sandy finished his perimeter check and came back and sat down in front of me with his tongue hanging out and a slight sneer on his face. Frank showed up with the same sneer.

"All right," I said, "do it your own way. *Dammit.*"

The dogs looked at each other and commented briefly that the young'un was showing some signs of sense, however feeble. Sandy stuck his head into the air and tested. Frank, the vice-president, chewed a cocklebur out of his fetlocks. Then Sandy got The Word. He pointed his nose toward a high hummock of piney-wooded land, a little island in the sopping straw. There was a sawdust pile just behind it. Holding his nose in the air like a society lady making an entrance, he walked, not ran, with Frank ambling behind him, to the high hummock, disappeared into the gallberry bush, and his bell became silent. Frank stuck his head into the bushes, liked what he saw, turned around, more or less waved, and told me to hurry up, that we were in business.

In business we were. Sandy had been stricken stiff on the side of the little hill. He looked like he had been shot out of a cannon and then arrested in mid-speed. He was so taut forward that he was nearly off balance. The great plumed tail was as rigid as a rudder. Frank had gone back into the bushes and was backing, his head leaning lovingly against Sandy's flank and his tail wagging gently and indulgently. When I came up to Sandy's head, he jumped right into the middle of the covey. The birds got up and flattened out over the sawdust pile in a perfect fan. I missed with the first barrel, shooting too quick, but dropped a bird with the second.

Frank lolloped up the side of the sawdust pile where the bird was fluttering a little bit. He took him by the head, bit his neck, laid him down, dead now, and then picked him up gently, carrying him, cradled in his lower jaw, with just enough pressure from the upper teeth to hold him secure. He came up to me and reared up on my chest with his front feet. I opened the game pocket of my old canvas hunting coat, and he nuzzled his head inside and dropped the bird in the pocket. Then he got down, spat out some feathers, and said, "Let's go, bud."

Sandy heaved a sigh, and the dogs consulted briefly. Frank said that the biggest bunch of them went thataway, where the branch crooks out in a gentle curve with a lot of high broom straw in front of it, and they're likely to glide right and spread out in that straw because the swamp is too wet to roost in. Sandy said no; in his considered judgment they turned left, and would be in that pine thicket. Frank made an impatient movement and said very plainly, "Just who the hell is the single-bird expert around here, you yaller-spotted wind-sniffer? I say they went to the *right*." "Okay," Sandy said, "it's your dice. Let's go."

It occurred to me that maybe the birds went straight, but neither one of the dogs asked me.

Sandy consulted again with Frank and then flashed off, quartering swiftly around and taking up a noble stand at the edge of the swamp. Frank plowed into the high, yellow, soaking grasses, hit a trail, shook his hips like a shimmy dancer, and fell dead on his belly. I could hear Sandy's bell on the far side of the broom, and I hollered, "Whoa!" He *whoaed.*

The bird got up, just under Frank's nose, and I nailed him in a shower of feathers. "Fetch," I said. Frank looked annoyed. "Don't be ridiculous," he said, and whirled, dropping dead again. The little brown rocket soared. I turned him over, and Frank looked pleased. He worked on for another few feet and sagged again. Two birds, a hen and a cock, got up and, so help me, I got one with the right and one with the left. Frank looked around and grinned. "That's enough," he said. "Break the gun, son, because five's enough out of any covey."

I broke the gun. Frank sent a signal to Sandy to the effect that even an aristocrat could do a little work, and I heard Sandy's bell again. Presently he showed up with a bird in his mouth. He dropped it on the ground and sat down. Frank had gone after the double. He came back with both at once and carefully nuzzled them into my coat.

We crossed over the swamp, and I snapped the little 16-gauge back into working order. Old Frank meandered out ahead of me, sniffing the fringes of the swamp, and all of a sudden he hit a scent. He telegraphed Sandy. Sandy romped up to where Frank was spinning around in circles, his tail whipping back and forth. "All right, genius," Frank said to Sandy, "take over. They came out here, and the wind is blowing right up that snooty nose of yours. Go earn your corn bread."

Up went that head, which, as I remember it, was more beautiful than any statue, woman, or painting I ever saw later on, and over the hill he went. Frank looked around and beckoned to me, and we strolled over the hill together. About two hundred yards away was Sandy, pale as a ghost at the distance, carved into marble at the edge of a clump of scrub pines.

One bird ducked around a tree as I fired. Another dived over a branch as I fired. No meat. The dogs looked sorrowful. "This lad is strictly an in-and-outer," Frank said sadly. "One minute he's a firecracker, and another minute he's a bum. Maybe we better build up his confidence a little bit." Sandy just shrugged. "I can't do it *all*," he said, very plainly, and lay down to investigate something on his stomach.

According to the consensus, in which I was not included, the birds had gone through the swamp and out onto a slope on the side, but a slope that was still thickly wooded. We went into the swamp and, as we crossed, a single flushed wild on the edge. I banged at the blur, and a couple more got up. Nothing whatsoever dropped. You could barely see them through the branches. Frank considered briefly and then detoured me around the bird area. He stationed me up on the hill, and when I started to follow him down he said, "No, boy, for the love of Pete. I'm trying to make it easy for you."

I stood on the slope. Frank sent Sandy down into the swamp. He worked the slope down toward the swamp. Neither dog made any effort to point. They found birds and flushed them, and when they flushed they were clear targets in the open. A short while later I had four more birds in my pocket.

We worked back toward where I was to meet Ma. Sandy spied another sawdust heap and marched off toward it. This time the birds were in a three-foot copse of sparkleberry bushes. Murder. The dogs had given me so much confidence by now that I just sort of casually raised the gun and collected a double with as much assurance as if I'd been a meat hunter with a sawed-off. Sandy sat down to investigate his rear end, a portion of which seemed to have been mislaid. Frank went and got the birds and stowed them in my coat. He looked up and told me that for a dumb kid I followed orders pretty good, and now let's go home.

I looked longingly over to where the birds had pitched in a field of broom straw.

Both dogs said, "No, remember the limit. The Old Man wouldn't like it." I said okay, let's go find Ma. The dogs never made a move to hunt, although I knew of at least three more coveys in the land we passed. They just trotted along at heel.

When we got back, the Old Man seemed not to be so near

death as before, because I could detect a slight odor of the medicine he always used to ward off the chills. It came in charred kegs and was colored a mahogany red and was illegal at that time. He seemed real pleased when I spread the ten birds—six cocks and four hens—out in front of the fireplace.

"Learn anything?" he asked casually, puffing on the pipe.

"Yessir," I said. "One thing I know is that after the rains you got to hunt the high ground, because quail don't like to get their feet wet, and at this time of the year there ain't anything for them to eat in the fields, anyhow. The birds are in the woods, eating the mast and what's left of the berries. Also, they seem to like sawdust piles."

"I dunno why," he said, "but seems to me I never recollect a sawdust pile that didn't have a covey of bobwhite using near it. Maybe they like to dust in it, or maybe they eat sawdust instead of grit to keep 'em healthy. Learn anything else?"

"Yessir. I learned that late in the afternoon, especially when it's wet, birds don't want to roost in a swamp, but will either settle down on the near side or fly through and put down on the far side. Also, they don't fly so far late as they do early. Also, that there's no point in trying to shoot in a swamp when you can stand on the side and send the dogs in to flush for you."

"*Send* the dogs in?" the Old Man asked gently, crinkling his eyes.

"Well, the dogs went in," I said, sort of lamely, "And they wouldn't let me go in with 'em; so I stood on the side and shot four easy birds."

"Anything else?"

"Well, I found out I can shoot pretty good when I'm out by myself. You don't have to watch for the other fellow, and you can take chances on birds you wouldn't shoot at ordinarily, and somehow you pick up some confidence as you go along, because you're relaxed and you don't want to disappoint the dogs."

"That all?"

"Well, sir, one thing more. I reckon that there ain't nothing anybody can tell a good dog that the dog don't know better than the man. I reckon it's the dog's business to know his business."

The Old Man smiled a big, broad, tobacco-stained, mustachy smile. "I was kind of hoping to hear that, son," he said. "So few people ever learn it. You take a dog and you train him right, and then leave him alone and you got a good dog. The same thing applies to boys. Spoil a dog early, and no amount of hollering will cure him. That also applies to boys. Beat him when he's bad, early, and you don't have to take a stick to him later. Did you have to holler *whoa* at Sandy?"

"Just once."

"Did he *whoa?*"

"He *whoaed.*"

The Old Man looked even more pleased. "Boy," he said, "I will tell you a very wise thing. If a man is really intelligent, there's practically nothing a good dog can't teach him. But a dumb man can't learn anything from a smart dog, while a dumb dog can occasionally learn something from a smart man. Remember that.

"And now," he said, and I knew what was coming, "go pick and gut the birds. Anything that's good enough to shoot is good enough to use, and the longer you put off cleaning a bird or a fish the harder the job is. Scat now, because I got a hankering for some quail with my grits. I don't believe I'm going to die tonight after all."

The winter had gone in a wild, cold flurry of nasty rain, and the sun was beginning to be a little more prevalent. It was too late to shoot and too early to fish, too hot for football and too cold for baseball. I had the adolescent nervous twitches. You know, when the house is too small and there doesn't seem to be anything around but school, with summer still too far off to be hopeful about. I reckon my behavior was not what the dictionary calls exemplary, unless it was a bad example.

The Old Man looked at me with some amusement. I was in

between engagements, so to speak, and he knew it. Maybe that's why he called me out to the back yard one day and showed me something. It was a pointer puppy, the saddest-looking pointer puppy I ever saw. It had feet as big as a grizzly bear's and one twisted ear, and was about half-dead from the mange, the hair gone off its hide and the skin wrinkled pink and ugly.

"This," the Old Man said, "is a damned fine bird dog. Pretty much in the rough, I'll admit, but a good dog nevertheless. I know about his parents. But he needs some work done on him, and the time to train a dog is in the spring, when you've got nothing better to do. The first thing we will do is get rid of this mange."

"Where'd you get him?" I asked. "I never saw such a homely critter."

"Don't let the looks fool you," the Old Man cautioned. "His blood is better'n yours. What happened was that the man that owns his mama had to go away for a spell, and he left the bitch with a share-crop farmer and the whole litter picked up the mange. Once we get this mange fixed, you will have yourself a dog. And now that you been pretty well trained by the old dogs, mebbe you'd better try your hand at training a puppy, so's you can learn some more about dogs, *from* dogs."

I grinned just a little bit, remembering the other day when Frank and Sandy gave me a kindergarten course.

"What do we do about this mange?" I asked him.

"Very simple," the Old Man said. "We go down to visit Gus McNeill at the filling station, and we beg some old used crank-case oil that he's got, from changing the oil in automobiles from winter to spring. Then we go see Doc Watson in the drugstore, and we buy a little sulphur off him. We mix the sulphur with the old crankcase oil and douse the puppy in it, and bimeby there won't be any mange."

The Old Man was right. We smeared the puppy with the mixture for a few days, and before long you could see the hair growing back, and it wasn't more than a month before he was haired out real nice and beginning to grow up to his feet. We named him Tom, for some reason or other, and I took over his education.

"A bird dog," the Old Man told me, "is trained in the back yard. There ain't no way in the world you can teach him to smell; so you don't have to bother about that. There ain't no way in the world you can teach him bird sense; so there ain't any use worrying about that. All you can teach this dog is a little discipline, so that he can use his talents to the best advantage. Like they're trying to teach you a little discipline in school. Whether you got brains enough to take advantage of it is strictly up to you."

"Where do you start?" I asked the Old Man.

"Well, there's all sorts of ways to train a dog and not break him. Don't you ever let me hear you use the word 'break.' You don't want a broken dog. You want to educate him, not crush him. A man who's got to break a dog don't deserve the dog. All you want to teach him is a little common sense and some politeness. The first thing you want to teach him is the difference between yes and no. We'll start with something basic, like food."

We only fed the dogs once a day; so they were pretty hungry. We fed 'em mostly table scraps and hard cold hominy and a lot of cold corn bread and turnip greens and fatback and now and then a can of salmon or some canned dog food, but not much. We fed them about five o'clock in the afternoon, and we always fed each dog out of his own tin pie plate, a few feet away from each other. I noticed neither Frank nor Sandy ever made a move at the dinner pail until the Old Man snapped his fingers and said, "Hie on." And right in the middle of the meal, if the Old Man said, "*Whoa!*" they quit eating. Old Frank was pretty cute. You could put a sliver of steak or some other tasty victual on his nose and he'd just sit there, and when you gave him the okay word he'd flip his head, toss the meat in the air, catch it, swallow it, and then sort of take a bow.

We trained the puppy very simple. We put his pan down, and when he lunged for the food I'd just grab him by the tail and say, "*Whoa!*" I would gentle him some and tell him he was a fine upstanding puppy, and then I would say, "Hie on" and let him go. It didn't take a week for him to get the message. He would head for his dinner, and I would say, "*Whoa*" and he'd *whoa*. He would turn his head and wait for the snapped fingers and the words, "Hie on," and then he would eat. In the middle of the meal I'd grab him by the tail again and say, "*Whoa.*" He learned that one in about two days. When I said, "*Whoa,*" even when he was swallowing, he would quit, haul back on his haunches, and wait the word again.

Like all puppies, he loved to go dashing after sticks or balls, and, like all puppies, he liked to run off with the stick or the ball and tease you with it. He was not what you'd call a natural-born retriever. He was a joker. The Old Man showed me how to lick that one, too. We bent a line on his collar and chucked out the stick, and when he picked it up and started off for the back forty the Old Man checked him in the middle of a leap with the rope and hollered, "Fetch!" Then he hauled him in so fast that he was sitting in front of us without his feet actually having touched the ground very often on the return trip. We added "Fetch" to his vocabulary in about three days. He quit thinking that this business of bringing things was a game. It was now a serious business.

"The thing about a dog," the Old Man said, "is that you got to teach him the difference between business and pleasure. And you got to keep reminding him of it. Like about rabbits. There never was a good bird dog that didn't like to chase rabbits. Rabbits are fun for him, where quail are just hard work. You can tell when a bird dog is pointing a rabbit, because he points all hunched up and with his ears cocked and his nose turned down kind of quizzical, and then he'll jump and look around at you like the village idiot that knows he's done something wrong but ain't quite sure what it is. The way to keep a dog from running rabbits is to discourage him early. We'll do this in the fall, before the bird season opens.

"In the meantime we will not let him run loose this sum-

mer, because a dog gets into a lot of bad habits in the summertime; and if you turn him loose to chase everything and anything, come autumn he has forgot what his real business is and
ain't much good for anything in particular. I don't approve of
chasing dogs except for a couple of things. One is running rabbits and the other is running up quail. A puppy is going to do
both at first, out of natural high spirits and just plain puppy
dam-foolishness. I wouldn't give you a nickel for a dog that
wasn't jealous about another dog over the quail subject, but
he's got to learn to control that jealousy, even if it drives him
crazy. Else you got no dog. You just got a ham actor that can't
be depended on."

We spent the spring teaching this pointer puppy Tom his
back-yard manners, and we spent the summer insisting that he
remember what we taught him in the spring. He learned
"Heel," and he learned "Down," and he learned that the back
of the car, not the front, was where he was supposed to jump
into. He learned "Fetch" and "Go" and "Hie on" and "Whoa."
He learned that a whistle was not a tin toy but had some
pointed meaning, and that when you waved an arm one way it
didn't mean that he was supposed to run the other way. All this
time he never smelled a quail.

The summer passed and the leaves turned rosy-crisp. It was
nearly time for the bird season to open, and here I had me a
puppy, almost grown up to fit his feet, that was like one of those
correspondence-course students who's learned it all by mail but
hasn't had a chance to practice his theories. I didn't know
whether I had an idiot or a genius, but at least his table manners were perfect.

One Sunday afternoon in early October the Old Man said,
"All the young birds are big enough now not to mind a bit o'
bother, and most of the snakes have gone to ground. Why don't
we take the puppy out and see if he's got any sense at all?"

We took him out in the back section where there was a kind
of tame covey of quail we could always locate, either in the
broom straw or the grove or in the peafields, that the Old Man

had taught me to shoot on and had always schooled the dogs on. We never shot it down under ten birds, and we always planted plenty of food for 'em and left plenty of cover, so that the birds stayed and stayed for all the years I can remember, sort of like being in the family.

The first thing the puppy did was point a rabbit, jump him, and chase him. He came back, his tongue hanging out, looking triumphant. All the *"Whoas!"* I'd screamed hadn't made a dent in his eardrums.

"Whip him," the Old Man said. "Whip him good. Wear him out. And say, 'No!' "

I cut an Indian-arrow switch and beat him pretty good. The next rabbit, he jumped at, ran a little ways after, and then came back and lay on his back, all four feet in the air, and said, more or less, "Beat me, boss." I beat him, but not very hard. And that was the last of the rabbit trouble. He had learned some early discipline in the back yard.

We steered him to where the quail had to be, and they were there. It was a funny sight to see. He was like a potential drunkard who had never tasted whisky before and had suddenly got the smell of it. He didn't know what he was smelling, but he knew he liked it and he knew he had something to do about it.

He approached very cautiously, cakewalking, and in the great moment of indecision, the moment he didn't know himself what he was going to do and when every inclination was to jump off and chase, he paid off his professors. He had a brief argument with himself, and he won it. What he did was stick his tail high in the air like a knobby flagstaff, and stiffen his body into a crouch, and raise his right front paw, and aim his nose right smack at where he thought something he'd never seen and never smelled was. And he stayed there, in that position, and he would be there now if I hadn't walked past him and kicked up the birds and said, *"Whoa,"* when he started to chase them, and he *whoaed* in mid-leap and watched them fly away. He watched where they pitched and went over and pointed five single birds, and never made a move to jump again. Maybe he was a miracle. I don't know.

But I do know that all the days he lived he never had another stick to his hide and rarely a command. He never ran another rabbit, and after the first "Whoa," when he was working with the old dogs, he never crowded a point. He would backstand until you needed a bulldozer to move him.

I took him out alone on the first day of the season, in another part of the country, with which he was entirely unfamiliar. He was less than nine months old. He went magically to the first covey, without fiddling, without fuss, without false-pointing. When he had it made, he made it, and lifted his fore-foot again to tell me about it. The birds rose, and I killed the first one and missed the second. He did not chase. "Fetch!" I said, and he sped straight to where he'd marked the bird—a bird whose feathers he had never tasted. He picked up the bird and brought it to me and laid it in my hand and spat out the feathers and said, "Well, boss, they went thataway," just like the old dogs did. And thataway was where they went, and where we went, and where the birds were, like he said.

I went home that day with a coatful of birds and a glowing progress report, but the Old Man wasn't the least bit impressed.

"I told you," he said, "that this mangy puppy had the right blood in him. When a dog or a person's got the right blood, all he needs is a couple of suggestions to use the blood right. I hope you turn out as well as the puppy, but, like I said, the puppy's bloodlines may be a little better than yours. At least, though, I didn't have to cure you of the mange."

9

All Colts Are Crazy
in the Spring

We were living at a place called Wrightsville Sound that spring, a most fascinating spot to be young in. It had numberless attractions for a boy. As is so much of the coastal South, it was semitropic. There were vast forests of gnarled, craggy live-oak trees, which were hung with Spanish moss, and tall timberlands of longleaf pine.

The Sound itself led to two inlets on a beach two miles away, and the tides brought ocean fish into the Sound and kept the water clean. There were little back bays that were full of fish, and in the winter, ducks. The woods were chattery with squirrels, little gray fellows and the big black-and-silver fox squirrels. There were quail in the brushy flats, and some deer, and rabbits untold. The trees were full of the bright blue jays I never seem to see these days, and the little bluebirds that have also made themselves scarce.

Even the wild vegetation was exciting to a youngster. There were whole groves of wild plum, and the wild asparagus shot up in the spring, and there were blackberries growing wild by the millions. There were sparkleberries and pawpaws and chinquapins—the little brown sweet nuts like chestnuts—and wild artichokes. There was almost no day in the year when a boy couldn't go out on an expedition of his own and make an adventure of living off the country. A bellyache usually accompanied the experience, but at least a man felt free of his parents and the necessity of carrying a box lunch.

At this time I was almost completely a young Tarzan. There was no house that could hold me. I swung through the trees like an ape, and generally managed to bust something about once a month. I had a tree house built high in the branches of a wild cherry, and an interlocking series of caves that threatened to undermine the county. My progress in school was deplorable, because I was just marking time for that last bell to sound and let me loose into the bush. There was a convenient stream—we called it a crick—near the school, and we would slip off at recess and go swimming naked. One day the teacher surprised the lot of us, and nasty notes were written to parents. I didn't know then who I was, but it was a cross between Tom Sawyer, Huck Finn, Tarzan, Daniel Boone, Buffalo Bill, and all the heroes of Ernest Thompson Seton.

I contracted ground itch and poison ivy and various wounds from fish hooks. Jellyfish stung me in the water. I played hooky constantly and acquired magnificently bad report cards in the process. My mother caught me smoking secretly, and there was a loud flap about that. My companions were mostly fishermen, and my language was shocking. I was about to run away and join the Indians—somewhere, I don't know where—when one day the Old Man looked at me sort of sardonically with one eyebrow cocked and said, "Hey!"

"Yessir?" I said.

"It's about time you calmed down a little, young feller," he said. "You 'mind me of a young buck Apache with no warpath to play with. I know it's spring, and all colts go crazy in the spring, but you need some sort of project to quiet you down. I think I got the answer: a boat. There's something about a boat that is powerful soothing to springtime hysterics. If you'll pay a little more attention to clean ears and arithmetic, I'll help you build one this month, and when school's over you can learn a whole lot of new things about fish and water this summer. You can also learn a whole lot about yourself. Ain't nothing like a boat to teach a man the worth of quiet contemplation."

The business of building the boat took the rest of the spring. The Old Man was working very methodical. He collected a great pile of planks and some sawhorses and stuck them in the back yard. What he was aiming for was a twelve-foot flat-bottom skiff, broad in the beam, that wouldn't draw any water at all and could be controlled by a boy, but that had room in it for at least three people and some fishing or shooting gear. She had a locker under the stern sheets to keep fish or lunch in, and a bait locker. I reckon this was the cheapest piece of construction that ever went into a boat, because he got the wood for nothing from his friend in the sawmill, including the hickory that went into the oars that he whittled out himself and fined down with sandpaper until they were as smooth as glass. He fitted the strakes so close that, once we stuck her in the water and let her seams swell, she never leaked another drop.

The Old Man scorned a two-piece keel. He went out into the woods until he found a piece of hickory—dead but not decayed —with the right curve in it, and he built the boat around it. Apart from the nails and the anchor, there wasn't a piece of metal in her. He despised oarlocks, noisy, clumsy iron things that were always falling overboard or being stolen or that you had to always remember to carry home. He whittled out some limber thole pins that cradled an oar like a mother holds her baby and did about half the rowing for you. We named her the *Charlotte Morse* after two strong-minded women we were both afraid of, and cracked a Coca-Cola over her for launching purposes. The Old Man had a slightly more serious snort. He wasn't one to waste good whisky by pouring it over a boat.

If I ever get rich, I may buy me a boat of some sort, but it'll never have the adventures that the *Charlotte* had. They were never big adventures. I looked for buried treasure on Money Island with her, and got blistered by the sun, but never found the pieces-of-eight. I fell out of her and stuck her on sand bars and had to swim after her now and again when she slipped her moorings. I shot out of her and caught fish out of her and got lost in her and durn near drowned alongside her. But like I said, she gave me some quiet adventure that you don't get out of the comic books, because none of it was vicarious, which means, I think, getting your thrills out of what somebody else has already done better.

When I was out alone in that boat, I never had to worry about amusement. I was Captain Blood looking for pirates, or I was actually on Treasure Island, running from Long John Silver. I was Zane Grey catching marlin off New Zealand—wherever that was—or I was a section of the Spanish Armada or I was Hawkins or Drake. Occasionally I was Robinson Crusoe, marooned on a little island and looking for a Friday. I used to take those books with me and read 'em while pulled up for lunch on one of the thousands of little sandy islands, and they meant a lot more than they did on the Required List at the schoolhouse library, with some four-eyed schoolmarm standing over me.

But mostly I learned about how much fun a man can have amusing himself, and about how exciting solitude can be if you play it right. I would get up early in the morning, row her out to one of the sand bars, jab an oar deep in the sand, and make her fast. Then I would kick around in the ooze, feeling for clams with my feet and looking for soft-shell crabs. When I had a mess of clams, I would take the cast net and prowl the shallows for mullet and shrimp for bait, casting the net in a great circular spread that drove upward sharp slivers of water as she settled, with the shrimp and the mullet bucking and arching inside the cords.

In time I got to know, just by experimentation, where all the better holes were—where the big blackfish lived, where the weakfish hung out, where you couldn't catch anything but spiny-backed perch. Sometimes I would take the boat around into the channel and have fun with the skipjacks, the little channel bluefish, and then I would tie her up under the channel bridge by the barnacle-encrusted pilings and fish very quietly for sheepshead. There were those big stone crabs, too, and to catch one of the big black-and-yellow fellows, whose claws were all white meat and whose body was practically nonexistent, was a big event.

But the best of it was at night, when you rigged up a jack light, took her out on a low tide, and let her drift gently while you looked for the shadow of flounders in the flickering yellow glow. You used a three-pronged harpoon and nailed the flounder to the bottom, and he flopped mightily when you dragged him into the boat. I used to sell the flounders, if I had a good night, and made what to me was a power of money, sometimes as much as a whole dollar.

Some of the best part of going out in the boat was eating the lunch I'd caught myself, pulled up to another little sand bar or a palmetto island. I kept salt and pepper and a skillet in the locker, and there was always driftwood for a fire. It occurs to me now that I was dining then off the things people pay a lot for in restaurants—fresh clams and oysters and broiled soft crabs, the freshest fish in the world. Perhaps it was cooked crude, but I've never eaten better since.

It was maybe a three-mile pull at the end of the day, with your lips salty and burned from the glassy bounce of the sun off the water and your back sore and your bare feet shriveled from the salt water. That last half-mile pull seemed like it was never going to end, and it was a great temptation to just beach the boat and leave her dirty and full of mud and fish scales. But the

Old Man had caught me at that a few times, and the weight of his scorn at filthy fishing was too heavy for me to bear. I would wash her out and make her fast, and string the fish and shoulder the oars, and stagger home so tired that I could have cried. Nobody had to whip me to get me to bed. I was plain-out beat.

By the time that summer ended I think I must have known every inch of that Sound, every fish hole, every sand bar, every creek and cove. I knew the tricks of the tides around the inlets and the rate the water would drop, according to how the wind was blowing. It was all trial and error, cut feet, bruised fingers, mosquitoes and sandflies and sunburn.

By the end of the summer I was considerably calmed down. Like the Old Man said, there is nothing like being alone on the water in a boat of your own to learn the value of peace, quiet, and responsibility. I found out you didn't need companionship to amuse yourself; that there are actually times when you can have more fun without people. A boy alone on a big water is a very small thing.

I didn't ever tell the Old Man about the time I got caught in the rip and was swept out through the inlet into the sea, and had to let the boat go out more than a mile on the ocean before I could get loose from the tow and beat her back to the beach. I didn't tell anybody about the dead man I found—what was left of him—jammed into a little wedge of marsh. He'd been in the water a long time.

Didn't tell, either, about the rusty nail I had to cut out of my foot with a pocketknife I had cauterized in a fire. I remember that very clear, sawing and hacking at the underpart of my big toe, with the nail run clean up under the ball of my foot, the knife dull and me alternately crying and cussing. Told my mother I cut it on an oyster shell when I asked her for the iodine. I guess I was afraid they would keep me out of the boat, and the marsh hen season was coming along, with the big swollen tides of the September northers.

When the tides covered the marsh grasses so that only the tips showed, the big rails had no place to hide and would flap awkwardly up ahead of you, birds as big as woodcock, with soft deer eyes. You poled the boat then, and they flew so slow that you could leave the pole stuck in the ooze, grab a gun, and still knock down the bird. Or sometimes you moored the boat and got out of her, prowling the edges of the shore line, where the birds had come in from their flooded-out home in the marsh. They flushed skittering like snipe, and headed for water, and it was fine shooting.

Schooltime came again, and the weather got colder, and we hauled the boat up and put her on rollers for the winter. I went back to school feeling a little more like a man and a little less like a boy. I reckon the Old Man knew what he was talking about when he said there was nothing like a boat to smooth the kinks out of a kid. This must have shown on the report card a little bit, because for Christmas that year there was a little one-lunged outboard motor under the tree. The Old Man said he guessed I'd earned it.

10

Lazy Day—No Women

It was one of those special days in May, when there was a
drowsy, almost-June feel to the softly stirring air. The little
warblers were twittering away in yellow clouds in the molt-
ing fruit trees, and a catbird was meowing softly in a hedge.
The sky was a pale washed-denim blue, and the sun shone down
gold and warm but not hot. It was a day to sit, maybe, or
perhaps a fishing day, but it was not a day to do anything that
might rile up the blood.

The womenfolk were housecleaning, flapping sheets and
dusting and sweeping and tormenting things, as women will,
and the Old Man was nowhere to be seen. The Liz was sitting
in the front yard, under the oak trees; so Himself couldn't have
strayed far. In our town there were only so many places where

he might be—the Cedar Bench, the pilot office, the poolroom, Uncle Jimmy's store, or Watson's drugstore.

I walked slowly down through the white oyster-shell street toward the water and took a slow sight on the Cedar Bench. It seemed to have a cluster of old gentlemen perched on it like crows, and amongst the old black coats, battered sea captain's caps, shapeless yellowed palmettos, and ratty old felts was the Old Man.

The Cedar Bench, I might say, was the exclusive property of the town's elder statesmen. It was a square wooden bench surrounding a wind-twisted, salt-silvered, ancient cedar. About equidistant from the pilothouse, the ship chandlery, and the shrimp dock with the shrimp houses, it wasn't too far from the fuel dock or the wharf where the pilot boat was moored, and the other docks where the pogie fleet tied up. The old Cedar Bench still hung together, but flimsylike, because it had been whittled at until parts of it were no wider than your hand. It had so much aimless knifework on it that the Old Man once remarked that if you sat long enough on enough sections of it your behind would eventually be engraved with the initials of everybody in town who was over fifty years old.

Nobody talked very much on the Cedar Bench, except around election time. It was a place of meditation. The Old Man was meditating real good when I arrived. He had his hat pulled down on top of his nose, like the pictures you sometimes see of Mr. Bernie Baruch sitting on a park bench. The Old Man's eyes were closed and his pipe had gone out. He had one knee cocked up, and his bony, brown-freckled hands were clasped around the knee. There was little sound except the scream of a sea gull, the hum of insects, and an occasional *splat* as one of the other elder statesmen ejected an amber stream of tobacco juice at an unwary butterfly. Some of those old boys could spit a curve against the wind and were deadly with the poolroom spittoon at ten paces.

I went and sat quietly down alongside the Old Man, and bimeby he opened first one eye, then the other. He kind of shook his head, as if to clear it. "Hello," he said. "What're you up to?"

"Nothin' very much," I said. "The womenfolk were cleaning house and it made me nervous."

"Makes me nervous too," he said, heaving himself to his feet. "I come down here for a rest—snuck out early when I heard the mops begin to swish and the buckets to rattle. Come on, let's walk down to the end of the dock so's we won't disturb these other gentlemen. It seems to be housecleaning day all over town."

We strolled down to the T-shaped end of the dock. The Old Man sat down creakily and leaned his back against a bollard, and I did the same. The gulls wheeled and curved and sailed on stiff wings, and the water was dimpled with the breeze, the sun striking tiny little sparks off the droplets.

The Old Man fetched up a gusty sigh and stuffed his pipe. "I reckon most folks would say we were just plain, cold-out, no-'count lazy," he remarked to one of the wheeling gulls. "It ain't necessarily so. Your grandma, if she ever saw fit to dirty her shoes on the water front, would take one look at the Bench and say something, with a sniff fore-and-aft of it, like: 'Look at those good-for-nothing loafers, so lazy that dead lice wouldn't drop off them, when they could be doing a hundred things we've been at them all winter to get done.' But, of course, that is women for you. It is the reason that, apart from having babies, no woman has ever done a first-class job of anything. They can't even cook as good as men. It's because they don't take the time to think. They're all like little old banty hens, scratching and pecking and looking around at every noise with a beady eye that's meant to be intelligent but ain't."

I had to laugh a little at that one. If you ever saw bantam hens, you'll remember that they're never still, always peering at their backs, looking for lice with their heads swiveled all the way round, or pecking at their chests or under their wings, or scratching, or flapping wings, or jumping up on something, and always cackling, either with indignation or in triumph when they've squeezed out another egg. Grandma—housecleaning, with a towel wrapped round her head, a dustcloth in one hand, and a feather duster in another—was just like a little-bitty old banty hen. She only paused to squawk.

"Now you take me," the Old Man said. "I'm not really lazy. A lazy man is a man who fiddles and fools around with a job he's supposed to be working at. I know a lot of do-less cusses like that. There is a difference between laziness and meditation, even meditation with the eyes closed. Just because I close my eyes and sit in the sun don't mean I'm triflin'.

"For instance," the Old Man continued, "today I am recovering from the rigors of the cold winter and the wet and windy spring. I am recovering from the past and storing up strength for the future. There ain't no telling what the next six months will bring that will call for full concentration and maximum effort. If I should git myself into some sort of big operation, such as inventing an airyoplane or running for Congress, it would be a shame to tackle it all wore out from last year's labors, and let some fresh, rested feller get the best of me."

I interrupted. "But you're a man grown," I said. (The Old Man didn't like anybody to refer to him as old, except himself.) "I ain't nothing but what Aunt Mae calls a shirt-tail boy. It seems to me that there is some sort of grown-up rule that rest is bad for boys, that they got to be doing something all the time. I never set down to whittle or snooze in the sun or fix a cast net that one of the women didn't come marching in with some chore for me to do, like going to the store or running over to Aunt Ada's for a cup of something or half a pound of something else."

"Unjust, unjust," the Old Man sighed. "Boys need more rest than grown-ups. Boys are busy growing bones and making meat to go on the bones, which is a full-time job in itself. Boys burn up more juice than grown-ups. Boys run a kind of a fever until they're past twenty-one years old. There seems to be some sort of deluded idea that boys were created to run errands for the old folks."

"Just like boys ain't supposed to like white meat." I was a little bitter. "Boys are supposed to like backs and wings and legs and the part that goes over the fence last. Grown-ups are supposed to like white meat. Boys are supposed to like to split kindling and clean fish and gut birds and go to the store and rake yards and cut grass. Speaking as boy to man, I would sure admire to say that the grown-up idea of what boys like is a sight different from what *boys* think boys like."

"True, too true," the Old Man said. "And unjust. But the grown-up's idea is that he's conditioning the boy for the toils and troubles of manhood."

"I'm going to be all wore out by the time I run into any toils and troubles of manhood," I said darkly. "I ain't got any time for what you call meditation, except when I'm hunting or fishing."

"I'd say you had enough time, then," the Old Man said tartly. "Seeing as how you manage to do one or t'other or both for about ten months a year, whenever you ain't in school. You never seem to be tired from rowing a boat ten miles or walking six hours in the rainy woods behind a bird dog."

"That ain't work," I said. "Work is doing what you don't like to do because somebody tells you to do it."

The Old Man ignored that for a bit. He chawed on his pipe stem and spat at a sea gull that flew too close. "Speaking of work," he said, "I am so rested up from this morning that I feel like a little honest toil wouldn't kill neither one of us. I'll make you a deal. You know that fishin' shack of ours took a powerful pounding this winter when we had them two hurricanes in a row. I figgered we'd build her back stronger this time. There's plenty of solid driftwood all up and down Caswell, big joists and logs and such as that. Now, if you was to stir yourself and walk—not run—up the street to your Uncle Jimmy's store and buy us a mess of provisions, such as sour pickles, johnnycake, a little fatback, some roofing nails, and some tenpenny nails, I might mosey over to the house and gather up the rest of the truck we need. We can spend the week end— The women are so busy getting everything antiseptic they'll never miss us."

That sounded like a fair-enough deal. I got up and stuck out a hand to the Old Man, hauled him creaking to his feet, and we walked off the dock. He headed home; I set a course for Uncle Jimmy's.

Now I could cheat and pretend that it happened to me, but it didn't. It happened to a little colored boy, and it was the standing joke around town. Most of Pa's family was pretty relaxed, but Uncle Jimmy was the champion relaxer of them all. He was relaxing when I got to the store, sitting on something on the porch, his hat over his eyes and his little fat hands folded on his little fat stomach.

"Hey, there," I said.

"Hey, there, son," he said. "You want something? Go roust it out and add it up on a paper sack and leave the sum on the counter." He closed his eyes to the bright sun. I snickered.

The story was that one day a little colored boy came to the store and found Uncle Jimmy in the same position.

"What can I do for you, son?" Uncle Jimmy kept his eyes closed.

"Papa sen' me say he need a poun' tenpenny nails, Mistah Jimmy. The back po'ch near 'bout fallin' down."

"You go look 'em, son," Uncle Jimmy said. "I think they're in the back of the store som'ers. Look som'ers around the pickle barrel and the overhalls."

The little colored boy disappeared and returned. "They ain't there, Mistah Jimmy."

"Well, son, try som'ers around the eatin' tobacco and the snuff and the two-for-a-penny cakes. You know, them pink ones with the coconut strings and the choc'late marshmellers."

The customer disappeared into the cool recess of the store, rummaged around, and reappeared. "I swear 'fo' Gawd and three 'sponsible witness, Mistah Jimmy, I done look high and I done look low, but I cain't fin' no tenpenny nails."

"You look 'round the yard goods and the bellywash and the

lickrish sticks? You look up high where we keep the Army shoes and the sardines?"

"Yassuh. I done look everywhere and I cain't fin' um."

Uncle Jimmy stirred, scratched his head, wrinkled his brow. "I know we got some," he said. "I ordered a mess from the hardware drummer last time he was around, and a whole shipment come in on the Willing But Slow the other day."

Uncle Jimmy let out a sudden guffaw and slapped his leg. "That's a joke on me, son," he wheezed. "Whilst we been talking about them nails, I been settin' on the nail keg this whole blessed time. Suppose, son," he said, closing his eyes again, "suppose you come back again *t'morrow.*"

That's what they told on Uncle Jimmy, anyhow. They said he was the first man in the business to invent self-service, which became so popular later on. Except he didn't believe in a cash business. He sent out bills once every so often, when he thought about it, and when small boys came to pay the bills for their people he was always good for a sack of jawbreakers or one of those mammoth, sickly sweet soft drinks he called bellywash. I knew where everything in the store was; so I made my purchases, scribbled down the total on a paper sack with a nubbin of a pencil, hooked a pink-striped peppermint, and went out into the sun. Uncle Jimmy grunted what was probably good-by and never opened his eyes.

By the time I walked most of the three long blocks home, the Old Man was in the Liz and heading in my direction. "Jump in," he said. "They're all cleaning like Old Ned upstairs and I give 'em the slip. Let's skedaddle. I left a farewell message pinned to the lamp shade in the parlor."

We bumped happily over the shell road and headed toward Caswell. As we came to the creek you could smell the pogie factory, and the odor of ripe fish meal was sweet to the nostrils, as was the hot smell of rotting marsh. The red-winged blackbirds rode the tops of the waving marsh grass, and away off a fish hawk was circling, looking for his dinner. The sun shone brighter, and the Old Man grinned. "How was Jimmy?"

"Just the same. All I got to do is look at him and I feel full of vinegar. I feel like work now."

"Me, too," the Old Man said. "But I wouldn't of felt like it if I hadn't of replenished myself this mornin'."

We pulled up to wait for the little ferry bridge to swing closed and let us over the creek. We weren't in no particular hurry to get there, and I noticed the Old Man had his hat tilted forward over his eyes again. His breath, or maybe the breeze, ruffled his mustache.

Today there's a lot of people who don't understand, when they see me sitting out in the yard in an easy chair, that I'm not really loafing. I'm doing what the Old Man said. I'm recovering from the past and storing up for the future.

11

Summertime, and the Livin'
Was Easy

June is a nice time of year, because school lets out and it
hasn't got real hot yet. The mornings are fresh and dewy and
everything is green and sweet-smelling, and generally the
mosquitoes haven't started and the nights are still cool enough
for covers. The nicest thing about June is that the awful
memories of school are behind you, and September is so far
away that it doesn't even count. The summertime belongs to
boys. Grown-up folks might play around at the beaches and the
country clubs and take vacations, but summer truly belongs to
kids. It's sunburn time and ground-itch time and poison-ivy
time. It's barefoot time and fishhooks-caught-in-your-ear time
and baseball time and whippoorwill time and bullbats-swoop-
ing-low-in-the-dusk time.

Seems to me the summertime had so much good stuff in it that it should have been made illegal for most people. You had all sorts of wonderful things to give you the bellyache—peaches and pears and wild berries and tame berries, such as raspberries and strawberries, and the big purple plums and the yellow-and-rose plums, and the figs, and the big cool green watermelons or the tiger-striped ones that you took out of the cold water in the springhouse and ate by just shoving your face in and chewing on through. Finally, as the summer would wear on and it began to smell a little smoky in the air, like fall was knocking, the grapes came—the big, fat, juice-bursting scuppernongs, white and chokingly sweet, and the slightly tart black ones, as big as golf balls.

In my town they closed up Sunday school as well as regular school in June, which suited me just fine. About all I ever learned in Sunday school was how to shoot craps down in the basement, a pastime so deplorable that Mr. James Stebbins, the sandy-haired Englishman (a foreigner!) who tried to domesticate us young demons, eventually renovated our shocking morals by ringing in a pair of loaded dice and busting us all for the spring term of religious worship. He was as steely as a professional bookmaker about the IOU's, and he put all his ill-got gains into the collection plate. I remember I was just paid out, and was feeling pretty religious about it, when the Old Man cornered me one morning after breakfast.

It was one of those days when a boy figures he's got to pop if something doesn't happen to him—something big, something adventurous, something stupendous, like saving a maiden fair from the wild animals that have busted loose from the circus, or rushing into a burning building to rescue a child, or something. Anything. Making tar balls out of the bubbling asphalt pavement wasn't enough. Eating plums that were too green or trying out a sneaky slingshot on a catbird wasn't enough. It was one of those days you maybe remember, with the bobolinks balanced on the bending grasses in the breeze, and the Baltimore orioles scattering notes around like millionaires throwing coins, and the wild cherries black and sweating sweet on the big leafy tree with the Tarzan house built into it.

The Old Man stabbed me with his pipe stem and his eyes. "I been hearing about you," he said. "I been hearing a lot of things about you—about how you cut Sunday school every other Sunday, and about that dice game you young hellions started down in the basement at Saint James', and it seems to me you are doomed for perdition. I thought I had you straightened out in the school business, but now I reckon I got to teach you a little humility."

Here she comes, I said to myself. I'm goin' to get preached at, or made to do something I don't want to without knowing why I don't want to. The Old Man was awful shifty when he come down hard with the parables according to Himself.

"What are you goin' to do?" I asked him.

"Fishin'," he said cheerfully. "We're just goin' fishin'."

Now, you certainly don't punish a boy for irreverence by taking him fishing; so there has got to be a catch in this one somewhere, I thought. But I had learned from the Old Man to play pretty cosy; so all I said was, "What kind of fishin'?"

"Fresh-water," the Old Man said. "Maybe catch us a big ol' bass or so, or at least a mess of brim. We'll take the Liz and rent us a boat from a man I know on Big Crick. Wait till I go get the rods, and while I'm after them you go roll over some rotten logs and see if you can turn your undoubted talents to filling a tin can full of worms."

I ambled down to the cow lot, behind which there was a low, wet swamp where the pigs rooted and the quail came to drink, and turned over a few old punky logs and filled up a big paint can with fine fat worms, just as happy as worms to be wriggling around in the loose, wet dirt I put in the can. When I got back to the house, the Old Man had produced a couple of light split-bamboo rods and a couple of little reels that I never had seen before.

"Where'd they come from?" I asked the Old Man.

"Oh," he said, "I've had 'em around for a long time. There's a lot of things I got you don't know about. I ain't a man to take every whippersnapper I meet into my confidence. I got plenty of secrets I ain't talkin' about. These rods are one of my secrets. On this coast it's supposed to be sissy to fish fresh water —either sissy or downright po' barkerish." A po' barker is the kind of shiftless white trash who would be so trifling that he'd have to feed his family off perch and catfish.

I cranked the Liz, and we snorted off. I never went off in the old Liz without snickering a little bit. The Old Man said only a monkey was fit to drive one of the old T-models. "You need both hands on the wheel, both feet on the pedals, and a tail to keep the door shut," he said. But they never built a better car. It would go anywhere that one of those Army tanks would go, and with about the same amount of noise. It rode high off the ground and looked like an old lady with her skirts held up off the mud, but it never wore out.

We drove about fifteen miles and came up to Big Crick. It had some other name, I suppose, but Big Crick was what we called it. Actually, it was a little river that connected up somewhere with the Cape Fear River. There were a boathouse and a landing and a few skiffs pulled up alongside the landing. When we got there, it was about four o'clock in the afternoon.

The Old Man paid fifty cents for the rent of a boat. He just indicated the oars to me with a jerk of his head, and I started pulling upstream in the slow, brown, leaf-dyed waters, against a lazy current that made little ripples and bubbles and sucking sounds as it ran over and around little rocks and old green-lichened snags. While I rowed, the Old Man fussed with the fishing gear. I noticed that he put a split shot and a single hook on one leader, and tied a bright red-and-white wooden lure with some pork-rind streamers on the other.

We came around a bend of the Big Crick, and the Old Man told me to head her into the bank, where there were a lot of lily pads and weeds and, it looked like, some fairly deep pools. He handed me the rod with the single hook and the little sinker on it.

"Now," he said sternly, "we will fish. You will use some of those worms you dug up and catch us a mess of brim. I will see if I can't do something about a bass or so. When you've caught us a bait o' brim, switch the hook and try for the bass yourself. They won't be bitin' for another hour or so, anyhow, until the evening fly hatch rises.

"Now, then, son," the Old Man said, "we ain't goin' to talk any, because fishin' is a silent sport and a lot of conversation scares the fish and wrecks the mood. What I want you to do is set there and fish, and when the fish ain't bitin' I want you to listen and look and think. Think about heaven and hell and just how long is hereafter. Look around you and don't take nothing for granted. Look at everything you see and listen to everything you hear, just like you were brand-new come from another world, and think about all those things and how they got there. Now let's fish."

I threaded a big, juicy worm onto the hook and flipped the line over the side, and in less than a minute a big fat bream had seized onto it and I jerked him into the boat. They only ran about half a pound apiece, but they bit like they hadn't ever seen a worm and thought it was candy. The Old Man was potting away at lily pads or close aboard them and flicking his line along the shore under overhangs of old logs or rocks, and wasn't catching anything at all.

I pulled in about two dozen bream, and then switched to a plug and started to imitate the Old Man. I had a little trouble with the wrist, but not much, because I had been doing a lot of salt-water fishing, and I'd learned to throw a cast net, and boys don't have much trouble learning anything outside of book lessons. Nothing hit my hook either. It was just flip, reel in, poise, flip, and reel in some more, with the bait hitting the water with a *plonk* and the pork streamers making a wriggle in the water like a frog kicking his legs in a breast stroke.

Well, sir, when you can't talk, you got to think and look and listen, and all of a sudden I was the lonesomest boy in the world. You know anything about what it's like in a fresh-water swamp in the South when the sun is starting to drop and the noises begin? Or what it smells like and feels like as it cools off from the heat of the day? And what sort of things are all around you?

I got to looking at the water. It was clear and clean, but as brown as your hat from the leaf dye, and when you scooped up a handful it tasted a little like leaves smelled if you crumpled them in your hand. And it was full of all sorts of little things—bugs that hopped and popped, little crawlers that left a tiny wake behind them, like a mink swimming. Fish swirled and rose to snap at the first beginnings of the fly hatch. A big bullfrog gave a loud, croaking *ker-tunk!* and leaped into the water with a splash. Over on the other bank a water moccasin slithered down the greasy earth and slipped into the water without a sound.

It was so lonely in that swampy river that it made you want to cry. All the sad sounds in the world suddenly started. A dove set up that woeful *oo-hoo-oo-hoo-hoo* across the swamp, and another one, sadder still, began to answer him back. They sounded like two old widow women swapping miseries.

In the utter hush a million noises intruded. A bittern roared. A heron squawked. A kingfisher rattled. A deer snorted and barked. A bird screeched. A crow cawed. Somewhere deep in the swamp there was a growl and a scream as a wildcat skittled a rabbit. A squirrel chirred and was answered. Leaves rustled. Things fell off trees. Bushes stirred mysteriously with the passing of unseen animals. Along the creek a piece a raccoon came down to drink, washing his little paws as daintily as a lady.

The sun sank lower, and the huge old live oaks, their Spanish-moss beards swaying down to the water's edge, looked as ominous as monsters. The cypress knees made all sorts of strange shapes. Along the banks the ferns grew—the delicate maidenhair fern and broader-leafed ones I didn't know the names of—in an indescribable carpetry of cool greenness. Little silly flowers poked their button heads up among the ferns.

Away off somewhere a cowbell tinkled very sadly, and you could hear a rich Negro voice singing its way through the frightening, falling shadows of the intruding evening. He sounded scared, and he was scared, and he wouldn't get any less scared until he sighted his shack with the fire going under the big black iron kettle. Now the cicadas and the crickets and all the other loudly vocal bugs were beginning to sound their eventide notes, like an orchestra tuning for the overture.

In my brain I looked at all of it—the trees, the grass, the moss, the bugs, the birds, the ferns, the flowers, the setting sun, the rising hatch of flies. I felt the dark creeping and saw the first shining speck of star and heard the mounting noises in the swamp. I felt cold in my bones from the rising miasma of mist as the air cooled. I was so lost in what was going on, in the million slivers of vibrant life, that when a big fish hit I lost him out of sheer panic.

The bass bit beautifully, there just at dusk, and we caught ten or so between us—not very big; but a two-pound bigmouth on a whippy rod is quite an order. When it got black-dark, the fish eased off and I shoved the boat into the stream and let the current carry us down toward the landing. The Old Man took in the lines and put the plugs back in the tackle box, and I just sort of warded the scow off the snags. The Old Man lit his pipe and puffed peacefully. He said nothing, nothing at all.

It was main late when we hit the landing. The stars had crept out bright now, and a little wedge of moon was slipping sneaky-like up over the trees. The frogs, the bugs, the night birds, and the animals were making a din. I got to thinking about eternity, and how long something that never ended would be, and I got to thinking about how much trouble Somebody went to, to make things like cocoons that butterflies come out of, and seasons and rain and moss on trees, and frogs and fish and possums and coons and quail and flowers and ferns and water and moons and suns and stars and winds. And boys. Especially boys.

Once we got back in the Liz, the Old Man didn't say any-thing for a few miles. Then he spoke, without turning his head. "You ain't said much. What do you feel like?"

"I feel like I been to church. I feel like I got—that word you said."

"Humility?" the Old Man asked gently.

"Yessir," I said. "I feel awful little and unimportant, some-how, and a little bit scared."

"You're beginning to learn, boy," he said. "You're beginning to learn."

Summertime seemed to be almost equally compounded of music and baseball. The Old Man and I used to sneak off into the woods some nights, when we could get out of the house without an argument, and just follow the singing until we came onto a big revival meeting, white, or a big camp meeting, colored, or a most amazing exhibition when the Holiness people got took down with the Sperrit, rolled and writhed in the sandspurs, foamed at the mouth, sang to Glory, and spoke in the Unknown Tongues. My Great-Uncle Wade was a Holy Roller, and when the Sperrit got a firm grip on him, he was a sight to see. He got trancified, and walled his eyes, and spoke in the Tongues, and when he really got to rolling, he didn't seem to feel the sand-spurs, which were nigh about as big as golfballs, with inch-long spikes.

The white revivals were a little depressing, because everybody including the preacher was full of sin and eager to admit it. Peo-ple I knew well who hadn't had a bad thought or committed an evil deed in forty years used to go to the bench and confess to the most amazing breaches of the peace of state and soul. I al-ways felt like they were bragging, so as not to be left out of things. One Sunday, though, we went to the Big Town and heard Billy Sunday produce a fire-and-brimstoner under a big tent, and I was powerful impressed, possibly because the Devil-hating Mr. Sunday had been a professional baseball player once. I didn't smoke for a week, not even corn silk or rabbit tobacco, for fear of hell-and-damnation. I even gave up baseball and fishing on Sunday for a little spell.

What I liked best—and so did the Old Man—were the colored folks' camp meetings. I reckon between us we knew every Negro in the country, old and young, male and female, ornery and exemplary. They would congregate in a clearing somewhere well out of town, with a thatched shelter over the big rough pine tables where the food was, and sometimes go on for days. The camp meetings had a lot of preaching and exhorting, and a lot of casting out of Satan, and a lot of mourning on the bench, and a lot of people reborn in the Lamb, but it was all much better-natured than the white folks' revivals. The colored folks seemed to be on a more intimate basis with the Lord. The backsliders were there to renew faith and acquire fresh hope, but the majority of the people who made up the congregation were there to have fun.

The smell of frying fish, and the spitting of the fish in the skillet, and the grease on hands and faces in the firelight, were part of it, as the watermelons and the lard cakes and the fried chicken and the rice pilaus were part of it. There was always some homespun corn whisky, and some home-stomped scuppernong wine too, which was as much a part of the festival as the music. I heard no music like that until I went to Africa a great many years later. When I first heard the Wakambas singing the working songs, and the lifting, toting songs, and the Waluingulus putting on a nocturnal meat-thanks concert in the bright of the moon, I could close my eyes and roll back thirty years to Brunswick County's camp meetings.

The singing would start out with a formal hymn, which would gradually syncopate into a chant, and would move easily from hymn to spiritual, with the African beat becoming more pronounced. The shuffling would become a stamping, hands would clap, and the first light stirrings would richen into a rolling sea of bodies, with the firelight flickering on grease-shining black faces. The voices of the women would separate into wailing minors from the deep rich basses and baritones of the men. Groups of singers would stray apart, answering and asking each other questions in song, blending in the refrain, pausing at the breath stops with deep-chested grunts from the men. (The old lion grunt is parcel to nearly all the African music I ever heard.) From time to time one of the women would let out a piercing, neck-hair-lifting scream, and throw herself on the confession bench, as the music took her and her sins welled up, to plead for purification. When Sister Mary had enjoyed her moment of full attention, Sister Kate would throw back her head and let out a screech, and in time all the good Sistren would have their prideful moment at the bench. Old Satan used to take a fearful beating.

The men very rarely were taken, but provided the constant chant. A good bass singer made the circuit of the meetings, and was nearly as popular as the preacher in terms of chocolate cake, fried chicken, and free access to the fruit jar. I remember the Old Man spotting a strange face in the crowd once, and asking the man where he came from, and why he was there. The man smiled, understanding our rather peculiar patriarchal attitude. "Ah comes from Onslow County. Ah come heah to drink whisky and sing bass," he replied in a voice that would have made Paul Robeson sound like a soprano. This fellow was very popular with the younger female set, and usually disappeared from view around midnight.

We never mixed into the festivities, of course, but sat at the edges, and were tolerated because we were the Cap'm and the Little Cap'm, and because my mammy, Aunt Laura, had been born a slave and wore a conjure bag until the day she died. We were kind of part of the family. From time to time somebody would fetch us a dipper of the scuppernong wine and a plate of fried chicken or some field peas with fatback. It was a mutually understood laissez-faire; the same shining black faces could be seen on the outskirts of the dancing when the white folks had their big square dances—interestedly watching the high jinks as the *bokra* (white people) leaped and cavorted and kicked their heels and sashayed in time to the fiddles. And I must say that a white-folks' Saturday night square dance, for action, might have made a Masai *ngoma* look tame, once the sweaty dancers got sufficiently lubricated on the white corn that burned a path down the gullet and landed with a fiery thump in the pit of the stomach. White music or black, summertime created a lot of vocal exercise, a power of banjo plinking and fiddle sawing.

The baseball was another thing entirely. The Old Man bought me a glove, a ball, a catcher's mitt, and a bat, which kind of gave me a corner on the two-o'-cat market. We pitched and caught interminably, under the shade of the big moss-bearded oaks in what was simply called "The Grove." We batted flies and rapped grounders on the one stretch of sidewalk in the town. This was perishing hard on the ball, which soon became scuffed, frayed its seams, and peeled its horsehide. The ball was then wrapped in bicycle tape, and landed in the glove with a leaden thump that like to have torn your hand off.

Walter Johnson was the big hero among the pitchers, and Babe Ruth was becoming so popular they named a candy bar after him. We, at least, promptly gave up O. Henry for Baby Ruth. Pictures of the stars came in cigarette and candy packages, just like the movie stars, and very brisk trading went on.

Saturday was the day of the big game between the town's pickup adult team and one of the surrounding hamlets. This game actually had as many as nine men on a side, and the catcher not only owned a "mast," we called it, but a belly protector and shin guards as well. It seems to me that a fellow named Fred Something played a fancy left-handed first base, and the two St. George boys, Donald and Bill, were the battery. They said that if Donald hadn't fooled around too much, and drunk a little too much corn, he could have pitched in the majors. I suppose there is always one man in every town who could have made the majors if he hadn't fooled around too much.

Saturday night in the summertime was when they swept the

small fry off the streets early, because the rival teams had a way
of canceling hostilities by burying their noses in the same jug,
and by midnight were apt to be burying blunt instruments in
each other's skulls. The word would go out that Tom or Joe or
Bill "was drinking"—they always used that phrase, "was drinking"—and sisters and mothers and aunts would hustle out like
agitated setter dogs to retrieve their wayward kith and kinry.
The fathers were known weaklings, and sometimes two members of the family would have to be fetched home; father and
son wrapped in each other's arms and either fighting or singing
lugubriously. We were not, as I recall, a breed of social sippers
in that day and age. When a man got his face stuck into a fruit
jar, he kept it there until paralysis set in.

The Old Man said that he approved of baseball because it
was the only neat sport he knew of—three strikes, out; four
balls, walk; fair and foul clearly marked; over the fence, a
homer; just so far around the bases; and always the same distance from the pitcher's block to the plate. But he did not approve of the wassail-all which followed the games, and his heart
nigh broke when the Black Sox scandals came to light. He
reckoned among other things that there had been too much
postgame drinking mixed up in it, and that was in some indirect way responsible for this breakdown of moral fiber in
Chicago.

Yet there never was a man who liked a toddy better than the
Old Man liked his. He just felt that if you were hunting, you
were supposed to hunt, and a cockle-warmer came at the end,
not in the middle of it. Same way about fishing, work, or
baseball. He made an exception in camp meetings, recognizing
that alcoholic incentive was part of the festivity.

There was a kind of unwritten rule in our town that nobody
was supposed to have any fun on Sunday, but was to stay home,
eat an enormous dinner, and spend the afternoon bored and
half-drugged from the monumental midday meal. The Old
Man took heavy exception to this. He said he had been clean
through the Good Book, and while he admitted that it came

out strong against working on the Sabbath, he couldn't see anything wrong in a man translating his day of rest any way it pleased him, so long as it didn't constitute a nuisance or offend other people's delicate sensibilities.

At this time there were very few privately owned automobiles, and one of the more barbarous customs was to pack the entire family into the Model T or the Locomobile and go for a grueling expedition called "the Sunday afternoon ride." For a youngster it was torture, packed in with the old folks and the musty smell of jet-beaded black funeral silk which constituted old ladies' Sunday uniform.

That's when we would slip quietly away after dinner and go fishing.

"The fish don't know if it's Sunday or Wednesday," the Old Man said. "It's all the same to a fish. So long as we are not catching fish for sale, which constitutes work, I reckon we are leaving the Sabbath intact according to formal rules. It certainly isn't any worse than racketing around in a car, or spending the afternoon playing this golf everybody's getting so crazy about, or just setting around the house trying to stay awake."

We never took very much trouble with Sunday fishing. If somebody else wanted the Liz, we just ambled down to the water, scooped up a mess of fiddler crabs, and sat quietly on the dock, waiting for the big sheepsheads to come out from their caverns around the rotted, barnacle-encrusted pilings. You caught more toadfish than sheepsheads, but occasionally there was a small blackfish to relieve the monotony. Now and again we shoved the skiff off the shingle and rowed half a mile or so to some holes we knew, close by an ancient wreck, stopping by the marsh on the way to net a few shrimp for bait. There was always a mess of croakers and the occasional weakfish to liven up the afternoon. Sometimes we just took the crab net and a piece of ancient meat and went crabbing off of one of the little piers. Or we'd rig up a light and a trident and pole the boat around after dark on low tide, stabbing the odd flounder. If the car wasn't working for somebody else, we might drive a few miles to one of the big fresh-water cricks and have a try at a few largemouthed bass when the evening cooled.

No, I reckon there wasn't very much to do in the summertime, but it got to be September before you knew it, with the big salt-water fish beginning to run, and the high, moon-swollen tides to make the marsh-hen shooting easy on the first big norther. And then the tortures of school and shoes began, and before very long the frosts had crinkled the persimmons and the hound dogs started running the woods by night, with quail and Christmas just around the corner.

But I still can't hear that "Summertime" song without fetching up the Old Man, as large as life, despite all he said about summers belonging to boys and the old folks standing aside. I reckoned for most of his days the Old Man figured he was a kind of overgrown boy himself.

12

September Song—II

Even for a young ruffian like me, getting back to school in September was a little bit of fun for a few days. You saw a lot of people you hadn't seen for three months, and the football practice was starting. In class there would be one or two new pretty girls, who had moved in from some other town. There would be a couple of new boys, too, and it took a bit of time and a fist fight after school to squeeze 'em into the pattern.

This was a pretty good September. Through some sort of accident I skipped a grade and was now a senior in grammar school—practically grown, I thought. There was a very pretty blonde girl named Rose Ellen sitting next to me, and I fell in love the first day. This didn't mean much because I'd started falling in love in kindergarten and had two or three seizures every year from that point on. I carried a mess of books in those days.

I was kind of in love double that year, because we had a red-headed, freckle-faced young sprout of a teacher named Miss Carrie Mae Knight, who was a real humdinger. You hear a lot about juvenile delinquents these days, but I'm here to tell you that if every classroom had a Carrie Mae Knight in it there wouldn't be any trouble with kids.

You never saw such a woman as this Knight female. Mind you, she was teaching a class that had boys in it older than she was, because she was only nineteen, and some of those big country kids were easily twenty. They got in one grade and just stayed.

Miss Carrie Mae Knight could do nearly anything we did better than we could. She coached the football team. She scandalized the principal by putting on pants and showing a great big clunk named Clyde Something how to really take a tackle out of play, and she rattled his teeth when she hit him. She could play any position on the baseball team, and when she pitched she came in with a high hard one that bore no resemblance to the crooked-arm way that most girls throw.

She never sent any ratty notes to your folks about whatever deviltry you'd been up to, and she never squealed to the principal or shifted her disciplinary responsibilities, which we called "being sent to the office." Nobody ever got sent to the office, not even when some big oaf she was keeping after school made a grown-up grab at her. She killed her own snakes. She hit him a punch in the chin with a straight left and crossed with her right, and never had any more trouble. I seem to remember that she had been raised with five brothers, all red-headed.

Carrie Mae—we called her Carrie Mae outside the classroom —had a big following at the parties, when we played kissing games, like post office and spin-the-bottle. She seemed to know instinctively how to hang onto kids, boys and girls. She was taking flying lessons, and she used to give us a half-hour fill-in on her progress—in the middle of the study period.

She read to us a full hour every day. It was never kid stuff, either. She read a lot of Mark Twain and Kipling and contemporary stuff from the magazines. To the best of my memory, nobody ever made a paper airplane or threw a spitball when Carrie Mae was reading. She was one of those natural-born readers who could lift you out of your seat. She even read us Shakespeare and made it sound like a Wild West story, and I still get hungry when I remember the first time I ever heard her read Charles Lamb's dissertation on roast pig. I knew about cracklin'; I'd been raised on it.

Carrie Mae was the first real contact I made with the outside world of adults. Of course the Old Man and some of his shooting and fishing friends were sort of buddies of mine, and I didn't think of them so much as grown-ups. I had a lot of adult friends among the fishermen and the Negro field hands and suchlike, but teachers and people like them were all enemies, guilty until proved innocent.

What really sold me on Carrie Mae was the day the Old Man drove up to the school and asked for me about ten o'clock in the morning. Miss Knight went out to see what the old gentleman wanted, and then she came back and crooked a finger at me. I followed her out into the hall. The Old Man was in the lobby, twisting his hat in his hands.

"Your grandfather," Carrie Mae said, "has got a crisis. He has explained to me that this is the day the dove season opens and he just got a message from a friend of his that there's a big dove drive taking place, away off in the other end of Brunswick County. He says that he doesn't think the entire progress of education would be ruined if I excused you from the rest of the classes today to go along with him. He's also asked me to dinner to eat some of the doves. You better run along. I'll need about two hours' help with some papers tomorrow afternoon, and you can pay me back then."

That was as close as I ever came to kissing a teacher, until several years later, of course. I made my manners and roared down the hall like a train with all boilers lit. The Old Man sort of grinned.

"That's quite a filly," he said. "If I was about forty-odd year younger, I'd choose her up myself. She's reasonable. A reasonable redheaded woman is hard to come by. Let's us go shoot some doves."

The Old Man had the guns and little Mickey, a golden cocker that I haven't told you about yet. Mickey was of the old cocker breed—pretty near as big as a springer, and an all-round hunting dog. She had hair about the color of Miss Knight's, and she had a good flat head and a square muzzle like a dog, not like some of the popeyed, pointed-headed idiots they call cockers today. They've bred all the sense out of most cockers and made sissy dogs out of them, but there was a time when a good cocker would rassle a bear and hunt anything that flew, ran, or climbed.

We drove across the river on Mr. Oscar Durant's old ferryboat and pointed the Liz in the general direction of the Willets farm, a big corn, cotton, and tobacco holding. The roads were made of corrugated clay, and it took time. We had plenty of time to get there for the afternoon shooting unless the Liz decided to throw a shoe. As we bumped along, the Old Man was lecturing a little bit, as he generally did when we took on a new subject.

"Doves," the Old Man began, "are the easiest hard shootin' in the world. Or maybe it's the other way around. Maybe they're the toughest easy shootin' in the world. I'm telling you right now, you figger to miss more'n you hit, and it wouldn't surprise me none if you didn't hit any for your first box o' shells.

"A cranked-up dove that's been driven is as fast and tricky as any bird in the world. He'll swoop like a swallow, and he'll change his flight pattern just when you start to pull. He's got more feathers on him—loose ones—than a feather-tick mattress. When he's going away, you can shoot off his tail and pull a pound of fluff off him, and he'll still continue on his errand.

"In all the ballistic computations of mankind, ain't nobody ever figured a way to lead a dove too far if he's going past you in a high wind, after he's been chased from one corner of a field to another. When he's coming straight at you, you got to throw some shot up where he's going to be a second later, and that seems like it's near about a quarter-mile away, sometimes. If he's quarterin', you got double trouble. My blanket suggestion is just to point the gun about twenty feet ahead of him, pull the trigger, sweep the gun around, and pray. Mebbe something will drop."

We finally got to the farm, and there were twenty or twenty-five men standing around in the clean-swept sandy front yard under the chinaberry tree, smoking pipes and chewing tobacco and spitting meditatively at targets. They all had guns, mostly rusty-looking old pumps and a few wire-wrapped single-barrels. There was a general air of festivity and an odor of crushed grain that was not unfamiliar.

They all said a hearty Hello to the Old Man and tossed a few jokes at me, such as, "Are you sure it's safe to hunt in the same field with this feller, Ned?" Or "Can we trust him not to kill all the birds and leave a few for us? That looks like a mighty potent hawgleg he's carrying, don't it?" Then they would slap their blue-jeaned legs and guffaw. The opening day of the dove season was a kind of community party, like a house raising or a cane grinding or a quilting bee.

The Old Man laid a hand on my neck and said, "Don't you worry about this feller. He'll wipe all of your eyes when he gets the hang of it. I'm here now. What're we waiting for? Let's go shoot some doves."

It was about four o'clock in the afternoon when we started to trudge out to the stubble field, a huge cornfield that must have been a mile across and two miles long. I had two boxes of shells for the 16-gauge. The Old Man said I'd need 'em. The cocker spaniel trailed along behind us, as though she knew what she was doing.

We came to a far corner of the field, and the Old Man pointed to a big hickory tree with some old dogfennel bushes under it. "Sort of scrootch down here," he said. "I ain't shootin' much today. I'm going to help Henry drive. The dog'll stay with you. Just tell her to fetch, if so be it there's anything to fetch." And the Old Man laughed loud—"Haw-haw"—and stalked off to crisscross the field, driving up the doves.

All those grown men were strung out around the edges of the field, partly hidden by trees or clumps of bush. Half a dozen were driving, and pretty soon you could see the doves whistling up, aimless at first, but working up steam as they got higher and leveled off. Then the guns started to go off, boom-boom here, boom-boom there, and now and again you'd see a swiftly darting dove crumple in a puff of feathers and drop like a brick, or slant or flutter down in a long glide.

The late sun was bright on their rosy breasts when a few came my way, and I tried to remember about leading 'em enough, and hauled down. I made quite a lot of noise, but nothing dropped.

Evidently the shooting addled the doves, because as the guns spoke all round the field they crisscrossed back and forth, flying higher and faster, darting more, dipping more, swerving and looping more. I shot. And shot. And shot, until the barrels were hot. Mickey, the cocker, looked up at me with a slight frown.

I had two birds on the ground—both straightaway shots, with no leadoff involved—when I scrabbled for more shells. There weren't any more in the first box. I had shot twenty-five times and had two birds and maybe a couple of possibles that the dogs would pick up later.

Ten shells later I had four birds on the ground—one killed coming straight at me, the other quartering away. And then a little machine clicked in my head, and the lead-off angles worked themselves out. I was leading passing birds as much as twenty or twenty-five feet, and they were coming down like hailstones. I was nailing incoming birds, and they were falling at my feet. Old Mickey was spitting out feathers and cursing dog language, but she was cursing at overwork. When I fired the fiftieth shell, there were fourteen birds on the ground under the tree; and my muscle was black and blue and red from the kick.

I felt pretty pleased. I had knocked down ten doves out of the last fifteen shells, and some I had shot at twice.

I stuffed the birds in my old canvas hunting jacket, picked up the gun, and headed off across the field. It was getting a little nippy, and the sun was red in the face and headed for bed. I reckoned the persimmons would be ripe in another month or so —and then it wouldn't be too long before the quail season started.

The Old Man was sitting on the running board of a car— cars had running boards in those days—and holding forth on something or other. I walked into the yard and inside-outed my hunting coat. The birds tumbled out, and the Old Man looked smug at his cronies. The men nodded and smiled, and one of 'em said, "I wouldn't be surprised if he ain't set a record." He was kidding, of course, because nobody paid much attention to bags on doves in those days.

"Like I said," the Old Man remarked as we drove bumpily home, "it's the easiest hard shooting or the toughest easy shoot-ing in the world. When you get it figured out, it's a cinch, but the figgerin' costs an awful lot of gunpowder before you'll admit that these things need all the leadoff you can crank into your head. The last ones come so easy you wonder how you missed the first ones—until next time, and then you wonder all over again.

"I must say, though," the Old Man said as we turned into home, "once you've got a dove on the ground, your troubles are over. You can breathe on 'em and the feathers will fall off. Sup-pose you go try to have 'em picked before suppertime."

Miss Carrie Mae Knight came over to the house for supper the next evening, and she ate three doves all by herself. She said she had never enjoyed any birds quite so much, because there were so few shot in them. I expect that Miss Carrie Mae Knight was righter than she knew.

I reckon the Old Man was about as queer as they come, a stickler for a whole lot of things that mightn't make much sense to other people. It was as if he had figured out a whole complete set of rules and regulations, according to his own ideas, which were good enough for him. You could do two things: you could play it his way, or you didn't play at all.

"I am an old boar coon," he told me one time. "I'm too old and sot in my ways to learn a mess of new teachin'. I have seen the elephant and heard the owl. I don't do nothin' I do except for a reason. The reason may not suit other people, but it suits me, because I have tried it all and made two mistakes for every mistake I didn't make. I am what you might call a monument to trial and error."

The Old Man had a lot of peculiar hates. He couldn't abide a loud talker, for one thing. He said a man that had to holler for emphasis was just echoing the wind that blew through the vacant space where his brains ought to be. He especially hated noise in the woods, particularly people that were always hollering at dogs. He said it not only confused the dog but confused him as well. It made him nervous.

He was a garrulous old man, and he loved to talk at length when talking had some point. But he purely despised idle chitter-chatter, people that just talked without having anything to say. And he hated to be interrupted. "The world," he used to say, "is full of fine fragmentary thoughts, killed at birth by the interruptions of damned fools."

The Old Man hated what he called uppity people, young and old alike. He had no time for a smart aleck. His friends were simple people that knew what they knew and kept their traps closed about things they didn't know. He hated discussions at the table, arguments, and problems and such. They interfered with his digestion. About the first thing I remember he ever said to me, when I was a very small boy, was that children should be seen and not heard at the table. This went for most adults too.

But he was a stickler for politeness. He claimed there was no excuse for impoliteness. He said that "sir" and "please" and "thank you, ma'am" were as cheap as dirt, and that ordinary good manners were a measure of the man, because only a dodlimbed fool was rude when he didn't have to be.

It was a long time ago, but I remember just as clear that one day when we had some trouble with what the Old Man called a Willie-off-the-pickle-boat. This Willie was one of those rich Yankees who had come into port with his ocean-going yacht. He had on a yachting cap and a double-breasted blue coat and white pants and pipe-clayed white shoes. There were another man and three women with him, and from the way they were carrying on in the stern sheets of that yacht they had been punishing the booze pretty frequent for some time. Between sunburn and whisky, the Willie-off-the-pickle-boat had a face like a beet, more purple than red.

I don't even know what the ruckus was about. I think it was something about the yacht being sloppily moored at a private pier that belonged to the Pilots' Association, and the yacht was beating up the pilot launch. The Old Man had some interest in the association, the pier, and the launch.

I believe he asked the Willie if he would kindly nurse his yacht around to another slip or sling his hook a little farther out so as to take up a little strain, or some such civil request. The Willie didn't take it kindly. He came bustling up on the pier, like he was about to pop, and started to holler and wave his arms. He said, playing it big for the womenfolk, that no old moss-backed yokel was going to tell him what to do with his yacht, and that if the Old Man didn't watch his step he'd buy the town, and so forth. The Old Man just stated his request over again, in a very mild voice, using "please" and "sir."

The Willie blew up. "Why, you old son of a bitch," using that Truman term which doesn't get you very far in an argument down South, "I've got a good mind to——"

Which was as far as he got, good mind or not. The Old Man. who was a good twenty to thirty years older, squared off and clouted him on the chin. The Willie staggered back and fell off the dock into the drink. His gold-braided hat went spinning downstream in the current. The Willie was about half coaled out, and he was flopping and spluttering in the water.

The Old Man hopped onto the pilot boat and grabbed a boat hook. He grappled the Willie in the seat of his flannel britches and hauled him aboard, choking and gasping like a big fish, and then being sick to his stomach. The Old Man never even looked at him.

He hopped back onto the dock and bowed to the women. "I wish to beg your pardon, ladies," he said. "I found the gentleman's language offensive in front of the ladies. Please accept my apologies." Then he turned to the other man. "And now, sir," he said, "*for the last time, move that boat. Please.*"

When we left the dock, the city slickers and the three women were moving the boat.

The Old Man muttered all the way home that he despised brawls, but there occasionally came a time and a place where politeness wasn't any good and you had to meet bad manners with worse manners.

"There ain't anything," he said, "that'll settle an argument as fast as a punch in the nose if you know you're right and the other feller knows he's wrong. But it sure is undignified."

The Old Man was strictly a shark on good manners in the woods. I have already told you how persnickety he was about cleaning up campsites and burying rubbish and washing down boats and keeping guns and gear clean and oiled. But he wouldn't hunt or fish with a meat hog or a rude man.

He used to shoot quail quite a lot with a man named Joe, a very pleasant fellow until you took him to the woods and let loose a couple of bird dogs. Then Joe changed coats and became a hog. He was one of those fast walkers, always right on the heels of the dog when it was working game. He was a fast shooter, too. A bird would get up, clearly in your quarter, and you would be taking your time to let the bird straighten out, and just as you were about to pull down, *pow!* Joe's gun would go off and the bird would fall, because Joe was a very fine shot.

I went along on a few hunts with Joe and the Old Man, not shooting, because the one thing the Old Man was adamant about was more than two guns loaded when you were hunting quail. Even not shooting, just watching Joe made me nervous as a fox in a forest fire. It made the dogs nervous too, because Joe was stepping on their tails all the time, and they didn't have a chance to work the birds properly. The dogs rushed the birds, and the birds flushed wild, and always there was Joe, right smack in the middle of the wild birds.

Even on steady points this Joe was a hog. Although they supposedly took turns on singles points, you'd never be surprised to see your bird drop before you shot, and Joe would say something like, "Well, I didn't think you were going to shoot," or, "I thought that palmetto bush had blocked off your bird."

The Old Man was deadly with his gun, but he never brought in more than half the birds Joe did. I noticed a lot of things. Every time they did get confused and both fired at the same bird, Joe would take the bird from the dog and put it in his pocket—even though it was the Old Man's turn. And when they got home, if Joe had fifteen and the Old Man had six, Joe would keep the fifteen, and there would be no mention of a divvy.

Finally the Old Man quit hunting with Joe. He said it took all the fun out of shooting. "Hunting ain't a competition," he said. "You ain't trying to win any prizes. Hunting is watching the dog work, and taking it easy, and shooting just enough, and walking slow, and enjoying the day. Damned if I figure to run any foot races at my age, not if I never fire off another shotgun. And if a man wants a bird more than I do, he can have him. But not in my steady company."

So the Old Man and I took to hunting regularly together, and we killed about as many birds as Joe did, but we killed them according to ordinary politeness and what the Old Man called protocol. We did it calm and easy. When the dogs would point a covey, I would stand to the left and the Old Man would take the right. If all the birds swung my way, he never shot. If they went his way, I let 'em go, and hoped a lay bird would jump up in front of me. Most of the time one did.

On single birds, we shot turn and turn about. If two birds got up when it was my turn, the Old Man never shot at all. He only shot if half a dozen jumped and one or two went away off to the right, 180 degrees from where I was pointing.

Quite a lot of birds got away from us, in one sense, but then quite a lot didn't. For one thing, knowing that you didn't have to compete with some itchy trigger behind you or on one side of you calmed you down. You'd let the bird fly and straighten out and kill him dead, rather than snap-shoot him and either miss him clean or blow him to pieces with the full charge.

And the difference it made in the dogs was unbelievable. The Old Man wasn't wrong when he said a nervous hunter can make even a good dog nervous, to where he starts crowding the bird and flushing him or running clean over a lay bird that he would have smelled if he'd been taking his time. I reckon we more than made up for the ones that got away with the ones we shot that we wouldn't even have suspected of being there if we'd been in a hurry.

After we'd put up a covey and shot into it and the dogs had retrieved, the Old Man would generally sit down under a tree, call in the dogs, and light his pipe. "Let's give 'em a little time," he'd say. "It'll take those singles ten minutes before they start to move around a bit and leave enough scent for the dogs to smell 'em out. A bird that's just hit the ground don't have hardly any smell at all. He has to move a little first."

Well, I learned something there, too. If you go crowding and stomping right into where you've seen the single light, you'll kick up bird after bird that the dogs have run smack over, especially if it's in thick grass. Lots of times the birds will get up again as a covey, or as two halves of a covey. Or if they've lit in sparse cover, they'll flush wild, whereas if you'd left 'em alone a little they'd have run for better cover and left a perfect scent for the dogs to follow, and you'd have gotten a stanch point and a good shot.

By just leaving them alone ten or fifteen minutes, when you did go to roust 'em out you'd have your dogs pointing a bird here, a bird there, two birds here, and each bird holding hard on the ground, even with the guns going off. The way the Old Man hunted singles, there was many a time we could have wiped out the covey, excepting that the Old Man didn't hold with shooting more than three or four birds apiece out of any one bunch.

I sat down one winter—we always kept strict account of the birds we brought in, and filed a report to the Game Department at the end of the year—and figured out an average bag for the pair of us. There was a fifteen-bird limit then, and we averaged twenty-one birds per hunting day for two guns. I missed a lot of birds, and I averaged eight birds per trip. That meant that, what with rain and snow and dry-nosed, sick dogs and just plain bad-luck days, we had to have a lot of days when we killed the limit, fifteen birds apiece.

But the important thing was that we had plenty of lovely time in between the actual shooting. So suppose it took us all afternoon to get a limit or a near limit? We had just that much more time in the woods, to see all the things a man can see in the woods if he's traipsing along slow and easy and taking his time. There's no fun going hunting at three o'clock if you're going to be back in the tin Liz at four-thirty, with the best part of the day still ahead of you.

In later years it seemed to me that this feller Joe missed all the important part of hunting, just from being in a hurry and greedy to see a little bundle of feathers fall. The Old Man said that hunting was not so much what you brought home in the bag as what you invested in it if you were satisfied to take a small return on your original investment.

"Otherwise," he said, "you might as well build yourself a

quail trap or take a couple dollars and buy a gross from one of these pot hunters. There just ain't enough meat on a bobwhite partridge to make it worth while to turn yourself into what that Willie-off-the-pickle-boat called me. I would rather come home any time with a few birds and a good day in the woods."

The Old Man was peculiar, all right. I wish there were more of his brand around these days. Maybe we'd have more birds.

13

Even School Can't Hurt October

It being Prohibition in those days, I had no way of knowing what brown October ale tasted like, but there were a passel of other things to recommend the month. I'm not referring to school, and wearing shoes again, because by October you'd got used to about six hours of torture and your feet had quit hurting. October meant a lot of things to me. It meant the oysters were prime again, and there was enough leaf off the trees so that you could see a squirrel. The big fish were beginning to run, and the first frosts had come, so that a fire felt fine in the evenings. And if October were here, why then it wasn't so long before the bird season opened, and once you had Thanksgiving settled you had Christmas practically made.

It was one of those nice bright Saturdays when it forgot to

rain. Speaking of rain, did you ever notice that for five school-days the sun always shone, but as soon as a boy got loose from learning and fixed his mouth to do something worth while with his time on a Saturday, it always poured rain?

Anyhow, this was one of those nice bright Saturdays, or promised to be, because the sun had just come up blood-red and was starting to turn gold, and the first mild frost was white and stiff on the browning grass, and there wasn't so much as a whisper of breeze to stir the trees. The Old Man had parked the Liz, and we were walking down a corduroy country road, heading for a big hickory grove we knew about. We were carry-ing a couple of .22 rifles and were accompanied by that fice dog, Jackie, the mongrel with the curled tail that swooped up in the air and came back to rest approximately between his shoulder blades. Jackie was dirty yellow and had a fox's face, and nobody could have accused him of having a hound's bugle, but there was one thing Jackie could do better than any other dog in the world. If there was a squirrel in a tree or rooting for nuts on the ground, Jackie would know about it, and tell you about it in a thin little voice that sounded like an angry woman quarreling.

"We'll just tie this masterpiece of bad breeding to a tree for a spell," the Old Man said. "All the squirrels are still in the trees, and we don't need no expert assistance until they come down on the ground. We will still-hunt 'em a spell. I reckon there's enough leaves off so we can see 'em."

We came into the hickory grove. It was as still as a cemetery.

"A great morning for squirrels," the Old Man whispered. "It's a waste of time to hunt them in the wind. They just don't move, and they don't feed much. Be quiet now, and let's walk soft and go sit under that big hickory yonder and see what happens. Ssshh."

We sat down, the Old Man on one side of the tree and me on the other. All over the grove you could hear the squirrels begin to talk. *Chirr* is about as close as you could come to the noise they make, but you can make about the same sound by sliding your tongue sideways across the top of your mouth. There was plenty of action going on this morning, I must say. You could hear them chirring all over the grove, and hear the click of their teeth on the nuts, and now and again you would hear a mild crash in the foliage as a big fellow traded trees and the branch he sailed off of would whip back.

I heard a chirr behind me on the ground, and a click, and I knew it was the Old Man talking squirrel. He was making the click with his safety. It sounded just like a squirrel bragging about the size of the nut he was tackling. Pretty soon there was a shaking in the branches of a tree just ahead of me, off to the right, and I sat still as a statue. Then there was some more shaking, and a head stuck out of a crotch. All I could see was head, but it was black-silver and it had to be a fox squirrel.

Bimebye I saw a tail flicker, and then the old fox slid round the trunk, flat-plastered to the bole. I let him come all the way round until his back was to me and he was peeping in the opposite direction. Then I raised the little .22 real slow, held high on his back between the shoulders, and squeezed her off. The long rifle hit with a thump, and Mr. Squirrel came down like a rock. He hit with a thud, kicked a couple of times, and quit. A soft-nosed .22 long rifle between the shoulders will make a man stop and think, let alone an old squirrel. From where this fellow lay, he looked as big as a tomcat. He was near solid black on top, with a lovely black-and-gray tail, and he was almost three times as big as a gray, or what we call a cat squirrel.

It wasn't long before I heard a rustling behind me, then a wait, and the Old Man's little gun spat. I heard a thump as something hit the deck, and judged the Old Man's gun eye was still working.

With the Old Man making his chittering noise, the squirrels came to that big hickory like they were cats and we had the catnip concession. First my gun would make its little *splat!*, followed by *tunk!* as the bullet hit, and *blump!* as the squirrel came tumbling down. There were mostly grays, but I acquired two more of the fox variety, one a lovely silver-gray and the other blacker than the first. The Old Man's gun was speaking pretty constant, too, and in less than an hour we had more than a dozen. Then I heard the Old Man creak to his feet and heard the rasp of a match as he fired up his pipe.

"Let's pick up and move on. We done wore out our welcome here. How many you got?" he asked.

"Seven," I told him. "Three foxes and four cats. How 'bout you?"

"I got eight," the Old Man said, "but only one fox. I missed another I coulda killed with a rock, if I had of had a rock instead of this cannon."

"I missed three," I explained. "I got fancy and tried to hit one jumping, and the other two I coulda caught with my hands. A squirrel looks like a mighty big target when he's flattened out or sitting up, don't he?"

We had a couple of towsacks with us, and I filled mine with my squirrels. Then I went around to where the Old Man had stacked his squirrels in a neat pile, and dumped 'em on top of mine. Fifteen squirrels in one sack is a powerful mess of squirrels. It was all I could do to heft the bag.

"Gimme," the Old Man said. "I'll just hang it up here in this low crotch, whilst you go let Jackie loose. It don't do to frustrate a dog, any more than you'd tease a young'un. He's been hearing the gun go off, and he's probably hung himself by now. We can still use a lot more squirrels. I promised a mess to half the neighborhood, and at last count Abner McCoy had at least fourteen head of young'uns to feed, and the boll weevils hit the cotton this year."

I grinned. The Old Man was powerful cute sometimes. Abner McCoy was as black as the ace of spades and he had a mouth as big as a scoop shovel. He farmed a lot of land next to the store, and he had more quail than anybody round. About a dozen fat squirrels would make a prime bait of meat for his family, and there would be enough heads left over for a proper squirrel-head stew. The squirrels would fix our hunting lease for another year.

There may have been a limit on squirrels in those days—I dis-remember—but we didn't hunt 'em much, and when we hunted we hunted serious.

So I rested my gun on my hat and trotted off to unleash Jackie, who was having a fit of nervous frustration and was foaming at the mouth. He nigh dragged me off my feet as we headed back to the grove.

"Turn him loose now," the Old Man said. "We'll go over yonder to that rise where all the scrubby oaks and chinquapins are. The survivors'll be on the ground. That's Jackie's business."

Jackie took off in the right direction, and presently we heard his squirrel-up-a-tree signal, a feverish yapping that would make you think he'd treed a panther or a bear, at least. He was standing under an oak—did I say standing? He was dancing an Irish reel and yipping his head off, with his sharp fox face pointing to heaven.

"You take that side," the Old Man said. "I'll take this. In a minute one of us will spot him."

Shooting treed squirrels is almost ridiculously simple. It is just a matter of knowing how to look for 'em. With two men to a tree, the squirrel, who is plastered to the trunk or squatting in a crotch or stretched full length on a branch, will move away from one side as soon as he is aware of the shooter on his side. That's when the guy on the other side shoots him.

Pretty soon I spotted a head sticking cautiously around the bole, and a gray body, stuck flat, eased around to my side. The little .22 talked some more, and down he came. Jackie raced over, picked him up by the back of the neck, gave him a sharp twist, and broke his neck. Then Jackie spat him out on the ground, barked a sharp bark of self-appreciation, and whipped off.

It went on like that until nearly eleven o'clock. I reckon Jackie must have netted us another two dozen squirrels, mostly cats, but at least six or seven more foxes. We filled the other bag, and it was so heavy that the Old Man ran a stick through a couple of holes in the hem, and we packed it out together.

When we got to Abner's, the Old Man dumped the first bag in Abner's clean, white-sanded front yard. Abner's vast, plumb-black face split in a grin as big and red as half a watermelon.

"Man, dat sure a bait o' skwull," Abner said. "What in de yudder crocusack?"

"More squirrels," the Old Man told him. "These fifteen are for you."

"Bossman, dat powerful neighborly. Us kin use some meat in dis house. Seem lak every day I count another young'un I didn't know us had, and de price o' sowbelly powerful high. Tell you what us best do," Abner said. "Dat too many skwull in de yudder sack for two people clean. I call my biggest chillun, and we set right down here and skin 'em now. You chillun! Come hope me and de Cap'm!"

Children of all sizes boiled from the little house.

"You, Woodrow Wilson, you go fotch de knives!" Abner ordered. "You, Hardin', you go tell Mama I say start de fiah and boil water in de hog-killin' pot. You just makes to sit in de shade, Cap'm, under dat chinkyberry tree, while de chillun fix de skwull. And if I ain't outa my station, Cap'm, maybe you like a little snort of somepin I found in de branch las' week, and de young Cap'm, maybe he like cool he th'oat with a little dipper scuppernong wine, yeddy?"

The Old Man said he couldn't think of a sounder idea. We sat in the shade, and Abner brought a half-gallon Mason jar full of white liquid, and a similar jar half-full of a darker liquid. The white liquid was sweet and cool from the well, and the brown liquid must have had plenty muscles in it, because the Old Man closed his eyes and his body contorted when he downed a dipperful. He wiped his mustaches with the back of his hand.

"How are the birds this year, Abner?" he asked.

"Never seen so many patridges in my life," Abner replied. "City man out here de yudder day, want pay me for huntin' rights, but I tell him I save my buhds for my white folks."

The Old Man looked at me and winked. It wasn't long before our two dozen squirrels, skinned, gutted, and washed, came pink and clean in the tow sack.

"I guess we better get on, Abner, and many thanks," the Old Man said. "Good-by."

Abner said good-by, and the chillun waved.

The Old Man drove slowly out of the yard. He turned and winked at me again. "There's more ways to kill a cat than to choke it to death on butter."

I reckon you all think I'm powerful concerned with food, because I'm always writing about it. I guess I've got to plead guilty, but it seems to me a boy lives mostly in his belly, and the Old Man said one time he didn't trust nobody that didn't like to eat so hearty that a nap was bounden necessary after Sunday dinner.

In those days we didn't have all the fancy outdoor barbecue rigs, with the host wearing a girl's apron and a chef's cap. Mostly what got cooked was cooked inside a house, on a slow-burning wood stove, by a slow-cooking colored lady who didn't want nobody messin' round her kitchen. The men didn't cook —least the men didn't cook public in town. But the sneaky spirit of the chef was always there, inside the hairiest of the roughnecks, and Christmas was a time of year when everybody who wasn't sweet as a peach (a Southport euphemism for being as drunk as a goat) was apt to be doing something in the woods or on the water. It was a kind of point of honor to go somewhere to spend a couple of days living off the land.

They still have them in my part of the South, but they've got a lot fancier now, and I'm talking about the old-fashioned oyster roasts. A roast was as much a part of the festive season as the Christmas tree, the holly berry, and the mistletoe. In these outdoor cooking sprees, the men mostly took over. The ladies had their hands floury enough from making the fruit-cakes, and they just sort of sat back, patted a foot, and let the boys be boys.

The first thing the boys did was go out in a skiff and tong up a bait of oysters and clams. The oysters in that neck of the woods were mighty fine. They were big—big as a bar of laundry soap—gray, striated, and shading to white around their wrinkled edges. The clams were nearly as big as tennis balls, purple-black on the shell and a plum-yellow solid globe on the inside. They came up muddy from the cold gray water, and when you swished the tongs in the clean water they tumbled onto the deck of the boat shining bright as jewels.

The fruits of the sea were taken to a proper oyster shed, which meant a lean-to under which a rough wooden table perched on trestles; the chairs were anything from camp stools to packing boxes. Kerosene lamps provided the light—I forgot to say that no respectable oyster roast was held in the daytime. It was not considered polite to get drunk in daylight, and a good portion of our holidaymakers considered oysters and corn liquor inseparable.

Wet-down moss would do, but a really top-grade oyster chef smothered his oysters in freshly gathered kelp. The actual oven was a simple compromise on a modern barbecue apparatus, meaning that three sides of stone or concrete held a sheet of heavy tin or galvanized iron on top. A slow fire was built under the metal sheet, and the oysters, blanketed in seaweed, were allowed to steam until the hinges relaxed and you could slide an oyster knife between the shell lips without cutting the valve. The smell is still vivid to me, because the oyster roast was held close by salt marsh, the scent of marsh and myrtle and beach pine mingling with the steam from the roaster.

You were supposed to tee off with either clam chowder or terrapin stew; you never got both at the same event. If it was clam chowder, it was very simple. The chowder contained no milk or tomatoes. It had clam juice and clams and diced Irish potatoes and browned fatback and onions and salt and pepper, and it simmered into such a delicious symphony that you had to hold yourself back, remembering the oysters. One of the ladies generally bestirred herself to make the chowder, for the gentlemen were always very busy with the oysters and with the half-gallon fruit jars that contained a white beverage which was known simply as mule.

But the oysters were the main operation. The chowder just paved your stomach for the real debauch. I don't care how they eat oysters today; there's only one way. As the Old Man said sometimes, "I value your opinion, but not when I know better. And in this case I know better."

First you take a bushel of oysters, smoky steam writhing, from their bed in the kelp over the slow coals, and you introduce them to a small Negro boy who is standing on your right with an opening knife in his hand. In front of you, on the rough pine planking of the table, is a bowl of red-hot melted butter and a wide, empty plate—almost platter size. For a condiment there is a thin-necked jug of pepper vinegar, with the little curled-up red peppers, hot as Hades, still inside. There is a platter full of johnnycake, corndodgers, or even hushpuppies in front of you. For a beverage, you drink Bevo, a concoction that was supposed to taste like beer but wanting a little needle to gain authority.

At the signal "Go!" the colored boy starts to open oysters, and if you are a man of control and high purpose you will allow him to release a dozen before you start to dip them in the butter, season them with the pepper vinegar, and put them away, mopping up the "gravy" of oyster juice, butter, and marsh mud with the already greasy johnnycake, corn fritter, or hushpuppy. Somehow, the tiny bit of remaining mud gives a flavor that is incomparable to anything, unless you know exactly what a Carolina marsh smells like with the wind in your nose and the water oaks shivering before the wind. You then lick your fingers and look reprovingly at the little boy if he has not managed to liberate another dozen oysters during your complete concentration on the first twelve.

The Old Man used to say, "There ain't no such thing as *enough* oysters—it's just that the human stomach was never really designed to handle a decent bait of them." My best record was four dozen, each oyster as big as a candy bar.

It was possible, of course, for a man to open his own oysters, but you lost something of glamour in the process, for the small boy was as much a part of a roast as the odor of steaming sea-weed, the smell of the sea and trees, and the scent of the roasting oysters as they reluctantly relaxed their valves under the steady pressure of the flame. You might as well have taken away the distant hoot of the owl and the hollow boom of the surf and the damp smell of the white beach sand, or the rustle of the sea oats that grew down on the dunes nearly to the water's edge.

There was another thing—two things, as a matter of fact. One was that a man opening his own oysters never had enough will power to unleash a dozen before diving into the butter. The other thing was that you robbed the little colored boys of a chance to bet their night's wages on which client could eat the most oysters. A man who was having his oysters shucked for him was duty-bound to founder himself, or it would cost his little assistant a mess of money, as much as fifty cents. The boys kept the shells as a tally. They rarely lost money backing my appetite.

There was a certain artistic elegance to this scene of gour-mandizing—the firelight red on the already-flushed faces of the cooks, glistening off the white eyeballs and black faces of the little Negro boys, shining greasily on the lips and the fingers of the eaters, lighting up the rough shed with weird shadows, and making weirder shadows of the angular, wind-tortured trees. The road to the roast was always of gleaming crushed oyster shell, which seemed fitting, and there was a bone-white, high-piled stack of shells off to the side.

This was the coeducational outdoor aspect of the holiday time.

The more intimate and cruder cookery by the gentlemen came on the two- or three-day hunting trips. Some of the richer men, off after ducks or deer, took along a cook. At that time there was a profession amongst the Carolina colored folks that possibly no longer exists, more's the pity—that of "sporting cook." He would be a man of the approximate moral equal of his employers, which is to say he wouldn't work steady if there was an excuse in the world to run loose in the woods and listen to that fine man-talk. Generally he drank—intemperately, sporadically—and so was adjudged a poor risk as a house cook.

I knew several of these fellows, and the best of them all was a paroled murderer who worked occasionally for my family. The name has gone away, but he was wizard in the woods. He did some things with a few rocks and an iron grill, shoved some oak chips underneath, with hard hickory to flavor it, and the venison chops that came off the grill would make you cry. Venison is a hard meat to cook, and a lot of people spend a lot of time basting it with this and that, and undrying it with jellies and wines, but this fellow would just toss it onto the coals, haul it off, and slap it steaming on the plate, and you always burned your tongue because you couldn't wait. I used to go to bed, full as a tick, already thinking about breakfast next morning.

Breakfast would be something special in fried eggs—he always toted an iron skillet, because he said you couldn't fry anything so a dog would eat it in anything else but an iron spider—and usually some broiled deer liver, and slabs of fried buttered bread, and maybe, if everybody was hungry, a squirrel fricassee. He made hoecakes, which are nothing but hushpuppies—meal and water and salt cooked in ashes. You scrape off the ashes, and there is a noble one-bite piece of ecstasy, especially if you've got some redeye ham gravy or fatback-flavored potlicker to dip it in.

I have never liked any egg, in any form, in a restaurant, but a fried egg in the woods, sizzled in bacon fat until its white edges turn to fine Belgian lace, grading up to brown, is a noble thing. And if it is accompanied by fried sowbelly and busted into a plate of fine-ground hominy grits, and the whole mess flavored up with grease, there may be indigestion around the corner, but it is not worthy of worry.

A lot of people won't eat a possum because it looks like a rat, but our cook could take a possum and nestle it in sweet 'taters and little onions and a few carrots, and I've never eaten anything in Paris, France, that could touch it. It wasn't fat and it wasn't lean. It was a kind of blend of both.

Remembering back to eating in the woods, it seems to me that the main staple, apart from coffee and sugar and salt and stuff, was corn sirup or molasses. A can of beans slow-cooked with molasses and onions and strips of bacon quit being just pork and beans. We used the long sweetening for everything —to sweeten coffee, drown the hotcakes, help the beans. We even combined it with ketchup on the spaghetti.

There are worse things than a duck or a fish caked in clay and set to slow-cook until the clay cracks, and when you peel it off the feathers or scales come with it. There are worse things than a chunk of fresh-killed deer liver broiled on a green stick around a campfire. Nobody has yet found a way to commercialize creek water, with its taste of brown leaf dye, but certainly there is no comparable liquid for making coffee in a tin percolator in a nest of coals.

Of course you realize all this was a very long time ago, and memory tends to make a man salivate. Youth and a body unjaded by whisky and tobacco are part of it, and of course the excitement of being out of doors. The only thing I can't figure out is that when I do it today it still tastes as good as I remember it, and very possibly a little better.

The first real concept of conservation that crawled into my head was fed me gradually by the Old Man, without his ever saying anything much about it. It took a period of years to develop, but one day it came into bloom like an autumn rosebush. There are a lot of things mixed in with keeping your game supply up to standard; some things that even a millionaire can't buy, such as friendship and cooperation.

Like most boys, I was as bloodthirsty as a cannibal. I got my first air gun when I was just six years old, and the robins and the blue jays and the catbirds and the rain crows really took a pounding. I shot everything from English sparrows to the neighbor's cat. When we had nothing better to do, my Cousin Roy and I went out into the woods and played Indians and shot each other from ambush. Why somebody didn't lose an eye will always be a source of wonder to me.

A big, old, sassy mocker lived in the magnolia tree alongside our house, and he used to sing late at night in the moonlight. He would scatter those notes around like one of the fishermen on Saturday-night payoff. He was a pet of my grandmother's; so it was natural that when I took down the Daisy one day and removed him from the concert business, the Old Man took down my pants and applied a very limber lath to my behind. It was one of the few times I ever had a hand laid on me, and it made an impression.

"Hunting," the Old Man said when my noise had slacked off, "is the noblest sport yet devised by the hand of man. There were mighty hunters in the Bible, and all the caves where the cave men lived are full of carvings of assorted game the head of the house drug home. If you hunt to eat, or hunt for sport for something fine, something that will make you proud, and make you remember every single detail of the day you found him and shot him, that is good too.

"But if there's one thing I despise it's a killer, some blood-crazy idiot that just goes around bam-bamming at everything he sees. A man who takes pleasure in death just for death's sake is rotten somewhere inside, and you'll find him doing things later on in life that'll prove it. I realize all young'uns get that first phase when they want to carve up desks and bust windows and shoot mockingbirds, but I aim to see you grow out of it, or I'll have every last inch of hide off your rear end.

"I want you to go to bed tonight and stay awake thinking about the mockingbird that sung so pretty and your grandma loved, and then think of that little mess of dirty feathers even the cat didn't want. And then think a little bit about this nice air rifle that Santa Claus brought you to learn to shoot with, and wish you had it back again."

Whereupon the Old Man took the little Daisy and busted it over his knee, and threw it over into the bushes where he had thrown the carcass of the mockingbird. That was Lesson One.

I went quite a spell before I got my first shotgun, and when the Old Man took me out to learn to shoot quail he spent quite a time reading me the riot act about how many quail a man could shoot out of a covey and still have some quail left to shoot next year and the year after. Like most kids, my idea of what to do, once you got birds scattered pretty, had been to shoot as long as the dogs pointed.

That sank in pretty good, because those quail and the Old Man had been friends for a long time; because he trained dogs over 'em, and knew to a bird what came out of the spring clutches. I didn't want him busting up my 20-gauge like he did the Daisy. And since he was my pretty constant companion in the woods, I couldn't have cheated if I had wanted to.

We hunted for quite a few years before it dawned on me that we had exclusive shooting rights to nearly a whole county. We shot land that said "Strictly Posted." But we shot it with the owner's permission, and we always started out with a word with the farmer, black or white, in his back yard, and always had a long, cold drink of icy well water out of the tin dipper. And when we came in tired and reached the house, we went in to warm chapped hands by the farmer's fire. Then maybe the Old Man would have a glass of scuppernong wine, and I would have a little bit too, and a handful of cookies or a doughnut before we got in the Liz to drive home.

This applied to both white and black. The colored folks were generally landowners, not croppers, and they had a big pride of land. I do not know how many little clapboard or log shacks I have been inside, with a roaring pine-knot fire actually showing through the house, the yard full of pickaninnies and yellow fice dogs, with some old woman always doing something over an iron pot in the yard—scalding a hog, doing the clothes, but always doing. When we went inside to warm up, the house was always neat and clean, with the walls papered in colored pages from newspapers, calenders, or sometimes just newspapers. Outside, the white-sand yard was always swept clean.

I had my first taste of squirrel-head stew in one of those little colored-folks' houses, my first possum and sweet 'taters. I still love the taste of fatback fried hard, and stewed rabbit to me tastes sweeter than any of those fancy French dishes. I called the older folks "Aunt" and "Uncle," and the middle folks by their first names. They called the Old Man "Cap'm," and called me "Young Cap'm" or "Mister Bobby." There wasn't any special servility, because the Old Man was always laughing and joking, and they always made a lot of fun of me, all loaded down with canteen and Scout ax and a gun as long as I was.

Old Aunt Florence, grizzled and bent, would sometimes say, "Cap'm, strange city man come out here the other day with some buhd dogs, and he drive up and ask me if I got any buhds on my place, and I say, 'Nawsuh. Ain't seen a single buhd since dem big rains come last spring and drownded 'em all. Anyhow, dis place posted. We got too many hawgs loose in de woods.' I knowed you wouldn't like no strange passer-bys shootin' yo' buhds. I sont him off."

Aunt Florence's little farm was so surrounded by coveys of quail, on purely public property, that she practically had to build a fence to keep them out of the yard. But the only way to the big timber leaseholds and swamps was through her yard, and she could look pretty fierce, surrounded by dogs that yapped ferociously at strange white folks.

Or we would stop to pay a call on big Abner McCoy, who was six foot four and had all those young'uns. Abner would grin horribly over his gums and say, "Cap'm, stay 'way from that covey over by de Old Church. There a den o' foxes over there been eating up yo' buhds and my chickens, and J got traps set thicker'n pine needles. Wouldn't like none o' yo' dogs to get caught.

"But the other day I was cuttin' some kindlin' over by dat ol' graveyard, between de graveyard and de old sawdust pile, and I jumped de biggest covey of buhds I ever seen. Dese is new buhds. Must been usin' cross de road, where dat loggin' goin' on, and plain couldn't stand de commotion. So dey come live with us. Wait a minute, I finish dis chore, I come show you exactly."

We never wasted any time finding birds, whether we were hunting on Sheriff Knox's big farm or Aunt Mary Millette's, who did the washing. Either the birds were here or they were there. If they weren't here, they had to be there. And you found 'em from one year to the next. We had peafield birds and swamp birds and woods birds that roved a little to eat the pine mast, but usually centered around a certain scrub-oak grove or a sawdust pile or a copse of gallberry and dead branches.

What is more, we had the whole county—a big county—to hunt in, and only one large estate was off limits. The rest was private shooting for the Old Man and me. One day it suddenly struck me that no millionaire could own that much prime shooting, and there must be a reason for it.

Well, there were a lot of reasons for it. For one thing, country folks in those days had no interest in quail unless they caught a covey running down a corn row and could kill the whole kaboodle for a stew. Or maybe to trap a few when times were tough and bellies growling. So they never paid any attention to partridges—which is what we used to call the bobwhite—and never made any effort to help them survive or to keep people from just killing off whole coveys right and left. There were pot hunters in those days, dead-eyed gents with pump sawed-offs, who could wipe out a covey in a day if the birds scattered right in the broom sedge.

The Old Man was pretty devious, as always. Everybody in the county knew him. He was in a position to give credit at a feed-and-grain store he was connected with, and in the hard years a lot of people planted on credit, and fed their cows on credit, and got their laying mash on credit. The Old Man could be counted on for one dollar's or two dollars' worth of personal loans, and at Christmastime he always went around with the flivver full of oranges and red candy. He had what are known today as connections at the source.

Well, when he started to circulate the idea among his friends that he thought right high of those little speckled partridges that ran together in droves and called to each other so mournful at dusk, he got action. He would tell one farmer that it would be a nice idea if he planted just a few black-eye peas down by the swamp, or another if he would let some stock stand here or there after the harvest, or not plow that field of broom over to the west if he didn't really need the space that year.

He said he'd give two shotgun shells for every tame cat gone wild that anybody brought him the tail of, and the same for hawks and foxes and similar varmints. He said he'd kind of appreciate it if the folks would keep account about where they flushed the coveys oftenest, so he'd know where to go look for 'em.

In return he was a sort of game scout, rounding up lost hogs and strayed cattle, and he was a terror about fire in the piney woods. Any time he came across a coon or a possum he would shoot it out of the tree and fetch it along to the nearest family. He usually had a few tins of snuff or a plug of Apple tobacco in his hunting coat for the old folks.

Well, sir, the upshot was that we had the primest shooting land around, and we had it pretty much to ourselves, and we had friends all over the place who looked after our game and kept down the brush fires and planted a little extra for the birds to eat. We had fires to warm us and cold water to drink and whatever there was in the pot to eat if we were hungry.

A long time later I read about conservation, but it seems to me the Old Man had it taped a long time ago. The only thing was, he didn't believe in sharing the wealth with every Tom,

Dick, and Harry. Only his friends and me, because he could control us. The Old Man reckoned that those birds were *his* birds, and not for nonappreciative short-time murderers to shoot into extinction. The more I look around at the opportunities for good shooting today, the more I think he might have been right on all counts.

14

Everybody Took Sick but Me

I suppose everybody has one little particular chunk of time he wishes he could get back and live all over again. The one fine time I remember best and most lovingly was when whooping cough hit the schools—all the schools. It was what they called an epidemic.

The epidemic struck about two weeks before the Christmas holidays started. First there was whooping cough, and then there was measles, and everybody came down with them except a few of us lucky ones. The teachers had them too—including the principal. There wasn't a thing to do but shut up shop and let the diseases run their course. By the time the race was run, it would be so close to Christmas that there wasn't any use in starting classes all over again, just for a few days. So they knocked off school for nearly a month.

I tried real hard to regret this unforeseen gap in my keen pursuit of such things as Latin and geometry, but it so happened I had enjoyed whooping cough and two kinds of measles, and I was salted. Maybe the other people were sick, but not me. I felt just fine.

The chances are I was grinning all over my face when I got home the day they announced the closing of the schools. The Old Man looked sharply up at me and asked, "What happened to start you grinning like a Chessy cat? Teacher break her leg?"

"No, sir," I said. "Better. They just closed down the schools until after New Year's. We got an epidemic or something. School's suspended. Hot diggety!"

"Look at you," the Old Man chided. "Happy as a dead pig in the sunshine. Here you are, going to grow up ignorant, and all you can do is grin. I'm ashamed of you."

"It's not my fault I already had whooping cough and the measles," I protested. "I didn't close the school. But as long as it's closed, I don't figure to cry myself to death. I think I'll just go and shoot some squirrels. You want to come?"

"Not me," the Old Man said. "This lumbago's got me. You're going to have to handle this misbegot holiday all by yourself. Just try to check in with me once in a while, so's I won't feel too left out of things."

The Old Man slid down in a chair and shoved his specs a little higher up on his nose and took to reading some book that must have weighed ten pounds. I changed my school clothes and went off to look for some squirrels. I didn't take the bird dogs along. I took old Mickey, the spaniel.

People today talk a lot about these German Weimaraners that'll hunt anything from rats to elephants, but I'll stack that Mickey up against any of them as a plain meat dog. She was a spayed golden cocker bitch, durn near as old as me and a whole lot fatter. She was a pure-T hunting fool.

Mickey was slow but she was certain. She would find a covey of quail as good as any professional quail dog. Although she wouldn't hold a point, she'd slow down enough to give you time to get up with her before she let out a yip and jumped.

She would run a possum at night or tree a coon. She was poison on rabbits, because, since she couldn't outrun 'em, she'd outthink 'em and run 'em past you. She loved to hunt squirrels, and she'd retrieve anything from a buck deer to a ground mole. She especially loved to go duck hunting, because the colder the water, the better she felt. One time I saw a big old bull mallard just about drown her.

I don't want to tell you any real big lies about Mick. She didn't run rabbits as good as a pedigreed beagle. She wasn't as dead on wounded ducks as a Chesapeake or a golden retriever. She didn't cover as much ground on quail as even a slow pointer, and she wasn't half the squirrel treer that little Jackie, the fice dog, was. But for most purposes she was the most all-purpose dog you ever saw.

As long as the Old Man was laid up I couldn't get too far away from base, because I wasn't old enough then to drive the Liz. And there weren't many quail around where we were living, so it was a waste of time to hunt much with the bird dogs. But there were a whole lot of little bits of game—a few quail, a few ducks, rabbits, squirrel, snipe. So for one solid month it was me and Mickey.

The cold had come, and there was a thin crust of ice on the ponds in the morning, not heavy enough to bear your weight, but enough to force the ducks into pools of free water. The leaves were off the trees, so that you could see the squirrels, and a lot of the underbrush had died, so that the rabbits were fairly easy. You could always find one in a brush pile. There were a few doves still in the fields. Shotgun shells cost a nickel apiece.

I reckon that this was the time when I picked up a very bad habit that has caused me a slew of complaints ever since. I wasn't then, and never will be, what is called a dedicated hunter, just burning to go and do one particular thing. I was

more like a highly trained quail dog that has slipped his leash
and is having a glorious time chasing rabbits. I liked to go out and
just sort of mess around, with some No. 8's in the shotgun and
a few 4's in my hip pocket and two buckshot shells in my shirt
pocket just in case a deer should run up and start out to trample
me.

One of the days I spent might have been typical of most of
the days, and I will try to tell you how it was. I was out of the
bed in the cold black night, with just a little glow in the old
square stove in the living room. I dressed as close to it as I could
get, and then went back into the kitchen and ate a cold
sweet potato, a pickle, a glass of milk, and some leftover pound
cake. I stuck a couple of apples and a bag of raisins in my hunting coat and didn't forget to grab a handful of matches on the
way out.

In addition to the gun and the shells, I carried a small belt
ax and a hunting knife and a light Army canteen. That was all I
needed to be Dan'l Boone. Missis Mickey and I started out to
conquer the country.

We'd go first, stumbling and half-frozen in the black morning, to a duck pond about half a mile away, and creep very
quietly in the dark down to the water's edge and hide in some
brush I'd stacked up to make a blind. When the first gray light
came, there would be ducks on that pond—some butterballs
and bluebills and a gray duck or a black mallard or so.

I knew what I was going to do as soon as there was enough
faint light to see by. I was going to pop off the first barrel at a
clump of them on the water and then bang at a flyer as they
went away. Mostly I was good for about four more shots,
because they'd circle the woods and come back again in small
bunches. On a good morning I was a cinch to bag about four,
five, six ducks, especially if I got a couple on the water.

This one morning I got only one on the water, and a wounded
one fluttered up and I gave him the other barrel, just so I
wouldn't have to go and hunt him in the woods. The ducks
made the first return run, and I knocked down another and

missed one going away. Then a fresh segment came in and I
was lucky. I got one coming and one going. The first one I hit
in the head. He went up about a hundred yards in the air like
a skyrocket and came plummeting down as dead as a mackerel.

Well, that was a fine start, I said to Mick as she plunged
into the icy water. One black mallard, two butterballs, a bluebill, and a gray duck. We will now hang these ducks in a tree
and go and investigate the squirrel situation. Mickey fetched
the last duck and looked at me as she shook herself. *That's
fine*, she said. *Man, that water's cold!*

We were just a few rods from a big stand of hardwood trees,
hickory mostly, with a few wild pecans that had sprung up
a long time ago when somebody was farming there. You could
almost always pull a few squirrels out of it, because there were
acorns and pine mast as well. We walked very slow and quiet,
and you could hear the squirrels chittering and making that
click-clack noise on the nuts, and once in a while that long,
metallic chirring sound.

Mickey and I hunted very scientific. If the squirrels were on
the ground, she'd chase them up a tree and raise the roof barking. The squirrels would watch her, and I would edge around
the other side of the tree and shoot. One morning I saw a big
black-and-gray fox squirrel go into a nest, and I shot into the
nest and four fox squirrels fell out.

This morning we didn't have that kind of rich luck. There
weren't any squirrels on the ground; so I told Mickey to hush
and we sat quiet under a tree and called the squirrels, slipping
the safety of the gun back and forth to sound like teeth on nuts,
and making that *squirrrr* noise with my tongue. A couple of
fool squirrels came skipping through the trees to investigate the
noise, and I collected the pair. We picked up one more by accident as we walked through the timber stand, heading for a
big deserted peafield that usually had some quail in it.

Mickey lumbered off to where she figured the birds ought to
be, and sure enough they were there. She shook her stubby tail
and wiggled her rear end like she'd slipped a ratchet some-

where, and the birds got up wild ahead of her. I shot twice and downed one. I reloaded, and two lay birds got up, and I killed one and missed the other. The birds went into a wild-grape swamp that was so thick they weren't worth following; so we quartered the field, and I shot one dove that got up ahead of me.

We were doubling back around to pick up the ducks and go home for lunch when Mickey cocked her ears and jumped a big buck rabbit, and I added him to the bag. When she fetched him, he looked bigger than she was.

I pulled out my dollar watch, and it was only ten o'clock; so I decided to stop and light a fire and clean the game. There wouldn't be any lunch for another two hours anyhow. I took the belt ax, and hacked off some pine knots and a couple of chunks of dead log, and built me a blaze. I shucked the squirrels and the rabbit and opened them up and started on the ducks. I had already eaten the apples and the raisins and I was still hungry; so I took one of the quail and plucked him and stuck him on a green stick over the coals. He tasted a little burnt-feathery and a touch raw, but he filled enough corners so that I could make it to lunch without starving. Mickey ate the innards, she being a rather indelicate bitch.

When I got home, I washed the ducks and the one quail and the dove and the three squirrels and the rabbit, and cut them up and put them in the icebox. Then I washed my hands and went to lunch, which was black-eyed peas cooked with sow-belly and hard country ham and bright golden cornbread and milk and apple pie with cinnamon dusted on it. Then I took a little nap, after asking big fat Lil, the cook, to wake me up at 2:00 P.M., about the same time I'd generally be thinking of getting out of school. I reckon I smiled when I slept, because all I had to do that afternoon was what I'd done that morning, only in reverse order—rabbits first, then quail, doves, squirrels, ducks.

I performed this routine every day except Sunday for three weeks. Christmas Eve came, and the Old Man, better now of his lumbago, asked me what I thought I'd like to find under the tree the next morning.

I didn't stop to think before I spoke. "Nothing that I can think of," I said. "I've had my Christmas. Except maybe I need some shotgun shells. I'm about shot out."

The Old Man grinned. He'd been watching me every day, stumbling home dead beat with a backload of game. "I sure am glad that epidemic of yours is about played out or there'll be nothing else left in this neck of the woods to shoot. Remember what happened to the buffaloes."

Christmas morning dawned bright and clear, but I wasn't there in the house to see it. I was down by the duck pond, with Mickey shivering beside me. I had clean forgot to look under the Christmas tree.

15

The Goat and I

There was one spring when everything seemed nice; it came early and stayed put, so that you got out the baseball stuff a month ahead of schedule and started to think about fishing and summer vacation, all in one bundle. And in addition to fishing and vacation, I started to plague everybody for a pony. I had read nearly all of Mr. Zane Grey's cowboy stories, and I was horse-minded. The Old Man was pretty unimpressed with my Riders-of-the-Purple-Sage stage. He did not care for horses very much.

"A horse," he said, "is the dumbest animal I know, and he takes a power of looking after. He's got to be fed and watered and curried and combed. He's always knocking a fetlock on the stall or something, and you need the vet to come running every whipstitch. He has to be looked after like a baby, and I don't know if you've got enough concentration to look after an animal that big after the first interest in getting throwed off him has dwindled down.

"Also, you know," the Old Man said, "his stall has to be cleaned and his saddle polished and his blankets aired. He needs fresh straw, and he eats a mountain of hay and oats, and he has to be walked to get himself cooled out after you've run him hard. You got to watch his hoofs and take him to the blacksmith. You got a bicycle; what do you need with a horse?"

I muttered something about every boy ought to have a horse, just like every boy ought to have a dog. The Old Man snorted. He said that pretty soon I would be telling him that every boy ought to have an automobile, and that some day I would be arguing that every boy ought to have an airplane.

"Tell you what," he said. "A horse is too large an investment for an unproven ability. We will just sort of try you out on a goat. Anybody that will look after a goat and cart will be a likely candidate for a pony, because nothing is quite as ornery as a billy goat. I know where there's one for sale. He's a real handsome goat, if you like goats, and I'll knock you together a cart and make you some harness."

We went to a place called Foxtown, where the colored people lived, and we stopped at the home of Albert Grey, the big colored boy who worked in the yard and told me fascinating stories to avoid doing any more work than he had to. Albert's aunt owned a goat. The goat was for sale for five dollars.

He was a real good-looking goat, young, fawn-colored, with a black stripe down his back, neat black hoofs, and a white star on his forehead. His horns weren't mature yet and hadn't curved out, and he had a forehead that was rock-hard. He had the worst disposition of anything or anybody I ever met.

We dragged—and I mean drug—Billy home, and he was protesting every inch of the way. He didn't want to leave Foxtown. He was happy in Foxtown, living under the house and eating anything that crossed his view. He did not want to go and live with the white folks. But we dragged him, and penned him up in the cow lot. The first thing he did was charge the cow, to the intense surprise of the cow. It was a big old creamy-yellow Jersey, with big horns, but that pint-sized he-goat had her scared stiff in five minutes.

We left Billy glaring at us through the fence and went off to see about the cart. The Old Man brought the tools out, and we got a big packing box and converted it into the body. The Old Man found some wheels somewhere, and we mounted her on the wheels, stuck some shafts on her, and painted her red, and she was a very handsome cart. Then he got some leather thongs and some buckles from the hardware store and produced a fine harness. He even made me a small whip. "You'll need it," he said, kind of mean. "A goat takes a lot of explaining to."

The Old Man said that any boy fit to own a horse and ride the range would have to train the critter himself, because no cowpoke worth his salt would ride a horse somebody else had broken. The same, he said, applied to a goat. I would have to break Billy myself, so that Billy would respect me and be a one-man goat. In later years I began to suspect that there was a lot of evil humor in the Old Man.

Bright and early the next day I set out to break Billy to his proper role of beast of burden. I went down to the cow lot and jumped over the fence, and Billy charged me like a lion. He hit me square in the stomach with that knobby skull, and I went over, all the breath knocked out of me. Billy backed off, sort of roared, and came again, like a cannon ball. This time I got out of his way, ran him down, got a strangle hold on his neck, grabbed an off leg like I'd read the cow hands bulldozed a steer, and spilled him on his side. He lay there on the ground and hated me with his cold yellow eyes.

Well, sir, trying to put a halter and a harness on that durn goat was a sight to see. I know it was a sight to see because a few minutes later, when I was red-faced and sweating and as mad at the goat as the goat was mad at me, I heard a chuckle.

There was the Old Man, leaning on the fence and laughing so hard that the tears were streaming down his face and running into his mustache.

"I don't think you're going at this exactly right," he said, "but I'm danged if I can tell you what you're doing wrong, unless it's that you ain't got but two hands and need six. Wait a minute. I'll help you hook him up."

Somehow between us we rassled the ornery beast into the harness and then tried to lead him to the cart. He sat down on his behind and braced his back legs, and when we pulled on the reins his eyes popped and he started to choke, but he didn't follow. He wasn't a very big goat, and the Old Man finally picked him up in his arms and toted him to where the cart was. Then we tried to back him between the shafts.

I heard somewhere about the camel and the needle's eye, and the camel had a cinch to get through. Getting this goat backward into the shafts was like trying to thread a needle with a snake. He blatted and kicked and butted and wiggled, but we finally got him in and secured—we thought—with the little hames on his shoulders and the reins threaded. I got into the cart and cracked the tiny little whiplash and hollered, "Gee haw," or some such. The goat looked around at me with the purest, most undistilled hatred I have ever seen in any eyes, and promptly lay down.

We would drag him to his feet, and as soon as I got into the cart he would lie down again. And then he started to twist and turn, and before long the harness looked like a backlash on a fishing line. Billy looked pleased. The Old Man shrugged.

"I think that's enough for one day," he said. "We don't want to rush his training. Let's drag him back to the cow lot, and we'll have another shot at him tomorrow."

We had another shot at him tomorrow, and it was the same old thing. This was a goat who wouldn't gee, wouldn't haw, wouldn't lead, wouldn't be dragged, wouldn't get up when he was lying down, and wouldn't lie down if he happened to want to stand up. He wouldn't go through the gate in the cow lot, which had a low fence; so I just simply took to throwing him over the fence. I had heard about Milo of Crotona in school, and I reckoned by the time Billy was a full-grown goat I could still heave him over the fence. I wasn't sure where Crotona was, but if Milo could heft a bull, full-grown, by starting out with him as a calf, I wasn't going to be backed down by any damn billy goat.

We worked on that goat for three months, and he never gave an inch. We had to battle to get him in the harness and battle to get him out of it. We had to run him down and catch him to get him out of the cow lot, and we had to throw him back like a fish when we were done with him.

I was getting no mileage and no amusement out of this goat at all. Then one day I found out by accident that this goat was a true warrior. He loved to butt and to eat anything that was regarded as inedible, but he had another vice too. He loved to wrestle. He would rear up on his hind legs and charge, and when I grabbed him he would twist and turn and do his level best to throw me. Fighting was the only thing he took any interest in except food.

The wrestling wore a little thin after a while because if a boy wants to wrestle he might as well find another boy; and anyhow, my mother was beginning to complain about my smell. This was a complete billy goat, including smell.

I tried everything I knew in the way of kindness to gentle him, and all I got was that yellow goatish glare. It isn't any fun to live with something that hates you and won't work even a little bit for his board and keep; so finally we took Billy in the Liz and returned him to Foxtown. He let out a happy blat when he saw his old home, and promptly dived under the house when we turned him loose.

I must have looked pretty downcast, because the Old Man stopped at Cox's Store and bought me a soft drink and a nickel's worth of candy. When we went on home he said, "Don't feel too upset. There are some things—some dogs, some goats, some people—that ain't worth troubling over. You can feed 'em and gentle 'em and worry over 'em and coax 'em and try to teach 'em, but they'll stay obstinate right on, like that damn goat. After a while, when you see it ain't any use, the only thing is to give up. The thing is to know when to give up—not too early, not too late."

I didn't say anything.

"You still want a horse?" the Old Man asked very gently.

"Not this year," I said. "I'm plumb wore out with that cusséd goat. This year I'm going to concentrate on fishing. At least I can manage a rowboat."

"Now there you are showing signs of sense," the Old Man said. "No man can do everything well. A lot of men spread themselves out, trying this, having a dib and a dab at that, never finishing what they start, and always trying to look for something new when they've failed. A smart man knows when he has a few things he can do well, and he's wise to do 'em, especially when he's failed at something. This gives him time to collect his wits and calm his disappointments, and then he's fit to go off and try something new again. I think the bigmouths might be biting tonight, if you'd care to try 'em."

The bigmouths were biting, and pretty soon my hurt feelings and frustrations cooled off and I wasn't mad at the goat any more. But I will never forget that animal as long as I live. He put a scar on my self-confidence, and since then I have met a power of people like him. When I run up against a person or a situation that has all the earmarks of Billy, that is when I quit and go fishing. Up to now it hasn't failed to help.

16

The Pipes of Pan

The first promise of summer was always an exciting thing to a boy—the spring winds eased and the sun burned away the April rains, the green pushed softly up and all the smells began. Mornings before breakfast were delightfully cool and breezy, and bred a restless excitement that made you want to caper barefoot on the dew-wet grass.

The smells were something. Down by the creek the dogtooth violets pushed up through the moss. The heavy tuberosy smell of the yellow jasmine filled the countryside, and the dogwood trees were white and pink with delicate bloom. In the orchards the early peaches and plums were breaking into blossom, adding their scents to the wild ones. The first tame flowers were popping out into the warmth, competing with the wild violets and the Johnny-jump-ups. I used to think that heaven would smell like this—cool and moist and very delicately fragrant.

You took to the woods then, not as a hunter or a fisherman, but as a naturalist. The Old Man was very firm about that.

"You're a bloodthirsty savage," he said, "like all boys are bloodthirsty savages. But there's a heap more to it than killing. Seeing the whole world come alive again after a long winter's nap and a wild, wet spring is more fun, 'specially as you grow older, than all the shootin' and fishin' there is. And I never was able to explain it, but the critters seem to notice this too. You'll see how tame everything is this time of the year, when it's wilder'n a buck rabbit in the shootin' season."

Maybe it seems a little dull today, but we used to go berry picking, after the blackberries had turned from green to red to purple-black, glistening on their thorny vines, and found it exciting. There were so many things to see and hear in the spring when you took a pail and went out berrying, to come home tired, with a crick in your back and your fingers and lips dyed purple from the juicy berries.

There were birds around that I do not seem to see so often any more—brilliant bluebirds, which came early in the spring and went away later in the summer. There were lots and lots of the big, fierce-looking redheaded woodpeckers; lots of what we called yellowhammers, another species of peckerwood known as flicker; the big cuckoos we called rain crows; the carnivorous shrikes with the bandit's velvet masks across their cold robbers' eyes; and hordes of the big, brilliant, raucously screaming blue jays.

The wet, plowed fields were crowded with teams of killdeers and the dainty-walking titlarks, racing along like pacing horses. The bobolinks were beginning to sway on the ends of high weeds, the stalks bending under their negligible weight. Soon the Baltimore orioles would be along, filling the air with sounds like the clinking of coins. The big cardinals were patches of blood against the dark green of the pines and cedars, and the scarlet tanagers darted like air-borne snakes.

When I think of it now, I think of it in terms of sounds and smells rather than sights. The catbirds quarreled in the low bushes around the house, and the big, fat, sassy old mocker that lived in the magnolia mimicked the catbirds. The doves cooed sadly from a great distance, and the quail called from the brushy cover at the edge of the cultivation. They came marching boldly into the strawberry patches, not in coveys but in pairs, walking through the back yard as if they owned it.

The killdeers wheeled and dipped in clouds over the wet fields, the skies filled with the mournful *kill-dee, kill-dee,* and the meadowlarks sang in the fields, and out of the wet places came the wild, sweet song of the woodcock. The crows and the jays raised general hell with everything, including the spring, and you could hear the rain crows' hollow *tonk* from some hidden position in a tall pine, and the solid knock of the woodpeckers, and the sweet chirrup of the little bluebirds.

This was the time of the year when the boys rushed out of school to swim naked in the creek at recess, and when it seemed impossible not to cut classes. This was the time of the bellyache from eating berries that had not completely ripened, from experimenting with stone-hard green peaches; and this also was the time of the lavish use of castor oil and calomel. It was impossible to concentrate in school, for the drowsy hum of June was just over the hill. Hence this was the time that boys were kept after school for throwing spitballs and making paper airplanes and dipping pigtails into inkpots. Summer vacation was yearned for by the teachers even more eagerly than it was craved by the students. Marks dropped terribly, and discipline teetered on the ragged edge of anarchy.

The Old Man said he reckoned the whole world went a little crazy at this time of the year, and he told me if I listened real close I could hear the piping of some old pagan god named Pan, who was half billy goat, away off in the wood. I told the Old Man that if Pan was anything like *my* billy goat I would just as lief have nothing to do with him.

"Be that as it may," the Old Man said, "that wood back there is creeping with all sorts of forest gods and spirits right now, and if we went and set quiet I ain't so sure but what we might see some. Hear 'em, anyhow."

The forest he mentioned was located back of the cow lot, and it was bounded by a big field of sedge where my pet covey of quail lived, and by a gully in which my secret interlocking caves were built, and by a big pond in which the diedappers swam and dived, and by a big soybean field that was full of doves in the fall. The forest covered about six acres, and was composed of towering pines and twisty live oaks and dogwood trees. Its floor was clean and mostly free of brush, a slippery floor of pine needles and jaunty wild flowers.

The Old Man and I spent a lot of time back there. We had to remodel some of the caves, which meant we needed fresh pine saplings for the front and some fresh beams under the heavy sod roofs; so some woodcutting was in order. It takes a lot of work to keep a cave in good shape, especially when there are half a dozen connected by long tunnels. The reason we needed so many caves was that I was then chieftain of a robber band, and in watermelon season the robbers needed plenty of sudden sanctuary.

Sometimes, when we got tired of working on the caves, the Old Man and I would sit down under a tree and lean back against the bole. He would light his pipe and tell me all sorts of wild tales about the Druids, who lived in trees, and the first Britons, who dug enormous caves called dene holes in the Kentish countryside in England, and about the bad spirits that lived in the Black Forest in Germany, and about the old pagan gods like Pan, who, I gathered, was a pretty fast fellow with the girls.

The Old Man had been near about everywhere, and I guess he had read just about everything, because anything I remember today I remember from what he told me. I always got pretty high grades in geography, because if they asked what country Kent was a county of, like New Hanover or Brunswick County in my state, I could always say "England," on account of the dene holes. I understood what a dene hole was because the Old Man and I had just dug us one.

We saw a lot of interesting things, just sitting quiet or walking carefully. One time I saw a rain crow, one of those big cuckoos, chase a dove off a nest and settle down in it herself. I went back the next day and shinnied up the tree, and sure enough, there was one great big egg laid in the clutch of smaller dove's eggs.

We saw the squirrels fighting and chasing each other through the trees, and once I saw two squirrels breeding. The rabbits hopped around softly and unafraid of us. Once a deer and a fawn walked right up to us and stared for a long time, and then the old lady sort of nodded to junior and they went off, not running, not jumping, just sort of frisking, with junior kicking up his heels.

I never did get to see Pan or any of the other strange people that live in the woods, but I swear I heard noises that I couldn't hook up to bird or frog or animal or insect, and soft rustlings that proved to be nothing at all when I went to look, my skin goose-pimpled and my neck hair lifting like a worried dog's when he hears a sound he can't quite figger.

What I did get was the feeling that there were spirits who lived in trees, and that there was something very special about an ancient wood, and that there was some peculiar magic about the late spring that has been justified by the behavior of beasts and people down through the ages. (This I learned later from books.)

There had been some talk among the grown-ups at the time about sending me off to the mountains to a boys' camp, and I was hot for it until the spring got soft and sweet and started to beckon toward the summer, and the Old Man and I made our daily pilgrimages past the cow lot and into the secret woods. But in May I would begin to weaken on this camp thing, and by June the camps had lost a customer. I knew when I had it good, because the Old Man always used to say that a smart feller knew when he was well off and was a goldarned fool to change it for something he didn't know about.

Then, too, you understand, I was too busy to go to camp. The Old Man and I had a lot of projects together, apart from the baseball and the swimming with the other boys. We had to get the boat in shape for the summer's fishing, and there was a puppy litter about due. We wanted to do some work on the duck blind, of course, and there was this billy goat to discipline—I guess you remember we failed on that one. And then there was fishing, of course, salt-water for blackfish and speckled trout and croakers, and fresh-water for bass, and by the time we got done fishing it would be September and the tides would swell, and then there would be the marsh hens jumping creakily out of the flooded marshes.

When we finished with the marsh hens, the bluefish would be along; and when we got through with the bluefish and the puppy drum, then the quail season would be on us, and before you knew it, Christmas holidays had come and gone.

We were sitting quietly in the secret forest one day, waiting to hear some word from the Old Man's friend, Pan, when he stabbed his pipe at me and said, "I suppose you're going off to camp this summer and leave me alone and unprotected with all the grown-ups, eh?"

"I reckon not," I said.

"Why not? They got all sorts of things up there in the mountains. They got counselors, and a swimming lake, and archery, and woodworking, and basket making, and lectures, and all sorts of things. You'll get to live in a tent and paddle a canoe and——"

"I been in a tent and I got a boat and I got the Atlantic Ocean and the Cape Fear River to swim in," I told him. "I got you for a counselor. I ain't interested in basket making or archery, because I got a shotgun and a boat that needs fixin'. I just ain't got time to play with children. The duck blind's a mess."

"But here it is just spring, with a whole summmer ahead of you," the Old Man was teasing me.

"The way I figger, I'm through Christmas already," I said,

"and by that time it'll be puppy-training time and we're right back in the summer again."

"I expect you may be right," the Old Man admitted. "Time just seems to fly away for a boy. That, I s'pose, is why one day you wake up suddenly and you ain't a boy any longer. Anyhow, I'm glad you ain't going. It gets awful lonesome around here with all them grown-ups."

17

Life Among the Giants

"Did you ever wonder why I spend so much time and trouble and accumulated wisdom on you?" The Old Man paused to look at his pipe as if it were a strange contraption he'd never seen before. He convinced himself that it was a pipe, the same old scarred, crook-stemmed, thick-caked pipe which smelled like an incinerator and which he had owned about as long as he'd owned Grandma. Or possibly as long as Grandma had owned him, which was more likely.

Now, honest to John, what is a feller going to say to this question? *No, sir? Yes, sir?* I didn't say anything except a sort of mutter with a rise on the end of it, like a bigmouth coming up to see but not to bite. "Yumph?"

"You're gettin' smarter already," the Old Man told me. "I liked that 'Yumph' you just did. You didn't give nothing away, and kept yourself covered at both ends. Like poker. You know, poker is like fishin', or mebbe more like waitin' out a deer stand or a turkey blind. Did I ever tell you about poker?"

"Numph."

"Hmmmm," the Old Man said. "I would judge you had kings backed, and maybe my queens ain't good enough. You're gettin' real cagey in your old age, ain't you?"

"Mmmmph." I was noncommittal-like. I had stepped in those traps before.

"Why," the Old Man asked me, "would you suppose that a man of my advanced years and general accomplishments would waste so much time trying to beat a little knowledge and a few good manners into the head of an unlicked cub? Is this personal conceit on my part, or what? I dunno. Am I trying to leave a memorial behind me? You tell me."

"I don't know, sir." I reckoned I had taken that "Yumph, umph, mmmm" business about as far as it would travel.

"I like the answer," the old gentleman declared. "Damn rare thing these days, in the age of experts, where a feller'll set down and say he don't know something. It's a smart-aleck age, full of Willies-off-the-pickle-boat, people that'll just spar for time while they're trying to figger out a way to conceal inbred ignorance. You ever notice I talk grammatic about one fourth of the time, and vulgar the other? It's because a man has to be able to talk correctly before he can allow himself the privilege of vulgar speech. You ever get curious about it?"

"Yes, sir," I said. "I wonder, because they're always at you in school not to say ain't and not to drop your g's, and not use double negatives. I find it kind of hard to follow you sometimes."

"You like crackling?" the Old Man asked. I could tell this was going to be a hard day. Crackling is the seared skin of a young pig. It is as crisp and tasty as the things they give you at cocktail parties today, and has more nourishment. But it had no point in the conversation.

"Yes, sir. I sure do. I like chitterlings, too, and scuppernong wine, and ham hock, and collards. And candy." I was getting a little mad. If the old gentleman was going to throw these things at me, I figured I'd heave a couple back.

"Only reason I asked about crackling," the Old Man said, "was that I was rereading that thing of Charles Lamb's—what d'you call it, *Dissertation on a Roast Pig*, or some such, I forget— and I got so dodlimbed hungry I couldn't stand it. They make you read that in school yet?"

"Yes, sir." I was very heavy with those "sirs." Once in a while the Old Man went big literary on me, and "sir" was the only way out. We got mixed up with some old Englishman named Chaucer once, and Chaucer and I went round and round for what seemed like years, until I "sirred" my way out of it.

"Well, all I got to say is, any man who can make you hungry after he's been dead a hundred years is a hell of a writer," the Old Man declared. "Where was I? Oh, yes. What you gonna be when you grow up?"

"Confused," I started to say, and bit it off. The Old Man liked to handle the flippancy business himself. "I don't know, sir. Maybe an artist. Maybe a writer or a sailor. Something—I don't know."

"Well, that's handy, not to know what you want to be until the time comes to be it." The Old Man liked that one. "Until the time comes to be it," he repeated, and kind of licked his whiskers like a happy cat. "I'm pretty well pleased with you today."

"Yes, sir."

"You can overdo them 'sirs,' boy," he said. "You ain't fooling nobody with that mock humility. So I will tell you why I spend all this time and conversation in my failing years, when I could just as easy be setting and rocking instead of talking. The reason is that all I got of me to pass on is you, and I know a couple or three things I like. I know quite a lot of goods and quite a lot of bads, and as long as I ain't got any money I would like to leave a few of the good things behind. You want some more of this?"

"Yes, sir."

"Well, now," he continued, "a gentleman starts down at his boots and works up to his hat. A gentleman is, first of all, polite. A gentleman never talks down to nobody, or even to anybody that says 'anybody' instead of 'nobody.' A gentleman ain't greedy. A gentleman don't holler at anybody else's dogs. A gentleman pays his score as he goes. He don't take what he can't put back, and if he borrows he borrows from banks. He never troubles his friends with his troubles."

It looked as though we had disposed of what a gentleman was apt to be made of. I didn't say anything.

"What is a sportsman?" The Old Man wasn't even asking me this. He nodded his head, as if he was giving himself a vote of confidence. "A sportsman," he said to nobody, "is a gentleman first. But a sportsman, basically, is a man who kills what he needs, whether it's a fish or a bird or an animal, or what he wants for a special reason, but he never kills anything just to kill it. And he tries to preserve the very same thing that he kills a little bit of from time to time. The books call this conservation. It's the same reason we don't shoot that tame covey of quail down to less'n ten birds."

This I could understand. We trained the puppies on those birds, and the birds always stayed put.

"I never knew a bad man who was what I'd call a sportsman," he said. "I never knew a true sportsman who wasn't a gentleman. So if you are a gentleman and a sportsman, you can't be a bad man. Is that clear?"

It wasn't, but I said it was. It seemed to save an argument.

"I ain't going to live forever," the Old Man went on. "So I would like to think that I cut a few scars on your carcass that maybe you could remember me by, like the old beaver trappers blazed trees to mark their passage. This is why I'm such a windy old bore. But up to now you ain't shot anybody or busted into a store, and you haven't even been expelled from school. If they keep exposing you to education, you might even realize some day that man becomes immortal only in what he writes on paper, or hacks into rock, or slabbers onto a canvas, or pulls out of a piano. You know," he said, "I really am getting old. I ask your tolerance and forgiveness for the lecture. I reckon I've started talking to myself. What would you like to do?"

"You wouldn't think I'm silly, would you, if I showed you something you don't know about that I been doing lately?"

"I wouldn't think that anything you ever showed me was silly if it was something you wouldn't show just anybody," the Old Man said. "Lead on, Macduff, and damned be he . . ."

Well, I have to write this kind of quiet, because I embarrass easy. The Old Man and I walked over to a great big wild cherry tree, about a thousand yards from the house, and I showed him the steps nailed neat onto the tree, plenty wide enough for hand-holds and footholds at the same time. The steps went up about thirty feet or so. Then in a big crotch of this tree was a house.

I had been reading *The Swiss Family Robinson*, and I had been fascinated with the tree house they built, that they called "Falconhurst," and I had built me one, as I said. There was a curious four-way spread of branches in this cherry tree, and it was pretty easy to make a house in the spread. It was a good house, although hoisting up the planks with a primitive block and tackle had been difficult.

In this house there was near about everything that I didn't want anybody to be prying at. I'd found some clay down by the creek, good potter's earth, and I had made a very sad stab at be-ing a sculptor. There was a bust of the Old Man I thought was right fair, but it had a tendency to crumble, and I didn't know the first thing about glazing clay. Then there were some awful drawings I had made with crayons of what I thought birds and dogs and deer ought to look like, and I had stuck them around the rough board walls of my Falconhurst. I had some pelts for carpets on the floor, some stiff-dried hides of rabbits and squir-rels.

In this tree house I had a bed of pine tops lashed with raw-hide over bendy branches. I even had a stove, which I had con-trived out of some old junk iron from the local dump, and which nobody could have cooked anything worth eating on.

In this house there were spears which I had made and pointed with tin, and a hickory bow, and a quiver of arrows. There was a bookshelf, filled mostly with things like *Robin Hood* and Ernest Thompson Seton's *Rolf in the Woods* and *Two Little Savages* and quite a lot of *Tarzan* and *Buffalo Bill* and *Treasure Island*, and even Sir Walter Scott. There were some arrowheads I'd found and the usual junk a kid will hive up when nobody's looking—sea shells and secret stuff he wants to keep away from grown-ups who'll be apt to discount it as childish. I was taking a chance on the Old Man when I showed him my stuff. Really, I shouldn't have worried.

He climbed creakily all the way up the tree, sat down in a little makeshift chair I had built onto the planking of Falconhurst, and panted a little while he fumbled some tobacco into his pipe. Then he looked around at everything and asked me, one question at a time, about how I got the things, and why I got the things, and especially if I had ever read anything about sculpture, because he recognized himself in the rough-thumbed clay fright-mask I had made of him.

He took the books down off the shelf, reverently I thought, and he rubbed his hands over the badly tanned skins, and he tested the bounce of the bed. He looked at the stove, and hefted the bow and arrows and the spears, and clucked appreciatively when he noticed that the bowstring was rawhide and not cord. Then he looked at me as though expecting me to ask him something.

"I suppose it's kind of silly," I hesitated, and he answered with something I'm never apt to forget.

"I wish I had me a house like this," the Old Man said. "It's got everything in it that a sportsman and a gentleman needs to be happy in. And now I have answered that first question I was asking you, about why I spent the time and trouble on you."

A lot of people said a lot of nice things to me since, but nobody ever beat that last remark the Old Man made before he climbed down the tree.

There is a time in the life of every Lilliputian when the gigantic grown-ups around him are very important. This is the time when the boy is not so very far away from being a grown-up himself, and the grown-ups are not so far away from being boys. What I mean to say, a certain politeness is indicated. There is a time when it is very bad to patronize a boy, just because he isn't quite a man yet.

The Old Man was a couple of hundred years older than I, the way I figured it; so we didn't have any conflict there. I mean, he was old and seasoned before I was born; so I was willing to take him like you accept the old dog that's too tired and too creaky to hunt any more, and just wants to lie in front of the fire. The Old Man was past proving anything. He had it wrapped up.

I've been lucky all the time I can remember. I was surrounded by adults who were sensitive to what small boys needed in the way of companionship. Looking all the way back as far as I can look, I can't remember anybody who ever made me feel as small as I was.

This was a mighty little town in the South, a poor little town, which had one movie—it's still called the Amuzu—and one restaurant run by a Greek named Pete, and two drugstores, and two grocery stores, and one undertaker who was also the coroner and who had an interest in one of the grocery stores. It had a couple of boarding houses and something that could have been called a hotel if you stretched a point.

I want to stretch a point for a minute and tell you a little bit about the town. My cousin Kate Stewart ran a boarding house, and she had a colored man who worked as waiter and whose name was Allen Jinny. He was named Allen Jinny because his mother's name was Jinny, and there weren't a whole lot of extra surnames to go around the colored population.

Allen Jinny had a deplorable habit. He drank. When he got drunk, he was liable as not to spill some hot soup down the neck of a customer who was spending a whole hard fifty cents on Miss Kate's cuisine, which was excellent if it was eaten instead of being worn. One night Allen Jinny was weaving through the dining room at Miss Kate's place on the water front, and he tipped a scalding tureen of soup down a gentleman's best boiled shirt front, and the gentleman raised a considerable ruckus. Miss Kate decided she'd better have a word with Allen Jinny. She took him more or less by the ear and led him aside to tell him the ancient parable about what happened to the man who killed the goose that laid the golden eggs.

Miss Kate was a lengthy talker, and she sort of overpowered Allen Jinny with analogies and things. She considered herself as the classic goose, and Allen Jinny's livelihood as the golden eggs, and she allowed as how that unless Allen Jinny sobered up and quit spilling soup on people the goose was going to quit laying those golden eggs. This appeared to interest Allen Jinny strangely. He went back to the kitchen. The cook was waiting, because you can always sense a turmoil outside a kitchen.

"What Miss Kate done say you, boy?" the cook asked.

"I dunno presackly," Allen Jinny said. "Something 'bout some silly son of a bitch want to eat a goose, but I don't know who de hell gone pick it."

That's the way the town was. If you mentioned a goose, somebody had to pick it, parable or no parable. And so my goose got picked pretty good by some grown-up men—who at that time couldn't have been more than twentyish to my teenishness.

I've already told you about Tom and Pete, the boys who pogie-fished some and made bootleg licker and drank bootleg licker and poached a lot and always wore hip boots in the woods and made like they always thought I was as old as they were. But my special grown-up friends were my Cousin Tommy and my non-Cousin Doonie and my non-Cousin Reggie and Dick, my Cousin Margie's boy friend, whom she married later. There was my Cousin Bonner, who run the shrimp boat, and my non-Cousin Willie, who was a little bit deaf in the ears.

We had quite a lot of Scandinavians around at that time, and some Portygees, but the Squareneck I remember best was my

Uncle John Ericsen, who is still alive and looks better than I, which isn't hard, come to think of it. I remember there was a time when John and another Scandihoovian were mistily trying to get aboard a boat that was swinging away from the pier, and the other 'Hoovian said, "Yoomp, Yon, yoomp!"

And John said, "Yoomp? How de hell can ay yoomp ven ay got no place to stood?"

John speaks elegant English now, of course, because this was so very long ago.

There was Will Sellers Davis, and Uncle Walker Newton, and all the St. George boys, especially Bill, who played catch on the ball club, and Donald, who was brilliant, but of whom they used to say he drank a little. And then there was my Uncle Rob. Uncle Rob was married to my Aunt May, and Uncle Rob was what we called chronically peevish. That's to say, nothing suited him, except maybe me; and me and Rob, why, we always got along good. Uncle Rob looked like a Scotch terrier, which isn't surprising, seeing as how his last name was McKeithan, and he had no truck with frivol or fancy. He was a fact man. I will tell you what I mean.

One time Aunt May trapped him into going to church. There he saw another one of my female relations who would win few prizes for prettiness. Rob took one look at her and muttered.

"That's the *ugliest* damn woman I ever saw in my life," he said, and in church, too.

"*Shhhhh*, Rob," Aunt May said. "The poor thing can't help it if she's ugly."

"No, but ding-dong and double-goddammit," Rob said in his fretful falsetto, "she *could* stay home."

There was another time I remember when my best beloved uncle came in one Christmas Eve just a little, you'll pardon the expression, fried to the eyes. He fell into the Christmas tree, toppled it over, busted the decorations, and set fire to the drapes. We used candles in those days. Uncle Rob pulled himself up out of the mess, scraped some tinsel off one ear, and brushed some powdered glass from the smashed ornaments off his coat. He glared mistrustfully around him.

"God *damn* Santa Claus," he said, and staggered off to bed, summarily dismissing Christmas for all time.

I hung around these men and they treated me like a man, and I never learned any nastiness from any of them. Doonie Watts wasn't a gift, I suppose; he was a seafaring man and a bit rough, and so was Reggie Pinner, but he and Cousin Tommy and the rest took us young'uns to raise. Right.

Doonie would fight, and Tommy would fight, when the mood come strong when the moon was right and the moonshine was wrong; but when they had to do with me and my Cousin Roy and Harold and George Watson, they were the best governesses you'll ever think to see. If we cussed, we got walloped, hard. The men didn't even cuss around us much, just an old damn or hell once in a while, and if us kids talked dirty, bam!

We went to the woods and on the waters whenever school allowed a breakout, and there was always a self-appointed chaperone to teach us caution and care with guns, neatness with camps, fire prevention, and love and respect for wildlife. They taught us such things as how to smother a grounder, moving up on it, beating it by one jump. They taught us a few knacks of aiming guns, and not shooting robins, and why a boat must be kept clean and the oars taken away and the boat dragged up on the shingle and overturned to keep the rain from rotting her innards.

I won't name any names here, but some were drunks and some were loafers and some didn't shave or wash very often, but from a boy's-eye view they were the best men I ever knew. Some are dead today and some have reformed, but I've got more sweet memories of a tender taking-to-raise from those men than you could find in all the schools and churches and contrived ways to give a kid a little dignity.

Maybe we have lost this a little bit today. In the older times the town characters showed a little special wonderful tenderness to the kids. My ma and the Old Man never had a qualm when I was off in the woods with one of the roughnecks. They knew that roughneck wouldn't come home except to die, rather swiftly, if anything happened to Bobby or Roy—or Ted or Harold or Tom or George.

And there were all sorts of things on the side. For instance, I learned about Kipling and Chaucer from one of the roughnecks who had, at one time before the bottle bruised him, graduated with honors in three years from a rather famous university. But he also told me about the *barrio chino* in Barcelona, and what it was like on the *grosse Freiheit* in Hamburg, and how to bust a bottle to use it fast if you needed a busted bottle in a brawl. He had been to two colleges—one literary, the other practical. I s'pose he was the one made me run away, eventually, to sea—but it was my Cousin Victor Price who saw that nobody bothered me when I was ordinary-seamaning around the tough ports of North Europe. He was an executive in the line I was working for.

The Old Man, in his vast wisdom, never worried about what would happen to my moral character so long as I was under the care of one of the hairy townsmen. The Old Man said once, "A boy has got to grow up to be a man some day. You can delay the process, but you can't protect the boy from manhood forever. The best and easiest way is to expose the boy to people who are already men, good and bad, drunk and sober, lazy and industrious. It is really, after all, up to the boy, when all is said and done, and there are a lot of boys who never get to be men, and a lot of men who never quit being boys."

I'm not doing a very good job of this, I realize, but the tremendous love I had for all those people when I was a kid prevents me from doing a very good job of it. You've got to realize what it means to a boy to be treated as a man grown by men already grown. You've got to realize what it is like to be gently carried along by rough giants who have so much built-in decency that they fear to bruise the stalk which is an adolescent, shooting up and subject to heavy impression, subject to hurt, as you might mishandle a gawky plant.

I reckon that 65 per cent of the men who took me to raise couldn't be admitted to a club, a church, or a tea party. I reckon that most were unread, most were profane, most broke laws, most didn't work, most drank too much, and most had dirty fingernails. And I reckon if we filled the schools with them as instructors today, and gave them jobs as cops, and set them up as tutors and baby sitters and camp counselors, we wouldn't have so much of a problem of delinquency.

In my life as a grown man I have managed to stay out of jail, pay taxes, and live a life in which the values are pretty clearly drawn. This makes me lucky, maybe, but it is also a reflection on the positive contributions of the Toms and Petes and Doonies and Johns and Bills and Reggies and Bonners and Robs and, of course, the Old Man—all of whom, in their own fashion, took me to raise.

I got mixed up sentimentally serious with the Coast Guard at a very early age, because around where I come from the Coast Guard was an industry as well as a luxury and a necessity. We lived in a little town where the Cape Fear River emptied out into the ocean, and there were Coast Guard stations on a big island called Bald Head and also on a spit of land named Fort Caswell. There was a lighthouse on Bald Head, and there was a lightship a little farther offshore, because we had some shoals called Frying Pan that were powerful treacherous.

There is something about real functional Coast Guarders that is maybe a little different from other people. They are a special breed; you could maybe call them a race. They mostly all seem to come from down around Hatteras and Ocracoke—so much so that we used to call them "down-homers." They were nearly all named Midyette, except the ones who were named Willis or Pickett or Barnett or Robinson.

These men lived with windswept loneliness and they lived

with cold wet death. They were veterans of battle with what somebody later called the cruel sea. They lived on gale-raked islands and rode patrol on the silent beaches on horses and mules always looking seaward for signals of distress. I remember well that the father of a friend of mine, named Bill Styron, was struck by lightning while riding beach patrol at Hatteras. The bolt killed him but didn't kill the mule, which tells you something about mules.

When the wind came furious and whipped up a stranger's offshore trouble, and a ship was fast aground or heading that way, when the lighthouse couldn't prevent it and the lightship off Frying Pan hadn't successfully done its job, friends of mine like Pete Midyette went into business. They had these double-bowed whaleboats, called surfboats, that nothing or nobody could capsize, and they shoved them through the mountainous black waves, straight off the beach into the cold, wet, enormous-waved nights to see what they could do about who was in seafaring trouble. To me they were greater heroes than anybody I ever met later, because they did their jobs when others would have run away to a snug bed and a fire. Quite a lot of them got drowned in a cold Atlantic Ocean, for very little money and practically no amusement at all, because those islands were bleak.

A boy named Dallas Pickett was a friend of mine when his old man was cap'n of the Bald Head station and an older friend of mine named Bill Willis was running Caswell. Bill was a pure down-homer, stringy and weatherbeaten and wrinkled, and in addition to his other duties he had to go out and knock off a rumrunner every now and then in the little cutter they gave him to chase rumrunners with. It didn't make no difference to me that they said Bill Tyce—that was his middle name, Tyce—never took on a booze boat until all his friends were fresh out of licker. The important thing was that he would sometimes take me with him when there was a rum boat to chase, and I learned a lot about fishing while we were chasing booze.

It was the same way with my friend Dallas Pickett's papa. He would let Dallas bring me and my Cousin Roy over for week ends to Bald Head, and we would stay in the big, bare, sandy-floored, stripped-for-action Coast Guard station. We would climb the watchtowers and make the beach patrol at night with the men, and we would go out in the heaving surfboats on practice beach launchings.

The Old Man encouraged these expeditions. He was a deep-water man himself, a sea captain and a licensed river pilot, and a fisherman too. In the off season he went to sea after menhaden, or pogies, the fat-backed fertilizer fish, in a creaky old boat called the *Vanessa*—and he liked me to know about water and what its chances of killing you were. Also he said he never knew a really bad waterman, and I could learn a lot by hanging around people that used the sea as a livelihood, always remembering it as an enemy.

In any case, I was over to Fort Caswell one time when Cap'n Willis, Bill Tyce, that is, broke out the rum chaser and said he heard there was a booze boat close at hand, and would I care to go help him chase the rumrunner. You understand the government boat was a rum chaser, and the quarry a rumrunner. This seemed to me to be an invitation worthy of acceptance, because I knew that on rum chasers there were machine guns and rifles, carefully cherished in scabbards of sheepskin with the clipped wool inside, well soaked in oil to prevent rust, and I knew the runners had the same armament, and once in a while when there was a disagreement between law and order and man's natural thirst, the guns came oily-wet out of the clipped-fleece scabbards and people started to shoot at each other. At my age, I hoped there would be a little shooting at each other and that possibly I could aid in some capacity in the shooting.

Well, we overhauled the runner off Frying Pan Shoals, and a sad little beat-up craft she was too. I have to report regretfully that there wasn't no shootin'. The Cap'n signaled her to heave to, and she plain hove to. She had a few cases of illegal booze from the Bahamas and a dirty, unshaven, scared crew of three, and so the Cap'n put a prize crew aboard her, and told the prize crew to take her in for the Customs to worry about and for the Federals to worry about. I think the prize crew was a man named Midyette, which is a safe bet, because the prize crew looked pretty thirsty.

Well, sir, with the business of law and order taken care of, no shots fired, we looked around. There the old chaser was right smack on the lip of Frying Pan. There are shoals, I swear, where a man who knows how to run a boat right can scoop up a handful of sand with his left hand and then jump over the side and drown himself on the starboard side, without changing course a half degree. What I mean, Frying Pan is tricky, and you may remember that tricky shoals breed fish.

Cap'n Bill announced that he hadn't had a mess of real fresh mackerel in a whole hell of a long time, and did anybody have any trolling gear aboard? The Coast Guard said yes, because in those days the Coast Guard was better prepared than the Boy Scouts ever thought of being. Cap'n Bill went for'ard and had a word with the Helm. The Helm knew his business. We started playing tag with Frying Pan Shoals. The Helm took the chaser so close to those shoals that you'd swear we'd smash aground if there was another knot in the breeze, but gentlemen, may I say, what fishing!

The gear consisted simply of hand lines and a couple of rods with reels older than Noah's original equipment. For lures we had quills run over the shank of the hook, or feathers, or a piece of sailcloth, or anything else that would create a ripple. You could of trailed a finger over the side and if there was a hook on the fingernail, you'd have caught a fish.

Now let me see if I can tell you what it was like. You had the white-gleaming shoals shimmering underneath a shining sun at about this time of the month, and you were a boy among men—a youth among warriors—and the sun and salt and breeze were fresh in your face. The water was the cleanest blue, clear, shading to green and finally to the white of shoal water, and in that roily water were fish.

They were maybe not the biggest fish a fellow ever caught,

but there were more of them than I can believe possible today. There were vast schools of blues—fat, greasy, jut-jawed blues— weighing up to maybe three pounds, and mean-frisky from the cold sea. There were gangs of Spanish mackerel, with a few bonito into the pot for variety, and even a horse mackerel or so. And they were hungry, eager for the hook.

I wouldn't say there was much sport in the actual catching of the fish, because all you did was throw out the line, let her trail a bit, and as soon as she was clear of the screw you had a customer on the other end. Then it was up to you to get the fish back into the vessel, whether you were hand-lining him or horsing him in on reels that wouldn't go either way, in or out, unless you fought 'em. And barked fingers.

The real sport was the job the man at the wheel was doing. He was playing the boat like it was a big salmon in tough swift water, on a four-ounce rod with a no-strain line. He didn't want to kill the fish, and to not kill the fish he had to slack his engines, and he had to fight those shoals with a knowledge of wind and water. I read some, later, about bullfighters. Never did any bull-fighter play a bull like this boy played that ship against those shoals. I swear, I yanked too hard one time and the fish flopped out on the beach. And we were deep-water trolling!

We filled that Coast Guard boat full of fish—brown-gray-green spotted mackerel, lean shimmering-steel blues with all the fat under the smooth submarine shape, and blunt-nosed bonito—and in a couple of hours we were headed home. I cannot remember the name of the man at the wheel, but he never touched a screw or a keel to those deadly shoals, and the ship frisked like a colt when he took her in to the last inch, and tossed her mane as she came away.

It was a tremendous thing to be a boy among men; and sitting in that rum chaser, sunburnt, sweaty, hot skin cooling from breeze, all full of righteous indignation that any bootleggers would even attempt to try to fool *my* Coast Guard, I was a young king amongst his faithful court.

It was *my* friend that drove the boat and kept her off the

shoals. It was *my* friend who was skipper, and who had kept the Atlantic seacoast free of the Demon Rum this day, while catching bluefish and mackerel besides. We were coming in triumphant after having saved America without firing a shot. The man at the wheel had headed the chaser home, and her prow knifed a clean line through the sparkling sun-kissed spray-tossed waters.

The things you see when you are going home triumphant are marvelous. I watched a gannet working on a red bank of menhaden. I saw the porpoise sounding and rising. The little ship bucked and pranced, full of rightful triumph. I was not even about to be seasick, because I was a man out with men, doing a man's job. Of course it is easily possible to say that a boy had no place, legally, on a rum-chasing expedition, and that a government boat that was coursing a bootlegger had no business to stop and go fishing, and that maybe the runner's cargo would most probably disappear, one way or another, before the righteous arm of the law could smash the bottles.

But there was one thing more: There was a boy's-eye view of men at work, but men with time to play, and men to make a boy feel a man. There was a Charlie Snow to ask you down to his house around Matamuskeet to teach you how to fool a goose. There was a Bill Barnett, a burly, red-faced man who was exec before Bill Tyce went off the station, who never made you feel a boy so long as you were with men, and who never expected you to act like a boy so long as you were with men.

These days I read about the delinquents and what causes delinquency, and I suppose you could say that a child as young as I was had no business combining rum chasing with fishing, that maybe I shouldn't have hung around the docks with people who cussed.

I don't know. Maybe my later character was imperfectly formed. But I tell you trolling for bluefish on the very frowning face of Frying Pan Shoals, after you've just knocked off a rum-runner, is a type of sport you aren't going to get out of comic books and television. And until a man has put his shoulder behind the sharp stern on a surfboat, to shove her in the black night through the shore-crashing seas, off the cold clean beach of Bald Head, with the gulls crying and a dying ship offshore— well. There are all sorts of ways to get to be a man, the Old Man used to say—and none of 'em easy.

The Old Man was fairly grumpy through the summer months, because the beaches were crowded with summer people and the bluefish knew it and stayed offshore. All our pet sloughs were full of swimmers, splashing and making noises, and if you tried surf-casting the inlets at night you had to pick your way through the neckers.

"Labor Day," the Old Man said, "is the best holiday of the year, because after it's over all the city people go home and leave the water to the professionals. A professional"—the Old Man grinned—"is the kind of damn fool who actually fishes when he goes fishin'. He don't turn it into a whisky party or an excuse to play poker, not that I'm low-ratin' either sport if taken in the correct perspective."

Some of the Old Man's feeling rubbed off on me. I could hardly wait for that first Tuesday in September, because the beach would be scrubbed clean of people by noon, the summer visitors having taken their hang-overs back to town for another year. Then and only then did the hardshells emerge—the year-rounders who were plank owners in the boardwalks. They were a grimy, grizzled, hard-bitten lot, including the few women who were admitted into the high society of surf casters. Then we owned the beach.

A beach suddenly flushed clean of strangers is a wonderfully lonesome place. All the boarding houses and summer cottages and hotels board up their windows against the first northers. The hot-dog stands close. The dance hall shuts up tight. The trolley service goes on winter schedule, and only the Greek keeps his general store open part time—I say part time, because most of the time the Greek is whipping the sloughs for the bluefish and sea trout and channel bass that come in close to feed off the minnows and sand fleas.

The weather knows it when the tourists leave. It invariably stayed fine for the long, noisy week end, but by Wednesday we generally had a gorgeous three-day norther started, and that norther was always the most exciting thing about the summer. An Atlantic beach in a norther is wild and exhilarating. The sky turns gray, and the wind drives the rain in angry gusts. The surf booms, and towering sheets of spume drive skyward as the waves smash onto the sands. Suddenly the tin stove earns its pay, and the driftwood in the fireplace burns blue and green. A sweat shirt and flannel pants feel wonderful, and there is a snugness to the little gray-weathered shingle cottage that is missing during the summer squalls.

For three days the wind screams and the water boils white, and then the best time of the year begins. The sun comes once again, warm and golden, and the skies are washed bright, but now the breeze is crisp and the air is full of wine. The water is not too cold to fish barefooted, but if you stumble and wet yourself all over, the goose-pimples form when the wind hits you. Give the waters a day to clear from the roily muddiness of the storm, and the fish swarm in to feed in the sloughs. The biggest fish haven't shown yet, and won't until late October, but the blues run to three pounds, and the puppy drum go up to fifteen, and there are always plenty of sea trout and Virginia mullet. All up and down the beach, toward the inlets, tiny, happy-lonely figures wade out and cast, walk backward and reel in as the rod curves and a bright sliver of fish flops through the shallows and onto the silvered sands.

That was a part of our September song. Another part was in the Sound, where the north wind raises the tides above the marsh grasses, and the mounting moon keeps the water high, until just the tips of the grasses show above the surface. That was when the Old Man's mouth cracked in a big grin and he took the shotguns from their cases and sent me under the house for the push pole and the paddles.

"Marsh-hen time," the Old Man said, and we dragged the old flat-bottomed skiff off the shingle, where she had been up-turned to keep her innards from rotting in the rain. We'd kick her across the channel with the little one-lung motor, and when we hit the grass we'd tilt the kicker and the Old Man would take the pole or—if the water was exceptionally high—paddle the skiff along like she was a canoe.

I don't suppose today that there is a great deal of sport in shooting the big rails we called marsh hens, but you'd be sur-prised how many you can miss. As the boat crept stealthily over the grasses, the big hens would spring creakily into flight, flop-ping low over the water and seeming slower than they actually were. The natural inclination was to shoot behind them, be-cause of the water-skimming lowness of their flights.

"Ain't but one man at a time supposed to shoot out of a boat," the Old Man said. "Otherwise you will be out with some blame fool some day and he will get excited and blow the back of your neck off. There's plenty of marsh hens to go round, and you can only eat so many."

So the Old Man would push or paddle and I would sit on the bow thwart. The hens would rise from under the boat with a cackle, and more often than not you'd have a chance to try for a stylish double. Then, after half a dozen birds were in the boat, I'd move aft and take over the propulsion, and the Old Man would creep gingerly forward and man the bow gun.

Poling after the hens was hard work; your boat was always getting stuck onto a mudbank, and there were still plenty of mosquitoes and other varmints clinging to the higher grasses. The sun smote down plenty hot, and your back ached like a tooth after hours of driving that skiff over what amounted to solid ground. But a boat full of the great, tawny rails, with their doe eyes and long legs and long, curved, mud-probing bills, made the blistered hands and sunburnt neck worth while.

There is no more fascinating place than a marsh anyhow. A marsh literally crackles and pops with life. Off yonder in a wide stretch of water, a thin ripply wake tells you a mink is swimming. An old blue heron looks grumpily at you and waits until the last minute before he flops away in swaybacked, ungainly flight. Over there a bittern booms like a tomtom, and the white herons sit silent and secure, because they know you won't shoot them.

Red-winged blackbirds love the marsh, and they swing like bobolinks from the barest ends of the swaying grass, hurling their joyful song into the air. The sky above the marsh is always full of crows, cawing angrily as they scavenge.

Along the edge of the mainland there was an enormous lightning-riven tree, where my private eagle always sat. The eagle, several times a year, was good for a fine show of aerobatics. There was a pair of fish hawks—ospreys—that haunted the area, and it used to delight me to watch them fish. You would see the male plummet down like dropped shot, smack the water with his outstretched talons, and struggle, wings flailing furiously, with a big bluefish nailed through the spine. As the hawk labored for altitude, Old Baldy would take off from his tree top and head for the stratosphere. When the hawk got enough height to level off and head for his nest with the flopping fish, the eagle, high above him, would fold his wings and come screaming down in a power dive. The hawk would make a few futile evasive motions, and then drop the fish. Usually the eagle, still screaming down, would flash by the hawk and sink his grapples in the falling fish before it hit the water. Then he would come out of his dive and leisurely flap back to his lightning-ruined perch. Then the hawk would go fishing again, and this time he would be allowed to keep his catch.

There were always 'gator holes to see, and occasionally you would see an old 'gator sunning himself on a greasy mudbank. The edges of the marsh were usually good for a coon or two, and the high hummocks close to shore were likely to yield you a brace of dark swamp rabbits. We 'most always took a couple of light rods and the cast net along, and when the water slacked off and began to drop so you couldn't shove the skiff over the grass, we'd take the net and seine a few shrimp and drop the hook by one of the potholes we knew by heart. These deep holes would give us a mess of croakers, blackfish, big sand perch, and now and again a weakfish.

Or, again, when we spotted a big school of fairish mullets, the Old Man swirled the cast net like a bullfighter's cape, hauled hard on the draw cord, and dumped a half-bushel of leaping mullet on the deck of the skiff. The big ones we kept for the skillet; the little ones made wonderful baits for surf casting.

Around the edges of the sand bars there were always clams in the mud—big purplish clams that came shining from the ooze. They tasted wonderful in the raw, the hinges smashed with the back of a fish knife, and eaten there on the spot. We always kept oyster tongs in the boat, and added a bushel or so of the big, briny ones to the mixed bag in the bottom. We'd roast these later, covering them with seaweed, and when you dipped them in melted butter there may have been better eating, but I doubt it.

The trip was never complete until, on the back leg, we chuffed under the bridge that spanned the channel and tied up in the swirling dark water next a barnacle-crusted piling. Here the huge, black, yellow-speckled stone crabs lived. Here the sheepshead swam close to the old pilings, and if you knew your business you could hook them in their silly little mouths that spat out a shrimp unless you fixed the hook just right.

By the time we got back home and pulled the old scow up on the shingle, it would take about three trips to the house to completely unload her. By the time the fish got cleaned and the marsh hens skinned and put in salt water to soak some of the fish out, it was dang near dark and time to get out the surf rods and fish the twilight into moonrise. It would be getting cold on the beach around dark, and I usually fixed us up a driftwood fire and set the oysters to roasting while we cast into the surf.

By eight o'clock the Old Man and I had just about enough

for one day. That's when you ran a stringer through the fish, carried the steaming oysters up to the house, pulled off your wet pants, and shoved the coffeepot onto the stove. The broiled marsh hens followed the oysters, and once in a while we barbecued a fish or just settled for a cold crab salad.

A long time after all this happened I heard Walter Huston sing "September Song," and the old man seemed pretty high on one of my favorite months. But he was thinking about love, mostly, and love ain't but about one-fifth of what September's really like. My September song is still based mainly on the fact that all the tourists went home and left the beaches and the marshes to the Old Man, the eagle, and me.

18

November Was Always the Best

A lot of people figure November to be a middling sad kind of month, with the trees showing naked against the leaden skies late in the afternoon, and the grass all crisp and brown from frost, and the threat of winter turning your ears red in the morning, and the evening cold making your nose run. The year has only one more month to live, and that is sad too, to some people.

But November was the month I aimed my whole year at, for the very simple reason that the bird season opened round about Thanksgiving, and if you lived in my neck of the woods, "birds" didn't mean canaries or parrots or bluejays. Birds meant quail. The Old Man was with me all the way on that one, but he liked to fuzz it up with a little philosophy. Like most pipe smokers, he needed some extras to hang on it to make it dignified.

We were talking about the seasons one time, and the Old Man said that if he had to he could do without summer and all of spring except maybe May, and he would be just as happy to settle for October through January, and give the rest away. He said he would pick November as the best one, because it wasn't too hot, and wasn't too cold, and you could do practically anything in it better than any other time of the year, except maybe get sunburnt or fall in love.

"Although," he said, "there ain't nothing wrong with November, or any other month, for falling in love if the moon's right. But mainly the reason I like November best is that it reminds me of me."

He stopped and struck another kitchen match to his pipe.

"Look at me," he went on. "Here you see a monument to use. I'm too old to fall in love, but I ain't old enough to die. I'm too old to run, but I can outwalk you because I know how to pace myself. I know when to work and when to rest. I know what to eat and what sits heavy on my stomach. I know there ain't any point in trying to drink all the licker in the world, because they'll keep on making it. I know I'll never be rich, but I'll never be stone-poor, neither, and there ain't much I can buy with money that I ain't already got.

"A man don't start to learn until he's about forty; and when he hits fifty, he's learned all he's going to learn. After that he can sort of lay back and enjoy what he's learned, and maybe pass a little bit of it on. His appetites have thinned down, and he's done most of his suffering, and yet he's still got plenty of time to pleasure himself before he peters out entirely. That's why I like November. November is a man past fifty who reckons he'll live to be seventy or so, which is old enough for anybody —which means he'll make it through November and December, with a better-than-average chance of seeing New Year's. Do you see what I'm driving at?"

I said, "Yessir," because I didn't want him to explain it all over again, and because I was worrying about a young pointer puppy who was going to have his first chance at being a working dog, and I was worrying over whether those late rains hadn't drowned off the whole second clutch of quail, and I was worrying over my shooting eye, which had fallen off alarmingly the final two weeks of the last season.

"What's your idea of November?" he asked, his eyes half-closed.

I wanted to tell him that it was mostly the opening of the bird season, and the Thanksgiving holidays, the persimmons wrinkled and ripe on the trees, when the weather was real nice, and it was hog-killing time in the country, and the punkins looked yellow and jolly in the fields, and the sun set good and red, and a lot of other things; but I couldn't manage to squeeze it all out because I had no way with words.

"The bird season," I said.

The Old Man looked at me and sighed. "I reckon I ain't ever going to make no philosopher out of you. Let's us go look at the guns and figger out where we'll best go tomorrow, when she opens."

The day and night before the opening of bird season lasts longer than anything, including the week before Christmas holidays. Awful, horrible thoughts keep you awake, such as will it be raining, or what if the dogs get hot noses or the quail have all moved? And then the next morning dawns clear and bright with just the right breeze, and it is another ten years until afternoon. I used to beg and coax to start in the morning, but the Old Man was stone-set against it.

"There ain't no point to hunting in the morning. Not quail," he said. "They don't feed out until nine or ten o'clock, and later if it's cold, and maybe not at all if it's too hot or raining. And if they come out at all, they don't go far away from the branches, and they head back before you can get the dogs calmed down. You'll find you'll kill all of your quail in two hours—between three and five o'clock—with very few exceptions. All-day hunting just tires you and the dogs, and if you do get lucky and find birds in the morning you've got your limit and there ain't nothing to do in the afternoon. No, morning is the time for deer and ducks and turkeys, but the bobwhite's a late-sleeping bird."

So we would mess around all morning, and then have us a light lunch about noon. By two o'clock we'd be where we had headed, with the dogs shivering and nipping from excitement and slobbering at the mouth, and me wishing I could. We had a lot of places where we hunted, but we usually started her off at a place called Spring Hill, which we had a lucky feeling for, after trying for three or four coveys closer in, just to let the dogs wet down all the bushes and get the damfoolishness out of their systems.

It is difficult, very hard, to try to explain what a boy feels when he sees the dogs sweeping the browned peafields, or skirting the edges of the gallberry bays, or crisscrossing the fields of yellow withered corn shocks, running like race horses with their heads high and their tails whipping. And then that moment, after nearly a year, of the first dog striking the first scent, and the excitement communicating to the other dogs, and all hands crowding in on the act—the trailers trailing, the winders sniffing high, but slow now, and the final eggshell-creeping, the tails going feverishly and the bellies low to the ground, presaging a point.

Then the sudden freeze, then the slight uncertainty, then a minor change of course, and then the swift, dead-sure cock of head which says plainly the bird is here, boss, right under my nose, and now it's all up to you. The backstanders edge closer, especially the puppy, and the Old Man says sharply, "Whoa!" You walk past the backstanders and then up to the pointer, who is still stamped out of iron, like an animal on a lawn. And you walk past him and kick, but nothing happens.

At this moment a blood-pressure estimate would bust the machine that takes it. Your heart is so loud it sounds like a pile driver. There is something in your throat about the size of a football, and your lips are dry from the temperature you're running, which is maybe just under 110 degrees Fahrenheit.

You are looking straight ahead of the dog—never down at the ground—and you are carrying your shotgun slanted across your chest, the stock slightly cocked under your elbow. Nothing happens. The dog changes the position of his head and creeps forward another six yards, and you come up behind him when he freezes again. This time he's looking right down at his fore-feet, and when you walk past him he jumps and the world blows up.

The world explodes, and a billion bits of it fly out in front of you, tiny brown bits with the thunder of Jove in each wing. They go in all directions—right, left, behind you, over your head, sometimes straight at you, sometimes straight up before they level. Then a miracle happens.

Out of these billion bits you choose one bit and fire, and if the bit explodes in a cloud of feathers you choose another bit and fire again, and if this bit also explodes you break your gun swiftly and load, figuring maybe there's a lay bird and you can turn to the Old Man with a grin, and when he says, "How many?" you can answer, "Three." More likely you'll answer, "One" or "None."

But the tension is over now, and you find you have broken out into a heavy sweat. If there's a crick nearby, you go and plunge your face in it, or at least you take a long drink from the water bottle. The dogs fetch, and there in your hand is the first bird of the year—the neat, speckled, cockaded little brown fellow with a white chin strap if he's a cock, a yellow necklace if she's hen. He weighs less than half a pound, but has just induced nervous prostration in a man, a boy, and two dogs.

This is when you first sniff the wonderful smell of gunpowder in an autumn wood, and notice that all save the evergreens have crumpled into red and golden and crinkly brown leaves, that the broom grass has gone sere and dusty yellow, and that the sparkleberries are ready to eat, the chinquapins ready to pick. The persimmon tree that always sits lonely at the edge of the cornfield is bare except for the wrinkled yellow balls that the possums love, soft and liver-brown-splotched now, and free of the alum that ties your tongue in knots and turns your mouth inside out.

The dogs are roving out ahead, and the Old Man says, "Well, we didn't do so bad for beginners. Anybody here notice where the singles went?"

"I thought about six went over there by that patch of scrub oak, just at the end of the broom," I say.

"Le's go have us a good look," the Old Man suggests. "The dogs seem to think you may be right. Old Frank has either found a friend or turned into a stump."

At the edge of the broom, with the scattered scrub oaks making a screen before the swamp, is old Frank, nailed to something. And over there, like a lemon-spotted statue, is Sandy, nailed to something else.

"You take this 'un, I'll take that 'un," the Old Man says. "We'll walk up together."

Two birds get up under my dog's nose, and I miss both clean, *blim-blam!* I hear the Old Man shoot once, and then the rest of the group explodes in my face, and me with the gun broke and both barrels empty. I load and another bird, a sneaker, gets up behind me, and I whirl and watch him drop off the end of my gun barrel.

"That's enough," the Old Man says. "We got three apiece. Le's go find another covey. There used to be one hell of a big one over the top of that rise that we never had no luck with last year. I was beginning to think they was bewitched when the season ended. Unless the cats and the foxes been at 'em, we could take the rest of the limit out of that 'un and not even make a dent in 'em."

The Old Man lights his pipe and I break an apple out of my pocket. I think I never really appreciated an apple until I ate it in the November woods, after the first covey of the first day of the year. We follow the dogs over the hill; and when we top the brow, there is the white dog stiff, the black dog backing, and the puppy sort of sitting back on his haunches, wondering what to do next.

This didn't happen every day, or even every year, but once in a while it happened like that, and I mean to say that the walk up to where the dogs were painted against the side of a hill was the longest, happiest journey I ever took in my life.

19

You Separate the Men from the Boys

I don't know why they didn't take February right out of the calendar, instead of monkeying around with it and making leap years out of it, because it is the worst-weathered of all the months, being halfway between winter and spring, with all the bad habits of both. I mean cold and rain and a little snow and a lot of wind and just natural nasty.

The trouble with February is that January's gone and March is coming next, and March is the most useless month of all, since there is nothing you can do in March except sniffle and wish the wind would quit blowing. All the hunting's over and generally it's too early to fish. There's still a long way to go until school's out, and "There ain't any wonder," the Old Man said, "that they told Caesar to beware the Ides of March." I didn't ask the Old Man what an Ide was. I was afraid he'd tell me.

But we aren't talking about March. The subject is February, and there's one thing you can do in February better than any other time of the year. That is shoot quail. For a long time I didn't believe it, but the Old Man always insisted that February was the best quail month of all.

I remember one day it was drizzling that slow, cold, nasty, steady sizzle-sozzle that is so cold it burns like fire and turns your ears into ice blocks and makes your nose run steady. The sky was a dark putty, and you could see the icicles hanging on the window frames and on the roof of the porch. The Old Man was sitting in front of a fire that was drawing so strong that she whistled as the flames sucked up the chimney, and occasionally he would cut loose and spit in the fire. It sounded like a black-smith tempering a horseshoe. *Hisssss!*

The Old Man stuck out his foot and nudged a log that had al-most burned through. It dropped in a shower of red coal to the bottom of the hearth and shot fresh slashes of flame up through the topmost chunks. The Old Man looked at me.

"There is always one way to separate the men from the boys," he said. "That is to watch and see if a feller'll do a thing the hard way, when all the other fellers are sitting around grumbling and quarreling that it can't be done." He cut loose another amber stream at the fire and looked at me with his head cocked side-wise, like a smart old dog. "Most people quit doing things as soon as the wire edge has worn off and it ain't fashionable or comfor-table any more. That makes it the beauty part for a few individ-ualists. Soon as the clerks run to cover, the big people got the field to themselves."

I didn't say anything. I knew the old buzzard pretty well by now. He was as tricky as a pet coon. All I had to do was make one peep, and he'd have me hooked. It'd be something he wanted me to do that he didn't want to do himself. Such as going to the store in the rain for some new eating tobacco, or going out for more wood, or having to report on Shakespeare, or something.

"You take quail," the Old Man went on. "When the season

opens around Thanksgiving, every damfool and his brother is out in the woods, blam-blamming around and trampling all over each other. The birds are wild, and the dogs are nervous, and they crowd the birds and run over coveys they ought to sneak up on. The ground is dry, and the birds run instead of holding. There practically ain't no such thing as good single-bird shooting, because the bobwhites take off and land as a covey, instead of scattering.

"Then along comes Christmas and New Year's, and the part-time quail hunter is tired of bird shooting, and it's too cold and too rainy, and he has to clean his guns ever' time he comes in to keep the rust off; so he ties up the dogs and forgets hunting until next year. This leaves the woods free of the city slickers and the ribbon clerks and the fashionable shooters. By this time the birds are steadied down and the dogs have had a lot of practice, and they've steadied down too. The young birds have been shot over and have grown their heavy feathers, and the young dogs have figured out that if they find birds the man will shoot some and they will bring them to the man, and that everybody—the dogs, the man, and the birds—is in business together. It ain't a game any more, like running rabbits. It's men's work."

I gave up. He had me nailed. "I'll go get my gun," I said. "You can drive me out and sit by the stove in Cox's Store while I catch pneumonia. That is, if the dogs will go out in this weather."

"They'll go out," the Old Man told me. "The dogs are professionals. They ain't part-time sports like some people I know. Go get 'em, and you better wear those oilskin pants and the oilskin jacket. The woods'll be sopping."

Man, I reckon I'm never going to forget that particular day. I sure was glad I wasn't a fish, because those woods were wetter than a well, with the little droplets clinging onto the low bush, the gallberries, and the broom grass, and the trees dripping steady. There wasn't a steady rain. It just sort of seeped down, half drizzle and half fog. My hands on the gun barrels were so cold that my fingers practically stuck to the steel. Rain collected on the gun sight and ran down the little streamway between the barrels. The dogs looked as miserable as any wet dog always looks, sort of like a land-borne otter.

Rain is miserable anywhere, but I expect there's nothing quite so cheerless as a wet wood in February. The sawdust piles have been soaked stiff and hard and dark brown. The green of the trees all turns black in the wet, so that you don't get any color contrasts, and the plowed ground is a dirty, ugly gray. The few shocks of corn that still stand are spotted and shriveled, and the sad little heads of cotton hanging onto the dead stalks look like orphans lost in a big city. But the good Lord put feathers and fur on birds and animals to keep them dry and warm, and life goes right on. Except that the Old Man is right, as he nearly always is. Wet woods make birds a heap easier to find, because the birds don't move around very much, and you can spot exactly where they're apt to be. And a dog's nose works dandy in the wet, just as a car runs better on a rainy night, when you get richer combustion.

I hadn't been out of the Liz for five minutes when Sandy, the covey dog, disappeared into a little copse of pine saplings half-way between a peafield and a broom-grassed stretch that led to a big swamp. Old Frank, the single-bird expert, went to have a look and then came back to give me the word. He jerked his head in the direction of the pine trees, impatient as a traffic cop who wants a car to move on, and then he dived into the bush with his tail assembly shaking like a hula dancer.

Maybe I have mentioned that I don't shoot very well except when I'm by myself or with the Old Man, because I'm not self-conscious in front of him and don't have to worry about shooting too fast or competing for birds. But when I'm by myself it seems as if it's almost impossible to shoot bad, because you shoot in any direction—backward, sideways, or whatever—without worrying about blowing somebody's head off.

I knew what old Sandy would be doing when I stepped into the dark, dripping grove. He would have suggested to the birds that they move to the outer edge of the pine thicket, so that they would have a nice clear field of soggy broom grass to fly over on their way to the swamp. I was pretty well trained by now. The dogs had been working on me for a couple of years, and the Old Man said he was surprised, that sometimes I showed as much bird sense as a half-trained puppy, and there was hope that I might grow up to where the dogs needn't be ashamed of me.

Sandy had herded the covey to the edge of the thicket, sure enough, and old Frank had come up on his right flank, inside the thicket, and was protecting the right wing. All I had to do was show a little common intelligence and walk along the left wing, outside the thicket, and when I came abreast of Sandy's nose Frank would run in from the right and Sandy would charge straight ahead and the birds would flush, leaving both me and the birds in the open. Then all I had to do was shoot some.

It was an enormous great covey—about twenty or twenty-five birds in it. Either it was two shot-over coveys that had got together, or one that had been missed entirely; I reckoned it was the latter. When Frank roared in from the right and old Sandy broke point and jumped into the birds, they got up in a cloud and fanned perfectly past me, giving me the best shot there is—a three-quarter straightaway where you lead just a little and let the shot string out behind your chosen bird.

This was jackpot day. Lots of times I had killed two birds with one shot, which is always an accident. You pick one out and aim at him, and the shot string knocks off another. I held on one of the front-flying cocks and pulled, and the whole doggone sky fell down. I stood there with my mouth open, just watching the rest of the birds sideslip into the edge of the swamp, and didn't bother to shoot the left barrel.

The dogs started to fetch—even Sandy, who doesn't care much about it as a steady job, because he reckons any damfool dog can pick up a dead bird and fill his mouth full of loose feathers. But they were interested in this job, because by the time they finished collecting the enemy I had six birds in my coat with one shot. The answer, of course, was very simple. Just as I pulled on the cock bird some of his relatives executed a cavalry maneuver and did a flank on him, and I simply fired right down the line, raking the face of the flank.

Sandy brought the last bird and spat him out on the ground and looked over at old Frank and sort of winked. *Lookit the kid,* Sandy was saying. *By the time he gets home, he'll think he did it on purpose. This time next year it'll be twelve birds when he tells it.* Frank laughed and nodded agreement.

We hunted through the sopping woods, and everywhere a covey of birds was supposed to be, a covey of birds was. I couldn't miss anything that day. I had to use two barrels on one single, was all, and I got that extra barrel back again a little later. It was just one of those days when all the birds got up right, pasted flat within an inch of the dog's nose before they rose. The singles clung to the ground like limpets, and you literally had to kick them up. Birds fly slower when they're waterlogged, and it was pretty near murder.

The extra barrel I got back, to make the score perfect for the day, was a present from Frank. I shot into the last covey and had fourteen birds in the coat with a double on the rise. Frank fetched both birds and then disappeared into the big, spooky black swamp into which the rest of the covey had flown.

A year ago I would have thought he was acting like an idiot, but, as I said, the dogs had trained me pretty good, and Frank, of all dogs, was no covey chaser. I reckoned that I had hit another bird and wounded him without knowing it, and that Frank had seen a leg drop, or something. I sat down on a stump and let the rain punish my face, and old Sandy sat down by me and shrugged his shoulders as an adult will when he cannot control a child. *If that damfool dog wants to go drown himself in that swamp on a wild-goose chase,* Sandy said with his shrug, *let him. Not for me, bud. There are too many birds around.*

Frank was gone for nearly half an hour. When he came back, he was wetter than a drowned rat, but he had a live bird in his mouth. He had evidently chased the runner for half a mile. I cracked the fugitive's neck and shoved him in my coat and went back to the store to collect the Old Man. He laughed out loud when we came into the bright warmth of Mr. Cox's potbellied stove. We must have been a sight—wet dogs, wet boy, wet coat full of bedraggled birds.

The Old Man is real clever. "How many shells?" he asked.

"Nine."

"How many birds?"

"Fifteen," I said, with pardonable pride.

"Don't tell me how it happened right now," the Old Man said. "I want to get you out of those wet clothes, and I reckon I'll need a little spot of nerve medicine to make me strong enough to listen to the bragging. But tell me one thing: was I right about February bird shooting?"

"Yessir," I said. "But then you ain't generally very wrong about anything in the woods."

"That," the Old Man declared, as we walked out into the rain and climbed into the Liz, "is a very sage observation from one so young, and I am highly flattered. If it'll make you feel any better, I made all my mistakes when I was young, which is the difference today between an old man and a boy. Youth is for making mistakes, and old age is for impressing the young with your knowledge. My Lord, it's an awful day, isn't it?"

"It's a beautiful day," I said.

20

March Is for Remembering

"March," the Old Man said, "is a fine month for remembering. I suppose that's because there is really nothing else you can do in it. Don't ever let anybody tell you that getting old happens in the autumn of your life. It happens in March."

The Old Man and I were sitting, just sitting, on a day you wouldn't want to give away to your worst enemy. The wind was blowing fit to split your teeth, so that your skin felt as if it was currycombed every time you walked out of doors. A few flowers had poked their heads up, and then a new frost nobody'd counted on arrived and the flowers ducked their heads right back again. It was just a touch too early for the geese to be flying north. Everything was finished—the quail season was over, and the fishing hadn't started, and in those days there wasn't any television.

I got up and started to pace, like a nervous cat when it's raining outside. The Old Man watched me walk a bit and then he sort of giggled under his mustache. He liked it right where he was. He didn't want to walk; he wasn't headed anywhere.

"Offhand," he said, "I would surmise there ain't nothing wrong with you that calomel can't cure. But if you'll settle down a minute, I'll read you a short sermon. It's this: Nobody ever got any younger, because if they had I would of heard of it, and maybe bought some. So what a man has got to do is take a little time off as he grows older, and devote the waste space to remembering the things he did that he maybe won't never do again. That's how you get your muscles back. It's also a fine preventative against the nervous indigestion. And when you get tired of thinking about all you've done, you can always use the time thinking about what you'd like to do in the future. You done anything lately you admired?"

I said, "Yessir, several things."

"Well, boy," the Old Man suggested, "suppose you sort of rehash 'em in your head and then tell me what it was like to do 'em. Just for instance," he said, "I bet you that you won't remember much of the little stuff. Suppose you start with those four geese you shot that day you came home full of the brags."

There had never been a day like the day I shot the four geese and came home full of the brags. I had had an accidental day with the fifteen quail on nine shots, but accidents don't count. Everybody touches perfection once; I touched it that day and knew I had it in my hand. But I hadn't tried to appraise it. I just knew I had it.

It happened like this: I was down in the east end of the state with some friends, down around Hatteras, and it was a fine big year for the old Canada honkers. By "fine" I mean nobody was shooting very many, because they would sit out there on the wide water until the shooting time was finished, and then they'd fly into the cornfields to feed. They must have been operating by stop watch, because you could hear 'em holler when the legal shooting was done, and then they'd come in to feed as tame as chickens.

Not having much else to do, I kept betting that some day they were going to get their time-check signals fouled, and some of those geese would flock in off the big water a bit early, and I would be there when they came. So I made me a nest in a ditch in the cornfield and waited 'em out with two shotguns, both 12's and both doubles. I didn't want to be undergunned when they did decide to arrive an hour early. I had both guns loaded with No. 1 bucks. In my youthful enthusiasm I reckoned that if No. 1's were big enough for a deer they were big enough for a goose, if you could hit a goose with 'em.

Every day I went and sat in my little hidey-hole in the corn shucks. Every day the geese came in just after the curfew. Every day I got up and went off with the two guns. The reason I didn't cheat was fairly simple. the Old Man said that if I ever had any trouble with the game wardens he was going to be on the side of the game wardens, and I could stay in jail and rot for all he cared. He said game laws were made on purpose, so you'd have some game to shoot next year.

There was that day I changed loads and shot a crow at a great distance because there weren't going to be any geese and I was bored. I shot him with an old thirty-incher double, full-choked, and he dropped like a stone at about sixty yards. There was another day I shot some doves, because the geese were still in a high V, talking, but not seriously, about dinner. But finally I learned the value of patience, and just sat there without shooting. I reckoned the geese would come some day, and they would be more apt to come if I didn't loose off at crows and doves.

It was late in the fall and the corn shucks were stained brown by frost, the crisp yellow leaves striped like streaks of nicotine. There were still a lot of yellow nubbin ears on the crazy-bending stalks, with the dried-out dark brown whiskers at the top of the ears and the husks split to show the seed inside. It was lone some, like it can get to be lonesome in a cornfield, because there is nothing I know of as shambly and dilapidated as an old cornfield. But there was still food a-plenty, and the honkers knew it. They wouldn't leave it until they finished it. And they hadn't even begun to finish it.

A late-autumn day is a wonderful thing, all by itself, because in hog-killing time the sun is bloody red from the wood smoke of a fire that's always going on somewhere. The ground gets gray and cold and hard in the late afternoon, and you find that your fingers stiffen from about three-thirty until you go home to the fire. All the lonesome sounds start earlier in the late fall: the scattered quail trying to call each other back into a covey; a cow lowing sad and hopeless away over yonder; even a crow's caw sounding wistful instead of ornery.

And then you have the goose sound. It isn't a gabble. It isn't really a honk. It just sounds like a goose, and it will never sound like anything else as the old gander lifts his gaggle off the lake or off the Sound and issues the correct instructions about where his herd is headed. A goose in the air is music. It is sad music when you know the goose is not apt to light, and beautiful music when he makes that big landing circle and stops his wings, holding them slanted in the cold, clean air, losing altitude and gliding down in a decreasing flight pattern until he drops his legs and bumps into a rocky landing.

The thing about a goose is he's a keen looker. He'll drop that snaky neck and shove his head down and check the terrain before he does anything at all about it. That is when you don't move an eyeball, not when a goose is looking. Yet he is stupid in one way. When I got a lot older, I shot blue geese in Louisiana, and they would even come in to a bad call, if they were young enough and had lost mama. They would also come in to a sheet of newspaper stuck on a stick or a dead cousin propped up on the ground.

But this one day I had in mind the geese left the water early. I held still in my cramped little hide-out in the ditch and looked at the three landing circles without getting nervous and without shooting too soon. I didn't move the barest part of a muscle, and when the old fifteen-pounder decided it was safe to land he said a word to the flock and they dropped in low.

I shot two coming. I dropped one gun and picked up the other and shot two going.

Possibly I never saw anything in my life like four geese, all seemingly dropping at once. They fell like shot-down aircraft and hit the deck with a thump like a bomb. Only one was wounded, the last one, and I shoved a fresh load into the gun I was holding and held the bead on his head, and he quit leaving the premises. The indignation in the sky was considerable. When the old gander came plummeting down and the other three fell out of the flock, there was a flat accusation of betrayal, and the survivors pushed on south, complaining bitterly as they flew.

I couldn't begin to describe the emotions. When you've got four dead Canada geese on the ground at once, you don't know which one to pick up first. I ran from one to the other like a nervous old lady, and then I decided I would just pick up the geese as I found them, starting with the first two that I shot coming, and winding up with the last one that I had to give the finisher to.

To me, a coat with ten quail in it is still a big event. But four Canada geese, four old ringnecks, is a feast, is a fortune, is a truckload of trophy. I cannot say how a small boy carried two big 12-bore shotguns and four mature honkers, but I managed. I think maybe I could have flown the load home with one hand.

To pluck a goose takes time, especially if you want the dry down to stuff a pillow with. To pluck four takes a lot of time, but somehow it was time I didn't mind spending. The old boss gander was tougher than whitleather, but I ate him happily. The others tasted not much better.

The guns, I thought, had a new dignity, because I had never met anybody who had killed four Canada geese in one salvo. I felt like a man who would never again shoot less than four Canada geese.

This is what I tried to tell the Old Man. "It was as if I had shot four elephants," I said. "I never had such a big day in all my life, with the exception of the one when we got the singles scattered that time and——"

The Old Man held up his hand, pushing it gently toward me. "No," he interrupted. "Don't remember any more today, or people will say you're a bore. You had enough remembering with the geese. You got to save some remembering for the next rainy day in March. But tell me one thing, what stood out the clearest about that day?"

"The day," I answered, before I thought. "All of it. There really wasn't anything bigger in it than all the little things in it. I felt lucky when I started it, sitting in the ditch in the cornfield, and I kind of knew that this was the one day for the geese to come in, and I knew I knew it. That was the only big thing. I knew it was going to be the right day for it."

"Well," the Old Man warned, "remember one thing. When you start remembering again, remember that there ain't anything in any one day any bigger than all the things that go to make up the day. This'll give you considerable comfort when you're as old as me. Do you understand what I'm driving at?"

"Yessir," I said, because this was getting too deep for me. "I sure do."

I sure didn't, actually. I just wanted to get off the platform. But now today I do. I remember very carefully, even a war, and there isn't any one event in any day I remember that was bigger than what I had for breakfast.

21

*You Got to Be Crazy
to Be a Duck Hunter*

The day was slaty, and the wind whipped the Sound into a froth. The clouds tumbled low and menacing, with a suspicion of snow to come. My ears seemed to catch fire when we came into the warmth of the house, and little droplets clung to my nose. My hands were wrinkled from cold water and as red as radishes. There was no feeling whatsoever in my feet, inside their muddy hip boots. I was never happier in my life.

"Just look at the pair of us," the Old Man said. "Froze stiff, probably going to die of the pneumonia, wet, muddy, and miserable, and both of us grinning at each other like Chessy cats. We're crazy as loons, but then you got to be a little crazy to be a duck hunter. Nobody in his right mind would get up before dawn to sit and freeze in a blind on the off chance that some old buck mallard full of fish will fly close enough to get missed."

We had had quite a day. The wind that tumbled the waters had broken up the enormous rafts of ducks—you know, the ones that sit so maddeningly in the middle of the bay on a bluebird day. The low ceiling had 'em well down within range, and the wind had also blown the water out of the little secret pools. As happens only once in a while, the ducks were hunting for a place to sit, and they came to the decoys like cats to catnip.

"There ain't nothing," the Old Man said, "as smart as a black mallard when the weather's with him. He can see from here to Japan, and he can spot a phony decoy from a mile high, which is generally where he's at. But you let that weather change and blow up a lot of wind, and mebbe a little snow, and there ain't nothing as stupid as a duck. That goes for geese too, and I reckon the old honker is generally smarter than the duck. You get the right weather, and you have to bat 'em out of the blind. How about that fellow today that lost his mama?"

The Old Man was talking about a two-thirds-grown Canada goose that had strayed off from the V, up there in the dirty gray sky, and was making pitiful sounds. The Old Man had snickered at it. "Some of them big fellows are tougher'n whitleather," he said, "but this little fellow will be real fine for your grandma's oven. See, now, how I call him down. I am going to make some noises like his mama."

He got out his goose call and began to talk like a goose's mama. I have no way of writing down the sounds, but you could see that lost goose stick his neck down as soon as the Old Man's wheedling call reached him. He dropped his flaps and came down out of the sky like a hawk after a fish. He came practically into the blind, and I took a whack at him and discovered I had done one of those things you do once in a blue moon—shot my gun dry and plumb forgot to load her. The goose took off, and the Old Man said, "Don't worry. Load her up and I'll call him back. Shoot him good this time, or we'll have him in the blind with us."

He set up a gabble again, and the goose turned and came

right back to the blind. This time I was loaded with 4's, and I delivered a mess right into his head and neck, and he came down like a rock.

"It's a mean trick," the Old Man said, "but you can always call a lost young goose with that mama noise. And they do eat better than the old ones."

The Old Man had shot behind live decoys in his time; it had been legal. You'd have a hen mallard tied to a stick that was stuck in the mud, and she had more conversation than a woman. She would stand on her tail and flutter her wings and talk sexy to the passing flocks, and they would turn on a dime and come in with their feet hanging out and wings cocked. There is no easier target than a fat mallard or pintail grabbing for water with his feet and his wings locked.

Well, the wind stirred the water to a devil's broth, the ducks poured in, and we filled our tickets. The mallards were the prettiest, of course, but it was the pins that the Old Man admired most. "The French duck is gaudy," he said, "with his yellow shoes and all those colors in his plumage and that big yellow shovel for a bill, but you can't trust him. He's a puddle duck, and if you don't give him enough grain he'll double-cross you and eat himself sick on fish, just like any old merganser. But not the pin. Look at the gentlemanly clothes he wears, while the mallard looks like a pool-hall sharpie. You'll never find a pintail eating fish. He'd starve first.

"I know you read a lot about the canvasback and how fine he is to eat, and how all the politicians in this neck of the woods won't eat anything but terrapin and canvasback at their big dinners, but the old can ain't got any more morals than a mallard about eating fish. The only big duck I can absolutely certify is the pintail. And amongst the little ducks, I never ate a fishy teal so far. As a matter of fact, when all is said and done, for the dinner plate you can't beat a teal.

"Ducks . . ." the Old Man said. "Now, take teal. They fly faster'n greased lightning, and on a teal in a tail wind you got to lead him thirty foot. But they will skitter in amongst the decoys right while you're blam-blamming at a bunch of other ducks, and swim around like they owned the pond. It don't make sense. Once you got a teal on the water, you practically can't scare him off it, 'less you shoot at him."

I mentioned casually that we seemed to waste an awful lot of ammunition shooting cripples, and that the few belts I had at teal, sitting, usually resulted in the teal's taking off to Mexico.

"I can't explain it all to you," the Old Man replied. "But you got to remember that a duck in the water is like an iceberg. About eight-tenths of him is under water, and water sheds shot like a tin roof. You practically got to hit him in the head to kill him, because his wings are folded and the wing feathers and the back feathers'll shed shot just like water. I've noticed that in all sorts of bird shooting it's a heap easier to shoot a flying bird than a sitting bird, all question of sportsmanship aside. A flying bird opens up his vulnerable parts, his softer-feathered parts, and he spreads his wings enough to give you a chance to bust one. Sitting, wings folded, he's damned near armor-plated.

"And there's one thing more: standing in a boat or a blind and aiming down at water does something to the shotgun pattern. Don't ask me what or how, because I dunno. But shotguns were made to shoot either up or straight out, not down. A smarter man than me could probably tell you. All you got to do to believe it, though, is to watch, on the next cripple, how irregular the pellets strike the water."

The Old Man and I were not steady permanent-blind boys. He was against it. Said the ducks got to associate the blind with noise and the sudden death of a relative, and would skirt it just enough to pass outside good range, unless it was such a dirty day that they completely lost their minds and became as crazy as duck hunters.

"The way to do it," he said, "is in a bateau. The Cajuns call it 'pirogue,' but bateau—which is French for 'boat,' my ignorant young friend—is a flat-bottomed skiff. You pole her out to where the wind and water seem right, and stick her in a bunch of reeds or rushes, and you cut yourself some *roseaux*, or *tules*—which is

French and Spanish, respectively, for 'reeds,' and build your blind around your boat. You always wear a khaki hat to match the reeds, and you keep your face down until you are ready to shoot, because anything but a teal or a bluebill will see your white face or bald head from as high up as he can fly, and all the decoys and calls in the world won't get him down—unless, like I said, the weather's so lousy they've quit caring. You peep through a little hole in the reeds, and you let them circle your blind twice, unless it's a very clear day, and on the second circle they'll decoy like cream.

"A man with patience will kill an awful lot of ducks, because when they drop those feet and lock those wings you get the first one automatic, and all you got to do is like the Cajun said—aim at the nose when the other half is climbing. A mallard looking for sky when he's just left the water is not really moving very fast, because he's fighting for altitude and his centrifugal force is all out of kilter."

I didn't ask the Old Man what centrifugal force was. Like I've said so many times, if you asked him he was apt to tell you, and it would take an hour or so, and everybody from Julius Caesar to Einstein would get mixed up in it.

The Old Man read me a lot of lectures about trash ducks and ducks that ought to be conserved. He wouldn't ever let me shoot a wood duck, because he said they were too pretty and too little, and besides, there weren't enough of them to go around. He never would shoot a gray duck or a spoonbill if anything else was flying, and when I complained that they looked like hen mallards at a distance he said I ought to sharpen up my eyesight or quit mingling with grown men. I took a crack at a swan once, and the Old Man took a crack at me. He said they weren't any good to eat and there were dodlimbed few of them around and what there was ought to be left in peace.

Come to think of it now, even in those days of practically non-existent game wardens, abundant game, and large limits, one thing stands out about the Old Man. He never willingly took more fish or game than we could eat or give away, and he never shot a gun—or allowed me to shoot a gun—just to hear it go off and kill something useless. He was absolutely firm about leaving a nucleus of game, whether it was quail or deer, and of never shooting females if the females were identifiable. This sex definition did not, of course, apply to quail or ducks, because unless it's mallards close at hand or a quail flying at you, there just isn't time enough to tell.

But it seems to me I've been rattling around all over the place, and what I really wanted to concentrate on was what the Old Man said first, which is that it takes a crazy man to be a duck hunter. As we stood in front of the fire, steaming out our wet clothes, after having risked death by drowning, exposure, and pneumonia, after having been up since black night, after having rowed and poled miles, after having frozen fingers setting out decoys and having frozen feet from inactivity—after having been uncomfortable constantly in the quest for a few pounds of bird meat that I didn't like to eat too terribly well, I concluded one thing: if you have to be crazy to hunt ducks, I do not wish to be sane.

22

X *Plus* Y *to the Second Power Equals Bluefish*

I think the subject came up because of some very bad marks on the report card, mostly having to do with algebra and Chaucer. Miss Hetty Struthers taught the algebra, and Miss Emma Martin taught the Chaucer, and I couldn't get anywhere with either one. My folks tore a small strip off me, and I was complaining bitterly to the Old Man one Sunday when we were going off to investigate the late run of bluefish.

"It don't make any sense to me," I grumbled. "What's the good of learning things like 'Whan that Aprille with its shoures sooty the droghte of Marche hath percéd to the rooty'? I can make more sense out of Geechee talk. At least when I ask a Geechee, 'Boy, where you get dem rope?' and he says, 'Man, I t'ief 'um off de dock,' I know what he's saying. I know he stole the rope."

"Well, everything's got some uses," the Old Man said mildly, tying a slipknot in a leader. "Maybe even Chaucer'll come in handy some day, although I must say I go along with you on this old English. We speak a lot of old English around here, such as 'holp' for help, and we call a bed a 'stid,' which I suppose is short for bedstead, and we say 'twig,' which I understand is Cockney for 'look.' "

"Yessir," I said, "but we're not pilgrims and we're not going to Canterbury, and we spell better than they spelled in those days, and I just don't see no sense in it, a-tall. How's it going to help me make a living?"

"Well, since time began," the Old Man said, "they have been jamming a lot of old stuff down young fellers because it is supposed to give 'em culture and make 'em think. What's your excuse for the 'D' in algebra?"

"Please, sir, you're not going to stand there and tell me that x plus y divided by z equals q? You taught me fractions by cutting up apples, and I understood that, especially when I ate the fractions. But this business of y to the third power is the cube root of p times 10 just don't rub off. What good is it?"

"I dunno," the Old Man admitted. "Maybe something will come of it, and maybe you ought to know something about it. You want to grow up stupid and work on a fish boat all your life?"

"*Yes*," I said stubbornly. "If it means Chaucer and algebra, I'd rather work on the *Vanessa* with Tom and Pete, and make liquor in the wintertime."

"*That* ain't any sort of an answer," the Old Man told me. "Mind, now, you're cutting that mullet too thick. You'll be going to college one of these days, and then you can study what you want to study, but first you got to get out of high school. And to get out of high school you got to make yourself do a lot of unpleasant things, which is how life works. It ain't all one way, you know. Hand me a sinker.

"Bear this in mind. Knowledge is an accumulation, like a pack rat hides things. Things you never knew you knew have a way of popping up later. You're supposed to fill your skull with a lot of things, against the day you might need one of them. And remember this, too: you can't pour a gallon of knowledge into a one-quart brain. The idea is to make the brain big enough and flexible enough to handle what it has to handle. I want to see some better marks next month, or we might just find ourselves not shooting any quail this fall. That ain't a threat. It's a suggestion. Let's go catch some fish."

We caught a lot of fish. The big blues had come in to feed in the sloughs, and so had the drum—the channel bass, that is— and there was a big run of enormous weakfish. We'd had a pretty good norther that had cut deep sloughs and firmed up the sand bar, and all you had to do was just give the rod a little flip, and the four-ounce pyramid sinker landed right in the mouth of something big and full of fight. I caught a thirty-pound drum that day, and the Old Man topped me with a forty-pounder. We quit when we were tired, and we had enough fish to fill up the back seat of the Liz. We went home dead beat, and for once the Old Man helped me gut and scale the fish. There were just too many for one boy.

We ate—not much, because I was tired; just some cornbread and milk and eggs and bacon and jelly—and I went to bed, but I couldn't sleep. Algebra and Chaucer kept chasing themselves round and round in my head, all mixed up with bluefish and channel bass and quail and camp making and horse riding and heaven and hell and how long is forever—one of those bad nights a kid'll have once in a blue moon.

About 2:00 A.M. I got up and dressed and called the dogs and went for a walk down by the river. The moon was nigh full, still sailing high and pretty in the sky, and all over town you could hear the dogs howl, like somebody was going to die and they knew all about it. I couldn't get one thing out of my mind: "You can't pour a gallon of knowledge into a one-quart brain," the Old Man had said. I wandered sad and lonely as a cloud—we'd had that one in English too—wondering if I was one of those people with a one-quart brain. One pint was more like it, I thought finally as we walked down to the wharf, and I sat and dangled my feet and watched the moon turn the water to milk.

Then I began to think of something else. I thought about how many things I already knew that the Old Man had taught me. These things skipped through my head helter-skelter. I knew how to train a puppy to be a good bird dog. I knew how to call a turkey or a duck. I knew how to row a boat and stand a deer. I knew about moon and tide and their effect on fish and game. I knew that a sea turtle wept huge tears when it laid its soft eggs in the sand. I knew how to hook a sheepshead with a sand fiddler. I knew how to make a camp and build a fire and skin a rabbit in one shuck. I knew how to cook in the woods and throw a cast net and lead a dove and grapple an oyster and draw a seine.

I suddenly decided I knew an awful lot about an awful lot of things, some of which I had been taught, some of which I had learned on my own. But mostly it seemed to me that what I knew—the odd pieces of information, like not calling the Aphrodite of Melos the Venus de Milo, and how the guano birds worked—all came out of the Old Man. It seemed to me that if they put the Old Man to work teaching school he could even make algebra easy. It also seemed to me that if a boy worked half as hard learning Chaucer as he worked hunting a coon, Chaucer would become a minor nuisance and could easily be got out of the way. Algebra wasn't any tougher than still-hunting a big buck deer, and probably had less mathematics to it. Whereupon I whistled up the dogs and went back to bed, and this time I slept.

Then a strange and wonderful thing happened to me in the schoolroom. I discovered reading. Real reading. I found out that Shakespeare had more muscles than Doonie Watts and was responsible for more rough characters than a water front. He knew more man-type jokes than the boys at Gus McNeill's filling station, and his language was frank enough to be of great interest to a boy.

I took on Shakespeare as I'd learned to build a turkey blind, and he was a cinch. I had more fun with Walter Scott than Ivanhoe ever did. I fell afoul of some naturalists like Ernest Thompson Seton, and some archaeologists, and some Gibbon, and I got so interested in Rome that I practically bought myself a toga. The Greeks and the Egyptians and the Phoenicians got to be personal friends. Robin Hood and *Treasure Island* and *Robinson Crusoe* were kid stuff now, although I must say that Mr. Defoe had a lot of know-how, and while Mr. Wyss' *Swiss Family Robinson* was a bunch of lies, mainly, it also had a lot of know-how in it. I mean about salting down fish and taming onagers and building tree houses and such as that.

The shock that I actually liked all this came one day when I was hunting with a friend of mine named E. G. Goodman, who was going to grow up to be a doctor like his dead daddy, even if his mamma, Mis' Eliza Goodman, had to beat him with a stick. The E. in his name stood for Erasmus or Erastus, I disremember which, but if you called him "Ras" you had to fight him.

G. and I had a real fine day at his farm. We hunted everything, like boys will—rabbits and squirrels and doves and quail. We were up before the dawn and bedded down early. We ate like starving Armenians and must have walked a hundred miles behind an old half-bred bulldog-plus-hound, who didn't seem to care what he chased.

That was the first day I really got into the texture of things. I mean, how big was a scuppernong grape, how much juice was inside it, what the moss on an old live oak looked like, the freckles on the leaves of an old cornstalk, the weight of a beefsteak tomato served with sugar and vinegar, the way a possum skin tacked to the weathered silver-gray boards of the smokehouse curled at the edges, the differing voice range of the bull hound when he was after a black swamp rabbit or was interested in a squirrel up a tree.

Inside the smokehouse the hams hung heavy and green-molded, hard-cured, and there was enough salt in the soil to assay at least 30 percent of the gross weight. The gourd dipper by the well was lumpy on its hard-dried yellow-green surface. The yard was clean-swept sand, like a beach, and the old house was stilted, like an old maid holding up her skirts when a mouse comes skittering into the room.

We hunted the swamp with one buckshot shell in the left-hand barrel, hoping to start a deer, and for the second time I truly knew about the solemnity of a swamp, green and cool and frightening, with the slow crick-colored brown from the leaf dye, the clusters of mistletoe high in the bare branches of the water oaks, the squirrels' nests brown and lonesome in the mizzen of the trees, and the high-cocked knees of the cypress. The mournful call of the dove came spooking, the last mournful cry of dove, plaintive whistle of scattered quail, the first wail of whippoorwill, and later the scary hoot of the elusive owl. Then the rise of moon and the devil shapes the trees made.

I had been living with this stuff all my life and had never completely noticed it before—never saw it, never smelled it, never heard it, never isolated it, never touched it. I had never thought of the curious fact that a drinking gourd was as rough as a file inside, or that magnolia blossoms turned brown if you touched them, or that the pomegranates that grew in Cousin Margie's front yard were composed only of hide and pulp and seeds.

I had given no real thought to the fact that the country at nightfall was so mournful that the Negroes whistled and sang to keep themselves company as they walked through the dark-ening woods, or that an iron caldron generally had three legs instead of four. The fact that smoke rose instead of falling had never touched my consciousness, or that frost was only frozen dew. I had eaten pork sausage and never noticed that the skin was mottled and generally made from intestines.

All this hit me that day at E. G. Goodman's farm, and in fairness I had to blame it on education. Without *The Decline and Fall*, without *Rolf in the Woods*, without Falstaff, without Lamb's roast pig (I had never even thought of what crackling really was, *mirabile dictu!*), without Chaucer and Macbeth and the crackling of prawns in a pot and that dreary dreamer, Hamlet—without these I would have passed through this fascinating life, accepting everything, seeing nothing.

The Old Man was old, but how much older was Cheops, whom I later came to know as Khufu. My house was old, but how much older Rome, how much older the Pyramids. "Rome wasn't built in a day" was a phrase we used as freely as "Sure as a gun's iron," and now I knew doggone well it wasn't built in a day. But I never did figure out how much higher it is than they hung Haman.

I have to admit I never made an "A" in algebra, but I passed it without cheating, and Miss Hetty said she never did see such a change in a boy. Miss Emma Martin was hard to convince that I wasn't cheating on Shakespeare, but I reared back and gave her a load of Chaucer one day and she had to hold still for the fact that I at least could memorize. Miss Claire Lathrop was flabbergasted when I turned up fairly sharp wih Julius Caesar in the Latin version, and she couldn't have known that the interest suddenly came via Shakespeare and the Old Man. I knew that all Gaul was divided into three parts, but I wanted the straight dope on why.

This is no advertisement for education, but I have to admit it had its points in teaching me what I was doing every day, with quite a lot of how and a little bit of why. Some of it came in real handy later, when I took up writing as a trade, but mostly it helped me heavy in the business of possum hunting and the anatomy of the large outdoors.

"Insanity," the Old Man observed, "seems to run in some families. It takes different forms. Some people bay the moon, and others think they are Napoleon. In my case, apart from being a duck hunter, I enjoy coon hunting. I even like possum hunting.

"Now, you just tell me," he went on, "why a man grown would admire to run around in the woods at night following a bunch of hollering hound dogs when he could be sound and warm in his bed. After a critter he don't really want. Insanity! Do you want to go coon hunting with me and the boys?"

"Yessir," I said. "I guess I've inherited it from you. When are we going?"

"Tonight. Tom and Pete and a couple other loose maniacs named Elwood and Corbett got some new hounds they went to try. Won't nothing much come of it except Corbett'll fight Tom and Pete'll be duty bound to take on Elwood—that's after they've got drunk—but if there's a coon or a possum or even a bear handy, we'll hear some music. In any case, we'll have some exercise."

I'd been around in the woods a lot at night, frog sticking and all, and early in the morning after deer and squirrel and turkey, but that is a kind of quiet operation. Coon hunting is a thing for bust-neck people who don't really care if they fall in holes and trip over briers and run against trees. Far as I know, a bone-bred coon hunter doesn't care whether he catches the coon or doesn't catch the coon. He just wants to hear the hounds make that music.

Even as a little feller I was always fascinated with woods at night. A wood in the daytime is a warm, friendly place, pierced with sunlight, splashed in the clearings with pools of light; but when she starts off to cool in the evening, she gets real spooky. Jungle isn't jungle in the daytime, but even a city park is jungle at night. The dogs know it, which is why they howl, and the colored folks know it, and even the sophisticated city folks draw the curtains and light up a fire.

To be in a forest by yourself at night is a large adventure in fear, but to be on a coon hunt with a lot of hairy men, most of whom have already been scarring their noses with the fruit jar, is another thing. People are stumbling around and falling and cussing and laughing, and all of a sudden the owl's hoot, the whippoorwill's wail, are no longer ghost noises but companionable accompaniments to the big spree.

The general idea of a coon hunt is you turn loose the dogs in a patch of likely cover, and then you run through the woods after the dogs. Maybe that is oversimplification, but it's about all I remember. On this particular night the dogs started a fox or so, treed a possum, and missed out completely on the coon. Another jumped a deer, and another took off after a rabbit, causing great disgust to his owner.

The possum I recall very well, because I was nominated to climb the old persimmon tree he was refugeeing in and to poke him out with a stick. The branch I was on busted, and the possum and I fell out of the tree at approximately the same time. We lost the coon in a swamp after he dang near murdered one of the dogs who was stupid enough to follow him into the creek. The deer went over to see friends in another county.

What I mind, mostly, is hearing the hounds on a night so clear and frosty sharp that the belling must have traveled miles; hearing the hounds crashing in the low gallberries and pine scrub, seeing the excited ring of hounds around a tree—from which the coon had departed—and the spectacle of a bunch of grown men acting so much like children that if they had been children other grown men would have tanned their britches.

I've got no real solution for what makes a man hunt coons at night unless he's crazy, like the Old Man said, but my mild idea today is that everybody, even a grown man, needs to get out of the house and cut up a little, just to ease his nerves. That's why the coon was created.

I don't know how many miles you travel on a coon-hunting night. The dogs circle, and you try to cut the circle, and you fall into the creek, and you lose people and lose dogs, and along about two or three in the morning everybody's had enough, including the dogs, the coon you didn't tree, and the deer that went over the hill. By some common accord everybody decides to quit. You know the hounds will come back, those you've lost, in a day or so. So you make for a headquarters, which would be Tom's place or Elwood's place, and you kick the sleepy fire into a blaze, and everybody lies around the kitchen floor while somebody else puts the coffee pot on the hob. Somebody else goes out to the smokehouse for a side of bacon, and somebody else disturbs a hen and brings in a gross of brown freckled eggs. Somebody else digs up another jar of hand-woven corn liquor, and somebody else gets out the guitar.

We sort of tended to the Elizabethan epoch where I was raised, and so all the songs you heard were old English folk songs that the hillbilly artists later made popular on the radio and juke boxes.

I don't know how or where the people learned the music. The Old Man, for instance, was a fiddler. First he carpentered his own fiddle, and then, seeing as how he had it made, he figgered he might as well learn to play it. Maybe he never played it very good, but he could squeeze as much emotion out of "Ol' Zip Coon" and "Pop Goes the Weasel" as anybody I ever heard.

Practically everybody played something. People that couldn't make anything more than a mark on a legal paper knew some odd things about harmony, whether they were playing a washboard, a jew's-harp, a banjo, or a mouth organ.

All the colored folks could play something or other too, if it was only the bones, and the singing you heard at the camp meetings and revivals, the old spirituals, had a beat that they're still struggling to put a finger on today. I can still get me a set of goose-pimples out of remembering what "Go Down, Moses" used to sound like when about a hundred colored voices took hold of it.

Seemed like nearly everything you did had some music in it. The dogs made music in the chase—rabbits, deer, coon—and it was sweet music. When the big, sweaty deck-hands were hauling seine in the pogie fleet, they used a chant with a "huh!" to mark the haul, a chant that I heard a lot of years later in the middle of Tanganyika. The chain gangs had their special songs, and the Cap'm in charge of the convict camps used to put on regular free concerts after the bad boys quit pounding on the railroad ties. The roustabouts around the turpentine camps had their song-and-dance specialists too, and altogether—rich and poor, black and white, chained and unchained—we made some mighty mellow music.

The square dances on Saturday nights were a throwback all the way to Sir Walter Raleigh. The music hadn't changed, and the intricacy of the figures hadn't changed much either. The best set caller in the county was a little, prune-faced, sawed-off fellow named Dan Ward. When he hit that part about "ladies in the middle, gents to the wall, take a chew tobacco, and balance all!" he used to leap half his height straight off the floor, kick his heels, and leer in a positively marvelous fashion.

I kind of got off the subject of coon hunting, but so did the coon that night. What I was generally aiming at, though, was the fact that so many good things were mixed up in whatever you did, whether it was a coon hunt, a ball game, a fish fry, or a camp meeting.

Whatever you did, there was music in it, and good food in it, and science and knowledge of a special sort; and there was always the fun of the firelight, and lazy rest when you were plumb beat. There was a slug of mule at the end of the day for the men grown, and maybe a sip of scuppernong wine for the boys. There seemed to be some sort of point to everything, a beginning, a middle, and an end.

The Old Man used to say that the best part of hunting and fishing was the thinking about going and the talking about it after you got back. You just had to have the actual middle as a basis of conversation and to put some meat in the pot. "Everybody," he said, "should be allowed to brag some about what he did good that day, and to cover up shameless on what he did wrong."

Lying around on the bleached white-pine floor of a country

kitchen, with the thin fat-pine walls literally vibrating with the heat of the roaring fire, the smell of eggs and bacon mingled with coffee and corn whisky, I heard all the stories that had become legend to the vicinity. All the past coon hunts were recounted. All the lies about hounds and bird dogs were retold, including the one about the setter who was so stanch on point that she got lost one day and was found a year later. There had been a change in the weather, and she froze to death. Her skeleton was found, still pointing at the skeletons of a covey of quail.

I heard Corbett tell all about the time he was "working for the state," a euphemism for a stretch in jail for bootlegging. I heard about the First World War. Crime and punishment, war and peace, came hand in hand with a coon hunt and a skillet of bacon and eggs.

It was bright light when the party broke up and we headed home, with one scarred dog and a possum to show for the evening's work. Sure enough, Corbett had got into an altercation with Elwood, and, being as how they were brothers, Tom and Pete had to show their sympathy by starting a private quarrel over who owned a cast net or a shotgun or something. Corbett swung at Elwood and missed and fell in the fire, and we had to haul him out. Pete and Tom took their argument out on the porch, and Pete dived at Tom and fell off the porch and just stayed where he was. Tom thought he looked lonesome; so he went and lay down by him, and a hound came up and lay down with the pair.

The Old Man shook his head and sniffed the bright morning breeze. "I'm telling you again," he said. "Insanity runs its own peculiar way. Coon hunting is a very strong symptom. In a way it reminds me of what life's like. You work and you fall down and you eat and you fight, and when it's all over you feel awful foolish. Because, generally, you ain't even got a coon to show for all the commotion."

23

The Women Drive You to the Poolrooms

It was one of those miserable spring days, with the wind whipping down in gusts and fetching the rain along with it, and nothing much to do. Too hot for a fire, and too cold not to have a fire. The rain rattled on the windowpanes, and the glass shivered when the spurts of wind struck.

The Old Man and I were just sittin', scratchin', and fidgetin'. Everywhere we'd light, in a minute Miss Lottie, my grandma, would be right behind us with a dust rag or a broom. If we sat on a chair, she'd come up on us and start to bustle around, like women will, and we'd know she was set on shifting the chair to some place else where it wouldn't look any better, but would give her some satisfaction. She kept hustling us from one stand to another until finally the Old Man sighed and said,

"Let's go down to Thompson's poolroom. At least there ain't any women in it. I am against poolrooms on principle, but there are times where there ain't any other place for a fellow to get away from his womenfolks."

About this time Miss Lottie came at us with the carpet sweeper, and we got up and walked the three blocks to the poolroom and sat down on one of the high-legged stools and drank a Coke and listened to the click of the balls and watched the players as they bent over the cool green baize of the tables in sometimes impossible positions as they shoved a bit of body English into the shots. Thompson's poolroom was full that day. "Evidently," the Old Man said, "all the local ladies have come down with the nervous wet-weather furniture-moving disease."

He pulled at his ragged mustache and lit up his pipe. Watching one of the players nudge the eight ball into a side pocket, he spoke more or less to himself.

"Women are the most curious of all the animal critters in the world. I have made a lifelong study of women, under all climatic conditions, and I reckon there ain't a varmint loose in the woods or water that takes as much figgerin' with no real answer. You can train a no-'count dog, or fool a fish, or outguess a fox, or outsmart a coon, or make a buck deer run your way, but there is no real past performance that you can use against a woman to cut her off at the draw. Just about the time you got her figgered she whips out a fresh bag of tricks, and you got to start all over again.

"Now, you take a poolroom," he said. "There ain't anything really sinister about a poolroom. I don't shoot pool, but the poolroom is where I come when I got a new dog to show off or some fresh exploit I want to brag about, because I know I'll find a lot of men to listen to what I got to say or see what I got to show. In a small place like this, a poolroom ain't a den of iniquity. It's the only refuge in town where a man ain't tormented by his womenfolks.

"Pool," the Old Man went on, "ain't nothing but heavy-ball

tennis, using a stick instead of a catgut fly swatter. When I was in England once, I looked and saw the high muckety-mucks playing pool in a couple of clubs I wangled my way into, except the Limeys call it snooker. But in our curious thinking, tennis is a ladylike sport and pool is bad. That's because the ladies can't get into the pool halls to bedevil their men, and the ladies resent it."

I watched Dooney Watts do a highly illegal jump shot. The cue ball leapfrogged over a blocking ball, picked up its target, and nudged it into a corner pocket.

"Pretty," the Old Man said. "Illegal, but pretty. Tells you what sort of a man Dooney is. That sign saying 'No jump or massé shots allowed' don't mean no more to Dooney than if it said 'Posted' or 'Hunting Strictly Forbidden.' Dooney ain't what you'd call a natural-born law abider. What was I saying? Oh, yes, I remember. Women.

"There ain't but one law you can use against 'em," the Old Man continued. "That's what I call the law of negative acceptance, or the power of reverse-English suggestion. You got to operate on the basic idea that they are two steps ahead of you, and then take a step back'ards and throw them off stride.

"Women are natural-born perverse. Anything a man takes delight in which they don't understand, and can't share, makes 'em mad. They keep trying to kiss their elbows and turn into boys, and when they can't be boys they don't like it; so they declare war on the boys at a very early age, and win the final victory when they trap themselves a wild boy and turn him into a house pet. Or try to.

"Boys like to cuss and chew tobacco and drink a little liquor and shoot pool and play poker and smoke cigars and go huntin' and fishin'. These generally ain't supposed to be sports the girls can share in; so the girls resent 'em.

"It ain't like any of these things was bad, if taken in moderation. I never knew no man to come to harm in the woods or in the water, or in a poolroom for that matter, if the man was a good man to start with. You have noticed that I smoke and take a little nip now and then, but no jailhouse ever knew me, and I pay what I owe and speak civilly to the preacher. You can overdo anything, including sweet charity and mashed potatoes, and turn a good thing into a bad thing.

"But the women automatically think it's bad if they got no part in it. An English fellow, name of Chesterton, once wrote a line that went something like this: 'There are three things in this world women don't understand: liberty, equality, fraternity.' I reckon that may be a little tough on the girls on the equality side, but on liberty and fraternity they ain't got a whisper of understanding."

One of the boys, maybe it was Bill St. George, did a three-cushion bank shot that nudged a ball out of a difficult lie and into the leather webbing of the pocket.

"That's how you handle 'em," the Old Man said. "Bank shots. Aim for about three extra cushions and they're so busy following the cue ball they don't see the main ball drop. They lose interest on the second cushion." The Old Man was pretty windy this day, and full of his subject.

I piped up, "I don't follow you. What do you mean, lose interest on the second cushion?"

"Come on home and I'll show you how it works. I taught you to shoot and make a camp and catch a fish and train a dog. I may as well complete your education with women."

The rain had stopped when we went out, and the wind was dying. The Old Man sniffed the air and grinned under his mustache. "She's going to be a good day tomorrow. What'd you most like to do?"

"I dunno," I said. "How do you figure bass'll be biting?"

"Fair," the Old Man reckoned. "Think we ought to go fishing? It's a week end."

"Yessir," I answered. "And we haven't done anything about fixing up the shack on Corncake. That'd be fun. I reckon she's in a mess, after the last blow."

"We'll see," the Old Man said. "We'll see how the land lays."

We went on into the house, and Miss Lottie fixed us with a wifely eye. "Where've you all been?" she asked.

"Down to the poolroom. You seemed awful busy, and we didn't want to disturb you."

"Taking that boy into the poolroom with all those loafers!" she said, and went on for about five minutes about how no good could come to anybody that hung around pool halls associating with riffraff, et cetera. The Old Man let her carry on till she was blowing like a winded horse. He never said a word, just let her have her head.

When she quit, he said, "Excuse me," and went out in the back yard and crawled under the house and got his cast net. He came back to the living room, spread it out on the floor, and sat down cross-legged and took a sail needle and started to mend it. He winked at me and whispered, "Go get the fishing rods. They need looking over."

I went and got the rods and broke 'em down and started cleaning the reels on a big spread of newspaper. Miss Lottie came in again, hopping mad when she saw all the truck over her fresh-swept rug. "What's all that mess you've got there? On my rugs!"

"Just the cast net and some fish poles, Lottie," the Old Man said, sweet as pie. "While we're at it, boy, you better go get the guns. This wet weather ain't helping them any."

"Yessir," I said and got up.

The old lady let out a screech. "You don't clean any guns on my clean carpet!" She was red and flustered. "Oil all over my ——"

"But, Lottie," the Old Man protested, "it's too wet to work outside, and since I took all them trunks up to the attic it——"

"I don't know who's the worst, you or the boy," she said. "Seems to me all you do is clutter up the house when I've cleaned it. Why don't you take the boy and go somewheres?"

"The poolroom?" The Old Man's eyes were wide and innocent.

"I don't care where you go!" Miss Lottie hollered. "Just get that much off my rugs!"

"Of course." The Old Man winked at me sideways. "There's so many no-'count people hanging around poolrooms that——"

"If you had any sense, you'd take the boy and go over to Corncake and fix that house you're always talking about," Miss Lottie told him. "You can make all the mess you want to over there, and at least be out from underfoot while I get on with my cleaning."

I started to say something, but the Old Man hushed me up with a wave of his hand.

"You know as well as I do, Lottie," he said, "it'll be cold and wet on Corncake, and there ain't any provisions in the house and we're apt to catch our death of cold and——"

"Oh, shush," she said. "You're a grown man, and you spend half your time either soaked to the skin or parboiled in the sun. There's plenty of driftwood under the house, or ought to be, and you can take some things to eat with you. You're always talking about how good you cook. Go some place and prove it."

"I don't know . . ." The Old Man shook his head. "My rheumatism has been pretty bad lately. I think we'd best just stay here. Come on, son. If your grandmother doesn't want us in the parlor, we can go to the dining room."

"You set foot in my dining room, and I'll—— You stay right here!" She rushed off toward the kitchen.

"Just set quiet and make a motion with that oily rag," the Old Man said. "She'll be back in a minute."

She was, too. She came back, bent over, carrying a big basket with both hands. "There's half a ham in here," she puffed. "There's three dozen eggs and some beans and bread and coffee. There's an apple pie and some oranges and bananas and part of a pound cake. Now, take that truck off my rug and go some place and play cowboys for a couple of days."

"I reckon we've been run off, son," the Old Man said.

"Gather up that gear and throw it in the Liz. Maybe we'll both get drowned; then she'll be sorry."

"Small loss," Miss Lottie snapped.

The Old Man sighed and went out the door. I was just getting into the Liz when Miss Lottie called me back to the door. She had a paper bag in her hands. It was hard inside and gurgled.

"He forgot his nerve tonic," she said. "If I was you, I'd try the bass first, before you go to the house. I think they might be biting." And she shot me a wink. "Stay out of the poolrooms."

When I handed the Old Man his nerve tonic, he sighed. "You see what I mean? There ain't no way to fool 'em. What'd she say?"

"She said go fishing first."

"Then we'll go fishing," the Old Man said. "But it would have saved us a lot of time if she'd come right out and said she had a hankering for fish."

24

Thar She Blows

In the old days the pogie-fishing industry was about as exciting a way to make a living as a fellow could run across. My first sharp awareness of the immensity of the sea, and with it the world, was when the Old Man decided I was big enough to pull a little weight on a pogie boat. A pogie is a very greasy, fat fish whose proper name is menhaden and which is used for fertilizer and fish meal and what not. You can do anything with a pogie but eat it, and I suppose if you were hungry enough to choke it down it wouldn't kill you.

Pogie fishing was big industry in my town. Between pogies and shrimp and the pilot business, we managed to eat. The Old Man had a pogie boat called the *Vanessa*. I suppose she wasn't the biggest ship that ever went to sea, but to me she was bigger than the *Queen Mary*. She was big enough to carry what seemed a million miles of seine, a flock of purse boats, a skipper, a mate, a winchman, a slew of strong backs, which were mostly colored—and a small boy.

The pogies went in shoals and they were followed by clouds of birds—gannets and gulls and such. They showed brassy in the sun, and you could see the big fish—the sharks and dolphin and mackerel—cutting into the bait, and the birds swooping and dipping down to grab a fish in their talons or beak.

My job was aloft in the crow's-nest. I was the lookout, the fearless fellow high above the decks. All alone up there in the boundless sky, I scanned the boundless sea, looking for an undulating shoal of fat-backed menhaden, to be seined and hauled silvery kicking aboard, then taken to Charlie Gause's refining factory and rendered into an awful smell that meant sowbelly and beans and long sweetening in the colored folks' houses and another installment on the flivver in the driveway of the white folks' houses.

"This is big business," the Old Man said. "You ain't just a kid wedged into the crow's-nest of a fishing boat. You are the economic difference in a lot of people's lives. You belong to see a shoal of pogue before the other lookouts in the other ships see 'em, so we can get to 'em first, or there may be no Christmas next year. See if you can't pretend you're Cap'n Ahab with your eye peeled for Moby Dick. After all, a good haul of pogies weighs as much as a whale, and is worth about the same amount of money."

One thing about the Old Man was that he always had a sort of play-toy approach to everything. A boy looking for a bad-smelling fish that is headed for a fertilizer factory is one thing, and pretty dull doings. But a boy with a title of Cap'n who is hunting a great white whale is quite another kettle of conditions. Man, when I perched up there high in the sky, with my eyes skinned for the fish, I was about as close to being lord of the universe as you're apt to get.

I'd spot a shoal of pogies and holler down, "Bridge ahoy!"

when I could just as easy have said, "Hey, Grandpa!" And I'd say, "Fish! Bearing two points off the starboard bow!" or some such formality, when I suppose all the time the Old Man had seen the fish before I'd sung out, and was just waiting on me out of politeness.

We'd cut off in the general direction of the fish, and the purse boats would swing over the side from their davits, and the great seine would be set from the bobbing boats. The enormous, shining, sweaty black deck-hands would heave and haul and grunt, and the fish would come with a surge into the hold of the ship when the donkey engine hauled the catch aboard, flapping and kicking, a treasure trove of marine organisms.

"Let's see what we got this time," the Old Man would say, and give over the wheel to Tom or Pete or somebody else.

That was the thrill, because you never knew what you'd be hauling out of the sea along with the pogies. There would always be sharks—hammerheads and shovelnoses—and once in a while a big one. Now and again a tarpon would find its way that far north, and there were always scatterings of the fine edible fish—mackerel and blues and dolphin. I had a new job then. With my feet shoved into rubber boots, I was down in the hold to plow through the surprise package and sort out the good fish, which the crew divided and sold fresh to the stores when we got back to port. I was allowed to keep my share of the money, and no questions asked about what I spent it on.

They were bright and golden days of sun and sea spray, the salt gritty on your lips, and your nose burning as the sun graved salt into your skin. There were so many things to watch: the way the birds worked the fish, the dorsals of the sharks slicing the water, the dolphins running a match race with the bow of the ship, the porpoises, jocular and friendly, cutting caracoles as they played around the boat, big clownish show-offs happy to have company.

There was always weather to watch—watching it breed and handling it according to whether she was squall, or storm, or dirty-mean with hurricane tendency. I had a small suit of oil-skins and a sou'wester and boots, and I loved it when the sky turned gray and dirty and the clouds lowered and the seas began to pile, sending great sheets of spray over the forecastle-head, even up to the bridge. There's always something wonder-ful about storm at sea, especially if you can trust the skipper to get you safely back to a fire and a clean bed.

The smells aboard a ship are special—oil and tar and clean hemp and canvas and salt, grease and fuel and paint. I first made the acquaintance of sujimuji on the *Vanessa*. It is a virulent lye concoction for the swabbing down of paintwork, and it burns holes in your hide. A lot of years later, when I went to sea in the merchant marine, I needed very few lessons concerning forecastlehead lookouts and the application of suji to paint.

The Old Man said that, as I was a common deck-hand (ex-cept when I was Cap'n Ahab looking for Moby Dick) I cer-tainly couldn't expect to eat with the skipper—himself. He said a skipper had a certain amount of dignity, which must be pre-served at all costs, even to eating by himself. So I messed with Tom and Pete, who constituted mate and bos'un. Seems to me we ate very high on the hog. Or maybe it was just hunger, be-cause fried salt pork, grits, eggs, salt ham, canned salmon, and fried fish, with coffee and sea biscuits, molasses for sweeten-ing, and maybe an apple, were about all we had to eat. I learned a long time later that if an army travels on its belly, the Navy lives off coffee. "Coffee time" has more significance in seagoing talk than "Damn the torpedoes!"

Best of all I can recall, none of the men, black or white, ever made me feel like a boy, or out of place, or a nuisance, or anything like that. They taught me things, but they were what a boy ought to know, such as not dumping a bucket of swill over the windward taffrail, and how to steer a bucking ship in a heavy sea, taking up two or three turns of slack in the wheel according to which way the wind and currents were driving you.

I got to where I could come hand over hand down the guy

line from crow's-nest to deck—or slide it if I had gloves. When the Navy got me years later, one thing I didn't have to learn was the difference between a clove hitch and a bowline, a square knot and a granny. Tom, or maybe Pete, taught me how to make a Turk's-head, handle a heaving line, and splice a spring line. I could run a winch and cast off or tie up without busting up the vessel or the dock.

All this may not sound as if it would ever come in handy, but there was one dirty night, a few years later, when the skipper, the mate, the cadet, and yours truly warped a full-sized freighter out of a dock in Hamburg and up the river to Bremerhaven when the crew and other officers were all drunk, and I was all by myself on the poop, handling two stern spring lines and two winches and saying profanely reverent thanks to the old *Vanessa* and its cooperative crew.

What I can remember best is the ghostly cold of a predawn sailing, the clammy dew on the tarpaulins—dew stiff-bristled on the hempen lines, cold-freckled on the deck, smeared across the glass of the bridge. I can remember the crash of sea against ship, the tremor all the way along her as she took a big one, the way anything that wasn't battened down took a walk when the seas were on the beam, and the crashing in the galley and the cursing of the cook and the smell of coffee grounds frying when the coffee pot up-ended on the galley stove.

I remember the bone-crushing fatigue at the end of the day, when you came bravely into port with your full-up flags flying, and the sun going down red, and the night chill coming on again. And the way the dock pitched when you tied up and your sea-limber legs hit firm planking again, and still continued to roll and pitch with the motion of the sea.

I saw an albatross before I read *The Ancient Mariner*, and what is more, I knew a boat that was named after one. I knew about the hunter home from the hills, and the sailor home from the sea.

The Old Man said one day, when I was taking a trick at the wheel, "I spent most of my life on the water, and so did your

Uncle Jack and your Uncle Tommie and your Uncle Walker and all the other ones ahead of us, and it looks iike we got a straight succession to blue water in you."

There was a time, somewhere east of Oran, during the late unpleasantness called World War II, when I remembered what he said, and wished we'd had a few more soldiers in the family.

25

Graveyards Are More Fun Than Sunday School

"It seems to me," the Old Man said one summer Sunday morning, "that it's about time you started teaching me something. This has been a one-sided operation for too long a time. What do you know that I don't?"

"Is there anything you don't know?" I countered.

"Don't be rude," the Old Man chided. "I was being serious."

"So was I," I told him. "Everything I know, you taught me."

"I wouldn't say that at all," the Old Man said. "An old codger can learn an awful lot of things from a kid. Except you're coming on for not being a kid any more. Seems to me you grow a foot a week."

"I seem to be mighty hungry all the time," I admitted, laughing. "Somehow or other, I never get enough to eat. You suppose I got a tapeworm?"

"Wouldn't think it likely. You couldn't eat enough for both of you. Stop fooling around and tell me something. Out of all the stuff I've rubbed off on you, what stuck the most?"

"Serious?"

"Serious."

"You'll laugh."

"I won't laugh. When did I ever? Out of place, I mean."

"All right, sir. Politeness."

"Politeness?"

"Yessir. And I bet you don't even know this about yourself. Everything we ever did together was mainly based on politeness."

The Old Man whistled. "Well, damn me," he said, and lit his pipe. "Proceed to inform me."

"I don't want to sound like Sunday school, but——"

"You couldn't ever sound like Sunday school," he interrupted. "You haven't spent that much time in it. I'll tell you one thing I've learned about boys before you continue. A boy who says he cut Sunday school to visit a graveyard because of its archeological importance is either going to be a chronic liar or a man of great vision. Proceed."

"It was a nice day, and I kind of like graveyards," I said. "Better than Sunday school. They're more cheerful. But if you still want to listen, what I was going to say is this:

"You taught me never to holler at another man's dog. You taught me never to hog a shot at a bird. You taught me that there isn't anybody who doesn't feel like he's a person too. I'm specially thinking about the colored people, like Aunt Florence Hendricks and Albert Grey and Mary Millett and Abner McCoy —all the people that let us shoot their quail and kind of look after us when we're in their neighborhood. I ain't speaking about 'yessir,' and 'please,' and 'thank you, ma'am,' and taking off hats and bowing and scraping, and children-will-be-seen-and-not-heard-at-the-table sort of things. But what I mean is I never saw you mean to anybody, including fice dogs, even including that Willie-off-the-pickle-boat you hit in the chin and knocked off the dock that day."

"That was a kind of special day," the Old Man murmured sheepishly. "A man hadn't ought to let his temper rule him. But I'd knock him off the same dock again, beggin' your pardon, and knock him further."

"You remember the time you whipped me for not fighting Wendell Newton?"

"That I do," the Old Man said. "I warmed your tail for fair, and I'd do that again too. Because you got up and beat the tar out of Wendell Newton, and have been fast friends since, with no worries about whether you're a coward or not. A lath on the tail has a certain importance in its place and time. Everything has its importance in its place and in its time. Including cussing. Sometimes you cuss and sometimes you don't. Sometimes you fight and sometimes you don't. You got to know when to pick your spots."

"How do you know when to pick your spots?"

"I dunno. I reckon you got your finger on it—politeness. When politeness gets infringed on, somebody's wrong, you or the other guy, and it calls for a fight, whether you're using words or fists."

"You'd be embarrassed," I admitted, "if I told you all the things you taught me. It'd get to sound like a lecture."

"Don't tell me," the Old Man said. "Just think about them, if they make you comfortable. I'm sorry I brought the whole thing up. The one thing I wanted to make out of you, apart from you not blowing your foot off with a shotgun, was a non-noble character. Our nation is afflicted with nobility, everybody wanting to reform somebody else.

"I take a little nip from time to time against the agues and aches, but your grandma thinks it's sinful, even though she'll take a little nip herself if she figures she's sick enough. But when I do it for fun, it's wrong, automatic. There ain't really a reason why anything that's fun ought to be wrong, but women are queer critters. I reckon you couldn't hardly call 'em human, but in the end they're necessary, or we wouldn't be here. But this is a distraction. What I had in mind was a simple injunction: don't be noble. It's wrecking the country."

"What's noble?" I asked.

"Well, it used to mean other things," the Old Man said. "It meant a man of gentle birth, which is to say gentleman, which is to say somebody whose papa had enough money so's he didn't have to soil his hands with toil. It was a part political, a part heredity, and a lot of who had what, such as more pigs than the next lad in the bog. Then it got degraded down to a mental level, with people thinking they were better than other people, due to having more pigs. Then they get a stern look on their faces and an urge to reform people who ain't as noble as they are, and bimeby somebody shoots 'em—somebody who ain't noble, I mean—and it all comes down to pigs. Do you follow me?"

"No. I ain't that noble."

"I see," he went on, "that you have picked up two deplorable habits from me—the use of the word 'ain't' and occasional flights of sheerest honesty. This will make you no friends, either, but will probably keep you from getting shot because of undue nobility. Are you tired of this?"

"Yessir," I said. "To be downright honest, you left me somewhere about halfway between Knox's Farm and Shallotte. About Lockwood's Folly, I'd say."

"Now there's a man I would of liked to of knowed—Lockwood," the Old Man mused. "I use the 'liked to of knowed' advisedly. Here is a man with a home on a crick and an urge to see the ocean in his own boat. So he spends years building the boat, and the boat is so fine and big he can't get it under the bridge on the crick, and it draws too much water anyhow; so he becomes immortal. They named the crick Lockwood's Folly. Such," he sighed, "is the material of which fame is constructed."

"How did we get started on this?" I asked.

"I don't really know," the Old Man replied. "I think I asked you an academic question, and got very little in the way of an answer. Something about politeness or some such. You wouldn't care to sneak into the attic, taking pains not to be seen by your grandmother, and get our fishing tackle, would you?"

"Yessir."

"That's what I like," the Old Man said. "A nice, polite boy who says 'yessir' to his elders. So many other boys would have said, 'No, sir. I want to go to Sunday school.' "

"It *is* Sunday, you know," I reminded him.

"If we play our cards right," the Old Man said, "we can get back in time for dinner, and tell Miss Lottie we went to church. Being noble, despite my warnings, has a certain amount of practical value, especially on Sunday morning when the fish are biting." He winked. "If we get caught, we can always tell her we went to the graveyard to study the archeological significance of early North Carolina tombs."

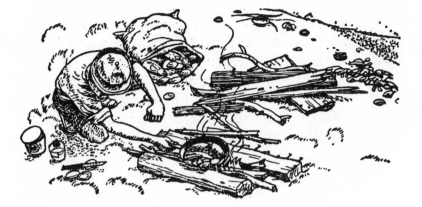

26

Christmas Always Comes Too Soon,
Which Is Ungruntling

The Old Man squinted at the sunny summer day, the washed sky lightly fleeced with cloud. He filled his pipe and lit it with great care. Then he puffed it into strong coal and pointed the stem at me.

"I don't care very much for you today," he said.

"What have I done bad now?"

"Nothing," the Old Man answered. "But you will. And that's got nothing whatsoever to do with the reason I'm not particularly fond of you today."

The Old Man raised me to be polite; so I was polite. "Why?" I asked.

"Because you're a boy," the Old Man said. "And I am an old man. And there are days when an old man looks at a boy and realizes what it is like to be a boy. And that makes the old man mad, because he can't ever be a boy any more."

Privately I reckoned that this was as useless a piece of confab as the Old Man ever unloaded. I didn't say anything at all.

"It's envy, of course," the Old Man said. "Just pure jealousy slightly complicated with rheumatism, sciatica, and the knowledge that all roads point only to the grave. I apologize for bringing up the subject. But I would like to leave you with one thought: Don't look forward to next Christmas. You'll just be six months older, and you can't get those six months back. And try to train yourself to milk the most out of any experience you're having at the moment, whether it's being kept after school or having the measles. Most of the things you do, you do only once, the right way, including whooping cough. I'll see you around."

The Old Man stuck his pipe in his mouth and stumped off. He was seldom if ever surly, but he was plainly what he called "ungruntled" today. He hadn't been really well for a long time, and I guess being sick was riding his nerves pretty hard.

All of a sudden I felt mighty miserable. You know how it is when you get used to a person—you can't see them change—and I was so used to the Old Man it never occurred to me that he was getting older all the time, and feebler, and maybe a little bit crankier. But now I watched him walking down the street, and he walked slower, and his feet sort of dragged, and his shoulders hunched more, and the thought suddenly struck me: He's getting *old* and so am I. It had never occurred to me, in a life where I waited for school to close, or Christmas to come, or the bird season to open, that I was merely marking time between one date and another, and wasting the hours in between. It never occurred to me that as the Old Man got older, so did I. All of a sudden the sun wasn't quite so bright, the sky was not so lovingly lined with soft cloud.

The Old Man used to say that most people looked but never saw anything. "Most people go through life," he told me once, "stone-blind with their eyes wide open. Anything from a chinch bug to a clam is interesting if you will really look at it and think about it." I was now beginning to understand what he meant.

I dived under the house and got the oars. I went to the attic and collected the cast net and a light fishing rod and the tackle box. I shouldered the lot and headed for the river. It never occurred to me that everything I did was dictated by something the old gent had told me. "Son," he would say, "when your heart is sick and you got some thinking to do, there ain't no substitute for a boat and a fish pole. Water eases the mind, soothes the eyes, calms the nerves, and you can always eat the fish."

I got into the boat and rowed out across the channel, the sun sparkling off the jolly little wind-tossed wavelets, and the smell of salt water and steaming marsh strong in my nose.

I don't know if you've ever been lucky enough to smell a salt mud marsh on a fresh summer's day, but this here Chanel No. 5 I read about can't smell near as good as just plain channel with the wind blowing off the marshes, fetching the smell of mud with a little bit of the cedars and cypress that line a sound mixed up in sun and grass and plain old mud full of sand-fiddler holes, oyster beds, and rotting clams. I never thought too much about a marsh, but it's really the richest piece of real estate in the world.

The life you don't see that goes on in a marsh is fantastic. There are little dark brown—almost black—marsh rabbits frisking about, and if you plod through the mud to a high hummock and turn a fice dog loose he will run any amount of rabbits past you. The quiet mink is hunting, stealthy as a serpent, and only once in a while you may see him swimming, making a tiny bow wave and leaving a neat and ripply wake behind him.

What I loved to hear was the bongo booming of the bitterns you never saw, and the cawing of the crows, and the occasional shrill scream of a lesser hawk as it swooped low and graceful over the tips of grass, looking, always looking, for something to swoop on and seize. The yellow-green of the marsh was spotted with great white herons, blue herons, and a rather droopy-looking heron we called a "cranky." The brilliant red epaulets of the blackbirds looked like rubies scattered in the grasses.

In the clear ponds the summer ducks paddled and dived, and the tiny didappers went under for unbelievable lengths of time. A long time ago I had given up shooting grebes and mergansers. They weren't any good to eat and no fun to shoot, and anyhow I'd rather watch them.

The sandpipers walked high-stilted along the edges of the sand bars, full of jerky dignity, and two oyster birds flew low along the water, big-billed and curious.

Just off the sand bars, in the mud, I drove an oar into the bottom and tethered my boat to it. Then I took the cast net and waded around until I saw a school of shrimp making little pops of water; two casts got me four or five dozen baits. A school of mullet was jumping—rather big ones, ten, twelve inches long— and the cast net took care of supper, even if I had no luck with the rod.

It was the time of year for soft crab, and I found half a dozen with my feet. A boy with nimble toes will always stumble over a clam or so, and by the time I got ready to unleash the boat, I had it pretty well stocked with crabs and kicking shrimp and mullet and big, blue-purple, white-lipped clams.

Don't let anybody kid you about a fishing hole. You can throw a bait all day long in ordinary water and get nothing but exercise, but if you know a deep sinkhole or an old wreck or some barnacled pilings, according to what you're looking for in the way of fish, you've got it fixed when you first drop your line. I rowed the little skiff to a hole I knew that was as certain a source of supply as a deep freezer, which had not at that time been invented. This hole was populous with blackfish and perch and an occasional trout—nothing grand, maybe, but powerful nice for the pan. I fished as happy as a boxful of birds for two hours, and filled the crocus sack I kept tied over the stern of the little boat. A half-pound of fish on a tiny rod seemed as big as a marlin in those days, and a two-pound weakfish was a whale.

In the boat's locker I always kept a frying pan, some cornmeal, salt, pepper, and vinegar. Driftwood was no problem on a sand bar, and I had myself a North Carolina approximation of a shore dinner when the fish quit biting and my stomach started to growl. There is nothing really wrong with soft-shell crabs, fresh clams, and fish that don't stop kicking until they feel the flame, not if you are a boy and starving and all by yourself in a boundless burning sweep of sand and marsh and sky and water.

When I washed the skillet clean with sand and salt water, wiped the grease off my hands and face, stomped out the fire, and got back into the boat, the tide was running strongly out, and shoving the skiff along was a job for a whole set of galley slaves. The sun was hitting like it always hits around three or four, hotter than the noonday sun, and by the time I got back to the shingle I was pouring sweat.

It was a simple enough matter to drag the boat up on the shingle and then walk down to the pier for a fast jump into the water. When I collected what was left of the fish and clams and crabs and shouldered the oars and the rowlocks and the cast net, I was just about barely able to make it to the house.

The Old Man was sitting on the porch, smoking his pipe and rocking gently in his favorite chair. He looked like he felt better. He looked younger. "What you been doing?" he asked unnecessarily.

"I went out in the boat," I said. "I went fishing."

"See anything interesting you want to tell me about?" he asked.

"Nothing very much," I said. "It was just the same old thing, marsh, water, fish, birds—same old thing."

"I am not being rude when I call you a little liar," the Old Man said. "It is a term of respect, not to say endearment. I apologize for this morning all over again, and I am no longer jealous of you because I am not a boy. Go wash the mud off you and come to supper. We're having steak, as I figgered you've had a bait of fish for one day."

The Old Man smiled. "I really wouldn't want to be a boy again," he said. "It's too much work."

27

Terrapin Stew Costs Ten Bucks a Quart

"Things," the Old Man said, "certainly ain't like they used to be. It's the penalty we pay for getting wise. About the time a man decides what he likes or don't like, either he can't find it, can't afford it, or can't handle it. I can sum it all up with the diamondback terrapin."

"Yessir," I said politely. It was September, and we were just setting around waiting for the moon to full so the tides would rise and give us some marsh-hen shooting. There isn't much else to shoot in September but doves, marsh hen, and the odd squirrel, but the leaves are too thick on the squirrel trees, and it's a little bit too hot to shoot doves.

"All the wisdom of the world is centered in the diamondback," the Old Man said. "If you ain't too busy, I will proceed to elucidate."

"I ain't too busy," I said. "School hasn't even started yet, and there's too many snakes in the woods to train the puppies. Pray do proceed," I said, and snickered. I had got a wayward *ain't* mixed up with some of the Old Man's occasional high-flung phrases.

"Well, even today, as poor as everybody is, with the depression and all, a terrapin stew costs you ten dollars a quart. In a hotel it'll cost you three-fifty a plate if you can get it at all. This means that I couldn't buy it, even if I could eat it. And I can't eat it, because it's too rich, for one thing, and another reason is that you have to make it with a decent sherry wine. With this goldanged Prohibition, you can't get any decent sherry wine. And if you could buy it, the doctors say it would be bad for my blood pressure or something. So between scarcity, poverty, Prohibition, and the gout, I am not a candidate for any terrapin stew. It shows you the futility of living too long."

The Old Man heaved a sigh.

"Boy, you know you're getting old when you start saying, 'Things ain't like they used to be.' But you're right, every time. Because things *ain't* like they used to be. There was a time when I was younger a Nigra never came out of a marsh without half a bushel of terrapin he'd dug out of holes, and he'd be happy to sell them for a nickel apiece—cows, that is. They are bigger than the bulls. Cows run about seven inches, and it takes them nine years to mature. Bulls never run more than about five inches across the belly shell, so the colored people would sell them for three cents. Now they get from three to five dollars for a grown terrapin, just because they got fished out in the nineties. Every rich politician that ever threw a dinner had to have terrapin as a staple."

The Old Man sighed again.

"I used to go up to Maryland to visit your Uncle Howard, when he had a lot of money and was consorting with governors and breeding horses. Seems like we never had but one type of dinner. After the early whisky they brought you Chincoteague oysters as big as a wharf rat. Then they laid on the terrapin stew. Then they fed you breasts of canvasback duck with stripes of red ham, and from there you went to the brandy and the cigars. I say canvasbacks, because you could buy a brace of four-pounders for two bits. It would have been an insult to feed a guest anything but cans, unless mebbe once in a while pintail. But now you're hard put to find a canvasback. The meat gunners shot 'em out because they were so popular."

"How did they shoot them?" I asked. "I mean how would you shoot them to sell for the pot?" I was always more interested in techniques than in the Old Man's philosophy. But I got pretty philosophic myself. I knew I couldn't have the one without holding still for the other.

"Well, they used punt guns, for one thing. They would take a flat-bottomed boat and secure a smoothbore cannon to her bows. They would load the cannon to the gunnels with anything you could imagine, from nails to stones to bullets. Then they would wait for a big freeze-up, so the ducks were rafted in little pools in the marsh, surrounded by paper-thin ice. They would go out at night, poling through the ice, and come up on a pool which would be jammed with ducks. They'd let fly with the punt gun, and the punt would jump, and there would be two score or more of dead ducks in the pool.

"Then, of course, they'd bait blinds, and then use hens to call in the high-flyers. The hen would stand on her tail and let out a chuckle-chuckle, and the men ducks would come down in swarms, and the pot hunters would loose off with 10-bores. Ducks used to be a lot stupider in those days, because there were more of them and fewer people were shootin' at 'em. Wildfowl was standard on any two-bit hotel menu. But we ate better in and around Baltimore than any place else I was ever at. It was a big part German, and Germans take a powerful fancy to their vittles."

"How did you cook the terrapins?"

"There was a lot of ways, but I still like the Maryland way

best. Saying you got two mature terrapins—and can afford them —you would get a pint, more or less, of meat. You pop in a pound of butter and a couple pints of Jersey cream, throw in a big slug of sherry and some seasoning, bring her to a boil—and, son, that is a stew that makes my gouty foot hurt just to think of it. They talk about turtle soup and stuff. Nobody ever touched terrapin for flavor and substance."

"How did you find them in the old days?" I asked. "Could I maybe find some now?"

"Not here, I reckon. They seem to have gone away. But away back yonder they had little feisty dogs they called terrapin hounds. They used to get them in the winter, because terrapins burrow in the mud and hibernate just like a bear sleeps away the cold months in a cave. They leave a little air hole in the mud, and dogs could spot it. This ain't surprising if you remember how many times you've seen a good bird dog false-point on a horse-turd terrapin or a snake. They got a definite musty smell. Then the darkies would dig 'em out and sell them. When I was a boy, in the slave days, seems to me I recollect they fed terrapin to the slaves because there is some sort of superstition that terrapins encourage breeding. Whether's anything to it, I couldn't say."

Being what used to be popularly known as a greedygut, I saw I had the Old Man going on food, and wished to keep him on the skillet and out of philosophy.

"Tell me some more about the olden days," I said. "What else was easy to eat that you can't get much of now?"

"Well, I never ate any buffalo hump, because that was before my time, and I got a hunch it was overrated. Also we never had too many buffalo in these parts. But I reckon you would have to go a far piece to beat quail on toast for breakfast, just the breasts of course, and a broiled soft-shell crab ain't exactly obnoxious. Today you can't buy quail except illegal. In the old times they didn't shoot them. They trapped them, and you weren't always digesting a No. 8 shot.

"I never ate any plover's eggs or hummingbird tongues, or anything fancy like that, but if you cook a rabbit right, it's hard to beat for tasty provender. I like 'em both better than venison, no matter how much wine and butter you shove into the saddle. To me the best venison is fresh-killed, with the chops and the liver broiled over hickory coals, when you're tired and hungry and just getting warm in front of the fire, after a couple of taps at the jug. Somehow venison in a hotel seems a little bit wicked. A deer don't belong in a hotel, dead or alive, but it was a poor hotel that couldn't give you the whole list of wild stuff, including bear steaks."

"What else?"

"Well, I suppose you know I fancy a little piece of whisky once in a while. Before that *man* Volstead put his act in, a man could buy a decent bottle of whisky for about a dollar, and if he drank in a saloon, he could get himself a shot of bonded stuff in quiet, refined surroundings, without any women in the bar, for ten cents. Not like this white poison they age with brown sugar and sell in fruit jars. A decent red whisky was a comfort to a man instead of an enemy. And the beer come honest out of a bung on a keg that the beer had got friendly with. It cost a nickel, and the free lunch was unlimited."

"I never heard of free lunch," I said. "What was it all about?"

"Free lunch was an invention of the angels, thought up by honest bartenders to encourage the purchase of beer and to prevent drunkenness in the clients, so they could buy more beer without making a nuisance out of themselves. When I was a younker a man with two nickels could feed like a king. The bartender was a little suspicious if you dug into the grub on the strength of one beer, but when you bellied up and ordered the second, you were a guest of the house and could eat your head off."

"What did they give you?"

The Old Man smiled wistfully, then blissfully licked his lips.

"Everything," he said. "There would be a big glass crock of pickled pig's feet, and a wooden pair of scissors to fish them out of the brine with. There would be a bowl of hard-boiled eggs, naturally, and another bowl of raw onions. Some barkeeps fancied hot roast beef, others liked cold tongue or cold beef, but they all competed to see who set out the best free lunch. There was usually a big loaf of salami, a bowl of mulligan, and nearly anything the Germans liked—sardines, herring, and all sorts of cheeses. A man drinking whisky could run the course. A man drinking beer had to pace himself a little, so the beer could keep up with the vittles.

"When Prohibition come, and they started making this needle beer and inventing whisky in the barn and sending people blind with the staggers, the country died. Whisky, legal, might come back some day, but I vow there won't be any more free lunch to go with it. Things won't ever be like they used to be."

"What went wrong with it all?" I asked.

"They shot off the buffalo, and they meat-hunted the game. They slaughtered the wildfowl, and they give the vote to the women. The women stirred up a ruckus about their menfolks spending too much time in the saloons, and so they got Prohibition and handmade corn whisky and what they call 'speak-easies' in the cities, where you can drink gin that was made out of embalming fluid and go blind for twice the price. They invented the automobile and the airy-o-plane and speeded everything up. They got mixed up in other people's wars and got to betting on the stock market and altogether they're in a hell of a mess. And *no* free lunch."

"Any cure for it?"

"Not much," the Old Man said. "People ain't like they used to be, either. A bunch of smart alecks, running around in circles like beheaded chickens, dancing the Charleston, and raising hell in general. They tell me some fellows won't dance with a girl without she takes her corsets off."

"I wouldn't know about that," I said. "But I do know I'm hungry, and that moon tells me tomorrow's high tide, and we'll be up early. Let's go down to Pete's and get a hamburger or something."

The Old Man spat.

"A *hamburger*," he said, as if it was a cuss word. "A *hamburger*, at my age. Like I said, things ain't like they used to be. But I suppose from some standpoints, they never were."

"I ain't been feeling so good lately," the Old Man said to me one day. "I think I need a change of air. I think I need to go to Baltimore for a physical check-up at Johns Hopkins. At my age a feller can't be too mindful of his health. And anyhow, Howard writes that the pheasant season is going to open next week. If you was to play your cards right I might talk your ma into forgiving you a week of school and take you with me. We can drive her easy in a day."

I had been driving the car for quite a spell now, although I wasn't old enough for a license, and nothing could have pleased me better than the idea of (1) missing a week of school, (2) shooting some pheasants, and (3) seeing some fresh real estate. The Old Man was always talking about Maryland, and he made it sound like the Promised Land. His friend, Mister Howard, had this big horse farm up in the Blue Ridge foothills, and from all I could gather from the tall talk, the pheasants and quail just about beat you to death when you got off the back porch.

The Old Man made some hocus-pocus with my ma, and somebody called school and got me paroled for a week, and we set off on my first big safari. You'd of thought we were going to Africa, instead of just Baltimore. We had a lunch packed, and the guns stowed, and road maps, and all sorts of clutter. I was strong for taking our dogs, but the Old Man, he said no, Howard had more dogs than he knew what to do with, and ours would just add to the confusion.

We set bravely off in the Liz, hoping she'd hold together, but glad we had a car of her virgin determination, because good roads were scarce in those days, and that Virginia red clay as you approach Fredericksburg and Richmond was a caution. Fortunately it was dry enough, but it rained on the way back, and it was as greasy as lard and twice as slippery.

It was a handsome piece of country then, with very few roadside advertisements to wreck the beauty of the rolling green hills, dark forests, and mile after mile of golden farmland. After you got out of Washington, heading toward Baltimore, it got prettier and prettier as it got hillier. Thinking back, Maryland looked more like a classic slice of English countryside than a classic slice of English countryside actually looks today. It was horsy country, and nearly every big holding had literally miles of white rail fences, with neat paddocks and immaculate barns and outhouses. The houses didn't just sit up naked in a flat piece of land, like they did in Carolina, but were kind of folded into the hills, and peeped through from thick trees. The miles of rolling pasture were either golden with wheat or brilliant, golf-course green—dotted here and there by golden or black-and-white cattle or grazing red horses.

Maryland was one of our very earliest "civilized" states, I suppose, and the English who followed the Calverts had plenty of time—and not too many angry Injuns—to make it into a graceful replica of what they remembered back home in England. And to a kid accustomed to live-oak and cyprus swamps, and clean-swept sand for front yards, and low, marshy mosquito-and-sandspur country, this was a picture-book adventure.

We stopped in Baltimore long enough for the Old Man to make his hospital arrangements, and then we went to some restaurant he seemed to know pretty well. He fished his greasy old wallet out of his pocket, thumbed through some bills, and nodded.

"You remember what I told you about terrapin stew and canvasback duck?" he said. "Well, it'll nigh break us, but I aim to have us a bait. Might be the last I'll have. It ain't on the menu, but if I know anything about this place, they'll have a duck or so on ice and some cooters in a barrel hid out in the yard."

He called the gray-haired Negro waiter, and whispered something, and I could see a bill pass and a flash of white teeth.

"Yassuh, *boss*," he said, and went flat-footed away. The Old Man grinned.

"I dearly love money," he said. "It'll get you so many pleasant things, and you don't have to rely on friendship. I took one look at that waiter and just naturally assumed that although that such-and-so of a Volstead run that Prohibition abomination through, they hadn't quit making red licker in Maryland. The grass here is just too good and the water too fine to pay any attention to the likes of Volstead. You're getting on to be a big boy, and I want you started off right on this grog business. What you are going to have is a proper Maryland old-fashioned, made with proper Maryland rye. We are going to have some sherry in the stew, and we will drink a glass of Burgundy with the duck. Thank God for Lord Baltimore. He could have been a red-nosed Puritan that thinks boiled salt cod is a banquet and rum punch fit to be a table wine."

The waiter shuffled back, grinning.

"Heah yo' *tea*, boss," he said, and put down two fat square glasses with a reddish liquid in them. "We always serves *tea* in glasses heah, boss," he said. "They tells me it is the fashion in Europe." The Old Man winked and the waiter guffawed. Then the Old Man picked up his glass, sniffed, smiled, raised it in a toast, and said to me: "Drink yo' *tea*, boss," mimicking the waiter. "But sip it, don't slug it down like an ignorant tar-heel from Brunswick County."

I sipped slowly on my first legal drink of illegal whisky. I had tried our local home-stomped scuppernong wine, and our local home-brew, and our local moonshine, but it was nothing like this mellow, charred-keg rye, with just a touch of bitters, a cherry, some sugar, and a slice of orange over the ice. I grinned and smacked my lips. The Old Man looked stern.

"You hold in your hand," he said, "man's best friend and worst enemy, depending on how you use him. He's been a firm friend of mine for over fifty years, but I never saw too much of him. Any friendship goes sour if you overdo it."

The waiter brought the terrapin stew, so hot it bubbled in the dish, and I won't even try to describe what can be done with butter, terrapin eggs, sherry, Jersey cream, and clear terrapin meat. Then the waiter brought in a brace of canvasback. "These powerful unusual *chicken*, boss," he said. He fetched a bottle of what I can only describe as another kind of tea, except this was red in color, and might have been described as having been made from grapes. I was in a state of complete contentment when we finished the coffee and headed in the direction of Ellicott City. The Old Man was driving, and it seemed to me that the Liz rambled a little.

I was sound asleep when we arrived at Mister Howard's place, and they just slung me into bed. I was lost for a minute when I woke up with vestiges of my first hang-over. I washed my face in the basin and put on some clothes and found my way downstairs. The Old Man and Mister Howard were already working on breakfast. They looked almost like twins as they shoved eggs and bacon past the same kinds of ragged mustaches. Mister Howard stood up and shook hands and laughed.

"You sure have come on since that last camping trip we made," he said. "Ned says you were pretty far gone in drink when you arrived last night. I thought it was for the young folks to put the old folks to bed, not the other way round."

"I was tired," I said defensively. "It was a long day."

"Well, have some breakfast," Mister Howard said, "and I'll show you around the place. And I wouldn't be surprised, if we had the foresight to take a dog or so and a gun, we might manage to produce a pheasant for you."

I gobbled some food and went to look at the house. Dimly remembered, it was the kind of house which was too good for women, if you know what I mean. Mister Howard came from an Irish aristocracy which thought horses and guns were more important than anything else in the world. The rooms were huge and filled with horse prints and hunting scenes, plus a few family portraits. The women were all pretty and the gentlemen all looked very well fed.

The sideboards and glass cases were filled with stuffed birds, everything from pheasants to orioles to quail to turkeys. The walls were dotted with foxes' masks and brushes, because this was prime fox-hunting country. There were portraits of horses and cows and bulls receiving blue ribbons, because Mister Howard's blooded stock committed suicide if it failed to hit a blue.

Everywhere you looked there was riding tackle—saddles and boots, surcingles, crops, spurs. The leather gear was old and mellow, as mellow as the hand-waxed floors. There was a wonderful smell of good pipe tobacco, saddle wax, and oily guns, and an even better smell of ancient leather-bound books, which were shoved by the hundreds into cases which covered whole walls.

There were guns everywhere—Revolutionary muskets, dueling pistols, modern rifles and shotguns, hung on the walls in brackets or standing in corners or lying in red-plush-lined cases in the halls. I remember that next to some of the guns and china figurines there were great flat silver bowls full of flowers, red and yellow roses mostly. The chairs, except for the polished mahogany of the dining room suite, were all of leather, deep, rump-sprung, broad-armed easy chairs and vast divans, some maroon, some deep forest green, some honest black.

Everything in that house had been lovingly used for generations—the heavy, worn silver table service, the old Wedgwood plates, the boots, the saddles, the guns, and the books—especially the books. There wasn't a book on the wall, whether it had to do with stock registration or the novels of Ouida, *Black Beauty* or the complete set of Dickens, that hadn't been rubbed smooth by handling.

In the center of each room was a fireplace a tall man could walk into, with enormous wrought-iron dog-irons and fireboxes and hobs to hold great kettles. Every bed I ever saw upstairs was a four-poster big enough for four people, and there was a fireplace in every room, including the bathroom. The tub, I recall, was an enormous thing, with the ceramic set into a huge walnut coffin sort of arrangement. The accompanying sanitary utensil was similarly set into walnut, with a removable bottom, such as today are expensively used to make liquor cabinets.

Outside, there seemed to be six acres of flowers, even though it was autumn. The green meadows rolled as far as the eye could see, until they hit the haze of the Blue Ridge. Streams cut through the pasture and paddocks, twisting silver threads among the green of the clovered paddocks, and accented, from time to time, by copses of trees.

The barns were a jolly hunting-coat red, and every fence was a glistening white, as clean as a dogtooth. There seemed to be about two acres of fowlyard alone, cut into littler paddocks, one for chickens, one for turkeys, one for ducks, another for pheasant, another for guinea fowl. Big black-and-white Holsteins and Jerseys the color of their own cream were in the milch-cow paddocks. The saddle stock was also confined, sixteen-hands-high Irish jumpers, but afar, in the vaster areas, barrel-bellied mares nudged their high-stilted colts, and yearlings gamboled like lambs. The breeding studs were in loose boxes with small yards, and the beef cattle, white-faced Herefords, roamed to the horizon.

Everywhere you looked there was a dog run. Hounds of all shapes and descriptions—bassets, beagles, Walkers. Spaniels, mostly springers but for a gross or so of golden cockers. Labradors—for this was duck country, down to the Eastern Sho'—and pointers and setters in legions. They set up a clamor fit to wake the dead as we passed, Mister Howard beating his riding boots with his crop.

The sky was a clear, sparkling blue, with a hint of cloud, and the morning frost had melted under the friendly sun. A small breeze stirred the trees. A quail called, and there was the harsh squawk of a pheasant. A horse whinnied, a cow lowed, and the dogs barked. Mister Howard pointed to a big black Gordon setter, and then to a husky black-and-white springer. "We'll just take Mac and Sue," he said. "Mac's the Gordon, of course. Between them, they invented pheasants. Get your gun and we'll put some meat in the pot. That is, of course, if you haven't lost interest in hunting?"

I declared firmly that the interest was undamaged, and I made a private reservation to have a house and property like that some day. Of course I never did, and never will, but in a way it's as well. For I can remember the house, and no pipes ever burst in my remembered house, no bank ever forecloses a mortgage, nobody ever dies, and no stranger buys the books and guns and saddles and beasts at a knockdown auction.

I still have clear title to the sight of the two old men, as we followed Mac and Sue over an undulating pasture toward a patch of bush where there would just naturally have to be a big, fat, sassy green-headed pheasant with my name on his tail.

28

But Not on Opening Day

Now you know your first big cock pheasant is a sight to see. There maybe ain't nothing as dramatic, whether it's an elephant or a polar bear. A cock pheasant is like a mallard duck. Maybe the pintail or the canvasback is better to eat, but there is nothing in the flying department as wonderfully gaudy as a cock pheasant or a he-mallard. Well, *maybe* a peacock, but we have so few peacocks around our neck of the woods.

You take a big cock pheasant, and you shoot him, you got a real bird in your hand. He'll weigh about four pounds, and he has this lovely long tail, and he has a ring on his neck, and he is colored green and red and brown and white, and he even has ears you can see. He is not so much dinner as trophy, but when he is cooked correctly, he is not so much trophy as dinner, if you see what I mean.

Mister Howard, he said to me after we quit looking around his farm in Maryland, "You don't want to make any mistakes about pheasants, boy. He looks like he is two yards long, and he looks mighty slow. But when you subtract his neck and his tail you are shooting at a pretty small target. He flies faster than a bobwhite, or so I'm told, and he sheds shot like a duck. I'd lead him pretty far and then double it. No man ever killed a cock pheasant by shooting it in the tail. All you get that way is feathers."

I can skip telling you about the first pheasant, since he is still alive, so far as I know. Mac, the Gordon setter, rounded him up for me in a patch of bush. He had a bell on his neck—Mac, I mean—and we heard it stop tinkling when he went into some scraggy sumach. Then he came out and kind of beckoned with his head.

"Got a bird," Mister Howard said. "You stand over there, and I'll put Sue on the flank and send Mac into the bush to flush him. If he tries to run, Sue'll nail him." Sue was a big springer who had a kind of casual air of saying, *What do we need a gun for, when we got me and Mac?*

The Old Man nodded at Mister Howard and winked when the Gordon setter dived back into the bush. I reckon the old boy knew what was going to happen.

There was an outraged squawk inside the brambles, a rapid beating of wings, and something—it might have been a bird or possibly the Graf Zeppelin—erupted in my general direction. It seemed to be less than a hundred yards long, and I could swear it was not actually breathing fire. Otherwise I never saw such a production in my life.

I shot at this thing twice, and it went away with very little damage, although one tail feather got dislodged, very possibly due to the imminence of the moulting season, or something.

Mister Howard looked at me while I was breaking the gun to recharge it.

"I told you," he said. "They ain't really that big. You just figure that you're shooting a teal, and we might eat tonight. Lead it. *Lead* it."

We walked across a meadow, were snubbed by several cows, and Sue, the springer, wagged her tail assembly and then fell on her belly. Mac, the Gordon, took a wide cast and came up in front of her, about fifty yards away.

"Now watch this," Mister Howard said. "You just stand behind Sue. I'll call Mac in, and he'll drive that bird right into Susie's nose. A pheasant ain't dumb. With Mac behind him and Sue in front of him and us here with weapons, he'll fly. But he'll fly slanchwise. To your left. And *lead* him. Three times his length, anyhow."

Mac came mincing in, putting his feet in front of him pad by pad. I looked at the ground ahead of me, wanting to see the pheasant before he flew.

"You *know* better than that," the Old Man said. "I *taught* you better than that. You look at the air where the bird's going to be when he jumps. What kind of raisin' will Howard think you've had?"

It was indeed a sight I never wish to forget. Mac came in so close that he was nearly rubbing noses with Sue. Somewhere in between a big green-headed cock pheasant jumped, squawked, and took off, like Mister Howard said, to the left. I hauled the gun ahead of him and squeezed off, and down he came like an aircraft, almost in flames. Sue went over and picked him up gently, fetched him to Mister Howard, reared with her front paws on his coat, and dropped the bird into his hand.

"Nice shooting," Mister Howard said. "You led that one, didn't you?"

"Yessir," I said. "May I touch him, please?"

"I forgot," Mister Howard said to the Old Man, handing me the pheasant. "I forgot how big a first pheasant is to a boy. It's kind of like an early squirrel. He is a little bit larger than a later lion."

If Christmas came on the Fourth of July and it also hap-

pened to be your birthday, you might have some idea of what
a first pheasant is like on a clear, crisp Maryland day, with the
hills behind, and the tender-green meadows reaching out to
black-green blotches of trees, and nothing very much to do but
watch a couple of expert dogs work over the noblest Oriental
stranger we have in our midst, while two mellowed old gentlemen do not interfere with a boy's passionate effort. They were
not shooting; they had been there before. It took me another
thirty years to find out how much fun you have *not* shooting
if there is somebody else around who wants to shoot it more
than you do.

On this day I wanted to shoot it more than they did, and
they knew it, and I think possibly the dogs knew it. They were
working for me like I was a corporation or something. It was
a conspiracy, the two Old Men and the dogs working to teach
me the pheasant business.

One thing happened I want to tell you about. I winged a
bird, and it flew into the side of a hill. There was a hole, like
a little cave, in the side of the hill. The big Gordon, Mac,
tiptoed gently on a narrow ledge until he got to where he could
see inside the hole in the hill. He dabbed tentatively with his
paw and found it dangerously awkward. He then walked backward, gingerly, until he achieved wider ground. Then he raced
over the top of the hill until he came to the ledge on the other
side of the hole.

This was a broader ledge. He walked now with assurance.
He came up to the hole, and he clawed in it with his right fore-
foot, and he brushed the bird out of the hole. The bird was
still very much alive.

Mac took the bird in his mouth and backed carefully down
the ledge until it widened into a safe position. Then Mac released the pheasant, which tumbled down the hill. Mac slid
down the hill on his backside, the bird scrambling along beside
him. They reached the base of the hill together. Mac pounced
on the bird, cracked its neck with one bite, picked it up gently,
and fetched it to Mister Howard. Mac—believe me, it's true—

shrugged his shoulders, as if to say, "For heaven's sake, from now on, kill 'em clean and save me some trouble. I'm afraid of heights, and this kind of work constitutes overtime."

We had quite a day. I hit some and I missed some, until we had accumulated six cocks. Six cock pheasants are a pleasant load for a boy to sweat back to the handsomest house in Maryland. The Old Man carried my gun. I insisted on carrying the birds. When my back began to creak I wondered how it was possible to miss something so big. I have been wondering about this for several years now. It's still possible.

There have been times since when days were especially special, when the sun was bright, the breeze fresh, and the dogs and the birds motivated by a general desire to please. But I cannot confuse those days with the sort of tender, happy sadness that I garnered from the Old Man and his final pheasant hunt, with a child he had raised from a pup, in the company of his best, most trusted friend.

I suppose I had the usual insensitivity of the child to possible tragedy, but it seems to me now that the Old Man knew that he had eaten his last terrapin stew and his final canvasback, and had seen his ultimate pheasant. This may sound silly, but you could kind of see it in his mustache, which appeared a bit wilty.

We went back, three grown men together, with the pheasants. I cleaned them and felt it a pity to remove so much beauty from a bird. I felt almost like a cannibal when Mister Howard said, "Damn this business of hanging them until they're rotten, we'll eat a couple tonight. They'll be a little tough, but jelly and wine and bacon strips can do a power of good to ease up the toughness."

The fire was lit and blazing chirpily in the stone fireplace when we returned. There was a tray of drinks on the table, and the Old Man showed no hesitancy in offering me a sherry. It was Bristol Cream. I had two. I was reaching for the decanter for No. 3 when the Old Man said, gently, "Let's not overdo it, son. You can't get to be a man in a day."

It was an enchanted week we spent, before we went back to Baltimore and Johns Hopkins, to find out what the Old Man knew all along was wrong with him. We got the doctors' reports and drove home. The old man was silent for most of the way.

When we got to a place called Jackie's Creek, where we had seen turkeys and shot quail, the Old Man said, "Stop the car. I want to look at it."

When we got to a place called Allen's Creek, and Moore's Creek, he said the same thing. We stopped and we looked. The Old Man nodded his head, and said, for no reason at all that I could think of, "I'm satisfied. Nobody owes me nothin'."

We pulled up in front of the live oaks that clustered round the house. The Old Man looked at the magnolia where the mockingbird had lived, and smiled.

"It'll last," he said. "It's a very durable tree."

We accepted congratulations freely for a safe return trip, and then the Old Man said, "Let's take a little walk and let the womenfolk get over their excitement. I got a thing or two to tell you."

We strolled down the street toward the Cedar Bench, next to the pilot office, where I used to steal the cream crackers and drink the hot tea with the sickly sweet condensed milk. We sat on the Cedar Bench, uncomfortably, because it was intricately carved with everybody's jackknifed initials.

"I ain't got to tell *you* that I am going to die," the Old Man said. "*You* would know it. You've had the best of me, and you're on your own from now on. You'll go to college next year, and you'll be a man, with all a man's problems, and there won't be no Old Man around to steer you. I raised you as best I could and now *you're* the Old Man, because I'm tired, and I think I'll leave."

My eyes blurted into tears, and I said all the things young people say in the presence of death.

"Leave it, *leave* it," the Old Man said. "Like I always told you, if there was a way to beat it, I would have heard about it. It'll even happen to *you*, unlikely as it seems."

"But *how, when, why?*" I said, for lack of anything better.

The Old Man lit his pipe very carefully and grinned under his ragged mustache.

"I promise you," he said, "on my word of honor, I won't die on the opening day of the bird season."

He kept his promise.

The Old Man's Boy
Grows Older

ROBERT RUARK

illustrated with line drawings

BY WALTER DOWER

This book is

for two grown-up small boys,

who once shared an idea in a rowboat.

I do not recall that we caught any fish,

but the idea was a beaut.

Contents

THE OLD MAN'S BOY GROWS OLDER

FOREWORD

A Word from the Boy

It's a popular pastime among adults, when the hair begins to gray and the aches of middle age grow more steadily persistent, to look back on the prodigious deeds of their youth and proclaim that we've all gone soft and that they don't make boys like that any more. The Old Man had a theory about this. He said that as a man grew older the miles that he used to walk to the Little Red Schoolhouse grew longer.

"I am convinced," he said, "that what schoolin' I had took place no farther than half a mile from the homestead, but the older I get the longer the trip seems to get. If you asked me right fast how far I walked through the snow I reckon I'd say ten mile without battin' an eye."

I wasn't paying too much attention to what the old gentleman was saying, except I caught the word "snow." It was steamy August, and I was torturing the crank handle of an ice-cream freezer. Or, rather, the crank was torturing me. Sweat was streaming down my face, and only the promise of being allowed to lick the dasher kept me grunting at the task, as the cream in the cylinder, surrounded by a mixture of cracked ice and rock salt, got stiff and stiffer.

When it became almost immovably stiff the ice cream was done, and I would be onto that smoothly creamy wooden paddle like a duck on a June bug, and there would be wonderful chunks of frozen peaches making lovely hillocks under the satin surface of the ice cream. This was known as solider's pay or extra incentive, and I was allowed an even start on the bulk of the ice cream with the family. I usually came out ahead despite impost.

It seems to me that this was the best ice cream ever tooled by the hand of man, when you consider the miracles one used to work with Jersey cream, sugar, eggs, and vanilla extract, with a few peach nuggets or cherries stirred into the mixture. They don't make ice cream like that today. They don't make life that way today either.

This sobering thought occurred sharply as I was smitten by a violent crick in the back the other day, when I was trying to recapture my misty youth by producing some home-churned ice cream instead of sending somebody to the store for a carton or merely reaching down into the freezer for a rock-hard package that generally tastes of the same old sawdust, no matter how brilliant the stripes.

I reckon that in recent years I've ruined an awful lot of good meat cooking out of doors in pursuit of youth. I will go fishing or camping just for the fun of being frozen or sunstruck, fly bit or mosquito chewn—anything at all as long as it's uncomfortable. I am a sucker for picnics, and savor anything at all to eat if it's either raw or burnt and has sand in it.

In recent years I have consumed elephant heart, raw antelope liver, and half-cooked sand grouse or gazelle chops—meat that had been flying through the air or gamboling on the plains a few short minutes before. Let me catch a fish and I'm not happy until I've given it a clay pack and shoved it into the coals. If it comes out half raw it doesn't hurt the taste, even on a tongue that may have been jaded by thirty years of nicotine and honed smooth by prohibition gin.

But it is true that things were different when I was a boy, and the Old Man represented the irretrievable mystery of yesteryear. I do not suppose that I would get very far in interesting today's crop of nippers in what to me was high sport and great fun some thirty to thirty-five years a-past. It was altogether too simple then for this age of television and ballet in the circus. Progress, like nearly everything else, is relative, and I often wonder if its benefits are entirely undiluted.

Most of the fine things we did in the long-buried days happened out of doors. The seasons were sharply etched on the calendar as to potential. Winter was the infrequent snow, with icicles to suck and snow ice cream to be made, and traps for rabbits and the little snowbirds and waxwings that miraculously appeared with the first powdering. The traps were simple. A box was tilted and propped with a stick that had a cord attached. A trail of bread crumbs led to the box, and when the prey entered the trap you gave the cord a twitch from your hiding place and the box fell, imprisoning your quarry. Then the only problem was getting the birds out, and they usually flew free.

A thin skin of ice on the sweet-water ponds made duck hunting easier, because the ducks rafted in clumps and bunches in open water and were loath to fly in the flurrying snow. Somehow all animals and birds seemed tamer and easier to hunt in the snow, and it was tremendous fun to track a deer instead of running him with hounds.

Springtime was strawberry time and green peaches time and bellyache time and—blessed of all the blesseds—getting-out-of-school time. As May nudged lazily into June and the bobolinks swayed atop the long grasses and the black cherries sweated sweetness as their trees oozed jewels of gum the medicine cabinet took quite a thrashing and the castor oil lowered its level in the penance bottle. And it was time to swim again, strictly against parental orders, so you swam anyhow, and the goose-pimpling waters were rendered doubly pneumonically delicious by their very illegality.

Summer, with the horrors of the schoolhouse all but for-gotten, was a steady diet of fishing and swimming. There were some summer camps, even in my time—up in the mountains mostly. These were basically created for parents who wanted their children out of their hair for six weeks or so, and so re-manded them to a kind of benevolent concentration camp with supervised archery, boating, swimming, hiking, campfire-mak-ing, basket-weaving, and suchlike.

The nicest thing about August was that it was a sort of preparatory school for September, when the real adult action started: when you started to train the puppies seriously, when the dove season opened, when the big nor'easters swelled the tides and fetched the marsh hens into sight, when the big blue-fish and the channel bass supplanted the inside fish as a point of interest.

October gave you squirrels and chinquapins glossy brown on the bushes, alum-tart persimmons wrinkling, and the quail call-ing sweetly in the dusk, still innocently secure from the fusillade that would greet them in November. That was when it really got frosty and the undergrowth withered. The necks of the buck deer swelled, and you could hear the big fellows scraping the last of the velvet off their antlers and snorting in the thick-ets.

I tried to put some of all this on paper, and once it got going it came with a rush. It was exactly as if the stuff had been locked away, waiting for someone to shove a key in the door and let it all come tumbling out. The first of this outpouring made a companion book called *The Old Man and the Boy.*

Often the material almost wrote itself. I suspect that in re-porting the fevered present I had somehow forgotten the old things: the smell of Christmas in a country house; the bugling of hounds hot after a coon; the sight of the wizened old Chinaman's face of a possum curled in a tight ball in a persimmon tree; a colored boy singing to keep off the hants as he drove the cow home through the lowering evening woods; the spumy smash of norther-driven waves on a lonely beach; the rich swelling of song at a colored camp meeting; the convivial gaiety at an oyster roast, when the fruit jar passed freely in the shadows and the square dancers struck up a slightly unsteady reel.

The Old Man and the Boy made me think, made me fine-tooth-comb my memory. The smell of Christmas is a case in point. The old-fashioned Christmas smell was predominantly that of crushed evergreens against the constant resiny scent of a snapping fire. One was a cool smell, the other hot, but both joined forces in delightful companionship. This aromatic backdrop was overlaid by the heady odors that drifted from the kitchen, the sage which went into the turkey stuffing predominating.

The whole was tinctured with spices and by alcohol, because brandies and wines were lavishly used in the preparation of sauces and in building the fruit cakes. There was, as well, an infusion of tropical scent, as the infrequent Christmas citrus fruits—the opulent golden oranges—added an oily sharpness to the mixture. This was counterbalanced by the clean, cidery bite of the hard, white-fleshed, scarlet apples. Bright Christmas candies—the clover-shaped and heart-shaped sugary ones you never saw at any other time of the year and the striped hard ones with the soft centers—helped the greasy Brazil nuts along, as did the winy aroma of the great clusters of raisins, sugary-sticky to the touch. The spices that went into the eggnog or the hot Tom and Jerrys stood off the warm friendship of the rum that gave character to the cream.

Now I had to turn back the clock a far piece to sort out all those various effluvia in my mental nostrils, and in the process I ran onto other stimuli. I could suddenly remember what it was like going to bed between icy sheets in an un-steam-heated house, and the torture of leaving a warm bed to crawl into your clothes in the black predawn of a duck-hunting day—of the tiny furnace that a hunter's big breakfast built in your stomach when your ears were dropping off from cold and your legs were numb from the knees down.

It was easy, then, to reconstruct the bright droplet that always hung at the cherry end of a boy's frozen nose, as he shivered in a duck blind and prayed for the mallards to come in. And such things as the dewdrops of spray standing distinctly on the Old Man's mustache, and the smell of an old man—"old men and old dogs both smell bad"—which seemed compounded of tobacco juice, corn whisky, open fire, and just plain old man.

I was moved to think again, for the first time in many a year, of just how hell-conscious a small boy can be, and of that frightening span of two or three years when I was sure I was going to hell for telling a lie or for cutting Sunday school or for saying damn, and of how I was sore stricken with the enormity of eternity. These severe strokes of conscience generally took hold during a late afternoon in a swamp, when the doves mourned and the early evening snaps and pops and hoots began. Even today, as an adult, during a late fishing afternoon in a darkly mysterious swamp, surrounded by cypress knees and Spanish moss, I feel something of the old fear of the wrath of God, and a chilly finger runs up and down my spine.

Practically nothing of what we did in the old days was artificial or contrived. I shot a bow and arrow, but I had made the bow and the arrows according to a recipe in a book by Ernest Thompson Seton. I didn't need a counselor to teach me archery. We could sling a hatchet, tomahawk fashion, and throw a spear, and make a deadfall, and hurl a knife, and row or sail a boat.

The barn walls in winter were generally tacked full of rabbit skins and the hide of an occasional coon or possum, and I daydreamed violently of meeting a bear to add to the trophies. I never did, but I saw one's tracks once, and that was almost as good as seeing him and shooting him.

There was also a secret life that adults never shared—a life of interlocking caves, of out-of-the-way islands where pirates

surely once had buried their loot, of tree houses and even log
cabins, their beams out of plumb, to be sure, but a power of
cozy comfort to the weary pioneer.

The train from Southport to Wilmington, North Carolina
(called the W.B.&S., which meant "Wilmington, Brunswick and
Southport," but was corrupted to "Willing But Slow"), consumed the best part of half a day to travel thirty miles, but the
trip was fraught with high adventure and a sense of vast travel.
The trip on the river boat, of which my Uncle Rob was engineer, took longer, but you felt pretty near like Columbus once
you passed the stinking fish meal factory. It took longer to
make that thirty miles than it does to fly from New York to
London today.

The Old Man and the Boy dealt with a small local segment
of the American scene, so it is rather strange and rather amusing
that its components should have been produced in practically
every corner of the world. The first two chapters were written
on a steamer bound for Genoa; subsequent ones were recorded
on an African safari. In the years that followed, *The Old Man
and the Boy* was written in such disparate places as the Hotel
Savoy in London, the Hadden Rig sheep station in New South
Wales, and in a camp in Goroka, high in the mountains of New
Guinea, as well as in Rome, Paris, Madrid, the Philippines,
Tokyo, Hong Kong, and a number of other places I won't take
the time to list. Altogether it has been one of the best-traveled
pieces of work in history, and it is odd that the only place in
which it has not been written is the locale where the incidents
happened—Southport and Wilmington. Most of the contents
of this book were written in Spain, Africa, and India, airplanes
being what they are today.

It is probably perverse and cranky of me, but I can't understand what the modern youngster sees of interest in rockets to
the moon and satellites and such when there are still so many
things to discover in the tangible sea. Nor how the extrava-
gances of television can claim precedence over camping trips, or
even over the limitless, understandable adventure to be found

in books that do not deal with space cadets and moon dwellers.

But as a boy grown old I do not seem to be lonely in this appraisal of things not being like they used to be. The weather's changed, and everybody talks about whether or not it's the atom bomb's fault. The safari business is booming, and is patronized largely by old boys with prominent veins and potbellies, men trying to torture themselves into a misty remembrance of things past. You never see any bluebirds any more, and the red-headed woodpeckers have joined the dodo. Things are definitely not the same as when I was a lad, and if you asked me right smart how many miles I walked to school through the snow I would probably top the Old Man and say, "Twenty." That would be a lie, because all the time I had a bicycle and the schoolhouse was just around the corner. It wasn't red either. That was the color of the seventh-grade teacher's hair at just about the time the birds and the bees took on a slightly different significance.

Come to think of it, they ain't making red-headed schoolteachers the way they used to either. Not the last time I looked.

1

All He Left Me Was the World

The streets filled as far as you could see; past the oak grove one way, down toward the river another way. Most of the faces were black, the black bulk accented here and there by a white face. There were dogs in the crowd, too, and children as well as adults.

They had come to see the Old Man off, to "say good-bye" to the Cap'm. The only face among his kinry that was missing was mine. I had said good-bye to him; he had said good-bye to me. I didn't want it all confused with a lot of mourners. I went and got the oars from under the house and rowed over to Battery Island. There didn't figure to be anything on it but birds.

There is no way, absolutely no way, to describe the desolation I felt. The Old Man was gone, and I was fifteen years old

and alone without a prop in a world that was too big for me
without the Old Man. I rowed the boat hard, trying not to
think of him dead, but not succeeding. Then I thought of what
had sent me onto the water—his old axiom that a boat and open
water would come pretty close to solving any problems you
had at the time, if only because water cleared your head, fishing
calmed your nerves, "and you can always eat the fish." I suppose that some people would think it odd that I skipped the
Old Man's funeral services and went fishing. The Old Man
would not have thought it odd.

I noticed that from force of habit I had brought the cast net,
and there were hand lines in the locker. I drove the boat over
into the shallows, jammed her into the bank with an oar, and
looked about the marsh for some schools of shrimp. In a bit I
had bait, and I pushed her free of the beach and went out to a
fishing hole I knew, where there were plenty of croakers and
often sea trout. I anchored, baited the line, and proceeded to
fish. What I caught I cannot say. I assume I caught something.
I usually caught something on these expeditions.

"March is an awful month," the Old Man used to say. "Best
you use it for remembering." So I sat in the boat and methodically fished, and remembered.

"I ain't going to leave you much," he had said, when it got
bad toward the end. "This sickness cost an awful lot of money.
The house is mortgaged, and there's a note in the bank, and the
depression is still on. There won't be much left but some shotguns and a cast net and a boat. And, maybe, a memory."

All of a sudden the sun came out in my head. What did he
mean, he wasn't going to leave me much? Who was kidding
whom? I was the richest boy in the world. Croesus was a beggar alongside me. I had had fifteen years of the Old Man, and
nearly everything he knew he'd taught me. I started to take a
check on my assets.

First he had raised me as a man among men, without con-
descension, without patronizing. He had allowed me companionship on an equal basis with himself and with his men friends.

He had given me pride and equality. He had taught me compassion and manners and tolerance, especially toward the less fortunate, white or black. That sea of black faces which appeared in the street had not heard desegregation or any other "ation" except starvation. They came because they loved the Old Man, their friend. All but the younger ones had been born of slaves.

The preachers, white and black, had been in the crowd. And so had the bums. These were the hairier types who had taken a part in my education, the drinkers and the fighters and the loafers. They were there, together with the city fathers, and the Coast Guard boys, and the Pilots' Association, plus the relatives and the hound dogs. I reckoned that the Old Man must have had something that rubbed off on people, including me.

What else was there?

Well, he had given me the vast gift of reading. He had made reading a form of sport, like hunting was a sport and fishing was a sport. He had unleashed all the treasures of the knowledge of the world, so that I always had my nose buried in a book. It didn't matter what kind of book so long as it had words in it. I was reading Macaulay and Addison and Swift and Shakespeare for kicks. I never read the Bible for religious reasons. Reading the Bible as a straight book, and not as a tract, I had found it to have more action than Zane Grey's woolliest westerns. I read history as avidly as fiction, and the ancient Egyptians got away with very little I wasn't hep to. Everybody else called her Venus, but I knew the lady that rose from the sea was called the Aphrodite of Melos a long time before Dr. Harland got hold of me in college.

So the Old Man had also given me the gift of avoidance of boredom. If there is any piece of paper anywhere, whether it's a patent-medicine bottle or a soap wrapper, and if it has words on it I will read the words and not be bored. I am well past forty now, and do not remember a moment of boredom, because, among other things, the Old Man also gave me eyes to see—to actually *see*.

"Most people," he had said, "go through life looking and

never see a thing. Anything you see is interesting, from a chinch bug to a barnacle, if you just look at it and wonder about it a little." Then he would send me to the swamps or out in the boat or off along the beach with a firm command to *look* and tell him later what I saw. I saw plenty and in detail, whether it was ants working or a mink swimming or a tumblebug endlessly pushing its ball.

I saw male squirrels castrate rivals in the rutting season; I saw a sea turtle laying eggs and weeping great tears. I saw the life of the swamps and the marshes, heard the sounds and watched the lives outdoors change as the climate varied. I learned to listen to the night sounds: the dogs barking in concert when the moon was right for it, the mournful hoot of owl and plaint of whippoorwill, the querulous yap of fox and the belling of a lonesome hound on a trail of his own devising. I learned to love the mournful coo of doves as the evening approached, the desperately forlorn call of quail as they tried to reassemble a scattered covey.

I became acutely conscious of smells: crushed fern, dogfennel, the bright slashes of split pine with the oozing gum, bruised Jimson weed—the little smells apart from the major ones, like jessamine or magnolia or myrtle. The smell of summer differed from the smell of autumn. Summer was languid and milky, like the soft breath of a cow. Autumn was tart and stimulating, with leaves burning, frost on the grass, and the gum trees turning. Spring was a young girl smell, and winter was an old man's smell, compounded of grate fires and tobacco juice.

Cooking? The Old Man had taught me that food can be something more than fodder to distend a growling gut. We had had as much fun out of preparing food as in the procuring of it with gun or rod. He had taught me to make an adventure out of cooking a catfish on a sandspit, of making an oyster roast or eating raw clams busted on the gunwale of a boat. I was proud of me as a cook—and grateful for the knowledge that hawg-and-hominy, if you're hungry, or a bait of turtle eggs or a fried squirrel or rabbit is better than the fine-haired saucy stuff you eat when you get wealthy enough to traffic with restaurants.

What else had he left me, apart from these things?

Well, good manners, painfully impressed, and once or twice with a lath. I said "Sir" and "Ma'am" and "Please" and "Thank you," and was more or less silent in the presence of my elders and at table. I didn't try to hog my shooting partner's bird shots, and I never infringed on another man's right to command his dogs. I was quiet in the woods, and I left my campsites clean, with all the refuse buried and the fire raked neat.

I could throw a cast net, shoot a gun, row a boat, call a turkey, build a duck blind, tong an oyster, train a puppy, stand a deer, bait a turkey blind (illegal), call the turkey to the blind, cast in the surf, pitch a tent, make a bed out of pine needles, follow a coonhound, stand a watch on a fishing boat, skin anything that had to be skun, scale a fish, dig a clam, build a cave, draw a picture, isolate edible mushrooms from the poisonous toadstools, pole a boat, identify all the trees and most of the flowers and berries, get along with the colored folks, and also practice a rude kind of game conservation.

That seemed to sum it up, as far as legacy was concerned; two shotguns, a cast net, a boat, and a house with a new mockingbird in the magnolia—a house that wouldn't be ours much longer. College just around the corner, if I could figure out a way to work my way through it.

I heaved up the hook, picked up the oars, and rowed home. By the time I got there the funeral crowd had dissipated, and there wasn't anybody there but a few relatives and close friends. Nobody appeared to have missed me.

I was hungry, and in the South funerals are always accompanied by food. The idea is slightly macabre, but everybody pitches in a cake or a turkey or a ham, and if you can conquer the funereal smell of the flowers the dining-room table is groaning. I made myself a ham sandwich and was pouring a glass of milk when one final thought hit me, wham!

On the rainy days or driving the Liz or rowing a boat or in

the off seasons where there wasn't anything to hunt or fish the Old Man had made a habit of what he called indoctrinating me into the world of human beings. This consisted of the sum of his travels and his reading. He was a shark on the old West, for instance, and he knew a great deal about Coronado's treasure and the people who had wasted their lives looking for it. He was a bug on the great trek westward, when the prairie schooners set out on a prayer and a venture. He knew all about what happened to the buffalo and about the passing of the carrier pigeon. He was an old-timer who was modern enough to know he was the last of the old-timers. He knew about all the world as well, whether it was ancient Egypt or Stanley looking for Livingstone in Africa, and he had fed me these stories like cakes ever since I was a toddler.

It suddenly occurred to me that I was educated before I saw a college. I made up my mind right then that someday I would learn to be a writer and write some of the stuff the Old Man had taught me. There was only one thing I had to do first, and that was to get educated and make enough money to buy back the old yellow-painted square house with its mockingbird in the magnolia and its pecan trees in the back yard.

This took a lot of time, and included a war, outraged peace, and a lot of written words. It included Washington and New York, London and Paris, Spain and Australia, Africa and India, lions and tigers, hope and despair. But the Old Man's house is back in the family now, and the mockingbird—lineal descendant of the one I once murdered—sings cheerfully on the moonlit nights in the magnolia, the pecans are bearing again and so is the fig tree. The oak grove hasn't changed.

There is gray in the boy's hair, but the Old Man persists, and you will be hearing more about the things he told me. And perhaps the gray will momentarily depart, and I shall not be the Old Man, but the boy again, because it is all coming powerfully clear.

2

Nobility Is Wrecking the Country

Some five years from the day I told the Old Man good-bye Mrs. Eleanor Roosevelt was saying—for about two hours—to several hundred bright-faced young people in the football stadium, ". . . and the future of the world rests solidly on your sturdy young shoulders," as the University of North Carolina prepared to thrust the graduates of 1935 out into the jungles of commerce.

Three of these sturdy-shouldered young men were not, I am afraid, treating the graduation exercises with proper respect. Among the three R's grouped together on the hard stadium seats was a scientist. Working secretly, just at dusk, he had managed to hide a large crock under the middle R. By way of individual rubber hoses, run from the crock underneath our scholarly robes, we could siphon sufficient home-brewed happiness to relieve the ceremony of some of its tedium. I am afraid that at least three young plumed knights wore their mortarboards at a rather rakish tilt when they marched bravely up to receive the sheepskin that declared them to be World Saviors (j.g.).

During the lengthy orations—or exhortations—I kept thinking how much more fun a colored camp meeting was, which conjured up the kind of graduation speech the Old Man might have made. Once he had said, "You're going to be a man soon. There never was anybody fit to tell another man how to be a man. Free advice generally accomplishes two things. If you take the advice and it turns sour you hate the man that gave it to you. If it works out sound you still don't like him for telling you how to run your life. And if you refuse the advice and make out all right he'll never forgive you for making him look bad." He paused to fire up his prop—the pipe.

"I plead guilty to having tried to teach you a few things I know, like not blowing your foot off or shooting me for a deer or killing all the quail instead of just a few. You were raised honest and decent to the best of my notion, and if none of it took, why, it's too late to do anything about it now. What you make of your early raising is strictly up to you.

"But I would ask your permission to throw a couple more thoughts at you, which might keep you out of jail or the loony bin. Don't be noble—it's wrecking the country. And try to remember that having a little fun as you go along ain't no sin. It's just as necessary as sleeping. Don't take yourself seriously, because you're competing with about a hundred billion people, including Chinamen and Ubangis, who think that they're just as important as the next Chinaman or Ubangi, and they never heard of you at all.

"Speaking metaphorically," he concluded with a flourish, "I will look down on you from wherever I'm at and smile if you manage to struggle through the next fifty years or so without setting fire to the bush, leaving a messy campsite, or hogging the shots from your fellow man. Selah."

The old gentleman had already read me a lecture on turning personal tragedy into high adventure (and sometimes low comedy) if you could only manage to regard yourself as somebody else, which I have found a handy aid over the last triple decade. At least if you can laugh instead of cry the troubles will either kill you or go away, and it is a bit better to die laughing than to die crying.

From the first days I was old enough to toddle into the woods the Old Man was able to make the tiniest occurrence—things that many people pass by—seem adventurous. He could find a symbol of life's struggle merely by watching a tumble-bug struggle with his ball.

"There," he would say, "is Everyman, trying to shove that ball uphill as a life's work and never quite making it. But you can't say the little devil ain't giving it his best effort, and he don't seem to be whining for any help."

He broke me into life as you'd teach a child to walk or a puppy to respect an older dog's point. He suggested rather than ordered, and he was diabolically oblique in his methods. Havilah Babcock once wrote a piece in which he cured an obstreperous puppy of breaking a back-stand by eventually beating the old dog that was suffering the indignity. The puppy's papa finally turned on the puppy instead of humoring him, and trounced the daylights out of the sinner. The sinner immediately conformed to the society of decent bird dogs. (The Old Man would have loved that piece as did I, because I could read me very easily into the puppy's part.)

The only thing the Old Man was intolerant of was intolerance. He construed intolerance as several things. Basically he was highly tolerant of other people's rights, whether it had to do with race, creed, or property. He respected POSTED signs, but sometimes, when he figured the end justified the means, he was not averse to calling another man's turkey across the road to where there weren't any POSTED signs—if nobody was shooting the turkeys anyhow. He was intolerant of impoliteness, whether it was in the house or in the field, whether it involved hogging a shot or leaving a filthy campsite or setting fire to a forest. He taught me humility in a darkening swamp, when the doves moaned and the shadows fell and all the spooky, late-afternoon swamp noises set in.

About this time of year, when I had been bucking and rearing like an overfed colt all spring, he calmed me down by letting me help him build a boat, and then sent me off for a summer on the waters all by myself. He was the original do-it-yourself inventor, especially if doing-it-yourself—such as scaling the fish or chopping the firewood or shooting quail in the rain—involved me.

"Boys," he would say, "belong to do a lot of men's work, out of respect to their elders' rheumatiz, and also as a kind of apprenticeship toward manhood. It's the price you pay for being a boy."

Curiosity, he reckoned, was one of the cardinal virtues of life. "They say curiosity killed the cat," he would opine, "but more likely it was an overdose of mice." He looked under logs and peered around the corners. He wasn't satisfied until he knew all there was to know about anything that crossed his path, and that included everything from Greek mythology to the nesting habits of a tomtit.

He had a strange sense of beauty and a stranger sense of humor. One time I deliberately stepped on a caterpillar.

"Don't let me see you do that again," he said sharply. "You've just squashed the daylights out of a diurnal rhopalocerous lepidopterous creature—a thing of beauty."

"A which?" I asked.

He grinned. "A butterfly that ain't born yet." He was full of that sort of foolishness, because while he used "ain't" and double negatives for emphasis he read encyclopedias for fun, and very early he had my nose stuck into Bulfinch's *Mythol-*

ogy, which I found fascinating. He had me reading Shakespeare for fun, instead of yellowbacks of blood and thunder.

"Shakespeare's got more blood and thunder in him than Nick Carter and Ned Buntline put together. And stay away from the Horatio Alger books. All them heroes are namby-pamby bores, and anyhow it didn't happen that way. Bosses are a little choosy about who marries their daughters. You can't build a life hoping to find a pocketbook on the streets so you can return it to the boss and get to be president of the bank."

Fun had several definitions. "No man belongs to play until the work's done," he would say sternly. And then slyly, "But there ain't nothing wrong in turning work into fun if you can get away with it. I see nothing wrong about pretending you're a high-rigger in an Oregon fir forest, two hundred feet above the ground, when all you're really doing is chopping kindling."

He dearly loved his toddy, but he was very stern about mixing up drinking with hunting or any other kind of sport or work that needed a keen eye and full concentration.

"You either come to hunt or you come to drink," he said. "It's all right with me if the drunks want to stay in camp, but I don't aim to have my head blown off by no damn fool in a duck blind. Drinkin's for when the work's done, too. Nothing I admire more than a cup of corn at the end of the day—or even," with a wink, "in the case of old men, when the morning's bitter and the stars are still up and it's colder'n a mile into an iceberg. But not while you're hunting. Or fishing. I know many a man to get himself drownded when he was drunk. Or fall off a hill and bust his neck."

He would continue on his favorite topic—fun. "Fun is a little present you give yourself as a reward for what you've earned. You can turn work into play, but you can also turn play into work if you don't balance it off with a little honest toil. You run out of things to play at, and you run out of play toys. Them rich playboys are as useless as tits on a boar. A bum is a bum, whether he's rich or poor."

On the topic of what constituted a gentleman: "A gentleman don't necessarily have to own a necktie or shave every day. There's some ruffians around this town that don't wash too much and might get drunk on Saturday night that I would call gentlemen. On the other hand there are some stiff-collared, nondrinking, church-going, clean-necked folks I wouldn't trust as far as you can sling an ox. A gentleman is what the word means, a *gentle man*."

The Old Man never held forth much on formal religion. He said he reckoned a man knew best what his own God was and how to work with Him, and he was never much of a reformer. He said he reckoned Somebody, no matter what name you called Him, was responsible for sun, moon, mountains, sea, stars, heat, cold, seasons, animals, birds, fish, and food—"even small boys, although that may have been a basic mistake"—and whether you called him God, Allah, Jehovah, or Mug-Mug didn't make much difference as long as you believed in Him.

On the sexes: "Man is a simple creature—a very small boy who wants to be patted on the head and told he's a good boy and a nice boy and a smart boy. You can lead him anywhere. But as for women, I don't know. They got a sort of contrary, different chemistry of brain and action from men, which makes them unruly and subject to strange fits. My only advice on women is to stay out of the house when they're cleaning and don't say yes too often."

The young people who are exploding forth from the citadels of knowledge in any lovely month of June will have a tremendous heap of exhortation flung at them, and they will be told, in varying terms, that the world's future rests on their stanch shoulders. They will feel, possibly, that this has not occurred before. But I can think they might do worse than heed some of the Old Man's advice.

I had no bad conscience that night more than a quarter-century ago, when the three R's inhaled a little home-brew while we sweated through the platform rhetoric. After all, the work of education had been finished and we were entitled to a little fun before we plunged into the future. I went to work that same week and have been steadily at it since. But it has not been work unleavened with fun. And I have heeded the old gentleman's advice as well as I have been able. At least, I haven't been noble, and so far I haven't managed to wreck the country.

3

Uncle Rob Had Humphrey Bogart Beat a Mile

The world of a boy who lives beside a river is limitless in
scope, if the boy is blessed with imagination and there is some
older, romantic head around to encourage the boy in what some
grown ups dismiss as tomfool daydreaming.

We lived by a river, and the river rolled snaking out to sea.
It was a broad, broad vista, seen by a boy's eyes, and the Old
Man's tales about what might lie on the other side drove me
into a frenzy of youthful torment. My people were born of the
river and of the sea, and they spoke a language which fed more
from seafaring English than Southern drawl. We drank strong
black tea and ate raisin duff; the surnames of St. George and
Newton, Adkins and Guthrie, Davis and Morse were only a
jump removed from another Southport in England. My rela-

tives ran the river, and some of them had strode the seas. My imagination surpassed them, until Samarkand and Far Cathay were at my beck.

All of this was fetched sharply home a few years ago when somebody steered me onto a moving picture called *The African Queen*, which had to do with Katharine Hepburn and Humphrey Bogart running a wild African river on a dilapidated old scow called "The African Queen."

All through the picture something kept bothering me, and it wasn't the fact that the director, John Huston, opened the action with Bogart's belly rumbling as some missionaries were leading the wretched heathen to the light. Nor, exactly, was it the anguished look on Bogart's face when Miss Hepburn threw all the gin over the side and Bogart watched each square-faced bottle as it disappeared to eternity in the "Queen's" bubbling wake.

What struck the basic reminiscent note was Bogart using his foot to kick the ramshackledy old engine into life and his primitive means of preventing the boilers from exploding. Whiskers and all, Mr. Bogart, now gathered to a land where the woodbine twineth around free gin bottles, drew me back to my Uncle Rob and some voyages I made with him when he was chief—and only—engineer of an old passenger tub called, I think, "The Steamer Wilmington." I could be wrong about the name as it was something more than thirty-five years ago.

Uncle Rob was my favorite relative, apart from the Old Man, but Rob was kind of a raffish relative, somewhat given to profanity and occasionally to strong waters. Not until later years was he addicted to steady work. Not that he was triflin'— far from it. Rob was a man of far horizons, but limited opportunity to reach them.

Uncle Rob, from young manhood until the day he died, looked like a whisker-shorn Scotch terrier, with a terrier's temper. He was a man of motion. When Rob was a boy his father would hitch up the buggy, and cart Rob off to some boarding school (his father was what was known in those days as well-to-do), and Rob would generally take a punch at the headmaster and beat the old man home, sometimes a distance of a couple of hundred miles. Rob did not lean kindly toward education, and education did not consider Rob a likely candidate for distinction.

But there was very little Rob could not do with his hands. They were strong, callused hands, with square-tipped fingers and nails that always wore a clean rim of grease, because Rob's hands were always plunged deep in the guts of an engine. He would tinker, and tinker, and if the cussed thing wouldn't go he would haul off and fetch her a kick. The motor would catch and settle down to a steady hum. They said Rob had "a knowing foot," and so he did.

Rob was blunt with a Scotsman's bluntness, which sometimes lost him friends. He had a habit of saying what he thought, regardless of consequence. On one occasion, when Aunt May had trapped him into going to church, he glanced down the prayerful aisles to a female relative who was somewhat lacking in beauty.

"Damn, that's an ugly woman," Rob muttered.

"Shhh, Rob," Aunt May said. "The poor thing can't help it if she's ugly."

"No, she can't help it if she's ugly," Rob muttered back, "but God dammit, *she could stay home.*"

Rob eventually turned highly respectable, and worked many years as chief engineer of government dredge boats on the Mississippi and elsewhere, and seldom jeopardized his professional standing on the strong waters without by his old fondness for the strong waters within—*within* Rob, that is. He kind of settled down after one bout with John Barleycorn caused him to lurch into a Christmas tree, scattering the burning candles and nearly setting the house afire.

"God*damn* Santa Claus," Uncle Rob muttered, and tottered off with something other than sugarplums dancing through his head. What pounded through his skull next day was a withering hangover and the combined censure of the steadier element of yuletide celebrants.

But somewhere in his earlier days of sketchy employment Uncle Rob enjoyed a brief span as engineer of this hand-knit passenger liner, the "Wilmington," and as his favorite nephew I was allowed to go voyaging occasionally with Uncle Rob. Thereby opened the vistas of far places, which have caused me trouble ever since.

I had some seagoing experience—as unpaid supercargo on the Coast Guard rumchasers and on the fertilizer-fish boat, the old "Vanessa," that the Old Man skippered from time to time in the pogy season. But I reckon my trip from Southport to Wilmington on the Cape Fear River was my first experience with a vessel on which people actually paid passage, and certainly it was my first run on the river.

I can clearly remember the thrill of being in the cabin (the cabin!) of the "Wilmington," and hearing the pulsing of the engines, and knowing that my Uncle Rob, greasy to the ears, was one-half of the human forces which kept us afloat. I was not concerned with the captain and the deck hand. The Cape Fear was wide enough to accommodate ocean-going freighters and needed little skill in the steering. What intrigued me most was that teakettle below decks, which kept me from the gaping maws of the imaginary hippos and crocodiles which undoubtedly thronged the river.

That first voyage was notable for the fact that I was deep in the vitals of *Tarzan of the Apes*, possibly the most fascinating book ever written for young or old. (I read it again with vast satisfaction the other day, and it loses nothing with time.)

In this instance the "Wilmington" had been renamed the barque "Fuwalda," by me, and I was John Clayton, Lord Greystoke, about to swim through the croc-ridden waters to the forbidding African shores. As a matter of fact there probably *were* a few sharks in the Cape Fear, and, as the water changed from salt to brackish to fresh, the odd alligator lurking in the rice marshes.

Uncle Rob cursed steadily and feverishly in the stinking heat of the engine room, and kicked the engine into sputtering life when its dying gasp was imminent, so I did not have to swim through the crocodiles and hippos into the waiting arms of shrieking savages and fierce beasts. And thus, with one of my first impressions of man against the sea, was born an abiding respect for anybody who could do anything with his hands which would make a piece of dumb machinery respond sufficiently to conquer the elements.

A trip down the river was quite a sight in those days. She is a strong brown river, the Cape Fear, roily with filth, and subject to whimsical current. The entry from the ocean, between the islands of Baldhead and Caswell, was jagged and marked by sand bars, to a point where the big foreign ships had to hang off the light and wait for the pilot boat to chug out, board a pilot, and then answer the pilot's con in the wheelhouse or on the flying bridge, as she ran the river to the discharge-and-loading port of Wilmington.

You would see the big ships, sea-weary and rust-scabbed, their stacks salt-grimed and their paint scaly, butting down the river. Their high poop decks bore their names in rusty gold, magical port names, "Hamburg" and "Liverpool," "Bremen" and "Antwerp," "Marseilles" and "Rotterdam." Wilmington was on the North Atlantic run, which touched Jacksonsville, Savannah, and Charleston, all names that were nearly as foreign to me then as the Rotterdams and the Bremens.

It was a powerful thrill, then, treading the quarter-deck of the stanch ship "Wilmington" to know that blood kin was driving the engine which throbbed and rattled beneath your feet, and that the guiding hand at the helm of the big, ocean-battered freighters that passed you belonged to another blood relative, Uncle Walker or Uncle Tommy or the Old Man himself, with a whole dynasty of younger blood relatives—someday, perhaps even me—coming up to guide the big ships and perhaps to sail away to the far places as master or man.

The entirely ersatz Africa of Mr. Edgar Rice Burroughs' Tarzan then seemed no more distant than the duck-tremulous rice fields of the fabulous Orton Plantation, with its moss-dripping live oaks and stately white-columned main house. A river is just as broad as a sea to a boy, and limitless depths of the ocean no more peril-fraught than a greasy, rolling brown river, which can wreck a big ship and has yielded its toll of bloated drowned men, just as dead as if they were swept ashore off Hatteras, the ships just as wrecked as if they were tolled to doom by the decoying lanterns of the wreckers at Nags Head.

My Uncle Rob—my Uncles Tommy and Walker, the Old Man, and me—were all part of what was a most exciting state, if only a boy realized it at the time. Blackbeard the Pirate was no stranger to our off-coast sea islands. British troops knew the old town of Wilmington, and old Fort Fisher had seen a power of Rhett Butlers running blockades. We had our own lost Indian tribe of Roanoke; we still had the Croatans upriver; and a solid reservation of half-naked blanket, bownarrer Cherokees upstate in the mountains.

Rumrunners used our coastal coves to dump their cargo, and our Coast Guard had a cutter, the "Modoc," which called Wilmington a home port. Baldhead and Caswell had its Coast Guard stations, from which beach patrol, surfboat patrol, and rumchasers operated. It was not unusual to see apprehended rum being smashed in the street in front of the Customs House, and I can remember the sight of one drunk dabbing the wasting rivulets of good whisky with a handkerchief and wringing out the booze-soaked cloth in his mouth.

Deeper, farther in the swamps, a few counties away, we had a strange race of people called Brass Ankles, a mixture of Indian, white, and Negro, who were as handy with knives as some of their relatives amongst the Croatans of the Lumberton area.

Not too far away, close to a township called Waccamaw, we

had the Green Swamp, big enough and impenetrable enough to be called abysmal. On some islands in this vast sea of tangled growth were clumps and clusters of humanity who had escaped first from the French Revolution to Haiti, thence from Haiti to Wilmington, thence from Wilmington inland to sanctuary in the swamps. Some were inbred and idiotic from isolation. Nearly all had French names and spoke a French patois not unlike the Haitian creole. In that swamp, the Green Swamp, there were panthers and bears and alligators, wild hogs and wild cats.

All of these riches, these excitements stretched before a small boy whose uncle drove the craft on which he strode the waters, whose other relatives piloted ships from far-distant places, ships whose crews gabbled in strange tongues and whose captains often gave the pilots a gold-foiled bottle of strange liquor or a sandalwood chest to take home as a souvenir of the trip down the river.

Yet for some reason, some obscure reason, only a handful of men from this area had been abroad, in the sense of having seen the Mississippi or the phosphate-loading port of Fernandina in Florida. They shrimped and they fertilizer-fished and they piloted other people's ships on the river, but they stayed home. One man named Lockwood built a boat on a big creek with some inchoate urge to take it down to the sea, but he built the boat too big for the bridge, her draft too deep for the channel. The locality is still called Lockwood's Folly, as an admonition to stay home and not go off mingling with the furriners.

My own people had been away and had mingled with furriners, but they had come home. Home was a salt-rimed fishing village, whose oak grove was called simply "The Grove," and any voyage to the post office or the store was called "going up the street." Even Wilmington, thirty miles away, was a foreign country, whose people spoke a different language, lived different lives, and were regarded with scorn as city people, fresh-water catfish.

Some of this must have rubbed off on me as I made my first run as a river-boat man with my Uncle Rob. Some of it must have bitten deeply as I breasted the bar with the "Penton," the pilot boat, went fish-chasing on the "Vanessa," or fingered the cold-greasy guns on the cutter "Modoc." Some of it must have itched and burned as we danced on the treacherous edges of Frying Pan shoals, sailing perilously close after bluefish and mackerel, within easy view of the lightship, a floating lighthouse, with its mournful bellow to keep the big ships away from Frying Pan.

All this, I suppose, came surging home when Humphrey Bogart kicked the engine alive in the moving picture *The African Queen*, reposing partially in the memory of Uncle Rob, who finally conquered a bigger river than Humphrey Bogart vanquished—a river leading to a considerably larger body of water.

But I will say another thing for Uncle Rob over Humphrey Bogart. Uncle Rob would not have stood idly by to watch Katharine Hepburn dump a case of gin over the side for the crocodiles to puzzle over. If Uncle Rob had been engineer of "The African Queen" Miss Hepburn would have joined the gin.

4

The Old Man Paid My Passage

The waves crashed against the bow of the ship, spreading sheets of water over the foc'sle head. The old Hog Islander was running bow on into the gale. As she plunged she suffered and creaked amidships, and when she buried her prow in a sea her screws came clear of the following waves and thrashed painfully half out of the water.

The night was blacker than the water and as cold as the Arctic that supplied the sea on this northern passage to Liverpool. The night watchman was braced against the anchor chains as they stretched taut from the chain locker to crimp round the winch. The night watchman was really two people—the Number Two Ordinary Seaman and the cadet. They each worked an eight-hour shift, from eight bells to eight bells, or from

8 P.M. to 8 A.M.—two hours on lookout, two hours stand-by, two hours lookout, two hours stand-by, seven bitter-cold nights a week, each week.

The night watchman wore smelly long drawers, two pairs of pants, two wool shirts, two sweaters, a sheepskin coat, oilskins, a knitted cap pulled down over his ears under the sou'wester, two pairs of socks, and hip boots. The sheets of water hit him full in the face, streamed back over the iced foc'sle head, and went cascading over the deck cargo of lashed-down logs, chained tautly to the hatch and bulkhead and tightened by turn-buckles.

The Ordinary Seaman, who was paid ten dollars a week, no overtime, who stood eight-hour watches at sea, who shortly would begin to rot his hands in a mixture of lye and water called *suji-muji* with which he cleaned the whitework, who helped shift the ship at night from dock to dock on his own time, who painted over the side in port, who swept the remains of sheep manure and phosphate rock and sulphur from the holds, who cleaned the stinking bilges in the deep tanks, who helped batten down open hatches in company-timesaving de-fiance of maritime law when the ship was already at sea, who was part of the poop-deck gang when the ship tied up or cast off, who had been shot at by strikers in Antwerp (strikers who had rifles and who climbed grain elevators for better aiming vantage), who ate biscuits from which cockroaches were knocked, who worked under a Danish bosun named Svendsen who hated him and was doubly hated in return, who lived with seven other men in one room under the poop next the grinding of the steering engine, who shared one toilet with the same seven men and washed out of a bucket into which a steampipe had been turned to heat the water, and who had been forced to fight half the men on the ship to defend his right to be a former college boy at sea during the great depression—this ordinary seaman walked into the crew mess and bled a cup of overboiled coffee out of the huge zinc urn in the corner, sat down on a bench by the mess table, observed that the "night lunch" had already been eaten, and lit a cigarette. Hungry, he cursed again —cursing ships and men and the sea and the spirit of high adventure that had gotten him into this mess.

The Ordinary Seaman Number Two was a little over twenty years old. He had been a college graduate on the bum for nine months. The year was early 1936. The Ordinary Seaman Number Two was me.

After I had my coffee I warmed my hands over the fiddley heat again, and then I got the *suji* bucket and the rags and went into the passageway to freeze my hands and open up the cuts the lye had already made in my fingers. I closed my mind to the freezing cold and the burning lye and began to think. I had found on the foc'sle head, where you weren't allowed to smoke, that I could control my thinking, and by channeling it along pleasant lines I could make the time pass more swiftly. Mostly I thought about the Old Man—not the captain of the ship, but *my* Old Man, dead now for six years.

"The Old Man got me into this," I used to say aloud. (You got used to talking aloud when they switched the watches to four on, four wheel watch and stand-by.) "He got me into it, and I might as well make him pay part of my passage."

He had, too, in a way. He had a master's license in sail and steam, and once he was on a trip around the Cape of Good Hope that took three years. He bottle-fed me on seafaring stuff. He told me all the hardships, all about the lousy food and some of the lousier people, and I refused to believe it wasn't romantic. I had one thing in mind: when I finished school I was going to sea. I was going to see the world.

"You ain't going to like it," the Old Man had said. "But you might as well try it and get it over with. You won't be happy until you do."

Oh brother, thought I, taking half a foot of paint off a plank with the *suji* rag and the same amount of skin off my hands, *he didn't tell me the half of it. He didn't tell me that the second*

*mate was going to wake me up once with a kick in the belly
or that I would ever entertain a serious idea about killing a
squarehead bosun named Svendsen in an alley with my bare
hands.*

I guess the Old Man saved me from being hanged for murder
at that, for when the mutinous madness came on I could drive it
off with the thinking. I thought of all the nice things we had
ever done together: the first shotgun, what Christmas cooking
smelt like. I thought about the first double on quail and the first
deer and how to make a good camp and how a bird dog looked
winding a covey in the broom grass. I thought about the quiet
of a Carolina swamp with the bass biting, and an autumn afternoon on a lonely beach with the blues ravenous and the wind
howling pleasantly outside a snug cabin whose walls shook
with the gale and trembled from a roaring fire, with ham spitting in the skillet. But I never thought about it all at once. I
rationed it. I would say: "All right, Ordinary, what do we
think about tonight?" and then I'd pick one thing and think
about every little bit of it. I suppose people in prison do the
same thing.

This particular cold night I was back in Louisiana, where the
Old Man took me on a duck-hunting trip. I was down a bayou.
We were living on a big boat with some of his friends, mostly
Cajuns, and I never saw duck hunting like this before. You
hunted in a singlet, and your face got sunburned, and all you
worried about was mosquitoes. We went to a lot of fuss over
blinds in the Carolinas, but here in the Louisiana marshes you
went to no trouble at all. You just climbed into a pirogue, with
the Cajun who poled it standing, from the stern, and the decoys
jumbled together in front of you. The Cajun could push that
flat-bottomed pirogue over solid mud, if it had a bead of moisture on it.

There were four pirogues in all, two men to a boat. We—or
rather, they—poled slowly down the bayou, letting the tide take
the boat, until we came to a kind of track that led into what

appeared, in the gray of the early morning light, to be a broad sweet-water pond set in the middle of the marsh.

My Cajun, named Pierre, shoved us into a patch of roseaux or reeds. He got out, in his boots, and then pulled the pirogue up onto a grassy tussock, where he braced her with the pole athwartships, each end of the skiff jammed into the reeds. Then he pulled the roseaux in bunches round us until we were beautifully hidden. He waded out into the finger-shallow water and flung the weighted decoys here and there. Across the pond I could hear the *skush* of the other pirogues as they slid across the ooze, and occasionally a muffled Cajun "By gar" drifted across the quiet water as the poler got his pole fouled in a water lily root. Then the splash of the decoys, and silence until the sky began to pink at the edges.

The most exciting sound in the world cut the stillness, and you forgot the persistent mosquitoes as the high wings whispered through the sky and dim shapes made faint marks against the low gray clouds as they passed out of range overhead. The torture was heightened by the thin whistle of teal coming by, low and turning, and the faint splashes as they set down among the decoys and the tiny gurgle as they swam. Then the watery flap of wings as one drake stood on his tail to challenge the world made the semidarkness well-nigh unbearable.

But the pink spread to red and crowded higher in the sky, and suddenly an enormous gray blur darted past the blind. I shot the blur more or less in the pants as it passed, and it fell with a soggy bump onto the water-covered ooze.

"Must of been a goose," I whispered to Pierre.

"*Non, man*, dat no goose," he whispered back. "Dat beeg bull peentail. Beeg lak a goose, though. Look, you, here come some more."

A flight of pintails came in and swirled, and I raised the gun, but Pierre touched me on the arm. "*Non*, don't shoot yet," he said. "Dey mak one more turn, den come seet down weeth decoy."

Pierre was right. They went away, turned, came in low and perfectly, and locked their wings. I shot at the feet of one big drake as he dropped his legs, dumped him, and pulled away to a fast-climbing bird—another drake. I aimed at his sky-seeking bill and dropped this fellow, too. I was out of breath—three big pins on the deck in half a minute—the most beautiful of all the ducks, with russet head and herringbone gray suit, showing white-breasted as they lay belly up, feebly kicking in shallow water. Pierre seemed impressed, although he said nothing, just nodded. He had a gun but hadn't fired.

Now the boom of guns was coming from the other blinds, and ducks were dropping out of the sky. You could hear the splash as they hit, and the rattle of shot on wing as some carried lead. It was full light now, the sun a red ball, a light breeze freshening and rippling the water, making the water lily pads bow their edges in a tiny little minuet. High against the cloud-gray were black strings of ducks, wedges of ducks—big mallards, more pintails. And higher still were enormous, endless V's of blue geese, honking mournfully as they passed.

The teal were working low, and Pierre touched my arm again. "When de teal dock come een, een a beeg ball," he said, "shoot de meedle. Teal docks don' count like beeg docks, but dey eat good for breakfast and mak' fine col' lunch. Shoot plenty teal docks for de cook."

A literal swarm of greenwings buzzed in and I fired across their bows with both barrels, and felled what seemed to be a bushel.

Pierre grinned a big gold-toothed grin. "*Bon, bon,*" he said. "Now we forget teal docks, shoot only beeg docks. De cook, he be plenty happy, you bet."

"Who's the cook?" I asked.

"De cook?" He punched himself in the chest. "I'm de cook, me."

A flight of mallards stuck their heads down as Pierre called plaintively. They turned, circled to reconnoiter, and Pierre called again. They swept behind us in a great curve and came around, intent now on decoying. Keeping my head down I moved the gun up higher and slipped the safety catch. . . .

A shrill whistle from the bridge hauled me swiftly out of Louisiana and back to a *suji* bucket on the hungry ship "Sundance" bound for northern European ports from Savannah. I ran up to the bridge. The mate was bending over the ladder, looking down at me.

"We've changed course," he said. "Trim the ventilators."

"Aye, aye, sir," I said, and went off to trim the ventilators that led to the cargo holds so that no nasty ocean damp would damage our lovely cargo of sheep manure, sulphur, phosphate rock, nails, and scrap iron for the Germans to make war with. The waves crashed over the decks as the ship changed course, and all the ventilators appeared to have rusted fast since they had been trimmed an hour ago. I thought, as I wrestled in the wet cold with the jammed ventilators, that Louisiana duck hunting was too good for this kind of work, and I would save the rest of it for the last two hours before dawn on that (unlimited stream of profanity) water-drenched, windswept, sea-tortured foc'sle head.

The foc'sle head was even colder, windier, and wetter after the change of course, and I had to wedge myself between the anchor chains to keep from being washed ten feet straight down into the well deck and onto the deck cargo of logs. It was still a couple of hours until dawn, the coldest, most miserable time of the waning night, when cold gray sky would merge with cold gray sea and there was nobody alive on the Atlantic but you. What they needed a lookout for I couldn't say, because you couldn't have seen the "Queen Mary" fifty yards ahead of you.

It was time to go back, mentally, to where it was warm, to the roseaux-reed blind off the Bayou Philibert in Louisiana, squatting in a flat-bottomed pirogue with a Cajun named Pierre. The sun was coming up, the mosquitoes were departing, and across the little lily-studded, sweet-water pond the Old Man's gun was booming. The sky was full of big ducks, and higher up a million geese were working. I wiped a gallon of cold Atlantic Ocean off my face with the back of a glove and longed then and there for Louisiana.

Somehow you don't associate fine duck hunting with warm weather and pleasant surroundings, but this Louisiana hunt the Old Man took me on was about the best I had ever seen up to then. We were living on a big clean launch moored at a Cajun oyster dock that stuck out of the levee, and poling out in the pirogues to hunt. There were eight of us—the Old Man and me, two of his friends, and four Cajuns who served as guides, cooks, and assistant gunners.

I thought Cajuns were just fine. They were originally the French people that the British deported from Acadia in the middle 1700's (Acadia now being Nova Scotia, the Old Man told me), and they still spoke a French-English patois that was pretty funny to the outsider. They were magnificent hunters, trappers, fishermen, and marshmen. A Cajun in hip boots could walk a marsh as though it were a sidewalk, when you would bog to your neck in the ooze.

My friend Pierre, my mate in the pirogue, was little, dark-sallow, bushy black-headed, and fox-faced. He wasn't shooting much, only when a big bunch of ducks came in to the decoys and then I could feel the rattling blast of his rusty old pump gun. Those were the days before you plugged them down to three, and Pierre could spout five out of that old sliphorn faster than most people play an automatic.

After the pintails quit flying the mallards took over. The Cajuns call a mallard a "French duck," possibly because the yellow bill and vulgar yellow shoes and green head and purple-blue wing feathers appeal to a certain Gallic appreciation of gaudiness. There was a sight of ducks flying, and we weren't having anything to do with little ducks or trash ducks. We let the shovelers and the goldeneyes and the broadbills alone, even though, there wasn't much attention paid to limits in the marshes in those days. A marsh was a far piece away from a warden. Wardens didn't have much truck with Cajuns anyhow, Cajuns being notably pepper-tempered and the malarial swamps and marshes where they lived a bit tricky for law enforcement. A fellow can get lost easy in those Louisiana swamps.

The French ducks were decoying well that morning. Allowing for the misses you make foolishly in an abundance of riches, by ten o'clock the marsh line, which surrounded the pond, was studded with dead ducks that the wind had wedged gently into a lee shore. Some of the ducks we would lose, as always—the runners that made the marsh only to meet a mink or a coon. Once that morning we saw a mink tiptoe daintily out onto the mud, seize a mallard by the neck, and disappear into the marsh.

It was almost pickup time when Pierre pointed to a lonely dot in the sky. The dot was making mournful noises and seemed to be mixed up in its directions. "Young goose. Lost hees mama," Pierre whispered. "You watch. I play the mama, call heem right eento blind. Hees eat very good, young goose. Not so tough lak hees papa, heem."

The seduction of a lost young goose is one of the simplest Cajun tricks, and one I was to see a great many times, but the first time is always the most impressive. Pierre talked that yearling goose out of the sky and down to the blind, which it circled three times. You might have killed it with a stick, but I settled for the shotgun. It fell with a crash, but I swear it wasn't any bigger than the first pintail I had taken in the early light.

"*Bon, bon,*" Pierre said again. "Dat cook, he be plenty happy, you bet you. I guess we pick up now and go back to boat." Pierre said as we watched the other pirogues snouting out of the impromptu blinds. "We got plenty dock today. Dees afternoon we go shoot plenty goose on de flat. I show you some treek, eh?"

It was tough poling—or it would have been for me, who couldn't even stand up in the skinny almond shell that is a pirogue—but Pierre leaned on his pole, standing erect in the stern, and shoved his boat full of boy, decoys, guns, and dead ducks along the bayou, against the surging tide, without working up a sweat. We pulled up alongside the launch and I looked at my dollar watch. It was just 10:30.

The Old Man was in high humor. "What do you think of *this* for duck hunting?" he asked himself, more than me. "Beats that freezing to death, don't it? You hungry?"

"I could eat a muskrat, me," I said. I was already about half-Cajun myself by this time. "What have we got for lunch?"

The Old Man winked at Pierre. "Well, the ducks won't be ready to eat before tonight. All we got is some sandwich truck and coffee and eggs and such as that. It seems to me it's up to you to provide the lunch, unless you'd rather stay aboard and gut about fifty ducks. Not that there's much trick to it, the way these fellows do it. Show him, Dedée"—this to another Cajun, the one who'd poled the Old Man's pirogue.

Dedée picked up a mallard and extended the anal vent with the point of his knife. He crooked a finger, stuck it inside the duck, and hauled the whole innards clear with one jerk. He shrugged, threw the guts over the side, and wiped the finger on the mallard's back feathers.

"Simple when you know how, ain't it?" the Old Man said. "But then, most things are. Tell you what. I'll go provide half the lunch if you and Pierre will furnish the main course. No, I forgot. Pierre's the cook and he'll have to stay aboard. You go with Anatole. But first— Dedée, where's that yellow stuff?"

Dedée grinned and went below. He came back with a half-gallon jar of light yellow liquid.

"That's Cajun orange wine," the Old Man said. "Have a sip, but don't let it get to be a habit. These boys make it, and it'll bust your skull if you take too much."

Dedée poured me out a dram in a coffee cup and I sipped it. It tasted innocent enough, and I drained the cup. Whatever it was it burnt a firebreak right down my gullet. My eyes must have popped and I broke into a light sweat.

"I told you," the Old Man said. "That's powerful stuff. Now get over the side and into that pirogue with Anatole. Whether you know it or not you're going fishing. Me, I got other chores. Come on, Dedée, let loose of that jar and we'll get to work."

Anatole and I drifted down the bayou a few hundred yards, and he worked the pirogue over to what looked like an enormous straight chair built into the water at the mouth of a smaller, excited stream, which came from a man-chopped cut about twelve feet wide that wound out of sight through the marshes. The rushing, eddying water made a roll where the stream met the bayou. Anatole jabbed at the bottom, and his pole went nearly its full length before he hit mud.

"You go 'long top," he said. "Here, tak' pole an' stringer." He handed me up a light rod with a small reel and a hook with a buckshot sinker. "You wait a meenit," he said. "I be back with bait." He let the pirogue drift and unfurled a cast net. Then he disappeared around a bend in the bayou, but I could hear the cast net splash, once, twice, three times. In a moment he came poling back. The pirogue's bottom was full of kicking, bucking little shrimp. He took a bailing bucket and filled it three-quarters full of the shrimp, and passed the bucket up to me.

"What are we fishing for?" I asked, perched on a crosspiece on the platform that obviously was intended to serve as a seat.

"Redfeesh," he said. "Red drum. Best feesh we got in bayou. You just steek shreemp on the hook, let her float in current and haul in feesh. Maybe you get a trout, maybe not. I be back in mebbe-so one hour, me. *'Voir.*" And he was off, around the bend again in his pirogue.

I baited a hook, paid out the line, settled back on the comfortable plank seat, braced my feet on the rough rails that surrounded three-quarters of the platform, smiled at the sun and fumbled in my pocket for a pack of cigarettes. I had been smoking about a year—legally, that is—but somehow I never smoked in duck blinds. I had just managed to get a cigarette lit when a bolt of lightning struck my shrimp and headed, I guess, for the Mississippi River. I fiddled with him a bit, but not wanting to foul up dinner I fetched him back as fast as I could. He was a big redfish, three or four pounds, well-hooked and swimming around at the foot of the platform.

I didn't have a net or a gaff, so I climbed down the crosspieces that made steps up to the fishing chair, holding the rod with the line taut in my left hand, the left arm crooked under a crosspiece to hang on. I managed to swim the fish in to where I could gaff him with my hooked fingers in the gills and jerked him kicking out of the water. I climbed backward upstairs to the platform and strung him on the stringer, then let him back into the water, where he seemed to be happy.

The sun was pounding down now and I took my undershirt off. I could almost feel the freckles pop again on my shoulders, where old-time blisters had been replaced by big blotchy brown spots. My nose and forehead were already beginning to pink. I threaded another shrimp on the hook and repeated the performance. When Anatole came poling back about an hour later I had six or eight big reds swimming on the stringer, and I'd lost as many as I caught.

"That's plenty for lonch," Anatole said. "Come on, we go back to boat. We got plenty odder t'ings for eat, us. Today we got jambalaya. At least we got de making, eef dat Pierre he don' wreck de rice."

I clambered down and we dragged my string of fish into the boat, where the big reds flopped and kicked on top of whatever it was Anatole had provided. What Anatole had provided was a bushel of big crayfish, another bushel of big shrimp, and about two bushels of clams.

When we got back to the boat, sitting clean and riding high and pretty, the Old Man was already aboard. He was perched on top of the cabin, shucking a mound of fresh oysters that reached nearly to his chin.

"Man, this is the land of plenty," he grinned around his pipe. "All you got ot do is stick down a tong and drag up a peck of oysters."

"*Oui,*" Dedée said from the stern sheets, where he was plucking ducks. "Plenty *huîtres.* Odder people's *huîtres.* You don't teenk deese tengs just grow *sauvage*, you? Steal de oyster very bad. Put you in jail plenty."

"Worth a stretch," the Old Man said happily. "Here, boy, have a dozen of these illegal critters to hold down your appetite until dinnertime, which is a good hour off yet. We got to get the raw materials ready for the cook. All he's done so far is fumble around with some rice and drink a quart of that jaundice-colored poison they make out of oranges."

The oysters, new-tonged from the mud and washed clean, tasted wonderful without salt, pepper, or sauce. There must have been a zillion-billion oysters in that bayou, because all the roads alongside were made of crushed shell, and right where the launch was moored were mountains of the bleached shells, just sitting like big white hills.

"Try some dees clam, you," Anatole said, dumping a dozen of the yellow-fleshed, purple-cornered, plump little clams onto my tin plate. "More better dan de *huîtres*, I teenk, me. Got more salt, heem."

Indeed, the clams tasted even better than the oysters. We all sat and worked now, me finishing up the fish and graduating to plucking ducks. Anatole tossed most of his clams onto the Old Man's dwindling pile of unshucked oysters and started preparing the shellfish. As the cleaned raw material mounted, somebody would take a batch to the cook. Certain smells began to drift out of the galley, wonderful smells. . . .

It was full light now and the ship was near awash, the deckload of logs loosened, the deep-cut well decks running with water. Eight bells hit on the bridge. I tapped the bells back. There was no need to yell, "Lights 'r bright, sir," because the running lights and the masthead lights had been doused. I could see the cadet stumble down the ladder from the wheelhouse. As soon as I'd hit the bells I secured my watch and picked my way over the loosely moored logs, climbed the ladder to the wheelhouse deck, and crossed the open midships deck to get back to the warmth of the engine room fiddley.

I peeled off my wet stuff and went aft to the crew's mess and what passed for breakfast. Breakfast would be half-baked, doughy biscuits and fried fatback and ancient eggs, badly scrambled, but at least the coffee would be fresh. But whatever it was we were going to have, if it had been plovers' eggs and caviar, I wasn't going to like it—not after what I had been expecting for lunch on the sunlit Bayou Philibert in Louisiana.

It wasn't really my fault that I got into trouble over the captain's night lunch. It was some my fault, because I was the actual thief, but mostly it was the Old Man's fault. He shouldn't have taken me to Louisiana, duck shooting that time, and the eight bells that sent me off watch to a filthy breakfast shouldn't have interrupted my train of thought. Smitty, the second cook of the "Sundance," was an enormous plum-black Negro, and a good cook when he had anything to cook. But like the old gittar song says, "the beans was tough and the meat was fat and oh, my Lord, I couldn't eat that"—which also applied to the eggs, which may have been extracted at gun point from the last of the dodos.

I guess it was one of those days. I couldn't seem to sleep in my blue-jean sheets back under the fantail, because the steering engine was making an ungodly racket as some poor freezing sailor tried to keep the raunchy "Sundance" on course. So I got up for lunch and we had curried-something, possibly ship's rat, and supper was worse. All through the three meals I had to look at Svendsen, the bosun, with his cigarette dripping out of his pursed mouth, the smoke floating upward past his squinted eye, as he held forth on the futility of hiring college boys as sailors when master mariners and chief mates were starving on the beach.

Then that night I came off the foc'sle-head lookout at midnight, frozen stiff and wet through. When I thawed out a bit I was hungry again. The night lunch wasn't much—coarse-grained cold bread, clammy salami, mummified bologna, and cheese a rat would refuse. What made it worse there wasn't anything left but crumbs, because the able seamen had eaten it all. My belly was singing a long lament, and I kept thinking about that meal I had in Louisiana, and this process led inevitably to the officers' night lunch.

I figured the skipper was in his sack, and I crept forward to the pantry. I opened the icebox and there it was, all the delicatessen my soul as well as stomach craved, and I ate hearty—stuffing it in with both hands. The stolen feast called for coffee . . . boiled-only-once coffee in a silver percolator, when I heard familiar steps. The skipper had been roused, by either intuition or hunger, and was heading for the pantry. I beat him out the door by a whisker, and for some stupid reason I was carrying the coffeepot with me. Thereupon began a chase that was never bettered by the Keystone Cops or the Ritz Brothers.

Still grasping that percolator I took off. The captain, wearing carpet slippers, took one look at his ravaged icebox, the door gaping open, and the gimbaled holder on which his purloined coffeepot once had rested. He let out a scream like a wounded banshee and took off behind me. Around, over, and practically under the ship we went, aft to fore and fore to aft, the skipper cursing, stumbling, and blowing his whistle for aid. It sounded like the Apaches had captured the fort and were scalping everybody.

I was pretty young and sure-footed and I knew that ship and its cargo as I knew my fingers, and what to me was a beaten track was an obstacle course to the captain, who ordinarily stayed close to the chartroom. He fell over deck cargo and barked his shins, slipped on the watery deck, collided with bulkheads, lost his footing on ladders, but he continued to blow his whistle and scream for assistance.

He got assistance, all right. He roused the off-watch mates and the steward's department and the deck gang and the black gang, and he also roused me. I had long since flung his coffeepot over the side, not wishing to be caught with the evidence, and I joined the protective coloration of the herd of drowsy men. I made myself busy at all sorts of things, like trimming the vents and slapping *suji* on distant bulkheads, and when the skipper herded everybody into the crew mess to sort out the culprit you might have seen the canary's feathers fluffing out of my lips.

There were over thirty men on that ship, and it's hard to pick a night-lunch thief out of thirty men, unless you stomach pump 'em all. Fortunately the "Sundance" did not carry a stomach pump, although I had a fleeting suspicion that the skipper might order the ship's carpenter to jury-rig a food detector out of the bilge pump. The skipper ranted and roared, and swore that he would keelhaul the guilty party when he caught him, and in the meantime there would be no pay when we docked and no shore leave at all. I suppose if it had been wartime he would have shot the entire crew. The captain ultimately lost his voice, swore a final husky oath of vengeance, and departed, croaking. Everybody went to bed, and I went back on the foc'sle head to announce colliding dolphins and reflect aloud that the lights, running and masthead, were bright, sir.

After the hare-and-hounds episode I had little difficulty concentrating on that midday meal on the Bayou Philibert, because I was stuffed with the skipper's night lunch and had scored my first and only victory over the anointed personnel of the wallowing bucket "Sundance" from Savannah.

I spoke aloud into the wind, addressing the Old Man, off somewhere in infinity. "I hope you're satisfied," I said. "You could have got me hanged from the yardarm. This'll teach you to expose me to Louisiana food. . . ."

That day on the bayou, after we'd finished preparing the ducks and the oysters and the fish and the shrimp and the crayfish, we saw the entire fruits of the morning collection pass down into the launch's galley, where Pierre was chef. I had stoked myself pretty well with raw oysters and clams, but there was still plenty of space in the boilers for whatever Pierre was making. What he was making was one big dish, and he made it in an iron cauldron big enough to boil a hog in.

It was jambalaya—call it *pilaf, payloo, pilau, paella,* or anything you want—but its main ingredients are rice and red peppers. Into this rice had been mixed shrimps, oysters, clams, crayfish, pork sausage, great white slabs of fish, a chicken for the stock, and the whole business cooked together until it was one great big wonderful adventure. Pierre had cooked the rice with saffron, so that it came out yellow, and the juices from the seafood and the chicken had got married in a tremendous soupy ceremony so that the rice, while dry by grain, was damp by volume, and the hunks of fish and the shellfish hadn't lost any of their flavor but were nuggeted through the rice.

He served all this with great big chunks of crusty French bread for mopping up and a gallon of homemade red wine, and we finished up with Louisiana chicory coffee that was so strong you had to cut it to drink it. Even with an elder gentleman's estimation of a young man's anaconda capacity I hesitate to recall how much I ate, sitting with a basin of this stuff in my lap, soaking in the sun, listening to the birds in the marsh, watching the fish jumping in the sparkling, breeze-ruffled bayou, and smelling the good smells of decaying oyster shell and marsh-grass mud.

Pierre observed the destruction of his masterpiece with proper Gallic pride, although he played it coy. "Dat only meedle-day snack, heem," he announced. "You tak' leetle sleep now and then go shoot goose. I theenk I don' go. I theenk I stay here on boat and mak' really good beeg supper, me. You got plenty of people for shoot goose."

The Old Man said he thought he'd grab forty winks below, and the other people said, "By gar, dat one hell of good idea," but I stayed up topside and just sort of snoozed on the cabin top. About three o'clock the Old Man stuck his head out of the cabin and announced that I better take some No. 2's along with the 4's if I intended to go shoot a goose that day.

"I already *shot* a goose," I said, "With a duck load."

"You shot a pinfeathered adolescent goose," the Old Man replied. "I'm talking about real grown-up geese, including maybe a honker from Canada. You don't want to mess around with 6's on these fellows. Buckshot ain't too big for a real hoary old gander. They can pack off a power of lead."

The Cajuns started piling stuff, including a bundle of reeds, into a broad-beamed, shallow-draft bateau, about the size of a surfboat but wider. It had a small engine in it. The bateau had been floating tandem to the launch.

"You don' need pirogue for goose," Anatole said. "You need beeg boat. We jus' go along bayou een dees bateau, then we park heem 'long levee, walk through muck, mak' blin', shoot plenty goose. We shoot off prairie."

We putted along the bayou for half a dozen miles. The flights of geese were enormous, and they settled in huge flocks on the water-soft savannas the Cajuns called prairie, semibogs covered with bright-green grasses. In the distance you could see the feeding geese, blue some, many white, as if they had changed their plumage with age. Once in a while a V-ended double thread of bigger, grayer geese entered the party—Canucks. I looked and saw no decoys in the boat, and finally screwed up courage enough to ask why.

Dedée laughed. "Dees ver' intelligent goose," he said. "Read all de tam'. We use *Picayune* newspaper, stick him on prairie, goose fly down to read all de news, shoot goose, bim, bam!"

I looked at the Old Man.

"You remember that time we were making decoys and you said they didn't look like ducks to you?" he said. "And I said they may not look like ducks to you, but they look like ducks to a duck? Same thing. You fold these papers, prop 'em up with sticks in front of the blind, and to a flying goose they look like a hull herd of geese feeding. You call the goose right, and the old stud gander will fetch his flock in."

We chuffed along some more, and on both sides of the bayou the geese rose with wild, annoyed honking in clouds of thousands, until the sky was filled with a hundred thousand. The noise they made was unbelievable.

Dedée, who was steering the bateau, finally nosed her into a cut, pushed a pole into the soggy turf, and announced it was firm enough to walk on. He drove his pole deeply into the turf, bent the bow painter around the pole, and let the bateau swing with the tide until she nestled against the bank.

"*Allons-nous,*" Dedée said. "We go shoot de goose."

We went off to shoot de goose, each man carrying his gun, each man with a couple of boxes of shells. I looked at the Old Man and saw he was loading his long barrels with a 4, right, a 2, left; and I did the same. I'd get mixed up later maybe, but at least I'd start right.

Away over yonder the ground was snowdrifted with geese. Flocks whirled and circled lazily and then dropped the undercarriage and slanted down to feed. Two of the Cajuns, Anatole and François, started splicing the reeds together to make small repairs to a blind that had been shot over before. There was a plank, a long one, mounted on saw-horse legs inside the blind.

"Better dan get the *derrière* wet seeting een dees prairie," Anatole said. "He's look dry, but he got plenty water under grass, heem." For the first time I really noticed that I was muddy past my shins. The water seeped up from the muck and came all the way through the grasses, when you put your foot down hard.

While Anatole and François were repairing the blind Dedée was out with the newspapers, which he had been folding into a very creditable representation of a goose—the wings cocked, so, the paper extended into a searching neck, scanning the sky, or a feeding neck, crooked over and inspecting the muck for nutriment. Even at a short distance they looked remarkably like feeding geese. From the air, I imagined, they would look exactly like feeding geese. Even to a goose.

"Ees not bad," Anatole said, "but ees not de best. When we shoot a few goose, we run out queek, us, and plant de dead goose in forked stick, so we have nex' best teeng to live goose. Den de goose he come plenty, heem."

Dedée finished his paper work, gave a look around, seemed satisfied, and scurried into the blind. We sat along the sixteen-foot length of plank, each man with his shell box opened in front of him.

"Who de goose?" Dedée asked. "I teenk you, François. You call de goose, you."

François scorned a mechanical caller. He cupped his hands around his mouth and yelped. He pleaded and cajoled and attracted the interest of a big flock of white geese. They circled three times, were not alarmed at the blind or the *Picayune* decoys, and sailed in for dinner. I performed in my usual fashion. I picked the biggest, oldest, toughest, grizzliest gander I could get under my sights and gave him two. He more or less cocked an eye at me and went swiftly elsewhere. I reloaded while I listened to the soggy thump of other people's geese hitting the prairie. One was a runner that got up and shook his head, and I settled his troubles for him, figuring I'd better contribute something to the party.

We let the dead geese lie. The Old Man had a smug look about his mustaches that indicated he had scored a double. All told, there were six geese down by seven shooters. Since I got none, and giving the Old Man two, the other five boys shared four. Somebody else missed too, I thought, and felt better.

François started to gabble goosy again, and before long in came another flock. This time I committed my second mistake. I let go both barrels at the entire flock, where it was biggest, and something dropped this time. A handful of feathers. Around me was the solid *thud-thud* of geese falling like sacks. I counted and now there were fourteen. Everybody was improving but me.

Dedée held up a hand. "Now we got de real decoy," he said. "Anatole, you help me feex, you."

They scuttled out of the blind, keeping low, and replaced fourteen folded newspapers with fourteen dead geese, their necks jammed in forked sticks, their wings braced in a flap or left to fold. Some had necks crooked, some extended. They looked like feeding geese. Even more so to a goose.

Back in the blind Dedée squinted at the horizon. A small V

of birds, bigger and blacker in the distance, was headed our way. "*Les Canadiens*," Dedée said. "My goose French she's more better dan you," he said to François. "I call dees cousins from Canada."

He changed the timbre slightly and began to talk. The Canucks halted slightly as the call touched them, and the lead gander inclined his head to look at the ground. He seemed satisfied and came on. The Canadas—big, gray, black-headed, with their white collars—came on, swept round in great circles, losing altitude all the time, and then came straight in like a great covey of aircraft. While they were coming I slipped the No. 4 out of one barrel and shoved in another 2.

This time, by gar, I wasn't going to miss, me. I still went for the gander, which flew almost into the gun barrel and then flinched, shuddered, and fell when the load struck him. I watched him drop from under the gun, and switched to a male friend that was struggling for altitude and led him too much for a big goose, but managed to put the full load into his head and neck. Down he came, like a rock, and while I did not blow through the smoking barrels I felt like it. I had *my* geese for the day. The other folks could mess around with blue geese and white geese, but I had a full bag of bull elephant. Blue geese me no blue geese. The pros shoot only the Canucks.

The Old Man looked at me and grinned. "There'll be no living with him," he said to nobody at all and shrugged. Then I looked at the goose-littered terrain and there were two more Canadas, both females, lying close aboard my ganders.

"Just call me a pothunter, not a hero," the Old Man said. "We got enough geese, boys. Let us *allons-nous* the hell out of here."

I'll say we had enough geese. We had enough for everybody to make two trips from the blind to the bateau. "Eet look like we shoot a snowstorm," Pierre ventured, "except for mebbe one, two leetle spots dirty snow."

My big gander weighed fourteen pounds. That is a very large gander. . . .

It was now about ten minutes, again, from finish-lookout and the same dreadful breakfast. As I sat down to the table my foc'sle-head mind raced back again to the dinner Pierre had smoking in the galley when we arrived triumphant with a bateau full of geese.

We had oysters on the half shell. We had a tawny-red soup called crayfish bisque, with the big crays, heads and all, in the sherry-rich soup. We had tiny teal broiled with bacon, like baby chickens, which fell apart in the fingers. Each man had a big pintail, cooked to pieces, with carrots and onions and potatoes and apples and sage shoved into its inside. We had that French bread and a chicory salad, and a side dish of redfish with a sauce of tiny shrimps and sherry and cream, which Pierre got the Lord knows where, unless he hijacked a cow. We had coffee.

"Tomorrow," Pierre said, "we have roas' goose. Weeth fresh goose leever for de hors de'œuvre."

The city of Hamburg, Germany, has a fine roast goose, and it is possible to buy a good goose-liver sausage, and if you are in funds a fine goose-liver pâté that comes from Strasbourg. When we docked there the skipper forgot the night-lunch-stealing episode and paid us off. Still haunted by Louisiana memories I went ashore and blew a week's pay on just one dinner.

It was then I decided that the Germans, when war inevitably came, would lose it. They couldn't have touched Pierre's goose with the business end of a pirogue pole.

5

How to Make a Hoorah's Nest a Home

Well, I been laying off to tell you about the spring when the Old Man and I decided to rebuild our fishing shack, which had been mauled by a couple of hurricanes. It never had been much of a shack, even for fishing every now and again—some four-by-fours and two-by-fours with a tar-paper roof and some warped, uncurried boards for walls. Everybody had used it and abused it, and even in good weather the inside looked like a tornado had struck it.

The Old Man used to grumble, "That's the trouble with be-ing nice to every Tom, Dick, and Harry that comes down the pike. They'd ride a free horse to death." Usually the place looked and smelled like a hoorah's nest—old tin cans, coffee grounds, papers, and rusty tackle scattered every which way;

the mattresses torn and dirty, and the lamp chimneys dyed black from smoke.

The last couple of big blows had really fixed her. Outside the shack looked like a bird's nest in a high wind—tar-paper blown to tatters, planks ripped off the sides, sand drifted up against the door.

"We'll salvage what we can and then burn her," the Old Man said. "It stinks like a cooter's den. Judging from the bottles the last few parties that used this shack didn't do much fishin'. Then we'll move over to another site and build us a proper lodge. We'll clap a lock on her, stick up a PRIVATE sign, and get the Coast Guard boys to keep an eye on her when they ride beach patrol. I hate to do it, but these days the only way a man can keep a decent permanent camp is to be selfish about it. Twenty, even ten years ago you could leave any door open and your provisions in the locker. People would come in, use what they needed, and leave the place clean. Later you'd find they'd put back what they used.

"It don't seem the same today, which is why, when you're my age, there practically won't be no such thing as common shootin' and fishin'. Everything will be posted and locked up, just for the protection of the farmer that's tired of having his pigs shot, and his hayfields burnt down with careless matches, and his property mucked up with old tin cans and filth. Dod-limb it," the Old Man said, "I'm just surprised this last bunch didn't set the place afire and be done with it."

The Old Man was striding up and down, mumbling and cussing under his breath. If there was anything he hated, it was a filthy camp. He was a real old maid about burning rubbish and burying leftovers and generally leaving a place cleaner and better than when he found it. I suppose a lot of it rubbed off on me, because even today a nest of beer cans and tumbleweeds of greasy paper can make me mad, just looking at the mess.

As far as we could see, up and down the beach, the shore was strewn with wreckage from the hurricanes. When she blows in that neck of the woods she rears back and blows, all the way from the Caribbean, past Hatteras, and right on up north. Anything that isn't secured pretty fast carries away. Most of it fetches up on the beach as flotsam, and a lot of it is usable. Where we used to call "down home," around Hatteras and Nags Head, the wreckers once made a considerable living gathering up the stuff that floated in off the ships that were wrecked, some by accident, some on purpose. The Old Man said Nags Head got its name from a cute little habit the natives had of hanging a lantern on a horse's neck and walking him up and down the beach during a storm. The distressed ships mistook the bobbing light for a signal light, plowed ahead, and broke up on the reefs. The flotsam came ashore, and when the weather calmed down the wreckers would go out in boats and pick the hulk clean, like buzzards. It was a long time ago, but that's how the story went anyhow.

The sand here was hard-packed, and we were able to get the Liz, the old high-axled Liz, down onto the beach. The Old Man had a coil of one-inch hemp in the stern sheets, and we went trundling down the beach looking for likely building materials. There was plenty to find: scantlings, a few tarry pilings where some fisherman's little dock had blown loose, a whole section of roofing—planks and joists and beams and the Lord knows what all in the way of innards—part of a staircase, ruined chairs, busted tables, even an old toilet seat.

A lot of it was no earthly good, but it was enough for a start. We made the line fast around what we wanted, piece by piece, bit by bit, and snaked it to the new building site, while the Liz panted and snorted and bucked and boiled over. I never saw such a car as those old T Models. They rattled and shook and made noises like coffee grinders, but they'd go places you couldn't get a team of horses in.

It took us the whole weekend to assemble the stuff and stack it in building order around the new site—one well back from the first line of dunes, one which grew enough sea oats to be anchored fairly permanent.

"We'll build her here," the Old Man said, "in that kind of

gully between the dunes. That way we'll get some wind protection. We won't have to worry about storm tides. What's more we'll set her up on pilings."

"How come pilings?" I asked. "Seems to me you're just shoving her up there in the air for the wind to blow over. Wouldn't it be better to snug her close to the ground?"

"I am no engineer," the Old Man said, "but I know a thing or three about building on a windy coast. A big wind don't fancy anything better than something that's nailed firm to a foundation, so's it can really bend a shoulder onto it and shove. I don't generally criticize the Good Book, but that business about the man who built his house upon a rock and the man who built his house on sand ain't strictly accurate for the Carolina coast. The principle is simple: You know how a big tree'll blow over and some wavy sapling will still stand in a gale? The limber log rocks with the gusts, the big stiff log or the pile of bricks tries to stand firm and shove back. One stays standing and the other blows down.

"There's another thing in favor of putting your house on stilts. It leaves plenty of space for the wind to blow underneath, and a lot of force gets diverted that way and passes on. The house'll rock a little and bend before the gale, but the gale goes round it and over it and under it. We'll shingle the roof. A blow might steal a few of your shingles, but you ain't apt to come here after a storm and find the hull roof carried away."

"It sounds reasonable," I said.

"There's still another thing you ain't spotted, from our standpoint, in terms of saving work. You know what I'm driving at?"

He had me stumped. "No sir," I said.

"Well, half or more of the work in a fishing or hunting camp can be better done under the house than in it. You can haul a boat up out of the weather for painting or repairs. It's cool underneath, out of the sun in the daytime. You can sort your tackle or mend a net or clean a mess of fish without cluttering up your house. You can stack your rods or your oars and leave your boots. You can dry your washing. You can tie your dogs under the house. All over the East and in the Pacific the salt-water people spend more time under the house than they do in it."

"You can't keep leaving gear and boats just loose when you go away," I said. "How you going to keep the stuff from getting swiped?"

"Simple," the Old Man grinned, "easy as pie. We build a lattice, about six-inch squares, all around the pilings. We put a heavy lattice door on it with a lock. I have noticed that while a man will use what's laid out handy and not nailed down he'll think twice before he'll batter open something that's got a door and a lock on it. We haven't got too many bad people around —just careless. Leave something loose and they may abuse it. Shove a lock on your gear, and tearing down the surroundings to get at it constitutes breaking and entering and maybe even burglary. We run powerful few burglars to a hill in these parts."

"All right," I said. "that's fine. You got me sold. But what about this business of the wind blowing *underneath* the house and passing on?"

"It blows through the *holes* in the lattice. The lattice'll be limber, too. So what does it matter if the wind rips off a strip or two? They're easy put back. So what you really got is not one house, but *two* houses. One is cool and shady to work in when it's hot, and the other is snug and warm to cook and sleep in when it's cold or rainy or blowy—all in the same space."

I don't know where the Old Man got all these ideas, except he had been nigh everywhere when he was younger, and he always had his nose stuck in some book that was too heavy to lift. But I must say most of his home-grown prescriptions for nearly everything had a practical side and generally seemed to work.

School let out in another week, and we went into the house-building business on a full-time basis. We took a little fly tent over to the island and some cooking gear and a cast net and a rod or so. We lived off the country. The big sea turtles were laying, and when you walked the beach in the moonlight it wasn't much trouble to get yourself a mess of fresh eggs for breakfast, if you just followed the big old herringbone marks the female made when she lurched across the wet sands to deposit her eggs. There were mullet and shrimp and pan fish in the creek, and an occasional puppy drum or little blue or Virginia mullet in the sloughs, working on the sand fleas. The big stuff was still up north or away off at sea using around the big shoals, but we made out. We had a hard-cured ham and some canned salmon and sardines and truck like that, and we ate pretty good.

Brother, we worked. The Old Man had sweet-talked somebody into sending over a truckload of stuff we hadn't been able to scavenge off the beach: cedar shakes for shingles, heavy-duty strips for the lattice work, creosote for the pilings, fittings for the innards. You'd have thought, the Old Man remarked, that we were building the Taj Mahal, which turned out to be some place in India. "But I must say," he said, "we'll take less time than they spent on the pyramids."

We sank the pilings about halfway to China, seeing as how I had to dig the holes, poured in a little cement to anchor the bottoms in the sand, and then built a platform across the top, which was the floor. There were good pine planks, and the Old Man shinnied up an improvised ladder and planed them smooth. He said his feet hurt bad enough without collecting splinters in his sock feet.

We reared the walls to six foot six, left room for a big window fronting the sea, and put what you might call square portholes on two sides. We installed a plank ceiling, and then built a shingled, pitched roof about a foot above the ceiling. The Old Man had got hold of some ratty old mattresses and he ripped the stuffing out of them and shoved it between the false roof and the regular roof. He said that was insulation and would keep the shack cool.

We cut the living quarters into two parts. One was the kitchen-living room, and the other was what the Old Man called the bull pen or sleeping quarters. The Old Man said he didn't like the idea of confusing slumber with grub.

He built—this called for fancywork—a hinged drop-leaf table that fell vertically against the wall and was out of the way when you weren't using it. He built cabinets all along one wall to hold the permanent stuff—canned goods, coffee, sugar, salt, pepper, mustard, catsup—that kind of camp truck. He built a perishable-food safe, with wire sides port and starboard, that fitted into one of the windows and could be hung outside in the breeze. We installed a two-burner cookstove that would feed off oil, and when it got hot it jumped up and down on its legs and filled the room with heat. Later on he arrived with two wicker rocking chairs—stolen from Miss Lottie, no doubt—and a couple of straight kitchen chairs. He built in lockers all around the room, for cups and saucers and frying pans and glasses, and he built one bookshelf the length of the room. We hung hurricane lamps from the ceiling. That was the living room-kitchen.

The bull pen was simple. It contained four beds—two double-decker bunks built right onto the walls on opposite sides of the room. Under each bottom bunk was a double set of lockers for clothes, and at one end of the room was a crosspiece for hangers. There was no running water in the shack, but in the kitchen he stuck a sink with a drain for inside dish washing and face washing.

It took near about all summer, building a rude staircase up from the ground, fitting the doors and storm windows, and building the lattice for the underpart. We sank a well about two hundred yards back toward the brush, and while the water was brackish it was usable. We put an old-fashioned stiff-handled pump on the well with a pumpshelf. Then he built a small rain water catcher—a reservoir—and put drains around the roof leading into it. He reckoned we could catch enough rain water to drink. About the last thing we constructed, back in the brush, was a two-hole privy with a deep trap. When we hung the Sears Roebuck catalogue on a nail we reckoned we had finished the job.

"She may not be much to look at," the Old Man said, as he dumped the mattresses into the bunks and hung the cups on the hooks and stuck the dishes in the racks, "but she's sound and weatherproof and she's ours. Anything you make yourself has a little bit more significance than if you got somebody to do it for you."

I rubbed a sunburnt nose with a palm that had long since seen its blisters change to horn. It seemed to me about the handsomest fishing lodge I ever saw—everything what they used to call shipshape and Bristol fashion. We had a power of fun in that little shack for as long as the Old Man lasted.

It's been about thirty years since we built it, and there have been a lot of hurricanes along since—Alice, Ethel, Helen, I don't know how many. But I am willing to bet that unless somebody tore the house down on purpose, the best part of it is still there. Certainly they haven't built a hurricane yet that would make it do anything more strenuous than take a bow.

6

If You Don't Care Where You Are You Ain't Lost

The Old Man and I were sitting in front of a driftwood fire we'd built down on the beach close to the water, and although it was late August the fire felt mighty good and looked prettier. You know how those old salt-sodden driftwood logs burn, light blue fairy flames that seem to dance over the wood, as alcohol burns. Sometimes you can't see the flickering flames at all the blue is so fragile against the night sky.

A sizeable mess of medium bluefish made silver stacks alongside the fire, and there were a couple of respectable puppy drum. An unseasonable nor'-easter, not due until September, had raised a ruckus and brought the first fish into the fresh-cut sloughs, where they were having a roaring fine time with the small bait and the sand fleas. We'd also had a roaring fine time with the feeding fish, until they knocked off biting when the tide came full flood. A little moon was shoving its way up over the horizon and any minute the water would start to ebb, and we figured we'd fish the ebb for another hour before we packed a mile up the beach to the shack.

"I wish we'd brought a wheelbarrow," the Old Man said, rummaging in the tackle box for his anti-sea serpent lotion. He found it, uncorked it, and blew drops of moisture through his mustache. "You're going to be powerful tired, sweating all those fish all the way back to the shack. I'd help you, but I'm too old and feeble and full of dignity to go around toting fish like a common peddler. Shouldn't be surprised if you didn't have to make two trips."

He snorted at his idea of a joke. I didn't laugh. I knew he'd help me lug the fish back to camp, but I had a strong suspicion about the identity of the fellow who would scale and gut 'em, and that fellow did not own a mustache or drink anti-sea serpent lotion out of a tackle box.

We sat quiet for a spell waiting for the tide to change, and the Old Man fired up his pipe and took another small precaution against moonstroke from his anti-moonstroke lotion. Then he hit me with one of his sudden questions. "What do you want to be when you grow up, now that you're past the policeman, fireman, cowboy stage? What do you want most?"

"I dunno," I said. "Money, I suppose. I want to have a lot of money."

"At least you're honest," he said, rubbing his chin with the pipestem. "Not that I admire it—your wanting to be rich, I mean. How do you figure to get rich?"

"Somehow. I dunno. But some way'll work itself out. I won't steal it, if that's what's worrying you."

"I wasn't worrying about you stealing it. You ain't got the makings of a good thief. You like to tell everybody your business too much. A thief keeps to himself. He don't gab. But he don't have any fun, either, because when he starts to spend what he stole and brag about it somebody ketches him at it. The lawyers get all the money, and he winds up breaking rocks in the jailhouse. What do you want to be rich *for?*" He threw that one at me hard.

"I don't rightly know. But there's a lot of things I want that take a lot of money."

"Such as?"

"Well travel, for one thing. I want to see all the things I've read about and you've told me about. I want to go hunting in Africa and India. I want to buy cars and guns and good clothes and houses. I want to send my young'uns, if I have any, to college, and I want to grow old without having to worry about it. That all takes money."

"That it does, that it does," the Old Man said. "But there's other ways of being rich without worrying so much about money. If you ever do get rich, and I ain't saying you will or you won't, but if you ever do you might find yourself worrying so hard about keeping the money that you wouldn't have time to do all these things. You know any real rich people?"

"Not firsthand, but I seen some. Them fellers that come in with the yachts from time to time."

"Willies-off-the-pickle-boat," the Old Man spat scornfully. "Drunk from noon on and working on their third marriage. Worried the whole time about Wall Street, even when they're out in their *yatch-its* all gussied up in brass buttons and captain's caps. They couldn't navigate a garbage scow from the pilot's dock to the quarantine station." That was about one mile over clear water.

"Well, how about those cotton people that own the big plantation? They're rich."

"Yep, they're rich, all right. I was raised with one of 'em. Used to hunt and fish with him when we were young'uns and he was still poor. He was crazier over fish poles and shotguns than you are. I bet he hasn't baited a hook or fired a shotgun in forty year—ever since he started getting rich. He don't even live on his plantation. Hasn't got the time. Seen him the other day in town and stopped for a talk. I asked when we were going to shoot some of those big turkeys on his place. His face lit up for a minute, and then dropped all the way to the sidewalk. 'I'd sure like to go again, Ned,' he said, 'but I never seem to get the time. You remember once, when we . . .' And then he looked at his watch. 'Oh hell, I got a directors' meeting,' says he, and rushes off like there was hounds after him. I never will know what he was about to remember. You know any more rich people?"

"No," I said. I was beginning to feel depressed.

"That's where you're dead wrong," he said quietly. "You know two rich people. You and me. We're both rich, right now. Richer than them Willies-off-the-pickle-boat. Richer than any of them cotton people. Stinkin', filthy rich you are, and so am I."

"What's rich, then?"

"Rich," the Old Man said dreamily, "is not baying after what you can't have. Rich is having the time to do what you want to do. Rich is a little whisky to drink and some food to eat and a roof over your head and a fish pole and a boat and a gun and a dollar for a box of shells. Rich is not owing any money to anybody, and not spending what you haven't got."

"It still takes money," I said doggedly. "It takes *some* money."

"Well, hell's bells," the Old Man said cheerfully, "anybody with the right number of arms and legs can make a *little* money. You take Tom and Pete. They fish some when the pogies are running, and manufacture a little moonshine in the winter. They trap a bit, and hunt a lot. They drink up most of the moonshine they make, but they take in a mite of money from fish and hides and guiding the sports from time to time. They live off a shotgun. They always got a smokehouse full of venison—most of it illegal, it's true—and other people's hogs that got lost. But their women tend the pea patch and the collards pretty good, and hominy don't cost much. They got a yard full of hounds and plenty of time to run 'em. I'd say they were pretty rich, wouldn't you?"

"I suppose so, if you look at it that way. But they won't never get to Africa or have a big car."

"For that matter, they won't ever get out of Brunswick County," replied the Old Man. "But the point is, they don't *want* to go to Africa, because they ain't got the right guns to shoot lions. They don't want a big car, because you couldn't take it into a deep swamp to tend the still. They got everything in the world they crave, including a set of cast-iron innards and the ability to sleep standing up. Many a rich city man would trade his millions for a house-broke belly that would let him eat a mess of fat pork and collards, chase it off with corn likker, and then lay down with the hounds and sleep ten hours in the yard. You know what I would of like to been, if I had been born in a different time?"

"No sir. What?"

"A kind of early-day Tom or Pete. One of them mountain men, they were called, about the time of Lewis and Clark and later Kit Carson and Jim Bridger and all those hairy old goats. The men that opened up the country west of the Mississippi. There's a lot of literature on the subject. Man, they were a rough lot of cobs. They thought they were lucky if they got back out of the Crow country with their hair on. They trapped virgin beaver streams and crossed mountains no white man ever crossed and charted rivers no white man ever seen. They were the advance people for traders like Frémont and Sublette and all those fellers, and they carved a trail through the Blackfoot country that left many a bone to bleach, but they wound up in Oregon and California.

"They were all rich men—not in their beaver plews, because they largely lost their profits gambling or pitching a big drunk when they come back to the outskirts of civilization—but rich because they were self-sufficient. They looked down on the traders and the soft city settlers that come later with the covered wagons, because the mountain men were a breed of he-coons apart. You interested in all this?"

I just nodded. The Old Man went on, dreamylike, and I could pretty near see it, the way he talked.

"Mountain men," the Old Man continued, in front of the blue-dancing fire, "were probably the most self-sufficient, uncurried boar hogs that ever lived. Most of them took to the small-bore, long-barreled rifle, with a cap lock instead of flint, after Dan Boone made the Kentucky long rifle a legend.

"Them fellers took everything the Injuns had to offer and improved the score considerable. They could throw a hatchet or a knife as well as any Injun or better. They rode bareback, Injun-fashion, with just a braided-hair loop around the pony's lower jaw to steer him by. They wore buckskins and long hair, and by the time they'd spent a winter in a buffalo-hide lodge, tanning skins and smoking themselves over a slow fire, you couldn't of told one from an Injun, either by sight or by smell.

"Some of them took squaws, if they were on good terms with the local tribes—Crows or Blackfeet proper or Shoshones or whatever—and the little, fat brown gal cooked their meat and sewed moccasins and chawed the buckskin to soften it for new clothes and scraped the beaver and the buffalo hides and slept 'em warm in the cold nights, even if the ladies were a little bit louse-infected. There was no disgrace attached to being a squaw man—that come later with the civilized back-easters, who wore linsey-woolsey and hickory shirts instead of buckskin. But some of the wilder mountain boys thought a feller who'd tie himself to a squaw and a half-breed family was going a little soft and sissy.

"These lone men were out in the West and Northwest for the spoken purpose of trapping beaver, but the beaver and the buffalo were just an excuse for roving free and unhampered by all the things they didn't like about law and order and rules and regulations. These fellers liked to get up on a bright morning in a place no other white man had ever seen, and look out to watch a million buffalo black on the plain as far as the eye could see, and to spin down a stream in a bullboat and take a prime beaver plew out of every trap.

"They lived off a steady diet of meat, when the shooting was good, and they never ate much fresh meat except buffalo hump, tongue, ribs, and what they called boudin—intestine stuffed full of chopped meat. The rest went to the wolves or got jerked into thin, dry strips, if there was a squaw handy. She'd pound a few dried berries into the pemmican and they lived off that all winter, that and a few carcasses shot during the cold and hung up in a tree to freeze. When they were off on the prowl they didn't need much provisioning. Buffalo chips made a fire to warm up the jerky, and if the jerky run out they could make it somehow on roots or prairie dogs or bear or mountain goat or whatever come under the gun sights, including horses and Injun dogs. If there weren't any roots or berries or prairie dogs they could make it for a spell on buckskin. Many a man ate up his last pair of spare moccasins.

"Where a man stood or rode or built a fire was home. He paid no taxes, saw no white people, obeyed no laws, spent no money. If his gun bust, he whittled a bow from wood or horn and strung it with a thong clipped off his hunting shirt; he chipped some flint and tipped his arrows. He only had two real enemies—Injuns and weather. Injuns could lift his hair, and weather could starve him first and freeze him second. But he never got lost, because a man that don't care much where he is ain't lost. He's exploring.

"They were a hairy, dirty, lice-ridden, mean, cantankerous, antisocial, and in some cases murderous lot of hopeless cases for civilization. When they come to the trading posts they spent their beaver money on watered-down trade whisky and foofaraw for their squaws, if any.

"They gambled and they fought with knives and cheerfully killed each other when the pannikins passed from hand to hand, and a man kicked his heels, let out a war whoop, and allowed he was a stud bear and could lick any other two- or four-footed animule that ever walked, crawled, or flew through the air. But when they got back on the plains and in the hills they owned all the space and sky and wood and water, and they were the freest, least dependent critters that God made recently. In that respect they were all rich."

The Old Man paused and looked at the sea. The ebb had started and the moon was riding high. In its light you could see the wet brown stain on the sand where the water had receded.

"I kind of got carried away," the Old Man said, a little sheepishly. "I would have probably made a terrible mountain man, and the first fat Kiowa that come along would have had my hair for a trophy. But it's nice to think about what it must have been like, especially if you never will see it again. That's where books come in handy. A man can be rich retroactively, if he can stand off the Armada with Drake and fight the Injuns with Jim Bridger. The water's going out. Let's try the fish again."

We walked down to the water's edge into the chill sea up to our thighs and cast. Each of us had simultaneous strikes. From the way the rods bent, we both had tied into good ones. We walked backward, reeling in, as the angry blues fought on the other end. The Old Man turned his head and asked, acidly, "You still want to be rich when you grow up?"

"That I do," I said stubbornly. "At least if I'm rich I can hire somebody to tote the fish and clean 'em afterward."

We toiled backward up the beach, and as usual the Old Man's fish was bigger than mine. I guess he might have made a pretty fair mountain man at that.

7

Stories Grow Taller in the Fresh Air

"A liar," the Old Man declared one day when I had stretched the truth a touch on some matter involving nonattendance at school, "is a person I cannot abide. He is like a suck-egg dog. You can't trust him out of your sight."

"Yes sir," I said, having been caught out handily.

"However," the Old Man said, gnawing at his mustaches, "there are certain exceptions to the rule."

"Yes sir," I said, looking hopeful.

"Now I wouldn't give a nickel for a truthful hunter or fisherman," the Old Man continued. "A hunter who ain't a liar, a fisherman who won't toy with the truth is generally the kind of man who will do you one in the eye on a cattle trade, foreclose a mortgage on a widder, and sneak stamps out of the petty-cash box. He will steal a horse and possibly kick his dogs. He will also have a small, tight, mean mouth and carry his money in a snap purse."

He fired up the pipe and shot one at me fast. "How much did that big puppy drum you caught the other day weigh?"

"Thirty-five pounds," I said.

The Old Man positively glowed with triumph. He cackled. "I weighed it behind your back," he said. "It weighed thirty-two pounds. You see, you're an automatic sporting liar, which I think is commendable. If it had been me, I'd of said forty pounds. But you're young yet and don't know the difference between a cheese-paring fib and a good, strong, hairy-chested falsehood. If you got to tell one tell a good one. I ever tell you about Elwood and Corbett and the doe deer?"

Elwood and Corbett were two brothers who lived near the Green Swamp and like many another, including my friends Tom and Pete, were known to make and sell a little white lightning, and thought that game laws were an invasion of civil liberties in Onslow County. They had a smokehouse that was full of meat the year round, and very little of it had ever seen an abattoir. There was a limit of two deer a year, and once I asked Elwood how many deer he'd shot so far (this being before Christmas). He scratched his head, and replied, "Well, I bought a box of shells in October. That's twenty-five, and I got two left. That means I must of shot twenty-three deer. No, dammit, I forgot. I had to shoot one deer twicet."

The Old Man went on. "I was hunting with the boys one day close to Waccamaw, and I was waiting on a deer-stand when I heard a gun go off. There wasn't any mistaking it, it was Elwood's; he was the only man around that had a single-shot .32 rifle. When I heard the crack I moseyed over, about half a mile, to help him skin and gut the deer. As I came close I heard voices, and there is this game warden talking to Elwood.

" 'You shot this here doe deer, Elwood,' the warden said.

" 'What doe deer?' Elwood replies.

" 'This here doe deer here. The one you just drug into the bushes and was fixin' to cover up with bresh when I come by.'

" 'I never shot no doe deer.'

" 'You must of shot her,' the warden says. 'Her neck's broke with a bullet and they's a .32 shell a-lyin' over there by that stand. The deer's here and the cartridge is here and you're here and you're the only feller around with a .32 rifle that always breaks deer's necks arunnin'. I say you shot this here doe deer, Elwood.'

"Elwood put another bullet in the rifle and hauled back the hammer. It made a nasty click. 'Warden,' he said, 'anybody that'd say I shot a doe deer is a suck-egg dog, and I'd *shoot* ary suck-egg dog I ever seen in the woods.'

"The warden looked at Elwood and then he looked at the gun and then he looked at the dead doe. He shuffled his feet and cleared his throat. 'I reckon you didn't shoot that there doe after all,' he said. 'But hit's a nice day, ain't it?'

"You know those cold gray eyes of Elwood's. He looked the warden straight in the face a long time before he answered. Finally he spoke. 'Hit *mought* be,' he said. 'Good day, Warden.'

" 'Good day, Elwood,' the warden said, and disappeared into the trees.

"Elwood got out his knife and started to gut the deer.

"Now that," the Old Man said to me, " is what I would call a very special lie, and one I don't approve of, because Elwood was wrong in the first place and he was backing up his lie with force. That's what starts all these wars you read about. A feller'll tell a lie and get caught at it, and then he's got to shoot his way out of it unless the other feller falls for the bluff. There's a little moral in that, too. There ain't any use bluffin' unless you're prepared to shoot your way out of it, and I am convinced that Elwood would of shot that warden. Those are hot-tempered boys down that way."

The Old Man got out a plug of tobacco and whittled a little clump of shavings into his hand. He stuffed them carefully into his pipe, after knocking out the dottle, and fired up the infernal machine.

"There's a lot to be said for some kinds of truth-stretching," he remarked vaguely. "A lot of mischief-making goes on from telling the pure-T truth that could be avoided either by keeping your mouth shut, giving an evasive answer, or telling a teensy little white one. This here kind of lying is called diplomacy, and is practiced the world round by diplomats and statesmen. At home it's a little simpler. I mean, if your ma asks me if you cut school the other day—which you did—I would merely say, 'I don't know. I haven't seen too much of him lately.' This would save you some trouble at home. But if I go running to your ma blabbering that you been cutting school, without her even asking me, then I am a meddlesome old man, but still I am technically telling the truth and should be had up for being noble beyond the call of duty. You see the difference?"

"As far as I'm concerned I see it," I said. "It's the difference between a week's lost allowance and a swat on the tail."

"It wouldn't be a lick amiss," the Old Man said.

"I know where you got that phrase," I said, sort of cocky. "You got it out of Tom Sawyer, when Aunt Polly whipped Tom when he really wasn't guilty."

The Old Man looked at me in amazement. He shook his head. "I cannot really believe that education is beginning to sink in, but there are signs—there are signs. Where was I?"

"Different kinds of storytelling," I said.

"Well now," the Old Man said, "we come to the sporting liar. He ain't really a liar. He is kind of an artist, like a painter. The difference between a photographer and a painter is that the photogtapher uses a machine that captures a subject exactly as it is. If the subject has got a wart on his nose the camera records the wart. But a painter only makes an impression—his impression—of what the subject seems like to him. If a man is painting a woman he loves or if he is painting for money and the woman has a wart on her nose or too many chins there is no law which forces the painter to leave the wart or dutifully record the chins. He can exercise a little artistic license because paint's cheap, as cheap as talk."

The Old Man yawned and scratched himself. "There are a great many fine things about hunting and fishing," he went on. "You can look at a deer-foot knife handle and remember what time the sun rose, how late the dew lasted, what the camp was like, how the food tasted, how the dogs sounded, when the sun set, when the moon rose, how the owls hooted, all the sounds and sights and tastes and feels. There is that moment of triumph when you boat the trout or haul in the bass or shoot the deer or score a snappy double on the birds. But it is really anticlimax to the other stuff. The adventure is ended with the bird in the coat, the fish in the creel, the deer gutted and hung in the tree. It is sad, a little bit, because all the anticipation is gone, the fact accomplished, the sport over. And that's where lying comes in.

"It is a sin to call it lying. It isn't, really. It's taking a piece of nice, honest cloth and embroidering a pretty design on it. You can't do the embroidery without you got the cloth first. You sit around and you remember and you talk in front of the fire, and gradually you swindle yourself into believing that the deer had eighteen points instead of twelve. You shot thirty ducks instead of fifteen. You only used half as many cartridges as you actually used, and all the fish were world records.

"This is a highly healthy thing. When you are a man grown you are too old for fairy stories, for folk tales, but any man is only a little boy with creaky joints and a bald spot, a mortgage and dyspepsia. He still needs to be amused, and this excessive use of imagination which we call fish stories is just an old little boy telling himself fanciful adventures to keep the hob-goblins away. Without these little embroideries life is mostly a matter of getting up in the morning, staggering through the day, going to bed at night, and thinking about the bills you haven't got the money to pay. When you get older," he said gently, "I think you'll understand what I mean."

"Where does it start and where does it stop?" I asked him. "Where does this embroidery leave off?"

"A man can overdo it," the Old Man replied. "I know a lot of bums who have managed to talk themselves into the idea that nothing's their fault, that they ain't lazy, and the world owes them a living. I know drunks that blame what's wrong with them on the state of the cosmos or the boss is down on them or their wives don't like 'em, when all the time they're drunks because they drink too much liquor. That is when you are really off with the birds.

"But a little self-delusion is good for the digestion, aids sleep, and improves conversation. It don't hurt a man to tell himself that things would've been different if the dog had a cold nose that day or the wind was right instead of wrong or that if he'd led it another foot he would have had it in the bag. And bimeby you believe it and are happy with it and it isn't a lie or a self-delusion any more. It's a fact, because you made it so by constant practice."

Of course, I see now that the Old Man was right, as he was mostly right. I have been to a war and I have written a great many words. I have hunted and fished and traveled the world. And I find that without any intent at real falsehood I have managed to embroider. So few true stories are letter-perfect. All need a little lacework, a little padding here, a little decoration there.

Recently in Africa I shot a leopard and that was quite a feat, if I do say it myself, as it had eluded the best six white hunters I know for a matter of more than two years. It steadfastly refused to appear in daylight. More by luck than design I got it to come to the tree in shooting light, nailed it precisely through the shoulders, and celebrated for a week.

In my mind that leopard is already becoming a legend. I did things to attract it that I really didn't do, but almost did—if I'd thought of the things at the time. The leopard has already grown about a foot in length and is easily another thirty pounds heavier. We stalked it a hundred yards at most but the distance has moved up to half a mile, and the other difficulties, from the pig as bait to bees in the tree, have grown apace.

A friend of mine shot another leopard, a big female, under most unusual circumstances on a recent safari. He shot it charging and growling and moving as only a hurried leopard can travel. Since that day I have heard the story about fifty times. (The exaggeration is mine—actually only about twenty-two times.) But the tale has changed as many times as he has told it. He is now referring to "she" as "he," and the beast has doubled in size, ferocity, and noise. We went together to the taxidermist one day in Nairobi and inspected a male leopard whose hide was as big as that of a medium-size tiger.

"I'd say mine was a little bigger, wouldn't you?" the friend said, believing it.

"I think yours was a lot bigger," I said, compounding the felony and believing it.

Back to the Old Man. I once declared my intention to hunt in Africa when I was a big boy, if the gods would so allow.

"I hope to live to see it," the Old Man said. "But most likely I won't. But I will make you a bet right now: By the time you get through talking about it and thinking about it, all the lions will be as big as elephants, all the elephants as big as houses, and when you go to sleep at night you will count the ammunition and find you never missed a shot."

The strange thing is that the Old Man was right. There was one day when I shot at a buffalo with a .318 and killed him and another standing behind him. Or was that a .300 Magnum and did it happen to Harry Selby?

8

Same Knife; Different Boy

Every time I pick up a paper and read about the teen-agers doing this and the teen-agers doing that and some young maniac shooting people or beating them up for fun I have a hard time reconciling it with the fellows I knew when I was a teenager. In days not so dead teen-agers meant somebody between twelve and twenty, but today it's gotten to be a term that certainly connotes problem and may connote criminal.

When I hear "teen-ager" today I almost immediately think in terms of switchblade knives, zip guns, gangs, rebellion, violence, and psychologic difficulty. The emphasis we put on certain examples of adolescence certainly far outweighs the indisputable fact that there are millions of good kids in jeans, who have a lot of fun with and without their folks, who know wind from water and how to build a campfire, run a motorboat, or catch a fish.

The Old Man had a saying about young'uns. He said they were fit to bust with energy, and unless you let the energy loose they *would* bust. The trick, he said, was to channel that energy down some road that wouldn't lead to window-breaking and car-stealing. He was a master at diverting energy and fetching the adolescent home so tired from the diversion that he didn't feel like getting into trouble.

I think today, even more than thirty years ago, that an interest in and knowledge of all dangerous weapons, including knives and pistols—brought out into the open and carefully supervised—is a healthy deterrent to misuse of those weapons. Possibly this does not apply to some social structures in the greater cities, but it never did really.

As the Boy I owned a knife from the time I was six. "The knife," the Old Man said, "is a tool, and a dangerous one. You ain't supposed to carry it open, and when you cut, always cut away from you. Keep it sharp, because if it's dull it ain't any use for what it's made for. But whittle *away* from you."

Thirty-five years later I still bear two magnificent scars on my left thumb. After acquiring those wounds I heeded the admonition and collected no more scars.

We all carried knives—starting with the twenty-five-cent barlow and working up to things with really wicked ripping blades —for skinning animals and cleaning fish. There was also a special saw-toothed, fish-scaling-and-bait-cutting knife in the tackle box, and as we grew a little older a sheath knife that we wore proudly as a sign of our frontiersmanship. But I would rather have gone without my pants than my pocketknife.

There wasn't a day when that dangerous weapon didn't come into use a dozen times—just plain whittling, cutting some cane to make arrows for the bownarrer, fixing a leader on a fishline, opening a can, cleaning fingernails (not very likely) or once, in my case, performing a bit of impromptu surgery on my own foot. I expect if you asked a really expert outdoorsman to name the last weapon he would abandon in the wilds he'd say, "Knife."

With a blade of sufficient temper there is nothing you can't do with a knife except shoot. And you can even make an acceptable substitute for that. The old Boers of South Africa used to kill zebra and wildebeest for their hides, meat, and tallow by riding in among the herds and stabbing them in the withers, a rather risky business if the horse stepped into a pig hole.

You can make a bow and arrows with a knife. You can literally make a canoe with a knife, and you can make a shelter with a knife, merely by cutting down small trees and using anything from a strip cut off your shirt to some tough twisted bark to tie the saplings and the sheltering foliage—whether it's palm frond or pine branches—together.

I reckon the stone knife was man's first important tool. It really became a weapon when he cut down a short sapling, whittled it smooth, and tied the knife onto the end of it, so he could throw it straighter. In a way, it was kind of a Stone Age zip gun.

When I was last in New Guinea a benevolent gentleman of the modern Stone Age, a former cannibal, gave me a magnificent ax. The blade is of greenstone and sharp enough to fell a tree, split the skull of an enemy, kill a pig, or build a house. The handle is shaped like a big T with a curved top, and is made from a single root or branch of hardwood. The greenstone blade was whetted by a warrior sitting in a river and using sand and rushing water to bring it to an edge. It fits into one arm of the T and is balanced by the branch that forms the other arm. The whole thing is bound together by a decorative cross-hatched sennit of the tough-barked *pitpit* palm, and is as tightly woven as cloth. The modern New Guinea Stone-Ager, discovered only in the mid-1930's, depends on this ax as the foundation of his entire economy.

Point is, it was put together with a knife.

The greatest archers of modern time I know are the Kuku-

kuku tribes of the New Guinea highlands. Their bow is a five-foot number made of black palm. It is strung with a fiber about half an inch wide. The arrows are unfletched, unnotched, untipped—merely fire-hardened. But they are deadly if only because of filth, and when fired in salvos they are something to see. I have watched one little black gentleman shove four into the air before the first one hit ground.

I have a spear from New Guinea and a shield made from a root. That shield will turn a bullet, unless it is centered dead on, and you can throw that spear entirely through a man's soft section. The spear is not tipped—just plain fire-hardened wood. And I have seen knives of tempered cane that cut beautifully.

Here again the knife, whether of wood or stone, made the other implements and weapons.

This is how I first came to regard a knife as something you used to keep the wolf from the knife-made door, not as something to stick into a stranger for fun. As far as I can remember us kids fought as kids will, but nobody ever drew a knife on anybody.

The same respect applied to guns. We started out at about six with a Daisy air gun, and by the time we hit seven or eight we graduated to a single-shot .22, and at eight or nine we got a 20-gauge shotgun. The care and feeding of these weapons, as I may have mentioned before, was forcefully impressed by a stout, whippy stick on the seat of your pants. In a very short time we learned to respect the tremendous power for harm, as well as the tremendous power for fun and positive enjoyment. I think the worst hiding I ever got was when the Old Man caught me and some cousins playing cowboys and Injuns by shooting each other in the pants with air rifles. My stern tingled for a time, and not from a BB pellet either.

Respect for what could kill you was hammered into our hides. Every summer, when the upcountry people came to the beaches, there was always somebody being hauled out of the water, drowned or half-drowned, because of being swept off-shore by the vicious currents that were formed by tide and two inlets to the major island. There is no such thing as undertow, but there are these currents, dictated by wind and tide and inlet, from sea to sound, and the wise guys always managed to die in defense of not appearing chicken, as they call it today.

My tribe comes from a long line of seafaring folk, and the first thing the Old Man impressed on me when I was a nose-holding, feet-first-jumping moppet was that the big stretch of blue stuff out there could kill unless you kept an eye on it every minute.

"Be frightened of it," he said. "It's a hell of a sight bigger than you are, and twice as ornery, twice as tricky."

Perhaps I am not very clear here, but what I am getting at is that my teen-age group possessed, legally, all the death-dealing, injury-wielding weapons that are now owned clandestinely by the "bad" kids. There was a certain pride in being trusted. My cousins and friends and I used to go off on a Saturday picnic into the local wilds with enough armament to conquer the county—rifles, shotguns, knives, scout axes—and were not regarded as a serious menace to the community. Or to each other.

It is perfectly true that we were free of the modern boons of child psychiatry, television, and progressive schooling. We denied ourselves much parental supervision, since we were out from dawn until dark. We cut Sunday school whenever possible, and the people we knew were rough—watermen, bushrangers, and city toughs. Mostly we came from medium-poor to poor families.

Why aren't we all in jail? I confess I have raided other people's watermelon patches and learned to chew tobacco at a very early age. I once jacklighted a deer and got into terrible trouble. But that seems a minor list of sins when you remember that I—and my chums—were all posssessed of formidable killing machinery. And if it came to racial tensions, God knows there were enough people of another color around to work out on.

We never traveled in packs. Cliques—yes. Three or four boys of an age group generally hunted and fished, and, when we were older and the sap began to rise, dated together. But the cliques never fought one another. Moonshiners and boot-leggers I knew by the score, yet they never taught me any nastiness. And then we came out of the teens in the teeth of the depression, which, Lord knows, showed a glistening set of fangs.

A moral is not intended here. I know a flock of modern kids with a cut of jib similar to ours, and they have been handi-capped by all the helpful aids to growing up that prevail in this decade. They still remain good kids, and do not run around killing each other for kicks.

. . . all of which leads me to the fact that during the summer they bagged John Dillinger in front of that Chicago theater everybody was making a lot of noise about this brave Robin Hood of the underworld and The Lady in Red and a lot of similar nonsense. You would have thought this thug was a com-bination of Davy Crockett and Mike Fink, and that his contem-poraries—Pretty Boy Floyd and Ma Barker and her brood—combined the nobler portions of Dan'l Boone and Hannah Somebody, who stood off the Injuns in the blockhouse raid.

I didn't take much stock in all the hullabaloo. The Old Man's memory was a bit too fresh—that and a dressing down he gave me one time when I did something bad. I disremember exactly what sin against the commonwealth I had committed, but the Old Man narrowed his eyes and sort of sneered.

"Who do you think you are?" he asked. "Judge Roy Bean? The law west of the Pecos? You make your own rules?"

"Who? What? No sir," I said.

"Your ignorance of your country's folklore is lamentable," the Old Man said, coming even closer to a sneer. "I don't sup-pose you ever heard of Joaquín Murieta or Billy the Kid or even Jesse James"

"I heard about Jesse James," I said. "He was an outlaw. He robbed the rich to give to the poor, and he was shot down in a dastardly fashion."

"Oh my God," the Old Man said, and clapped his brow. "In a dastardly fashion.' A *dastardly* fashion. You know what dastardly means?"

"No sir," I said. "I read it somewhere."

"You get a dictionary for Christmas," the Old Man said grimly. "But right now you get a little lecture."

I settled down for the long winter.

"I called you Roy Bean because there was a hanging Judge by that name one time, when the West was rough and they were building railroads with a lot of ignorant riffraff. There was so much murder and mayhem about that there was a saying: 'No law west of the Pecos.' So a scallywag named Roy Bean—a gunfighter, drunk, cowpoke, blockade runner, and saloonkeeper—set up shop in a place called Langtry, Texas. He opened a saloon called 'The Jersey Lily' after Lillie Langtry, and got appointed justice of the peace. He held court in the saloon, and announced that *he* was the 'law west of the Pecos.' In a way he was, because he would try you, fine you, and hang you all in the same motion. He set himself up as law, and justice didn't enter into it."

The Old Man snorted through his mustache.

"This bum was a hero when I was a boy," he said "We are a peculiar people, us Americans. All a fellow has to do is take the law in his own hands and we make a hero of him. Like this Billy the Kid. A nasty little bucktoothed rat, who'd shoot his mother in the back, who wasn't even a very good murderer, and who got killed by Sheriff Pat Garrett when he was twenty-one. Now they got songs about him.

"And this California bandit, Murieta. He is still famous, since 1853, but they ain't even certain it was him they killed and cut the head off of to exhibit around at the fairs. There was about five Joaquíns—all bums, all rustlers and back-shooters—working at the time, and they seized onto the first Mexican they could bushwhack who looked like his name might of been Joaquín.

"One thing you will find running through all these tall stories about bandit heroes. They were all supposed to be kind, generous, handsome, happy, chivalrous, kind to women and children. They were all supposed to be forced into a life of crime because of some outrage society dealt 'em off the bottom of the deck. I don't know what it takes to make a legend, but honesty, decency, and a reasonable obedience to law and order don't seem to qualify."

"How about Robin Hood, from the olden days?" I ventured. "I read a lot about him, how he robbed the rich to give to the poor."

"Fiddlesticks," the Old Man said. "There never was a highwayman would give a plugged nickel to a blind beggar. As for Mr. Robin Hood, he got in trouble first because he was a poacher—a rustler, if you will—and stayed in trouble because he couldn't keep his paws off other people's pokes. His pleasing personality was an invention of time and people with vivid imaginations."

"How do you know all this, for sure?"

"I *don't*," the Old Man said, "but it figures. When a man sets himself up bigger than the society he lives in anything he had nice for a start wears off him as he goes along, and he winds up a rat in a hole until somebody removes him from serious consideration."

"There must of been somebody from the last hundred years you admired," I said, figuring that the Old Man was so mad at Roy Bean and Billy the Kid and Robin Hood that I was off the hook for my own misdemeanor.

The Old Man smiled. "I kind of fancied a couple folks," he said. "I reckon I would go along with Jim Bowie. He was wild but he wasn't no outlaw, and he died with the knife he invented in his hand in the battle of the Alamo. Like everybody else in the fort. You must of read about that in the history books, General Santa Anna and the siege and all?"

"Yes sir, we had a chapter on it."

"Well, that chapter didn't tell all about Bowie, not by a durn sight. This was a cold-eyed, soft-voiced gentleman, from all accounts, and a real ring-tailed wildcat. He was born gentle and raised rough. He rode alligators for fun in Louisiana, and he had slave dealings with Jean Lafitte, the pirate, on Galveston Island. He was a colonel under Andy Jackson. He ran wild cattle and speared them, and he was a great dark-room duelist with that wicked knife he thought up. He was maybe the greatest Injun fighter of them all. One time a hull flock of Comanches aimed to ambush him, and he and ten men accounted for fifty dead and thirty-odd wounded, against one white man dead and three hurt. The books say there was a hundred and sixty-some Injuns against the eleven whites. He was a sick man at the siege of the Alamo, but they say there was Mexicans stacked up like cordwood alongside his bunk before they finally got him.

"No man I ever heard about lived as big as Jim Bowie. He married the prettiest girl in San Antonio, a Spanish gal, daughter of the vice-governor when the Mexicans still had Texas. He went out and got himself adopted by the Lipan Apaches. These Lipans did a heavy traffic in silver at the trading posts, and Bowie had himself a keen eye for old Spanish treasure.

"He worked hard at being a good Injun. He was a fine shot and he killed a lot of buffalo and fought a lot of the Lipans' enemies. He stood so high with the chief and the tribe that they finally showed him their treasure. The historians don't quite agree as to whether they showed him a galore of smelted Coronado ore or an ocean of natural veins. But they showed him something that drove him mad, and he spent the rest of his life trying to locate the lost San Saba mine.

"Some think he found it, but didn't have time to exploit it, or else he was biding his time until he could work it without cutting the country in half. But the Texas War of Independence came along and Jim Bowie died with all the other men in the Alamo. Even today the Texas people around Santone think he died knowing the whereabouts of the San Saba treasure, whether it was smelted ore or natural vein. And they're still looking for the lost mine."

"Your Mr. Jim Bowie sounds about as raunchy as the others you're so down on," I said. "I mean he was a killer and a slaver and a real roughneck."

"There's a difference," the Old Man said. "Bowie was a gentleman and most of his legend is founded on fact, not on what a bunch of latter-day sentimentalists and maudlin outlaw-worshippers wove around some drunk cowpoke, who managed to shoot six Mexicans and make himself a reputation as a bad hombre. Most of the Kids and Jameses were just murderers and stick-up artists, before they hung halos on 'em. There's been more lies told about the olden days and the tough guys that inhabited those days than I like to think about. Seems like all a fellow's got to do is die with his boots on and he gets to be an archangel, when all the time he was just some ignorant bushwhacker with a mean streak."

"How do you account for all the hero worship then, in modern times, if they're all so no-account?"

"Son," the Old Man said, "a fellow named Thoreau once remarked that the mass of men lead lives of quiet desperation. The average fellow is stuck so firm under the thumb of his wife and his family and his job that even a hyena sounds romantic, if it happened to holler yesterday. These hairy ruffians would have seemed pretty commonplace, disgusting, and possibly full of lice if you'd lived in the same neighborhood with 'em. When they got drunk you ducked out of their way, and wished they'd move off someplace else."

"All the same," I said stubbornly, "I would like to have lived in those days."

"I do not doubt it in the least," the Old Man said. "You would have been one of the first victims of the James boys or of Billy the Kid, due to being a basically law-abiding type and a little slow at fanning a gun."

About that time a female voice sounded strong on the evening breeze.

"That's your grandma requesting that we wash up for supper, Judge Roy Bean," the Old Man said. "I'll say one thing. If she'd of been around in those days, there would have been law west of the Pecos, and they wouldn't have made a legend out of your namesake. She'd have made a great peace marshal without firing a shot."

9

You Got to Hurt to Be Happy

It was one of those freezing Southern days, with the wind slapping harshly against the clapboards and riffling the green shingles on the roof. The house seemed to shake a little as the gale buffeted the tiny town, and there was a flurry of snow amongst the magnolias. The Old Man hunched his rocker a little closer to the fire, and we both listened to the wind screaming down the chimney and raising tiny cyclones of loosely shifting ash. The Old Man mock-shivered and hunched his shoulders. He was wearing a ratty old gray sweater hauled up under his chin.

"If you pinned me right down to it," the Old Man said, "I don't like nothing very much but a hot fire and a warm bed and a quiet woman to fetch me my food. I can generally manage the first two, but I been looking constantly for the basic ingredient of the third. Quiet, I mean.

"What I really like is more or less bearish. I mean a cave, a snug, warm cave. Let the winds howl and the snow fall and leave me safe inside my cave. The bear is a mighty intelligent animal. He's got sense enough to come in out of the winter weather and wait for the pretty flowers in the spring." The Old Man spat a sizzling jetstream into a fire that was fairly shaking the chimney.

"Listen to that wind," he said. "It'll have the planks off the house by tomorrow. Nobody but a damned fool or a hungry Eskimo would go out in weather like that. You better go to bed early tonight, boy, or us damned fools will be late for the ducks." He grinned and spat again. "Try to remember you're a hungry Eskimo when the alarm clock rousts you out tomorrow. It makes more sense than being an idiot."

That was the Old Man for you—full of contradictions. He would be praising the comforts of the fireside one minute and then deviling you to buck weather that would have put old Peary off his program.

The Old Man had a lot of favorite topics, and one was that a hunting-fishing fellow hated comfort, that he welcomed pain, that he was never so happy as when he was miserable. He was like the gent in the old joke who kept hitting himself over the head with a hammer, because it felt so good when he quit. The Old Man ranked duck hunters with mountain climbers for damfoolishness; said he never climbed a mountain and didn't want to. He hadn't lost nothing up there in those clouds.

The Old Man had stomped in with his pipe frozen solid, rime on his mustache, and his nose a brilliant cherry red. He seemed as bright as a boxful of birds at a time when the dogs were indistinguishable from the logs on the fire, they were that close to the blaze.

"It's a lovely day today, ain't it?" said he, shaking the snow from his overcoat and warming his chapped hands before the fire. "And by all indications it'll be lovelier tomorrow."

Grandma regarded her mate with disapproval. "Quit dripping all over my rugs," Miss Lottie said. "A lovely day for what? Pneumonia? Hang that wet coat on the back porch."

The Old Man smiled. "It's a lovely day for ducks," he said. "I never saw a nicer day for ducks. The wind will break up the rafts, and the snow and ice will freeze up the big ponds. The ducks'll fly low and come into any little pothole that isn't frozen tight. They'll decoy to anything that looks free of wind. If I was a meat hunter I'd make me a fortune in the morning, just creeping up on a few unfrozen patches and letting fly with a 10-gauge or some other murderous weapon. Slay 'em by the hundreds."

The Old Man scowled at the idea. "Fortunately," he said, "I ain't a pothunter, and I don't own no 10-gauge shotgun. But all the same I intend to take advantage of the weather and shoot rather selectively with that old pump gun that's standing in the corner. Tomorrow I shoot nothing but canvasbacks, bar the occasional pintail and a Canada goose or so. Have I got any takers or are you just going to sit here and shiver and feel sorry because it ain't April?"

The Old Man used to reckon that one man's weather is another man's poison. "The only way to handle weather," he said now, "is to know what you want to do with it and use it accordingly. Quit complaining about it and put up with it for what it's worth. And be prepared for it. The trouble with city people is that they freeze when it's cold and boil when it's hot, because they dress the same way for all seasons. An Eskimo knows it's going to be cold, so he stokes himself up on boiled walrus or blubber, builds a house to match his mood, and only interrupts the long dark winter to thaw out another chunk of seal. The African savage knows it's going to be hot the year round, so he wears a strip of banana leaf to hide his nakedness and seeks his coolness under a palm.

"You get a big unseasonable snow like this, and the man who owns a pair of long-handled, red-flannel drawers hollers hooray and goes for a sleigh ride. The fellow that's still stuck into summer BVD's whimpers and wails that the weatherman's betrayed him personally. There ain't no such thing as bad weather, if you come right down to it. Some's just better than others, as there ain't no such thing as a real ugly woman. Some are just prettier than others."

I had seen that pointed pipestem before. He strictly wasn't aiming it at Grandma.

"What time do we get up?" I asked. "Before dawn, as usual?"

"Let's don't overdo it," the old buzzard grinned. "It'll be black night until seven o'clock, and they'll fly all day in this wind anyhow. I should remark that if you had breakfast ready by six-thirty we'd have ample time to cope with all the necessities. But dress warm, boy, dress warm, and don't bother to get me up till the coffee's boiling. I aim to sleep in my long drawers, too. That way you start off warm."

One thing the Old Man taught me: You dress warm from the inside out, not the outside in. You start with a hot breakfast—ham and eggs and toast and a lot of coffee—and then you surround the breakfast with long drawers and a soft sweater and a couple of flannel shirts and two pairs of socks. A pair of woolly britches over that, and hip boots to keep the wind and water off you, and an oilskin jacket and a cap with earmuffs, and you don't need a bearskin coat. Once that inside furnace starts working you find you can sweat in a blizzard.

"I know it sounds kind of sissy," the Old Man said, as we mopped up the remains of the eggs with the toast, "but certain creature comforts can make a power of difference in how good you shoot. You go get that little kerosene stove we used on the beach this fall, while I tend to the coffee thermos."

He tended to another kind of thermos, too, but I suspect it contained no coffee. It didn't *sound* like coffee. It sounded thinner to the naked ear, and possibly contained a vitamin tonic whose sale, at the time, was highly illegal. In any case it was too special for boys.

We had two or three blinds to be used according to wind and weather, and this freezing morning we chose a nearby one, with me poling the boat and freezing my fingers through the mittens, my nose running droplets onto the scarf around my neck, the marshes cold and gray and windswept, as only salt marshes can be on a day like this. As I shoved the skiff up the little avenues of what was water day before yesterday the boat's keel made a crackling noise, forcing its way through the thin crusting of last night's ice. The narrow lanes were frozen bank to bank, but when we hove onto a semisweet-water pond it was only iced around the edges. A mighty flock of mallards took off with irritable quacks when we approached the blind, and the darting *squish-wish* of frustrated teal swept low as we shoved the skiff into the little tunnel behind it. The Old Man more or less slung a dozen decoys into the water helter-skelter, with nothing of his usual attention to meticulous placement.

"Today," he said blandly, "they'll decoy to a couple of old tin cans and some milk bottles. Fire up that stove, sonny, and hand me the jug—the *other* thermos."

I swear we could have gotten a limit of anything with a couple of old brooms and a slingshot that day. It was almost—but not quite—as if the ducks were trying to come into the blind to get warm. You know Canada geese as wary birds. We collected our limit of the old honkers in two flights, and didn't even bother to change to goose loads; they came in that close.

The roaring wind had filled the skies with disturbed birds, all looking for a place to set. None of the usual artifices which the Old Man employed, and which I knew by now, were necessary. It was a mere matter of choice of breed. We got so persnickety at one time that we made a bargain: I would shoot only canvasbacks and the Old Man would specialize in pintails. We sneered at mallards—as it was late in the season, and we suspected a tendency to fish eating—and simply stood up and shooed away the teal and the goldeneyes and broadbills and trash ducks that fought their way to the little space.

Time has passed, but I would swear we were out of that blind with the boat loaded to the gunwales and the special jug only a quarter diminished before an hour was up. I have only

seen it that way once since, when an old friend named Joe
Turner, a Washington rasslin'-boxing promoter, and I dared
a snowstorm on the Eastern Shore of Maryland. You had to
look between the snowflakes to see the ducks, but Lord save us
there were more ducks than snowflakes.

Well, the Old Man and I snuffed out the little kerosene stove,
broke the skiff free of the ice that bound her, and shoved happily off for home and fire. The snow had started again but the
wind had dropped, and the sky was still filled with enough low-
flying ducks to have provided a hundred years' imprisonment
for a man who wished to overshoot his quota. When we dragged
the boat up on the shingle and shouldered the strings of fowl
and the guns the Old Man smiled sort of sardonically at the
putty-gray skies.

"Your grandma ain't going to believe it," he said, "but I think
this was one of the prettiest days I ever saw in my life. Any argument?"

"No sir," I said. "I ain't arguing. You can have them bluebird
days."

I don't ski, as I would rather contract pneumonia without
breaking my back in the process, but I can see now where a
snowfall that wrecks a city's transportation can be a thing of
beauty to a man who straps staves on his feet and goes hurtling
down a hill to sudden dissolution.

The older I get and the more places I have hunted, the more I
figure the old man was dead right, as usual, about suffering.
Ernie Pyle, the late war correspondent, once wrote that he had
been sicker in more hotel rooms than any living man, and I
swear I have been scareder, hotter, colder, dizzier, more exten-
sively bug-bitten, sunstricken, breathless, witless, and generally
unhappier than any of the old Penitentes, who used to climb
mountains wearing hair shirts and beating themselves rhyth-
mically over the shoulders with whips for fun. And all in the
name of happy outdoor sport.

I get vertigo just crossing a plank bridge over a six-inch-deep creek, but now it seems everything I hunt is placed on top of a peak that would make a molehill out of Everest. I took up grouse hunting once because I thought a moor was a kind of lowland bog—at least a marsh—and found out that a Scottish grouse moor is always placed on the highest peak of the highest range, and that no matter how the cards fell for the draw of butt position I drew the one nearest the top.

I took up elephants as an art form once because I thought you could find them on level ground. You *can* find them on level ground, all right, but you've got to climb Mount Kenya first and then walk a rough hundred miles before you discover that the owner of the big fat track you've been following has only one lousy tusk.

In the hunting business there seems to be no pleasure without excruciating pain. You got to hurt to be happy.

I was mixed up in an Alaska brown bear hunt not too long ago, and it seems to me all I did was crawl through thick bush on my belly, trying to make the summits of mountains I never cared for even pictorially, in order to sit glumly in the rain and let the mosquitoes bite me. I had heard of Alaskan mosquitoes, but never believed they actually carry four motors. They do.

I shot a bear eventually, and nearly got hit on the head by it. I shot it in the heart, and it had enough adrenalin left to run straight away from me up the face of a mountain for about sixty yards before it decided to die and come roaring down again like a Sherman tank out of control. One thousand pounds of bear bounced between me and the guide, and later I reflected that this would have been a silly way to die. Sample conversation around the cracker barrel:

"What happened to Ruark?"

"Oh he was hit in the head with a bear. Always said he'd come to a bad end."

Whoever might have made this snide remark would not have included the fact that in order to get hit in the head with a bear you have to push a skiff about half a league in shallow water, breathing the delightful aroma of rotting salmon, and then stumble another half a league onward over moss-slick stones, feeling the gruesome, fleshy squish of the same rotting salmon under booted foot, before you get to the base of the mountain you must climb in order to see the bears in a nine-foot jungle of lush grass.

A bear is not a bear; it is a far-distant black grubworm on a piece of ragged yellow carpet, and shortly it will go away never to be seen again. That's if it is worth shooting. You fairly have to fight your way through the she-bears with half-grown cubs, each of which could throw a horse over its shoulder and gallop it a country mile. But the big boys are all mobbed up in the hills, eating blueberries and playing poker.

The thing most nonhunters don't realize about the artistic pain that goes into filling four ounces of flesh-and-feathers or seven tons of elephant with the correct prescription is that when you walk out thataway you got to walk back thisaway. Non-fishermen don't realize that the current is likely to run steadily in one direction, and if you float downstream, eventually you have to fight your way upstream. From rabbit to tiger, from bobwhite to buffalo, from sand perch to marlin, there's no such thing as a free lunch.

And the animals have us always stopped on a simple axiom: Nothing moves very much except in early morning or late afternoon, which means you leave camp in blackest freezing dawn and return—cursing, stumbling, bone-sore—in the chill of even blacker night. Except that now you are thorn-wounded, stone-bruised, ankle-wobbly, nose-running, lip-parched, bug-bit —and nearly always without the thing you went after in the first place.

I do not know how many dusty miles I have driven in Kenya and Tanganyika, in North Carolina and Texas, how many bogged-down vehicles I have rescued, how much mud I have slogged through, how many busted axles, how many tsetse-fly bites, how many wait-a-bit thorns, how much blazing sun or how much grinding monotony, aggravated by cracked lips and blistered feet. I do not remember the pain when I see a noble head on the wall, whether it's a whitetail or a really good buff. I just remember the triumphal coming into camp with the horn beeping and the promise of a cold Martini before a hot fire.

But I do remember the aching agony of my legs on a little twenty-mile jaunt after elephant, when we had struggled through the highest, closest-clenched grass and past the ugliest, nearest rhino I ever hope *not* to see any more to finally achieve the blessed level calm of a railroad bed. I sighed and thought, *Now we're home*, but a sadist named John Sutton smiled brightly and said, "Well, we're *almost* there. It's only another seven miles." I made it, God knows how, but the elephants have been safe from me since.

The most self-punishing hunters I know today are millionaires who have been and been and *been*, who've shot it all and don't really want to shoot any more. They just want to see and to suffer. One is just back, after searching a couple of months for what is, in these times, the almost mythical grail of an elephant that will go a hundred and fifty pounds or better per tusk. I doubt he shot anything larger than a sand grouse during the trip, because he is not interested in killing just to hear the gun go off. But he must have been spending a minimum thousand a week just to walk in foot-sucking sand, following seductive tracks through razored dwarf palm, only to end up in daily disappointment and the long trek back.

What makes them do it? Why go to all that bother? It isn't entirely curiosity, because the guy I have in mind has made at least eight safaris.

It must get back to the Old Man's theory that you ain't happy unless you're hurtin', and that somewhere in the hurt you cleanse yourself of a lot of civilized nonsense that spreads a thick veneer on the hides of people, like a scabby overpaint when what you really need first is a scrape job or a blowtorch. You scrape it off, you sweat it off, you walk it off. Your head gets clearer, your senses sharper, and when you do come back—blistered, thirsty, too tired to be hungry, too weary to wash—some of the nonsense of today has been burnt away.

Some beauty has been observed, some hardships overcome, some sympathies established, and there is a wondrous satisfaction about honest fatigue.

I remember once I took a hard-core city slicker—a man who did not like dogs, who knew nothing of guns or game—on a pheasant hunt in Connecticut, which was blanketed with a light early-autumn snow. The fellowship in the snug cabin was excellent, the food fine, and the next day the dogs worked beautifully. The birds were plentiful. We had what is generally described as a magnificent day in the blazing autumn woods, and the bourbon was beneficent when we came in, beat, with a lovely bag of birds and memories to the beckoning fingers of the fire.

Our man had missed manfully; his Stork Club training had done little for his wind as we trudged the snowy hills. Finally, if only to vindicate himself to the dogs, he more or less accidentally killed a magnificent cock pheasant and insisted on carrying it personally all the weary way back to the lodge. He leaped immediately to the phone and called all his acquaintances —and they are widespread, including Europe and Mexico—to declaim his prowess over the rumpled bird that he still stroked mentally as he talked.

He finally sat down, emotionally overcome. "How long has this been going on?" he asked. "And where have *I* been all my life?"

I don't know. Possibly somewhere beyond the point reached when the first cave man did in the first hairy mammoth for food and clothing, and then was constrained to scratch its picture on the wall. Something between gratification of the hunger pangs and some essential element of esthetic conflict between man and animal, man and bird, man and death took over to build hunting into an art form of appreciation and self-sacrifice, of a willingness to punish the hunter's body to make a point of personal egotism; with, finally, a possible tangible reward at the end—a plume to deck the cave lady's head, a fine tusk to turn into a rude plowshare.

And always the fire, the snugness inside to hold the elements aloof once the dreadful travail of the day was done. And then the old boy can sit down with the braggies to tell all the cave kids how good Papa done that day with his spear.

It is, I suppose the Old Man would say, a form of crawling back into the cave, but all I want ahead of it is a long, hard day's work in the woods, so that I'll feel I've earned it when the cave lady brings me some dinosaur broth or even a Brontosaurus hamburger. Quietly. On time.

10

Hang Your Stocking in August

"Christmas," the Old Man once said, "is a damned dull day, and generally raining. But preparing for it is more fun than a barrel of monkeys." And as a Texas friend of mine once opined, "It ain't gettin' ready that's the most fun. It's the gettin' ready to get ready."

It is maybe August elsewhere—just plain August—but in England it is something else. You can throw away all those trite flights of prose about the trees being lushly heavy with August, the lazy buzzing hum of August. In England during August a lot of people are whetted to a fine edge and are busier than they were in the blitz.

There is a day in August that is called simply The Twelfth. Nothing more, but nobody ever asks, "The twelfth of what?"

Because the Twelfth is when the grouse season opens in Scotland. Ever since the season closed last fall all the wine-purpled gentlemen with ersatz healthy complexions have been preparing for this day. Sherlock Holmes deerstalkers have been carefully rescued from the moths, tweed knickers and canvas gaiters have been hauled out of the attic, shooting sticks have been furbished to a high-silver shine, and the matched Purdeys and Greeners and Churchills have been exhumed from their plush-lined cases and searched suspiciously for a minute speck of dust. The square leather cartridge cases come out of the attic, and the state of the world is neglected. What the gentry wants to know is the condition of the heather, the amount of the hatch, the abundance of the vital quartz; and Nasser can go and be damned, together with all the Russians. I rather like the idea.

All this came up because I more or less tore off an arm one time just before the quail season opened. A recent split finger, in the middle of a working project, fetched it back strong. Just before I was supposed to leave for a safari I helped Mama in the kitchen, and wound up with a hand that was grease-crisped to the bone. I had been preparing for that safari for eighteen solid months. During the first two days I had to shoot an elephant and a rhino under rather tense conditions, and the second finger of the convalescing right hand was split open like a frankfurter that had tarried overlong on the grill.

In the strange thinking process of a small boy August was the big month, because August prepared you for September. September whipped you into shape for October, and October was the trial run for the best of them all: November. After that December and January were a cinch, and all you had to do was sweat out February and March, and then the fish bit again and school's recess was just around the corner.

In August I was sick to death of summer. I was weary of summer as a man tires of too many gooey desserts, and craves the peasant companionship of hard ham and hominy, the smell of wood smoke, the invigorating thrashing of a salt breeze, or the nip of frost that wrinkles the persimmons, browns the grasses, and pulls the leaves off trees so you can see the squirrels. Along about August summer took on the aspect of a pretty woman who had let herself go and was beginning to bulge over her girdle as a result of too much fudge.

Enough of those flowers, boy; let's hear a little hound music bugling in the piny woods.

The Old Man had said that if you just confined life to preparation you'd never really be disappointed when the actuality arrived. This was soundly cynical, but it was true—if you can accept a poet's negation of the harsh bitterness of reality. Stars in eyes have never been practical, but sometimes are more comfortable than a speck of actual grit.

It would not be very long before the bluefish were running close to the coast. One big norther in September would bring them along for you. So a man had better get up to the attic or into the closets, and see what shape the fishing tackle was in. It is amazing what manner of demons infest the secret places in which a man hides his fishing gear. They perform strange feats of tangling lines, misleading leaders, warping rods, and jamming reels. So if August had no other value it was a fine month for straightening out the mischief the leprechauns had wreaked on his salt water tackle over the winter.

The season for squirrel, marsh hen, and dove would suddenly be upon you, and the dogs had gotten awful lax. The bird dogs and the duck dogs had a little more time to be lazy in, but it certainly was time to ginger up the hounds and beat a little nonsense out of the utility crossbreeds, the squirrel-chasers and the rabbit-coursers that had done nothing but sleep under the house all summer and eat themselves out of shape.

Come to think of it, I know of nothing as shiftless as a working dog when there's no work. The finest pointer in the world, the best-bred setter, the most dedicated hound, the infallible Chesapeake, all get to be bums over the slack months. Maybe they are like writers who make sudden money and don't have to write for a while, for they sure do get out of the habit of earning their keep. When you finally kick them loose from lethargy they look at you as if you were asking them to stick up a bank or volunteer for a trip to the moon.

"You know," the Old Man used to say, "I never knew anybody who really liked his work. I knew a lot of people who *said* they liked their work, but I disbelieved it. Take one of these dogs. The setters were created to find quail. The retrievers were made to fetch ducks. The fice dogs were accidentally provided to tree squirrels and jump rabbits. But damme, none of them are satisfied. The bird dogs want to run rabbits, and the junk dogs want to be pointers. The duck dogs want to sit in the blind and shiver and look at you with them appealing brown eyes, like Eliza being sent out into the snow and ice. Any man or any dog really needs a boot in the behind to set him about his appointed task."

Part of August's preparation was to take the dogs into the woods and cure them of laziness, rebellion, and the idea that the world owed them a living. It is possible that a whippy stick laid smartly on the behind is mildly brutal, but you could more swiftly reimbue a lazy dog with fresh interest in his work by use of a switch than by all the preacherly persuasions in the world.

At that time you really had to reindoctrinate the quail in the idea that they were not nightingales paid by the state to thrill the world with song, but five-ounce packages of dynamite that shortly were going to be working on their own time, and that men, dogs, and guns were portion to their soldier's pay. I will entertain arguments, but I swear you could train a covey of quail to kind of behave at the same time you were schooling the newest puppy and informing the elder canine statesmen that they really were not Winston Churchill after a long stretch on the Riviera. You could accustom the bobwhite to use in a certain place at a certain time, and there were always some coveys that almost left you a note in a cleft stick if they decided to go someplace else to spend the afternoon.

Man, but that August was busy, and a lot of it was waiting for the drowsy heat to depart and the first bracing chill to come.

It seemed like September would never arrive, and in the meantime you had to put up with all the people who cluttered the beaches and jammed the streetcars under some sort of mistaken idea that they were having a vacation. August was a time of strangers—sunburned, pink-blotched people, people you didn't know and didn't want to know. Strangers far from home, cluttering up the local facilities.

On a hot day, with the asphalt oozing under bare feet and the air dripping humidity, the thoughts of autumn crispness became well-nigh unbearable. The dogs' tongues lolled and they panted in the heat. The sea was a solid shimmer of sun, unlike your angry gray friend that crashed onto the beaches and communicated its leashed fierceness to you, promising lean, mean, undershot-jawed bluefish and solid silver slabs of sea bass, while the gulls screamed.

The flies all came into the house in August, as I recall, and the mosquitoes, sensing winter death ahead, tried to eat everybody before they died. While scratching bites you kept telling yourself that Labor Day would bring that norther and the mosquitoes would die and the people would go away and a man might breathe again.

August was really the night before Christmas. I was not seeing the steaming, traffic-cluttered city streets or drowsing to the hum of cicadas or hearing the plaint of the whippoorwills at night. The mockingbird in the magnolia bored me with his silvery night song, and I wished he would shut up. He sounded too much like summer, and I would have preferred to hear a turkey gobble.

What I was really hearing was an angry squawk as a marsh hen flapped ungainly from the tips of the marsh grass, almost covered by the swollen tides the full moon and the northeaster brought. I was hearing the harsh whistle of duck wings as they arrived from Canada. I was seeing the dark frieze of geese before a full moon, the night trembling with honking. I was hearing a coon dog belling in the woods, and my mouth was watering, because when you could hear the hounds hog-killing time was close, the frost was on the punkin, and oysters were fit to eat again.

Then I was thinking that the summer calling of quail changed, abruptly, and that the classic *bob-white, bob-bob-white* changed to a lonely *who-he, who-he,* as the scattered coveys remustered in the dusk. I was already cupping an ear for the snort of a buck whitetail powerfully overcome by nipping frost and his own importance, his neck swollen with lust and his eye walled for all the pretty girls in a twenty-mile area.

And all the time it kept on being August, August, *August!* Where was September, the golden month, the threshold of the fine times, the wondrous days when the leaves turned gold and red and the pine woods assumed dark, spicy importance again? Where *are* you, September? Possibly you don't recall the frustration, the oil-smelling frustration, of cleaning a gun you know damn well you can't use for another month. Or you may not remember just how long it can be until the quail season opens in November. Time drags. The days, for a boy, never end, although the days end very swiftly in the three months you are allowed to shoot quail. Then it is barely morning before it's dark. Weeks tumble into one another, telescoped like an accordion. This is not all boy feeling; some several hundred years later as a man I went on my first African safari, and I swear it was over before I got there. Or almost.

But in one way August may be the best of all the months. It holds the promise of autumn, the breathless excitement of what is just around the corner, and if autumn falls down on you you have at least experienced delicious anticipation. Even if it rains on a future autumn Saturday, even if it's too calm for the ducks, even if the dogs' noses go hot it has not happened to you *yet.* What you experience in August is a future millennium, where the ducks always decoy well, the geese always come in to feed before the legal shooting hour expires, and where no dog ever runs up a covey of quail because of a dry smeller.

Whether you are shooting grouse with a thousand-dollar Purdey in November or just whistling up a yellow fice dog to go look for a squirrel with your mail-order .22 it is always nice to remember one thing: No matter what happens that day, good or bad, you really paid for the day in August, the bridesmaid of all the months, the bridesmaid who will never be a bride.

11

Good-bye, Cruel World

My boy Mark Robert, godson to me and son to a friend, has a tent pitched in the yard outside his pappy's house in Limuru in Kenya. Mark is six years old. He has his air gun and his cooking equipment and most of his lares and penates in the tent. But up to now he is afraid to pass the night in the tent, although Mummy is within easy hail and he has his lion dog, Sam (part dachshund, part cocker), to keep the carnivores at bay.

"But don't you want to spend the night in the bush in that tent all by yourself?" I asked young Twain, who is called Twain because his first name is Mark, if that makes any sense.

"No," said young Mark Twain.

"Why?" said I.

"I'm too scared," said young Mark, a tad of appalling frankness.

I admire honesty in the young, and this particular spate of a rare commodity reminded me of some days when I had a tent pitched under the magnolia tree in Southport, North Carolina, to which I retreated when the adults became too heavy to bear. It was a tent quite like young Twain's tent, and no more distant from the house.

We had a difference of opinion, as I recall, my people and I, and I determined to run away and embark on a life of piracy, rapine, and highway robbery. I was a red-hot six years old, and the Irish was showing. The whole world was wrong, and you could have called me Parnell.

"Good-bye, cruel world," I said, more or less, and departed for a life of shame.

I must say that the Old Man took it in stride when I announced my intention to trek. "You sure you going to give us all up and run off to live with the Injuns?" he said gently. "I mean, we don't get no chance to mend our ways and maybe keep you with us until you get out of the sixth grade?" The Old Man had a dirty twinkle, but this was dirtier than usual, and made me even madder.

"You'll be sorry when I'm gone," I said. "There won't be nobody around the place to fetch the firewood and run the errands and clean the fish. You'll be sorry, all right."

The Old Man heaved a sigh. "That's what I was afeard of," he said. "Without I got you, *they*"—he gestured in the general direction of Miss Lottie and the other grownups—"they'll be making *me* do *your* work. Maybe I could run away with you?"

"No sir." I was very firm. I figured even at my tender age that running away was something a boy had to do all by himself or it didn't count.

"No sir," I said. At the time I had not encountered Mr. Dickens and his Sydney Carton, and the bad gag about "it is a far, far better thing that I do" had not crept into my working vocabulary, but I was thinking it all right.

"I'm going now," I said, full of dignity and trepidation.

"Well, good-bye," the Old Man said. His tone was solicitous.

"You got everything you'll need? Matches? Hatchet for fire-wood? Air rifle to shoot birds with? You better take some eggs and bacon to tide you over until you start living off the country. And be careful of snakes. If you do get struck try to cut a cross over the bite, tie on a tourniquet, pour in some gunpowder, set it afire, and if you can find somebody to suck the poison out of the wound do so. Gettin' snake-bit is a messy business when you're off on your own, because you generally can't reach the place you're bit to suck out your own poison."

The Old Man fired up his pipe and looked at me under low-ered lids.

"You ain't going to find it very comfortable," he said. "I mind well I run away once when I was a kid. Of course, we ain't got any Injuns now, except some tame ones in Robeson County, but in them days the place was populous with redskins. A man come home with his hair on was an exception. I knowed one feller, he got scalped before he was dead. The Injun run off with his hair, and when the man come to he was prematurely bald. Had to buy a wig to cover his shame."

"There ain't any Injuns around now except some Brass An-kles," I said. "And they ain't really Injuns."

"True," the Old Man said. "But you want to watch out for such things as wild hogs and wild cats and the stray panther now and then. That air rifle is all right for robins and such—like that mockingbird you killed that made your Grandma so mad—but a BB gun don't stack up very high against a wild boar. And when you're reduced to eatin' what you can find in the way of herbs I suggest you watch out for the poisonous toadstools and the berries I don't even know about myself. What might seem like a sparkleberry to you might be something en-tirely different when they do the autopsy."

"You're just tryin' to scare me," I said. "I'm leavin'. Good-bye."

"Would you mind shakin' hands?" the Old Man said, and shoved out his paw. "We may never meet again in this life."

Feeling very noble, I took his hand, shook it, and went off

to the wilds of my tent. I figured I would mount the expedition from the tent, straighten out my gear, pack my rucksack, and depart before dawn.

"Good-bye sir," I called and choked back a sob. Frankly, I was on the hook and there wasn't any way to get out of running away except to run away.

You know how lonely it can be in a tent, even in the side yard, when the night falls and there's no place to go except the tent, with the world opening up ahead of you and no point of fixed destination?

Yes. Just about that lonely. The house was maybe thirty yards away. It could have been a million miles, because my pride had removed it from my ken. There were lights and laughter, but I, the outcast, was now not allowed to share either lights or laughter. I was stuck in a tent, ringed round by loneliness.

Night noises came on. Late-blooming mockingbirds tuned in. Bugs zoomed and swooshed and plunked against the canvas. Frogs croaked. The whippoorwills made a symphony of sadness. Things popped and cracked and boomed and snapped and crackled—and stalked by on careful feet. Over there an owl hooted. Over yonder a dog howled, which meant somebody was dead. A lonely, frightened colored boy started a sad song to stave off the demons of the dark until he got home to Foxtown.

And me? I had acute claustrophobia complicated by active fright and a vague guilt consciousness. I was trapped in a tent, and over thataway lay the far shores. And I didn't know precisely how I was going to achieve those far shores. Certainly not in the middle of the night, with all the sounds and the things—all the birds, bugs, and beasts—against me.

But I couldn't leave the tent, although the rustle I had just heard was certainly a moccasin, an adder, or a rattler. A man has his pride. Once you start to run away you got to run away. I peeked out of the tent flap and the house had never seemed brighter, gayer. Life was in the house, and there I was dead stone cold in the dark in a tent.

"Make a fire," I said aloud. But then I considered that I would have to go and rob the house of firewood, which was a poor way to start a life of crime. Also, there wasn't any flue in the tent.

Anyhow, it was too hot for a fire, although a fire might have been a heavy help against the mosquitoes, which were now beginning a concerted dive on my carcass.

Now I was hungry. Figuring that I would live off the country I had spurned the Old Man's suggestion about bacon and eggs. There was no country I could live off of at this moment It was the wrong season for figs and grapes and pecans, which were all we grew in this plot.

The mosquitoes buzzed and my belly growled. Lone and lorn in a tent, with civilization thirty yards away and me too proud to compromise. The owl hooted louder, the whippoorwill keened. The dead-man dog howled.

Footsteps padded softly across the lawn. "You all right in there?" The Old Man's voice was soft. "Anything I can do?"

"I'm fine," I said. "Don't worry about me," and I must have snuffled back half a sob.

"Well," the Old Man said, "I'm kind of a committee. I'm speaking on behalf of your ma and pa and grandma. They reckon that maybe there was wrong on both sides, and if you could see your way clear to make a parley we might be able to straighten things out.

"Mind you," the Old Man said, "we ain't askin' you to give in on anything that offends your sense of what's right and wrong. It's just that we're havin' deep-dish apple pie for dinner, and it seems a shame to waste the spare slice. You reckon you could come in under a flag of truce and we could work the whole thing out tomorrow morning after the ham and hominy?"

Even at six years old I wasn't no fool. I knew a concession when I saw one. I stuck my head out of the tent. My relieved soul wanted to cry, but I made the voice cool and bored.

"I'm willing to talk business if you are," I said, when what I wanted to do was jump up and wrap myself around his neck and weep out of sheer relief, not knowing then that the old gent had really pulled me off the hook and left my self-respect intact.

That's why, I suspect, I'm glad my boy Mark Robert was honestly scared to spend the night in that tent in Limuru. He didn't have to go through that horrible evening I spent before we called the conference next day. There is nothing as lonesome as a tent when the home fires are burning within spittin' distance, and I do not recommend running away unless there is a circus handy to join.

And there are so few circuses handy these days that running away seems scarcely worth the effort, especially if they are having deep-dish apple pie on the night of departure.

Thinking back on my first journey into fear, when I holed up in the tent, I was suddenly reminded of the second time I absconded. I don't recall now exactly what I was sore at, but I was mad as a wet hen at something, very possibly school, my parents, or the weather. Also, I had been reading *Huckleberry Finn*, who had run off down the river with the slave Jim. This is heady fare for a young man resentful of the adult currycomb. My heart was sore and my disposition desperate.

"What's graveling you?" the Old Man asked. "You look like you're about to cloud up and rain."

"I am," I said. "I think I'll run off. Don't nobody around here understand me."

The Old Man sucked on his pipe and crooked an eyebrow. "That's a prime pity," he said. "I know how you feel. If I wasn't so old and rheumaticky I'd run off with you. Miss Lottie . . ." He shrugged. "But I guess I'm too old and sot in my ways. However, you don't want to take this runnin' away too light. An absconder burns his bridges behind him, because once you've lit out there ain't no returnin'."

I muttered something about I didn't care if I never saw nobody I knew again, except maybe the Old Man, and I guess I just put that in to be polite.

"Runnin' away from your responsibility takes a power of

preparation, not to mention precautions. The old Injuns used to tie a tree branch to their horses' tails and sweep away the hoof marks as they moved camp. And any hobo'll tell you that you got to travel light, but you still got to carry most of the things you need when you're alone in the woods in the night. Seems to me we better practice a little before you run off permanent. You gonna take your gun?"

"I better. I'll have to live off the country. I better take some line and some fishhooks, too."

The Old Man looked at me. "You ain't very big yet," he said. "A gun, even that little 20-gauge, can get powerful heavy. Or was you planning to steal a raft like Huck Finn and live on that for a spell? A boat ain't goin' to take you no farther than Wilmington, unless you care to ride these reefs here on the ebb tide and hit the open sea for Charleston."

"I'll hoof it," I said, mean and stubborn. "Don't you worry about me."

"I'm not," the Old Man said, a little too cheerfully. "I just don't want you to be ashamed in front of the other hobos, for running off without the full kit. Of course, you'll need two blankets, a hand ax, a knife, a canteen, a skillet, a coffeepot, some iron rations, and some pepper and salt. With that gear you ought to be able to live off the country. Any idea where you're headed?"

"No"—even more stubborn than before. "West, maybe. Maybe to Canada. I dunno, and I don't care."

"Well, if it's Canada you got in mind you better take more than two blankets. I'd say about six. It's cold in Canada. Was you planning to live with the Eskimos, or the Indians and be a trapper, or will you fetch up as a cowboy? That's if you decide on the West."

The Old Man never cracked a smile, but I could see he was up to his old tricks of going along with my tantrums, and this made me even madder. "I'm going somewhere, all right," I said. "Maybe one day I'll write and tell you where I wind up. If I ain't too busy."

"They're a little short on communications in the Arctic," the old buzzard said. "But I would appreciate a birchbark postcard once in a while, if you can rassle down a caribou and ride it to the nearest trading post. But in the meantime we better get you outfitted, because there's no tellin' how long you'll be gone. In fact, you may be gone for good.

"Now we'll do a kind of checkoff list, and I'll see can I get you geared up for the road. I'll even do more than that. When you're all ready to roam I'll drive you a half-dozen miles out of town in the Liz. This is kind of covering your trail. People won't reckon you're running away. They'll just think you and me are going huntin' or fishin' like we used to before you got restless." The Old Man stared at the sky. "I'll miss you, you know. You got your faults, but you were a pretty good huntin' and fishin' partner. I guess I'll have to stir around some and dig me up another boy."

I ignored that one. It hurt, but I let it fly by.

"Well," the Old Man said, "there's no time like now for running away. It's pretty late in the afternoon, but it might be raining or even snowing tomorrow. It's a chance you have to take. Now you go collect all your gear, and mind you make them blankets into a tight bundle so you can strap them on your back. And you're goin' to need a belt strong enough to carry your ax, your knife, your canteen, your coffeepot, and your skillet. These things don't pack so good. Too much bulk. And then, of course, you're goin' to have to tote your shotgun and a knapsack full of things like fresh socks and underwear and a little salt pork and flour and sugar and salt and coffee. You can't hit the road without the basic essentials. You can't go off half-cocked. Get movin' now."

Well, sir, I was a sight for sore eyes. I must have weighed about ninety pounds stripped. The gun weighed six, and by the time the Old Man had strapped a blanket roll and a knapsack on my back, and draped a cartridge box around me like a bandoleer, and hung things onto one of those World War I web pistol belts with the hooks on I must have weighed two hundred pounds. It was a pretty hot day for winter, but the Old Man made me wear my Mackinaw too, because he said you never could tell when it would turn real chilly, and catching pneumonia when you were all by yourself in the woods with nobody to nurse you was even too much for a Blackfoot brave.

"We lost more Injuns from the *p*-neumonia than we ever did from the cavalry," the Old Man said, as he helped me, clinking and clanking and sweating, into the Tin Liz. "Seems like most Injuns suffered from a weakness in the chest. That and diphtheria, not to mention starvation when the big snows come and the buffalo crop run short. If I was you—after you decide roughly what you want out of life—I'd head for some place like Mexico, where you can always eat lizards and sleep out of nights if the Aztecs don't sacrifice you to one of their gods."

Not once did he twinkle. He was as stony stern as the preacher when he talked about hellfire and damnation. Mostly I could surprise him in a twinkle, but not this time. No twinkle. Nothing.

He had to help me into the car; cars had high running boards in those days and boys had short fat legs, and this boy resembled a walking hardware store more than he resembled a boy. I sat down with a clank and a rattle, and all you could see out of this mess of equipment was my face and my feet. Somehow I didn't feel like Leatherstocking or Dan'l Boone.

The Old Man cranked up the Liz and off we went, me rattling inside and the Liz rattling outside. The Old Man was garrulous as we rode. He pointed to a cornfield off to the right, with a stand of second-growth pine trees on its rim, and sighed.

"We had us some mighty good times with the dogs there, didn't we?" He was talking to himself. "I'm sure goin' to miss opening day of the quail season, with you not here. I may not even hunt. Huntin' ain't much fun by yourself, and I suspect I'm too old to break in another boy, no matter what I said earlier. Maybe I'll just give up huntin' altogether. I'm a little old to be alone in the woods, with nobody to run for help if I fall into a stump hole and bust a leg or something like that. The woods can be mighty lonesome by yourself, and if you get into trouble, well . . ." His voice trailed off.

We drove about five miles and he stopped the Liz by a creek. "You know where you are now. You've got plenty of water, and the campsite where you and me and Mr. Howard shot your first deer ain't more'n a mile off yonder. I guess I taught you enough about camping to where I ain't got to give you any advice about not setting fire to the broom sedge and leavin' a clean campsite for people who ain't so fortunate as to be running away."

He got out of the car, opened the door, and helped me out. Weighed down as I was, I couldn't have made it on my own. He clapped me on the back.

"So long, son," he said. "And good luck. If you find the time drop me a line once in a while. I'll be here if I ain't dead. And don't worry too much about me and your folks. We'll all make out."

He banged me on the back again, got back into the car, turned her around in a little sandy cut off the main road, and headed back to the village. Dusk had dropped swiftly, and I could see him switch on his headlights. The taillight winked like a malicious red eye.

I stood in the middle of the road in the night, and watched the taillight disappear over a rise. I have been lonely since, but never quite that lonely. And I often wondered if the Old Man forgot to include a flashlight on purpose, because suddenly the night fell like a great black blanket and there was no moon to lead me to the campsite. Walking through the bush was impossible, encumbered as I was by all the tinware the Old Man had tied to me.

This was, I believe, the first time I ever realized how big the world, how absent the moon, and how lonely the loner, not to mention how long was eternity, a problem that had been bothering me a lot.

There was nothing to do but make the best of the mess I'd landed myself in. I clanked a couple of hundred yards off the main road, found myself a little bare patch of ground, and un-slung about a hundred pounds of accouterment. Cursing myself and the Old Man for not remembering the flashlight I lit some kitchen matches, and managed to scrabble up some pine cones, which made the beginnings of a fire. In the faintly flaring light I was able to pick up a few dead branches, and I found a fat pine stump that granted me a few slivers of lightwood. Then, with the fire blazing, I was able to accumulate a few dead logs. Well, I thought, I had man's first friend—fire.

I took the hatchet and went round the perimeter to the little longleaf pine saplings, and cut myself sufficient butts to make a springy basis for a bed. I spread one blanket over the pine branches, weighting its corners with stones, and pulled the other blanket up over the bottom covering. At least I had a fire and a place to sleep.

But a sudden pang in the pit of my stomach told me that I didn't have anything to eat. There was about half a pound of side meat in the knapsack, and that would have to do. I put the fat pork in the skillet and browned it, mentally deploring the waste of grease, and chewed on enough of the fat meat to quiet my belly.

The stars were out now, and I lay down on my bed. The pine boughs were not nearly so springy as I remembered, and some of the butts gouged me in the back. Owls hooted, and there were the usual myriad night noises that are so terrifying unless you have company.

Dew fell, and the blankets were stiff with it and my face was wet-cold with it. The fire was flickering low, casting eerie shadows into my imagination. I was a big boy. I was big enough to shoot a gun. I was big enough to run away to the West or to Canada. But I was not too big to cry. I cried myself into a semblance of sleep. It was just dawning when the rattle of a car stopping roused me from a nightmare-ridden slumber.

In a few minutes I heard footsteps out in the brush, and an occasional curse. It was the Old Man, standing over me, looking down at a very lonely lad.

"I wouldn't of come back," he said, "but when I was helping you out of the car I lost my best pipe. You see anything of it?"

"No sir," I said, scrambling out of my uneasy bed, "but if you like I'll help you look for it."

"All right," the Old Man said. "It's a little dark yet. Where's your flashlight?"

"We—I forgot to bring one," I said.

"Well," the Old Man said, "*I* didn't. Suppose you use mine. And the next time you run away be damned sure you're fully equipped for it."

Of course he never lost a pipe, and he did not insist that I strap myself back into my running-away kit.

"I told your grandma you'd gone camping with some of the other boys," the Old Man said. "If I was you I'd keep my mouth shut about this."

"Yes sir," I said.

This is the first time I've opened it, but since everybody's gone but me it don't make no difference now.

12

It Always Rains on Saturday

The rain sheeted against the panes. Recurrent blasts of wind shook the house, rattled the doors, struck wildly at the windows. A draft crept down the chimney to loosen the ashes, to drive smoke snaking into the room, and to spread a chill around the ankles.

"It's Saturday," I said to the Old Man. "Why does it always have to rain on Saturday?"

My voice was bitter. The good Lord above had betrayed me. Here it was Saturday, and the bird season freshly opened in midweek, and I had been to the wholesale grocery where my Pa worked, and had bought some shotgun shells, and now my mind was out in the country. The soybeans were velvety gray capsules on their stalks, and the black-eyed peas had succumbed to frost, and the field peas—the peanuts—were clustered lusciously on their stalks atop the moist red earth, lying helpless where the plow had torn them from the earth. A feast lying fallow for the birds.

If it had not been for the rain—the dratted rain, the pounding, slashing, miserable rain—I would be out there on the back forty. I would be picking a handful of chinquapins and cupping a mouthful of sparkleberries, and it would just be a matter of where I sent the dogs. The quail season had opened, the dove season was still on, fall plowing was finished, and the birds would be pinpointed. All you had to do was wave at Frank, whistle in Sandy, or just nod at Tom, and you could predict to square yards where the birds would collect. Except for this rain — this I-wish-I-was-bigger-so-I-could-come-right-out-and-say-it rain.

"I go to school all week," I said to the Old Man. "Monday through Friday, I go to school. I study Latin, which nobody speaks, and algebra, which I will never understand, and read that Chaucer foolishness—you ever know anybody who went around saying, 'Whan that Aprille with his shoures soote'?— and Miss Emma Martin says I'm goin' to flunk English, and Miss Rachel Clifford says that I ain't got the right interest in Charlie-Main and the Saracens. The sun shines bright all week and then it sets red and clear on Friday, and I got a pocketful of shells and three bird dogs, and look at it! Rain! "Aprille with his shoures soote," my foot! It's plain old rain—rain on the only day I got off!"

"Here, here, calm down," the Old Man said. "Take it easy. You ain't Noah, and this ain't an ark. It's rained before and it'll rain again. What do you want me to do, ask God to stop it so that one little microbe on the face of the earth can go bird huntin'? I thought you were bigger than that by now."

"Well, it just don't seem fair. I don't care if it rains from Monday through Friday and on Sunday, too. I don't care if it snows or sleets. But Saturday is the only day I get off, and it just ain't supposed to rain on Saturday!"

The Old Man looked at me with his eyes sort of sleepy. He rubbed his nose with one finger. "Son," he said, "when you're as old as me you'll realize that it always rains on Saturday. That's the tragedy of bein' alive. Saturday is for rainin', like work is for doin', like cryin' makes up for laughin'. Believe me. From now until the day you die it'll nearly always rain on Saturday. As far as I know, Noah couldn't lick it, and he had the Lord and all the animals goin' strong for him. When he cut loose that dove . . ."

I was still mad. I had got to where I could handle the Old Man's philosophy in small swallows, but just hearing the word "dove" made me sore as a boil. I thought about all that corn still standing, all those soybeans, all those peanuts and black-eyed peas, and all those doves I wasn't shooting, and I didn't want any lectures about olive branches. The rain kept pounding down, and I thought about how long it was going to be until next Saturday.

The Old Man always enjoyed seeing me heated up, and he liked to keep it going. He had a lot of sayings that were just calculated to rile me. And he could make his voice kind of mincing, sissylike, like an old-maid schoolteacher's.

"Remember," he was singsonging now, "April showers make May flowers. It isn't rainin' rain to me, it's rainin' violets. That ain't really rain out there. That's violets, daffodils, and maybe pee-tunias."

Then he snickered. I guess the word "pee-tunias" got him. "All right," he said. "I'll let you up. I don't like rain no more than you do, because I got joints with aches you don't know about; but if you're ever goin' to be big enough to call yourself a man you got to remember one thing: There ain't any use developin' ulcers over what you can't help. Few things in this life ever work out the way you had them figgered. And there are certain things like wind and rain and high tides that you just can't control, even if you beat your brains out. Might help you someday, when you're older, to remember it. If you can't beat it, join it—or least don't try to fight it."

I'm not going to sit here and tell you that I felt any less mad at Providence for keeping me nailed to the hearthside on a day when I had my mouth fixed for bird hunting. I paced like a nervous puppy, and when the Old Man suggested I try a book I tried it, but I couldn't concentrate, even though it was a book by a man named Selous, a hunter who seemed to know an awful lot about what he was writing.

And I didn't feel any more kindly disposed toward Sunday, when the dawn broke clear and I took all the dogs out—without guns, of course, because I wasn't allowed to shoot on Sunday—and we found every covey I knew we should have found yesterday, and put up enough droves of doves to have reassured all the Arks that ever was or ever will be. I guarantee that the sun shone all through the next school week, although somebody made a bargain with me and carried it over through Saturday. It rained real hard on Sunday, and I didn't have to leave the country to go to town to Sunday school.

"You can call that a bonus," the Old Man said. "You see how everything works out for the best?"

I was prepared to agree. I had indulged my blood lust to a limit on everything but people the day before. Coming back to the house I had even shot a coon, and was figuring to make myself a cap out of the hide, like D. Boone, who "cilled a bar" on that tree. That was the kind of day when I envied a man who had not been subjected to sufficient schooling to know how to spell "killed" and "bear," and so could hunt seven days a week. At least, I thought, he could spell better than Old Man Chaucer, him and his "droghte of March hath perced to the roote." I'll take Dan Boone and that bar he cilled on that tree every time. "And bathed every veyne in swich licour," Chaucer said. I bet Dan Boone just had him a drink of hard corn likker and went out looking for a fresh bear.

Somehow I survived the educational processes, although some people would say you'd never know it, and went on to other things. I didn't really start to think about rainy Saturdays and Noah's arks and *The Canterbury Tales* until one day in

Tanganyika, a great many years later, when a Mr. Frank Bowman and I got mixed up with nature the hard way. And believe me, getting mixed up with ordinary nature in Brunswick
County, North Carolina, is one nest of eggs, and taking on
nature in Darkest A. is quite another.

Frank Bowman is a professional hunter, a slightly testy gentleman, and he has fought sufficient elements in Australia, where
he came from, and in Africa, where he works, to know that
you can't do much better than you can do. But he'll still quarrel
with the process. In Swahili it's *"shauri a Mungu"* or God's will,
and Frank's willing to argue the point.

Frank and I had been away up in Tanganyika in a place called
Singida, shooting—or trying to shoot—greater kudu, a creature
that is considerably larger than a quail or a dove. We had a
variety of ornery vehicles: one jeep that eventually got put out
of its misery and a big fat English truck that had a wistful habit
of catching fire every time you spat.

Through some arrangement with the hunters' gods who control kudu I had shot me a nice heavy-horned fellow along about
the same time a large black cloud suggested that if we did not
plan to spend the rainy season in and around Singida we had
better up-anchor and get the hell out of there right now. That
Africa, as somebody once said, is a large chunk of real estate,
and we were a fur piece away from where we were headed.

There were certain obstacles before our arrival at the promised land. One was a greasy clay hill straight up the side of a
mountain, that is so bad you are not allowed into the area if it
seems dubious that you can make the climb. But once allowed
in and up it, you still have to go down again, whereupon you
are confronted with a desert. This desert is largely surfaced
with cotton soil and lava dust, in which your happy little axles
can sink. It's only about sixty-five miles wide, the Serengeti, but
I have heard tell of another time when one of the best hunters
in east Africa spent an unhappy three weeks just simply bogged
down and cussing.

In an operation of this sort rain is your active enemy. And

what makes it especially your enemy is that you can see it, see it in the black clouds speeding up on you, so that if you blow a tire, if your engine catches fire the rain is right on top of you and you can see the track turn to muck, turn to sticky goo; and all of a sudden, a profane sudden, you are just as immobilized, just as lost, just as planted as if somebody had stolen your wheels.

Also, there's precious little firewood. You are marooned, and what makes it doubly ironic you are not supposed to shoot, either to feed or to protect yourself, since it is a government park. The fact that it is a native poachers' paradise does not concern you. You are not supposed to shoot, even to avoid starvation. The sixty lions over thataway, eating their heads off on the game that blacks the plains, are a thumbed nose at your integrity. The alkali lakes are also an insult to thirst.

Certainly that last hill behind you, that one you just came slipping down, sliding slantwise from the greasy red clay to the greasier, more-suckingly clinging cotton soil, is a frightener, and then that menacing black cloud that hovers, that follows, that threatens ahead—rain? Man, nobody who ever got thwarted on a Brunswick County Saturday ever even heard about rain.

In the case of Brother Bowman and me, we were lucky, just plain-out country lucky. We slid down the mountain backward, the truck slewing in circles, and beat that rain all the way across the Serengeti. I will permit Bowman a small knock against me about our spending one extra day shooting the guinea fowl, and all would have been well if we had left a little earlier on the way from Singida; but then Bowman must yield on the fact that we constantly had to send people back for extra motor parts because the lorry kept catching fire. Bowman kept cursing the Kipsigi driver for unwarranted use of overextended intelligence, such as throwing sand on the wrong side of the truck's engine at about twelve thousand feet, with a rainstorm hotly pursuing us.

Running a forced foot race with rain in Africa is one of the most unrewarding sports I ever got tangled up with. As we crossed the desert it would look for a minute as if we'd make it, and then something would happen and it would look as if we wouldn't. If we didn't . . .

We did. We got to a river called the Grummetti just as the rains clashed, one behind, one ahead of us. We barely crossed the river with all the vehicles just before it went into flood—in flood behind us, in flood ahead of us in its other branches. Brother Noah, perched high atop Ararat, was never more precisely marooned than Frank and I. Fortunately, just as the cloudburst started, the boys managed to wrestle the tents up and hoe drainage ditches around them. Fortunately, too, *shauri a Mungu* touched my trigger finger and I accidentally managed to shoot an impala for camp meat. When I pulled the trigger the rain was coming down so hard that I couldn't have seen through a scope with windshield wipers.

We collected the poor critter and barely squished through the mud back to our dreary camp. There was no such thing as a real fire; the wood was sopping and the rain was coming down so hard that it was falling sideways. Somerset Maugham once wrote something called *Rain*. After a week in that downpour I am here to tell you I could write a series of clinical novels called *Rain*.

Brother Bowman and I had a real good time, though. For some reason we never snapped at each other once. The cook made sufficient pathetic fire to feed us fresh meat until we ran out of impala, and then he started hacking at the tins with his panga, and corned willy is not really unpalatable. I got out the Swahili dictionary and increased my vocabulary by another six or seven words, and wrote some stuff on the rusty typewriter— stuff that I would have to write someday anyhow, even when the sun was shining. The radio didn't work, but nobody cared much.

Bowman had recently come back from crocodile shooting in northern Australia, and I was not so long out of duck hunting in Spain and tiger shooting in India. We managed to sit and tell lies to each other very profitably for a week.

The rain hit that canvas like a giant slapping it with the flat of his hand, and you could hear the small roar as it went by the tent in runnels to spill into the almost raging stream below. (I will tell you a little more about African rain. In the *lugga* country of the Northern Frontier I have seen huge trees cast as high as thirty or forty feet above the banks of the river bed, and the whole Northern Frontier District is off limits, from Isiolo all the way to Ethiopia, during the wet season.)

Finally the rains stopped and the sun came out and the river shrank and we could move the vehicles again, and I was almost sorry. Frank and I had both learned a lesson in temper control. We had both learned some sort of lesson about *not fighting city hall.*

I know I tend toward the Pollyanna approach sometimes, after the temper's done, but hunting and fishing are at least two things that you can't do much about if the boss weather-maker decides adversely. And to sit in a soppy tent, with everything clammy damp—clothes, equipment, everything—is a thing to try a good man's patience, soul, and cussing vocabulary. The only answer, which I believe the Old Man seeded in me at an early age, has been aptly phrased by sage counsel to a man just joining the Foreign Legion. The old Legion hand told the recruit, "When things are bad, *bleu*, try not to make them worse, because it is very likely that they are bad enough already."

If there is a moral in this tale it is that the sun came out in many more ways than one. For the next six weeks I never had more fun or better luck, and at the end of the safari there was no bitter recrimination to spoil the good-bye part. I suspect the Old Man would say it's merely a matter of growing older, or just growing used to being wet on Saturday.

13

The Trouble with Dogs Is People

"The trouble with dogs," the Old Man once said, "is people." We had been through the dog business thoroughly—how a dog was like a boy, you had to wallop it with a stick once in a while to make it behave; how a dog could accumulate bad habits unless corrected; how a dog needed gentleness in its early months and stern discipline thereafter. Foxhounds, quail dogs, retrievers—I thought I had a graduate degree in dogs. Then he hit me with the people bit.

One thing I learned as a kid: You must play your cards right with adults when they come up with a sweeping statement that exacts attention. No adult goes around muttering wise words on his own time. He demands a question, so he can make the answer run awful long.

"Yes sir," I said. "I been thinking the same thing for a long time. What I always say is—all right, you got me. Why is the trouble with dogs people?" I gave up without firing a shot.

"The horse," the Old Man said, "ennobled man, and when you debase a horse you debase mankind. The same thing applies to dogs. In a way the trouble with people is dogs."

And in a way he was right.

Every time I see a bug-eyed, narrow-headed cocker spaniel today, all ears and hysteria, every time I see an Irish setter, nothing but red coat and stupidity, every time I see a collie, bred out of working into a mere mattress for ticks and other debris, I recall the dogs of my tenderest youth. And I think how the people have degenerated too.

Every time somebody's "tame" German shepherd snaps a chunk out of me from sheer nervous reflex, every time a dachshund disputes my right to sit down on the sofa, every time I meet a dumb French poodle I think about dogs in the days when I was not so old and you could kind of count on a dog by his brand name.

I know I must sound like the Old Man in one of those things-ain't-like-they-useter-be moods, but I swear to John I'm right. Cocker spaniels today, for instance, ain't much better than bugs for any practical purpose. They yip and they yap and step on their own ears and they got these big stupid eyes and pinheads, and if a rabbit snarled at them they'd have a fit of high hysterics.

The cocker has been ruined by mankind in exactly the same sense that the Irish setter has been turned into a kind of Liberace-type dog—all adornment. I am so old I can even remember when an Irish setter was used to find birds, and we didn't care too much whether his tail was plumy or his fetlocks feathered. He would work for you, if you conquered his Irish arrogance with an occasional whack on the behind when he ran up a covey or failed to honor a point. Now he isn't anything but the memory of Errol Flynn in a red jacket.

We had a cocker named Mickey, who was the best all-round

working dog I ever saw in my life. She was sort of sand-colored
and wasn't overlong in the ear department, but she had a head
as square as a cigar box and brains inside it. Her muzzle was as
heavy as a boxer's. She would run a rabbit or course a deer. She
was death on ducks, and she had a radar nose for quail. She
would sit quiet if you were shooting doves, and she treed a real
fine squirrel, possum, or coon. If there ever was an all-purpose
bitch, old Mick was it.

Mickey died an honorable death under the careless feet of a
speeding motorcar at about the same time cockers got to be
popular, and when fanciers started breeding them to type.
Twenty years later they had wrecked a sturdy working dog
and turned it into a kind of beetle that couldn't find its way off
it's mistress's lap, like a pug or a Peke. Except that the Peke did
keep its lousy disposition; all that was left of the cocker was
whine. And yip. And yap.

We had Irish setters before they got to be stylish, and though
they needed a touch of reeducation after a long hot summer
they were fancy in the field. They were prone to moodiness,
perhaps, and not so day-in-day-out steady as a Llewellin or an
English cousin, but they also had occasional flashes of genius
that allowed them to find all the birds on a particular afternoon.
Like most redheads they figured to be a touch temperamental.

I would invite correspondence, all adverse, on this statement:
I don't believe there's a good, dependable Irish setter or an all-
purpose field cocker at work these days. The springers seem to
have resisted the new look and can be depended on to fetch you
a duck or a grouse. But cockers—I didn't even see one working
last year around the grouse moors of Scotland or the partridge
shoots in Spain. And I haven't seen a dashing mick on anything
but a leash in twenty years.

The French poodle was a spaniel by original intent, and was
one of the finer hunting dogs. They came into France by way of
Germany, and their fancy hedge-clipping dates back to hunt
masters who cut their coats in various designs for identification

purposes, much as you'd brand a cow-brute. The lion-mane trim evolved as a thumbed nose by France to the British lion, when the kids were having hard words across the Channel.

Offhand I would hazard that the French poodle of twenty-some years ago was the smartest of all dogs, in the field and out of it. But association with people—too many trips to the beauty parlor, too much time waiting for Mama to finish girl lunches, and too much inbreeding to cut down their size—is really making a stupid dog of the poodle. The little ones are nasty yipping beasts, nervous as the well-known lady fox in a forest fire, and the larger ones seem to have forgotten that they got their working papers in a peat bog rustling up blackcock.

At least I can say one thing without stirring up an argument: For ten years I have owned a beautifully bred standard French poodle bitch, who is unqualifiedly the dumbest dog I ever saw in my life. And before you start in to write I offer this for free: It is undoubtedly from long association with her master.

Hewing to the Old Man's thoughts about dogs being spoiled by people, I know one kind-of collie whose life has been wrecked by being named Lassie. The fact that this Lassie is male and does not want to be called Lassie has inverted him to a point where he is a mass of jangled nerves. Don't tell me dogs aren't subject to psychic pressure. I once had a male pointer named Tom, whose voice never changed, and the girls hated him, and, so help me, he committed suicide.

The only dogs I know who have successfully resisted people are the halfbreeds, the nondescripts. The best deerhound I ever saw was half bulldog. The best quail dog, for finding, stanch pointing, and gentle but ardent retrieving was a dropper—half pointer and maybe half setter, with possibly a slight infusion of cur.

The only people I ever knew who successfully resisted the blandishment of dogs were people I did not choose to know much better. There is, to me, something distastefully peculiar about people who are afraid of dogs, who dislike dogs. And the dogs know it right back.

The dogs I miss most today—and seldom seem to see around —are the true Huckleberry Finns; the part Airedale, part fox terrier, part plain fice, with shoebrush coats and back-curled tails. The old-fashioned cur seems to have vanished from the land. For sheer street-gamin intelligence, good disposition, and proficiency in any kind of field work the mixed-salad pariah was the most. I got more hunting mileage out of a yellow semijackal named Jackie than all the purebreds I ever associated with.

The Old Man was right. The trouble with people is dogs, and the trouble with dogs is people. But somehow, one breed can't seem to get along without the other and still call it a life.

Which brings us to Sam, an animal whose very uselessness has made him an all-purpose paragon of necessity around the house. Sam is the. property of a godson of mine, and he has been named Samuanensis Horribilis by the father of the godson, and I resent it. He is not horrible at all. Sam is one part cocker and one part dachshund, and he inherits the decadent qualities of each. He has long hair like a cocker's, is colored black and russet, and has a cocker's ears, a dachshund's snout, a cocker's plumy tail, and a dachshund's undercarriage.

Sam is the best all-purpose, useless dog I've ever met. He is small enough not to knock the glasses off a coffee table with a swishing tail, but not so small so that you are always stepping on him. He is an inveterate hunter of lizards in the flower beds, but is not large enough to wreck the posies.

Sam loves cats—he has three large playfellows named Simba (lion), Chui (leopard), and Somali, which is coal black. They are all as big as Sam or bigger. Sam hates strangers and loves friends. From time to time he will absorb a snifter of gin (which makes him sneeze), but steadfastly refuses whisky or beer.

As mentioned, I don't care much for either dachshunds or cockers today, but in the case of Sam the twain have met and produced something delightfully impractical, as in the case of H. Allen Smith's dream of an all-purpose animal called a bouncing pussy-pup.

Under the influence of a late night on beer (the United Press was not paying much in salaries in those days, certainly not enough to afford whisky for its serfs), Author Smith dreamed of a charming creature that was half cat and half dog. You bounced the cat once on the floor, and it became a puppy. You bounced the puppy, and it turned back into a kitten.

Smith was inordinately proud of his dream. He made the mistake of confiding its basic ingredients to a colleague, Henry McLemore, also a slave of the U.P. salt mines, and Henry promptly claimed the dream as his own, and went around promulgating the idea of a bouncing pussy-pup as the solution to all pet problems. This caused an estrangement between Messrs. Smith and McLemore, since there is no way to copyright a dream. Result was that the two didn't speak for a year or so, since both stanchly protested that the bouncing pussy-pup was his own personal dream property.

I feel more or less that way about Sam, as if I'd invented him myself. I didn't, but I would answer for trouble if someone attempted to take him away from me—in a purely vicarious sense, that is.

Having been owned by many dogs, I have a memory that's always pleasurable and nearly always on the semidisreputable side. We had the usual number of pureblooded setters and pointers when I was a kid, but whenever possible I hung out in the back alleys with the waifs and the strays and the odd amalgams.

For downright street-urchin intelligence, such as is seen among Arab children and young Parisiens, there was never a peer of Jackie, a cross between a fox terrier, a jackal, a raccoon, and a skunk, judging from the smell of him. He was colored a dingy yellow. His tail curled so far over his back it almost touched his neck. His specialty was squirrels, but he would bravely bay a bear if called on and would run a deer if there wasn't a hound handy. He would retrieve a duck, hating the coldness of the water all the time, and find, if not point, a covey of quail.

He was entirely a professional dog. You could not get him inside the house, and apart from coldly and balefully accepting his tin plate of scraps he had no time for the human race. Jackie was completely without racial prejudice: He hated people, black or white, and bit them indiscriminately. He only associated with people in the field, and his allegiance was to the gun.

Jackie was one. A boyhood friend of mine named E. G. Goodman had another mongrel, which defied description. It seemed to be part hound and part bull, with heaven knows what else cranked into his chromosomes. I can't remember the name of this beast, but I can remember that one day, in Goodman's precinct, we shot quail, dove, rabbit, coon, one possum, and buck deer over the noble efforts of this large assortment of nothing that owned a hound's bugle, a bulldog's tenacity, a retriever's sense of where it dropped, and an over-all sense of what-the-hell-boys-hunting-is-fun. This character is long gone to his fathers, but he was a power of dog.

Perhaps the greatest mongrel of them all was a dog that became named, late in life, Bonzo. This dog was basically bull terrier, with one red eye and one black eye. He had lived all his life on his own, until one day he pitched up on the veranda of the Norfolk Hotel in Nairobi, in Kenya, where a sign plainly declared that all dogs were forbidden.

He was scarred and flea-bitten and hungry. His ribs washboarded, and he had more than a touch of mange. The manager of the hotel wasn't feeling so well himself that day, and just as a big porter was about to kick the dog back into the streets the manager said a loud no, and carried the animal off to his cottage.

Some days later Bonzo emerged looking considerably better. His mange was gone (burnt crankcase oil and sulphur), and he had filled out the wrinkles in his belly. And he took over the hotel. The service, which had been drooping, improved, because Bonzo bit the waiters if they were tardy in feeding him. Bonzo improved public relations, because he had an unerring instinct for sorting out the poor types, to a point where he sometimes stood on the register and refused to let a suspicious character sign in. He treed a couple of Mau Mau in the back compound.

As Bonzo increased in power so did the manager. The manager found a better tailor and ran a better hotel, and soon became general manager of the entire chain.

Bonzo had only one failing. He was dame-happy. He would take off occasionally and come home full of battle scars, as a result of love's labors lost. His interest in the other sex finally got him gored to a point where, in his boss's absence, the assistant manager had him destroyed. It is interesting to note that the assistant manager shortly thereafter took off with all the available funds, a weakness that Bonzo must have suspected.

But Bonzo's picture hangs today in the head receptionist's office a few feet away from a sign that says "All Dogs Strictly Forbidden," because there will never be another Bonzo in anybody's time or heart.

The theme of the boy and his dog has been badly overworked and I do not propose to thrash it to bits, but I have observed my young godson with Sam, and am prepared to propound the idea that a youngster is better off with a mongrel in his early formative years than with a haughty something with Ch. in front of his lofty handle.

There is a curious communion between a runny-nosed tad and an animal out of the back drawer, a sort of Tom Sawyer-Huck Finn relationship, where the urchins share a small world of their own. My young man is learning to clean and maintain a weapon, to shoot a BB gun, and to absorb something about the fields and streams. Somehow Sam fits the apprentice pattern better as an intrepid lizard-courser and toad-nagger than if he were the best of show in any category at the Westminster Kennel Club show.

Small boys are little beasts at best, and need careful nurturing to introduce them to adult responsibility. The mongrel—the "Please, can I keep him, Mommy?" pup—fills in a gap between babyhood and boyhood, because a puppy is a puppy, whether it's human or canine.

The Old Man used to have a saying about that. "There ain't

much difference," the Old Man said. "They both need worming at regular intervals. They both need to be housebroke, with a smack on the behind to teach 'em manners. A combination of castor oil and birch tea will work wonders with any boy and any dog, because there comes a time when everybody has to learn the difference between running loose and walking to heel."

I observe my boy Mark and his dog Sam with great pleasure. Through keen parental perception and discipline both are learning the difference between running loose and walking to heel. And I think in the process, as a result of association with Sam, young Mark will grow up one day soon to deserve the companionship of a purebred.

14

Cooties in the Knight Clothes

I was reading a divorce story the other day in which the aggrieved husband called his wife's boy friend a "sugar daddy," while the wife's counsel hailed the other man as a "knight-errant who rushed to Ellen's protection after her husband deserted her."

I laughed right out loud. The last time I got mixed up with knights-errant was via the Old Man. He had a salty way of disposing of popular error, and since that particular day I have never felt quite the same about chivalry.

It was the kind of day you've got to expect sometime in May—cold, rainy. The Old Man was resigned to sitting it out, but I wasn't.

"I want to *do* something," I complained. "It's too late to

hunt and it's too cold and rainy to fish and it's too late for football and too wet for baseball."

"You could try studyin'," the Old Man said. "The last look I had at one of your report cards tells me you could do with a small bait of application. You want to grow up ignorant?"

"I don't care if I do," I said, stubborn as a billy goat. "There ain't anything for a boy to do today. You can't run off and join the Indians or take up with a circus or be a cowboy or a knight in armor or anything that's fun—and gets you out of the house."

"I think maybe you need a good sound worming," the Old Man said. "You got the nervous twitches, like a hound dog with a tape. But it's odd you mention bein' a knight in armor. All along that's just what I thought you was practicing up to be."

"How could I be a knight in armor?" I said, kind of cautious. "There ain't much call for that kind of work these days."

"Oh I don't know," the Old Man said. "You just kind of strike me as a natural-born knight. Or a highwayman. They were about one and the same thing. Maybe bum would be as good a name as any. What would be your idea of a knight-errant, for example?"

I was trapped, and well I knew it. There was going to be a moral hid out in this one, like a rattlesnake, and I knew who would get bit, and it wasn't going to be the Old Man. I'd been there before, but it seems I was never going to learn to keep my mouth shut.

"Well, a knight-errant was a kind of hero that practiced chivalry. He wore armor and rode horses and lived in castles with portcullises and a donjon keep and drawbridges and things. He had a sword and a lance and he rode around the country righting wrongs and saving maidens and killing the savage infidel and slaying dragons and giants and all like that."

"Somewhere between a Boy Scout and William S. Hart, I wouldn't wonder," the Old Man murmured. "Chunk another faggot on that fire, varlet, and I will see can I straighten you out a little bit on knighthood. The ignorance of young people these days is something fierce.

"First place, chivalry and chevalier don't mean exactly what you said. They came out of the French word for horse—*cheval*. You could apply chivalry to a hostler in a livery stable just as easy as to a knight. Chivalry just got mixed up to where it meant anything that wasn't walkin'.

"Knight started out to mean boy or manservant, and got graduated to mean a mounted man who had a shootin' license, so to speak. He could tote arms when most of the other people couldn't, and it give him a superiority complex, even though it might take half a dozen stout yeomen to raise him and his armor onto a horse's back. Once he fell off chances are he'd just lay there and kick and cuss until somebody set him on his feet again. That cast-iron suit he wore weighed more than the man."

The average knight, the Old Man went on, was nothing much more than a paid fighter when a local war sprang up, and in between wars he hung around the castles, tickling the ladies fair, getting plastered twice a day on some sort of moonshine they called mead, and lying his head off about all the brave deeds he performed last time out against the Saracens or mayhap the next-door neighbor.

A knight-errant wasn't anything better than a knight out of work. After his liege lord got sick of listening to all the gassing about how many dragons the knight had fetched with his lance and how many heathen he'd done in with his sword, after he got tired of the knight eating him out of castle and home and swilling down all the best liquor and kissing the prettiest maidens, the lord would spot weld the knight into his cast-iron overalls and gently indicate the drawbridge, with the suggestion that travel was broadening and that maybe King Theobald the Unwashed, down the road apiece, hadn't heard all of Sir Bohort's latest best stories.

"A knight-errant," the Old Man said, warming up at the mention of mead, which appeared to be some sort of nerve balm constructed mainly of fermented honey and malt and fit to blow the vizor off a headpiece, "a knight-errant was nothin' better than a bum. Him and his squire—if he had one—rambled around the countryside beggin' a handout here, stealin' a shoat there, kissin' the pretty milkmaids, and now and again moochin' a meal and a night on a pallet in front of the fire in a castle or an abbey. Often as not they slept out by the crossroads or in a pigsty or a barn.

"They had fleas in abundance in them days, inside the castles and out, and you can bet that the average knight-errant was pretty lousy too. You can imagine the fun a flock of fleas and cooties might have inside that iron undershirt, with no way for Sir Lancelot to scratch less'n he had a blowtorch with him."

Castles, the Old Man continued, were powerful short on central heating, inside toilets, and general comfort. They were drafty and kind of noisy, what with generally being overrun with the ghosts of all the people that had been locked up and died in the donjon keeps.

"At best," the Old Man said, "knights were a feisty lot, and would steal anything that wasn't red-hot or nailed down. They were either chronic liars or must have suffered from the D.T.'s, because they were always seeing bare hands clutching swords coming out of lakes or ladies rising up in the mists or evil sorcerers changing people into unicorns and such as that. They must of smelled pretty rank, too, as I believe they only washed every other year when the armor got rusty and they had to be fitted into another suit. You still want to be a knight?"

"I'm losing my interest in the proposition," I said. "But how did you get to be one in the olden days?" And then I could have bitten my tongue right off at the roots, because I saw he had me. The Old Man licked his chops, spread his mustache with his thumb and forefinger, and let me have it.

"Well, good blood or bad, a fellow with a hankering to be a knight got sort of sold down the river at the age of seven. He left his happy home and got removed to the castle of his future boss or patron, as they called it in them days. And oh my, didn't the fur fly for a spell! They called this little shirttail boy a varlet, which ain't anything but a corruption of valet or servant.

The varlet had to wait on tables and shine up the ironmongery and empty the slop jars. He only et what the master didn't throw to the dogs. He fetched wood and drew water, and if he didn't bow down to everybody he got a hiding. He also had to go to Sunday school every day. That was called teaching him politeness.

"In his spare time he had to learn to dance and play the harp and sing and carry on. He had to learn to stick pigs and ride horses and work with falcons and boarhounds. He had to wrestle and tilt at other varlets with sharp sticks instead of spears.

"When he come fourteen he graduated into being an esquire, and then the heavy work really begun. He was supposed to be able to fork a horse on the gallop, wearing a full suit of boiler plate, and jump streams and scale walls and such strenuous things as that, all under full armor. They used to lose a lot of esquires that way, because if a guy tried to jump a deep stream and didn't make it he plumb sank. And when a wall-scaler missed his foothold, all you heard was *clank!* and somebody had to fetch the royal can opener to recover the corpse. Next to the king the most important man in the castle was the blacksmith. He was kept busy pounding dents out of the armor after they had subtracted the esquire.

"These little chores occupied the squire until he was twenty-one, and when he wasn't too bruised he had to learn to bow and scrape and kiss hands and wear handkerchiefs tied to his tin hat and carry on with the girls. Finally he became a knight. And no sooner did they smack him three times over the shoulder with a sword than they handed him his bonnet and said, 'Git out there and play knight-errant. Go kill a dragon or something or don't come back, because we've wasted a power of time and money on your education.'"

The Old Man stopped talking and stirred the fire with his toe. He sat for a moment staring into the flickering flames. Finally he said, "You still want to be a knight?"

"I don't think so. It sounds like an awful lot of hard work

with not much reward at the end of it, now that you've trimmed off all the feathers. Maybe I'll forget it and take up some other line of work."

"I was hoping you'd say that," the Old Man said. "When you're as old as me you'll generally find that when you trim the feathers off anything there ain't much underneath but hard work and hard times, so you'd better kind of concentrate on what you got in the present and not go mooning around wanting to be an Injun or a cowboy or a lion tamer. Dogs and boats and guns and fishing rods and books—yes, I said books—ought to be enough to hold you for the present. Where do you think I learned so much about knights, for instance?"

"Books," I said. "I guess, books." He had me, right and proper.

"All right, varlet," he said. "On your way up to my bedroom to retrieve a book called Bulfinch's *Mythology* for your liege lord you might look in the closet and locate a bottle of mead. I think it's stuck in the left leg of a hip boot. Mind you don't drop it, and don't you dare to sample it. Mead ain't for varlets. It ain't even for esquires. Mead is only for liege lords and kings, and for knights when they come in from playing hooky and fetch back their first legal dragon."

15

You Don't Have to Shoot to Go Hunting

The Old Man had kind of eased up on heavy hunting and fishing in his declining days. He would say, "I think I'll send a boy
to do a man's work," and run me off to the fields or waters,
while he snugged himself with a dram in front of the fire. When
the Boy would return, half-frozen or as wet as a drowned rat,
the Old Man would smile benignly and say something cynical
like, "Old and creaky as I am, I get my fun out of thinking
about you freezing to death in the rain, missing those birds
right and left, and wondering why I took so much trouble to
teach you to hunt."

As I approach senility I find that now *I'm* the Old Man, and
I get my kicks out of *not* hunting, but of making it possible for
other people. Not that I sit by the fire, but I still receive more

satisfaction in watching over people new to the business enjoy themselves—and incidentally make all the mistakes that I once made—than I used to when I was playing the lead myself.

"The best thing about hunting and fishing," the Old Man said, "is that you don't have to actually do it to enjoy it. You can go to bed every night thinking how much fun you had twenty years ago, and it all comes back as clear as moonlight.

"You can listen to somebody bragging about the fish he caught or the deer he shot or the day he fell in the duck pond, and it is a kind of immortality, because you're doing it yourself all over again. In the meantime—and I don't mean to sound like a Pollyanna—you actually *do* feel that it's better to give than to get. Also, a little healthy sermon on game conservation creeps in here, because if you've done it once and done it twice and done it three times then what's wrong with knocking off and leaving some of the raw material for the other feller?"

The old gent's sentiments kept coming back when Mama and I first took some tenderfeet to Africa. Apart from taking necessary camp meat and doing a little bird shooting I never fired a shot. Bob and Jane Low were the guests, and if you take a poll on Low I think he will sound off strong for the safari business. As for the blonde and beautiful Jane, a lady you'd more expect to see in a slim black dress at the 21 Club, well, you never saw a woman fall more speedily and permanently in love with African bush. Bugs, dust, rain, stuck vehicles, and all, the elegant Tia Juana never mouthed a complaint that I heard.

Her husband was a daily delight. Nobody else had ever been to Africa before. He discovered elephants and lions and leopards. He was the first living man to see a green plain dotted with a million antelope and gazelle. Nobody else had ever laid eyes on a buffalo. Such a small thing as the taste of an orange squash became more potent than champagne. He was nearly incoherent for a week after he killed his leopard under rather unusual conditions.

The leopard, it appears, went into a piece of bush in broad daylight, and Low and the gunbearers dived in after it. Then the leopard began to track Low (later I found its footprints atop Low's big pug marks). They beat the bush three times, and finally the leopard tore out into the open—with the gunbearers just ahead of him.

The boys turned right at flank speed, and the leopard turned left, also flat out. Low executed a snappy shoulder shot, and was back in camp by 11 A.M. with his Land-Rover full of lovely spotted cat. I had about five other toms feeding from trees, but this one had been reaped by *Bwana Mkubwa Sana Kabisa* Low on his own, all by his little self, and he was fit to bust. He broke out in a rash of babble, and I was looking over his shoulder to see how big the slain *chui* was.

Low grabbed me by the collar and shook me violently. "You're not listening to me!" he screeched. "You're not listening to me! And then the boys went back in for the last time and fired some shotguns and the cat came . . ." And so forth.

At the end of a conversationally leopard-drenched week the girls and I came to a solemn conclusion: that we wished the leopard had shot Low. But you must consider that while Low was having this high adventure, which has traveled verbally from Africa to Spain to America to London to Paris, I had more fun listening to it than if I'd committed it, having just shot a difficult *chui* myself the month before Bob arrived. I plain didn't *need* any more leopards for myself. It still pleased me to know that if Bob hadn't shot his cat on his own I knew enough about baits and the right trees to drape 'em in to have had four or five big ones coming earlier and earlier every day, so drunk with power over that reeking big pig were they.

I found that cutting down a stinking, maggoty, half-eaten wart hog can be fun. I knew that nobody else would poach on my tree, and that the leopard would be saved for another year.

Possibly I inherited a malicious sense of humor from the Old Man, but I never laughed so hard in my life as I did on Bob Low's hunting debut in Africa. I had sent the trucks and jeeps on ahead, and we flew in to a makeshift airstrip, whose boundaries were marked by strips of toilet paper held down by rocks, and the wind direction indicated for the pilot by a green-wood smudge fire. Bob and Jane literally flew from starkest civilization into darkest Tanganyika bush country.

The camp was made and ready in a beautiful new site I'd found a month before, and all the boys said, "*Jambo, bwana; jambo, memsaab.*" Low had on his new bush clothes from Ahamed Brothers and my floppy Texas Stetson with the leopard tail hatband, and he looked exactly like a white hunter as played by Stewart Granger with a mustache. The tables were set up in the mess tent with an array of bright bottles, and the refrigerators were humming happily, and the bantam chickens we used as alarm clocks—Rubi and Rosa—had already settled in, and Rosa had deposited another egg behind the refrigerator. The Grummetti River chuckled happily, the trees were green, and the fresh-mowed grass was a velvet carpet in front of the tents.

Low was fairly panting to try out his—or rather, my—weapons; so we exposed him to a topi and a tommie, and after the usual trial and error he was blooded. He came back to cool drinks and dinner, convinced that somebody had made a mistake, that we had blundered into the Waldorf, which had suddenly been moved to the Bronx Zoo.

The first serious hunting day was miraculous. We picked up fourteen lone buffalo bulls, all shootable. They galloped into a small piece of bush. Low went in after them like a little man, and he could not know that in that patch of bush were a couple of lions, a herd of buffalo, and a cobra. He also could not know that the bullets for my .450-400 double had gotten confused with the bullets from Don Bousfield's .450-400, and that our guns were chambered differently. Low was forced to wait until one of the boys hared back to my vehicle for fresh asparagus, so to speak, leaving Low more or less naked in the presence of many large, hoofed, horned, fanged, toothy things—now wondering to himself if Africa was always this way.

Eventually organization triumphed and Low shot his buff. But I shall never forget, as an innocent bystander, the picture of

Low, all the buffalo, all the lions, and the cobra suddenly spouting from the clump of bush.

I must say in behalf of Low, he quailed not and neither did he flee. He was a touch ashen at the end, but that sweet .450-400 spake happily, and Low managed to collect a better buff on his first day than it took me two safaris and six months and about a thousand miles of unpleasant walking and crawling to find. He was no good at all for anything the rest of the day, when the enormity of his achievement dawned.

I do not know many of the details, except secondhand, of the good *bwana's* achievements in the veld, as I was chief baby sitter for two girls, and it seems all I did was pour gin and tonics, explain whistling thorns and why they whistle, and whomp up birthday parties. Mrs. Low passed another milestone —I believe twenty-one is the accepted age for all ladies—and I laid on a flock of ex-cannibals to do her honor.

It was quite a birthday party. First I had to explain the basic ingredients of "happy birthday to you" in Swahili to Matisia, the Low's personal boy, who is a Wakamba. Matisia then retired to the bush to retranslate the ditty into Kamba, and emerged, beaming, with a series of grunts which ended: "Dear Janey to you."

Meantime, while the birthday toasts—Martinis, very dry— were being hoisted I managed to smuggle seventy-five Wa-Ikoma warriors into a patch of bush nearby without the knowledge of *Memsaab* Low. This is a very difficult feat, for the gentlemen had been painting themselves for three days past, wore lion-mane headdresses, had iron rattles bound to their legs, carried knives and spears, and were all slightly drunk and in a most festive mood.

They erupted as a Masai war party descending on the Kikuyu, and for the first and only time in my life I saw the cool Madame Low shaken out of her calm. Seventy-five war-painted Ikoma lads in full fighting regalia is not a sight to sneer at, especially when it erupts into your lap. I suppose a birthday party in

Tanganyika is as much a part of hunting as a fish fry or a picnic, as the lion Low did *not* shoot is a part of hunting.

We had special permission on some lions for Bob, but after he made friends with a few of my leonine friends he flatly refused to shoot one. This suddenly raised him in the community concept from tenderfoot to a member of the old gentlemen's club.

We had been more or less shaking hands daily with a couple dozen of the gracious, lazy, blasé beasts, including two youngsters that were the most beautiful things I have ever seen on four feet—one so dark he was almost blue, and the other blond as Marilyn Monroe.

"My God," Low said, "how can anybody shoot one of these lovely things? Be like shooting your best friend. No, thank you very much, no lions for me."

To see a man go from gun-happy to conservationist in a week is quite a thrill. The average first-timer says something like: "How *many* of *what* can I shoot today?" and the professionals look at the gunbearer and shrug slightly. I couldn't have been prouder as the father of twins than when Low turned down the easy lions. The entire atmosphere of the camp changed so that you could almost taste it.

It changed some more when John Sutton took Low on what John calls a "reccy-run," to see what had happened to the elephant concentration that had been disrupted and widely scattered by unseasonable rains. Fifty miles over no track is a long journey in a Land-Rover. Sutton, a serious professional hunter, conducted Low on a jaunt of over *six hundred* miles with no camp and no sleep. If Sutton was a basket case when he veered the jeep into camp, Low was an uncomplaining corpse. I felt fine. I had been bird shooting with the ladies, and Rosa had laid another egg.

But Low returned from the dead and got onto his shaky feet and took off next day with the other hunter, Don Bousfield. Living under a poncho on short ration, he didn't come back until he had a beautiful pair of tusks. This was the diploma. We packed up and went to Mombasa and then to Malindi and simply went fishing.

Low's safari gave me more satisfaction than any of my own. He shot out the license in both Kenya and Tanganyika inside four weeks, and did not acquire an inferior trophy. He never shot once to hear the gun go off. As with ships, safaris can be difficult tests of friendship, and in the month we six white adults—me, Mama, Jane, Bob, Don, and John—were together there wasn't a cross word. And I have known fast friends of years to cease speaking after three days in the bush.

My most serious hunting throughout all this was a private vendetta with Rubi, the bantam cock. Rubi and I hated each other on sight. He would leap onto my camp chair, crow, and deposit droppings. Then he would crow sneeringly and swagger off to peck Rosa on the head. I armed myself with a siphon bottle and stalked him relentlessly. I may not have collected anything for the wall, but there is one bantam rooster that knows when he's met a better man. I got him one day in full flight, using a duck-length lead with the soda bottle, and shot him down in extremely moist flames. Thereafter there was no doubt in Rubi's mind about who was running the show.

The Low safari worked so well that I decided to test my luck a little more. I had a Spanish chum, and I thought I knew him pretty well. I'd take a chance on Ricardo and . . . Well, we'd see.

The Old Man had some pretty firm ideas about friends in fresh circumstances. "A man," the Old Man once said, "ain't no built-in hero in the woods or on the water. I don't care if he's got ten million dollars and six yachts. He ain't a hero to his dog if he shoots bad. And he ain't a hero to his friends if he hogs shots. You give me just one weekend in the woods or on a boat with a man, and I can tell you if he beats his wife or is likely to run off with the company's money."

This was not the first time it had been said, but the truth persists. It takes anywhere from two days to two weeks to prove it, but in the end it always comes out. The city veneer wears thin, and the man who is a big wheel in his main line begins to whine over a visitation of gnats. The man who might appear to be a surly heel on his native heath suddenly exhibits traits of alarming humility and tremendous consideration of others in the party.

Thinking back to when I was a boy, and the Old Man was not only younger but remarkably spry for his then considerable age, I can recall that we broke off diplomatic relations with one of his best friends. It was a simple matter of politeness involving quail. The friend was a shot-hogger, and he was always so close on the dogs' heels that if a bird got up you had a simple choice: Don't shoot or else shoot the friend in the back of the neck. When you walked into a covey past the pointing dog the friend would fire across your bows if the bulk of the birds went your way.

"I spent half my life teaching dogs to honor a point and behave like decent human beings," the Old Man said. "Now I got a friend who don't even know how to behave like a decent dog. I think maybe we don't hunt with Joe no more."

And we didn't. We spoke politely to Joe on the streets, because we did not actively dislike Joe on the streets, but we didn't hunt with Joe no more. Apart from his other unattractive habits he claimed every bird of dubious ownership, and never once, at the end of the day, had he made even a feeble effort to whack the bag fifty-fifty.

Perhaps the greatest strain on personal relations I know of is a boat trip or a hunting trip of more than one day. Perhaps the boat trip is worse, because you are a captive guest in an alien sea. However, a safari, which can stretch into weeks and months, almost invariably winds up in strife. The communion is too close, the community too big, and, generally, the people too small.

I have usually come out pretty even with the people I have taken on safari, because they have been more or less pretested under other circumstances. That's to say I've hunted and fished or visited with them before, and that way you get a pretty fair idea of what you're liable to buck.

But you still can't plan on the outcome. I've known people, who went out only to photograph, suddenly to develop a blood thirst, and people who started out wanting to shoot the entire list to wind up as bird watchers. Africa, as any reader of Ernest Hemingway will know, has a tremendous effect on personalities. The brave become cowards, the cowards become brave, the bore becomes interesting, and the practiced charmers become bores.

And it doesn't really need Africa to dredge out the true insides of a man or woman. You can do it as easily in North Carolina as on the Northern Frontier of Kenya. Somehow even the birds and animals seem to sense it too, and certainly the natives know. I was on a grouse shoot in Scotland a couple of times, and after the first day or so the local gillies could give you a pretty fair run-down on the general character of the clients involved. It would not surprise you to know that it was only a matter of time before Margaret would divorce Peter, or that Ian would abscond with his bank's funds.

And you can't depend on precedent or type or previous condition of servitude. We'd been lucky with Bob and Jane Low. Now I was taking out this Spanish friend, Ricardo, with Harry Selby and John Sutton. Again I wasn't shooting anything but birds and camp meat, and so this Spaniard had the rare opportunity of having the two best professional hunters in Africa (in my opinion) at his personal beck.

If you can meet the right people Spanish shooting is fabulous, and these people like to keep a brace of guns hot and a loader busy. I just kind of wondered if Ricardo would want to shoot the first elephant he saw or a maneless lion or a lousy buffalo, just to hear the gun go off and collect a batch of flesh.

I should not have had the reservation. Selby and Sutton said later that this was the best safari—and Ricardo Sicrè of Madrid the best client—of their combined experience.

Let me explain Ricardo. He is a millionaire and he made all the money honestly, while he was in his mid-thirties, from a standing start of two hundred dollars cash. He had a fabulous war record with the British and the Americans, when he ran the underground in southern France. He is a good writer, a fair bullfighter, a good horseman, a good shooter, an art connoisseur. He has an enormous yacht and he knows everybody of much importance from New York to London to Monte Carlo to Paris to Madrid. If ever a man had built-in possibilities to be a bum in the bush it was Ricardo.

Not a bit of it developed. From the day he hit Nairobi—with his face beat up from an auto accident on the way to the airport in Madrid—Ricardo was a smashing success. My old friend Selby has a pair of perpetual pistons for legs and the burly body of a bull buffalo. Ricardo had been sick, apart from his accident, and wasn't in the best of shape. Selby damn near worked him to death.

They were up at 3:30 A.M. every morning to drive a couple of hours to make a morning approach to a lion kill. When each of these approaches proved abortive they spent the rest of the day tracking elephants. They generally arrived back in camp, where I was living in opulent ease, about 9 P.M.

We were far north, in Kenya, and the sun smote mightily down. And the bugs bit and elephants invaded the camp and the vehicles got sick. But nary a word of complaint from Ricardo, who never had a decent lunch in camp the whole trip. He and Selby would shoot something, a bird or a small animal, and broil it on a green stick.

We—they, mostly—looked at a hundred and fifty mature bull elephants before they finally decided to shoot one. If there had been more time they'd have looked at a hundred and fifty more, on the off-chance of finding a really superb bull. As it was they collected an eighty-pounder.

They tended that lion kill and the leopard kills as reverently as though making obeisance at a shrine. They averaged two hundred rattling miles a day in the hunting car and about twenty on foot. Ricardo almost fainted from the heat one day, but he didn't beef. He got up, mopped his pale brow, and went back for more.

I confess shamelessly that most of us, when we are shooting guinea fowl or spur fowl for the pot, brass off into a clump of sitting birds with the idea of collecting meat, and we do the sporting thing with the other barrel when the birds take off. This is intelligent, because anybody who has ever hunted a running bird knows that you can't run fast enough to flush them yourself. Not within gun range.

But Ricardo would have none of this firing into a flock. He'd loose off one barrel into the air, and then take his chances with the fliers. (He was pretty lucky one day. Some birds crossed his pattern and he knocked off eight with one salvo. *Flying.*)

It is possible to murder thousands of sand grouse if you let them come close enough, tornado-twisting like teal, to the lone water hole they are forced to patronize for their daily sip in a desert land. One shot and you've got ten, twenty, thirty grouse. Ricardo shot only at the high-flying doubles, triples, and quartets. And a sand grouse, flying high and jinking, is the fastest bird I know outside the peregrine family.

Ricardo finally shot his leopard just at dark, and shot it through the left eye. He took his buffalo on the high slopes of Mount Kenya in the last half-hour of his last day. He shot the buffalo running and dropped it in its tracks.

During the entire month there was no hint of impatience, no complaint about the tremendously hard work, no whining when killing effort turned into failure. He could have shot a half-dozen lions, but none were good enough. So he didn't shoot a lion. He could have shot up the countryside, and didn't. He became so firmly fixed in the affections of the white and black hunters that Swahili is now being spoken with a Spanish accent. And we all laughed constantly, which is terribly important. I was very proud of Ricardo, and my old friends seemed a little proud of me for having produced him. I gained local status.

It seems to me that the basic theme of hunting is that word exactly—*hunting*. Not killing. Whether it's a good pair of tusks or a cloud-touching mallard or the quest of something special in any bird or beast there is a certain imponderable that separates the man from the boy. Call it a grail complex, if you will, but it sure shows up on the face of the hunter and the people around him.

As the Old Man's boy grows older he finds less and less fun in killing, and more and more fun in taking people hunting. We collected two magnificent lions in Uganda a while back on another safari, in a year when lion hunting was almost impossible in terms of mountable results. By safari rights both lions belonged to me, since they were shot on my kills—baits prepared by me and Harry. It was nice to give those lions away. It was nice to see that everybody finally had his leopard and buffalo and waterbuck and all the rest.

It was also nice to know that I, too, collected a magnificent trophy. It was a rather large rabbit, and I had to give him both barrels, but it had been a long time since I had shot a rabbit, and at least it was something to have my picture taken with. The satisfaction I got out of this rabbit fetched back acutely a remark the Old Man once made: "It's twice as much fun to see others do it if you've done it yourself, and done it well enough to where you don't have to do it again."

It occurred to me that I had had enough tigers and lions, and that I would rather watch the elephants than shoot them. Unfortunately, this does not apply to quail. Concerning quail I am still as bloodthirsty as the day my first bobwhite scared me so bad I threw up and had to be put to bed for two days.

Well, now I had two down, and another upcoming. Bob and Jane Low had departed with our friendship still firm, and Ricardo had passed all the exams. Now we had another kettle of conditions coming hard after Ricardo. Now it would be Mike and Jill from the Middle West, and a fairly difficult one to run a test on, because Mike knew a lot about his own bush country. The simon-pure amateurs put themselves wholly in your hands, and if anything goes wrong it's your fault. Sometimes the people who know a lot about their own back yard try to convert that knowledge to Africa, and in the process they do foolish things. Everybody makes mistakes, but they seem to hurt more in somebody else's country.

On this one we were in the high hills of the Masai country of Kenya, where the tame, wild lions keep you alert at night, the hippos splash in the Mara River, the tsetse flies engrave their initials on your hide, and the hyenas remind you of Saturday night in a madhouse. It was a happy camp until that day when one of the jeeps rolled in bearing a tale of tragedy of the highest order.

The Old Man had quite a few trenchant things to say about hunters, and one thing that sticks in my mind was, "No man can call himself a pure hunter until he has committed the damnedest mistake a man can make at a time when he least wants to make it.

"They laugh and carry on a lot about the big fish that got away," he'd elaborate, "and they kid you about having buck fever or forgetting to load the gun or forgetting to slip off the safety catch. But if you will prowl into the life of any man who has spent considerable time hunting and fishing you will find that everybody, at one time or another, has made a mistake that caused him to kick himself in the behind for the rest of his natural life. And it's never a big mistake. It's some damn silly little blunder that the average backward child wouldn't make, and it always happens to people that ordinarily know the hunting and shooting business backwards."

I believe I mentioned at the time, with the arrogance of youth, that so far this boy hadn't made any such stupid mistakes, and didn't think it was likely that he ever would.

The Old Man grinned his shark's grin and blew on the inside of his mustache. "You ain't home yet, son," he said. "You got another sixty years or so for the law of averages to catch up with you."

It turned out he was right, but this is not my story. It is the story of this friend whom we are calling Mike.

Mike is a man of middle years, and most of those years, since he comes from the West, have been spent hunting and fishing when time allowed. He says he does not shoot until he knows he can kill, preferring not to shoot at all rather than wound. He also wears Apache moccasins to ensure quiet stalking.

As a matter of fact, Mike is more a maniacal fisherman than a possessed hunter, and one of our more adept dry-fly flingers. But he likes bird shooting, and he has killed his elk and his mule deer and antelope, and he has caught very large angry fish on very fine thread. Mike, largely because of me, became deeply bitten by the Africa bug, and this bite festered when his charming wife Jill expressed a desire for a leopard to spread in front of her fireplace.

This Jill is a very determined woman, being of Nordic extraction, and when she sets her mouth for something to happen it had better happen. This is how Mike and Jill came to go on safari with a fiercely determined aim: Mike would shoot a leopard and Jill would unfurl it in front of the fireplace for the puppies and the children to roll on, and occasionally a Martini might be mixed to recall the good old days in the African bush. Then Jill would tell all and sundry how her man Mike dragged this lovely spotted pussycat out of the bush by his tail, just because Jill wanted a rug for her tepee.

Well sir, the safari traipsed all around, up from Kenya to darkest Uganda and then back to Kenya—long, dusty, tail-wearying miles—just to see if somehow we could not collect a leopard for Mike. Animals were dispatched and slung into trees and left to ripen enticingly. Blinds were built. Drags of defunct animals were made, the better to diffuse the scent. Water holes were inspected for leopard tracks. We constructed morning approaches and evening approaches, and crawled miles through safari ants in the blackest, bone-freezing predawn, and sat up untiringly, bug-devoured, for three hours in the afternoon, each afternoon, to jounce home, kidney-shaken, murderously weary, and fantastically filthy, ready only to stagger off into bed dirty and arise with the waning moon to do it all over again.

Weeks passed. Foot-loose lady lions climbed trees and ate Mike's leopard baits. Once a surly rhino—the only one in the neighborhood—chased a leopard off a kill and evidently scared it so badly that the *chui* never returned. But Mike was a dauntless leopard hunter, and a dauntless leopard hunter is at least one part idiot. He crawled out of bed in the freezing Masai dawn to go and inspect a couple of feeble, tawdry kills to see if any mentally retarded leopard might be feeding, and he cruised the country endlessly on the off-chance—a one-in-a-million shot —that a nocturnal slinker might stay up too late some night with the boys and go wandering home to his lair in the bright morning sunlight, when all good dues-paying leopards should be snugly abed in a thorny thicket.

Mike had been shooting a .318 Westley Richards of mine very well. It's a very flat rifle that throws about two hundred and fifty grains of lead. He had come to trust this gun, for it had killed him a fine lion. He was not really interested in the lion until he saw it sitting underneath a leopard bait, and I do believe he shot the lion so it would not hamper the leopard's chances of coming to the tree-strung kill.

The story might meander on, but I will shorten it. Clean living and high purpose paid off, and the day came when Mike had been riding along the flat top of the Trans-Mara escarpment, checking to see if any leopards (faint hope) had been feeding on a couple of topi kills. And then the million-to-one-shot hit.

A big, very big, dog leopard—an eight-footer, perhaps— meandered across the track and sauntered into a small patch of bush in broad Masai daylight. Now the search for the spotted grail was at an end, because the patch of bush was very small indeed, and the leopard could easily be driven out of it. Mike's professional hunter stopped the car, and they strolled along to the piece of bush.

Inside the bush they could hear the leopard growl. The hunters stood with guns ready, and the gunbearers began to fling chunks of wood into the clump. Out came the leopard, broad on, not hurrying but more of less meandering, presenting a target (for a man who shoots as well as Mike) as big as a spotted house. Up came the trusty .318. Jill, who was watching the show, already saw herself serving Martinis in front of the fire while sitting on this splendid, very dark, golden leopard skin.

Mike held the leopard firmly in his sights at about twenty-five yards and squeezed. The logical sequence was the sharp bark of the .318, a final growl, and a mighty leap of the leopard; then conjugal kisses, hearty congratulations, and the triumphant end of the hunt. Jill would have her rug and Mike would stand proud and tall among his clan brothers.

There was a dry half-click. The leopard melted into thick bush and was no more seen, because a leopard melting into thick bush is untrackable unless he is wounded and spraying a blood spoor. *Kuisha chui.* Leopard finish.

Mike stood there looking, as at a stranger, at the gun in his hand; this trusty gun; this marvel of rifled craftsmanship by one of the best gunsmiths in London; this burled walnut-stocked gun whose prototype has been known to speed a solid bullet all the way through an elephant, penetrating completely from stern to bow.

What had happened was simple—one of those little mistakes the Old Man had mentioned. Some years back I had affixed a very low-mounted scope to this rifle. The scope interfered with the Mauser-type safety catch, so I had the catch taken off, intending to install another type of safety. But time passed, and it scarcely seemed worth the trouble, because complete safety could be maintained when a bullet was in the chamber by leaving the bolt handle only half-thrown. All you had to do to shoot was to slap the bolt handle firmly into its bed, and she would be in vicious business.

In the truly magnificent spectacle of the leopard erupting from the bush Mike, really unaccustomed to the rifle, had forgotten to snap the bolt handle all the way home. And with leopard you are not allowed mistakes. Not even one. Not the littlest one.

There is really not much you can say to comfort at a time like that. I claim I helped some. I mentioned to Mike that he was only an amateur in the frustration league, because anybody who knows me might remember the painful story of the tiger that got away.

This particular tiger was the biggest of three in the Madhya Pradesh of India, and I killed it just as dead as I had slain the two others. He was a huge old tiger, a cattle-lifter, and I shot him, smirking the while, through the neck. He collapsed and my shikari and I congratulated each other. The shikari suggested a second, make-sure shot, but I waved him off. What need? We smoked a couple of cigarettes and had a pull at the flask. It was then that the tiger got up and slowly walked away. We never saw him again.

The tiger story helped Mike some, but not enough. The Old Man said once that you never forget a mistake that cost you dearly; so when somebody said that Mike's leopard would be a mere memory on the dewy morrow I said, No. No sir. That leopard would continue to grow, and Mike would still be hating himself twenty years hence.

"That's the real beauty part of hunting," the Old Man had said. "A hunter still finds it possible to kick himself in the tail after everybody else has forgotten the tragic incident. That separates the men from the boys in the hunting business, because a casual gent will pretend that it never happened, and even if it did, it was somebody else's fault. The mark of the true man is will he continue to hunt, instead of busting his gun over the nearest tree."

But Mike has the mark of the true man, and I was perfectly certain that before we removed ourselves from the Loita Plains he would have his leopard, and Jill might one day be able to sit on the skin in front of the fire and whip up a batch of Martinis, extra dry.

Like the Old Man said, it ain't so much talent as energy, and the bad breaks can't go on forever. The Old Man just claimed that the stature of the man was measured by how much he could smile when fate was beating him over the head with a stick.

Mike shot a big leopard later. But it'll never be as big as the one that walked across the road.

16

Lions and Liars

There is a saying among the Masai of Africa—or maybe it's the Somali—that a brave man is frightened three times by a lion: when he first sees its track, when he first hears its roar, and when he first sees the lion in the flesh. It's a pity the Old Man didn't live to see me get to Africa, because I wish to add to this generalization and I'm sure he would approve.

The first time a man comes in contact with a lion he automatically turns liar. If there is a tiny, faint shred of mendacity in a man his first lion will bring it out. This applies in a similar, if lesser, degree to male deer, giving rise first to an ague-making malady called buck fever and later to delusions of grandeur accompanied by faint falsehoods. These expand into outright fantasies that might even be medically described as an early journey into schizophrenia. Every day becomes April first.

In the bird world I believe that the bobwhite quail has done more to corrupt man's truce with fact that any other feathered friend, although a duck liar and a wild turkey liar enjoy certain phases of the moon when they take an adverse view of temperance and truth. In the exotic fields I suppose a tiger liar is almost as good as a lion liar, and the African elephant as a liar-breeder stands all by itself.

This, of course, refers only to low-level lying. People who climb mountains in search of such rich fare as ibex, tahr, mountain sheep and goats, chamois, and greater kudu are not to be included among the sea-level liars, because the altitude obviously affects fantasy. Rarefied air has a tendency to loosen the centers of imagination and also the tongue, because there are often very few witnesses to call the liar a liar. This is what generally gives rise to legends about Abominable Snowmen and such.

The Old Man had some definite ideas about sporting liars. He claimed that in his better days, weight for age, no holds barred, he could outlast anybody he knew in the solid construction of an airproof lie, although he was not so much for the gaudy fringes. The Old Man believed that when you got your mouth fixed to lie you ought to start at the ground and work up, and that a soundly planted liar didn't need a lot of fancy trimmings.

"A sporting liar," the Old Man once said, "is a truthful man turned dishonest by circumstances beyond his control. There is no real malice in him, and he is unique among all brands of liars, because with practice and careful handling his lies eventually become unshakable truth. This applies to all sporting liars except dog liars. I wouldn't believe anything a man said about his hound, his Labrador, his pointer, or his setter, sworn before a notary on a stack of Ken-L Ration."

The bare anatomy of nonmalicious lying is a complex thing. First, a silent self-deluder doesn't count, because such deception is lying on your own time and creates no harm save personal confusion, such as fanning yourself with a fly swatter. Fishermen are also excluded, because a fisherman starts lying to himself before he takes down the rod and chases the kittens out of the creel. It does no real self-eroding damage for the self-liar to add a pound to the fish or an inch to the horn or a brace to the bag.

If controlled, this self-deception is difficult to detect. You look at a pair of elephant tusks framing a fireplace and the owner says calmly, "A hundred and sixteen and a hundred and twenty." He knows better than the elephant's ghost that one weighs a hundred and ten and the other weighs a hundred and twelve, but something impels him to add a few pounds to the trophy, even though it makes no difference in their appearance or to the facts of acquisition, and his latest target for untruth has no way of weighing them anyhow.

They say that tusks have a habit of losing weight after they are thoroughly dry. My best pair is unique. Standing for the last half-dozen years by a roaring fire that operates six months a year those tusks have gone from a hundred and ten and a hundred and twelve, wet, to a hundred and twenty and a hundred and twenty-five, dry. I suppose as I grow older they'll eventually weigh a hundred and ninety-five and two hundred respectively.

An elephant is the biggest land-bound animal in the world. Conversely, the bobwhite quail is the smallest ferocious bird I know. But the quail outweighs the elephant as a corrosive influence on ordinary truth. I have long believed that one day I killed fifteen quail with thirteen shots. This is an outright falsehood, although I tell it frequently. It actually happened, but it happened to Mr. Bernie Baruch. I stole it callously, and I don't know why, any more than Henry McLemore knows why he stole H. Allen Smith's dream about the bouncing pussy-pup.

I have shot exactly two elephants, two tigers, and two lions in my life. I have shot exactly five leopards. But wind me up, boy, let me ramble, and I make Karamoja Bell and Jim Corbett look like pikers. It is a strange thing, but the tendency to outdoor falsehood generally touches on quantity rather than trophy weight or actual size. What I mean is I have hunted massive concentrations of elephants on a control operation that was supposed to thin the herds by three or four hundred beasts. Actually I never fired a shot, but unless you listen closely you might believe that I fetched back three hundred jumbo tails, was hailed as Protector of the Poor, and was duly decorated.

One of the more unusual, unvarying, and untrue aspects of big-game tale-telling is that nearly all bull elephants are rogues, and that all lions, tigers, and leopards brought to bag are man-eaters. I know there are rogue elephants. There must be, because so much is written about them. But I never saw one. Certainly there are man-eating cats, but the outsize pussies I have fetched home never sampled so much as a rasher of bacon off Homo sapiens. The leopards all seemed to relish pork, preferably maggoty, and the lions and tigers generally chose an animal like a jackass, a zebra, a young buffalo, or a cow—something with much more eatin' meat on it than a skinny human.

Possibly the main thing about lions' effect on liars is that very few people you will meet in your daily life ever saw a loose lion. This more or less prevents challenge on your veracity or lack of same. The mere fact that you are within a few feet of the unfettered king disarranges the chromosomes of your soul and everything thereafter seems bigger, more profuse. Once you've seen a wild lion at close hand, once you've shot a lion at a range of thirty yards or so your perspective changes, even when you speak of such innocuous fluffy beasts as bunnies.

I have noticed recently that I retroactively tend to shoot all lions and elephants at a range that is never greater than ten yards. Up to now I've not shot either animal from the hip, but I'm gaining, men, I'm gaining. A fellow named Harry Selby did have to shoot a wounded buff from the hip not so long ago, and I see no real reason not to steal the experience from him.

The lion that sent me darting off the narrow path of truth

was almost, but not quite, the first thing I ever shot with a rifle larger than a .22 I have to admit to a couple of zebras and a wart hog on my first day of safari, and some shocking misses on Thomson's gazelle. But I actually did shoot the lion the morning of the second day out, and a second-day lion is heady fare for a tenderfoot who is not quite sure how to load a magazine rifle. I clobbered this slightly moth-bitten old fellow medium-clean and semitruly through the ear, and he spread out into a rug midly studded with camel flies. On advice of Master Selby, who even at the age of twenty-four was a cautious professional, I walloped him again behind the shoulder before I walked close enough to pose with a prideful foot on his neck.

We slung Simba into the back of the Land-Rover, suitably padded by hastily hewn grass, and jounced merrily off to camp to show Mama how brave her little man was his second day in Africa. Mama got out of the sack to admire the beast, and I was accorded to be quite a fellow by the black boys, who had a keen nose for baksheesh on a triumphant day and broke out the formal celebration.

We propped *Bwana* Simba's chin on a rock, and Mama unlimbered her cameras. Then *Bwana* Simba's eyes opened wide, his ears perked up, and he let out a soul-shattering roar. Never before have so many people so swiftly and successfully climbed so few trees, thorns and all.

Now the truth is that the lion was stone-cold dead from the first .375 in the ear, and even deader from a second slug through the heart, and had been dead for two hours by the time we got him to camp. The opened eyes, the pricked ears came from some sort of muscular contraction as he prepared for rigor mortis. The roar was nothing but a sudden release of stomach gases.

But you check back a couple of paragraphs and you will see that I have a dandy story—if I skip the explanation. The thing is to tell it modestly and mention quietly that you ran to the jeep and got a gun and shot the lion again. (Which I did, because I hadn't figured out what made him come alive and roaring after having been dead for two hours.)

About a week later we had another bright day of derring-do, which combined the slaying of a kind of champion waterbuck in the morning, a very fine lion in the early afternoon, and a very big leopard (the first) toward evening. The lion was accompanied by several lionesses and cubs. It seems there were six or nine or twelve lionesses. I think six would be the more accurate figure, but these days I just settle for two dozen and let it go.

I wouldn't know today what happened on the rest of the trip if I hadn't written some modest pieces for *Field & Stream*, and later a less modest book about it. I find a streak of basic honesty in a writing-sporting liar. If he records the facts at the time he will be scrupulous in his adherence to basic truth—at the time. I never told any major fibs in print. My conscience dwelt among the scribbled notes. It is only age and distance that lend an added luster to the unvarnished fact.

The Old Man said he blamed whisky and open fireplaces as much as anything else for the decay of probity. Also he said no outdoor man ever touched his peak performance for tall stories before he was forty-plus.

"Lies," the Old Man said, "are like whisky. They go down better after having been aged in the wood."

I came up in a little town where the expansive yarn would have made a Paul Bunyan blush. I couldn't have been more than six when I heard the one about the bird dog who was so stanch that he froze to death on point, and when the thaw came the next year his master found a skeletal dog still standing a covey of skeletal quail. And, of course, there was one character in our town who was such a smooth and adept thief that he slid into a house one night and stole a lamp so fast that its owner kept right on reading after it was gone.

As to dogs, I certainly do not care to say whether I am an accurate witness on the prowess of some of the beasts I owned. I think it highly unlikely that any dog of mine ever pointed a live bird with a dead bird in his mouth and one foot pinning down a cripple, but wouldn't it be lovely if it were as true as it sounds when I tell it?

Sometime, when you've got a minute, remind me to tell you of the whitetailed deer I once shot in Carolina. The hounds coursed it through a friend's back yard. I shot it, and its dying leap carried it through the door of the smokehouse, and when we got inside it was hanging there, its horns caught on a hook.

17

Fishing Is a State of Mind

"The only thing crazier than a duck hunter or a mountain climber," the Old Man repeatedly said, "is a really dedicated fisherman—a man who will fish where he knows there are no fish, just as long as he's fishing. In fact, the dedicated fisherman is Simple Simon with a license."

I didn't believe a word of this, of course, because I was kind of partial to fishing myself in those days, but only when I could catch fish.

"In fact," the Old Man went on, "I think the dedicated fisherman really hates fish. Take Cap'n Ahab. You perhaps know the story of *Moby Dick*. I don't suppose you could actually call a whale a true fish, but let's say that at least a whale can't walk, and concede that he's got fins and flippers and lives in the water. Well, this here Cap'n Ahab was a clear case of a man who hated fish, and one fish in particular. This hatred for fish ruined his life and lost him a leg."

The Old Man was drawing the longbow, as usual, but there was a seed in what he said. This came to mind the other day in Spain, when a neighbor dropped in of a Sunday and announced proudly, "I caught another fish." You'd have thought he'd just won the Nobel prize.

A fish hooked this character two years ago when he moved to my occasional neck of the woods. Using a borrowed rod he landed a three-pound *dorada*—a very fine sort of sea bass. From that point on he was lost. He had a seagoing monkey on his back.

Every Sunday since that awful day he has fished, when he was in the little town of Palamós, up and down the beach in front of my house. He bought rods and reels and lines and tackle and one large milk can to keep his bait alive. He had more bait than the professionals, and more equipment than Ernest Hemingway.

Two years he fished, and the other Sunday he caught his second fish—another *dorada*, weighing a pound and a half. That, you must admit, was a long time between bites. It took him two years and three hours of lonely fishing to snag this critter, and he was late to lunch and got chewed out at home. Then he gave the fish away to a neighbor (not me).

There are a passel of fish in Spain, and in my neighborhood fishing is the major industry. But it is big-boat, deep-sea stuff with seines. Angling off the beach you might just catch a tourist or find yourself tied onto a bikini. But this does not discourage my friend Ted. He once had a hell of a day with a submerged auto tire. He is as trustingly tireless as the poor souls who fish the Seine in France. One day, the Parisian thinks, I'll catch a tuna that has strayed from the Strait of Gibraltar, or at least a large sardine.

A slightly more successful slave to the foul fishing habit is another neighbor, Artie Shaw, the reformed clarinetist. He lives on a lofty mountaintop a league or so away, and he has more equipment than Abercrombie & Fitch. He ties his own flies, hand-wraps his own rods, and makes regular pilgrimages to Austria and France and America to see what's newest and most expensive in the angling equipment dodge.

Shaw threshes the streams of the Pyrenees and the small rivers in our neighborhood. He can flick your eye out with a fly, wet or dry, at fifty yards. He hunts fish nearly every day, and from time to time he catches something, be it nothing larger than a whiskered minnow. But since he has one whole room in his castle devoted to fishing gear I keep asking him where he is going to use those platinum-mounted mammoth reels that are suitable for the tuna tournament in the Bahamas. He just mutters and ties another fly.

About the only notable trophy I ever took with a fly rod was my own ear, but occasionally the poison that invaded my veins when I was a kid in Carolina seeps back, and I can still handle a spinning reel or the old-time surf rod without seriously wounding anybody. And I came down with a craving for fishing recently that probably qualifies me to become president of the Idiots' Club.

As seems usual these years, I was in Africa, and I was sick of safari. "Let's go fishing. I need a rest," says I to Harry Selby, my professional hunter friend, and to Brian Burrows, who runs some hotels out Kenya way.

"Sure," Selby said, "I know just the place. Lake Rudolf. You'll find it fascinating. We got a permanent camp up there I built a couple years back, and a motor launch that I transported nearly six hundred miles over land. She'll do nicely if she hasn't sunk, which is entirely likely."

The difficulties involved in transporting about thirty-eight feet of specially built lake boat, on the order of the "African Queen," across the Northern Frontier District of Kenya atop a lurching lorry add up to a logistical feat comparable to carrying a ton of coal to Newcastle on your head, and I will not bore you with the harrowing details.

They even had to build a slipway to launch her and a dock to shelter her. Every nail, every plank, every piece of equipment, except thatch, came up from Nairobi by truck, for Selby to rear his village for a scientific expedition that was intent on charting the lake, its fish, and its birds.

"How long does it take to fly there?" I asked.

"Oh, 'bout an hour and a half," Selby said. "Maybe two. But we can't fly. We haven't any vehicles up there. Everybody's left, and we'll need some food and some transport for the boys. Anyhow, it's terribly interesting country, and the fish are something really extraordinary."

He cited me some statistics. One day very recently they had boated fifteen Nile perch—only one under twenty-five pounds and the rest ranging from twenty to sixty—in three-quarters of an hour. Some other people had caught sixteen perch over one hundred pounds at the south end of the lake. The record was two hundred and forty pounds.

"Sounds like action," I said.

"You'll like it. The air's so dry that you really don't mind if it gets to be a hundred and twenty degrees around midday."

Brian Burrows, an Irishman who sunburns easily, paled a mite at this information, but he had already signed on for the trip. Our noble caravan, consisting of a Dodge Power Wagon, one Mercedes diesel truck, and a dozen unhappy natives, set off to catch a fish. To catch a fish you drive about ninety miles from Nairobi until you turn right at a place called Gilgil. This road eventually brings you to Thomson's Falls, about a hundred and sixty miles from Nairobi.

If you're a lucky little chap you can go from Thomson's Falls to Maralal, another seventy-five miles, before you pitch your camp after dark. You have sent the lorry on ahead and you camp at the foot of the mountain, because it's about fourteen thousand feet high at the top, and though it is cold at the bottom it is considerably colder at the top—even in the daytime.

You will have inhaled plentiful dust and suffered a great many bumps on the base of the spine, and seen a power of dull, drab country. Juma and the other boys have made a fire, and you thank heaven for it when you dismount from the Power Wagon. You have just left a luxury safari, with iceboxes and pretty girls and mess tents and forty-odd assorted attendants. You have shot nothing, and you pitch no tents. You dine sumptuously off hot whisky, cold beans, and clammy bread, and hit the feathers without benefit of any tentage whatsoever.

Nothing is as unhappy looking as a bunch of freezing Africans loading one lonesome lorry in the cold gray crack of dawn, feeding you makeshift ham and eggs, and literally whisking the chair out from under you in order to cram it onto the truck. Nothing is as miserable as three white fishermen, who have slept in their clothes and have decided that teeth cleaning can wait for a hotter clime. Nothing is as miserable—until you check with me later.

So now we tackle the escarpment, which is really a very lovely thing, if you like driving a clanking vehicle straight up to the sky around impossible curves. We hit the summit and paused to see the view, but the wind blew us right away from the view and suicidally down a hill that twisted around the badly sutured scar of the Rift, product of a great volcanic upheaval.

We clambered down the escarpment and stopped for a drink. Burrows was pale and so was I, because no parachutes had been issued with the Power Wagon. A young Samburu warrior, who looked like Lena Horne's twin brother, stopped to pass the time of day. He asked, in Swahili, where we were going.

"Fishing," Selby said.

The Samburu *moran* shook both his head and his spear. He had now heard it all. He looked around him at the lava-strewn desert, at the escarpment behind us, and toward Baragoi, which he had left a couple of days earlier, about sixty miles t'other way.

"I have never seen a fish," he said. "I don't think you'll find any around here. Perhaps if you go far enough, my father says, to the other side of Baragoi, you will come to a great lake. Perhaps there will be fish there."

We gave the Samburu warrior a candy bar and bade him fond adieu.

"Let us press on, men," I said. "The fish are waiting." And I knew I would hate myself in the morning. I did.

We stopped off at Baragoi village to buy some gin, which the *dukah* owner naturally forgot to put into the truck. We had a small libation of cold beer and then took off, ginless in Gaza, so to speak, figuring that we would lunch when we got down the hill.

Immeasurably cheered by a couple of beers I asked the Scoutmaster how far were we from our destination, where we would fish.

"Only sixty-five miles or so," Mr. Selby said, taking a hairpin curve that headed us back to Baragoi. "It's really nothing until we come to the Valley of Death. That's something. The nice thing, though, is that we'll do it after dark. You won't be able to see where I'm driving." He chuckled darkly. "But then, of course, neither will I," he said.

I could hear Burrows gulp.

We progressed until we passed a place called South Horr. There is another place at the other end of the lake called North Horr. We played tag with a herd of elephants, and we had what could be called a miserable lunch. This was about the time we discovered that our friend in the *dukah* had forgotten to pack the gin. Even the Horr Valley, which was pretty green, was still miserable country.

"There's a police post up there," Selby said, pointing to a mountainside. "Once in a while there is a pretty good chance of getting through to it on the radio. If you have a two-way radio, of course."

"Do we have a two-way radio?"

"No," Selby said.

"That's nice," Burrows said. "It's one thing we won't have to worry about if the Gelubba come over from Abyssinia to kill us."

"Oh," Selby said, "they'd have to pass the police post at North Horr first. Unless they decided to by-pass it. They do that, you know. They can move about forty-five miles a day on foot, and generally strike and move out before the police find out about it."

"We could have fished the streams in Nanyuki," I said.

"The fishing's pretty good down Mombasa way," Burrows said.

"Oh," Selby said, "but it doesn't have the stark drama of the north. In 1957 and '58 the Gelubba concentrated on the western shore of the lake. About a hundred and sixty deaths among the Turkana were reported. There must have been more. Tomorrow, when it's light, I'll show you a hill called Porr where they wiped out a whole tribe of Turks in 1954.

"It's rather a rough bit of country," Selby went on, narrowly avoiding a plunge to our mutual deaths. "Anything bearing arms on this side of the Kenya-Abyssinia boundary, up to a line between Porr and South Horr, is shot on sight. Any government official making his rounds on the other side of North Horr must carry an escort of ten men. This makes it a bit sticky when you consider that there are only forty-eight Kenya police for all of the Marsabit District, which includes Lasames—you know how far away that is, Bob—and the whole eastern shore of Rudolf. But, of course, there's the *recoup*."

"And what exactly is the recoup?"

"A sort of flying squad, a camel corps, made up of Somalis, Wakambas, everybody—fighting people. It's an elite troop. You can't do much with vehicles around here"—for emphasis he rattled our teeth on a block of stone—"because of the lava rocks. The recoup takes off in the black dawn to the trouble spots, siestas in the heat of the day, and generally arrives at its destination from nine to ten at night. More or less like the spahis in the old *Beau Geste* books. Tell the truth," Harry said, "we are not terribly civilized around here."

"The catfishing is pretty good on the Mara River," I said.

"Malindi's nice," Burrows said. "The fishing's fine in Malindi, and you can always hop over to Zanzibar or up to Lamu to watch the dhows smuggling the elephant tusks. I hear the fishing is fine around Malindi."

"Ah, but they haven't got the real sense of the country any more," Selby said, feeling the bitter hatred that swirled around him and loving every moment of it. "Too many tourists. Not enough mythology. Now you just take the goats."

"What goats?" That must have been me speaking.

"The goats on South Island. South Island is kind of haunted. Nothing on it but goats—great big goats—and nobody really knows how they got there. Goats and ghosts. But they're there, all right. Seen 'em myself, the ghosts, and shot some and trapped some. The goats, I mean."

We clanked along in the mobile iron maiden, while Selby elaborated. "The locals," Harry said, "they believe that South Island was once connected to the mainland by a peninsula. At the base of the island was a spring where the Samburu cattle watered. The spring was sacred, and everybody was forbidden to tamper with it when it dried. But one day a pregnant Rendille woman came along with a flock of goats and started digging for water, and the spring burst forth and swallowed the whole countryside.

"She climbed the hill with her goats and eventually gave birth to a son, who, the natives said, later married his own mother and had children. As a matter of fact somebody *did* live on the island, because Sir Vivian Fuchs, in 1921, found remnants of huts and quite a lot of artifacts. And goats. Some other scientists—two men—tried to go over there and were never seen again. But George Adamson and his wife—you know him, Bob, he's the New Frontier District game warden who has the tame lioness—were over there about three years ago and they found a cairn of rocks and a whisky bottle, so the two scientists must have been lost on their way back to the eastern shore.

"Also," Harry said, "you can see firelight over there, although there's nobody living on the island."

"I don't want to see any firelight on a place nobody lives on," said I. "How about the goats?"

"You wouldn't believe them," Harry said. "They got horns twice as tall and beards twice as long as any goats I ever saw. Sort of trophy goats."

"I believe the fishing is wonderful on the Athi River," Burrows said. "And it has the advantage of being very close to Nairobi. Very few goats, though, I'm told."

"We'd better stop," Harry said. "It's about nighttime and that damned lorry seems to be too far behind us. A pity, really, that we have to get there in the black of night. As a true experiment into fear that descent into the Valley of Death really wants seeing by day."

We had come through some more horrid country and were now perched atop a high hill. Hill? Hell's delight, it was a mountain. We looked hopefully for the flickering yellow tongues of the lorry's lights. Nothing showed. The wind howled.

"I wish I was back there with the camels," Burrows said. "They at least look like contented camels." We had passed through a vast herd, numbering into the thousands, of Samburu wealth, which in that area is camels. For pure wealth you can't beat a camel. You can milk it, eat it, wear its hair, ride it, make it carry your belongings, and it has the definite advantage of getting fat on thorns and only drinking every other semester.

"Here comes the lorry," Selby said finally. "Brace yourselves, chaps. Into the Valley of Death."

It was midnight when we hit the camp on the little sweetwater stream. It had taken us fourteen hours of driving to cover sixty-five miles. The last three hours was absolutely straight down a lava-strewn mountain, with the vehicles hanging onto the rocks by their heels—like klipspringers. The last few miles were along the lake's beach, which was composed of slippery shale on which the autos skidded as though on ice.

"Home," Harry said, as we came up to what appeared to be a thatched palace. "I'll just go cut in the generator and we'll have some lights."

In a moment he was back, smiling cheerfully—the bearer of ill tidings. "The generator won't cut in," he said. "I guess we'll make it on the hurricane lamps."

Juma, the headman, came in and said something rapidly in Swahili. I could sort out the word "Ramadan," used several times over.

"Boys ain't pleased," Harry said. "It gets hot here, and on the Moslem national holiday month, Ramadan, you can't drink or eat from dawn to dusk. Also, most of the blokes spent six months here with the expedition, and they've been out with you for three months. Juma's face looks like an old boot."

"So does mine," I said.

"I hear the fishing is very good outside of Denver, Colorado," Burrows said. "In the time we've spent we could have gone there."

"Ah, you'll love it by daylight," Harry said, "when the freezer gets going—that's if the generator works—and we go out on the lake in the boat. Her name's *Lady of the Lake*—that is, if she's not sunk."

"Let's eat something before we turn in," I said. "What've we got that is quick and easy?"

"Well, I know there's some tinned salmon and some sardines," Harry said.

That's when Burrows and I both bore him savagely to the floor, intent on murder. *Fish.*

"Well," I said when Juma came early next morning with the tea, "so this is where we are. Finally."

"*Mbaya*," Juma said. (In Swahili *mbaya* means "bad.") "Rudolf *mbaya*."

"*Hapana mbaya,*" I said. "*Hi m'zuri sana.*" That means, "Very good, any amount."

"*Fish!*" Juma said, making a cuss word out of the noun. "All this way to go fishing. When I could be with my wives. I have been here before. I have been here for maybe six months before. The face of the place doesn't change, the water doesn't change, and the people don't change. *Mbaya kapisa sana.*"

This was the third phase of one of the longest nonfishing trips in history. We were now into the third day of torture and we had not yet wet a line. We had not seen the lake, which is a lake that very few people have seen. It is by survey 365 feet deep in spots, and 135 miles long by 35 miles wide at its broadest. It is crammed with leaping tiger fish, Nile perch, and *tilapia,* a very fine-tasting fish. Supposedly.

"*Mbaya,*" Juma said, all the laughter gone from his snub-nosed, half-Congolese Arab, half-Kikuyu face. "Bad people the other way. Gelubba that kill. Rendille that kill. Turkana that kill. Borron, bad. Samburu, bad. Locals, stupid. All bad. Also too hot. Hot as a fire all day and the *Muslimi* can't drink." Juma's face now looked like a melted rubber boot. "Not until sundown the *Muslimi* can't drink."

The staff was not only beat but frustrated rich from a year's steady safari employment, and no chance to spend any money; beat and wanting to go home to their wives and cattle and goats. Beat and not wanting to be again in the haunted hot country with its strewn lava rocks that looked like the mountains of the moon, its mysterious tricky lake full of crocodiles and hippo, and the murderous tribe called Gelubba just around the corner in Ethiopia.

"You won't like the people here," Juma said. "All *shenzis. Burri.* Fisheaters. Savages."

"But the fishing's good," I said. "And it's very comfortable here."

"I would rather live in a tent with the hyenas and the baboons outside," Juma muttered, and shuffled away in his working clothes.

The camp was the former site of a scientific expedition mounted by the University of Miami, and as far as I was concerned, when we got around to inspecting the area, an absolutely charming camp, by far the most lavish I have seen in Africa. Harry Selby and John Sutton, in the interest of the expedition, had created a palm-and-grass-thatched paradise in the middle of nowhere, with a chuckling stream running coolly through the middle. Great palms shaded the enormous main hut; its ridgepole must have been twenty-five feet high. There was a lab where the scientists had worked, a great dormitory for the men, a lockable kitchen, and several scattered cottages for married couples and the occasional female guests.

The generator was cut in now; the freezer and the refrigerator were humming, and all the lights working in the various buildings. The showers functioned, and the radio brought the BBC news from London. Selby and his assistants had built themselves about the deluxiest fishing camp in show business. There was even a barber's chair with a prospect of the lake and a magic island in clear view.

"We ain't so crazy," said Brian Burrows, the hotelkeeper, "now that we're here. I ain't going home no more." He gestured at the vast, cool main building with its low-sweeping eaves, designed like lifted skirts so that a constant breeze was swept in and over the thwarts to circulate air in the room. "Even if there ain't any fish," said the Liverpool Irishman, "I ain't going home no more."

"There will be fish," said Selby, appearing well-shined, shaved, and showered. "Don't fret your heads about the fish. How do you like my layout?"

"Great," said I, "if I can fly in the next time. And if there are any fish. I have to wait until I see the fish."

"You'll see the fish," Selby said. "We'll go down to the lake in a minute and see if the *Lady of the Lake* is still with us. If she's sunk we can still surf cast. The big ones come into the weeds anyhow. All you have to do is mind the crocodiles. They come into the weeds too."

"I think I shall stay clear of the weeds," Brian Burrows said. "I ain't lost nothing in them there weeds."

"Somebody's going to have to teach this chap to speak English again," Selby said. "Ever since he's known you he's a vast discredit to his rearing."

"Look who's talking," Burrows said. "I mind well that an 'ain't' or so creeps into your occasional context, me beamish boy."

"I ain't knockin' the word 'ain't,' " Selby said. "Ruark makes money off it. Let's go fishin'."

The *Lady of the Lake*, after having her bilges pumped, was an agreeable girl. We endowed Selby with the title of the Cautious Captain, because he was unwilling to go outside El Molo Bay. And smartly so, because Rudolf runs up a wind you wouldn't believe until you picked up your teeth.

"Inside is good enough for me," I said. "I ain't lost nothing outside that big hill."

Evidently we were a caravan of cowards. Nobody dissented, including Metheke, my old and trusted gunbearer, who wouldn't get on the boat at all. This gap-toothed Wakamba, who may be the bravest man I ever met, said that he was an elephant hunter and a cannibal, but he hadn't lost nothing on that big *magi* either. Metheke would sit at the shore and pluck the whistling teal and the occasional knob-nosed goose I had shot. He was content to watch the boat from a distance. He had been along when they freighted her overland. Metheke is very rich, and has a lot of wives, sheep, goats, and cattle. He wanted to live to enjoy them.

You might possibly have seen pictures of Selby and me, but I must describe Burrows, the vagrant fisherman. He looks like a cross between Brendan Behan and an Assyrian emperor, and when you deck him in shorts and the kind of floppy straw hat that Jamaican peasants wear the ensemble is, in a word, horrid. He is one of the truly brave people I know, and has the disposition of a baby lamb, or he wouldn't be off in the wilderness with me and Selby in the first place.

During the Mau Mau emergency a busload of nice old ladies arrived at Brian's hotel just as a Kenya settler shot a running native across the street in front of the opera house. One of the horrified old ducks turned to Brian. "Tell me, young man," she quavered, "is this a safe hotel?"

"Great God, no," the manager said, stripping off his jacket to display bandages. "Look what the blighters did to me last night!"

And they had, too. Old Beebee got mashed up three times in the peaceful administration of his business.

We proceeded to fish. Burrows got stuck into something we all decided was a rock, because nothing moved, even when the Cautious Captain gave the "Lady" full speed ahead. Aly, the only competent sailor among us—he's a Swahili from Mombasa, and so knows boats—went over the side and into the dinghy to see if he could unsnag the line, and then the rock came alive. Burrows had been pumping steadily for fifteen minutes on what turned out to be a sixty-pound Nile perch that had merely decided to lie doggo.

We caught fish, all right. I caught two: a tiger and a perch. I lost a mess, because these tiger fish have a way of digesting tackle. We caught more fish in the shallows. That was because we sent the local laddybucks, the Molos, fishing with nets. We wanted to freeze some fish to take home to various Mamas, and the freezer was working wonderfully.

It was working wonderfully, because we suspended fishing the following day so that Selby and Metheke could dismantle the generator, which had become temperamental again. It does not take much to please Selby. Get him greasy to the ears and surround him with displaced bits and pieces of an engine and he carols like a lark.

Once he got the generator sorted out we didn't go fishing again, because of one thing and another in the pursuit of culture, such as literary talk and the adjustment of the windsock at the airstrip on the off-chance any pretty girls might fly in to visit us. This consumed the best part of a day, and nothing ever came of it. The only pretty girl I saw was on the way home, and she was twins. I started to buy both of them as a house present for Mama Selby, but decided against it. They were more or less naked Samburu maidens and entirely too pretty to be an acceptable house present.

The generator on the boat—the "Lady" had a refrigerator too—was a bit dicky also, so that took some work, and one of the reels jammed and that took some work, and then I decided to go duck hunting and that took some work, and then we went croc hunting and that took a lot of work.

I will tell you a thing about Selby. Passing a camel through a needle's eye is child's play alongside hunting anything with Selby. If he hasn't got a mountain to walk you over he will take the year off and build one.

You would think that croc stalking could best be done in a boat. That is not so. We landed the boat around the corner of a mountain and stalked carefully over the king-size cobbles until we were in a position to miss the crocodiles and still have a decent excuse to fetch back to Burrows, who was now flag admiral of the *Lady of the Lake*, as she tugged at her anchor and threatened to break up on a lee shore.

I will say one thing for Selby, the Cautious Captain. He can shoot. He is currently in love with a tiny little toy, a Winchester .243, which has the flattest trajectory of any rifle I ever saw. Shooting well downhill off this mountain at a target area no bigger than a tangerine he nailed one croc under the bumps at a good five hundred yards. It made the water, but only barely, and surfaced at six hundred yards. Harry now had a target area the size of a small lemon, and when he squeezed off the croc turned over and showed a lot of white belly and a death thrash.

Turned out not to be the same croc. The first one was sick enough to make the same lee shore the "Lady" was headed for I took the dinghy and went away to dispatch him, and learned a cardinal truth in croc shooting. The real place to aim for is not under the bumps, but just behind the smile, where the wicked mouth turns up at the end of the long, lascivious grin.

I got a solid rest on my knees and popped the gentleman behind his smile, and you could see complete paralysis set in as his four legs spread and one long ripple went through his body. Even so he was far from being a pocketbook. I finally beached the boat and walked up and blew the top of his head off at a range of one foot, and now he was a pocketbook. We towed him home and gave him to the Molo to eat, and that was the end of another day's fishing.

The next day there were pictures to be taken and the rains were moving closer and the lodge had to be neated up and the provisions battened down and the generator secured and the local troops paid. All this time Juma and company were sulking because Ramadan isn't any fun even when it's cool, and Lake Rudolf is certainly not cool if you're not drinking ice water. We had a freezer full of frozen fish the Molo had caught for us, and a few whistling teal, which make the most delightful eating of any fowl I ever tasted. I had caught two fish, Selby had caught none, Burrows had caught three, and the Molo boat boy, using a hand line, had caught several.

The time had come to leave. We struggled painfully straight up the Valley of Death, made a camp outside of Baragoi, and it was in Maralal that we saw the twin Samburu chicks, and everybody said, "*Wacha!*" at the same time. "*Wacha*" means "No!" We had been away from home too long, especially the multiple-wived Moslems.

We developed a blockage in the oil feed that caused several pleasant stops, and some years later we arrived at Harry's farm in Limuru, magnificently filthy, bone-weary, and green-whiskery.

Mrs. Mickey Selby met the heroes at the door. "Catch any fish?" she asked.

"Some," we said. "Enough."

Next day in Nairobi everybody said, "Where have you chaps been?"

"Fishing," I said stoutly, ready to swing on anybody who would say me nay. "And I never had a better time in my life."

It was true, because as the Old Man was often heard to say, "Fishing doesn't actually happen. It just goes on in your head."

18

Voodoo in the Skillet

Along about September, when the first tart whisper of coming autumn crisps the breeze and the dogs begin to stir restlessly, I always seem to get hungrier than usual. As Havilah Babcock says, "My health is better in November," and my stomach starts to grumble a bit more vociferously when October beckons.

It is not that summer's butter beans and sweet corn are inferior to a pumpkin, even with frost on it, or that the stanch line of rich, red-fleshed tomatoes and an infinite variety of sea food are not nourishing fare, but they lack the tang of autumn, the crackling authority of anything that is flavored with wood smoke. There is still an excitement to camp cookery that cannot be counterfeited by all the back-yard barbecues in the world.

"If I had it to do all over again," the Old Man once said, "I would like to be born black and be a professional hunting cook. Seems to me that apart from being a dead pig in the sunshine there ain't a healthier way to work your way through life. And it's a heap more practical than being a pioneer."

They may possibly have disappeared from the scene, but there used to be a considerable fraternity of outdoor professional chefs. They worked only when fishing and hunting were at their height, which is to say about six months a year. They "laid up" the other six months and lived off their fat.

The specialist was by no means a servant. His cook fire gave him as much professional recognition as attaches to a good guide in Canada or a professional hunter in Africa. He was an autocrat of his outdoor kitchen, brooked no interference, took no advice, and was likely to be severely critical of the hunting or fishing techniques of his clients.

The closest modern parallel is the seasoned African safari cook, like my Aly or Mwende of recent experience. Aly is a coastal Swahili, a good part Arab, and a man I would choose to be my father if I needed a spare. He's as wrinkled as a prune, a sort of medium brown in complexion, and I should say is possibly the best cook for my tastes in the world. Mwende, who is a Wakamba, has been around so long that he was second boy when Philip Percival first took Ernest Hemingway safariing about thirty years ago.

These are Africans of great dignity, professionally grave and almost winsomely charming, as opposed to that rogue Juma, who looks like a carbon of Mickey Rooney and is a kind of priest. He is currently wearing a new set of gold front teeth, shamelessly wheedled out of me on the last expedition. This was his due, he said, because when he went methodically through my box I had brought along nothing worth stealing this trip. At last count Juma owned more of my clothes than I did.

But whether they come from Mombasa or Machakos or

Southport, North Carolina, these outdoor African chefs have a special thing in common. They can take a tin cracker box, a shovel, and a heap of glowing coals, and turn out a meal to make a French chef commit suicide out of sheer envy. I don't know how they do it, but they do.

My old Aly, for instance, uses heaps of coal of varying intensity of heat, depending on what he's cooking. He bakes a crusty, light-golden loaf in one cracker tin by heaping the coals on its top. He sears a piece of meat on a hot flame, then moves it to a back burner of damped coals, while he broils a fowl on another fire, cooks a game leg-enriched soup on a third, boils spaghetti on a fourth, or uses still another to render a chunk of fresh-killed eland suitably tender for tomorrow's broiling.

My wife is a good cook, with a lot of experience and a great deal of imagination, but she had only one try at reforming Aly's kitchen techniques. When his version of her mother's molasses-*cum*-bacon-*cum*-onion special beans turned out better than the old lady's she tossed in her chef's cap and left Aly to his own devices. In the screaming middle of Tanganyika Aly gives you breast of guinea under glass and has been known to produce a soufflé so light that you have to put weights on it to hold it to the table top.

When I was a kid in Carolina we had a succession of Alys. One, I remember, was a paroled murderer, but what he did with fresh-killed venison chops over hickory coals was worthy of official pardon. He could also stick an unplucked duck into a clay mold and cook it until the clay cracked; you peeled off the clay, which took the feathers with it. He did the same thing with a fish, and its scales came off with the clay. I don't know the details of this gentleman's fit of ill temper that sent him to the jug for a spell, but given enough corn whisky and a free hand he could turn an aged shitepoke into a symphony.

Several things distinguished cooks who worked only for sporting gentlemen. I never knew one, not one, who didn't operate in a vapor of alcohol—except of course the Swahilis, who are Moslems and are not supposed to use booze. But mainly, the drunker they got off hand-hewn corn or home-stomped wine the better they cooked.

Another thing: They couldn't stand anybody in their alfresco kitchens. You went back to the cook fire and made some mild recommendation about the quail stew or the rabbit ragout, and you got a less-than-mild admonition to confine your energies to missing fewer quail or to bringing home a better brand of bunny. And there was generally some pouting crack such as: "Mah mouth waterin' for some deer liver, but ah notice ain't no-body fetched in no tender spike buck yet. How y'all gentlemen 'spects me to cook what ah ain't got ah is hard put to say. . . ."

Properly chastened, you went out and clobbered anything with horns, even a stray goat, just to keep the cook from sticking out his underlip.

If you were hunting anywhere at all close to salt water oys-ters always figured heavily in the menu—oysters and any fish, like a blue or a mackerel, that was fat enough to sputter his own grease into the low-blue-tongued broiling fire. The oysters got roasted in a kelp blanket, and sometimes when I think about those oysters, drowned in a peppered sea of heat-bub-bling butter, I just want to sit right down and cry. There'd be a fat mackerel, his hide cracked from the heat, much of his surplus oil dissipated in his own cremation, falling apart from the sheer thoroughness of his preparation, with only a sprinkle of pepper and a slight douse of vinegar. . . . Brother, pass the plate.

Somehow the coffee made from leaf-dyed branch water had an extra-special tang, and enough smoke got mixed up in the eggs and bacon—not these silly, slim strips of bacon, but a de-cent hunk of hog meat—to make an adventure of it. And the sowbelly that flavored the beans had enough character to trans-mute a string bean into an art form.

Possibly the idea of a possum may revolt you, because he's certainly a filthy beast and horrid to look at, but a Mose or an

Ike had a certain talent for bastioning the rendered-down mar-supial with enough sweet taters and onions to make an innocent believe that he was eating his way across France. In the same vein, I shunned wart hog for a long time until the white hunter Don Bousfield conned me into trying a young one. It makes American pork repulsive by comparison. Since the African wart hog is an active animal it doesn't run to fat, so the meat is as lean as fowl.

I would like to insert here that I have eaten elephant's heart, and found it nothing much but rubbery and tough. The foot tastes like pickled pig's feet, and has the same gristly cellular structure. And when once I presented my idea of how to grill a kudu fillet to Aly, even the hyenas spurned the refuse. But roast grasshoppers ain't bad; taste kind of like shrimps in batter.

I think that the bread the old-timy hunting cooks used to produce was possibly the best flour or corn-meal combination I ever encountered. There was a large, plum-black gentleman named Joe, who worked for the late Paul Dooley in a snake-infested camp in the Everglades, and he could make a golden corn bread on an open fire—a corn bread that had the consistency of cake. Joe was kind of handy with hush puppies, too, and when you scraped off the ash they went away in a bite. A hush puppy (which ain't nothing but a hoecake) dipped into the mud-and-oyster-flavored butter in which the oyster has bathed is a kind of gastronomic experience that is too good for most people and should be licensed.

Joe, like most hunting cooks, was a lover of extreme scope, but instead of orchids he took rabbits to his ladies fair. We always went hunting at Grapefruit Gulch with a stern admonition from Joe to assassinate a mess of rabbits, because he had his eye on that fat gal over the hill.

One day Paul and I, with Lee Hills and Walker Stone (the latter two sort of disreputable newspaper executives), went out in the swamp buggy and put the hounds onto an Everglades wild boar. They fetched him squealing by the ears, and we shoved him—he was only a shoat, really—into one of the boxes in the back of the buggy.

Then we went back to camp and told Joe that we'd bad luck with the rabbits, but the dogs had caught one alive and he was in the beverage box in the back of the truck. Joe went out to retrieve his long-eared calling card, and came back stricken sore and almost gray.

"Ah open dat box and de rabbit *roar* at me," Joe said. "Ah don't want no truck wid no roarin' rabbits!"

Joe had a hard time out of us ruffians. Dooley took him to the Bahamas on his boat one time, and the weather was awful. Joe got so sick that his normal purple coloration doubled.

Later he said to me, "Ah swears 'fo' Gawd and three other 'sponsible witnesses, ah ain't nevah goin' to sea wid Mistah Dooley agin!"

Joe's off-duty hours were devoted to romance, although in the Bahamas he had no rabbits to serve as entree. But shortly after he recovered from his mal de mer, a certain covey of comely maids were in evidence. I asked Joe how he arranged this collation of beauty so swiftly.

"Ah tells you, Mistah Bob," he said. "It *so* simple. Ah jes goes asho' and makes a play fo' de old, ugly gals, and in no time de word jes' spreads."

The world is so full of nobility and stupidity and other "itys" these days that I have almost forgotten the wonderful simplicity of a hickory-chip-fire smell, the tiny beacon of light presaging a massive breakfast sandwich of hot egg and bacon on fat-fried bread, with a rich African voice singing something like "Go Down Moses," and the dogs whimpering with eagerness to be off, the coffee bubbling, brownly inviting, the smell of greased gun, and the last star dropping in the sky. The whole promise of a great day was before you, the dew was wet and so were the noses of the dogs, and any one of fifty Joes was going to do something miraculous with the skillet by the time you'd come home, dead tired but almost blissfully, impossibly happy.

You know, I think the Old Man had a good idea. I can't wait to be reborn black, but I think I'll get myself a job with some rich folks as a hunting-fishing cook and lay down this weary writin' load.

19

Dogs, Boys, and the Unspared Rod

Every time I see in the papers where some young thug is up for casual murder or senseless assault and every time I see a picture of a man who has just made chairman of the board from a standing start of nothing I get the same sensation: a distinct tingling in the caboose or rear end. It dates back to being a boy and having a respect for law, order, and eventual achievement imprinted onto my behind with a stick, switch, or limber lath. I sometimes think we don't beat our children, wives, and dogs frequently enough these days, or there'd be fewer creatures who mug strangers, get divorces, and jump onto gentlemen wearing blue suits.

That notion came into my head the other day when little Satchmo, just turned three (which is twenty-one the way humans count time), got all excited because it was the heat season around here, and Satch hasn't met any girl dogs, formally or informally. Satchmo is a boxer who looks just like his namesake, one Louis Armstrong, who plays a trumpet and sings in graveled tones.

This juvenile delinquent Satch got all excited about a bitch across the street being in season, and he took it out on his toothless father in a completely senseless but very fierce attack. I suddenly found myself in the midst of the fray, beating a three-year-old boxer on the back of the neck with my bare fist. The beating didn't have much effect on the boxer, although I came out of the incident with jammed knuckles, a swollen hand, and two very decent accidental bites.

But what did have an effect on the sap-risen little man was a session in the back room with a very heavy Texas-type belt. It has been a long time since I really walloped a dog. I had forgotten that dogs and children can use a tanning once in a while, when they get too big for their britches, and my own rear end tingled as it remembered a few unpleasant afternoons I had experienced on the receiving end of the strap in the woodhouse. "Spare the rod and spoil the child" was a phrase I heard quite often around my house when I was a young'un, and I can assure you I was not spoiled.

Satch isn't spoiled as of today, either, and I can practically promise you that he isn't going to be chewing on his toothless papa any more. But the strange thing is that one sound licking has made a new man out of what had been a shamefully pampered puppy. Satch has fresh dignity. He also responds to commands. He also doesn't get on the wrong sofas or jump up on the guests. And he seems to look at the boss with a new, if rather puzzled, respect. I wonder if I wasn't a couple of years late with the belt business.

The two people who knew most about dog training—working dogs, I mean—that I ever met were the Old Man and a fine black gentleman named Ely Wilson. Wilson was better than the Old Man, if that's possible, and I seem to remember now that he used to cut himself a whippy switch when a particularly headstrong puppy persisted in running up birds or failed to respect another dog's point. Ely, a very kind man whose animals adored him, would take this limber switch, and in the words of the Carolinas simply "wear out" the youngster while saying, "Whoa!" with every lick.

This was momentarily unpleasant to the puppy, but very shortly, when Ely hollered, "Whoa!" the dog associated the word with a limber stick and whoaed. His dogs still retained the high spirits that made them superb in their business, which was quail finding, but they now worked as executives instead of free-lance hot-rodders with strange haircuts.

The Old Man had a trick about retrieving that was also a little hard on the animal at the time, but generally turned out feather-perfect retrievers. It was more or less a gradual process, such as teaching the Boy to be careful with a gun first, before he taught the Boy the business of ballistics and lead-off angles, by merely making the Boy try to hit a running cousin with a stream of water from a hose. (The Boy, I might say, grew up to be a gunnery officer in the Navy, and had remarkable success in teaching lead-off angles to green gun crews with the old hose technique of pointing ahead of what you want to hit, so that the target and the water merge at a logical time and place.)

"This puppy"—Sam or Pete or Tom or Joe—"is a mortal cinch to chew up the first quail he ever lays mouth to," the Old Man said. "So first you catch him in the act. You have already taught him to fetch a stick or a ball, even if you have to wind him in on a length of rope. Now you got to convince him that this bird you shot is not a stick or a ball, but somethin' you want delivered intact when you holler, 'Fetch!' "

"Yes sir," I seem to remember saying. I had been taught to say, yes sir and please and thank you, and I knew that little boys should be seen and not heard at the table. I had been taught this painfully, as I had been taught to fight a plaguing little monster named Wendell, who wouldn't let me out of the yard. I would run and cry when Wendell fell upon me. The Old Man took a stick to me. "It's just a matter of who hurts you the worst," he said, "me with this stick or that little boy you run from. Because every time you run from Wendell I'm goin' to lay this lath on your backside, until you go back and fight him."

Wendell and I have been friends now for about thirty-eight years, give or take a month. The battle could have been called a draw. The Old Man broke the stick over his knee and gave both us battered kids a nickel to buy ice-cream cones.

"Now," the Old Man said, "in this business of training a puppy to bring you back the bird with its feathers nice and dry and the meat unchawed there ain't no sense beating the dog for mouthing a bird. The dog is a young'un and the bird is still warm, maybe even still alive a little bit. If you beat the dog he'll figger that you're beating him for getting the bird for you. What do you do?"

"I dunno, sir," I said. One of the things you learned around the Old Man was that a confession of innocent ignorance was very often to be preferred to smart-aleck error or even to smart-aleck nonerror. The Old Man was like a boy in a way: He didn't want to be deprived of a chance to show off once in a while.

"Well I'll show you. Now, suppose you see if you can hit the next bird the dog points, and after you've shot hang onto old Frank with one hand and the puppy with the other, and let me be your bird dog."

Frank stood a covey, and I hit with the first and missed with the second. The first bird fell in a shower of feathers in an easy patch of ground peas. Frank was trained to hold a point until the fetch command came. I hollered, "Hold!" and made a dive for the puppy, managing to collar both dogs.

The Old Man went over to where the drifting feathers had settled on the peanut stalks and bent over the dead bird. In a minute he said, "Now hang onto the old dog. Holler 'Fetch!' and let the little feller go!"

Off bounded the puppy, looking for the bird, while the Old Man said steadily, "Dead, dead, dead." And the puppy located the bird and pounced on it with a hard mouth, full of sharp puppy teeth. The puppy bit down on the dead bird and let out a horrified yelp. He dropped the bird, spat out some feathers, and stood looking at the bird with his ears cocked.

"Now fetch dead," the Old Man said. "Bring it here. Give it to me. That's a good boy." These were commands the puppy had learned in the back yard training sessions, over the tin pie plate of food. The puppy picked up the dead bird very gently now and brought it to the Old Man, as if he might be very happy to get rid of it.

The Old Man handed me the bird and grinned. He had used one of the oldest dog-training tricks in the world, I guess. He had merely taken a broad rubber band, studded it with needle-pointed tacks, and slipped it around the dead quail's body. When the puppy chomped down on the dead bird the bird more or less bit back. Puppy's teeth are sharp, but half-inch tacks are sharper.

"He might forget and mouth a bird again," the Old Man said. "I doubt he will, but you keep this rubber band handy in your huntin' coat, and if he does mouth a bird again give him another dose of the same treatment. About two doses is generally enough. Dogs ain't generally as big fools as people."

The Old Man entertained some sort of premise that it was nice to try to reason with a dog or a boy, but if the dog or boy didn't listen to reason then you had to find some way to impress him that wrong was wrong, good was good, and black was not white. He was all for the initial ounce of prevention, but he generally had a long ton of cure in reserve.

I don't know if he invented the choke collar or not. But we had a magnificent lemon-and-white English setter named Sandy that had a nasty habit of stealing other dogs' points, breaking to shot, and occasionally running up coveys out of sheer jealous arrogance. The Old Man went to the local blacksmith shop and had a short consultation with the boss, and eventually, in a shower of sparks, emerged with a slip-noose collar that seemed to be constructed of sharp-nailed fingers.

"Next time Frank points and Sandy starts to steal it I'm going to drape this thing around Mr. Sandy's neck. When he bolts you'll hear me holler, 'Whoa!' Don't pay no attention. Just go ahead and shoot. I'll be in command of the rest of the situation."

It was sort of difficult to work this mousetrap operation with coveys, because Sandy was a winder and a far-ranging, high-headed genius with a radar nose. Frank was the single-bird expert, and a lot of his careful, close work was wasted by the arrogant Sandy's rushing around fool-headed in close cover. Sandy could generally manage to run up more birds out of shooting range than Frank could nail with his Swiss-watch accuracy in finding singles, after the flushed covey scattered in the broom or on the edge of the branch.

It came about one day that Frank pinned a single in a patch of scrub pine, and Sandy came up behind and—as easily, as gently, as craftily as a cat burglar—began to encroach on the point. He was so intent on theft that he paid no attention when the Old Man more or less lassoed him with this strange, cruel-looking collar. All of a sudden he made his pounce, flashed by Frank, and flushed Frank's private bird. I shot and killed the bird just after I heard the Old Man yell, "Whoa!"

Then I turned and saw the Old Man hanging onto a lead, with a half-choked lemon-and-white English setter, his eyes bugged out, on its other end.

"I believe that if there's crime there ought to be punishment," the Old Man said. "Sandy is a criminal. I have just taught him a lesson they used to teach highwaymen in England. If you steal you hang. Hanging is not pleasant, is it Sandy?" He slacked the line and took the choke collar off the dog's neck. He patted Sandy on the head. "The next time I holler 'Whoa!' you'll whoa, all right. And," he said to me, "the next batch of singles we hit we'll slap this collar back on Mr.

Sandy again, and see if we can't restrain his high spirits by exerting just a *gentle* pressure on his neck with my tailor-made gallows rope. Just sort of play him out a little bit, like you'd play a fish."

I came up through several dynasties of dogs: pointers, setters, spaniels, just plain fice dogs with back-curled tails, and even one hybrid that seemed to be at least one part muskrat, judging from his appearance. They all worked well. They answered the whistle and brought the dead birds—even doves, which they hated because of the free-falling feathers—and they back-stood each other and slowed down on singles and watched where the ducks fell and responded to a waved hand when they were hunting very far out.

Only one I remember as a natural. The rest learned it through the tough back-yard discipline: first the commands with food and the tossed ball; next the switch; and finally through such refinements as choke collars and tack-studded rubber bands. Mainly they were dogs to be proud of, and they seemed to be proud of themselves once they worked the orneriness out of their systems.

"You can't give a dog a nose," the Old Man said. "Only God can teach him to smell. But by the Lord Harry, you can teach him decent manners, and you can teach him to use what nose he's got to the best advantage of all of us.

"You might remember," the Old Man continued, "when you grow up and have some young'uns of your own, that the word *whoa* is a valuable word for a child as well as a puppy, since children ain't nothin' but puppies anyhow. And that a lecture accompanied by a sharp rap on the rear has more weight than a lecture without the sharp rap on the rear. I will ask you a question to prove it. What should little boys be at the table?"

"Seen and not heard," I replied. Man, I'd been through *that* one before, and I didn't need a choke collar.

A few years ago the first view halloo over the pooch the Russians sent winging into outer space in the sputnik aroused a strange reaction around the world. Possibly the Arabs were not concerned, since to the average Arab a dog is a miserable *miskeen* of a creature fit only for kicks and slow starvation.

But the rest of the world, even the Russians themselves, suddenly got all upset over this poor Fido whirling around the globe in an ersatz satellite, eating when his Pavlov-developed reflexes answered a bell, and finally dying in his unearthly kennel. Now indeed, in human indignation, was science fiction married to fact. Somebody was mistreating a dog. The outcry was loudest in Britain, but most of the world's journals abandoned scientific speculation for front-page evaluation of the pup's chances of homing back to this globe.

It was touching and shocking, in that it took a small bitch to bring the world face to face with reality, and all of a sudden the Old Man's figure towered tremendously in my mind over Khrushchev, Einstein, and all the scientists and technicians everywhere, who dealt in armament larger than a twelve-bore shotgun.

The Old Man would have been real mad about this mutt being perverted into a dog in the moon. He had very strong ideas about dogs, and none of them included putting a pooch in a pressureproof kennel and shooting him out of a rocket into the stratosphere to die in loneliness with no fleas to scratch and no human hand upon his head.

"Dogs," the Old Man used to say, "are a cut better than people, and should be treated according to their station and their worth. Even a trash dog has got a certain nobility about him, and should be allowed to pursue happiness in his fashion."

A trash dog, by the Old Man's definition, was any dog who had no real function by which he earned his food. A Dane, a Peke, a poodle, a pug, each was trash in the Old Man's reckoning. A yaller cur that would run rabbits, a back-curl-tailed fice that would tree squirrels, any bastard brindle of bulldog-*cum*-hound that would run a deer, even a hearty cocker spaniel that would work in the woods were borderline between trash and quality.

The quality started with purebred Walker hounds, big

springers, Chesapeakes, and beagles, hovered momentarily over setters of all breeds except Irish ("You got to relearn the dod-limbed dogs every year, and they're as flighty as a red-headed woman"), and wound up with pointers. The Old Man mightily fancied pointers, and was willing to argue that while the Caro-lina briers would leave a pointer's tail bloody he was better fitted for hot bush work than a heavy-haired setter. He made only one exception: our big rangy Llewellin setter named Frank, a blue-ticked genius that knew integral calculus where quail were concerned, and was haired almost as thinly as a pointer.

I reckon the old gentleman owned as austere a set of ideas about dogs as anybody I ever met. I do not say he was harsh, but he was powerful stern.

For instance, he refused to pamper a working dog—a hound or a bird dog—by turning it into a house pet. He would com-promise with a retriever, though—a spaniel or a Labrador—because the retriever's work was actually fun and couldn't be spoiled by steam heat or female coddling.

"A hound dog or a bird dog belongs to live outside the house," he said. "Bring him into the house except for an occasional visit, like Christmas, and you lose a good workman and get yourself a dodlimbed lap dog that won't hunt unless he feels like it, because he thinks he's as good as you. A good hunting dog is kind of religious. You ought to mortify his flesh a little bit to keep him in line. You keep him penned so he won't waste his energy ambling around aimless, and when you turn him loose he knows he's in business. Also, you keep him a little bit thin when he ain't working, so he won't be wheezing when the season opens. Then you feed him strong, because he'll run off what extra vittles you shove into him."

I don't know what the fashionable fare for hunting dogs is today, but we never had any cases of malnutrition on a more or less steady diet of table scraps, cold hominy, green vegetables, and corn bread. Old Galena and later Big Lil used to make enormous pans of corn bread for the animals, and to the best of my memory it tasted just as good as what we had on the table.

They were fed once a day, at 5 P.M., and they were fed together but in separate plates. Mostly our dogs were males, but there was no fighting. The Old Man discouraged fighting from puppyhood, by rebuking the combatants personally with a stick and then removing their meal.

"A greedy gut," he used to say, "has got more sense than a brain."

We gave them the cheapest butcher's meat once or twice a week, and once a week a can of salmon, which at the time cost about fourteen cents. For a treat there was an occasional tin of prepared dog food, and oddly enough (for this was well over thirty years ago) the Old Man dosed most meals heavily with fish oil. This was easy to come by and cheap, too, because we lived in a community that produced a great deal of fish-scrap fertilizer from the enormous shoals of pogies, or menhaden, that provided the village with a major industry.

It seems heretical now, but we also fed them whole fish and chicken bones. The Old Man's justification was simple.

"What is a dog?" he would ask himself rhetorically. "A dog is a descendant of a wolf. A fox is his cousin. What does a wolf eat? What does a fox eat? What he can catch: rabbits, birds, small game. In Alaska the huskies eat a steady diet of nothing but fish. All of this stuff has got bones. A dog's got enough quicklime in his digestive apparatus to melt an iron bar. If he gets something stuck in his throat he just throws up. You let any one of these modern pampered critters loose, and he'll eat or try to eat anything he comes across in the woods. He'll eat it, dead and rotten—fur, feathers, bones, and all. I never knew of a dog dying of indigestion, and up to now I never heard of one choking to death on a chicken bone."

It is very possible that I learned my first lessons in general sanitation, apart from discipline, from the Old Man and the dogs. After I graduated from being Mammy Laura's "do' boy," which meant that I was vice-president in charge of holding the kitchen door open for my ancient mammy, a former slave, I achieved the adult position at the age of about six of being the dog boy.

The dog boy's job was to see that the animals got fed promptly and to train the puppies not to attack their food until the command, "Hie on!" was given. Undue exercise of appetite was prevented by holding the puppies firmly by the tails and saying, "Whoa!" when they bolted for the food. In a week's time they ate on command.

Another chore of the dog boy was to see that every kennel was aired daily and that the pine straw that made the bed was replaced weekly. We built simple kennels—a big packing box, stilted dry off the ground on bricks, with a flap top that could be turned back on its hinges to let the sun in. Pine straw, I do believe, is still the cleanest and warmest material for a dog nest, as it seems to have some sort of aromatic resistance to insects. Also, it was great fun going out once a week in the towering (to a small boy) forests to sweep bagfuls of the clean brown needles in the hushed cathedral of the pine groves. If I was feeling especially virtuous I would also lug home a crocus sack full of the fallen cones, which made magnificent kindling and issued a lovely, almost incenselike smell—to grownups, that is. Me, I preferred the smell of baking bread.

The dog boy was simultaneously in charge of defleaing, and in the rare instances when mange crept unbidden into the run it was the dog boy who cured himself as well as the afflicted animal with a tremendously potent mixture of burnt crankcase oil and sulphur. Neither the dog boy nor the dog smelled so good as formerly, but the mange generally departed.

Today I know that most things seem better in retrospect, but I cannot begin to tell you the thrill there is in taking a hand-trained puppy, a puppy you've sweated through babyhood, adolescence, manners, mange, and his natural exuberance of spirit, into the woods and have him make *you* look good in front of your elders.

"Dogs are kind of like people," the Old Man said once.

"You generally get out of 'em what you put in 'em. There's good dogs and bad dogs, dumb dogs and smart dogs that are actually too big for their britches, but, mainly speaking, you can correct up or down and get yourself a decent four-legged citizen if you go about it right. A taste of the switch and a little explanation as to why, and you got yourself a dog that won't run rabbits and a boy that won't stick up banks."

Every time I read a new headline about that poor dog in the sputnik the Old Man kept coming back stronger than the beep. It had nothing to do with the sacrifice of dogs for science or any undue sentimentality about animals, as we know that a great many animals have died that people may live. It was just a sense of outrage at the unfitness of things, at the futility of using a dog—good, bad, or indifferent—where a dog didn't belong.

"A working dog," the Old Man said, "don't belong to live in the house. A pet dog don't belong to live outside the house. A pet dog is different from a work dog, but all dogs have a dignity that ought to be respected. And any lost hound worthy of his grits will eventually find his way home."

I guess what made me real mad was that this critter wasn't ever going to find her way home, and the fault was not hers. Somehow a dog has too much dignity to get her tail caught in any kind of machine away up yonder where she can't hear a whistle.

20

Second Childhood Is More Fun than the First—I

A fellow I know turned forty the other day, and it had him mightiful down. Forty is a kind of rough year for a man. It is an October sort of year. You still wear the scars of old summer mosquito bites, but there is a prickling of frost on the pumpkin and there is more than a clammy hint of the winter crouching just behind the hill.

"I dunno what there is about forty," the Old Man said once, referring acidly to the antics of some male relative, who seemed to be trying to convince himself that his capacity for the local corn-squeezing was limitless. "Seems to afflict most fellers about the middle of their thirty-ninth year. Sort of a final fling before they give up what they think is youth and force themselves to settle down with the idea of livin' with a potbelly and a shiny head. You hear a lot of talk about women actin' flighty when they start to crowd thirty. I tell you the honest-to-John truth, a woman on the edge of what she calls middle age ain't half as fidgety and worrisome as a man."

The Old Man grinned, and fired his pipe. "Ever occur to you that you'll be forty someday?"

I guess I was about fifteen at the time, and sweating out every day that stood between me and a driving license, which became legally possible at sixteen. The idea of anybody being forty was outlandish, except for *old* people like my pa, who was nudging that ancient estate himself. It never occurred to me that the Old Man was any age at all. He had worn the same battered hat and the same shaggy mustache ever since I could remember. Even the yellow nicotine stains on the mustache hadn't changed since we started knocking around like men together, when I was summ'at sixish.

"No sir," I said. "It's too far off."

"It ain't as far off as you think," the Old Man replied. "You'll find out that it's just around the corner once you pass twenty-one and the years start to sneak up on you. The whole point, though, is not to miss nothing as they pass you by, and when you hit that real middle age don't let it fret you none. I reckon the years between forty and sixty are the best a man's apt to put in. He can do dang near anything as good as he could when he was a youngster, and what he can't jump over he's smart enough to walk around. Which would you say's the best dog we got, Frank or Sandy?"

"Frank," I said. I didn't even have to stop to think. "Sure, Frank." Our blue belton Llewellin had more bird sense in his backside than most dogs wear in their nose.

"Well," the Old Man said, "Frank's pretty near as old as me, if you average dog years into man years, and I sure ain't no spring chicken. What is the main thing you notice about Frank when he hunts?"

I thought for a minute. "Well," I said, "he don't make many mistakes. And he takes his time. And he don't run all over the

place like a blame-fool puppy, pointing larks and chasing rabbits. He sure don't waste many steps, come to think of it."

The Old Man smiled approvingly. "There you got it in a
nutshell. Now that Sandy's a good dog, and he'll steady down
someday, but right now he's got to run a mile and a half and
lift his leg on every bush in the neighborhood before you can
impress on him with a stick that he's in the bird-huntin' business.
When he runs up a covey it ain't because he don't know any
better or hasn't been taught that it's wrong. He's just full of
vinegar, and he hasn't learned to put the brakes on his spirit.
When he cocks his ears and half-points a rabbit he's still playing.
He knows damned well it's a rabbit and he's not supposed to
notice it, but the puppy in him is just crying out loud for foolish
expression and the rabbit is it."

It was beginning to look like a long day. Also it was in
between seasons: too late for doves and too early for quail and
ducks. It wasn't that I didn't like to listen to the Old Man, but
when he started to philosophize somehow it always seemed to
wind up with work, with me doing most of it. I looked hopeful
and kept my trap shut.

"Sandy reminds me of you," the Old Man said. "Fit to bust
with useless energy. He ain't happy with today. He's always
over the next hill, looking for tomorrow. Right now you're
fretting yourself sick about getting to be sixteen, so you can
drive the Liz *legal*." He stressed the word "legal," knowing
very well that I had been driving that old tin tragedy on the
sly since I was twelve. "Sixteen'll get here fast enough, and so
will twenty-one and so will forty and so will eighty, and then
all of a sudden you're dead before you realize what happened
to all the time you wasted worryin' about next Christmas when
you ought to be happy with the Fourth of July."

The Old Man rubbed his pipe on his nose, and looked at me
like he was expecting me to say something. I didn't oblige him.
There didn't seem to be much point to me worrying about
being forty or eighty. It was still about thirty-seven days, six
hours, and forty-two minutes until the bird season opened, and

about forty-nine days, seven hours, and nine minutes until school let out for the holidays, and my birthday would come during the holidays. . . .

"I know what you're thinking," the Old Man said. "You just can't wait for the time to pass until something that you can't do now gets to be possible, and then you'll worry about how long it is before you can do it again. You start to fret on Christmas Eve, because it'll be three hundred and sixty-six days until next Christmas. You ain't like me and Frank. We don't false-point and we don't run all over the place chasing stinkbirds, but we come home with the bacon more often than not, and we ain't all wore out when we get home to the fire either. You bleed for an hour if you miss a bird, and you're so busy worrying about the last one you missed, you miss the next one as well. There ain't no such animal as hindsight positive action. All you can do is wipe up the spilt milk and try to do better with the present, and let the future come up sort of gradual. You got to learn to live with what you got."

I begun to fidget. You can stand just so much high thinking on any given day when you are near-about sixteen. I wanted to *do* something.

The Old Man heaved a mock sigh. "I can see my fine-haired conversation is wasted on you," he said. "Suppose you just run upstairs to my room and get me another tin of Prince Albert, and then we'll go get arrested or something."

I came back down with the tobacco. "Let's go," I said.

"Where?" the Old Man asked. "You call it."

"Africa," I said. "I want to shoot a lion. Or India. I want to shoot a tiger. I want to do it today. I don't want to wait until I'm forty. Now, like you said. I don't want life to pass me by."

The Old Man grinned. "Purty sassy, ain't you? I reckon we don't run much to lions and tigers around here, but mebbe I can provide something in the way of one of them what-do-you-call-its for you. About time you blooded yourself on dangerous game." He grinned again and this time it was wicked.

"You ever read anything about them Bengal Lancers—the

British soldier fellers in India that go wild pigstickin'? Well, wrap a rag around your hat and call it a *puggree*, I think that's the name, and we'll go boarstickin'. Except in the case of this pig I expect we better use buckshot. We'll need some dogs. Just run over and ask Sam Watts if we can borrow a couple of his hounds. Bell and Blue'll do."

We tied up the bird dogs and slung the hounds in the back of the Liz. They lay flat on the back seat and drooled, their tongues lolloping sideways. Old Blue perked one coon-chewed ear. Cars meant guns, and guns meant hunting.

The Old Man looked at me kind of curiously. "Where's the tents? And the salt and pepper and fat back and coffee and sugar? What kind of pigstickin' expedition is this, anyhow? You don't expect to stick a pig and come home the same night, do you? It might take five, six days. You might even have to miss a little school. I reckon that'll worry you nigh to death, but sometimes you have to take the bitter with the sweet. And how about all the beaters and gunbearers and such as that? This ain't just any old kind of pigstickin' expedition."

"I don't know any beaters and gunbearers," I said. The Old Man had me on the run. "This is all new to me."

"I don't see nothing wrong with some of Big Abner's young'uns for beaters," the Old Man said, more or less to himself. "He can easy spare half a dozen. And I reckon Pete and Tom'll have to do for gunbearers. You better run down the road and tell them to be ready in half an hour. And tell Tom to bring his rifle. You can't tell what we'll run into in the jungle. Maybe a bobcat or a panther. Pity we haven't got any tigers, but I reckon you'll have to blame it all on geography. Somebody got careless and didn't apportion none of them critters to these parts."

Somebody must have got careless with Tom and Pete, too. I guess I've told you about them more'n once before. They were both lean, lantern-jawed, black-whiskered woodsmen, that some people said had a smidgen of Injun in them. They wore hip boots like other people wore shoes, in town and out, and they chawed tobacco constant. They made corn liquor in the winter, and drank it up in the spring. They fished in the summer and hunted in the fall. They worked a little bit when the menhaden—the pogies—were running and Mr. Charlie Gause's fertilizer factory was standing in the need of fish scrap. I reckon they forgot more about woods and water than most fellers ever learned, and they weren't above sharing it with me. They kidded me along, but it was gentle kidding. Pete was my special buddy. Tom, he was kind of surly sometimes. People said the Injun showed more strong in Tom, who could be a ringtailed bear cat in a rough-and-tumble, when a little homemade whisky took a firm hold of him. I never saw him cut up nasty any, though. Mostly what I remember about Tom and Pete was that they were in on the death of the first deer I ever shot, and they stuck my face into the deer's green, fodder-filled paunch.

"What's Ned Hall up to now?" Pete said, when I panted up to the house, after running all the way. The house was a weathered-gray, ramshackledy house, what paint it had flaking off in scabby stretches. The porch had a hole rotted in one end of its planking, and the steps sagged sort of slanchwise. Tom and Pete were squatted on the steps, whittling and spitting tobacco juice in the sandy yard. Seems like I never saw either one of them when they weren't doing something with a knife or a gun.

"He's decided to go pigstickin'," I said, out of breath. "You know him when he takes a notion to do something in a hurry. He said to tell you to bring the rifle, we might need it."

Tom looked at Pete, and Pete looked at Tom.

Tom grunted. "Pigs, huh?"

"That's what he said. He said you and Pete could be the gunbearers, and we could use some of Big Abner's young'uns for beaters. Something about the Bengal Lancers, I dunno, but he said get a move on."

Pete looked at Tom. He winked. "We was layin' off to fix up

the porch some," he said. "The old woman's been after us to
hit a lick and fix it. You reckon . . ." He let the words drift.

"I reckon," Tom said. "It's been needin' fixin' for nigh onto
three year now, and if she wasn't hollerin' about that it'd be
somethin' else. Come on, Pete. If the old gentleman wants to
stick a pig I reckon we best go help him out. Tell Ned we'll be
ready when you come by."

I dashed off over the sand hill again, and I thought I could
hear the men snickering as I ran. I didn't care if it was a snipe
hunt. It was action, if it had Tom and Pete and two hound dogs
mixed up in it, let alone pigs and Bengal Lancers.

The Old Man was pretty near ready when I got back. There
was a stack of tentage and blankets and cooking equipment
piled in a heap around the Lizzie.

"I already made some peace with your grandma," he said.
"Go get your huntin' duds, and then help me load up this car.
The boys coming? They ain't drunk or in jail or anything like
that?"

"They're coming," I said. "They said they'd be ready when
we drove by. But they seem to think there was something
awful funny about this trip. Is there?"

"Not that I know of," the Old Man said. "Pigstickin' is a
very serious business. A feller can get hurt with the right pig
unless he handles him careful. Come on now, let's run off before Miss Lottie changes her mind."

We picked up Tom and Pete and crammed them, somehow,
into the back seat of the Liz with the dogs and guns and pots
and pans. We jounced along on the corduroy road on the way
out of town, and suddenly the Old Man started to laugh. He
laughed so hard he had to stop the car until he got his breath
back. Tom and Pete, they begun to laugh with him. I sat
there kind of hurt, because I didn't see anything to laugh at. I
guess the Old Man must have noticed that I looked put out.

"Don't take it to heart," he said, "but does anything strike
you as unusual about this trip—more than usual, I mean?"

"No sir," I said.

"Well then," the Old Man said, "look at us. Four grown men, past prime, two old flea-bit hounds, and a shirttail boy, all heading off to the jungles to play Bengal Lancer and stick pigs—at our age. I ain't apt to see seventy again any time soon, and if they'd of kept records when they whelped Tom and Pete they'd be easy fifty, fifty-two. And Bell and Blue are mighty near as old as you are, which makes them about a hundred years old apiece as dogs go. But away we rush off to the woods, like a bunch of young'uns playin' Injun. Remember what I told you earlier today about being forty years old ain't quite the end of the world?"

"Yes sir," I said. "I sure do." I looked around me at the Old Man and Tom and Pete and the dogs, and for a minute I felt older than any of them.

I told all this to my aging friend, the one who turned forty the other day, and was down in the dumps about it. He seemed to brighten considerably.

"Did you get any pigs?" he asked.

I said sure, we got some pigs, but I would tell him more later, after I soothed my old bones with a little painkiller.

You see, the Boy, which is me, had just turned forty-five, and was feeling his decrepitude in the joints.

21

Second Childhood Is More Fun than the First—II

The Old Man had squirreled away a supply of hand-hewn philosophy to fit most moods and conditions, and he was very fond of saying that a man was nothing but a boy grown old. He liked to say that if a feller was raised right it was powerful difficult to beat the boy out of him no matter how many hard knocks he absorbed in the painful process of achieving maturity.

"The measure of a grown man," the Old Man said, "is just how much tomfoolery he can get away with when he's got gray in his whiskers, without appearin' to be a damned fool. I ain't referrin' to coon chasin' and suchlike, because anybody that runs around tearing up his clothes in the woods at night behind a pack of hounds on the off-chance they'll tree a coon is just lookin' for an excuse to get drunk and fall in a briar patch."

The Old Man did not utter these sage words, however, when he and Tom and Pete, the half-Injun woodsmen, decided to quench my thirst for youthful adventure and whip me off on what he referred to as a pigstickin' expedition. We were, as I was saying, supposed to be what he called Bengal Lancers, and we were going to hunt pigs the hard way. Not sticking them with a lance, on horseback, as the Lancers did in India, but using hounds to course them, and after that it was every man—and pig—for himself.

In our neck of the woods we have what is called a razorback, a tame pig run wild and breeding to more wild hogs until he produces a wild animal every bit as mean as anything that started off in the swamps. He ain't so big as one of those Russian-y boars they have in the mountains, but he's just as ornery. He's spread out through the east Carolinas all the way down through the Everglades in Florida.

The first thing we did on this notable expedition was to stop at Big Abner's farm. Big Abner looked to be about seven feet tall. He was sort of purple black, weighed around two hundred and fifty pounds, and had about twenty children, or so it seemed. He also had several coveys of quail that used around his pea fields. He had some deer and turkey and foxes and wildcats that hung out in the big branch—swamp, that is—which ran through his property. And he had pigs. His eyes lit up when the Old Man asked him if he'd seen any lately.

"Yassuh, Cap'm," he said. "Sho is. Dey's a passel on 'em usin' down in de branch. One big old boar, too. I run him up t'other day, when I 'uz mindin' some traps, and he roar at me lak a lion. Got tushes on him turn right back to he eyes. Dat a mean hog. Got some mean sows wid him, too, and a whole mess o' shoats. I lak mighty well git ahold a couple of dem shoats befo' dey tough up lak de old feller."

"We thought we'd give the boy here a pig hunt," the Old Man said. "We got the hounds. But we need some mules and some young'uns. Come on over to the well and we'll work this thing out."

(The well, I knew, was where a half-gallon jug of scuppernong wine dwelt in the cool depths. By-and-by the grown men came back smiling.)

"We'll make us a camp," the Old Man said, "and we'll start out bright and early in the morning. We need a good night's rest for this business. You have the young'uns ready before light, hey Abner?"

"Yassuh, Cap'm," Big Abner said. "We be's ready."

We got back in the Liz and drove off the main road a few miles to a place we'd camped before, when we were after turkey or deer. It was on Abner's land, and it was a place nobody else ever used, because Abner was very strict about keeping his land posted. He leased a lot of land, mostly for the turpentine rights, and he didn't hold with strangers who were apt to set the broom grass alight with careless cigarettes and burn up a whole lot of valuable pitch pine.

It was lovely hunting country. There were big stands of tall longleaf pine, their boles chopped to make the pockets in which the big, waxy, grapelike clusters of sap gathered. If you knocked off one of these knobs of congealed sap it had the same consistency as chewing gum and was cleanly aromatic on the tongue. These big piny wood stands had very little undergrowth beneath them, because their tall umbrella tops shut out the sun. The ground underneath these great trees was strewn with long brown needles, as clean as a carpet and as slippery as glass. The sun made little golden pools and flecks of light on this carpet, but mostly the shade was as somberly solemn as a church. It got very spooky along about dusk, when the doves began to complain and the night air started to turn gently cool.

The tall pine thickets held to the high ground, but their outskirts were cutover patches of scrubby oak and seedling pine, with a lot of old dead stuff on the ground, making little hummocks and high ridges of fallen trees, lichened stumps, and shiny green gallberry bushes. These islands, for they were literally islands, were where you found most of the quail, after you'd started them out of the broom grass or the corn fields or pea patches.

Vast sweeps of broom sedge, dotted with the occasional islands, made up a rolling yellow sea. The quail roosted in the broom, away from the varmints that inhabited the swamps. Sometimes they flushed from the fields and scattered in the broom, and anybody with a good single-bird dog could shoot his limit if he was a mind to and didn't care about leaving anything for next year. But mostly the flushed birds pitched on sides of the swamps in the little islands, or sometimes flew straight through and dropped on the scrubby hills on the other side. They seldom lit in the big pine thickets—no cover—and even less seldom in the swamps—varmints.

But the deer and the wild pigs and the occasional wildcat haunted the swamps, as did the rare black bear. The deer and the pig fed out at night, wrecking the corn fields and rooting up the goobers. The pigs were particularly death on the pea fields, both peanut and black-eyed field peas, while the deer gourmandized young corn and the tender green rye.

"The plan of campaign," the Old Man was saying now, "is to pick up some pig sign and start the dogs. Then we'll send the pickaninnies in behind the dogs, some of them, and stake out some more on the flanks, and we'll beat them pigs right out into the open. We'll run 'em into the grass and ride 'em down on the mules. You, Boy," he said to me, "you're the head lancer. You're the boss pigsticker."

"What'll I stick him with?" I asked. "I plumb forgot to bring my lance."

"A pitchfork is plenty good enough to start with," the Old Man said. "If a pig gets close enough to bite you a pitchfork is all you'll need. Come in handy, especially if you fall off the mule."

"What'll *you* use?" I asked, kind of nervous. "Another pitchfork?"

"Nope," the Old Man replied. "I'm the head *shikari* of this shebang. I'm the native gunbearer. I'm too old for pitchforks. I'll stick to this old pump gun of mine. Tom's got his rifle and Pete'll back you up with his double barrel. But a real classy pigsticker shouldn't need any help from guns. It ain't supposed to be sportin', not the way I've read about it. Kipling wouldn't approve of it for certain."

Then everybody but me laughed again. It seemed to me that there was an awful lot of unnecessary laughing going on for a bunch of grown men. Mostly they were serious hunters, when it had to do with deer or ducks or quail or turkey, but every time anybody said "pig" somebody else snickered.

I won't trouble you with the camp making, because one good camp is just like another. That is to say, I did most of the work, such as chopping wood, splitting kindling, going for water, and cutting pine tops for beds, while the men lazed around investigating something ripe-smelling in a fruit jar. We had a fine meal of corn bread, fried ham and eggs, and I went to sleep wondering what devilment these grown-up children had in store for me.

I only had a short dream to wait before somebody shook me awake in the chill dawn and I scrubbed the sleep out of my eyes with my knuckles. By the time I'd been to the branch for water Big Abner and his tribe had arrived. He had evidently drummed up some nieces and nephews, for what appeared to be an army of young black faces swarmed around him. At least a dozen dogs of indeterminate breed accompanied Big Abner's relatives, and they were snapping and snarling amongst themselves. Old Bell and Blue, our borrowed hounds, looked sleepy-eyed and bored as the curs scuffled and yipped. Four mules, their ears drooping in the dawn's shifting light, were wearing battle array of wooden working hames and saddle blanket, with the reins looped over the hames. I noticed then that each of Abner's troop had a tin pot or pan of some description, and each carried a short club.

"Now," the Old Man grinned, "the idea is that you and me and Pete will ride out to the far end of the swamp, and take up stations in the broom grass. Tom will take Bell and Blue and go to the pea patch and pick up some hog sign. The hogs will naturally go into the branch, and then we'll turn the beaters and the other dogs a-loose. The beaters will pound on the pans and the other dogs will take up the trail, and if all goes well we'll beat the pigs back out into the clear. I think." The Old Man said in a loud aside to Pete and Tom, "I think this is the way you are supposed to do her. Personally, all I ever did was read about it in a book. If things go wrong I ain't responsible."

"What do I do in all this?" I asked. I wished I'd kept my mouth shut about wanting to go off to India to shoot tigers and Africa to shoot lions before I was too old to enjoy it.

"Why," the Old Man said, "it's the easiest thing in the world. You just kick the mule in the ribs and charge the pig. The pig will be charging you, of course, if he's worth the salt to cure him into a ham, and when you and the pig meet you kind of lean over the mule and stick him with the pitchfork. With all them hayfork tines I don't see how you can miss him. If you should fall off the mule I'd try not to lose a-holt of that pitchfork. These pigs can turn mighty nasty if they think they got you cornered."

I was mumbling when I climbed aboard the mule. Under that blanket the mule had a backbone any razorback hog would have been proud of. The mule turned his head and looked at me. He shook his head in what seemed to be disgust.

Tom took his mule by the reins and the dogs by their leads, and went off toward the pea field with his rifle tucked under one arm. Between the two hounds and the mule and the rifle he seemed to have considerable on his hands.

I had considerable on my hands, too, with this consarned mule. I never did put too much trust in horses, and none at all in mules, and this wall-eyed son of a roving jackass seemed to sense my lack of appreciation of his nobler qualities. He reminded me in some ways of a billy goat I had once, only he was bigger. And constructed a heap higher off the ground. They say mules have sure feet. This big gray critter stumbled and almost fell every time he took a step. It looked like half a mile from his back to the ground. Clutching the pitchfork with one hand, it was all I could do to hang onto him with the other.

We shambled along to the bottleneck end of the swamp, where the thick stuff cleared and emptied out onto the broom grass, and Pete and the Old Man didn't seem to be doing much better than I was. Mules, I reckon, ain't built to be ridden as a steady thing. Not even by Sancho Panza.

We got to the end of the swamp, and heard the dogs tune up and then settle into a steady belling as they hit a hot trail. The tune was loud and clear, and then suddenly was punctuated with angry growls and barks. Two rifle shots snapped in the keen morning air, and then there was a whole lot of yipping and yapping. Then came an unholy sound of pans and buckets being beaten with sticks, the clattering and banging relieved by squeals and growls and barking and yelling. I never heard such a mess of assorted noise in all my born days. There was a crashing of brush in the swamp on top of all the other noise, and I heard the Old Man let out a whoop and holler: "Get set! Here they come!"

And here they came, indeed. A couple of lengths ahead of the mob was a big old sow, with Blue hanging onto one ear and old Bell dug into another. The sow was making pretty good way in the grass, though, and she was squealing her head off, swinging her head from side to side while she tried to dislodge the dogs.

Behind the old sow came a litter of half-grown pigs, all squealing, and behind the pigs came all the fice dogs the Abner children had imported, and behind the dogs the Abner children were running, beating on the pots and pans and hollering fit to kill. Puffing behind the young'uns was Big Abner, and behind Big Abner was Tom, cussing steady and hauling away on his mule, which had its front feet braced and was giving Tom quite an argument.

One of the bigger pigs spied my mule and more or less charged it. I made a frantic stab at it with the pitchfork and missed, of course. The squealing pig ran between the mule's legs and the mule bucked and I flew through the air to land with a thump on the ground. Just before I was engulfed by a flood of pigs, dogs, and Negro children I heard the Old Man yelling: "Whoa, you dumb fool!" and some more sulphury cuss words before he hit the ground with a thump, too. I didn't see this happen, of course, being submerged in pigs and dogs, but Pete's mule got its head and run off under a low-hanging tree branch and scraped Pete off, knocking him cold for a minute.

It was quite a party, I reckon. Some of the smaller dogs took ear-holds on some of the smaller pigs, and the squealing increased. The problem of separating the dogs from the pigs seemed insurmountable until Big Abner produced some crocus sacks, and the pigs were sort of decanted from the dogs into the tow sacks, where they continued to kick and squeal. The big dogs, Bell and Blue, finally slowed the old sow down to a walk. She was too big to handle, so Big Abner hit her over the head with a club and tied her feet while she was dreaming. All told it was a pretty good haul: a half-dozen prime pigs and one sow for Big Abner to pen up against hog-killing time.

"Where's the boar?" I asked Tom, who finally came up without his mule. "Where's your mule?"

"Tied the damn thing to a tree," Tom said. "Shot the boar. He was too big to play with. Somebody might of got hurt. Wait'll you see them tushes. Big as a elephant. Lay a dog—or you—open like you'd rip into a sack of meal. He took two, Ned," Tom said to the Old Man. "I reckon him to be tougher'n a bear to kill dead."

"Jest as well you shot him," the Old Man said. "Our Bengal Lancer here, he fell off the mule right off, lost his lance, and got run over by the whole passel of hogs, dogs, and young'uns. I reckon that big old boar would of et him alive."

"I reckon I ain't the only one fell off a mule," I said. "I saw you fall off, and Pete got scraped off. I reckon that big boar would have et you-all, too, if Tom hadn't shot him in self-defense."

"It was either that or climb a tree," Tom muttered. "And not the first time, neither. I'd as live take on a panther as a big pig."

It turned out that the Old Man had told Tom to shoot the boar, because fun's fun and he didn't want any dogs or boys hurt in this horseplay, or pigplay, I reckon you'd call it. I understood why when we skinned out the pig. He had a hide on him nearly an inch thick. It was white like coconut meat under the thin black hair, but so tough Big Abner had to keep whetting his ripping knife when they were shucking off the hide. His tusks *did* curl up nearly to his nasty little eyes, but the tusks, Pete said, weren't what did the damage. He dug with his tusks, but fought with a jaw tooth that whetted itself sharp against the underside of the tusk, and would slash you like a knife. With his bristly reddish mane that stuck up from behind his big head and ran all the way to his haunches down his sloping spine he was as nasty a looking wild animal as ever I saw.

I guess I was a pretty sight, when we got the mules, pigs, hounds, fice dogs, pickaninnies, and other hog hunters back to camp. I was full of mud where I'd been run over by the pack, and owned a fresh set of bruises where I'd been tromped on. Tom and Pete and the Old Man seemed to think I was a very funny sight, and they kept kidding me about losing my pitchfork until the joke wore itself out.

"I reckon this boy will never make a real pig hunter in the classic tradition," the Old Man said that night, while fire warmed his feet and something else warmed his innards. "Some people are just born pig hunters; others ain't. Our young feller here just ain't a real dedicated pigsticker. We better give him back to the easy stuff, like birds. Certain sure thing I wouldn't trust him with tigers and lions."

I didn't say much then, but I was thinking just how little it took to amuse grown people. I was thinking the same thing not so long ago in Africa, several lions and tigers later not to mention years. I was having a high old time trying to get a wart hog to come out of a hole, and I wondered bitterly how the

Old Man would have managed it. This occurred to me when I was halfway up a thorn tree, after the pig *did* decide to come out of the hole. I reckoned I had finally become a pig hunter in the classic tradition, even if it was a little thorny coming down out of that tree.

22

Hold Perfection in Your Hand

There is a state of mind called October that always makes me remember a thing the Old Man once said about Christmas. "Christmas," he said, "is best remembered as the day after tomorrow."

A wealth of worldly sadness went into that one, but more than a treasury of truth. For some years now I have had my Aprils and Augusts, my Septembers and Februarys, but the only truly perfect month is October, because it is close enough to summer and close enough to Christmas and still not near enough to March to be rendered miserable. October is truly the month of the day after tomorrow.

I have been sitting here trying to recapture the elation of October and have been stumped. Do you base it on carven pumpkins or the slavering eagerness of hunting dogs who can't work until latish November or the fact that your pants hold their crease now that the unseasonable September weather has settled into cool crispness; persimmons wrinkling, perhaps, and the leaves glowing scarlet and gold against the pine green and the last of the grapes on the vines?

The Old Man said that October was the only perfect month of the year, because it was a month that really didn't have to *do* anything to justify itself. All it held was present perfection, beautiful memory, and magnificent promise. The Old Man was a great hand for cataloguing the seasons, and I'm afraid some of it wore off on me. What he really hated was March, and he was kind of bored with August until it turned into September and all the summer people went back to where they belonged.

October in my neck of the woods was a time when you had got used to the calculated torment of school once more; I mean, to where education didn't physically hurt you any longer. The football season had started, but you could still play a little side-bar baseball if you wanted to, because the World Series was still topical. And it was cold enough for a ceremonial fire at night.

We shook the bloom off the doves in September, but the trees were dropping sufficient leaves now so that you could see a squirrel, instead of just knowing he was there. We had had the big rails—the marsh hens—in the first nor'easters with the full-moon flooding tide. A few transient ducks—teal—were beginning to drop in, and you knew that the first really cold snap would fetch a mess of mallards.

Out in the back yard the dogs were going noisily, frustratedly mad. The high grass was dying, they knew, and the quail were calling, and the dogs were being restrained from hearing the pleasant sound of gunfire and savoring the wondrous odor of burnt powder on the late-afternoon air.

October was the month for torturing the young dogs. You took them out and worked them on quail, using a choke collar if necessary, and firing a pistol to get them to hold to gun. But we never worked the old pros, because they had enough problems when the season started just before Thanksgiving, and we didn't want to confuse the reflexes. Sometimes I wondered who'd go crazy first, me or the old dogs. You would nail a covey in a patch of peas and the birds would hold to a point perfectly and then fan out into an ideal singles situation in a pasture of broom grass. And there you were, stranded with a .22 pistol, a choke collar, and a puppy.

The old dogs would know it when you came back and they'd snap at the young'uns, and then you would go and take down the shotgun and inspect it for the merest fleck of rust. You'd groan and think, would it never get to be November so you and the old dogs could go out and deal with these speckled bombshells properly? It would get to be November, all right, but it would take six centuries, so in the meantime you sort of had to do something after prison hours, when Miss Clifford or Miss Struthers turned you loose on the free world.

So you took a man's knife with a sawing edge for scaling fish on its blade top, a fishing rod, and a tackle box full of such things as four-ounce pyramid sinkers and long wire leaders, and you went to the beach to start a rumble with the bluefish, which were, by now, invading your turf.

A Carolina beach in October is a thing that would have captured Van Gogh's tormented paintbrush. The wind-tortured little scrub oaks all bend in the same direction. There are long dunes of really high hills with crape myrtles helping the tiny oaks. There are vast rolling waves of sea oats, like wheat rippling in the wind, and over-all an air of wonderful loneliness that is invaded only by the silvered gulls, slanting in the breeze, and the saucily tipped-up sandpipers. And then there would be the fish.

The nor'easters start in September, and by the time October rolls around in its golden glory the wind-built tides will have cut tremendous sloughs between the protecting barrier reef and the beach proper. All manner of small fish and a great many sand fleas inhabit these sloughs. The water was icy around our knees when we stepped in to cast, because we scorned waders in those days—I doubt if they were even made, though hip boots were made—but we slung that four-ounce lead pyramid out into that slough and we didn't have to wait long for action.

We always used diagonally sliced strips of salt mullet for bait, because it would hang onto a hook, whereas the crashing waves would disengage a shrimp, a feeble creature at best. A good slab of mullet, with the hook worked through it three or four times, would withstand a typhoon. We used a double leader with two baited hooks, and when the dark evening came and the moon began to peep the local suckers came to call.

Any man who has ever tied into *two* channel bass ranging up to twenty pounds each will carry the memory of it to his grave. The big white fellows with the black spots were there, and so were the speckled sea trout, and so were the big, mean-mouthed bluefish that later sputtered so happily in the pan. A couple of three-pound blues, striking at the same time and heading in opposite directions, could create considerable diversion for the gentleman with his hand stuck into the reeling apparatus of an old-time surf-casting rig. Not so much diversion as would the puppy drum—the channel bass—but enough to stifle a yawn.

There was usually a well-weathered shack nearby, with a tin stove that was dangerously heated by its kerosene fuel. And around ten at night, with your hands freezing red and wrinkled from the sea and your body just one big goose pimple, the snug harbor of that salt-rimed shack was like a preview of heaven. But if there wasn't a shack at close hand you dragged together a pile of driftwood and built a fire on the beach, and thawed yourself out before the leaping blue flames of the salt-impregnated fuel. Hunger clutched at your belly and the cookin' was easy. You gutted a bluefish, stuck him on a stick, and let him baste himself with his own fat. His hide cracked as he cooked, but inside he was sweet as peaches.

Apart from the cold it was marvelously spooky on an October beach, with the warped, stunted oaks casting strange shadows in the fitful moonlight and the wind soughing sadly through the myrtle. All the ocean was out there, broad-striped by a moon path, and it stretched across all the world, the world you were mad to see but never really reckoned you would. Over there, somewhere, were Europe and Africa and China, and underneath the surface of that wind-tossed silvered sheet were all the secrets you would never know: sunken galleons, treasure troves, great fish, sea serpents. . . . You shivered deliciously, and not from cold.

This was a part of October. A better part was the opening of the deer season, when you took a stand in the autumn-changing woods and listened to the hounds, the bugling ever closer, now fading as the running buck changed course, the belling now rising, now falling. You always knew that the deer would be a half-mile or so ahead of the coursing pack, but you never really expected to see him when he burst out of the bushes, his rack laid back as he split the breeze.

What I mean is, it was asking too much to really *see* a deer. Other people did, maybe, but it could never happen to you. Until it did. And then the buck fever, as you stood there gawking like an idiot and just watched the deer run, with the dogs panting up a couple of minutes later looking pretty sour, because they'd done their job of work and had expected to hear rewarding gunfire at the end of it.

There was the business of retrieving the hounds that never quit running a deer until he hit the lake and left his pursuers frustrated at the edge. Sometimes one of your best hounds wouldn't show up for a week or you would get a phone call from a farmer in the next county saying that Old Bell or Old Blue had arrived in a ramshackledy condition and would you please come fetch your dog?

Come to think, there was so much to *do* in October, while you waited for the serious business of the quail and the ducks to start in November, if it was only playing Tarzan in the shrimp house. And thereby hangs the major tragedy of a life that has known considerable pain.

It was the end of October, and the dogs were fighting fit and the puppies behaving well, and soon the bird season would open. (In North Carolina when you said "bird" you meant one thing—quail.) Soon the bird season would open, and I had spotted the using grounds of every covey in Brunswick County or almost. We had a limit of fifteen in those days, and I figured that if I hunted six days a week I would average out at ninety birds a week until March 1. You cannot call me bloodthirsty; I was just optimistic.

October birds have a way of knowing when the season starts, and coveys that come when you call in October decide to spend the winter in Cuba or Jamaica or some other exotic place. No matter where or how closely you had them taped, come that fateful day of legality they leave a Miss-Otis-regrets note, and all you rouse is a fieldful of larks. No matter. Eventually you catch up with the little brown scoundrels and miss them to your heart's content.

My tragedy was this. In a spate of boredom we were playing Tarzan in the shrimp house and swinging from rafter to rafter in the best approved manner. I missed a swing, and when I got up off the floor my left wrist had a most curious-looking sag in it. It didn't hurt, but it sure was busted.

I began to cry, because here it was the end of October and November was just over the hill, and I wasn't going to be able to make opening day of the bird season. Not with this busted wing, I wasn't. I recall I cried some more when it *did* begin to hurt, but the tears were not half so hearty as when I realized that I had used October, the golden month, to cheat me of the serious business of the day after tomorrow.

23

To Seek a Bear and Find a Boy

The expectation of excitement, the Old Man used to say, is better than the fulfillment thereof, or in his precise words candy in the window is better than candy in the belly, because you can't catch a bellyache from just looking.

"But," he said, "there are certain differences between eager anticipation and ducking responsibilities. The happy medium is to approach the candy with caution, enjoy it, and avoid the bellyache. This is a perfection that very few colored folks and no white people at all ever achieve."

This had come to be known to me as November talk, when my mind was not really on algebra but was sweating profusely over the imminence of the hunting season. My nose was hot and I had a tendency to quiver, like a pointer dog that can't wait to get out of the kennel on an autumn Saturday afternoon.

"There ain't but two things really worth-while," the Old Man continued. "Anticipation and remembrance. But in order to remember, you have to include execution of the anticipation. This means, roughly, that you got to take the dare. You got to bet your hand. You got to put your courage on the block and invite everybody to take a whack at it. And a brave coward is like a force-broken retriever. He may not like his work, but he'll force himself to do it, even if he's gun shy too."

This came back to me as I was headed for Alaska to shoot a bear, and was wondering slightly if I hadn't stretched my luck a little. After achieving the untender age of the mid-forty's I have never been disappointed in anything that ever happened in the field or on the stream, and I didn't want this bear, to whom I had not yet been introduced, to let me down. He was to be the last big bugabear that I intended to shoot, except in self-defense, and I must confess I was quivering as eagerly as on the eve of opening day of the bobwhite season.

The Old Man could get real windy on occasion, but mostly there was a solid kernel of sense in his vocal finger exercises. "What you remember," he said, "is the end result of practiced anticipation. Nor do I mean just triumph. That kind of remembering is bragging. Any bum can brag, because all you have to do is remember the girl you kissed and forget the one that slapped you flat. Experience comes from an acute recall of your mistakes as well as your successes."

I caught a fair point there. That last year I had started off with a flashy streak of quail shooting. Man, I had that quail thing down to a point where all I had to do was close my eyes and loose off both barrels and at least three birds would fall into my coat pocket. Then I hit a slump. One day I missed thirteen straight birds, one of which was sitting in a tree. Old Frank, the setter, took a final disgusted look at me and went home.

Then the panic set in. Just walking up behind Frank or

Sandy or Tom was such a venture into terror that I began to invent excuses *not* to go hunting. I even mentioned that I was behind in my schoolwork, which fooled nobody at all, since schoolwork ranked next to embroidery in my disesteem file. The Old Man scourged me into what the Spaniards call the "moment of truth," and literally forced me at gun point to walk up behind those damn dogs—which I now regarded as enemies every time they pointed—and blast away. Fortunately, finally, my timing came back, and I executed what could only be called a snappy double, and then went on to fill my limit with a minimum of misses. The jinx was broken, and I was okay again.

But I noticed that I refused to remember the series of raging misses. All I wanted to recall was the first part of the season, when I could have shot a teal with a slingshot. That, as the Old Man said, was the bragging section. I had closed off the failure, in my own mind, as securely as if I had slammed and dogged down the door.

I believe that one of the first signs of mellowing is when you start remembering your failures—remembering not only with honesty but with pleasure, because they were as much a portion to the day as the mad triumphs or the competent performance. For instance, I have two enormous tiger trophies, and the bigger of the two gives me a tremendous lift every time I see him or even think of him stretched skyward on my wall. But my favorite tiger is the one that is stretched skyward only on the wall of my memory. Because he is the one that got away.

This is the one that has now grown in my reveries to be at least twenty-two feet long, with teeth like railroad spikes, and a ruff twice the size of a zoo lion's mane. It must be true, because I killed that tiger and he was dead for at least twenty minutes. Vanity prevented my giving him the other barrel as he lay slumped over the carcass of a buffalo, but I didn't want to spoil the hide. And he was dead, wasn't he, shot precisely through the neck just like the other two?

So I thought. So thought Khan Sahib Jamshed Butt, who was perched with me in the tree in the black night of the Madhya Pradesh. This tiger—at least forty-four feet long from nose to tail tip—was stone-dead, with his face pillowed snugly on the buff's behind. Khan Sahib informed me that I was a Sahib Bahadur, the greatest tiger slayer since the late Jim Corbett, and I agreed with him freely.

And then this tiger, which was eighty-eight feet long if he was an inch, got up, snarled, and disappeared. It was a very long walk home, because the cobra-filled jungle now contained a wounded tiger, and anyhow, I am afraid of the dark. I was even more afraid of facing the two Texans sitting on the veranda of the dak bungalow, who would be certain I had missed the tiger when they heard only the one shot.

It has taken some time, but I find I can now face the memory of this beast, which was a hundred and sixty-six feet long and weighed over ten tons, without cringing and even with pleasure. Because the tiger has grown and I have gotten older and can realize that a damn fool is a damn fool, and also that foolishness does not necessarily spoil the entire picture of the trip.

I could cite you some more of the same sort of stuff. I was shooting *perdices*—the big, fast Spanish partridge—a while back, and missing everything that passed. On my right my friend Ricardo Sicré was keeping two guns hot and nailing everything that approached. Señor Sicré and I had shot grouse earlier in Scotland, and here, too, I was the bum, Ricardo the star.

But late that afternoon I shot a passing bird over my shoulder, going fast and far away, and the tumblers clicked and I was on the beam again. On the last drive of these transplanted Hungarians I was zeroed in and pulled twenty-two birds out of the flight.

Now, this is nice to remember. But what makes it so nice is that I remember the morning when I couldn't have hit a trapped elephant, and the Scottish trip, which cost a fortune and from which I accumulated little but embarrassment and a magnificent hangover from dancing on the green with the locals. When I finally started hitting again I was so relieved I really enjoyed recalling the shocking state of my shooting hand before.

This also applied to greater kudu. I have spent the last seven or eight years doing everything possible wrong with that magnificent, double-curl-horned African antelope, and now that there's a decent one on the wall I remember all the mistakes and tragedies and grim post mortems, but also the beauty of the days in Tanganyika and all the wonder of the birds and animals.

I think it really takes a Pollyanna to be the kind of hunter or fisherman who gets the most out of the expedition, rather than the result. I don't think the result, though necessary, is one-half so important in retrospect as all the side-bar fun and the little incidents that go to fill in the holes. I was certain that Alaska, which I had never seen, would be fabulous.

The bears might possibly eat me, and the fish might get away, and I would fall off a mountain or into a stream, and the geese might nibble me to death, but out of the whole ordeal was sure to come a series of possible triumphs that would plant the forty-ninth state more firmly in my memory than an oil strike or a gold mine.

Whatever the outcome the Old Man remains firmly in my head. "You can't enjoy it or be sorry about it unless you try it," he said. "Whether it's bobwhites or possums, whether it's a war or a job, you got to be in it to know about it. And unless you know about it, it didn't happen, and there you are as lonesome as an old maid who never got off the front porch for fear she might meet a man."

The Australians put it more succinctly. Around the race courses in Sydney there is a saying, "You've got to be in it to win it," and a common phrase is "I'm in it," no matter what it applies to.

I was in it in Alaska, and a most unusual thing happened. I ran into a kid, who but for a change in time might have been me.

I became very young this time in Alaska, when I met a youngster named Jerry Chisum, age about fifteen. He was a quiet youngster, good-looking, blondish, blue-jeaned, and competent to be a man with a gun or an airplane or a hunting camp.

Jerry's father is Jack Chisum of Anchorage, Alaska, who runs a flying service and an earth-moving operation with his brother Mark. Both are veteran bush pilots and sourdoughs in the better sense of the word, hunters and fishermen, hard-working, gnarled-fisted men who can grease an airplane into a tricky landing as easily as they might once have handled a sled and a team of huskies.

We were goose hunting together, after a chance meeting in, of all places, a bar. I had met Jerry's father earlier in Kodiak, where I was shooting a brown bear. When we bumped into each other in Anchorage it seemed natural enough to climb into a plane and ramble off to an island to belabor a goose or so. The other members of the party were Mark Chisum, young Jerry, and Paul Choquette of Homer on the Kenai Peninsula.

We took off from Anchorage in a float plane with added wheels, a Cessna 180, and because the water was rough we switched to a true amphib, a Widgeon. And we hit a hunting camp that carried me back about thirty years. It was a rough shack, comfortable enough, with crude bunks and a heat-quivering stove, and there were the usual hurried preparations for food and drink in the local store at Homer. Nobody had shaved that day, but I noticed the pilots had taken not so much as a short beer for a minimum twelve hours before flying. Bush flying in Alaska is a sketchy business at best, and a hangover doesn't help you much when you are flying mountainous passes in a float plane or landing downwind from necessity in rough water.

At first I was a little surprised to see the kid, carrying his full share of the duffel, scramble into the plane, and figured him for a passenger. Then something struck me as vaguely familiar. The kid, young Jerry, was a full-fledged hunting partner, a man among men. Apart from being taller and better looking and of course apart from using aircraft instead of T model Fords, he might very well have been me, thirty years ago. That is, if Alaska in any way resembles Southport, North Carolina.

His father and his uncle made no patronizing effort to explain him. Conversation was earthy, and none of it was curried because of Jerry's presence. We drank and told men's stories in camp, and there was none of this "not in front of the boy" business. Young Jerry performed a certain number of chores, in perhaps a little heavier ratio than the grizzled men; but apart from the utilization of his young legs for a little firewood fetching, apart from the fact that he was not invited to share the communal jug, he was one of the bunch, equal before the law and hunting society.

The birds were not flying overmuch that weekend, and much of the hunt was conducted in the warmth of the shack. But young Jerry was off prowling on his lonesome with his gun on the odd chance that there might be some action, while parents, so to speak, slept. That struck a reminiscent chord too. One of my brightest young dreams was to slope off, while the grownups tackled the fruit jar and told stories, to come triumphantly back with the biggest gobbler, the hatrackiest deer in the entire history of hunting. This dream never matured into reality, but it was not for lack of sturdy legs and sturdier effort.

I became interested in Jerry, who is an only boy in a family that includes three sisters. It seems he has been naturally accepted as a mature man since he was about six, and has known how to fly a variety of planes since he was eight or nine. There has never been any effort by his pa and his uncle to make an outdoorsman of him, apart from certain instructions in gun handling and hunting etiquette, and a full expectation that he'd carry his weight in the camp chores. Association with the hairy adults doesn't seem to have damaged his character any, and though he is not profane I imagine his retentive store of colorful language is considerable.

Mostly I was impressed by the way the adults kidded him, and by the way he returned the kidding without being either overbrash or what might be called smart-alecky. They joshed him as a man, and he joshed them right back on their own grounds, also as a man. He was polite to me as a guest, but not oversolicitous because of the difference in our ages. He was, in short, completely integrated to adult society and responsibility, and some credit must go to his father and his uncle for making a man of a boy in easy, exciting stages.

Jerry Chisum's world is a world of modern outdoor glamour, since his vehicle is the aircraft, as everybody's vehicle in Alaska is the aircraft. Where I once saw quail and squirrels he sees ptarmigan and geese. My biggest game was whitetailed deer and an occasional wild hog. Jerry has been teethed on brown and grizzly bear, moose and wolves. He has seen perhaps the finest fishing in the world, where I perforce settled for smaller fry. But there is not much basic difference in the way we were raised.

Perhaps it was luck that kept a lot of us country boys out of jail, but I like to think that a considerable part was played by the horny-handed adults who raised us as equals and imbued us with a love for the bush. Pool halls and corner gangs never interested us. A knife was not a weapon but a handy utensil that must be kept sharp and could cut you if you whittled toward you or otherwise used it carelessly. A gun was for killing, and at all times had to be considered a deadly weapon. It also had to be kept clean. Camps were to be left neat, and in a permanent camp a certain amount of basic supplies was to be left for the next occupants.

All these rules still apply to young Jerry Chisum, but in addition, today, he knows that nobody but a fool will fly a plane with a screeching hangover or a snootful of booze. He checks the instrument panel as automatically as his pilot-father does. He knows that lack of meticulous maintenance of that aircraft will surely kill him, for he pilots in the strange and wonderful weather that makes Alaskan flying a science unplumbed by ordinary aviators.

In my day we watched wind and weather too, but mainly for its effect on game. In Alaska wind and weather are active enemies, positive friends. There used to be a saying among the old bush pilots that you carried an anchor in the plane. When you were flying in heavy fog you dropped the anchor, and if you heard it splash you knew you were over water. Modern navigational aids—a full instrument panel—have changed that somewhat, but even today the standard plane for travel is a single-motored job which is little fancier than the old Tin Liz of my time.

When I see a kid like young Jerry I have little use for the beat generation and not too much time for the massed delinquents of the cities. If such kids were subject to heady fare—a land where you wash gold out of the creek, wolves howl, bears rob the meat safe, tough people abound, and the close recall of the dog-sled, gold-rush days is something more than just a legend —I'm sure they'd get carried far away in the opposite direction from beat.

There is as much temptation in a frontier nation as there is on a city street corner, and an incipient bum makes his own community. I am no psychologist, but I do think that a certain rule of thumb on child-raising can be made. Give a boy a sense of fitness, of belonging, and impress him with the responsibilities that go along with that belonging, and the transition from boy to man comes without a wrench.

My early mentors—God bless them all, black, white, drunk or sober, educated or unread—never once diminished my enthusiasm because it had all been done by them before. My first deer was, in their eyes, bigger than a mastodon, and my first fox squirrel achieved the proportions of a black leopard. A coon was a tiger, a rabbit a lion. I remember being violently sick to my stomach when I shot my first quail over a pointing dog, but nobody laughed—and nobody ventured that I probably fired at the whole covey (which I undoubtedly did) and dropped a bird by accident.

There was considerably more to my inclusion in adult hunting and fishing parties than an education in caution. A lot of
practical conservation was hammered into my knotty skull because, as the Old Man used to say, if you shot it all there
wouldn't be any for next year, and if you were careless with
fire and burned down the woods there wouldn't be any forest
to hunt in.

Mainly, though—and here we depart from the modern "progressive" child and certainly from the delinquent—I think that
good manners were as vital as any aspect of our training. You
didn't hog a quail shot. You didn't loose off a gun across your
partner's bow. You didn't deafen him in a duck blind by exploding a shell in his eardrum. The left-hand man took the first
duck, and in case of a possible tie on a single bird or animal you
honored your partner's presence.

"If a dog can be taught to honor another dog's point," the
Old Man used to say, "there's no reason for a man to be a game
hog."

I like to think that the time and trouble my elders took with
me on etiquette and caution, on conservation and just plain
good manners may have kept this particular youth out of the
Jimmy Dean set. It is not terribly difficult to translate the first
basics of the woods and waters into drawing room or business
behavior.

As I mentioned earlier, the association needn't be on a
Fauntleroy basis. I could have cussed as good as any stevedore
when I was ten, because I knew all the words. Whisky, I knew,
was for drinking, but somehow it seemed a little impolite for
me to be in a mad rush to cuss and drink in front of people
until I had earned the right in terms of years. My hunting
partners were often crude men, fisherfolk and sailors, but a certain gentleness pervaded and always a certain discipline obtained.

I had a plain wonderful time with young Jerry Chisum and
his folks in Alaska, although no trophies resulted from the
weekend hunt. In this age of jets and rockets to the moon, of

juvenile gang wars and what seems almost total confusion it was wonderful to see a modern rerun of what I remember so clearly as the Old Man and the Boy, even with the bird-dog homing device on the instrument panel replacing the bird dog on the ground.

24

Nobody's Too Old for a Physic

A few years back, in the Central Provinces of India, yr. ob't sv't had just climbed up a tree in the black of night. He had walked through a few miles of cobras to achieve this tree, quaking in his boots all the way, because a jungle is scary at night, even without snakes. But there was a natural kill near the tree—a big domesticated buffalo that the biggest tiger in the world had knocked off that afternoon. He had been driven off his kill before he had a chance to get stuck into it, and it was a cinch he'd return.

They still do a lot of night shooting in India, sitting up for tigers and leopards over baits, shooting indiscriminately from cars, with lights, and I didn't like it; even when hunting villainous varmints—and this particular tiger was a veteran cattle-lifter that was decimating the Gond villagers' herds and would certainly turn into a natural man eater when he got too decrepit to kill animals or eventually panic-kill a herdsman and develop a swift taste for man meat.

I was crouched uncomfortably on a rough tree-branch machan, forbidden to smoke, scratch, cough, or think, but as the mosquitoes chawed me I broke one rule and began to think about the Old Man and why I didn't care for night hunting and never would.

"If you want to hunt, hunt," the Old Man once said. "If you want to be a murderer, be a murderer. Buy yourself a cheap flashlight or a headlight for the car and drive easy through the rye fields or the corn. Pick up some green eyes with your light, fire between the eyes, and when the eyes go out pick up your deer—you won't know whether it's a buck, doe, or fawn—and sneak it home. Venison's venison. Tastes the same to a hunter or to a murderer. Only don't let me catch you at it. You might as well take up highway robbery. You ain't too old yet for a touch of hickory physic." Hickory physic was a whippy switch across the bottom.

The Old Man was a fanatic on conservation of game and obedience to the game laws, which he said were the first three rungs on the ladder of conservation. Oh, maybe we might have committed a little indirect poaching, such as the calling of somebody else's turkeys from across the road into legal no man's land which I've already mentioned, and I used to be pretty handy poaching squirrels off some government property, but the squirrels weren't doing the government any good just sitting there eating up the pecans. But by and large we were kind of model hunters, even to keeping a season tally of birds shot, and this at a time when the meat hunters thought nothing of exceeding the limit a dozen times over or murdering the best part of a covey of quail on the ground.

But like all young'uns with enough pimples to rate a driver's license I hit the nocturnal daredevil stage, and one night a bunch of us hellions decided we would go jacklight a deer, just to see what is was like.

We rigged a big searchlight, which we "borrowed" from the pilot launch, onto the new Model A Liz, loaded the shotguns, and went on the prod. Not too far out of town there were some rye fields, fresh and green, where whole herds of deer came to graze the winter crop, and we told each other that we were really doing the farmers a favor; you know, St. Patrick chasing out the snakes, St. George knocking off the dragon.

We cruised along, flashing the light across the level fields, and after an hour or so we hit onto a constellation of eyes that showed green and sometimes red under the lamp's beam. A sizable herd of deer had come out from their lying-up beds in the swamps to take on the night's provisions. They stopped grazing and stood transfixed, pinioned in the yellow trap of light. We drew alongside and I picked out the closest pair of eyes and fired between them. They went out like a suddenly extinguished bulb. At the sound of the shot the other lights disappeared and you could hear the crash of antlers as they hit the nearest brush.

The flashlight showed us a nice young spike buck, stone-dead on the ground. The Model A coupé had a kind of luggage compartment in the back. We opened it up and slung the murdered animal into it. Then we drove back to town feeling like a bunch of thugs, who had stuck up a bank and killed the teller as well.

As we hit the town we saw that the car needed some gas. Just as we pulled up to the pump the damnedest *baaaa—blattttt!* you ever heard came out of the hind end, and there was enough thumping and bumping and thrashing around to wake the dead. *Baaaa—blattttt!* Bump! Crash! Wallop! *Baaa—blatttt!* Obviously our corpse had been merely stunned and had just come alive.

The filling-station attendant looked as startled as we did, and as for me the neck hairs stood up like tenpenny nails. Old refrains of "Birmingham Jail" and "Prisoner's Song" and "In the Jailhouse Now" began to creep into my subconscious as we gunned that Model A out of there for the deep timber. Naturally we ran out of gas.

Now here was the predicament: black night with no gas on a country road and a live buck deer threatening to tear the Liz to tin shreds, and suddenly the brave freebooters were three scared kids facing a life in jail plus an extra life of shame. But in the meantime, how do you get a live deer out of the tail end of a Model A Ford coop?

When you are a criminal you seek a partner in crime. A case-hardened crook turns always to his own sort for comfort. I inspected the terrain and remembered that about a mile down the road there dwelt some gentlemen who lived by the manu-facture and sale of an illegal specific against nervous tremors, namely, white mule. If one or both of the brothers were not off "working for the state," as they called a jolt in jail, we might expect some criminal assistance, since their smokehouse generally contained venison that had not been acquired under the law's strictest letter.

Junius, a lean, lantern-jawed, bristle-chinned buccaneer, was cradling a jug on the front porch of his ramshackle cabin. Eph, he informed us, was off on a romantic errand involving the nearest neighbor's daughter, Miss Sary Jane, aged sixteen, and "he'd be back when he got done." We dispatched a courier to the tumble-down manse of Miss Sary Jane, aged sixteen, and tore Eph from the arms of his beloved, for this was a tricky, technical job. Junius loaded a spare demijohn of gas into his creaky old T model, and the task force proceeded toward the liberation.

It was quite simple, actually. Eph crawled up on the top of our car with a noose in his hand. Junius opened the back end cautiously, and when the young buck stuck its head out Eph snagged it with the lasso, drew taut, and Junius dropped the compartment top back on the buck's neck. For a split second—

until Junius cut its throat with one slash of a clasp knife that had been so frequently honed that its blade showed an inner curve —the buck looked like a picture of a mounted deer head, only the wall was the tail end of a car.

"You fellers want this critter?" Eph asked.

Three of us hollered together, "No!"

"We'll take him, then," Junius said.

We drove silently, guiltily back to town, and dispersed without saying good night. I avoided the Old Man the next morning, after a sleepless night, but just after the noon meal— which I picked at—he collared me.

"Any truth in this stuff about the deer you fellers jacklit that come alive in the car? There's different versions all over town."

I saw there wasn't any use trying to lie out of it, because the Old Man had a beagle nose for news. "I'm afraid it's true," I said. "It ain't gonna happen again."

The Old Man gave me a look that would have put out a forest fire. "I'll say it won't," he snapped. "Not unless you can manage to break jail to do it. Come on, murderer," he said. "We're going to see the warden."

We got in the car and drove off. The warden was in the poolroom. The Old Man waited until he finished his game, and then he said, "Jack, if you'd step outside a minute."

When the warden was outside the Old Man said, "I just caught a criminal for you. Do your duty. You got any handcuffs?"

The warden said no he didn't have any, but he could borrow some mighty quick if the criminal was dangerous.

"I think he's dangerous," the Old Man said. "He's an accessory to murder, car theft, night hunting, and the use of a stolen searchlight on the murder car."

"Maybe he's repented," the warden said. "This is a first offense, ain't it?"

"Yes, I suppose so," the Old Man said, "unless you count them watermelons he stole a couple of months back—also at night."

"Well hell," the warden said. "I got a bet on this next game. I parole him into your custody, Ned, and you can deal with him as you see fit. All right?"

"If you say so," the Old Man answered. "It'll save the state some money."

He never spoke all the way home. He said, when we got there, "You go back to the garage and wait for me." Then he went into the house and came back with a whippy Malacca cane somebody'd given him. "Take down your pants," he said, "and bend over."

Sitting in this tree, waiting for this tiger, my behind began to hurt double, and it wasn't this makeshift machan that made it hurt. The Old Man really laid into me with that cane, but even that didn't hurt as much as his icy contempt, which lasted three or four days until he figured I'd served my sentence and was due to be admitted to society again.

That cured me of night hunting until now, when Khan Sahib punched me. The tiger had come silently to the bait. We let him feed for ten minutes, and then Khan Sahib snapped the flash on him. He had a head as big as a bushel basket, and his enormous ruff was bloody. He looked balefully into the light. I drew a bead on his neck, as he lay on the buffalo eating from aft to fore, and the .470 boomed. He collapsed without moving —a rug, with his head pillowed on the buffalo's hindquarters. I started to shoot him again.

"No," Khan Sahib said. "Don't spoil the skin. He's dead, like the others." He yoo-hoo'd for the distant boys to come let us down out of the tree.

This was Tiger Three in ten days—all big, but this the biggest, and the only one shot at night. I forgot the Old Man. This was the biggest tiger I'd ever heard of, from his pug marks and the sight I had of his head. I had a flask in the tree. We celebrated.

"Let's look at him again," I said, about twenty minutes later.

Khan Sahib snapped on the light. There was a growl and I saw a tail disappear into the high grass. The tiger that had been dead twenty minutes had come to life. He'd been creased and only stunned.

We hunted that tiger for two days with buffalo, and never came close. He'd quit bleeding inside a hundred yards. The late Jack Roach of Houston, Texas, saw him a couple of weeks later, and Jack said that as far as he could make out, through the glasses, the cat had a fully healed scar a mere hair off the top of the spine.

It did me no good to reflect that Karamoja Bell, the famous elephant hunter, once cut the tail off a brain-shot bull and returned a few hours later to find the bull had got up and gone, tailless, and that everybody who ever hunted has made at least one damfool mistake. All I could think of was that buck deer carrying on and blatting in the back of the Liz, and the Old Man's rattan walking stick swishing on my backside.

From that point on you could offer me a hairy mammoth and a saber-toothed tiger staked out and tied to a tree at night and get a very sharp, profane "No!" for an answer. Daytime hunting is for hunters, and nighttime hunting is for animals. But wherever the Hunting Grounds the Old Man inhabits, I'll bet he was laughing fit to kill the night when that big tiger got up and calmly walked away.

25

Only One Head to a Customer

This happened in the Suphkar Range of the Madhya Pradesh, also in the Central Provinces of India. The dak bungalow stood on the summit of a slight hill in rolling country, beautiful country, whose crisp greens and yellows and reds were reminiscent of Connecticut in the fall or of a bright autumn day in the Carolinas. You expected to hear quail calling as they mustered scattered ranks at sunset. Instead there was the raucous *me-ow* of peacocks, the croak of ravens, the belling of a sambar stag startled by a tiger, or the sharp, biting yap of the barking deer. In the dak bungalow, which the government kindly leases to tiger hunters who rent shooting blocks, there was a kerosene-operated refrigerator and a whole sideboard of tinned delicacies and condiments.

In the main room guns were stacked aimlessly in a corner—a .470, a .308 with scope, shotguns, a scoped .220. Every time some Indian visitor would come to call—and, the good Lord knows, enough curious locals dropped in—somebody would pick up a gun and snap it at the floor or at somebody else's foot. The camp was equipped with camp managers and secretaries and clerks and a variety of nondescripts who just came to rubberneck. They all were fascinated powerfully by the guns.

The guns were not mine, but rented, and fitted tolerably well. I had already had some experience with them, especially with the .308, a really dandy little middle weapon. Dandy, that is, except I couldn't hit anything with it. This is not unusual in my case, except that once in a while the law of averages says that you're supposed to hit something if you blow off enough powder, and I was ringing up exactly nothing with the scoped weapons, including the .220. I asked the head shikari, "Anybody sight these scopes in? Graticules all checked?" And got a blank look.

"You know," I said, "scopes have to be checked—atmospheric pressure, joggling around in jeeps, too many rounds of ammunition fired, that sort of thing. They get out of alignment."

Blank look. Never heard of it. A scope is a scope is a scope. Tie it onto the weapon with a bit o' string, and the scope will kill, just as in Kenya, where the natives still believe largely that the noise kills.

"We'll stick up a target," I said, "and sight them in."

Wistful shake of head at European whim, but up went the target, a hundred paces off on a tree as big as a baobab. From a steady rest on the cushioned hood of a jeep I hauled down on the target and took a piece off the side of the tree. Repeated the shot and duplicated the hit. The gun grouped beautifully, if you liked it a foot high and two feet wide. I tried the .220 and missed the tree a couple of times.

I unscrewed the sighting apparatus and looked at the downs and the ups on the graticules, and discovered that if you wanted to shoot around corners these were the most murderous weapons I ever saw. But unfortunately if you aimed at something close-hand you were likely to kill the shikari's cousin in downtown Gondia. Evidently nobody had reshaped the sights since the scopes had been sewn on, possibly on the other side of an ocean voyage. I made the few adjustments on the screws, fired a few more sighting shots, and when the guns were on I set the sights solidly by rapping the pan with the butt end of a .470 bullet. This appeared to be magic, especially after I downed a peacock at a couple of hundred yards.

This had nothing to do with mechanics, of course. Magic. The aboriginal black Gonds and Baigas didn't believe in guns anyhow. They were very heavy on rocks and trees and iron adzes and phallic symbols, but guns, no.

"Oh my God, Old Man," said I, "you told me one day I would go to shoot tigers, but you never said it would be like this." (*This* was the shikari's venerable .577, which was wired together with baling wire.)

That business of the sighting finished, we shot some chital and sambar and pigs and one tiger. The guns were always carefully stacked in the corner of the room. One day I had a look at them and could barely fetch a mite of daylight through the muzzle.

"For the love of the Gautama Buddha and any pagan gods we have handy," I hollered, "don't nobody ever clean no bloody rifles around here?"

"Oh yas, sahib, we are cleaning immediately," and off went the artillery. To the laundry, I suppose, because the caste system would certainly demand that a dhobi (professional washerman) have charge of the cleaning detail.

Back came the guns, cleaned, to be stacked in the corner. I took them out of the corner and laid them on a table. I went to have a nap and read some enchanting fifty-year-old prose from *Blackwood's Magazine*, and when I got up there were the guns, stacked in a corner again. About the time I was smiting my brow I spied a hawk circling over the trees in front of the bungalow, and suddenly it lit. Without taking my eyes off the hawk I snatched the .220 from the nest in the corner and stalked as best I could, using trees for cover, toward the hawk.

Something of my African chum Harry Selby may have rubbed off, because I made it to easy shooting range without alerting the hawk. As is customary I started to snick the safety and discovered the safety done been snicked. I drew back the bolt to charge the magazine, and, bless pappy, I heard a tiny *chink* as a live round was ejected from the chamber. I didn't even bother to shoot at the hawk, I was that rattled. I turned and dashed for the dak bungalow.

Every gun in the cluster in the corner was loaded. Every rifle had a live round in the chamber. Every safety was off. The double .470 had two large cordite-charged softpoints in its barrels. I let out a scream that the Old Man must certainly have heard, Upstairs or Downstairs, wherever he be.

I do not believe in raising hell except when it's necessary, but the idea that anybody in the hunting business could be such a bloody fool as to stack charged weapons in a corner for any idiot to point at his foot and snap—*boom-boom*—made me so mad I went white and shaky. It was an affront to decency, as if a maiden of impeccable virtue had suddenly been accosted as an easy lady.

"Grandpa, Grandpa!" was all I could think of to say, between curses in all the six languages I swear in. And who was cursing louder than me was my wife, who had been so painstakingly trained in safety with firearms that she was almost afraid to shoot when the critical moment finally came. I never quite forgave the Indians after that one.

I went all the way back to Carolina, that first day of the gun, and remembered. The Old Man and I were out to shoot us a quail—my first. I was eight years old.

"In a minute," the Old Man said, as the dogs fanned out, "I aim to let you use this thing the best way you can. Your mother thinks I'm a damned old idiot to give a shirttail boy a gun that's just about as tall as the boy is. I told her I'd be personally

responsible for you and the gun and the way you use it. I told
her that anytime a boy is ready to learn about guns is the time
he's ready, no matter how young he is, and you can't start too
young to learn how to be careful. What you got in your hands
is a dangerous weapon. It can kill you or kill me or kill a dog.
You always got to remember that when a gun is loaded it makes
a potential killer out of the man that's handling it. Don't you
ever forget it."

I never did forget it.

During the course of my apprenticeship the Old Man ate me
out. He put me through a course of fence climbing that would
make the old Marine boot training look easy, and he was as
mean as a drill sergeant.

"Whoa!" he'd say, like he was calling a scatterbrained dog
that had just run through a covey of quail. "Now ain't you a
silly sight, stuck on a bob-wire fence with a gun waving around
in the breeze, with one foot in the air and the other on a piece
of limber wire?"

Or: "Now, what kind of a hunter have I got here, his gun
propped against a tree for any fool dog to run against and explode in his face?"

Or: "What kind of a damfool hunter stacks his gun in a corner when he comes in from hunting, so some young'un can take
it to play with and blast a hole in his mama?"

And I would say to the Old Man, "But Grandpa, it ain't
loaded."

"Who says it ain't loaded?" The Old Man was scornful. He
walked over to the gun, took it out on the back porch, and
pulled. *Bam! Bam!*

"Not loaded, huh? What was that, *mice?*"

Of course the old monster had framed me again, and stuck a
couple of shells in when I wasn't looking, which was his way of
making a moral lesson. He had done it before, the first day of
my new gun, when he palmed a shell into the spout and told
me to dry-fire to improve my aim, after I'd missed my first
quail with both barrels. I cut down on a pine cone and *"Blim!"*

the gun went off and near scared me to pieces. Then he took
my gun—*my* gun—away from me, and killed a quail with it,
just to teach me a lesson. I was so mad at him I would have
liked to palm a shell in and shoot *him*, except for the fact that I
loved him and knew instinctively that he had a point. In later
days my wife confessed to a desire to shoot *me* in the pants for
the same reason.

But in my early pre-teens the Old Man made me uncouple
the gun every time we moved from one hunting sector to another in the car. And the first thing I did when we came in,
dead-beat in the evening, was to take down the piece, clean it,
and stow it in its case.

The Old Man, smiling smugly over his first snort of the day,
would say: "Take a mighty clever young'un or a mighty pert
dog to undo that case, snap the gun together, load it, and then
shoot you accidentally with it."

It may sound old-maidy, all this caution, but I confess to a
breach of it. I fix my safety catches on my big guns—the double rifles, that is—so they won't slide back on to safe when the
gun is broken, because I don't want to worry about forgetting
to slip the automatic safety catch back on if I am reloading
again in a hurry to keep something large and ugly from stepping on me. For the same reason I don't use automatic ejectors
on a double express rifle. It's just one more thing that might
jam when a jam is not precisely what you crave at the moment.

But one day I had to change crews and I forgot to tell the
new gunbearer about this peculiarity. We were hot after an
elephant and I told the boy to load the *bundouki* and he did,
and when we came up to the jumbo he handed me the weapon.
I automatically tried to push the safety forward and it seemed
stuck, so I jerked it back and couldn't fire, because now it was
on safe. In a moment of panic that lasted a thousand light-years
and took a sixth of a second I fought mechanics. What happened, he had broken the gun to load it, and the safety went
forward and *stayed* forward on fire, as per arrangement. I had
hustled five miles through bush with that loaded cannon point-

ing at my head over his shoulder, and all he had to do was step in a pig hole and *"Karaam!"*—richest widow in Palamós, Spain. So the next day I took the whole safety apparatus completely off. Now when that lovely little Jeffery is loaded it shoots, and it is in my hands, and I am in front of the bearer.

It's a far cry from the Old Man and BB shots in the eye and people blowing off their heads crossing fences, but shooting some grouse just the other day in Scotland there was such a fanfaronade of pellets falling in the butts that I got down in the bottom of mine and gave up sport for the moment. The week before, one of the more tempestuous French clients had loosed a load at a grouse crossing the nearest butt, and one pellet nicked a gillie less than a quarter inch below his eye. A quarter inch higher—being one-eyed is less fun than being two-eyed.

That's why I got so tarnal mad in India, I guess. If we'd have had the Old Man for a shikari I bet you there would have been a lot of sore tails in the Suphkar camp, because the Indians have a chastising instrument called a *lathi,* and if the Old Man could lay on a *lathi* as well as he could flourish a common American stave I'd feel a touch less afraid of the guns than I was skeered of the tigers. Come to think of it, I didn't waste much time being afraid of the tigers. I was too busy keeping an eye on my friends and employees.

26

Greedy Gut

We have a shambling little orchard out in the back yard. It has
an aversion to bearing anything much except spotty plums and
the occasional fig, which the birds generally beat me to. But I
noticed when the plums formed this year I was out there beating off the birds for a whack at the early crop. The same applied to the seldom strawberries that poke their heads up from
the unwilling green around the drive. The house was a crying
admonition of bellyache, but I was munching happily away.
There is nothing really wrong with adolescent plums and pale
pink strawberries. Even today I prefer them to their full-blown
brethren. I guess it's a childhood habit I'll never kick.

"I am always surprised," the Old Man said to me once long
ago, "that there is such a thing as an adult. I am surprised any

young'un ever grows up to votin' age. Boy young'uns and billy goats, maybe, got less regard for their innards than anything I know of, including hogs, and a hog will eat anything, including its own pigs."

This homily was designed to justify a large dose of castor oil as antidote for the consumption of a large number of green peaches. Green peaches do not give you the bellyache as alleged; castor oil does. To my mind someone bigger than me was compounding the felony, with me as the victim.

"Green peaches, green plums, green backberries, green figs, green grapes, green apples, green pears," the Old Man said in a sing-song voice. "Why do all boys *have* to eat things when they're green? They can't taste good and they tear up your stomach and you get punished besides. Why?"

"I reckon I just can't wait," I said. "They always look so *good* when they're green. I even like the way they taste."

The Old Man grunted in disgust. "It's *your* stomach," he said. "Go ahead and wreck it."

He stalked off, muttering. I knew what ailed the Old Man. The doctor had nailed him with some sort of light diet for a stomach disorder, and had put him plumb off fried foods, desserts, and almost anything else he liked. The Old Man wasn't mad at me for eating the green peaches; he was mad at himself for not being *able* to do what he wanted to any more. He reckoned somehow that reducing him to an infant's diet was a reflection on his age.

Looking back, I expect I must have had a zinc-lined stomach, at that. I still have one today, and can only credit the early practice I had with inedibles, or a mixed bag of what was supposed to be inedible, in combination.

As a man I have withstood the kind of food you get at cocktail parties—the kind of canapés that would gag a goat. In a restless itch to stride the world I have rambled Mexico without succumbing to what is commonly called "Montezuma's revenge." The tourist in Europe generally falls afoul of what the Spaniards called the *turistas*, and blames it on a change of water, a change of diet, the local cooking oil, strange sea food, green vegetables, bad ice, peculiar wine—anything at all.

I really can't say why nothing upsets my stomach, unless it was the early training of that poor repository of juvenile whim to expect and accept anything at all. I could and did chase sour pickles with ice cream. They said you shouldn't mix sea food with sweets. If they had made a shrimp-flavored ice cream I would have been the first to ask for it. You supposedly couldn't combine watermelon with certain things, and garlic with other things. I combined watermelon with everything and I can still munch garlic by the clove. I have eaten sheep's eyes with Arabs, raw sea food with Japs, fried grub worms with Africans, and all manner of strange exotic fruits everywhere. I do not recommend this as a diet for everyone. All I can say is that nothing I eat makes me sick.

As a kid I had a sort of inventive mind. Nobody frowned on eating raw clams and oysters, fresh and salty dripping from their beds. If clams and oysters were sea food, I reckoned, then so were fish and crabs and shrimp. I never went to sea (going to sea was shoving the dinghy off the shingle and ramming home the oarlocks) without a plentiful supply of salt and a bag of fruit. The fruit nearly always included lemons and limes against the scurvy, because a solitary seafarer never knew when an exclusive diet of salt horse and hardtack would breed scurvy and inspire the crew to mutiny.

I had not read at the time that lime juice would cook fish if left alone, in the Polynesian fashion, but it did not take me very long to discover that raw fish and raw shrimp and raw crab meat were delicious if well-salted, sprinkled with lemon or lime juice, and left a short while in the sun. I got particularly fond of mullet, which we used for bait when we were surf casting. The Old Man complained bitterly that I ate more cut bait than the fish did, but the half-dried, heavily salted mullet was delicious, particularly if accompanied by a chocolate bar.

A quarter-decade later I encountered biltong in Africa. Biltong is made by slicing thin sheets of meat and spreading it on bushes to dry in the sun. It turns black and is almost un-swallowable, but is a power of comfort to chew and is most nutritious. The old Boer voortrekkers used it as a staple, much as our coon-capped trail blazers dived into the wilds with a bag of pemmican or jerky, which is practically the same thing. A really well-cured biltong will break off in short sticks, like crumbly candy, and is delicious as well as sustaining.

Biltong came as no surprise to me, nor did dried fish in the Pacific and Japan. They only tasted vaguely familiar, as if I had been there before.

As a kid I cooked the fruits of my gun about as sketchily as any savage. We made long safaris on Saturdays, which were as full of adventure as any major safari I made in later years. Even in the air-rifle stage we had attained considerable skill with the Daisies, and later the fifty-shot BB pump guns. Robins, song sparrows, jorees, thrushes, woodpeckers, and the big flickers—the yellowhammers—were regarded as major game, and the occasional dove, rain crow, or once in a long while a quail or marsh hen were placed in the elephant, lion, buffalo category. What we shamelessly slew we cooked over a hasty fire—sketchily skinned, hastily gutted, and unwashed—impaled on a green stick and merely scorched. But it tasted good at the time, and oddly it tasted just as good later . . .

. . . such as a couple of years ago in Africa. One day on a long walk after elephant we got hungry at midday, and nobody carries a chop box when he is fighting high grass after moving elephant. We called a halt, and somebody shot a small antelope, a gerenuk, I think it was. We whipped off the hide and emptied the stomach. We ate its heart and liver raw, and it was delicious. We roasted a few chops over a hasty fire. It may sound horrible, but the animal was still hot from life and tasted great after being liberally salted.

We performed a small series of experiments thereafter, and found that all birds and most small gazelle tasted wonderful, if you got them onto the fire while they were still warm with recent life. It was only after they cooled out and rigor mortis set in that they had to be aged and otherwise kitchen-treated to provide tenderness.

The birds were particularly good. We would shoot a batch of sand grouse, young guinea, doves, pigeons, or francolin, clean them while they were still quivering, impale them on a green stick, and pop them over the coals, and they were great. And these were no savage palates, either. We would go home to camp that night and sit down to a dinner which might include caviar, breast of guinea fowl, asparagus, and fresh fruit, washed down with a French wine such as Mouton-Rothschild or Chambolle-Musigny. One of the heartiest eaters of the half-cooked, only-just-dead birds was a Spaniard, who made annual pilgrimages to France merely to eat his way across the countryside and who was an expert on wines and sauces.

It did not really seem to matter what you ate, as a youngster, if you were actually hungry. One of the palatial meals I shall always remember (and still eat, when I am lucky enough to find an old-fashioned country store when I am quail hunting in the Carolinas) was what we had around noontime, when the birds had fed back into the cool of the swamp and the dogs needed water and a breather before hunting resumed around three-thirty.

A gourmet would shudder at this, perhaps, but what we ate was canned salmon (the same as we fed the dogs), canned sardines, oyster crackers or plain soda crackers, gingersnaps, and rat cheese. This was washed down with one of the enormous bottles of soft drinks they used to sell for a nickel, grape- or orange-flavored, and twice the size of a Coke. The Old Man called it "bellywash," and so it was, but it made a delicious accompaniment to the sardines, gingersnaps, and rat cheese. If belching is a sign of politeness in some countries we were more than exceedingly polite.

All through the woods in the afternoon I gnawed on dirty— and sometimes bloodstained from the pockets of my hunting coat—peppermint candies and hard cooking apples from the barrel, with perhaps an enormous, bumpy, brine-rimed sour or dill pickle from the keg that stood in the cool of the store, amongst the kegs that held the various sizes of nails, under the shelves which contained the overalls and hickory shirts. If I was in funds I might also buy a bag of assorted cakes from the slanting stand that held them—crumbly vanilla johnnycakes, as big as coffee saucers, round sticky black chocolate cakes with vanilla goo between the cake halves, and great pink things with sparse slivers of white coconut glued to the top pastry.

To go home to an oyster roast, with that sort of backlog of fodder, did not seem strange, although roasted oysters are held by some to be indigestible enough without the aid of the earlier accompaniment, without the cool-of-the-evening swill of scuppernong wine at the nearest colored man's farmhouse when your whole body is still hot from hunting.

And speaking of wine, for a man who in later life learned a little of vintage years and brand names, I was in on the birth of some of the more bizarre home-stomped beverages that ever assaulted a palate. *Or* a stomach.

With no regard whatsoever for the Volstead Act we young hellions pounded juice-oozy wild cherries into goo, fattened the mixture with sugar, and strained the fermented leavings into what we fondly believed was wine. Some wild and savage voodoo experiments were concocted in the cool of the caves we built—hideaways against the onslaughts of hostile Indians, parents, and if we had thought about it, revenooers. Dried apricots and raisins made an acceptable mash, as did grapes and fresh peaches. Mostly the stuff was nauseating to the taste, and usually contained collections of dead beetles and woozy flies, but the mere idea that we were doing something unsanctioned was sufficiently intoxicating.

I really do not know how we all lived through it. We chewed sour grass and smoked rabbit tobacco in our totem pipes. We combined sparkleberries with green persimmons and richened the mixture with all manner of nuts, from the rich tame pecans to wild hickories and chinquapins. Uncle Jimmy's all-purpose store contained penny candies that must have been confected of equal portions of ratsbane and sugar. Irey Ivans, in colored town, specialized in Brown Dogs, which seemed simply to be made of peanuts and burnt sugar. The colored folk did interesting things with blackstrap molasses in candy form, which I loved. And I never turned a hair when confronted by roast coon or a mess of chitterlings or squirrel-head stew.

We ate these oddly assorted vittles avidly. I can remember clearly drinking stickily sweet condensed milk so thick you could cut it; and the yams we roasted in the woods were notable more for their content of ingrained dirt and wood ash than for their half-raw innards.

We had only one rule on food: If it grew wild, was bought in a store, or was condemned as unfit for consumption by parents it had to be delicious. Some of the less hardy scientists occasionally went green in the face and became ill. They were greeted with jeers, the same unfeeling juvenile taunts that were hurled at the timid souls who got seasick.

When I grew older I graduated to the vile corn liquor and the viler home-brew of the prohibition era, and never batted an eye. I survived Tunisian *eau-de-vie* (ugh!), Australian whisky, South Sea jungle juice, and some illegal seagoing mixtures of compass-cleaning alcohol and grapefruit juice. I have sampled Kaffir beer and Tanganyika *pombe*, which ferments *after* it hits the stomach. And I have survived, although the Lord in His wisdom only knows why.

When he discussed the range of my gustatory habits with something more than admiring disgust the Old Man dusted off the old chestnut about curiosity killing the cat. "But in your case," he said, "it's a very large cat, and anyhow you ain't home yet."

The Old Man was generally right about most things, and these days, on some mornings, I have a queasy feeling that his record for accuracy is still unbroken, even if it's taken a long time to jell.

27

Snakes Ain't Hostile in November

Like I say, the Old Man infected me early with a feeling for
the seasons of the year, and he divided the year sharply according to what the seasons had to offer. This, the Old Man said,
was the way the Greeks did it. There was a season for plant-
ing, a season for harvesting, a season for suspicion and worry,
and always a time to love and a time to die. March, the miserable month, had its ides, against which even the great Caesar
was warned. June was soft and sweet—a woman's month—
and October was full of promise and present perfection.

But the big month, at least for this boy—and I think for the
Old Man—was November, a harsh, rough, tough man's month,
with the threat of winter ahead but a marvelous sense of
weathered magic in the woods. The quail now called only

when they were scattered from flushed coveys, and you could hear the rutting snort of the buck deer as his neck swelled and see where the velvet had rubbed off—in tatters—his fighting horns.

Everything happened in November. The quail season opened, around Thanksgiving time, and the deer and turkey seasons opened. The days were crisp but still red and golden in North Carolina, and the nights were sparklingly cold and made welcome a roaring blaze. The ducks were flying legally, and sometimes it seemed that there was just too much action for one boy to stand.

Even the fishing had improved. The summer fishing was gone, but the big stuff had come in from the skimpy schools of September and early October, and November was the time for the really big jut-chinned blues and the heavy channel bass. The gray seas were chill and sad to see, but the fish flocked in close in the deep-cut sloughs, which were now almost bayous banked by a barrier reef, and the fish took up housekeeping in the sloughs.

One of the keenest memories I have is of a big shark, run almost aground and stranded on a reef when he sought to cross the barrier reef that lay between him and the feeding blues and trout and Virginia mullet. His dorsal fin wavered out of water as he literally pulled himself over the shallows on his belly.

After my first few bucks I was never much of a deer shooter, but to me November meant the beautiful belling of the hounds in the dim distance, growing and swelling to the full strength of bass and cello, almost in your lap, just before the buck burst out of the gallberries.

The dogs knew November: Jackie, the upcurl-tailed fice that was an expert on squirrels; the deerhounds, Bell and Blue; and the quail dogs, which had hunted themselves lean in early practice and now were deadly in diagnosis and steady as rocks to shot. Six days a week saw me in the woods or on the water, and if it had not been for a certain stuffy attitude about Sunday shooting I would have compromised the Biblical injunction about working on six days and resting on the seventh.

Maybe I'm too much the old man now and too little the boy when I say that modern kids—those I know, anyway—don't feel as deeply about the wondrous works of God in the forests and fields and waters; that they are completely unconscious of the present unless it involves a TV show or a red-hot car. Am I becoming an old fuddy-duddy—one of those when-I-was-a-boy types?

Perhaps, but I still think that modern kids are cheated of sensation that is not contrived. I occasionally try to talk with some of the spawn of my friends, and get the feeling they are very far away from kinship with adults. It seems to me that as a boy I didn't have many friends of my own age. My friends were mostly adults, black and white, and they raised me without recourse to hot-rods or rumbles. I can swear that the month of November was rendered delightful by my association with a bunch of hairy characters, who would be ruled off the course as improper associates in this era of the switchblade knife.

My guys fought among themselves when they got drunk on a Saturday night, and some of them manufactured illegal whisky, besides drinking it. But mostly they seemed to possess a tremendous gentleness and understanding for small boys who tagged along with them in the woods or on the boats. I can even recall one compulsive thief who threatened to beat the bejabbers out of me if he ever caught me stealing anything.

These people were as much a part of November as the sleepy possum in the persimmon tree; the cold, clotted lumps of earth in the sere cotton fields; or the delicious, frightening loneliness of the swamp on a deerstand; or the burning cold of a turkey blind on a cold morning as you waited for the big toms to come.

Perhaps I spent more time with the Negroes than with the whites, largely because in my neck of the woods there were more Negroes than whites. I was at home in the abodes of Big Abner and Aunt Florence, and they allowed no stranger to trespass on my quail reserves. I ate with them, and on occasion when caught out too late to get back to the Old Man's house slept in their tiny clapboard or rough-log houses. I suspect we were pretty well integrated before they made a law of it. At least nobody ever brought up the subject of who was white and who was colored, when we shared the squirrel-head stew or the possum and sweet taters.

The crowning aspect of my November was the big camping trip, when the Old Man and a couple of cronies permitted me— if I had been a good boy about splitting kindling and cleaning fish and gutting ducks and plucking birds—to go along sometimes on a week-long campout, where I would split kindling, clean fish, gut ducks, and pluck birds, with a few additional duties, such as skinning deer and squirrels and fetching water and washing dishes. This was now the perfection of a boy included in an adult world, where men cursed openly, told man-type stories, drank whisky, and appeared to accept the boy as a man, while tactfully forbidding him to cuss, drink whisky, or tell off-color yarns.

The fruition in weather and sport was something unbelievable. October had beckoned, but November delivered. Only a true idiot can appreciate the predawn misery of a duck blind. Even in the South—as far south as Louisiana—it is black and miserable in the morning, with the cold graved into your bones, and the torture of whistling wings of unseen ducks is something more than exquisite. Then comes the faint dove's breast pink of dawn, and then the rosy red, and then you can see the ducks. You can shoot. And miss. And occasionally hit.

Perhaps jubilance is the word that describes it all. There was the nocturnal stupidity of coon hunting, when the hounds were as apt to raise a skunk as a coon. The tumbles we took seemed fun, and certainly the streams we fell into were part of the obstacle course.

I was one time in a friend's house in Texas, where the doves were swarming like locusts and the wild turkeys consuming a ton of purloined food a week, just waiting for Thanksgiving. I was prowling around, bird-dogging some dead doves, when a remark the Old Man once made struck sharply home. I had turned up a rattler the size of a log, and just before the lady with me blew its head off with her new gun I remembered the ancient remark.

"In November," the Old Man said, "even the rattlesnakes don't like to bite people."

28

Stoicism Is Bad for Boys

"The accumulation of laughter," the Old Man said, pacing up and down in front of the fire with his hands behind his back, "comprises an aggregate of wisdom." It was raining to beat the band.

"Huh?" I said. "What was that again?" I was looking hopefully out the window, and not paying much attention to the inside of the house.

"The accumulation of . . . you heard me the first time," he said. "How did it sound?"

"Fine," I said. "What does it mean? And who made it up?"

"*I* just made it up," the Old Man said. "Maybe I might of read it somewhere, I disremember. Seneca or one of them other old Romans. Somebody or other."

"Seneca?" I said. "I always thought Senecas were a tribe of Indians, kind of like the Iroquois." If this was going to be one of those days when everybody was flinging knowledge around I was going to crowd right in there with my share.

"There's a lot you don't know," the Old Man said. "Seneca tended store somers about thirty or forty years A.D. He got famous for being a Stoic."

"A what?"

The Old Man held up his hand. "A Stoic. A Stoic is a man who practices and preaches Stoicism, which is another word for grinning and bearing it, no matter how rough times get. You could pull the toenails out of a real Stoic before he'd let out a whimper. He was calm in the face of adversity. He could stand there and take it, even though his whole life was crumbling in ashes all around him. You got to be a Stoic these days to get along in this world."

I noticed the Old Man wasn't dropping his "g's," a sure sign of something about to happen that I wasn't going to like He had a habit of leading up to these things kind of sneaky more or less for his own amusement. The Old Man was about the kindest man in the world, but there was a streak of bad boy in him still. He liked to tease me, and that's what he was doing now.

"What does it mean?" I asked again.

"It means," the Old Man said, "that it ain't going to quit raining today and if I were you I'd start practicing being a Stoic right now. I'd try to think about all the funny things that've happened, and this way you wind up wise. How's your stiff upper lip?"

When I looked out the window my lip didn't feel very stiff, and I didn't feel either funny or wise. It was raining pure pitchforks, and each driving tine stabbed my hunter's soul. I had waited nine months—and one five-day century—for this Day. Very seldom does Opening Day come on Saturday, but this year it did, combining permanent Christmas with a blue moon and a month of Sundays, with hell about to freeze over for good measure.

Now then, me and the weather had come to grips before. I had been rained out of more than one Saturday, but generally I found something to do with it that did not involve robbing a bank. Being rained out of *any* Saturday would stab you to the heart, and all the Old Man's favorite quotes about life being just a rainy Saturday didn't help much.

But I had never been rained out of a Saturday which was also Opening Day before, and I had been planning this one since I put my gun away when the season closed last February.

I had been to the hardware store and bought the shells. I was spending Saturday night out in the country, at Sheriff Knox's house. Apart from the Sheriff's birds, there were Mrs. Goodman's birds, and Aunt Florence Hendricks' birds, and Big Abner's birds, and Aunt Mary Millette's birds, and Lyndon Knox's birds, and some vagrant perimeter birds, all waiting to be shot at on this Saturday by me. The dogs had dry-hunted every Sunday since the weather turned cool, and were panting for the smell of powder. There was one six-month-old puppy who promised to be the best quail dog that ever hit the piny woods.

Monday had been bright and golden, the sky blue and un-specked by cloud. Frosts had come and killed the undergreen-ery. The corn shucks were sere and liver-spotted, and the per-simmons were sweet enough to eat without turning you into a Chinaman. A fire felt cozy-comforting at night. The last Sunday, the dogs had worked well on the tame coveys we kept around the house for training purposes. The dogs were sharp and ready, and so, I thought, was the hunter.

Tuesday was bright and golden. So was Wednesday. So was Thursday. So was Friday. And tomorrow would be Saturday, with no school. *And* Opening Day!

But now the rain pounded down in drops as big, it seemed, as baseballs. Then the wind rose and drove the drops savagely in thin arrows against the walls and windows. The panes were steadily bleared by water, as it cascaded down in clear sheets against the sills. The rain had come about breakfast time, teasingly at first, each big drop making a little dimple in the clean-swept sand of Sheriff Knox's yard. Then the dimples turned to holes, and then the holes to little gulleys, and finally the gulleys spread to small lakes. Noah never saw a meaner rain than I had to celebrate that Saturday, the Opening Day.

Breakfast was warm inside me—a big breakfast of oatmeal and ham and eggs and hominy and coffee. The fires burnt bright in the fireplaces, but a steady gust of rain drove through the breezeway that cut the old-fashioned country house in half, and little creeks of water ran in the uneven flooring.

I opened the front door against the solid wall of sheeting water, and went out on the wide veranda. The rain was not so heavy you couldn't see across the road to the soybean field where all the doves hung out. The dogs started to follow me out of the warm sitting room, but the wet wind smote them and they huddled back against the door. The guinea fowl that always ran loose committing suicide in the road had crowded under the house, and were standing, ruffled and angry clatter-ing, with their feet hating the wet sand.

I fought the door open again and the dogs and I went back inside. The Old Man and the Sheriff were sitting companion-ably in front of the fire, which hissed from the trickles that drove down the chimney. I was dressed for the wars, but neither of the old gentlemen had bothered to put on boots. They both wore the soft-sided Congress gaiters, and you could see the white legs of their long-handled drawers pulled down over their sock tops. They hadn't even bothered to put on the long red-topped wool hunting socks they wore with their boots. The Old Man shook his head.

"You might as well take off some of that regalia," he said. "I don't think you'll hunt any birds today. How about it, John?" he turned his head to the Sheriff. "That rain looks like she's here to stay, eh?"

"Yep," the Sheriff said, spitting an amber arc into the fire. "You won't see sun today. I thought for a while she might fair off, but I don't think so now. And even if she did, the woods are too wet. Birds are all in the branches, huddled under some brush. They wouldn't of fed out, and it's too wet for the dogs to smell. No scent on a day like this."

I was all for dragging the dogs out by main force and fighting my way into the wet, but the Old Man shook his head.

"Waste of time," he said. "All you'll do is rust your gun and catch a death of cold. You might as well resign yourself to the fact that this ain't your lucky day. Even the dogs got better sense than to go out on a day like this. This day ain't good for nothin' but ducks, and the duck season ain't open yet. Be a Stoic and count your past blessings."

The Old Man was right, of course. Some of the best bird shooting in the world happens in the right kind of rain—a slow drizzle that moistens the dry ground and helps a dog's nose function, like a wet night makes combustion better in an automobile motor. The trailers can trail and the winders can wind, and the coveys hang closer together. Also the singles have a way of sticking to where they hit, so you can make them better, and they don't flush wild all over the place when you shoot over a point.

Some of the best shooting I ever had was on a half-wet day, when the boys got separated from the men and the lazy hunters stayed home by the fire, but this was not going to be one of those days. I would have needed a boat to make it to the nearest pea patch.

The Sheriff and the Old Man kept talking interestingly enough, I suppose, all about war and politics and crops and the last deer drive, but I couldn't work up an appetite for what they were saying. I was someplace else, with the sun shining and the dogs fanning the fields.

The Old Man watched me fidget for a while, and then he said, "Why don't you go do something with the girls and leave us in peace? You're about to wear out the rug. This ain't any way to be a Stoic, and anyhow you're making me and the Sheriff nervous."

Now as a rule I ain't got anything against girls, especially today, when I'm a sight older. But right then the only time I had for women was when they were in the kitchen cooking something that smelled good and that I would eat later. About all girls were good for was to tattle and giggle and cry if you looked cross-eyed at them. I never knew a girl who could throw a baseball without snapping her elbow, and there seemed to be a general suspicion that all girls were good and all boys were bad.

The Sheriff had a flock of gal children, and Ethel and Sally and Annie Mae and Gertrude were all twittering around about something or other, and all I could think of was that they sounded like a gaggle of geese and didn't seem to accomplish much outside of confusion. The dogs were no help, either. They just lay by the fire and looked as mournful as I felt. Altogether it was the finest study in frustrated indoor activity I ever run onto.

Lunchtime came and the rain still walloped down, hitting as hard as hammers. We sat down to eat a big country lunch—dinner, it was called in those days—but I didn't have much feeling for the fried chicken and the venison and the apple pie, the big sugared tomatoes and all the other stuff I usually loved.

After lunch the Old Man looked at me sharply, and for one of the few times in his life his voice matched the look. "All right, all *right*," he said. "Get your gun and the dogs, if you can find one that's damned fool enough to go with you, and go hunting! Anything to get you out of the house before you drive us all crazy."

I put on an old oilskin over my canvas hunting coat, got the gun, and stirred up the dogs with my foot. They were not enthusiastic about leaving the fire, and I had to drag the old boys out the door. Only the puppy thought it was fun enough to come along under his own steam.

The rain still sloshed down by the bucketful. I trudged through the soybean field, hoping to rouse a dove or so, but nothing was feeding. The gray-topped cotton soil was pure muck, now, and it stuck to my boots like cement, leaving black patches of soil underneath. Just walking in the gumbo was an effort, for your feet weighed a ton each.

Two things, I learned that day, are not improved by bad weather. One is open ocean. One is woodland. Of the two the weeping woods are sadder than the sea.

I still don't know what happens to most outdoor life when it rains. I suppose the rabbits dive into their burrows and the birds perch in the trees or huddle under brush heaps. No sign of life appeared in the dripping woods, in the sodden fields, in the soaked prairies of high grass. The dogs were draggled, cockle-burred, and shivering. My old oilskin provided small protection. Rain got into my eyes and blinded me. My nose ran in time to the dripping of the trees, and the wind howled and the rain slashed down.

I forced the dogs down into the swamps, figuring it would be dryer under the heavy trees, and perhaps we would stumble on a covey of quail. We stumbled on nothing shootable, although I did manage to slip in the mud while jumping the small creek and made myself a little wetter, but not much.

After two hours or so I gave up. The dogs and I trudged back to the farm, as cold and miserable as dogs and boys are likely to get. We must have been a sight as we trudged into the breezeway.

The Old Man must have seen us coming, because he met us in the breezeway. "Get out of them wet clothes," he snapped, "and then come in to the fire. But mind you dry them dogs off before you turn them into the house. They'll stink bad enough half-dry, anyhow." Then he turned and stumped back into the sitting room where the fire was.

I nearly froze changing from wet clothes to some dry ones, and I was afraid to go in to the fire until I had rubbed the dogs with a couple of dry tow sacks from the smokehouse.

"Get any birds?" the Old Man asked sarcastically, as I stood with my back to the fire, waiting for the heat to burn my backside before I gave it a chance at the front.

"Nosir," I said.

"See anything?"

"Nosir. Nothing."

"I thought not," the Old Man said. "You feel any better for flounderin' around in the wet for the past few hours?"

"Nosir," I said.

"Prove anything?"

"Nosir."

"Have a cup of coffee," the Old Man said, "and listen to the Sheriff tell about that bad field hand that killed his wife with an ax just back there close the road near to the graveyard."

After the Sheriff had finished his tale, which was sufficiently gory to hold any boy's interest, the Old Man got up and walked to the window.

"Looks like the rain's slackenin' off," he said. "I wouldn't be at all surprised if the sun didn't set fair. Tomorrow'll likely be a nice day. Pity it's Sunday."

I muttered something, I dunno what, but it wasn't very stoical. Then I sneezed.

"You're as butt-headed as your mother," the Old Man said. "And she's as butt-headed as *her* mother. I reckon if being butt-headed means anything you got the makings of a pretty good Stoic. I don't see you handing out any accumulation of laughter, but if an aggregate of wisdom comes from being butt-headed I guess that sneeze tells me you've learned something about beating your head against a stone wall. Time and again you've heard me say that bad weather's all right if you know how to make it work for you, but on a day like today the best way to make it work for you is to stay home in front of the fire with a book."

I sneezed again.

The Old Man cocked his head. "Go get one of the women folks to give you some cough syrup and tie a rag around your neck," he said. "A sneezing Stoic is an abomination before the Lord. And anyhow, if you get sick from being foolish you won't be able to go hunting tomorrow. Tomorrow's dead certain to be better, because I can see the clouds lifting and the sun coming out."

"But tomorrow's Sunday," I said. "And I ain't allowed to hunt on Sunday." This time I managed to snuffle back the sneeze.

The Old Man grinned. "You can carry Stoicism too far," he said. "We're out here in the backwoods and you're visitin' the Sheriff. You've got the Law on your side, and I shouldn't wonder if the good Lord wouldn't make an exception in your case this time, if you don't go telling everybody about how you broke the Law. I reckon with it raining on Saturday *and* Opening Day you been punished enough, and you got a little something coming from On High."

I let out a whoop, which might have been the first symptoms of pneumonia, but I didn't care. That was the Old Man for you. He was tricky as a pet coon. One thing I had added to my "aggregate of wisdom" this day was that if I lived to be a hundred I'd never figure him out, but right then I wasn't inclined to argue. I felt so good with my accumulated laughter that I even helped the gals wash dishes that night after supper and didn't bust but one.

29

The House Comes Home

When the Old Man decided to lay down the load, a whole lot of
years ago, it was depression time, and he like nearly everybody
we knew had stuck a whacking big mortgage on the House.
It wasn't much of a mortgage for these times, but it was com-
puted in thousands and was as hopeless of repayment as if it had
been counted in millions. Anybody in those days who had a
cent squirreled off in the much-darned sock was a very rich man.
Anybody who could command a certain amount of skinny credit
at the store for the basic beans and fat back was richer than most
folks. The earliest thirties were not a time for mortgage lifting,
even if the bank that held the mortgage wasn't bust.

So when the Old Man decided that the thing he had would
kill him—and it did—and with Miss Lottie already gone ahead

of him and everybody broke and discouraged, the rich old fellow who held the mortgage just naturally foreclosed it, as was his right. The man who foreclosed it, some said, was a skinflint, and maybe he was.

Well, the family busted up and scattered every whichaway, and nobody looked like ever making any money at all, so the old fellow who now owned the House decided to rent it, after a decent period of mourning, but he swore he'd never sell the old place to anybody but a member of the family, so long as he lived. He loved the House, too, most as much as and maybe more than some of the people who had eaten and drunk in it and hunted and fished out of it.

It was a fine old House, and most of my life with the Old Man was spent in and around it. It was located in Southport, the sleepy little North Carolina town I've written about so much; the town with the cedar bench where the old men loafed to whittle and chew tobacco and argue; the Pilots' Association, where the men sat with spyglasses and gazed out past Battery Island and Caswell to the sea; Mr. Rob Thompson's pool parlor, where the racier element hung out on the rainy days; Mr. Price Furpless's picture show, the Amuzu; Watson's and Leggett's drug stores, and Gus McNeill's filling station; all social centers of a town which had an oak grove called The Grove and a street called The Street.

The House was square and in those days, so long ago, was painted yellow. It sat on a corner next to a smaller oak grove where we played one o' cat. It was right next door to Uncle Tommy and catty-cornered on the street from Uncle Walker, and right across the street from old Sam Watts, who had the best deerhounds in town. Some people said Sam set more store by his hounds than he did his young'uns.

The House was set up on brick stilts, and I spent many a rainy day under it, rummaging through the trove of generally nonfunctional treasure a small boy is apt to find under a house in the days before they had basements to store truck in. There were exciting things like the Old Man's hunting tents, boats hauled up from the water for a recaulk, busted oars and ragged cast nets, and crates of old yellowing magazines, and even Miss Lottie's moldy old sidesaddle.

There were some pomegranate bushes by the front door, and in the back yard behind the kitchen was an arbor with the first big Malaga grapes I ever tasted, although I had plenty of experience with black-and-white scuppernongs—experience which included the bellyache, and later a dipperful of cool, tart, homemade grape wine from the springhouses on the little farmsteads I shot over. Also in the back yard was a fig tree with huge black figs that broke open in sticky white cracks and attracted hordes of birds and June bugs and bumblebees. And a towering pecan, which hailed storms of rich nuts in the fall.

I never spent much more time inside the House than I could help, but it was very comfortable for that time. It had a big Kalamazoo stove in the parlor, where nobody but the preacher ever sat, and an awful picture of a big St. Bernard dog looking after a little girl. It had a big kitchen where Old Galena, the cook, was queen, and off the kitchen there was a pumpshelf with a graniteware basin and a dirty roller towel. On the ceiling near the pumpshelf was a rafter with two holes bored in it, where my Aunt May had a swing when she was a little girl. The holes are still there.

As a matter of fact, the whole House is still there. It was made out of fat pine so hard you had to bore holes to drive the nails in. Not being very firmly anchored to the earth it could sway its hips in a storm without sagging out of plumb or blowing away. That House is about a hundred years old, and it has weathered all the hurricanes—Alice, Ethel, Helen, and lately, Donna—that have come along since hurricanes became latterly fashionable along that part of the rugged Carolina coast. Maybe we would lose a gross of shingles, perhaps, while the modern houses with basements were skittering off in the breeze, but the Old Man's House kept stubbornly standing, as did the handful of other old houses lovingly shaped before man discovered the shoddy speed-up.

During the depression years, during the war, and after, I had a fixation about that House. It had been rented to a variety of families through the lean and the better years to follow; families careless of the love that went into its construction and the solid fun that was parcel to its planking. I saw it a few years after the war, when I went South on some business or other and took my dog Schnorkel with me. It was a sad House.

It was a sad House as so many houses become pathetic, when they are no longer filled with tumbling children and sprawling dogs. The Old Man's house had been filthed and abused. For seventeen years the strangers who lived in it beat it up. The rose-bushes died and the chandelier, with the tinkling glass prisms, fell down—that chandelier which had seen Christmas dinners with loaded boards of wild turkey and venison, standing just a whiff away from Galena's kitchen, whence came the odors of spicy fruit cake and frizzling ham and baking cookies.

The ancient slatted shutters were sagging crazily from the broken windows, banging in the wind, and the porch had rotted and fallen in. The roses were gone from the side yard, replaced by sandspurs and dandelions, and the neat borders of perennials were long-withered or shrunken brown stalks. But the magnolia was there, bigger and taller than ever, with one of a succession of mockingbirds still shouting his silver serenade on the moonlit nights. The grape arbor was gone, its framework collapsed, but there was the stump of the fig tree and the tall bole remaining of a sick pecan.

At the time, the Boy was having his troubles in a man's world, but the sight of that House made me fair sick. I didn't have any loose money and I was living in New York and traveling all over the globe. I think having the dog with me did it. I got to thinking about all the things that had happened to me with that House as a base; all the things I had done, all the things I had learned in that House and from that House. Most of the things that I value today had started in that House, started when I was a small, fat, cowlicked boy with lop-ears,

spending as much time as I could in it. That House combined
Christmas and Thanksgiving and Easter and summertime, in an
ordered world of guns and dogs and boats and fish and ducks
and quail. It was a cathedral of ancient times, when children
were accorded dignity according to how they earned it, and
adults were merely small boys grown older. That was not just
a House; that House was Me.

I had fallen out of the magnolia, and had shot one of the
mockingbirds—for which I suffered both physically and emotionally. I had gathered the pecans and fought the birds for the
figs. The oak grove was still there by the side of the House,
the gnarled old branches still hung with Spanish moss, and I had
played baseball under its shade. Over the hill was The Cottage
and Beaver Dam and Dutchman's Creek, where I had safari-ed
before I knew there was such a word as safari. From the front
yard there was the water front with its Cedar Bench and the
row of salt-silvered old houses, and I bet myself that I could
still find the old wreck close to where the fish always bit well.

The dog ran into the weed-grown yard and laid his black
square muzzle flat on the ground and stuck his bobtailed behind
into the air, waiting to play. There was still a mockingbird; it
attempted a scherzo. In the oak grove there was a flash of blue,
a scuff of wings, and the harsh calling of a jay. The wind came
up freshly from the water with its burden of salt and tar and,
faintly, fish.

It was October, 1949, and the squirrel season was on. The
hounds would be belling in the crisp October woods as they
coursed the big buck deer, whose necks were swelling as the
frost brought the rutting season and its disregard of consequence.
On the beaches at Baldhead and Corncake the blues would be
running in the sloughs, and occasionally the big silver slabs of
channel bass would be striking. There were still quail in these
parts, and the season would be opening next month, and the
dogs would be whining in the back yard. Possums would be
curled in gray balls in the naked persimmon trees, and the woods

would be full of blue-drifting wood smoke and the evening cries of the colored children driving the cows home. Hog-killin' time was just around the corner. . . .

I was wearing a Countess Maria necktie and driving a blue Buick convertible. I was writing a syndicated newspaper column and selling stuff to magazines and going to the Stork Club and Twenty One for lunch. Toots Shor called me by my first name, and I was living in a penthouse and owed money to the bank.

And I felt like a complete fraud. I felt like I was wearing somebody else's clothes and driving somebody else's car and going around under somebody else's name, so long as the Old Man's House stood there empty and sad, lonely and despoiled of firelight and laughter.

So of course you know what I did. I had the mockingbird, and I had the magnolia, and all I needed was the mortgage.

I went to see the man people called a skinflint, and told him that I was the Old Man's boy grown considerably older. He said he remembered me; I don't know if he actually did. But this old man—he was sere and crisp-frail as a leaf before it falls —that people called a skinflint said he would be glad to sell me the House back, and for exactly as much as the amount of the mortgage for which he had foreclosed it!

Perhaps he *was* a skinflint, but he could have gotten three times as much as the mortgage warranted, for the country was fat with postwar prosperity and housing was acutely short. Skinflint or not, he had awaited death on the strength of his promise to keep the House in the family. I bought back the House, not because I could use it but because I needed it.

The House sits proud and freshly painted today on its corner. Its flowers are cherished, its interior restored. A woman who was born in the House, my mother, is its chatelaine. My father watches television in the back living room, where the Old Man used to listen to the lugubrious whine of "The Wreck of the Old Ninety-Seven" on one of those long-horned gramophones. The little girl who swung on the back porch, a grandmother for many years now, lives "down the street." There are lights and voices in the House again, and from time to time, dogs and children. Rich black laughter is heard in the kitchen, and the old-time smells still come tantalizingly into the dining room, where the old glass chandelier used to swing. Corn and butter beans and hot biscuits are still cooked in that kitchen, and the brandy is soaked into the Christmas fruitcake as in times past.

It is amazing how the time passes. There was a letter the other day from the bank that holds the mortgage, saying that we don't owe any money on the Old Man's House any more. The Old Man's House is free of strangers, and makes a happy harbor for cheerful ghosts. The magnolia and the mockingbird are safe again, and the flowers bloom, and I somehow thought that the Old Man might like to know it.

30

Even His Runts Were Giants

The death of an old dog is comparable in heartache to the death of any person, young or old, and in some respects produces more pain. The dog has been dependent, totally, and has become an extension of the man, closer in companionship than humans and certainly more blind to the master's faults. The loss of a dog is felt more keenly because a portion of the human dies with the beast, or so it seems to me.

You maybe remember that the Old Man said, "Old dogs and old men both smell bad and are better out of the house." He also said, "Watching something die is not a very pleasant process, especially if it's you."

He was referring at the time to a beast that was somewhat overdue. All we could do was make him comfortable. Then

one day he died, and he died in the knowledge that he had
not been abused in sharing the life of people whose lives he
had richened in the sharing. When the Old Man died, he did
it the same way.

Ever since I can remember I have been enslaved by dogs, and
not particularly in the sentimental lap-dog fashion. Dogs and
people vary in intelligence and personality. My Mickey, a
cocker bitch, was meaner than a Doberman. My Frank, the
blue belton Llewellin, was such a wencher that he hanged himself on a fence trying to chase a new girl, and he was well past
the age of such shenanigans. My Tom, a liver-and-white pointer
was the best bird dog I've ever owned, and he was queer. His
voice never changed from the treble, he shrieked at the idea of
being bred, and the real he-dogs never even bothered to bite
him. And then, of course, there was Sandy, a lemon-and-white
English setter with as foul a disposition and as accurate a nose
as ever I encountered. And there was Jet, a Gordon setter who
spent most of his life asleep on the sports desk of the Washington *Daily News;* and the setter twins, Abercrombie and Bitch;
plus a big, rangy Rhett Butler kind of pointer named Dude,
who ran away from his happy home. And finally the current
crop.

The current crop is worthy of consideration. There is a
spayed standard French poodle bitch named Miss Mam'selle
Señorita Fräulein Memsahib, who is possibly the only stupid
French poodle in the world. This one really hasn't got sense
enough to come in out of the rain. There was, until recently,
Schnorkel, the Old Man of the bunch, who was possibly the
only brilliant boxer I have ever met. I cannot say this for his
son, Satchmo, or Satch's sister, Mrs. Gwendolyn Wentworth-
Brewster, otherwise known as Wendy, or some of his half-
brothers and sisters, named variously Rufus and Ella and Lena.

Schnorkel, who was pressing thirteen years of dignified age,
was a Warlord of Mazelaine offshoot, and like that grand old
man he always bred true. There are more half-bred boxers with

white shoes and white chest blazes running around Spain than you can shake a muleta at. This is known as outside work. Actually my old gentleman has been married only four times, producing forty-two pups out of the brief honeymoons. The last time—we had the bride flown in from Madrid to Barcelona —he managed to sire eleven, which is pretty good going for an old boy with a hoary face and the Reaper just around the corner. And as somebody once said of Schnork, even his runts are bigger than most people's giants.

Except Satchmo, of course. Satchmo takes after his Spanish mother. But he makes up for his smallness by being perhaps the silliest beast I've ever met. He is a comic dog on the order of a young Mickey Rooney. He sleeps on a split level and sulks if I forget his morning kick. He helps the gardener at work by biting his ankles, and suffers horribly from sinus. I can tell when the weather's changing, just by hearing Satch wheeze. I would give him away, as I gave his sister Wendy away, but nobody intelligent enough to feed him will have him. So I'm stuck with an idiot child.

It is not so bad when they are run over or succumb to distemper when they're too young to be part of the family, or even when they garrote themselves like old Frank did. But we were just in the process of watching Schnorkel die, slowly, and it was a terrible thing.

I bought this ten-week-old puppy as a gift for my wife. Paul Gallico, the writer; Bill Williams, the editor; a nonclassifiable friend named Bernie Relin; and I went puppy hunting one day after an exuberant lunch involving Martinis. We wound up in Long Island and were introduced to the baby's family. His old man, of whom the baby was the spittin' image, was unleashed and he cuffed every puppy soundly. Only one pup bared his milk teeth and charged back at Papa.

"I'll have that one," I said. "The scrapper. What's his name?"

"Chip," the owner said. "He's the dead image of his father and his grandpa. Chip off the Old Block is his square handle."

I had just made a week's run as the first civilian to test a schnorkel submarine. "His name is Schnorkel," I said. "He looks like a dog who would be named Schnorkel."

While he was kindly disposed to most people and all children this puppy was the worst dog-fighter I have ever seen. I had to pull him off a full-grown Doberman when he was just over six months old. His feet were hanging clear of the ground, but he had a tooth hold on the throat, and there was very little the Dobe could do about him until I got a stick and pried the puppy's teeth out of his neck.

This was on the same weekend that Schnork gained a lasting aversion to water. I was out fishing in a boat on a lake in New Jersey, and the puppy was on the dock. I called him, and he thought what was in front of him was pale-blue sidewalk. He strolled off the dock and damn near drowned.

From that point on all water was his enemy. You can't tell me that this is a boxer trait, because his offspring, Satch, can barely be restrained from swimming daily to Africa with old Miss Mam'selle. The Spaniards where we live had a name for Schnork. They called him *el Salvavida*—the Lifesaver. That's because he used to roam up and down the beach wringing his paws, frothing at the mouth, and beseeching people to come out of that wet old mess before they drowned.

Schnorkel was a puppy when we lived in Greenwich Village, and he had a strange set of social values. There was a nice hoodlum around the Minetta Street area, a nondescript little man who liked dogs. He approached me one day in his quiet hoodlum manner and said tightly, out of the corner of his mouth, that he had heard we had been refused insurance on personal belongings because the neighborhood was so tough.

"Don't worry," he said. "Nobody lays a glove on your joint. Leave the door open. I run this end of the town. No bum lays a glove on your joint." I waited for the kicker. "You wouldn't mind sometime if I walked your dog? I'm a sucker for pooches and I love this dog."

I said, "Fine." From time to time there would be a ring or a knock or even a lightly cast pebble against a window, and there would be Mr. Hoodlum in his form-fitting overcoat. I would shove the puppy down the stairs and the two mobsters would go for a walk.

At the time I was working late at night, and occasionally Ginny Ruark would have to walk the dog. I didn't worry about her safety in murky back alleys at 2 A.M. I had looked out the window one night. As she went into the street with the dog a shadow detached itself from a deeper, darker shadow. It flitted shadowwise down the tiny street, always melting into tiny corners.

"You shouldn't worry if your missus walks the dog late nights," my tight-mouthed little man said one day. "My boys are always around." He paused. "They got nothing better to do," he said. "Can I walk the dog now?"

Schnorkel became perceptive early. He was part of the mob, but he didn't like outsiders. It is necessary to explain here that he once owned a tame duck, and baby-sat a cat named Short-change. This did not mean that he liked either ducks or cats. He just liked one duck, and one cat named Shortchange. The same with our tame mobsters.

Some penny-ante boys tried a heist in the neighborhood one night when Schnork was off leash, and he treed the interlopers on a fire escape. They say boxers can't smell very good, but they can sure feel. When we became a little more affluent and moved uptown to Fifth Avenue he chased one set of thieves right up on top of an outbuilding. And he really distinguished himself one night as a house detective.

This was a penthouse apartment, and the elevator opened directly into the foyer. We were having an intimate little gathering of a hundred and fifty-two people, a business-cocktail do, and Schnork leaped happily into everybody's lap. Let's just say he enjoyed meeting a hundred fifty-two people, including the cat lovers who wore blue suits and hated dogs.

All of a sudden my wife came to me in a far corner. "Schnorkel won't let two people off the elevator," she said. "He's got them bayed, like he treed the burglars. I suppose they're some loaded friends of yours that you picked up somewhere, but you better come explain it to the dog."

They were smooth enough in appearance, certainly slick enough to fit in with the other guests. But Schnorkel, legs braced and teeth showing, was having none of them. I had never seen the bums before in my life.

"What do you want?" I asked.

"Well," one said, "we thought it was some kind of club. We saw the lights on late every night, and tonight all these people came, and we thought you were maybe running an after-hours club."

"You want to go back down in the elevator or will you have some dog?" I said. "I couldn't care less."

They chose the elevator, and then Schnork went back to mingle with the party and rub his hairs off on the gentry's blue suits.

Schnorkel and Mam'selle had been Europeans for eight years when the old boy cashed. Schnorkel spoke French, Spanish, Catalan, Swahili, and English English; and Mam'selle still doesn't know her name. The help called Schnorkel *el Cocinero*, the cook, because he was always in the kitchen. Mam'selle does not associate with the help. She also refused to drink water out of anything but a bidet, which is a Latin bathroom fixture.

Both dogs were quite well traveled. They alternated between Palamós and Barcelona, and we spent one summer in Tangier in North Africa at an appalling cost in time, trouble, and money, because there was no housing readily available in Barcelona except the Hotel Ritz, and the dogs didn't care much for the noise the tramcars made outside the Ritz. So we went to Tangier and shacked up in the Hotel el Minzah and I overdrew my account again, while being involved in cat fights and the beginning of the Moroccan rebellion.

They have been well pleased with life in Spain, since they have slaves to do their bidding and a large yard in front of two houses. The yards are filled with flowers on which they make water. In front of one house there is a beach that is filled with tourists. Schnorkel, being a Kraut, was allowed to snarl at the French; while Mam'selle, being a Frog, barks at the Germans. Satchmo usually just bites me, being too lazy to *heraus* the Krauts.

You will have noticed a forced light touch to this piece. I'll tell you why. Schnorkel was gray, and he walked spraddled-legged, weak in the hindquarters, and his teeth were worn down so he couldn't even fight his son any more, and noise bothered him, and his hide was abraded, and his eyesight was going, and he had forgotten his last girl friend. My old puppy, my dog Schnorkel, was dying, in the midst of all the love he had mustered since he was ten weeks old.

It seemed to do nobody any good to see the old boy as what he was, gray and feeble, finished and useless to himself and to the others, the dogs and the people. All the ham actor was gone out of him, all of the sense of humor, all of the bounce, and all of his considerable dignity. He had a stroke and he walked around with his head down, bumping into things, and toward the end he kept fumbling for corners to die in. The facilities for modern dog destruction are few, in the backwater section of Spain I live in. We dug him a grave under some pine trees and I borrowed a pistol from one of the Guardia Civil *carabineros* and took my old dog out under the trees and shot him. The cook and the Guardia Civil and I tossed some earth into the grave, and we buried a good portion of me, that sunny morning, with the big, cockaded yellow hoopoe birds looping from pine to pine and the Mediterranean lapping softly blue almost in the front yard. We were all glad to see the old dog go, because this way we got the puppy back.

What we didn't get back was the years since the puppy came into the little flat in Greenwich Village in New York and decided to stay. We didn't get back the years which took me uptown and then Europe, to South America and Africa and India and Japan and Australia and China and New Guinea and all the other places I had hankered to see.

In his lifetime Schnorkel lived a hundred years of man's span. My grown-up friends were his grown-up friends, and so very many of Schnorkel's friends got old and sick and tired and died of it too.

I measure most of the importance of my adult life from the time I got Schnorkel until the day I buried him. I wasn't much more than a boy when I got him, just a few years out of the war and still puppyish with all the cocky confidence of youth that had been momentarily interrupted by the war. Schnork and I started growing up together and the developing project continued until time, which expands the years of a dog, stopped the dog as a wise old man and left the graying humans to profit by his past presence.

I was glad that Schnorkel had been with me the day I drove down to North Carolina and bought the Old Man's House back, not because I could use it but because I needed it. Schnorkel was still alive when I finished paying off the mortgage, and so the Old Man had his House back, as I had a good deal of my boyhood back. In between there had been a lot of living and a great deal of work, a lot of departures and homecomings. Once I was gone for nine months on a swing around the world; the welcome was the same as if I'd just strolled down to the post office.

After I wrapped my old friend in a bathrobe and put him in the earth the Guardia Civil man and I came back to the house and had a drink to the dog. The Guardia Civil looked around at the working room with the big fireplace, with some African game heads on the wall.

"He was a good dog," the *carabinero* said. "A good person. He lived a good life in a good house."

I reckon the Old Man wouldn't have minded that as an epitaph for himself.

Robert Chester Ruark born in Wilmington, North Carolina, in 1915. He began his writing career as a sports writer and columnist for the *Washington Daily News* and produced a total of 4,000 columns for the United Feature Syndicate. He wrote several best-selling novels, including *Something of Value, Uhuru,* and *The Honey Badger. The Old Man and the Boy* is his most widely known and perhaps best-liked book. Robert Ruark died in 1965.

Peter Hathaway Capstick is the author of *Death in the Long Grass, Death in the Dark Continent,* and *Safari: The Last Adventure.* His latest book, *The Last Ivory Hunter,* is a biography of the African hunter Wally Johnson.